Theirs was a world of peasants and princes, of dazzling beauty and savage brutality, and to them was entrusted the monumental task of immortalizing their age in towering works of mortar and stone, the grandeur of which the world had never seen—and would never see again.

STEPHEN OF DUNWICH—The illegitimate son of a Suffolk peasant, he was possessed by his visions of architectural glory and obsessed by his passion for a beautiful woman— only to find he must choose between them.

MAUD—Poor and uneducated, she was forced to make the most agonizing decision a mother ever has to make—and she paid the price with her soul.

BROTHER DANIEL—A harsh and forbidding master, he would leave his searing mark on a young boy's soul—and carry his own guilty secret to his grave.

AUDE—The beautiful, barefoot girl from the fens, she could give Stephen everything he ever needed—but not the one thing he most desperately wanted.

KAMIL—The crown prince of Cairo, he would command Stephen to build him the most dazzling palace the world had ever seen—in exchange for the young architect's freedom.

JOKAI—Irresolute and sardonic, this dashing Hungarian count would inspire the spectacular cathedral that would prove to be Stephen's masterwork—the greatest House of God ever built by man.

BIANCA—Jokai's stunning, Venetian-born wife, she made no secret of h_____ emier master builder—_____ hem both.

D0711478

A
BRIDGE
TO THE
SKY

Margaret Ball

BANTAM BOOKS
NEW YORK • TORONTO • LONDON • SYDNEY • AUCKLAND

A BRIDGE TO THE SKY

A BANTAM BOOK / JULY 1990

All rights reserved.
Copyright © 1990 by Margaret Ball.
Cover art copyright © 1990 by Sanjulian.
No part of this book may be reproduced or transmitted
in any form or by any means, electronic or mechanical,
including photocopying, recording, or by any information
storage and retrieval system, without permission in writing from
the publisher.
For information address: Bantam Books.

ISBN 0-553-28137-2

Published simultaneously in the United States and Canada

Bantam Books are published by Bantam Books, a division of
Bantam Doubleday Dell Publishing Group, Inc. Its trademark,
consisting of the words "Bantam Books" and the portrayal of a
rooster, is Registered in U.S. Patent and Trademark Office and in
other countries. Marca Registrada. Bantam Books, 666 Fifth
Avenue, New York, New York 10103.

PRINTED IN THE UNITED STATES OF AMERICA

RAD   0 9 8 7 6 5 4 3 2 1

A BRIDGE TO THE SKY

PART I

The Monks
of Ely

◫

1208–1216

CHAPTER

1

◻

The bells of Dunwich were ringing once again.

The previous year had been full of strife between the English king and the Pope. The antagonism concerned who should be archbishop of Canterbury, the King's candidate or the Pope's. The fisherfolk of Dunwich had known little and cared less about the King's quarrel; what was it to them who was elected to the see of Canterbury? But in March 1208, the Pope struck at all of England to bring King John to submission. He proclaimed an interdict. As result couples married without the church's blessing, sinners went unconfessed, the dead were buried in unconsecrated ground. In Dunwich, as everywhere else, the church's doors were closed, the bells silent until this stormy autumn dawn when they rang out again with a call more urgent than prayer. The wind from the east was driving the tide higher than it had been in living memory, and the strand of Dunwich, where the fishers built their huts, was lashed with waves: a drowning tide, a death tide they would call it. From the seven church towers, from the monks' cell of the priory of Eye, and from the three round watchtowers built in the days of the Danish invasions, all the bells of Dunwich swung in cacophonous, panic-laden strife: the deep tones of Great Michael and Old John, the high sweet tenor of Little Tom, and the three cracked notes of the three Bartholomews. The clashing tones jarred and deafened the townspeople scrambling from their beds, drowned out the babble of questions and hasty replies.

Farther out, beyond the sloping shingle beach, the roar of waves coming in to shore drowned the clamorous ringing of the bells. The fishermen who'd set sail the evening before in hopes of a good herring catch would be far beyond the sound of bells now; unless perhaps, as the legends said, they heard them still beneath the sea.

The boy had been dreaming of those bells under the water and of the sea-drowned cities of the fairyfolk when his mother's hand shook him half awake, and he felt the cold of the water creep into his floor pallet. At seven he had already learned the meaning of saltwater on the floor and bells shaking the darkness; she didn't have to tarry on explanations. But he was still dazed from the dream. Kneeling in the salty mud, he fumbled on his clothes too slowly to suit her. An impatient jerk brought him to his feet and out of the hut in one stumbling motion, his shoulder wrenched with the force of her pull, and he blinked in sleepy surprise to see the beach already covered knee-deep with water. The gray half-light of early dawn softened everything into a vague amorphous mass of shadowy shapes, beach and water and tumbledown fishing huts, but the sea pulled at his ankles with a hungry sucking sound that frightened him.

"'Twill have our house this time, I know it," Mam sobbed as she pulled him along behind her, laboring along the sandy path with a bundle of clothes perched on her hip. She kept up a quiet keening whine, cursing equally the rich burghers who wouldn't make room on the high ground for poor fisherfolk to build, the folly of her man in going out after herring in storm-season, the high tide that was nibbling away at the shingle behind them, and the God who'd sent such a tide to plague poor helpless folk.

The loose, sandy soil above the beach was so soft that their feet sank into it with each step. The cool damp grit of the sand felt good between the boy's toes, but his mother pulled him along too quickly for him to enjoy it. Behind them, the hut they'd left was already swaying in a two-foot depth of water, and the ground was bordered with a line of white foam that edged forward almost as quickly as they hurried ahead of it. Before them, the rising waters curled round the base of the sandy knoll where the church stood, already foaming across the path that led upwards to the safety of the high town. Mam was panting for breath by the time they reached the low flint wall set round the churchyard, but the muttered complaints never ceased, even when she rested with one hand on the wall.

The Church of St. Michael was a small square building of flints set in mortar, hardly bigger than the hut they'd left, with a sodden roof of plain thatch. The wooden bell tower stood apart from the church and slightly higher on a rounded ledge that had been eaten away underneath by years of storms like this one. Its hammered flat tin bell made a sad clanking sound, hardly audible over the deep sonorous clanging of the cast bells in the richer churches within the town walls. While they rested by the church wall, the other refugees from the fishing shanties below pushed past, almost trampling each other in their eagerness to get to the shelter of the tower. As they pushed in, the tower shook with the weight of all those bodies crowding up the stairs.

"Look where you're going, you greedy swine!" Mam cursed a neighbor who shouldered them aside to wheel a barrow full of his leather hides up to the church tower.

"Not my fault if some had no goods to save, nor nought in the house save their stinking bodies!" the tanner shouted back over his shoulder. He was naked but for a cloth tied around his loins, and the muscles under the rain-slick skin of his back were bulging with the effort of pushing the barrow through mud and sand.

"A fine one to talk about stinking, you with your hides!" Mam screeched at his retreating figure and her cry broke in the middle. "Come on, then, you," she sobbed, gripping the boy's wrist and pulling him across the churchyard toward the tower. He hung back, digging his heels into the soft sand, and she slapped him.

"Y'are too old for such games! Come on, or we'll be last—they'll not let us in—"

Her eyes were wide with fear of the rising waters; already the tide was at the base of the flint wall. When the boy looked back, he could see that their house was trembling as the water ate away the shingle on which it stood. He looked back at the wooden tower and saw the same trembling, like the waver of summer heat over a still pool. The creaking of wood being tortured out of shape came clearly to him over the deep-throated roar of waves and the clamor of bells.

"Not there, Mam! Not there!"

He couldn't find words to explain his certainty, and she was too frightened and angry to listen. As she let go his wrist to deliver another slap, he darted away from her toward the empty church. The stone path was slimy with rain, and his bare feet slipped, bruising his toes. But the small squat church was before him, its dark open door offering safety from everything that had terrified him this morning—the hungry waves, the bells and the crowding, pushing, angry people, and most of all, the high shrieking song of the tortured bell tower.

Inside the church, it was quiet. He squatted on the floor in a corner and watched the water that trickled slowly in through the open door. His heart was thudding against his ribs, but he felt safe now, even when Mam splashed heavily in and called his name.

"They closed the tower door. Stinking peasants. Dunwich men, won't give an inch to a poor lass from Bliburgh. If my man was here they'd not ha' shut us out." She swung her bundle of clothes down on the altartop and sat beside it, her legs swinging free. "See what y've done? No safety for us in the tower now. We'll likely drown in here. If the waters come up any farther, they'll pull the church down."

She spoke wearily, without anger, as though it wasn't any use being angry with him now that their fate was settled. He came out of his hiding place and leaned on the bundle of clothes beside his mother. The stone square of the altartop was cold but the bundle was warm from his mother's body and smelled like her sweat, like his Da coming home from the sea with the smell of herring clinging to him, like their small stuffy hut.

"Mam? We could go on higher up. To the town. We don't have to stay here, Mam."

Wordlessly she pointed toward the open door. The boy stared out at the sheet of water that stretched out over the churchyard, covering the sparse knobs of pale grass and sucking away at the sandy foundations of the wall. She didn't have to say anything. The church was higher than the path that led on up to Dunwich town. They'd have to wade through rising waters to get to safety now, with the tide pulling at their legs, hungry, greedy to pull their bodies down beneath the sea.

"I wish the bells would stop ringing!" Mam said suddenly. "If there's anybody below who's not waked by now, 'tis too late for them to hear the bells."

"I wish my Da was here."

"So do I, Stephen. So do I." With a deep sigh, she pulled her shoulders back, brushed the damp pale strands of hair away from her cheeks, and forced a smile. Stephen felt the softening in her and leaned into her lap, comforted. This was his Mam again, strong and in control; not the sharp-voiced frightened woman whose fear made him feel that the whole world was washing away. "Let's us try to think about something else, that always helps when you're troubled. You tell me 'bout the Bible pictures on the wall."

"Don't want to!"

The mural opposite them was a violently colored representation of an old man being swallowed up by a fish. The tail of the fish curled into the corner of the wall and blended with the foaming waves painted beneath it.

"All right," Mam conceded. "Say a prayer, then." Her lips moved, the words of the rote prayer drowned out by the storm, and the boy tried to follow in his head. But the sound of the sea kept getting in his way, and soon he gave up the pretense at prayer. They huddled together on the altar, watching the steady rise of the waters that had never yet quite covered the Church of St. Michael By The Sea.

The sky lightened and the water crept higher.

The two feet of water that now stood in the church were not quite enough to float the priest's tall wooden reading-stand. But the water made the stand light enough for a woman and a small boy to maneuver it across the church to the square western foot with the round open arch above it. She lifted him to safety first, then gripped the ledge and scrambled up herself. The narrow lintel was an uncomfortable seat, but from here they could look through the open arch and measure the progress of the water against the churchyard wall. Rain and salt sea-spray beat against their faces when the wind gusted toward them.

Mam gave a sharp sigh when the water covered the rounded flints at the top of the wall. "It's never been so high before. Church is like up to its knees in water, isn't it?" She peered through the arched window, twisted her body against the stones, to look at the tower. The monotonous clanking of the bell had stopped some time ago. "Hope they're all warm and dry in there, selfish sods."

"No." Stephen shook his head. "I mean, we're better here. I mean—" He screwed his face up, trying to find some way to explain to Mam what he felt and heard so clearly, the thin anguished singing of the wood that set his teeth on edge. "The tower's not safe."

"Higher than we are."

"Yes, but—" He shook his head so violently that he almost lost his balance. Mam caught him round the waist and pressed him against her.

"Be careful, you little fool!"

"It's not safe in the tower. The water is coming up under it. Can't you see?" It was like a quiet, continuous, soft slurping noise in the back of his head, the way the rising tide swirled and sucked at the ledge underneath the bell tower. And the timbers creaked once, then again, crying out like afflicted living things. "Can't you *hear*?"

"Who can hear anything in this?"

The wind had gathered force; it battered at the church and the tower, throwing saltwater at them, tugging at the corners and shrieking round the edges of the buildings. The people in the tower were screaming, praying, blaspheming. Over and through it all, Stephen could still hear the high discordant music of the tower itself. He clenched his own body, wanting everything to hold, to stay in place, and feeling each sagging motion of the tower as if he were there himself. His arms and legs trembled with the effort of holding still. The tower was leaning now, the walls canting slowly to one side, even Mam must see it—

The snapping of timbers and the crash of falling walls and the screams of people inside the tower masked the last, doomed ringing of St. Michael's bell. Mam's arms were tight around him again, hurting him, and in the gray dawn the churchyard was momentarily full of white startled faces, limbs cast up by the water, sodden garments dragging their wearers down, foam, floating splintered timbers, and waves splashing up against the church wall. The church itself seemed to crouch lower, groaning, as the pieces of the shattered bell tower struck its corners.

Stephen could feel the shocks of the blows vibrating deep within the church, transmitted from the carved freestone corner blocks to the body of flints and mortar, quivering and dying out deep in the solid strength of the rounded arches that rose above the flood.

Then everything was gone, tower and bell and all the folk within swept away by that last great wave, and the wind was dropping too as though it had done its task for that day. The lightening sky shone through gray clouds and a fine intermittent drizzle of rain succeeded the storm. Mam released him, and she edged away from him as though she didn't want to sit too close on this narrow ledge that they both shared. "How did you know?" she whispered. "You saved us, Stephen—us alone, out of all the folk as come to shelter here. How did you know?" And then, on a higher, more despairing note, "And what good will it do? Where will we go now? Everything's lost."

He knew then that his Da wouldn't be coming back, tired and cold and taciturn, with his clothes stiff with sea-spray and glittering with fish scales. He didn't need the long day of waiting that followed, the discovery of one fishing boat drifting keel-up off the sands of Walberswick, Mam's awkward explanations. Three days after the storm, they were still living in the empty church, and she was still trying to reconcile Stephen to their loss.

"God took your Da."

"The sea took him." Stephen scowled at the placid expanse of blue water, now calm and sparkling with sunlight, and at the shingle littered with wreckage. Some of their neighbors, the lucky ones who'd made it to the safety of Dunwich before the tide was too high, were already collecting the remnants of beams and thatch and good smooth stones to build their houses again. Mam wouldn't touch the stuff, even though some of it might well have been theirs. "Dead men's bones," she said listlessly, and sat staring out to sea from her post on the churchyard wall.

"Mam. We have to have a *house*. We can't go on living in the church."

"Why not? God's not using it these days." The church had stood empty and neglected since the interdict was pronounced in March, while the priest lived comfortably in the upper town on the rents of his fields.

But somebody told the priest of St. Michael's that

people were living in his church, and he emerged from his safe house in the town to tell them the church couldn't be used as shelter for poor families that had lost their homes. It was God's house, even if He didn't use it at the moment. They would have to move on and rebuild their lives as others were doing.

"Perhaps," he suggested, "you'd like to go back to your family for a while. Until you find . . ."

"They're dead. Alwin's folks, too. We was alone in the world—as you should know. How many years have I been coming to Mass here?"

The priest shuffled and coughed into the long sleeves of his tunic and looked sidelong at Stephen, almost as if he feared him. "Well . . . there's been talk about you in the town."

"About the miracle that saved us?"

"Some folk," said the priest, "don't call it a miracle. . . . You can't stay here. I was only trying to help."

Mam gazed at him with wide, blank eyes and said, "Oh, yes, it was a miracle. God saved us. My son had a vision."

"What's that to do with—don't blaspheme. Visions are for saints."

"Maybe he's a saint. Or going to be. He saw St. Michael himself standing on the church tower, waving a fiery sword and telling us not to come in. That's why we took shelter in the church and were saved when all those selfish sods who'd pushed ahead and locked us out drowned. It was God's will."

"Well, now—"

"It was a miracle. You won't put us out of the church yet, Father?"

Her insistence, and maybe the fear that if he tried to throw her out she'd wail and make a scene, bought them a few more days of shelter. Then the story of the miracle spread, and those who'd lost families or friends in the crash of the bell tower began to mutter that some might call it God's help and some might call it a witch's doing. What could you expect of a stuck-up piece from Bliburgh who'd always thought herself above her neighbors, though she and her husband were the poorest of the very poor?

And the boy, now. Hadn't they always said there was something queer about the lad? The woman had insisted on teaching him his letters, which wasn't seemly for her to know or for him to learn. He was big for his age, with yellow hair and those light sky-colored eyes—not much like his father, Alwin, who'd been small and dark like most of the fisherfolk. The fat alewife who brewed for East Dunwich said that the boy's pale eyes gave her a turn, and such people oughtn't to be allowed around honest folk. Who called that storm up, anyway?

The whispers didn't mean much to Stephen until the day when his Mam was away, looking for work in Dunwich, and a group of boys caught him alone on the beach and chased him home with a cruel, taunting rhyme.

> Ely for a Bishop,
> Bungay for the Poor;
> Southwold for a Drunkard,
> And Bliburgh for a Whore.

He ran home, crying with anger at words he did not quite understand, and found his Mam standing outside the church door with her bundle under her arm. She had a cut on one side of her forehead, blue at the center and scabbed over with dried blood.

"What happened, Mam?"

She shook her head and gave an angry sniff. "Doesn't matter. There's no work for me in this town, not even at the alehouse. Fat Letselina said I was too old for 'er customers. Me! Do I look old?"

She looked worse than old at that moment, with her pale hair strained back, the red swelling on her forehead, and her eyes darting from side to side as she spoke. "*He*" she jerked her head toward the church, and Stephen understood that she meant the priest, "—he says we have to go, no matter if I've found a place or not. He says there's talk in the town of witches. They say someone put a spell on the tower to pull it down, and the one who did such work should be dunked for a witch and held under until the evil bubbles out of their mouth. He says he doesn't know whether it was God's work or the devil's that saved us when everybody else drowned, and he can't protect us if there's trouble." She sniffed, hitched the bundle up on her hip, and grabbed Stephen's hand. "Come on. I'm not one to stay where I'm not wanted."

"Where are we going, Mam?" Stephen asked as she led him up the steep path toward the upper town.

"Home. Bliburgh. To a priest I know—knew. He'll help us."

The priest of St. Michael's hadn't helped them. Stephen thought about that but decided not to say anything. His Mam was strange these days, staring at nothing, and suddenly overcome by fits of anger that left him bruised and her sobbing with remorse.

They dared not go through the town for fear of the townsfolk with their whisperings of witchcraft. Instead they walked around the town and back to the ferry over Dunwich River. Stephen's legs were aching by the time they reached the ferry. And they still had the long walk up the coast and inland to Bliburgh. But by then he'd thought of something comforting to say.

"You're not a witch, Mam," he said. "*I* know you aren't."

She swung her bundle to the ground and stared past him while they waited for the ferryman to amble out of his hut and set the sweeps going. "Not me," she said at last, still looking past him. "It's not me they want to drown for witching. It's you."

The next few days were a jumble of quiet misery and confusion for Stephen. The two of them were always on the move, and his Mam's voice was sharp and impatient, and there was never very much to eat. A few scenes stood out in his memory. There was the small priory of the Austin Canons at Bliburgh, where a tonsured monk shook his head in answer to his Mam's query. "Brother Daniel? No longer with us. He joined the Black Monks—the Benedictines."

"Where?"

"At Ely. It's a cathedral city, you know, and the convent is well endowed." The monk went on talking quietly, as if to himself, while his Mam shifted from one foot to the other. "The Benedictines usually do well for themselves. I expect the opportunities for advancement in that order are considerably greater, but then—" He broke off and looked directly at Mam for the first time since she'd pulled at the iron ring on the priory door. "Don't I know you? You were a local girl. Mary—Margaret—"

"Maud."

"Oh. Yes. Married a Dunwich man?"

"He's dead now." His Mam hesitated, twisting thin hands around her bundle. "Could you tell me how to get to Ely, Father?"

"It's too far, Maud. Why do you want to go all that way?"

"Just—tell—me—where it is."

The directions meant nothing to Stephen, but the desperate, hungry look in Mam's eyes when the monk closed the door frightened him. "Mam? Are we starving, Mam?"

She forced a laugh and stopped in the middle of the road to pull out a crust of dark bread from their bundle. "Of course not. Here, chew on that if you're hungry. I'll always see that you're clothed and fed, Stephen. *Always*. Remember that." She knelt before him, hands tight on his shoulders, eyes burning into his. "That's a promise."

Stephen was afraid to tell her that he didn't want the bread, not just then; maybe they should save it for later. Instead he sucked on the dry end of the crust as they walked along.

In the days that followed, Stephen lost all sense of time and direction. There were long dusty roads and villages where the dogs barked at them, and usually the doors slammed shut when Mam approached with her hand out, speaking softly of alms and charity to poor pilgrims. The storms that brought the disastrous flood-tide to Dunwich had flattened crops in the rest of Suffolk, and most people were looking ahead to a hard winter with little to spare for their own, let alone strangers.

As they drew closer to Ely, the road became a narrow, raised ridge between flat sheets of water, green with algae and choked with sedge and reeds and shoots of alder. A damp fog came out of the waters at night. Mam coughed into the stained hem of her kirtle whenever she thought Stephen wasn't looking.

On the last day of their journey, Stephen could see their destination rising above them like a great ship that rode the fens. The high arched walls of the cathedral seemed to rise directly out of the mist, a ship of gray stone, light as the soaring lines of its arches, sturdy as the columns on which it floated. He kept his eyes fixed on the cathedral as they walked, and the road seemed softer underfoot and his legs didn't ache so much.

Once they crossed the River Ouse, his view was reduced to the lanes lined with daub-and-wattle houses, the legs of hurrying strangers, and the occasional long robe of a monk or a burgher. He held on to Mam's kirtle, resisting the temptation to suck his fingers like a baby, and followed her blindly through the narrow, winding lanes. More than once she stopped to ask her way, and Stephen waited, numbed by the unfamiliar sights and sounds as by fatigue. He made no sense of the names he heard: Wynferthing Lane, Monk's Hithe, Steeple Row, they were too far away from the shingled shore, the narrow church, and the leaning fishermen's huts that were his world. He was past making any effort to understand this new world, too tired and dazed even to look up at the cathedral. All he wanted was for Mam to finish her business here so they could go home again.

"Brother Daniel? And what would one like *you* be wanting with the cellarer?"

The old man who kept the gate at Steeple Row looked Mam up and down with a dismissing glance. "It's the almoner you'll want to be seeing," he said more kindly. "Bread, and a night's lodging for Saint Audrey's sake, is it?"

"Brother Daniel, who was an Austin Canon at Bliburgh. Tell him Maud of Bliburgh is here. He'll see me."

The man they'd come to see didn't look to Stephen as if he would be much more help than the priest of St. Michael's Church who'd turned them out at the first rumor of witchcraft. Tall, with a bony beak of a nose and a ring of sparse, pale hair showing around his tonsure, he had come upon them at the gate as swiftly and silently as a stooping hawk. He did not look pleased to see Mam, and Stephen thought they'd only been allowed within the grounds because Brother Daniel didn't want the bypassers on Steeple Row to see him talking with a poor woman and her child. He led them straight to the cathedral, through an open rectangle where masons were levering new-carved blocks of stone into place, into a silent and empty nave where shadows fell about the columns like the black drapes of the monks' robes. Even the merchants' wooden stalls lining the aisles were deserted: no one came to trade in a cathedral under the interdict.

"You choose a strange place to be private." It was Mam, challenging the cellarer in a voice Stephen had never heard her use. Her back was straighter, too, and she'd left their bundle at the porter's lodge.

Brother Daniel gave a thin smile. "As private a place as we'll find in England, until this King of ours repents his ways. No one uses the cathedral now except for priests saying their daily mass in private, and they're all in chapter at the moment."

"Oh, aye. Even us poor folk in Dunwich have heard of the interdict. Church bells are as silent in poor villages as in great cities. I haven't blistered my feet and dragged the boy all these miles to talk treason about the King."

"What did you come here for?"

Now Mam would have to beg for food and shelter, be reduced to a humble mendicant again in front of this tall lean man. Stephen shut his eyes, not wanting to see her shrink before him. But instead of hearing her voice, he felt her hands grasp him by the shoulders and shove him forward to stand before the monk.

"He'll be eight years old come Candlemas."

"A sturdy boy. You're blessed."

The monk's voice was indifferent, but when Stephen met the man's intense stare, Brother Daniel folded his hands in the sleeves of his habit and looked back at Mam.

"He's a bright lad. Knows his crisscross row already, and his prayers." Mam paused, and when the monk didn't respond, she went on. "His name's Stephen. You could school him. He'd be a credit to you."

"Scholars pay fees. Novices bring a dowry to the church to help pay for their subsistence. We don't just take in anonymous boys off the streets."

"A-non-y-mous." Mam repeated the word slowly. "That means nameless, don't it? I wonder you'd have the gall to say that, Brother Daniel."

"What do you mean by that?"

The monk seemed to grow even taller; Mam shrank back into herself. "I—I only meant—I was married proper. In the church. You know I had a man."

"Alwin, wasn't it?"

"Good of you to remember." Mam's voice was stronger again; Stephen felt that in some way he couldn't understand, she was taking strength from the black monk. "He's dead now. There was a bad storm that washed away our house and all. I can't hardly keep myself—and there's the boy. Will y' see him tramp the roads as a beggar?"

"It seems," said Brother Daniel, "you are already doing that. You should have spoken to our almoner, Brother Gilbert. He dispenses charity to the deserving poor."

"I don't want charity!" Mam's voice was shrill in the silent nave, echoing off the stone columns and dying away in the shadowed clusters of arches. Her hands were tight on Stephen's shoulders, thin fingers digging into the muscles of his neck. "He's not just any bright boy. God's finger is on him. He saved us from drowning in the flood. Most of Herring Row went under. Other folk took shelter in the bell tower of St. Michael's, but the boy wouldn't let us go in there. He saw Saint Michael himself, with a great flaming sword just like he stands guarding the gates of Paradise, and the holy saint told him to go into the church. The church stood against the floods, and the tower was swept away and all the souls within it. Why d'you think God saved us? Not for *me*, you know that. This boy is going to be something special."

Everytime Mam told the story it got better. And by now Stephen himself was feeling confused as to just what had happened. Had he really seen a vision of a saint with a flaming sword? It seemed so clear when Mam was talking. But when he shut his eyes and tried to remember, all that came back was the deep instinctive fear he'd known when he looked at the sodden wood of the bell tower, and the cold clammy feeling of his sea-wet clothes clinging to his legs.

The Black Monk knelt before Stephen and held his arms. The very touch of his hands was cold. Stephen stood quite still, wishing the man would let him go. The monk's light eyes searched his face with an intensity that went beyond curiosity.

"Is it true, what your mother says? Did you see a vision? Has Our Lord spoken to you?"

Stephen could feel Mam beside him, silently willing him to affirm her story. The strength of her wanting was a force that flowed through him, almost as clear as the lines of force that pressed down through the interior of the cathedral: the high small triple arches at the top, then the larger double ones supporting them, and finally the great single arches thrusting their weight down into the floor and sideways into the shafts of the piers that bound them. Stephen could feel them both, his Mam's wanting and the weight of the stone, and himself poised between them.

The stone was forever. Mam would stop pushing at him when something else caught her attention.

"No."

His voice was so low that the monk bent forward.

"I didn't see an angel."

"Then how did you know the tower would be washed away?"

Stephen shook his head. "I just—it didn't look right."

"Did you see something?"

In Stephen's memory, the wooden tower quivered around the edges like the air over water on a hot, still day. But that hadn't been what made him run away. "I... heard something." The thin, high, crazy music of timbers bent slowly out of shape, skewed and twisted with the weight of so many people.

"A voice, then. A voice of warning."

Stephen opened his dry mouth again, but Mam had taught him not to contradict his elders. The monk stood, looking satisfied. "You were always given to exaggeration, Maud. I believe the boy did experience God's grace, though you have embroidered the story past all recognition."

"Somehow I thought you'd say that. Once you saw him. He's eight years old come Candlemas." Mam's shoulders were slumped, as though she'd given up the fight in the moment of victory. But what were they fighting about? His vision?

"There are some details to be settled."

Stephen stirred restlessly beside Mam, shifting from one foot to the other on the hard stone floor, and she looked down at him. "Stephen, go outside and play. Brother Daniel and I have to talk."

He'd been longing for freedom to explore the cathedral, but now he felt shy of venturing into those vast shadowy spaces. He backed away from Mam and gazed about him, trying to get up the courage to explore.

He was standing at the end of the long nave with its columns leading down on either side to the distant altar. If from the outside the church had resembled a ship, from here it was more like a forest where ancient trees grew smooth and tall, their branches interlocking overhead to form a gracefully arched canopy, a forest that had been growing undisturbed for centuries.

The clatter of falling rubble outside, the voice of the master mason raised in anger, and the scrape of a shovel upon stone broke Stephen's reverie. He turned to look at the workmen, but all he could see through the open door was an arch of bright light and a man's shoulder as he bent over, laying the great stones smooth and true. Stephen sidled away from Mam, down the aisle toward the light and the cheerful noise of the masons at work. While he watched the men, Maud and Brother Daniel continued their discussion in low tones.

"I can't pay you now. I can't even keep myself. But without the boy—there was an inn at the ferry—the woman said I could work there helping her with the customers. Only she won't let me keep him. And truth to tell, it's no place for a boy—you know what I mean?"

"The Bush and Barrel? You'd work there?"

"I told you, I'm not askin' charity. Not for myself. You've done enough already. Just keep the boy, and when I get paid I'll bring you money for his schooling an' all. He's a bright lad. Do you credit, he would."

The cellarer shook his head. "No."

"You want him. I know you do."

"Not like that. Not with a woman who works at the Bush and Barrel for his mother, coming to give him worldly ideas, taking him away when it strikes her fancy. I could hardly persuade our abbot to accept a scholar with such a...dubious...background."

"What will I do? I can't keep us!"

Outside, the stonemasons' tools chinked with a bright ringing sound, and Stephen laughed at something.

"There is another way," Daniel said finally. "Somewhat out of favor these days, but it has been done in the past. It was how I entered the church. You can offer him to us, give him to God. Promise that he will make his life in the Church. It's called an oblation."

"You couldn't just take him and school him for a few years? I thought—I might get a good place where they'd let me have him with me—or I might marry again."

The cellarer shook his head sternly. "No, Maud. If the boy is to be offered to God, you must make the offering with a whole heart. God is not cheated. You cannot hold back half your gift."

"Fine words!" Maud spat back at him. "And you're a fine one to speak of cheating God!"

The monk slid his hands into his sleeves again and stared, a black column against the white stone columns of the nave. At first she stared back, defiant, but finally her eyes dropped and she bowed her head. "All right," she muttered. "Maybe 'tis for the best."

"It is."

"You'd—let me see him sometimes?"

"It would only disturb the boy. A monk has no family but his brothers in God."

"An' you don't want me coming back to Ely! You want him all to yourself!"

"That is the price." The monk seemed neither disturbed nor angered by her accusations.

Maud bowed her head. "I promised," she murmured to herself, "that the boy would not go cold or hungry or lack a roof over his head."

"In this way you can keep your promise. The Church looks after her own."

"Are we going home now, Mam?" Stephen asked when his mother called him back into the church. "Are you finished?" Her eyes were red around the edges, and her face looked even more pinched than before. He had known this monk wouldn't be any help to them. When would Mam learn to stop trusting priests?

"We're—almost through, Stephen. But we're going to stay to hear a mass. You'll like that, won't you? It's been long since Mam has been to church," she coaxed.

Brother Daniel and an older monk celebrated the brief mass while Stephen watched at his mother's side, stiffly rebellious. If Mam wanted to waste time in church, that was her business, but why couldn't she have left him to play outside until she was ready to go?

After the gospel, Brother Daniel held out the shining silver cup and Mam pushed Stephen toward him. "Go and give the cup to the prior," she whispered.

Stephen took the heavy silver cup by both handles, careful not to spill the wine, and carried it the few steps from one side of the altar to the other. When he had handed it to the older monk, he looked back at Mam for congratulations, but she wouldn't look at him. The mass was over now, Stephen knew that much. Why was everybody still looking so serious?

"Stephen? Give me your hands." The prior whisked the embroidered cloth off the top of the altar, wrapped it round Stephen's outstretched hands and quickly undid it. "The promise must be signed and witnessed," he said, almost in the same breath. "Read the statement to the woman, and let her make her mark—"

Mam bobbed her head. "I know my letters, Father. So does the boy."

"Oh? And you can read Latin, too? I thought not. As I said, Brother Daniel will interpret the statement for you."

"No need. Not in front of—" Mam jerked her head at Stephen.

"As you wish, then."

Stephen decided he did not care for the fussy, self-important prior. Even Brother Daniel's harsh coldness was better than this man's patronizing air. And he was proud of his Mam for insisting on signing her own name to the document, whatever it was. She labored long over each letter, tongue sticking out of her mouth, but the writing came out firm and black and clear.

"Very well. That's all. Unless you'd care to see him tonsured and put into his robes?"

"No—no, I'd best be getting on." Very slowly, she detached Stephen's hand. She reached toward his shoulder, as if to push him to the monk, but she did not quite touch him. "Stephen? You're to stay here. Be a good boy, and do whatever Brother Daniel here tells you, and—and—be a good boy," she repeated before she turned away.

"Mam!" Stephen grabbed at the edge of her kirtle like a baby. "Mam, aren't we going home now? Mam, I want to go with you. Mam. . . ."

The Black Monk's hand was heavy on his shoulder, holding him still while his Mam walked toward the archway opening onto the west porch, growing smaller and smaller until she was just a black line against the sunlight outside. "This is your home now, Stephen. Your mother has given you to the Church, to be educated and to become one of us when you reach years of reason."

The prior tapped his other arm. "She felt it was the best thing for you. You'll understand when you are older, boy."

He understood now. He was too little. He couldn't work and help Mam, and it was too hard for her to feed him. He hadn't been worth keeping. Stephen swallowed hard and stared down the nave of the cathedral. When you're frightened or unhappy, Mam always said, think very hard about something else.

The columns rose in three levels of arches, each level repeating the curves of the arches below, the shafts clustering and growing ever more slender, like the branches of trees reaching to the sky. The painted wood of the ceiling showed pictures Stephen could not read, haloed saints and angels with fiery swords. The stones pressed down into the earth in driving lines of force that he could almost see and hear, deep bass mutterings that held the universe rock-hard and steady. The stones didn't crumble and give way, no matter how much force was placed on them.

He would be a good boy, like Mam said. He would do whatever they told him to, and when she came back for him, they would tell her how good he'd been and she would keep him always.

He would not cry. He would not.

CHAPTER

2

◘

*E*very morning that Stephen woke up in the unfamiliar
narrow bed in the novices' dormitory, he went through
the same aching sequence of recollection and loss. First he
was momentarily confused by the clean coarse sheets
under him and the sight of high groined vaults overhead,
so different from the cozy darkness of the fishing hut.
Then he remembered where he was and scrambled out of
bed in the hope that today would be the day when Mam
came back for him.

Before his feet touched the stone-flagged floor, the rest
of memory returned in a rush too painful to be borne at
first waking. She wasn't coming back. She had left him
here. He must have done something terribly bad for her to
leave him this way; and she hadn't even given him a
chance to ask what it was, to tell her he was sorry and he'd
never do it again.

If he cried once he would not be able to stop. The other
novices and scholars would scorn him, but that wasn't what
he feared most; it was that he would dissolve into his own
tears, leaving nothing but the aching, hollow, black grief
inside him. In defense against that terrible pain of Mam's
disappearance, against this hard, cold unloving place where
he was shoved into line and hushed into silence and
flogged for putting a foot out of place, he was beginning to

make himself anew. He would be as strong as the stones that raised the great cathedral and as silent and unmoved as the stone. He would raise walls of stone all around his grief so that nobody would ever guess that he was really a bad, worthless little boy whose mother couldn't be bothered to keep him.

In those first lonely days, the rigid routine of the convent was like a second set of stone walls, constricting his movements until he sometimes felt he could not breathe. The "day" began a little after two in the morning, when the monks and novices arose and marched to choir in their night shoes to pray and recite the fifteen psalms of the night. After the psalms, they sang the service of Matins, Lauds of All Saints, and the prayers for the dead. Then they waited in chilly silence for dawn, the signal for Prime.

From Prime to eight o'clock, they read in the cloister; then they returned to the dormitory in two long lines. They washed, put on their day shoes, and went to the chapter for Terce, which lasted until nearly nine o'clock.

The day crept forward in a rhythm of long chanted prayers: Sext at noon, Vespers at five, Compline at six, and back to the dormitory at seven. In between were short breaks for the monks' simple meals and longer breaks for periods of manual labor as prescribed in the Rule of St. Benedict. Gone were the free hours that Stephen used to spend wandering by the seaside, dreaming, watching the fishermen, building little cairns of pebbles, and begging Mam for stories.

Mam was gone. And the sea, too, was very far away. There was nothing familiar in this strange cold world, nothing to which he could cling except the walls he built up around himself.

Sometimes his walls of stone worked; sometimes they crumbled under assault, and he had to start building them up again. On the first morning, before he had time to recover from the first dazzling rush of memory and sorrow and loss, his thin new walls went down temporarily under the jabbing questions of one of his new fellows.

Among the dozen novices with whom he slept and prayed and took his meals, there were two older boys being schooled by the monks, neither of whom were destined to join the convent permanently. Joscelin was a brilliant scholar whose aunt wanted him trained for one of the universities, and Drogo had been sent to the convent to get him out of his family's way.

Stephen met Drogo first. He was a fat boy of eleven who introduced himself by asking Stephen if it were true his mother had been a Bliburgh whore who dumped her unwanted child on the church? Why had the brothers consented to take him when he couldn't pay for his schooling or bring a dowry to the convent? Was he a charity boy? Or—this with a knowing leer—was one of the monks his dad?

"My Da's dead."

"Ha. I'll wager your father was three sailors from Southwark."

Stephen didn't understand the insult, but he knew that it was one, and he had the satisfaction of driving his fist into Drogo's squashy nose before the other boy saw that he was under attack. After that first blow, it was a one-sided fight, consisting mostly of Drogo sitting on Stephen and hammering his head against the paving stones until someone dragged him off. Stephen heard a shrill argument going on. "Let the poor little bastard alone, can't you, Drogo?"

"He hit me first," Drogo muttered. One hand covered a rapidly swelling nose that had already drenched the front of his tunic with dark-red blood. Above him stood a dark, self-assured boy who looked to be even older than Drogo.

"Well then, he's plucky for such a little one. Come on now, the bell for chapter's end is about to sound and we'll all get a flogging if we're not in our desks. And do something about that nose, I won't have you bleeding on our book. You come with us, young Stephen. I'm Joscelin of Cressy, so if it's true your Mam was from Bliburgh, we're neighbors of a sort. My aunt's Lady Margery. She owns Bliburgh."

Somewhat dazed by the fight and by this invitation to join the young lordlings, Stephen stumbled after the other boys with his head still ringing from the pavement. Stone, he told himself. I am stone, I am as hard as the pavement, so nothing can hurt me. By the time they reached the refectory, he almost believed it.

That encounter set the tone between the three of them for the years that followed. Joscelin led the way, lordly and self-assured by virtue of his age, his scholar's brain, and the riches of a quarterly allowance paid over to him personally by Lady Margery's steward. Drogo didn't insult Stephen directly again, but for some years he took pleasure in provoking Stephen into fighting. By the time Stephen was eleven, and big for his age, he did not always lose the fights—not immediately, anyway—and Drogo's interest in the subject of Stephen's mother seemed to fade.

By that time, Stephen had almost stopped looking up hopefully whenever the porter's bell rang to announce an outside visitor. In all these years he had not heard from Mam, and the prior claimed he did not know where she had gone from Ely. He ought to be grateful to the monks of Ely for taking him when nobody else wanted him—this was another favorite theme of Drogo's—and to God, who also wanted him. According to Brother Coluin, the aging monk who heard the boys' reading and taught them grammar out of Donatus, God loved everybody, but boys like Stephen who had vowed their lives to God were specially dear to Him. And wasn't God's love, which was eternal and unbounded, far better than the earthly, limited love of mother or father? Stephen must work hard at his books and look forward to the day when he would take holy orders and join the community of the monks forever. Had he memorized the third page of Donatus yet?

Brother Daniel was less calm than Coluin and seemed to expect far more of Stephen. He had no direct hand in the novices' training, but Stephen felt he was always there, watching lessons, swooping from around a corner to interrupt a game of jackstraws with reminders that it was time for some dreary prayer, wasting Stephen's few precious minutes of recreation time with a pointless lecture on the need to give himself fully to God or, worse, giving Stephen an examination on something he was learning.

"How many parts of speech are there?" Brother Daniel would demand, breaking up the first decent game of catch-me-who-can Stephen had had in weeks.

At least he knew that much from studying the manual of Donatus, who in the fourth century had written down the minimum of grammar that a boy must know before advancing to more interesting studies. "Eight."

"What are they?"

Out of the corner of his eye, Stephen saw Joscelin and

Drogo sidling away to continue their game somewhere else. Perhaps if he answered quickly enough, he could get back in time to join them. "Noun pronoun verb adverb participle conjunction . . ." he gabbled in one breath. Only six! If Brother Daniel would just give him a minute to think . . .

"Preposition, interjection. You haven't been studying hard enough. I will give you extra tuition. You must know Donatus by heart before you advance to the next stage."

There was no hope, now, of getting back into the game before the bell rang for prayers. "Don't much care if I *never* advance to the next class," Stephen muttered in English. Brother Daniel's hard, flat hand came down with a painful smack against the side of Stephen's head. Stars danced in front of his eyes, and water filled them, but he did not cry.

"Never say that again! You must be the best scholar, the best monk, the greatest man in this convent! I will not allow you to waste your brains like this!" He took Stephen's ear in a pincer grip and towed him into the narrow cell where the accounts were kept. "Now. We have a few minutes before Sext. Let us continue the study of Donatus. What is a noun?"

"A part of . . ." Having to do all this in French was another stumbling block to Stephen's tongue. He'd never spoken anything but English before he came to Ely. But the other novices came of the upper classes and spoke Norman French, the language of the conquerors who'd taken England a hundred and fifty years earlier. All the classes of the *trivium*—grammar, rhetoric, and dialectic— were conducted in French. Worse yet, the higher classes of the *quadrivium*—arithmetic, geometry, music, and astronomy—were taught in Latin, the international language of all churchmen and scholars. Stephen knew the Latin prayers and songs required in the monastery by rote, stumbled despairingly through his grammar lessons, and devoutly hoped he never advanced as far as the *quadrivium*. He would happily leave its mysteries to true scholars like Joscelin.

"A part of speech with a case, properly or commonly signifying a body or a thing," Daniel snapped impatiently. "Repeat that! Were you paying attention?"

The bell for Sext was a welcome release.

Day by lonely day, the convent routine of prayers and lessons moved Stephen through childhood, until Mam was a faraway memory and the sea echoed only in his dreams. The dull, lonely years of study and singing were occasionally enlivened by rumors from the outside world that reached the convent like light filtering through a thick, dirty pane, dim and distorted. One October, just before the fair of St. Audrey (or St. Etheldreda, as the monks correctly but unpronounceably named her), the moon turned bloodred in the autumn sky and then disappeared entirely. That winter, there was a shower of blood seen in Normandy; a monk who had been studying at Caen told them about it. Some said these portents foretold the death of King John, now excommunicated for his obduracy in the matter of the archbishop of Canterbury. Others said they meant disaster for the children in France who had been seized with a mad desire to go on a crusade like their parents. They might have been right, for none of those children who marched singing to Marseilles was ever heard from again.

While the English barons warred and the French children marched for Jerusalem, Stephen memorized Donatus and moved on to the more complicated textbook of Alexander de Villa Dei, who wrote in excruciatingly boring Latin hexameters. He advanced through the four minor orders of ostiarius, lector, exorcist, and acolyte, and he learned to assist the priests, who each had to say a daily private mass. Brother Coluin explained to him how lucky he was to be able to hear mass at all, when the common folk who lived outside the cathedral grounds had been deprived of the consolations of religion since the ninth year of King John's reign.

There was talk of a French invasion. Joscelin went to stay with his aunt at Cressy for some weeks, and came back to report that the merchants of Dunwich were grumbling over being taxed and, worse, being forced to provide ships for the King's fleet.

Stephen learned by heart the twenty-six hundred hexameters of Alexander's *Doctrinale* and began studying dictamen, the art of letter writing, and verse making. He began composing a short hymn to the Virgin, praising her selfless love for the Son whom she gave up to God, but after a few lines he grew depressed and put the work away. Letter writing was a more practical skill anyway.

Brother Daniel was advanced from cellarer to treasurer, with responsibility for the finances of the entire convent. On the occasion of his promotion, he dropped in on Coluin's lessons, as he frequently did, and pointed out to Stephen how a worthy and clever man could do well for himself in the service of the Church. Coluin said it was kind of Brother Daniel to keep an interest in the child oblate whom he had accepted in the convent's name, but could the boys please finish their recitations now?

The threatened invasion never happened; in the year when Stephen turned thirteen, before the French could land, the King's messengers came back from the Pope with word that the King's submission had been accepted. The interdict was over, the excommunication raised. The monks of Ely were jubilant, not only for the reconciliation with Rome, but also because the cathedral and monastery would be rich again. Part of the King's agreement had included heavy payments to Ely and other religious houses, in recompense for the unlawful fines and taxes he'd levied during the years of separation from Rome.

What would the new move mean to England and to the barons who'd been seeking to take away the King's rights? That was hard to say, and in the meantime the monks of Ely had more pressing considerations. They had to dig up all the monks who had died in the last six years and rebury them in consecrated ground, with the appropriate prayers. Stephen assisted at seven funeral masses in one day.

One of the monks, who had been carelessly buried, lost some of his finger-bones on the way to the new grave; Stephen had to collect them and drop them in on top of the shroud. The bones were light, and they rattled in his hand like seeds in a drying pod. They had no odor of mortality about them. He hid one in his sleeve and dropped it down Drogo's back during lessons, for which he was flogged and made to do penance on his knees in the refectory for a week. But it was worth it.

Bishop Eustace came back from France, where he'd been in exile during the interdict. He had been one of three bishops to sign the decree of interdict, and although the King had not forgiven him, he would not dare to move against him now. Eustace was an old man; there was talk that the years of exile had been too hard on him. "He won't last long," Brother Daniel once said in Stephen's hearing. "And the prior's old, too. You mark my words, before next summer there'll be two elections held. It's time some new men took over here. The basis of everything we do here is the treasury, managing the convent's income. It's what gives us the strength to stand up against the King's exactions. We're rich now, but we must manage our new wealth wisely. What if there's another quarrel with Rome? What if the King seizes our property and taxes us as he did before? We need leaders who understand money, who can build wealth from wealth until we have enough gold to stand against any wicked king." He spoke as if gold were a living thing, a loved thing.

Stephen paid little attention to this or to any of the political talk that dipped and swirled about his head like currents of air. That summer, when the interdict was lifted, he had discovered something solid and real and worthwhile, something that made him finally able to love his life at Ely as he'd always been expected to do.

The masons had come back to finish the west porch.

The building work that Stephen had seen on the day of his arrival had been the last that was done on the porch for some time. In the years of the interdict, the cathedral had been pinched for money, with no masses to stir up the hearts and purses of the faithful, with the King's exactions on their lands cutting into the rents, with Bishop Eustace himself to be maintained in France. There'd been nothing in the building fund; the masons had moved on to other projects.

The summer the first installments of King John's gold arrived, the masons came back to put up the last wooden centering frames under the vaults that were to roof the galilee porch. It was fine, tricky, painstaking work, cutting the wedge-shaped voussoirs to follow the arching lines of the vault ribs and filling the space between ribs with a web of rubble and concrete. Stephen did not see how something so thin could stay up once the wooden frames were removed, and he was fascinated by the process.

Hubert, one of the oldest masons, who couldn't climb up on the scaffolding with the vault-setters, tried to explain it to Stephen. "'Tis like an eggshell, lad. Think of the strength of that thin little shell. Because it curves, see?"

Stephen felt that Hubert's explanation lacked some-thing, but when he got permission to climb up the scaf-folding and look at the curved top of the vault, he began to understand. The thin strong lines of the ribs pressed down and outward in perpetual tension that was barely restrained by the buttressed walls. The shell-thin web between the walls pushed all ways at once, and so there was nowhere it could tear.

It was a great summer for Stephen. For weeks after the commencement of the work, masons were drifting in from all corners of England and even from abroad. Sunburnt men with strange accents, some of them unable to speak English, communicated with their strong hands that held their tools and struck the stones of Purbeck marble into the curved shapes of the master builder's wooden tem-plets. Some came without tools of their own, and a scowling Master Brito had to assign them stone axes, chisels, and punches from the common store. Stephen asked him why he was angry—it seemed to him that there were plenty of tools in the lodgeshed that had been unlocked with the resumption of building work.

"Aye, lad, but some belong to the convent and some to me, and all must be accounted for properly and the men who took 'em must pay for any broken stuff or have it taken out of their wages, see? And I'm no scholar." Master Brito scowled at the parchment before him and laboriously drew a crude outline of a scabbling hammer next to a scratched sign that looked like a bent pitchfork. "That's his mark to remind me he's got a scabbling hammer on loan from the convent's store. Now, how many hammers is that I've got out?" Brito ran a finger down the page, stabbing at each little drawing. "Hant, tant, tethery, futhery, fant; sarny, darny, downy, dick; hain-dick, tain-dick, tuthery-dick— No, that's not a hammer, it's a claw chisel. St. Bartholomew's bones on a dungheap! Now I'll have to start over. Hant, tant, tethery..."

"What are you doing? Why don't you just count them?"

"I *am* counting. Don't know your Latin names and numbers, do I? My old dad was a shepherd and he taught me to count the way he counted the sheep into the fold. Now don't interrupt. Hant, tant..."

"I can write. And I know arithmetic." Stephen dropped back a little and lowered his eyes. Something warned him not to sound too eager. One thing he had learned in his years at the convent was to approach what he wanted in an oblique fashion. If you made it too obvious that you wanted something, somebody—usually Brother Daniel— was likely to make it his business to stop you with some prating about your soul's good. But Stephen had never wanted anything the way he longed to be here with Master Brito and the masons, learning to build in stone as he'd built the walls in his head. Keeping the desire out of his voice was harder than keeping silent during a flogging. "I could keep all those records for you and reckon up the men's wages, too."

"Can't pay a clerk."

"Oh, I couldn't work for *pay*. The convent would never allow that." Don't beg, Stephen told himself fiercely. *Don't beg*. He'd begged Mam to stay, not to leave him here, but she went away anyway. People don't care what I want, they only care about making things comfortable for themselves. I have to make Brito think how nice it would be for him to have me here, then maybe he'll help me. "It would be good practice for me, that's all. Too bad I have to spend the afternoons studying verse with Brother Coluin. I could do your accounts every day after dinner. . . ." Stephen shrugged. "No, there's just not enough time in the day. Too bad."

He drifted away then, leaving Master Brito staring at his own ink-stained sleeves, and waited to see if anything would happen.

"What's the matter with you?" Joscelin asked. "You've been staring at that wall all day."

"I think I've found something I want as much as you want to get learning."

"How nice for you. Are you going to get it?"

"I don't know. It depends on other people." How he hated that. Stephen had never consciously thought it before, but one of the things he hated worst was always having to wait on somebody else's good will, following somebody else's rules, trying to hold onto a little bit of himself in the chinks between rules and hours of prayer and the convent's constant insistence on God's will.

"Wouldn't hurt to make an offering to Our Lady about it," advised Joscelin.

But that would be like begging, wouldn't it? No. He

would just wait, and maybe he could nudge Brother
Coluin in the right direction while he was waiting. That
much he could do for himself. And if he could get assigned
to work with Master Brito, he would learn and remember
everything and he would have it all to think about in the
long cold winters. That would be another little piece of
himself to wall-away from the convent's rules and Brother
Daniel's pale eyes.

At the afternoon lessons he casually mentioned that the
convent was always in need of monks who could help the
obedientiaries keep accounts, and it did seem a pity that
he couldn't get more practice in such work along with the
traditional studies of verse and letter writing and grammar. "I know what you're up to." Coluin looked stern.
"You made three grievous errors of quantity in your last
exercise. Maybe you need to write out Alexander's *Doctrinale*
from memory instead of playing about with the masons.
We could use a fresh copy of the *Doctrinale*."

"That would take all summer!" Stephen was horrified for
a moment; then he realized that Coluin was trying not to
laugh.

"Master Brito already spoke to me about you. It seems a
reasonable plan. Better than hiring a clerk for him—it's
clear the man's no scholar, not like the builder who
originally designed the porch for us."

"Why isn't he here to finish it?" Stephen asked, momentarily sidetracked. It had not occurred to him before that
some man's mind was responsible for the dark shimmering
beauty of the porch, that the columns and arches he
admired had been raised in someone's head before they
were carved in stone. How wonderful it would be to meet
the man who'd conceived this perfection!

"He's dead. The work was started fifteen years ago,
before you were born, and the man who did it was old
then. Anyway, about Brito..."

Coluin paused, and Stephen thought he could hear his
own heart thumping with eagerness in the long silence.
"Yes, he'll need help, and Brother Daniel is already worried that the sacristan will overspend our building fund.
And it will spare me listening to your atrocious quantities
for a while. You've permission to spend the afternoons
working for Brito."

Day by day the painstaking, slow work of erecting the

porch went on, and Stephen was there to watch and glory in it all. Partially dressed stones from Barnack quarries and dark marble from Purbeck came in flatboats, one stone to a boat, to be swung ashore at the quays by cursing day laborers while the machinery that deposited the stones in carts strained and creaked. The plain stones for the courses were dressed at the quarry, but the shaped corbels and capitals had to be done in the lodge, following the lines of the wooden templets cut by the master of works. Only the most skilled masons were entrusted with them. Once a dark journeyman from Italy, who had much to say about the superiority of Continental craftsmen over these stolid English, applied his skill to a half-cut corbel during the masons' dinner break. He cut a longer and smoother curve than the templet called for, and when Master Brito came back from dinner, Stephen's vocabulary was enlarged by a number of new and interesting words in both Italian and English.

The summer did not end for Stephen until mid-October. Three days before St. Audrey's fair there was a light frost on the grass at dawn, and on the morning of the fair the water in the mortar tubs was glittering with frost crystals. Master Brito decreed that it was time to stop work for the winter. Frost would interfere with the setting of the mortar and might crack the newly quarried stones that still held earth's moisture. Besides, the vaults were up.

The masons scattered like birds flying south, each man gathering his tools or returning borrowed ones. Stephen skipped the singing of Vespers at five o'clock to finish recording the returned tools, the fines for breakages, and the final wages for each man. He didn't quite realize how completely the work had come to an end until he looked up in the gathering dusk, the last line of accounts transcribed in a fine, neat, clerical hand, and saw that he was alone with Master Brito in the open lodge. Over the master builder's shoulder, the west porch glimmered, blue with shadows, and shining from foundation piers to springing arches. The tops of the vaults were now covered with a temporary thatch of sedge and old rushes against the winter's frost. Master Brito drew a deep breath of satisfaction and wheeled to take the rolls from Stephen.

"That's it, lad. Work well done. A pity you're set on

being a monk—I could use a lad like you in my winter business, down Dunwich way. Got a little yard and a covered shed where the men can work inside all winter, carving stone angels and what-not for country churches. And keeping the accounts, on piecework like that—" Brito sighed again and ruffled the long hair around Stephen's tonsure. "Well, never mind. This convent of yours raises good clerks. If you ever have a schoolmate who wants work, tell him to look me up. There's the wagon to carry my tools. I'd best be on my way. God keep you. We'll see you again in the spring, God willing."

Then he was gone, but before Stephen had time to feel the emptiness of the abandoned lodge, Brother Coluin came trotting out of the cloister, thin shoulders stooped beneath his black habit and long sharp nose dripping a little in the frosty evening air.

"Master Brito spoke well of you," he told Stephen. "It's a feast day, did you forget? We're to have a pittance of apple pancakes in the refectory, before Compline. Come along now." And then, as Stephen tried to uncramp his legs from the rungs of the high stool where he'd sat all afternoon, "Well, don't just sit there looking as if you'd lost a penny and found a salt herring, boy! The masons make pretty things, but it's only earthly work they do. You and I, we're about God's work, which will last forever."

Coluin's well-meant words of comfort stayed with Stephen during the long singing of Compline and psalms that evening. He recited the words, but his mind was with the masons tramping home in twos and threes to farms or shops or winter businesses. The black-browed Italian, the one Master Brito had sworn at, said he meant to go to the Saracen lands beyond Jerusalem, where a man could work all year long without fear of frost if he didn't mind working for the heathen kings.

Coluin said this chanting in choir was God's work, and would last forever. The music was almost as beautiful, in its own way, as the cathedral itself; both had the same ordered rhythms, the same feeling of reaching for something too high for men to grasp. When the Office was finished, the monks stopped singing, and the high pure notes faded away. But the choir was still there, its pillars carved at the top in shapes of beasts or demons with the long nave stretching away into darkness, and the new porch casting shadows beyond the western door.

After St. Audrey's fair the convent went on the winter schedule. They rose later and went to bed earlier and the hours of study and singing filled the day completely. During the first days back in the dull routine, Stephen dreamed of running away from the convent to find Master Brito's shop where the journeymen and apprentices carved stone angels all winter long. These dreams ended badly, with black shadowlike robes swooping over him and enveloping him in their darkness, drawing him back to the convent where he belonged. Or he dreamt he was wandering in an icy wilderness, starving and unable to find the warm safety of the shop.

Drogo complained that Stephen was keeping him awake at night with his tossing and mumbling. "What are you dreaming about anyway? Girls?"

Stephen shrugged. "It doesn't matter. Nothing." He hunched one shoulder against the expected jeers and pretended to study his book. In the pale, cold daylight he knew that he would not leave the convent. He could not. Unlike the other novices who came to study and make their vows, or, if they found they lacked a vocation, return to their former lives, Stephen didn't have a life in the outside world. Nobody wanted him, not even Master Brito—he was just being kind, trying to ease the pain of parting. And his vows were already made. It didn't matter whether or not he had a vocation; he belonged to the convent.

But how would anybody find him if he ran away? That is, if anybody did want to find him. Stephen found that his hands were trembling. He laid his fingers flat on either side of the book and stared at the black letters before him until they danced in front of his eyes like swarming bees.

In November, the bishop made a hasty journey to Bury St. Edmunds. He came back shaking with indignation and fear. The gossip in the convent was that King John had affronted the monks of St. Edmunds, lecturing them in their own chapter house about his right to control their choice of an abbot. After the King's departure, there had been a meeting of the great men of the land, and treasonous talk about forcing the King to confirm the liberties they demanded.

Of more moment to Stephen was the fact that the bishop took Drogo with him, and left him at St. Edmunds to go home with his older brother. He was to serve as his brother's seneschal, to keep account of the estates. A pity, said Coluin, that Drogo didn't have something of Stephen's gift with numbers.

After Drogo left, Stephen's life was more peaceful. His dreams at night might have disturbed Joscelin as well as Drogo, but Joscelin never complained. He was perfectly happy to soar into the higher realms of logic and disputation with Brother Coluin while Stephen plodded behind, copying out an example of a letter from a poor student asking his father for supplies, and aching as much with boredom as with cold.

"You should have been the monk instead of me," Stephen said after Joscelin and Coluin had missed dinner without even noticing, so caught up were they in disputing whether an imaginary white horse or a real gray one had more of the quality of whiteness.

"I'm going to be a great lawyer. Or a great churchman. Or maybe both. The Pope studied law at Bologna in his youth, did you know that? Maybe I'll go to Bologna." Joscelin chinned himself on the tracery of an arched window in the cloister, pulled himself up, and sat on top of the carved cupboard where the monks kept their books.

"How much learning do you want?"

"As much as I can get." Joscelin drummed his heels on the cupboard doors and amended his statement. "As much as Aunt Margery will pay for. . . . I'm to study with a master of dialectic at Cambridge next year, did you know? Brother Coluin says I have as much learning as he can give me. And you're to study accounting with our pinchpurse treasurer. They think you have a gift for it. You certainly haven't a gift for verse! Brother Coluin says he doesn't know how anybody as quick to learn languages as you can have such a tin ear for their rhythms. Maybe you'll like numbers better. Will you like learning from Sour Daniel, Stephen?"

"I'll miss you." He didn't want to think about the rest of it. It wasn't the treasurer's fault that he had been the monk to whom Mam handed him over like an unwanted parcel. But Stephen could never look at Daniel's long face and pale eyes without feeling a chill of desolation around him. "Maybe he'll be too busy soon," he said, more cheerfully. "He's expecting to be elected to replace Bishop Eustace. Everybody says the old man can't last much longer."

The bishop died in February, but Daniel the treasurer was not elected in his place. The monks chose a man from outside the convent, Robert of York, who was openly for Louis of France and the rebel barons. Not surprisingly, the King refused his assent to the election, and Ely remained without a consecrated bishop for a time. Robert of York, like Eustace before him, found it wise to retreat to France, and Brother Daniel took over much of the management of the bishop's affairs anyway.

In the same month, old prior Hugh died, of the same cold winter cough; Roger de Bergham was elected prior in his place. It was rumored that immediately after his election he had sent for the treasurer and assured him that he would always have an honored place at Ely; men of affairs were needed in the convent's business life, Roger had explained kindly, but for spiritual leadership a different sort of man was necessary.

The gossip was probably true: Daniel the treasurer had a temper like a nestful of spitting snakes after the double election, and Stephen carried the marks of that temper on his shoulders after most of his lessons. He didn't mind the floggings as much as Daniel's cold insistence on perfection, not only in matters of sums and accounts but also in every detail of Stephen's life—from his intonation of the daily prayers to the way he walked when he entered the refectory.

"It's not enough to do well. You have to do brilliantly. You could have a great career ahead of you, Stephen, if you'd only apply yourself. You're not going to make the mistakes I made."

Daniel didn't specify what those mistakes had been, but he was explicit and unremitting in pointing out Stephen's errors, and the resulting tongue-lashings were usually underlined by the rod he kept in a corner beside his writing desk.

"Now then. What are the four sources of the convent's income?"

"Temporalities, spiritualities, trade, and gifts."

"What is the difference between temporalities and spiritualities?"

"Temporalities are income from our landed estates, such as rents, tolls on traffic passing over the estates, mill rights, fishing rights . . ."

"And spiritualities?"

"Income from the parish churches that we own."

"What are the convent's holdings in Stuntney?"

"Oh, *God*," Stephen muttered under his breath. Did Brother Daniel really expect him to know by heart every cottar, villein, pig, and stick of eels owned by or owed to the convent? On top of his Latin grammar and rhetoric?

Brother Daniel did.

"You had those rolls to study during your recreation time all last week." The rod was in his hand, cracking down across Stephen's shoulders with a sharp sting on each sentence; one blow was nothing, but they built up until Stephen could hardly hear the treasurer's voice for the buzzing pain in his flesh.

"Stuntney has land for three plough teams." Crack! "It maintains six villeins—five cottars—and three serfs. It renders—twenty-four sticks of eels—and eighteen shillingsworth of fish—yearly."

Brother Daniel lowered the rod and nodded something like approval at Stephen's defiant face. "You didn't cry. You have strength. When you have learned to apply that strength to God's will, the Church will have a worthy servant. Tomorrow you will know the renders of Stuntney, Chettisham, Alleford, and Little Alleford, as well as the stock grazed by the convent on each of their meadows."

"*He* isn't perfect," Stephen grumbled later to Brother Coluin. The novicemaster had found him inspecting his latest stripes and, without comment, brought a bowl of salve to rub into the bleeding weals. "Why do I have to be?"

"We are all commanded to be perfect in Jesus Christ. You should be grateful that someone cares so much for you, Stephen." Coluin's voice was mild, but he rubbed the salve in too hard and Stephen had to grasp the edge of his stool with both hands to keep from wincing.

When Stephen went to the cloister for afternoon studies, two lay brothers were busy removing the wooden shutters that kept out drafts and light during the winter. The square walkway with its border of carrels lay open to the interior court. A chilly breeze whistled through the colonnade, turned up the hem of Stephen's robe, and numbed his fingers so that he could barely write. But there were tentative shoots of green in the courtyard, and there was a smell of growing things and fresh-turned earth in the cold wind. Spring was almost here. The masons would be coming back to finish the porch. How he looked forward to that.

CHAPTER

3

◻

When the masons did come back, it was only for a few days. The toolshed adjoining the lodge remained locked, the benches where they carved stone were left inside, and Daniel brusquely refused Stephen's request to help Master Brito with the accounts as he'd done last summer.

"There's not that much work to be done, lad," Brito explained when Stephen stole a moment to visit the porch. "Almost through, we are. Just got to take down the centering and see if the mortar on these vaults set all right in the winter."

The removal of the wooden centering that supported the arches during construction, Brito explained, was always an anxious moment. If the lime mortar hadn't dried out thoroughly, if the builder had miscalculated the stresses on the arch, the whole vault could collapse. Stephen counted it well worth the probable cost of a beating to skip his accounting lessons to watch these final steps.

As the wooden forms came down, each carefully disassembled by men hammering out the wedges that held it in shape, the porch was revealed as the master builder's mind had conceived it more than fifteen years earlier. The true work of building was finished: the great entrance arch and the two smaller arches within its graceful curve, the vaulted bays and the blind arcades on either side, the tall supporting shafts that rose to meet the vaulting of the arcades. All stood straight and true.

Brito said that the next few months would be the true test of the design. A poorly shaped arch, or one that took too much strain from the outward thrust of the weight it supported, would begin to show hairline fractures along the mortar, and would eventually crumble. But the design wasn't Master Brito's problem; it had been sketched by an architect on loan from the King's works, and the preliminary work had been overseen by that same man. Brito wasn't a learned man who could make his own designs, just a competent contractor with a good team who could be called in to finish another man's plan. Now that his part in the work was done, he had to move on to other projects.

Fortunately, there was work awaiting him. The lord Stephen Ridel, whom he had met at Bury St. Edmunds when combining against the King, had vowed to raise a church for St. Jude if he and his friends succeeded in getting their charter of liberties from King John. That very month, in Staines Meadow, the King had signed the charter; and the new prior of Ely had suggested that Alleford, one of the poor marsh villages that paid a rent of eels to the convent, could benefit from a new church. The revenues from the church could be evenly divided between Ridel and the convent, thus pleasing everybody and fulfilling Ridel's sacred vow.

"It's not far, lad," Master Brito told Stephen. "Maybe you'll come and see how we're getting on, if you ever get a holiday."

Between grammar with Coluin, accounts with Daniel, and the everlasting round of prayers and masses, Stephen didn't see how he would get so much as a free hour, let alone a whole half-day to visit Alleford.

A few of the masons went with Master Brito, but there would hardly be work at a little place like Alleford for all the craftsmen who had been at Ely last summer. Most had not even come back this year, knowing that the work was near completion. The skilled stone-carvers, whose talents would not be needed for a simple village church, stayed to turn the rough surfaces of the porch's piers and arches into a wilderness of twining vines. While two men covered the capitals on either side of the entrance with flowers and leaves and grotesque figures, a third carved elaborate tracery between the pointed tops of the double arches and the peak of the single enclosing arch. Their slow painstaking work with the small chisels had its own beauty and dignity, but it did not satisfy Stephen as much as the actual building of the porch had. The sculptors' lines were whimsical curves, dictated by nothing more than a man's vision on a given morning. They didn't have the true, irrefutable force of the arches and shafts, held in place by the weight of stone pressing down and out and forced back by the will of the builder.

The summer Stephen had awaited so eagerly crept by in a leaden succession of hot blue days. Coluin might have permitted him an occasional day's freedom, but Daniel had no such laxity in him.

"The masons are a distraction. You have better things to do with your time. You have a brain, Stephen, and God doesn't want you to waste it. Do you know how much power a man of learning can command in the Church? Look at Bury St. Edmunds. The old abbot didn't understand money, and by the time he died, the convent was so deep in debt there were moneylenders wandering around the church during mass and pricing the sacred vessels. It's taken Abbot Samson fifteen years to set matters straight. If I weren't watching over our accounts at Ely, we could be in the same situation. Someday they'll appreciate what I've done for them. And you can do better than I, because you're not going to waste any time. Your time belongs to God! Think on that and don't waste your immortal soul yearning after stones and dust!"

Then it was ten more pages of the custumal of the abbey, with tolls, mill rights, and fishing rights to be learned by heart, and a flogging if his mind wandered. Afterwards, there was singing in the choir, praying for the dead, filing into the refectory, reading during the meal, and then more lessons. Stephen had managed the mind-numbing routine all winter in the expectation of spring. Now what was there to look forward to?

July passed, and there were rumors that the King was sulking after his defeat in Staines Meadow. Robert of York, the unconsecrated exiled bishop who waited in France, sent word to expect him soon; young Louis of France had plans to invade and take the English crown for himself, and Robert would come in his train as one of his valued supporters.

"We'll see," said the monks without great excitement. There'd been talk of invasions before, but war never touched the sheltered isle of Ely, protected by its surrounding marshes. Rumors of war were no excuse for neglecting the daily round of prayer and study. Stephen began studying the duties of a subdeacon. That was the lowest of the major orders and the first irrevocable one; when he became a subdeacon, he would be vowed to chastity and to the Church forever. He made slow going of the lessons.

"You're already vowed," Joscelin pointed out. "As an oblate, you can't ever leave. What difference does one more set of vows make?"

Stephen shook his head. "The only vows I've taken of my own will were for minor orders, and everybody takes those. That doesn't bind me to staying in the convent."

"The oblation ceremony does."

"I didn't know what that was!"

"That doesn't make a difference in canon law."

In August, King John ordered the merchants of the Cinque Ports and those of Dunwich and Yarmouth to provide him with ships, and he raised another tax to hire mercenaries from the Low Countries. Ely was taxed twice, once for being a rich foundation and once for having elected a rebellious bishop. It was said even this money wasn't enough for the King; he had gone to the moneylenders also.

Robert of York, the elected bishop of Ely, did not come from France that August; nor did the French army under Louis. In the time of waiting, Brother Daniel was sent to London to persuade the King that Ely simply could not find the sums of money he demanded in taxes. On the day after Brother Daniel left, Stephen woke to the dazzling realization that his morning was free and that no one would be expecting to see him before the noon meal.

Master Brito might have considered Alleford close to the cathedral city, but to Stephen it seemed an incredibly long way. First he walked, then he ran with one eye cocked on the progress of the sun. As the land gently sloped down to water level he lost himself in a maze of winding paths where the clumps of alder and buckthorn and the tall green reeds grew over his head, and the black peaty soil squished under his bare feet. By the time he reached a patch of slightly higher ground where he could see over the tall reeds, his chest burned with hard-drawn breaths and his legs ached with the unaccustomed exercise. He'd passed the village in his haste; it was behind him, a clump of low wattle-and-daub houses with a cleared space at the edge where the new church was going up. He would have to retrace his steps. Time wasted—and the sun was already high!

The church was a poor, mean building compared to the Galilee porch, just a rectangle of thin masonry walls filled with rubble. But a graceful pointed arch that had already been set in the west wall showed that Master Brito had learned something from his work on the cathedral's west porch. But where were the masons? Stephen skidded to a halt and looked around him in bewilderment. To one side of the church stood a ramshackle shelter, no more than a thatched roof on four poles, and under the shade of the roof he saw the benches and bankers where the masons set their stones for fine carving. Yet there were no tools hanging on the walls, no men in leather aprons chiseling the stones and coughing with the fine white dust they raised, drinking ale to lay the dust, and quarreling cheerfully with their fellows about the best way to cleave the face of a quarry stone or to lay out a perfectly square courtyard.

One old man sat in the far end of the lodge, polishing his tools with a scrap of soft leather and humming tunelessly to himself. Stephen recognized him from the crew that had worked on the Galilee porch.

"Hubert. Hubert of Walsingham?" he called softly, over the raw burning in his lungs. "Where is everybody, Hubert?"

"Downed tools and went fishing. There's talk of an impressment."

"A what?"

Hubert of Walsingham put down his scrap of polishing leather and beckoned to Stephen with a gnarled finger. "Don't know much about this business, do you, lad? An impressment is when the King decides he wants a bit of work done—or one of his friends wants a bit done—so they send out the sheriff of the county with a writ to take skilled men and send 'em to work wherever the King wants. Or in our case, here on the Isle, the bishop's officer holds the writ instead of the sheriff."

"Oh!" Stephen knew that theoretically the bishop of Ely

was as powerful as any landed magnate. He had not thought about what happened when the bishop's rights conflicted with the King's over some small matter. He knew what happened, of course, when it was a great matter; the bishop went to France. "What if the bishop and the sheriff both want to impress men for different tasks?"

"Depends where they are, I guess, and who's got the most soldiers. They'd probably argue it all the way to the King's court—but meanwhile the work would be done. It's better to work for the King, generally—the pay's not bad. But the King's purse-pinched these days, and they say all his gold is going to pay those foreign mercenaries he's hired to keep the barons down. They want us to work a castle up north for nothing. Out of love for the King." Hubert spat into the dust at his feet. "So the gentlemen of the lodge are taking a few unofficial holidays."

Stephen nodded slowly, swallowing his disappointment. "When will they be back?"

"Few days. Whenever they stop looking for men. Word gets around."

"What about you?"

"Me?" Hubert cackled as if Stephen had said something highly amusing, coughed in the middle of his laugh, and slowly wheezed his way back to regular breathing. "Bless you, lad, I'm in no danger of being pressed. Got the dust-sickness in my chest so bad I can't even set a stone, got my hands so knotted with the damp I can't carve a fair straight line. Brito never would say it, but he only keeps me on because I worked for his dad. Charity. King's men don't know charity; they wouldn't have an old shriveled-up soul like me. I'm too old to go off in the fens and get marsh-fever. I'll just sit here in the sun and tell lies to the press-officer when he comes."

Hubert turned the tool in his hands over and over. The pitted surface of the metal gleamed where he had polished it. "There was a time when these hands could coax a fresh-quarried stone to open for me—or a woman, which takes more skill yet. You wouldn't know about that, would you, boy? Maybe you should take this holiday to find yourself a girl, seeing the monks let you loose for once!" He elbowed Stephen and went into another paroxysm of wheezy laughter and coughing.

"I'd rather work on the church."

"A true monk!"

The old man's friendly mockery didn't bother Stephen. A brilliant, consuming thought had seized him. "Do you think the bishop's men will come today? Would they take me? If I stayed here and worked on the church? I know how to do everything, I watched all last summer—"

Hubert shook his head slowly, sadly. "Maybe you know the work in your head, in your eyes. You think that's all? That's how you clerks are—if you can explain a thing in fancy Latin words, you think you know all about it. To be a mason, you have to learn with your hands. Those 'prentices spend seven years cutting and dressing and laying stone. You couldn't even split a quarry stone straight, you with your soft monk's hands."

"I could so!" Stephen felt sure of that. He'd watched it done a thousand times, knew exactly how the mason knelt before the stone, set his chisel at just the right angle, and struck the soft tapping blows that found the hidden stresses and fractures within the rough-hewn block.

"Could you? Well, then, show me. Here's a spoilt block, I was to turn it into rubble for wall-fill while the men were gone; won't hurt if you make it rubble 'stead o' me, I suppose. Take my tools, boy, show me what a monk's learning is good for."

Once in his hands, the chisel felt different, cold and heavy and awkward. When he squinted at the rock and tried to set the blade of the chisel at the right angle, it slipped and left fine slanting scratches on the surface. The head of the hammer seemed impossibly small. How could he hit the top of the chisel with any force? The slightest slip, and the hammer would smash his hand into the rock. He tapped tentatively and the chisel slipped out of place, leaving only a small white scar on the rock.

"Go on, lad! Give it a good blow!"

Hubert was laughing softly behind him. Stephen clenched his teeth and swung the hammer with all the force of his arm. The head glanced off the end of the chisel and bounced off his knuckles; the chisel went flying out of his bruised hand, and a very small chip of rock flew the opposite way and stung him on the cheek.

He wanted to fling the hammer after the chisel, to cry, to kick the rock, and to kill Hubert, who was laughing at his humiliation. Stephen spread his trembling hands on the rough surface of the stone, feeling its warmth from the sun, until the mist before his eyes cleared and he could look quite objectively at the blue-edged bleeding slash across the knuckles of his left hand.

"You're right," he said when he found that he could speak normally again. "I don't know what I'm doing. I suppose I'd best get back to my grammar studies. What else is a monk good for?"

His throat threatened to close up on the last word and he jumped to his feet, head down, and ran back the way he came. It would be the ultimate humiliation if Hubert of Walsingham reported to his fellow masons that the little novice from Ely had cried over a scratch on his hand.

Squinting hard to stop the tears that prickled behind his eyelids, he crashed into the reeds and set off along the path away from the village. He ran until his breath was burning, his blood pumping loud in his ears, his knees trembling, and exhaustion consumed all feelings. The reeds were high about him now, a merciful green and gold curtain shielding him from the scorn of masons and villagers.

He was completely lost. If this had been the same path he took to reach the village, he should have been back on the high ground of the Isle by now, with plowed fields on either side and the cathedral rising before him in the distance. Instead he was beside the water. No, almost in it. There was water on either side of the narrow path, and nothing around him but soggy black soil and more reeds blocking his vision.

It would be humiliating to return to the village, but Stephen knew no other way to go. Perhaps if he walked slowly and watched where he was going this time, he would be able to see the village through the screen of reeds and work around it until he found the way home. Stephen retraced his steps, thinking very hard about the way his bare feet sank into the peaty soil, and the way the light came through the reeds gloriously tinged with green and gold. He thought of anything that would keep him from remembering the ridiculous failure in front of old Hubert.

The path branched at a clump of alder, and branched again a few paces farther on. Each time he kept to the left, the direction in which he thought the village lay. But the sun was getting too high for him to judge directions, and the narrow path turned and curled so many times that he could no longer be sure where he was going. He pushed the reeds aside; they were so close now that they brushed against his arms and closed off the path ahead of him. Grasses poked up through the path, mixing with pale pink marsh orchids and the green leaves of bog pimpernel. When Stephen turned to go back, he saw only the wall of reeds, and a flat sheet of water.

He was very thirsty. He knelt among the marsh orchids, crushing the pale pink flowers and mottled leaves under his bare knees, and cupped his hands to drink. The water was warm from the sun, and it smelled of the greenish algae that bordered the mere, but underlying that was a sweet taste and a hint of colder water below the sun-warmed surface.

The sun danced off the water in thousands of dazzling, broken shards of light and drops that spilled from his hands fell back into the mere like rainbows that were instantly swallowed up. As the surface calmed, Stephen studied his reflection with interest. He had never seen himself before, except in the distorted curved reflection of the polished silver vessels he held when serving at mass. He had yellow hair growing too long over his forehead, light eyes, and a white face. No wonder Hubert had called him a soft-handed little monk, a learner of grammar and a chanter of prayers!

His reflection was framed in green and amber reeds, soft with the trembling water and light with the sun. Then the reflected reeds parted slowly and another face appeared above his own: a brown, triangular face, with large black eyes and a pointed chin. Framed in a halo of green reeds that shimmered in the sun, the face seemed to be floating, bodiless. Stephen couldn't tell whether it was in the water or in the air behind him. He grew very still where he knelt, hardly breathing. The lay brothers and the monastery servants told stories of the flickering fairy lights that could be seen in the fens at night, of the mere-maidens who lay in wait to drag unwary travelers down into the icy, muddy depths. "St. Michael, keep us—" breathed Stephen, the fingers of his right hand flickering over the water in a barely perceptible cross.

"Ey! None o' thy magic!" came the shrill cry in peasant English.

Stephen swung around, still on one knee, and looked up

at a palpably human and very muddy girl no older than himself. She was wearing a ragged tunic, indecently short, whose muddy-brown hue blended perfectly with the water, the reeds, and the brown-stemmed alder shoots. Her bare legs stuck out under the torn hem of the tunic and the neckline slipped off one shoulder, showing that the skin underneath was as brown as her face. She had pushed her way fully through the reeds when he breathed his prayer. Now she was waving a tall spike of greenish flowers at him as if she thought he meant to attack her, and the flowers would hold him off.

Her feet were not webbed, as the mere-maidens' were said to be. The bare toes were quite separate, and quite dirty.

"I wasn't doing magic," Stephen said. "That was a prayer. I'm an acolyte."

"Oh? We had one of those, but me father broke it."

Stephen started at her. Who was this strange creature, and why was she talking gibberish?

The girl giggled at his blank look. "That's a joke. Just means, you've no call to use funny words. I know who you are now. You're a monk, aren't you? Shaven head an' black robes an' all."

Stephen's hand went involuntarily to the smooth tonsure at the top of his head. "I haven't taken orders yet."

"Coo! I take orders all the time, if me Da can get ahold of me. Course, usually I stay out of his way."

Clearly there was no use speaking of adult things to this girl. "Are you going back to your father now?" If she lived in the village, maybe he could just walk along with her, without exactly asking for her help.

"Maybe, maybe not," she teased, waving the stalk of flowers back and forth under Stephen's nose. "You're lost, aren't you?"

"Certainly not. I was just resting."

"Oh, aye? Been resting in circles for the last hour, have you? I been watching you. Pushing through the reeds and puffing enough to drive all the fish into hiding. You don't know much about how to live in the fens."

Or how to carve a block of stone into shape, or anything else that anybody would care about. Stephen clenched his hands at his sides and stood up slowly. "All right. I'm lost.

Will you show me the way back as far as Alleford? I can find my own way from there."

"Maybe, maybe not."

Stephen wheeled and started out at random, pushing the reeds aside with his clenched fists. The ground under his feet sank with each step, sucking at his bare ankles with moist slurping sounds.

"Ey! Stupid monk! Don't go drowning yourself in a temper. You want to go back to the village, I'll take you."

"I haven't lost my temper. But I'm in no mood to play games with a little girl."

"A minute ago you thought I was a mere-maiden," the girl teased. "Maybe I am. Maybe you'd best watch your tongue if you don't want to go down under the waters— deep down in the cold mud, where the soldiers sleep in their mail coats and the eels swim in and out of their ribs." Her voice dropped on each phrase, until she was almost crooning at the last.

"What soldiers?"

"Them as drowned in the days of Hereward the Wake, when he fought the Norman soldiers here. Don't you know anything, little monk? I know where Hereward had his castle, and where the Norman soldiers tried to cross and drowned, and where the witch fired the reeds—bet they don't teach you anything like that in your convent! An' I could show you where they lie, too, all dragged down in their metal coats to sleep under the waters—but you want to go back to the village."

Stephen cast a regretful glance at the sun, now high above his head and beating straight down on them. Even if he ran all the way, he might not make it back to the convent in time to slip in among the returning lay brothers. "I have to."

"Oh, aye. I didn't think a monk would be afraid of dead men's bones."

If he stayed out the whole day, he would certainly get a beating when he returned; perhaps more than one. Stephen shrugged and felt the rough cloth of his tunic rubbing against the welts on his shoulders from his last beating. They were almost healed now. If he didn't get beaten for running away from his lessons, it would be something else—dozing in choir, or whispering to Joscelin during the long hours of silent prayer. "I'm not afraid. Take me to see the dead knights," he ordered. "And stop calling me monk!"

Her name was Aude, and her father was a wild-fowler who lived on the shifting, quivery surface of the fens, in land that didn't officially exist and so belonged to no one. Besides, Aude said, people could not find their hut unless her father, Edric, chose to show them the secret winding ways over the surface of the bog.

Aude had once seen the cathedral city from a distance when she and her father took a basket of eels to the market inside the city gates; but they'd been turned back at the gates for lack of the clay stamp that would give them market rights, and she'd never gone that close to the city again. Stephen was able to recoup a little of his lost dignity by telling her about the wonders of the soaring cathedral, the carved and painted designs, and the glowing jewel-colors of the stained-glass windows. But they were very much in Aude's territory now, and she did not let him forget it for long.

"Step after me. Lightly now! D'you want to startle them?"

A flock of white-winged marsh birds rose from the tussocks ahead of them, whirring and filling the air with a dance of white feathers. Aude blamed Stephen's clumsy, splashing steps for setting the birds off, though he privately thought the sound of her voice might have had something to do with it.

"Here's where they sank. There wasn't a causeway in those days, and the Normans tried to get over to the Isle on a bridge of floating logs. Only they crowded in too close, greedy souls, all wanting to be first to the gold and silver in that church of yours, monk, and the weight of their bodies sunk the bridge and the weight of their armor dragged them down—and here they lie now!" Aude flung out her arm over the mirror-bright surface of the water with a dramatic flourish.

"I don't see anything." Stephen lay on his stomach, chewing on a sweet stem of marsh grass while Aude embellished her story. The reflection of sky and sun and clouds was so bright that Stephen couldn't see below the surface, couldn't guess how deep the channel was or what might lie beneath the brilliant reflections. Nor did he particularly care.

"D'you want to see them? Do you want me to raise one of them, all dripping green slime out of his empty eyesockets, marching over the surface of the water to—get—YOU, Stephen of Ely!" Aude extended her hands, fingers bent like claws, and dropped her voice to a menacing growl. On the last word she pounced at Stephen. He put out his own hands to stop the mock attack. It was like wrestling with Joscelin and Drogo, play-fighting, but he wasn't going to let a little girl see that she'd startled him. He found her thin ribs under the tunic and tickled her until she shrieked and fell over, dragging him with her. They rolled in and out of the muddy water, giggling and tickling each other, until Stephen's weight came down over Aude and held her still for a moment. He braced himself against her, expecting her to throw him off, but she only looked up at him without struggling or laughing.

Not so very much like Joscelin or Drogo, after all. Not at all. Stephen burned with the difference, and his face moved closer and closer without any thought. Her lips were cool and smooth as the water of the mere, but the browned skin of her cheek was warm with the sun. Stephen's head swam and he suddenly felt weak, so weak that he couldn't stop Aude when she pushed him away and sat up.

"Monks don't do that sort of thing."

"I'm not a monk. I haven't taken my final vows yet."

"You will, though. . . . Come on. I'll show you something prettier than your old glass windows!"

Catching his hand and dragging him after her, Aude stepped across shaking tussocks of grass in the water until they came to a reed-enclosed bog where pink and purple marsh orchids were scattered across an expanse of brilliant green moss. Jewel-winged dragonflies, glittering like gold and silver wire, buzzed over the surface of the bog.

"Is that what your cathedral windows look like? All colors, and light shining through?"

"Yes . . . but the windows tell a story. Something out of the Bible, or the life of a saint. Something to edify the people."

"So does this tell a story," said Aude, "but you can't read it, for all your Latin."

"Maybe I could learn."

"Maybe, maybe not." She thrust a spray of pale green flowers into Stephen's face and was off again, leaping from grass to moss to semisolid land while Stephen splashed to keep up with her.

The cottage where Aude and her father lived was scarcely distinguishable, at a distance, from the clumps of dwarf willow and buckthorn that rose at intervals out of the reeds, wherever a small island had established itself in the fen. The cottage was humble, hardly higher than the tallest reeds, irregularly shaped, and covered with twigs. If Stephen hadn't known it was there, he'd never have noticed it; as they drew closer, the bushes of the fen concealed it entirely. Aude insisted that he follow exactly in her footsteps along a twisting path that she took without hesitation. Puddles of water shimmered where she had stepped, and once, when Stephen tried to cut across a black, boggy patch of ground that she had skirted, his feet sank into the damp peaty soil and the mud sucked at his ankles. After that, he followed her steps with so much concentration that he didn't even notice the hut until she stopped and told him to go in. Then Stephen realized that what he'd taken for a tangle of small trees was in fact a heap of branches daubed with clay and roofed with bunches of sedge.

Inside, the walls of the hut sweated with the moisture of the fen, and the fire in the center added to the stifling heat. Aude's father, Edric, a lean, taciturn man dressed in stiff home-cured leathers, acknowledged the visitor with a nod and ladled a portion of dark stew into a third bowl. Stephen looked doubtfully at the unidentifiable contents of the bowl.

"Eat, lad. We've plenty more where that came from. One thing comes in plenty here is eels."

Stephen dutifully dipped a wooden spoon into the bowl and tasted the broth. It was rich and salty, with flavors of fish, of sweet grass like that Aude had given him to chew, and of earthy peat. He emptied the bowl without thinking and sucked the last of the broth off his spoon while Aude chattered to her father about mere-maidens, marsh-lights, and the waterfowl they'd disturbed earlier.

"Come again," Edric offered when Aude's chatter turned to guiding "my little monk" home before a marsh-goblin rose out of the evening mists to snatch him. "My daughter's lonely. Don't see many folk here. Better for me—not for her," said Edric.

His words came out like rusty nails being pried from stone, as though he'd seldom strung so many sentences together in his life. Probably he was a runaway villein afraid to move into a village where he would have to give account of himself. Stephen wondered where they'd come from and what had happened to Aude's mother. It didn't matter now; certainly it wasn't worth the risk of upsetting them with too many questions. He liked Aude, even if she did keep calling him a little monk, and he would come back to see her and Edric if he could get away again. That would be a while. The monks would surely have noticed his absence by now; he'd earned a flogging, and maybe something worse, like extra Latin to translate. He didn't mind. It was worth a flogging to have had this day of feeling like a normal human being and to have found friends.

He explained that he couldn't say exactly when he would be able to come back, but Aude must believe he would try. He would certainly be watched closely after this escapade. "Oh, aye, you'll come in your own time." Aude nodded, and went on to chatter about the birds that clustered in the marsh in spring and darkened the autumn sky with their passage south. She moved to a different rhythm than Stephen's convent world; her life had never been bound and sectioned by bells and hours of prayer. Even if he couldn't come for a while, Aude would still be there.

Walking on the path around the village, they could see the unfinished church door standing like a black arch against the evening sky. Aude slipped away into the reeds between one word and the next and Stephen walked on slowly, chewing a stem of sweet grass and watching the reeds blaze with amber light as the sun set. Before he was out of the fenlands the sun had sunk below the horizon, and he moved through a darkness broken only by white bands of fog where the water channels lay. The mist clung to his tunic in droplets and chilled him from bare legs to tonsured scalp. Night birds cried out with shrill notes that made him jump and stumble on the path. He was glad to see the dark shape of the cathedral rising before him, black and solid against the fog, ringed by a cluster of small houses and shops that made up the town of Ely. Glowing cooking-fires lit the open doors of the houses, and candles burned in the cathedral as the monks made their way into the choir. They were about to begin singing Compline—it was even later than Stephen had thought.

He was braced for a beating and an inquisition, but when he slipped in to join the evening service, Joscelin caught his eye, winked, and mouthed "It's all right."

"I told them Master Brito needed help with his accounts," Joscelin explained when they were alone in the dormitory. "Coluin looked surprised, so I said, 'Didn't Brother Daniel tell you?' Coluin said he supposed Daniel wanted you to get more practical experience while he was away, but he was surprised the treasurer was willing to let you associate with secular people so much. He said that you really should have told him before you left and that he would have worried if I hadn't explained where you were."

Stephen looked at Joscelin with surprise and admiration. "And you want to be Pope someday! Telling lies like that, you'll more likely be unfrocked and cast onto the streets."

"I didn't lie. I'm sure Master Brito does need help with his accounts, and it's not my fault if he didn't have the sense to send for you himself. I never told Coluin that Daniel had sent you to the village. I asked if Daniel hadn't told him so. A question isn't a lie."

"Well, you'll make a good lawyer someday, anyway."

For the next few days Stephen was cautious, expecting that the monks would hear how work had stopped on the church at Alleford and that Joscelin's carefully erected structure of nonlies would come crashing down. But nothing happened. After three days, Coluin asked if one day's visit had been enough to straighten out Brito's building accounts. "Because if you're not going back, I really should find something else for you to do since Brother Daniel has been delayed."

"I'm supposed to go two full days a week, and make up the time lost from Latin lessons on the other mornings." Stephen decided to borrow from Joscelin's tactics. "Didn't Brother Daniel tell you?"

After that, he was committed. He had to find something to do outside the convent on Mondays and Thursdays, or confess that he'd been lying from the beginning. And since

the masons never did get back to working on the church—
some were caught and impressed, others drifted off to
other jobs—he wound up spending a succession of golden
days in the fens with Aude, learning to read the book of
the marshlands under her tutelage.

August mellowed into September, and Brother Daniel
sent word that he was further delayed in London. Those
monks who did not love him whispered that he had not
even been given audience with the King, and made merry
over the notion of their harsh treasurer pacing impatiently
in the King's antechamber day after day. Stephen simply
said a brief prayer of gratitude and enjoyed the passing
days as an unexpected gift. The marsh birds flew south,
darkening the skies for an hour at a time with their
feathers. Stephen made one or two attempts to kiss Aude
in the shelter of the reeds where they lay watching the
migrating birds; she pushed him off, laughing, and said
she was too young for such games.

"Come back in two years," she teased. "I'll be fourteen
then. Da'd be proud to have a lettered man in the family."

"And I'll be sixteen," said Stephen gloomily, depressed
as always when he thought about his future. "I'll probably
be a deacon in two years or maybe even ordained priest."

Aude shrugged and rolled over to stare at the sky. "Is
that what you want?"

Her little breasts poked through the thin cloth of her
single garment. Stephen remembered when he'd pinned
her in mock-wrestling, and felt the smooth coolness of her
lips and the warm life in her body. "Do you know," he said
slowly, "I don't think anybody's ever asked me what I
wanted."

But the vows had been made. He belonged to Ely and
he knew that Brother Daniel, with his cold ambition and
his insistence on Stephen's perfection, would never let
him go, especially to marry a fowler's daughter in the
fenland.

The days grew bright and thin as the chill of cold
weather settled in. Brother Daniel still did not return
from London and the half-built church of Alleford stood
silent and empty. Wagonfuls of trade goods creaked into
Ely in preparation for the great fair that began on St.
Audrey's Day. Aude said wistfully that she'd never seen a
fair—Edric didn't like the city.

The opening day of St. Audrey's fair fell on a Thursday, and Stephen arranged to take Aude to the fair and return to the fens afterwards. Joscelin, who had been excused choir duties to study for the Cambridge examinations, cheerfully agreed to take Stephen's place at choir, padding in his robe to simulate Stephen's broad shoulders and pulling his hood down to cover his own dark curly hair. A straw dummy dressed in Stephen's second-best robes would satisfy the *dormitarius* when he checked on the sleeping boys. Stephen promised on St. Audrey's bones to be back before dawn, when Joscelin would have to show up for studies in his own person.

He met Aude at the quay by Bridge Mead, where the horse copers' tents were already set up. The air was alive with the shrill cries of hot-pastry vendors and the bawling of animals being dragged to market.

"Good fortune for St. Audrey's Day." Stephen essayed a sweeping bow, imitating the nobles who sometimes stayed in the prior's guest rooms, but the folds of his black habit billowed over his head and spoiled the effect.

"Good fortune for S't'Audrey's!" Aude slurred the saint's name the way the unlettered country folk did, making it sound soft and pretty. When Stephen straightened up, she handed him a roll of patched brown cloth. "Da says you can't wear black robes around the fair, and it's too cold for you to strip down to tunic. He said you sh'd borrow his good cloak with the capuchin."

Stephen managed the exchange of garments in a stable off Potter's Lane, leaving his habit rolled in a tight ball under some wisps of hay too old to tempt even the hungriest horse. With the hood of Edric's cloak over his tonsured head, he hoped that he would look like any common peasant boy. Edric had been right about the cold: his bare arms prickled with goose bumps during the brief moments of changing clothes, and the shadowed corners of the stable were as chilly as the stone-floored cloister in winter.

There would be night frosts soon. This might be his last chance to escape the confines of the monastery until spring; even dear vague Brother Coluin would be aware that masons didn't work through the winter. Well, if it were his last day of freedom, he might as well make it a good one.

Neither Stephen nor Aude had so much as a clipped farthing to buy a ginger nut, but the sights, sounds, and smells of the fair were free to all. Aude's father had supplied her with a packet of greased cloth that contained smoked goose and brown bread with goosefat. As they ate, they watched a woman dancing on her hands with two knives balanced on her feet, and another who could juggle while crossing a loose rope hung between two wagons. Then they teased the man with the tame bear about his pet's sleepy eyes until the mastiffs came for the baiting.

Aude looked sick and wanted to leave. Stephen lingered; it seemed a shameful thing to be fourteen, nearly a man, and never to have seen a fight or a bearbaiting. It wasn't what he'd imagined, though. The bear's chains were drawn so tight he could hardly move; Stephen could see the links cutting into his skin. The bear growled and shook his head impotently while the dogs leapt at his chained hindquarters and came away with gobbets of flesh. As Stephen pushed his way through the gathering crowd, he heard murmurs of protest. The bear-leader planned to do away with this sickly old beast, and had sent his boy to announce a fight to the death. The audience expected a much livelier show than this half-hearted growling. One of the men in front had an iron-shod staff with a sharp point. As Stephen left, he was jabbing at the bear's face to make it fight better.

One of the men on the fringes of the crowd gave Stephen a hard look, and Stephen thought he recognized one of the laborers from Swalugh Lane. He pulled the hood of his borrowed cloak down over his eyes and pushed past with a surly mutter.

Stephen found Aude entranced by the antics of three skinny black pigs on one string. Squealing and complaining, the pigs were dragged along, their limbs and snouts so tangled in string that all they could do was sit in the mud while the old woman who'd brought them cursed and tried to untangle them.

"Aren't they sweet, Stephen?"

"Too lean to make good bacon," said a man who stood behind them. "Have to feed 'em up for a year before you cut their throats."

Aude winced. "Let's go look at the fairings."

"You're squeamish today, for a lass who puts the bird-lime on her Da's nets," Stephen teased as they wandered toward the high ground away from the river where the peddlers' booths were set up. "You don't make pets of the wild fowl, why be so fond of a piglet?"

Aude glanced sideways at him, and he noticed how long and thick her dark lashes were. She'd grown during the summer; her thin dress was tight on her. "I don't like killing things, even when it's necessary. I'll do it, with Da, because that's how we live. But I don't have to like it, or waste my fairday watching dogs rip a poor old bear to pieces!" She marched on ahead of Stephen, and the autumn wind caught at the hem of her kirtle and pulled it taut behind her.

He caught up with her at the crest of the hill where the merchants' booths began. "Here. It's too cold for you in nothing but that thin dress." He held out the width of Edric's capacious, patched cloak and drew her in close under the shelter of his arm. Her bones were so light and fragile, it was like holding a bird in his cupped hands. There were two men in black robes to the left, inspecting a spicer's wares. Stephen escorted Aude down a narrow line of booths where gaudily painted wooden toys and gilt cakes hung. At the very end was a peddler with a tray of lace necklaces.

"Buy a S't'Audrey's necklace for your lady?"

St. Audrey had scorned her father's jewels, refusing to wear any finery except a lace necklace that she knotted with her own hands. This legend had been one of Stephen's first reading lessons, and it was immortalized in two sculptured capitals and one stained-glass window in Ely Cathedral. It was also the subject of the daily reading in refectory at least three times a year. Stephen was heartily sick of St. Audrey and her humility, but the delicate spirals of fine white lace would look beautiful against Aude's sunburnt skin. She was staring with parted lips at the cheap trinkets, as though she'd never seen anything so fine before.

And Stephen couldn't even give her one. The vows he was to take had never troubled him much before, except that they would commit him irrevocably to a monastic life. But today both chastity and poverty bothered him. As for obedience, that had flown out the window at the beginning of this magic summer.

"When I'm a journeyman and have my own wages, I'll buy you all the St. Audrey's necklaces in the fair," he promised Aude.

"Go on!" She gave him a friendly shove under the cloak. "You're goin' to be a monk. You won't never have more money than you have today."

"No." Stephen felt a dizzy exultation as the words came to his lips. Somewhere this knowledge had been building within him. Each sunlit day with Aude another course of stones laid smooth and true on his foundations. "I'm not going into the Church. I don't have a vocation, and surely they can't hold me to vows made when I was too young to know what they meant." He felt a quiver of uneasiness, remembering Joscelin had said that made no difference in canon law. But surely they would make an exception for Stephen. "I'm going to ask them to apprentice me to a stonemason. I'll learn the trade, and when I'm a journeyman and can keep myself, I'm going to marry you."

"Oh, aye? And what d'you think I'll be doing all those years when you're a poor 'prentice in some mason's yard?"

"Waiting for me." Stephen looked into Aude's eyes repeating his statement as a question. "Waiting for me?"

Aude caught her breath, and Stephen saw his own reflection in the dark centers of her eyes. "Oh, maybe— maybe not!" She slipped out from under the shelter of his cloak, tweaked his nose, and ran back into the hurly-burly of the fair. Stephen ran after her, never noticing the two cowled men who stood at the brow of the hill watching him.

Sunset, and the convent bells ringing the monks to prayers, caught Stephen and Aude unawares between the rope dancer's tent and the flat meadow where the horses showed their paces. The pure tones of the bells rang out over the flat fenland all around Ely, echoing off the surface of the water like more bells ringing from below the mere. Stephen stood holding Aude's thin brown hand, caught between the convent bells and their ghostly echo, the red glow of the western sky, and the white mists already rising from the marshes.

The final low ringing note died away, and with it the last light left the sky. The fair had changed character subtly in those few minutes, and when Stephen looked back, he saw shapeless huddles of tents and stalls, shadows where things

moved, flaring torches whose uneven light turned peddlers' and jugglers' faces into deformed jokes. The laughter
around the rope dancer's tent was louder now, and the
men who gathered were more interested in tweaking the
rope to make the girl fall off and show her legs than in
letting her demonstrate her balancing skills.

"Aude—"

"I know. 'Tis time for you to go back." Aude withdrew
her hand.

Stephen wanted to say that he would not go back, that
he would run away to the marshes to live with her and
Edric. But even as the words rose to his lips, he knew he
was being childish. Edric could barely keep himself and
Aude; he didn't need another mouth to feed, especially
not a clumsy, town-bred lad who would be no help hunting
in the marshes. The monks would come for him, and then
there would be trouble. Stephen felt he'd never get trained
as a builder since he had no way to pay anybody to take
him on as an apprentice.

"I have to go back for now. But—we'll meet again?"

"How? You said yourself, this has to be the last day. You
can't pretend to help Master Brito build his church when
there's frost in the ground." Aude's voice was muffled, and
she gave a sharp, uncharacteristic sniff on the last word.

"I'll think of something. Anyway, I'm taking you home
first, so this isn't farewell." Not quite yet. He would have
these last hours. On the way, Stephen thought of a crack in
the convent's winter schedule. "If you come to the ferry at
Monk's Hithe on Wednesday morning, I've got an hour
between choir and lessons when I'm supposed to be reading Latin with Joscelin—but he's leaving next week to
study at Cambridge and the monks won't think to change
my schedule, they never do. Meet me then and we'll work
our something else."

In fact it was Aude who led Stephen home. Even after a
summer's practice of threading his way along the decep-
tive, quivering paths at the edge of the fens, Stephen had
enough trouble finding Edric's hut in daylight. By night,
with the moon turning reeds and water a uniform, silver
color, he might have stumbled a dozen times if Aude
hadn't been stepping light-footed before him. And even
then, she wouldn't let him go the last few hundred yards.

"You'd be going back alone, and 'tis near moonset, and

you'd drown for su.e," she told him flatly. "Even those as live here all their lives aren't so marsh-canny as my Da, they'll wait for one of us to lead them. And you—ah, I'll not have a drowned monk on my conscience."

"A drowned mason," Stephen corrected her.

"Well, when you know which it is, come back and tell me!"

He'd thought to have one kiss of farewell from her, but she pushed him lightly and flitted through the reeds before he could stop her. One minute he saw her slender form bending the reeds aside, the next there was nothing there but a wavering column of mist.

By the time Stephen returned to Ely, the fair's night-time gaiety was over, and the narrow streets were dark. The cathedral's stained-glass windows were black, empty eyes reflecting the night. It was the dead time between Compline and Nocturns, a time when the monks retired to their dormitory and lay still, each one careful not to make any noise that might disturb his fellows.

The ordered stillness of the convent enclosed him, walls within walls. Joscelin had left open the low casement window in the boys' sleeping room; Stephen felt for the sill with both hands, swung himself up, and banged one knee on the wall in his hurry. After a quick scrabble in the darkness, both legs were over and he dropped to the floor. The smooth stones jarred his heels all the way up to his teeth, and while he was recovering from the drop, a blaze of torchlight dazzled his eyes.

The cowled monk who had been waiting for him raised the torch as it flamed into life. Stephen, half blinded by the sudden light, recognized Brother Daniel's dry voice.

"So. The penitent returns. And your habit?"

Still in the shed on Potter's Lane, Stephen supposed; he'd entirely forgotten that he was wearing Edric's patched cloak over his own sturdy undertunic.

There didn't seem to be much point in trying to make up an explanation, nor did Daniel seem particularly interested in hearing one.

"You were fortunate," said Daniel, almost mildly, "that I returned from my travels in time to discover this tissue of lies that you and your friend have been weaving. If you had escaped undetected, your soul might have been lost forever. Lying to your masters, evading your assigned work, whoring in the streets of a filthy city!"

Stephen's body tensed at this last insult. "Don't bother denying it!" Daniel went on before he could speak. "Your friend told me where you went."

There was a rustling movement in the other bed. Stephen squinted against the torchlight and saw Joscelin's face, pale and unhappy. His eyes were red. "I couldn't help it, Stephen," the older boy said. "They said—he said—he could stop me going to Cambridge. That a criminous clerk couldn't be sent into the world. You know I have to have learning, Stephen!" His voice cracked like a much younger boy's. "I have to learn! I couldn't give that up, could I?"

Daniel's eyes took on the yellow-flame color of the torchlight. "I've been watching you all day—playing with that slut of a peasant girl, disappearing into the fens with her. Do you want to damn your soul for eternity? Do you want to ruin your chances within the Church?"

Stephen's mouth was dry; the words came out in a husky whisper, unconvincing. "I'm not going to join the Church. I don't have a vocation."

"You have no choice." Daniel's voice was as calm and certain and heavy as the incoming tide. Stephen felt that certainty smothering him, swallowing him up until he could no longer remember what it was like to draw a free breath. "The vows of oblation are irrevocable. That was explained to your mother when she gave you up, and she consented in your name."

Stephen stared at the wall behind Daniel's cowled head. The coursing was uneven, and in the torchlight he could see where the mortar had cracked slightly. That would be from the pressure of the arch that rose above this room, carrying the vaulted ceiling. The foundations hadn't been laid right; there was a flaw in the design, and the wall was slowly crumbling from that original error. It wouldn't last. Someday the whole building would have to be torn down. It was better so; flawed and broken things weren't worth keeping and patching up.

CHAPTER

4

◘

The fog that crept in that winter was so dense that the monks walked with outstretched hands at midday, feeling their way along the cold, damp buildings. During the night, frost settled in the cathedral, leaving sparkling ice crystals at dawn. The running sores on Stephen's knuckles cracked and bled every morning, and Brother Coluin's cough worsened. One of the monks from Yorkshire said that Ely was lucky: the water in the marshes kept the air from getting really cold. In his home convent, the washing ewers would be covered with half an inch of ice every morning.

"It's cold enough here to satisfy us," said Coluin with a dry laugh that turned into another cough.

In the cathedral, any heat rose to the high ceiling and escaped. Services in choir became an icy penance, with numbing cold creeping slowly from the stone floor to feet and legs. Stephen imagined Aude and her father huddled in their clay-walled hut, crouched under a pile of ill-tanned skins, tending the fire that left the walls smoky with soot, and waiting for spring just as he did. For them, February would be just another cold month of waiting until the first warm breeze softened the land. Their life would begin again when they saw green shoots poking out from the brown, barren fens. But Stephen would not see those signs of spring. For him, February meant the feast of Candlemas, his fifteenth birthday, and the vows that would seal his fate.

Stephen had given up fighting now. He was watched every minute since the day of the fair and there had been no opportunity to meet Aude at Monk's Hithe. What was the point in breaking free again, anyway? Joscelin had betrayed him as his mother had done. Stephen's mind skittered over the surface of that memory but found only a child's confusion, a desolate world in which the monks' harsh rule was the closest thing to kindness. Daniel was right—the Church was his only home. If he saw Aude again, she too would desert him. It was better to stop now, while he could warm himself with the memory of her friendship.

There was no one at Ely, that winter, to break through Stephen's lonely misery. Joscelin had been sent to Cambridge immediately after the fair, before he and Stephen could repair their broken friendship. And Stephen had been removed from Coluin's gentle tutelage to join the monks in their daily round of liturgy. It would keep him out of trouble, Brother Daniel said.

Brother Daniel was quite right. The endless repetitions of prayers and psalms that filled the monks' "day" from the middle of the cold winter night until long after sunset of the next night, the prescribed movements of filing into and out of choir and kneeling and bowing and clasping hands, the pressure of being constantly surrounded by his fellows, all these things dulled Stephen's thoughts and drained his energy until nothing was left but a kind of dumb acceptance. Reality was this cold, dull world where every word and every step was governed by ancient rituals. Stephen had no more thoughts of escaping reality—this was to be his life. Only in his dreams was he still free to choose.

In time, as the words of the liturgy became automatic, he discovered he had the ability to withdraw his thoughts entirely from the icy choir and his own shivering body, to erect castles in his mind where he and Aude strolled in the warm light of summer. Sometimes he amused himself by picturing the interior of the cathedral in detail. Forbidden to lift his head, Stephen made a game of seeing how well he could envision this place he'd seen for so many years. In his mind he built it from floor to ceiling, from the springing columns of the thirteen bays to the light pointed arches of the triforium and the ribs of the vaulted ceiling; then he tore it all down and began again, mentally opening the walls and making the massy columns into slender shafts and tearing away the weight of stone to admit pure winter-white sunshine.

The prior and the obedientiaries, who were excused from the hours in choir on account of their administrative duties, paced in the winter-chilled cloister or warmed their hands before the fire in the prior's private chamber. Politics and rumor mingled to create a vague sense of worry that seeped into the convent, and the monks' words drifted to Stephen's ears as he sat in Daniel's room.

"He's a desperate man, our King. He'd not have submitted to the Pope if the barons hadn't been pressing him close."

"Not to be King much longer, they say. There's been talk of young Louis of France. They say John's broken his pact with the realm."

The prior made an impatient gesture. "He was anointed and crowned. How can that pact be broken?"

"He'd be wise not to go hunting alone."

"The barons—"

"The King—"

"Louis and his fleet waiting for a good wind—"

"And we're caught in the middle."

"Safer there," said Daniel. "One side or the other will pay dearly for this conflict. Probably both. God send our rebel bishop stays in France until it's over!"

By January, it was impossible for the monks of Ely to stay on that safe middle ground. King John's army was pressing the rebellious barons close, harrying the north while his mercenaries swept the south. And Ely, the traditional refuge of rebels, was an attractive sanctuary to men whose castles had fallen and whose families had no other home. They came for Christmas mass and for Epiphany, stayed in the town and filled the guesthouse of the convent. They lodged their retainers in the crumbling castle. There was more gold than anyone could recollect in Ely that Christmastide, flowing from the pockets of great men who were lavish enough with what they might soon lose. Merchants and innkeepers pocketed the gold with a sour smile at the innocence of these lords who thought they could stave off misfortune by paying like princes for a new-stitched saddle, for silver bells for a falcon's jesses. The island's natural defenses were strengthened. Day laborers ventured out in the damp, clinging cold to build trenches and set up sharpened stakes of wood across the three causeways that led over the marshes to Ely. And everywhere, the whispers gathered and grew force.

Some said the King was at Nottingham, keeping Christmas feast with the view of men he'd hanged from the castle walls to cheer him. Then he was said to be at Berwick, harrying the Scots and far away from Cambridgeshire; but the monks of Ely had barely relaxed when the isle was swollen with new bands of refugees from Bury St. Edmund's. Brother Coluin was called to help the infirmarian tend to the frostbite and infected wounds of the refugees, and he brought Stephen to hold the bleeding-bowl.

"Who cares where the King is?" growled a middle-aged tradesman whose fur-lined robe trailed incongruously over bare legs and soft night-slippers. "I'll tell you where Walter Buc is—him and his damned Flemish mercenaries— that's more to the point. King John hasn't the stomach to do his own fighting, so he hired foreign soldiers to put down Englishmen—and they're raping the countryside where they pass. They're the ones you want to watch out for."

"All right," said Brother Coluin. "Just give me your feet while we talk. Those cuts will fester if they're not salved. This is not the season to go running barefoot."

"Those who stayed to put on their shoes," said the merchant, "had them taken off again by Buc's mercenaries. And their feet were roasted over the fire until they paid the ransoms he wanted. That's who you should be worrying about—Walter Buc—to hell with the King."

"And where is Master Buc's army now?"

"Marching this way, for all I know. You should be able to trace his path by the burning farms. I hope your knights are prepared to defend this place."

Coluin wrapped a linen bandaging around the merchant's torn foot and stood up. "While the causeways are blocked, you're safe enough. William the Norman never got across the marshes into Ely except by treachery, and even then half his knights sank into the marshes and drowned in their armor. The fishers still bring up bits of mail in their nets from time to time. And from all accounts, our King isn't half the campaigner the Norman was, and his mercenaries don't know the territory. If they don't want to feed the eels and tangle their armor in our fishers' nets, they'll stay clear of the fens." He gave the merchant a hard look. "Most of the able-bodied men in town have given their time to working on the causeway defenses."

"My feet..."

"And the rest have contributed to pay for materials and labor, as have the cathedral clergy and the monks of this convent."

The merchant took the hint and reluctantly gave a few coins from the purse he'd evidently had time to fill before he fled in the path of the mercenary army.

Daily the refugees limped over the causeways, filling every wretched corner of the isle and begging for alms and shelter at the convent gates. The almoner gave bread and thin, weak soup to all who came, but turned them away to seek their own shelter in the town.

"Couldn't we at least find room for those in most need?" Stephen asked one evening when the almoner had turned away a woman close to her time, with rags tied around her feet. She had thanked them profusely for the warm soup that was made thinner every day, and hadn't even asked for a place to rest.

"And just where would you have me put them?" Brother Gilbert dropped his metal ladle into the empty soup cauldron and beckoned two of the lay brothers to carry it away. "Already a man can't walk from choir to cloister without tripping over a dozen painted lordlings and their women. All we need is to fill up the odd corners with stinking peasants and we'll have a city of our own within these walls."

But there was always room, it seemed, for a merchant who contributed well to the defense of the isle and to the various funds of the cathedral. The lord Stephen Ridel, who had offered a church, was sumptuously lodged in the prior's guesthouse with his train of servants and pageboys, his wife and her women. Strangely enough, he was the only one who seemed to understand Stephen's unease with the convent policy. He had been silently watching, while Stephen helped the almoner to ladle out soup for the poor who streamed through the outeryard of the convent; he heard the almoner's snappish reply and caught Stephen's eye as he slouched away.

"It seems unfair to you, doesn't it, lad?" A careless hand ruffled Stephen's hair. "Well, and it is unfair. But we're sleeping close-packed as eels in a pot, even in the prior's guesthouse. And remember, if King John's mercenaries attack the honest Englishmen who've taken refuge here, it won't be the peasants who defend us. It'll be men like me and the knights in my train. Does that even the balance a little?"

The lord Ridel was taller than Stephen, golden and glowing even in the gray dampness of this January evening. Stephen felt slow and stupid before him, his thoughts as clumsy as his winter-numbed fingers. If Stephen Ridel and his friends hadn't taken refuge here, Ely would be in no danger from King John's soldiers. Why couldn't they fight their battles with the King somewhere else? But then, what place would welcome these rebellious barons?

"My lord," Stephen mumbled at last, "you don't need *my* approval to stay here."

"Stephen, stop bothering the gentlemen and come inside. I need your help with the accounts!" Brother Daniel moved smoothly between them, with a word of apology to Stephen Ridel and a firm hand on his novice's shoulder.

Stephen's fingers were too cold to hold a pen. He warmed them over the single candle in the treasurer's room while he scanned the close-written pages. With the influx of refugees, it had been some time since he'd worked with Brother Daniel, and there were many new entries to be copied and balanced. Lord Ridel had promised the income of his two farms in Lincolnshire to the cathedral. Three gentlemen in the service of Oliver de Vaux had given the convent a mark of silver in de Vaux's name. The lady of Walter de Mauduit gave three serfs skilled in carpentry and leatherwork; Maurice de Gant renounced his rights to the eelery of Gantston in the name of the convent of Ely; others gave silver pennies, gold for church vessels, rings, rich embroidered cloths of assorted value, depending on the amount of gilt-work.

"I certainly understand why we cannot *afford* room for the poor who come to our gates."

"You understand nothing, or you wouldn't be so sarcastic. Great religious houses have been dragged in the dust before by men who kept their eyes on the stars and let the gold of the house trickle through their fingers. If we hadn't built up our funds cannily in Richard's day, we'd never have survived the taxes and fines John laid on us. Be quiet now and copy the new entries."

"And what cash value," Stephen inquired after his pen had scratched busily for a few minutes, "shall I put on the prayers of that pregnant woman who blessed me for giving her a cup of soup tonight? Or the curses of the crazy man before her? The one who saw his children hung upside down over a fire to make him give the army gold he didn't have? He hasn't wit to cover his head, and this rain will turn to sleet before morning."

"You shall be grateful that you aren't out there with him. We've enough to do, with the King fighting the barons again and new fines and taxes levied every day. We've enough of a task just to take care of our own. And you don't know how well I have taken care of you today."

"I don't think the lord Ridel was any danger to me." There was a rough spot on the parchment, indicating that the sheet had been carelessly prepared. Stephen took up the crescent-shaped scraping blade and smoothed the sheet until the surface was even enough to take his writing.

"Not Ridel, no. It's your soul I've been preserving. That little slut you were with last fairday came begging entrance, or rather some man was begging it for her, in your name. Fortunately you were in choir at the time. They were such nuisances the almoner finally sent for me to make them clear off." Daniel smiled thinly. "You should have seen the precious pair. It might have made you bless the chance that keeps you safe in God's service, to see what you could have turned into if I hadn't been watching over you. The girl was nothing but a smelly bundle of rags with sharp bones sticking out, and the man was worse—a real wild man from the marshes, hung with stinking leather and eelskins. How she could endure the embraces of such a one escapes me, but I suppose the peasants don't feel these things as we do."

Stephen's hands closed round the half-moon shape of his parchment scraper. The sharp edge stung the insides of his fingers and helped him keep a calm tone. "That would be her father Edric. Why were they here?"

"I told you. Like everyone else in three counties, they wanted to hide behind our walls for fear of the army. At least I think that's what the man wanted." Daniel shrugged under his loose black robes. "His thick accent was hard to understand, and he kept jabbering some nonsense about the geese flying away, and the color of the clouds. Half crazy, I should think. He was shoving the girl at me saying, 'Keep the little maid! Keep her!' as if this were a keeping house for peasants. I finally made it clear that we had no use for such trash, and that you didn't want to see the folk who'd nearly seduced you out of God's house, and eventually they took themselves off."

"You told them I didn't want to see them." There was a roaring like the tide coming in, a white mist rising between the two of them. Something terrible was going to happen—he didn't quite understand what.

"You shouldn't want to see such folk and when you belong to God, you won't."

"It was a lie." The tide was higher now, cold between his teeth. Aude was turned away from the convent gates, thinking he'd forgotten her—betrayed her.

"It was a kindness. We pray not to be led into temptation; like Our Father, I sheltered you from it. I'm not going to let you ruin yourself because of adolescent urges toward some peasant slut. You have a greater career ahead of you in the Church."

"Doing what? Counting great lords' donations and kicking the poor in the teeth? No, thank you." Stephen felt calm now, as if the waves that roared in his ears were lifting him up. It was quite simple. Nobody wanted him; he understood that. It wasn't important. What nobody had thought to ask was, whether he wanted the Church. And he didn't. It was as easy as that.

"You grow insolent!"

"Yes. I'm growing." Stephen pushed the writing stand away and stood up. One carved wooden foot caught between two uneven planks of the floor and the stand slowly toppled. Stephen made no move to catch it. The inkhorn slid out of its round hole and splattered the floor with brownish black droplets that rolled away over the planks. The heavy stand seemed to take forever to fall, and when it hit the floor, the crash of wood on wood echoed in the back of his mind with a high, thin whining. The last drops of thin convent ink spilled out of the inkhorn and collected among the unevenly worn floorboards.

Daniel remained where he was, back to the window, one hand thrown up as he'd raised it in the first moment of surprise.

"You like being cruel." Stephen heard his own voice, high and surprised. "I didn't know that. All this talk about doing this or that for my own good, or for God's service. But you like hurting."

"We've turned others away. There was nothing special about those two, save for the danger they posed to you."

"Perhaps not." And wouldn't they be as safe from the soldiers in their secret hut, guarded by the black quaking bog and the labyrinth of paths, as these great lords crowding into the convent grounds and praying the causeways could be defended? Stephen shook his head. "But you didn't have to tell Aude that I didn't want to see her. And you didn't have to tell me about it. You enjoyed that."

"I will do whatever is necessary to bend your stubborn neck to God's will. Even hurting you, yes, if that is necessary. You will keep the vows that were made in your name."

"Words." Stephen said mildly. He could barely hear his own voice, let alone Daniel's thin justifications. The screaming sound of wood twisted askew was loud in his ears, and beneath that was a roar like the rush of an incoming tide. There were voices, weaving in and out of the rushing waters. *Be a good boy now. Mea culpa. When your mother gave you to us. Little monk.* "I don't think I care about words anymore. And if God wants me to practice your brand of charity, I don't care about Him either. I'm leaving. And nothing you can say will stop me."

When Daniel moved to intercept him, Stephen swung out with a closed fist and saw the treasurer stagger back with his hand clasped over his cheekbone and blood oozing between the white thin fingers. "Lay brothers! Jude, Aluric, Stinewulf!"

"He's got a knife," Daniel panted as the men burst into the room. Stephen tried to squirm out between them. "Get it away from him—first—then—"

"I'm sorry," said Stephen. "I forgot I was holding the scraping-blade. Look, it cut my hand, too—"

A jolting blow to his midsection knocked the breath out of him. Stephen fought to stay on his feet, cursing the weakness of his convent-bred body. Hours in choir and scriptorium were no match for the days of shoveling earth and carrying burdens that made Aluric's body hard and massive as a tree trunk. Stephen got in a few weak blows that went unnoticed before he was wrestled to the floor. With a swollen eye and a split lip, Stephen met Daniel's cold gaze.

"If I reported this episode in chapter," Daniel said, "you would be flogged, set a penance, and probably forbidden to take your vows in February. And the record of this would follow you all your days. One mistake can mark a man's life for good, in the Church or out of it. I will not let you make that mistake. For your own good, I'm going to flog the sin out of you now, in private, so that the chapter need hear nothing about it."

Jude pulled Stephen's habit and tunic over his shoulders while Brother Aluric grasped his wrists in one hand and dragged him across the overturned writing stand. Still sick and wheezing from the blow to his stomach, Stephen didn't resist. His bare skin prickled with goose bumps in the damp air, and inwardly he shivered at the thought of Daniel's long smooth cane falling across the half-healed weals from his last flogging. But he managed a semblance of a grin through swelling lips.

"*In nomine Patris*—" the treasurer began, as if pronouncing a blessing.

It was worse than usual; Daniel struck not with the restraint that was enjoined for a flogging in chapter, but with the full force of his bitter, frustrated anger. Stephen hissed with pain when the rod came down over the cuts that had been laid open in the first few minutes.

"Do you repent? Do you repent?"

At first Stephen could think of something annoying to say each time Daniel asked that question. Later he could only shake his head and grunt a denial through clenched teeth; still later he was unable to make any response at all. Somehow the beating had ceased to hurt. His back was covered with burning coals, but it wasn't his anymore, and he was floating somewhere outside the scene, watching objectively as Daniel laid on the rod with growing frenzy.

If he keeps on, the muscles will be stiff for life, he thought, objectively, as though he were watching somebody else. And then, wondering at the strange floating softness that surrounded him, *Is this a miracle? I don't think I'll make a very good saint. They'll have to change the story somewhat.*

CHAPTER

5

◻

*H*e woke to darkness and a dull ache that filled his body. When he raised his head, fire rippled down his back and he cried out involuntarily at the sudden sharp pain.

"Are you conscious now? Here, drink this." The soft globe of light from a single candle hovered at the edge of his bed. A hand raised his chin and the cool edge of a glazed cup touched his lips. Something bitter, with the tang of strange herbs, trickled into his mouth. Stephen coughed with surprise, spat out the mixture, and recognized Coluin's gently chiding voice. "Now, lad, you need the good herbs. 'Twill help you rest and heal."

To please Coluin he swallowed a few mouthfuls of the bitter infusion before laying his head down on the pallet. The smoothness of linen under his cheek, the scent of rosemary and lavender rising from the folds of pressed cloth, puzzled him for a moment. He turned his head to seek out Coluin, gritting his teeth against pain caused by the movement. "Where—this isn't the dormitory?" The candlelight revealed a small room, not the long high-roofed hall he was accustomed to. There were no monks silently awaiting the call to Matins, still as carved effigies on their separate pallets. There was no watchman with his lantern keeping watch against undefined evil practices.

Privacy was a thing Stephen had longed for as an unattainable luxury; why had it been given him now? he wondered.

"Not the dormitory, no. I asked for permission to tend you in one of the small cells off the infirmary, so that we shouldn't disturb anybody if you woke in the night. Now let me look at your back."

Stephen gritted his teeth as Coluin lifted the bandages, but the pain wasn't as bad as he'd expected. Something made him feel light-headed and pleasantly detached from his body—it must have been Coluin's bitter herb tea.

Coluin clucked his tongue and muttered disapproving words under his breath. "Brother Daniel is too zealous. Will he save the boy's soul by killing him?" The first touch of Coluin fingers was agony, but then the salve took over; it was cool and smooth, taming the fire and sting from the cuts.

Stephen closed his eyes and the fire receded into darkness. He conjured up a picture of the infirmary: a long vaulted hall with aisles on both sides. On one side the aisle had been blocked off into little cubicles like this one. The west door of the hall opened onto a long columned passage overlooking the garden, and the garden's low wall bordered on Oyster Lane. On the other side of the lane was a vineyard. No one would be working in the garden or the vineyard in this bitter weather. It would be easy enough to get away unobserved. Just thinking of the plan made Stephen feel stronger. It was a good thing he'd been brought here, rather than back to the monks' dormitory where someone would be watching him constantly. "Good," he murmured. "Better here . . . easier to . . ."

"Feeling easier? That's good."

He must have spoken part of his thought aloud but not all of it. Stephen started to thank St. Michael for that before remembering that he had renounced God and His saints. It would be easier to escape from the infirmary. And another good thing about this location was the almoner's ambry, with meats and bread for the poor, just down a narrow corridor from the infirmary. Beside the ambry was a chestful of worn clothes taken in charity from the townspeople, washed, mended, to be given out as part of the convent's alms to the poor. As soon as Coluin went to sleep, Stephen could slip away, with food and worldly clothing to make his escape from the convent easier. . . .

Stephen slept fitfully, dreaming he was already free, running through the secret, winding ways of the fens to find Aude. It was high summer, and his forehead was beaded with sweat from the sun perhaps. But why did the sun hurt his back so? A thin, high voice filled his dreams. Though the words were unintelligible, he recognized the sound of despair. The marshes were deep and black and he was sinking in them and Aude was laughing far away. . . . He moaned, turned, and heard Coluin's voice. "The man's mad. Did he want to kill the boy? *No*, I'm not having him here to look at his work. See how the sound of voices upsets the lad?"

Later, "Drink this . . . good boy," and he was a child in a hut on the shingle beach of Dunwich, fretful with a baby fever and praised by Mam when he swallowed the bitter gruel of herbs and meal.

Night came, then dawn, and the cries of wild fowl passing overhead entered Stephen's dreams as he remembered something Edric had said. "When they don't winter over in the marshes, we know there'll be ice over the meres before Candlemas." He was supposed to do something at Candlemas—something that would be a terrible mistake—but that wasn't why he was afraid. There was something worse than his final vows, something creeping cold and dark over the ice that Edric prophesied.

"No!" he cried in his sleep, and never felt Coluin's patient hands replacing the blanket that he'd thrown away in his delirium.

When at last he woke, the cell was dark but the slits where the warped shutters hung loose let in the gray light of a winter morning. It was not the morning after the fight, Stephen knew that, but he could only guess how much time had passed while he lay in the infirmary.

The cold was an enemy slipping in through the cracks of the shutters, relentlessly seeking out every weak place in Stephen's defenses, trickling under the blanket when he moved. It burned in his lungs and bit at his exposed nose and cheeks, and when he sat up suddenly, it rushed in under the bandages, awakening every throbbing weal to a new kind of pain. Stephen hissed under his breath and glanced about the narrow room.

Coluin was nowhere to be seen. It was morning, so he must be in choir. How long had Stephen been dreaming?

That medicine, whatever it was, had worn off now, and so had the fever. He felt weak but clearheaded, and he had a plan of sorts that had grown out of the nights of dreaming. Hadn't Master Brito said he could use a likely lad to reckon up accounts in his marble-carving business? First Stephen would find Aude, then they'd make for Dunwich and he'd get work in Brito's stoneyard. Edric could come too, if he dared leave the marsh. They'd find Mam, too, and she would explain why she hadn't been able to come back for him. All would live together while he worked in the stoneyard and learned a proper trade. It would work out perfectly. But the first thing was to escape; and now, while the monks were at Prime, was the best chance he was likely to get.

The passageway from the west door of the infirmary opened on one side to the garden. The fresh, clean smell of the air made Stephen feel awake and alive, despite the warning stiffness of his back. He slipped on a patch of ice where someone had spilled water between two worn stones, caught hold of a column to save himself and gasped aloud when the sudden movement pulled loose bandages that were stuck to his skin. He stood quite still waiting for the red haze of pain to fade.

It was strange that his foot hadn't gone through the thin crust of ice over the puddle. He put his weight on it and nearly skidded again. The water was frozen solid. Stephen grew hopeful, knowing the marshes that surrounded Ely would also be frozen solid. He could escape over the ice. Without having to pass one of the guarded causeways and risk being challenged.

Stephen had found a warm hooded cloak, threadbare at the hem but good and solid around the shoulders, and had rolled up a bundle of bread and scraps in a patched tunic, when he heard the shouting. It was coming from some distance south of the convent. At first it was just a series of muffled noises, then he heard the neighing of horses and a woman's shrill scream.

"The ice," Stephen whispered to himself. He wrapped his arms tightly round the bundle of stolen food and clothes. What a fool he'd been, not to think of it at once. The trackless bogs and the secret, sodden marshes were Ely's protection. The hard frost that turned them to ice left the island open to attack from any side. King John's mercenaries had not needed to fight their way over the barricaded causeway this morning. They simply rode over the ice to take the little castle below the convent walls, while the defenders slept and the monks chanted the last of their night-to-morning prayers.

Stephen had to see what was happening. He must move quickly, before the monks heard the noise over their chanting and came pouring out of the cathedral like bees from an overturned hive. He tucked the bundle into the wide sleeve of his habit and skidded through the monks' cemetery, tripping over headstones and sliding on icy patches, until he reached the high walls of the cathedral. Through an inconspicuous outside door he reached a network of narrow spiral stairs and galleries that the cleaning people and repairmen used.

The pathway that threaded along the clerestory level was covered with dust and no one had cleaned the windows in years. Stephen had only a dim view from the glass which was rippled with arcs and dense with rich colors. He squinted through a pattern of green diamonds at a saint's feet and thought he saw armed men filling the narrow streets and surging toward the cathedral like a foaming flood. But the green glass distorted everything and he couldn't be sure.

The crash of the heavy cathedral doors interrupted the monks' monotonous chanting. Stephen wriggled behind a pillar and stared down at the floor of the cathedral. People scurried across the floor like toy soldiers; he recognized Lord Ridel in a furred bedgown, his bright hair mussed with sleep. The woman who clung to his arm had skin like snow and smooth dark hair that tumbled down her back. She was crying. From his lookout Stephen saw her rounded red mouth and heard the muffled sobs that she was trying to control. Behind these two came a fair-haired page boy about Stephen's own age, expostulating with his master that he should be allowed to go with the knights instead of staying behind with the women.

"I need someone I can trust here," Ridel interrupted, and the boy stood a little straighter and squared his shoulders.

A monk was coming forward from the choir, gliding across the cathedral floor with the smooth unhurried pace favored within the convent.

"Brother, there is fighting in the town," Ridel said before the monk could speak. "King John's soldiers must have crossed over the ice. Let my people take refuge here. Surely the soldiers will not profane a house of God."

"Will you leave knights to defend them?"

"My knights are needed elsewhere. And I too—God's bones, Brother, I haven't even had time to arm yet! Listen, you'd better bar the cathedral doors."

That would hardly be possible. Even as they talked, more lords and ladies were pushing their way into the nave, men and women clutching night-robes around themselves, waiting women crying aloud, barefoot servitors hopping up and down on the cold stones—all these rich merchants and nobles who had demanded lodging in the convent were now crowding into the cathedral. The mosaic set into the paving-stones of the nave was entirely covered now, and the cathedral was as full as ever it had been for Christmas mass or St. Audrey's feast day.

Still the doors were pushed open, but the people thronging into the cathedral now were a humbler sort. Stephen recognized the shoemaker who kept his stall on Steeple Row just outside the convent gate, and the smith from Monk's Hithe with a leather apron flapping incongruously over his naked chest. With them were crying women and children.

They must have forced the convent gates, he thought, leaving them open, like an invitation. . . .

The clang of mail and the sound of horses' hooves on stone completed Stephen's thought for him. Right on the heels of the last refugees came the mounted men in armor, swords drawn and already bloody. The women sent up a high shrieking that drowned out any other noise, and people pressed to the sides of the nave to get out of the mercenaries' way. The merchants' wooden stalls were crushed, and those who slipped and fell were trampled in the rush. Stephen saw Ridel's page boy turn and throw out his arms, trying to shield his master and mistress. The lead rider, a black-clad mercenary whose head was encased in a box of steel, struck him down with one blow and grabbed the lady by her long black hair. His horse's hooves smashed the page boy's head and Stephen thought he could hear the crunch of the boy's skull being crushed. There was too much screaming and too much blood. . . . The horses were screaming now. One of the burghers was swinging a jagged wooden plank torn off the front of a stall. He was clearing an arc of space where three terrified women huddled, and the raw splintery ends of the plank had scraped across a horse's nose and sent it wild. A pike came out of nowhere and pinned the merchant to the wrecked remains of his stall, and then there were figures in black tunics and gleaming steel on top of the women, and the screams were worse than ever. . . . Stephen buried his head in the crook of his arm and lay still, sweating in the cold cleaning-gallery, choking on the gray rolls of dust, and trying to block out what he saw and heard below.

At one time he heard Lord Ridel's voice raised in a shout of protest, then in promises of ransom—his plate and furs, all the gold he possessed, even the woman who waited on his wife. . . . Stephen remembered his deep, confident voice saying, "If the King's men come here, it'll be men like myself and the knights in my train who defend us."

He had no idea how long it was before the commotion stopped. When he dared to look around the column again, the cathedral was empty but for some piles of blood-soaked rags scattered on the floor. No, not rags, but limbs. Stephen swallowed hard against the bitter rush of bile in his mouth and forced himself to look. A few men were still standing in the nave, close to the carved wooden screen that separated the monks in the choir from the profane worshippers in the public part of the church. There were three armed men in black surcoats and iron helmets. One had removed his helmet to talk to a monk. The Flemish soldier was a middle-aged man, red in the face and going bald on top. Take away the rattling cage of mail that protected him, lengthen his black surcoat and add a hood, he would look no different from the monks. They were men who'd done this—not demons.

The mercenary gestured at the wooden choir screen, then at the carved capitals of the piers. Stephen caught the words "should fire the church . . . punishment for re-sistance . . ." in a strongly accented voice.

The monk put one hand on his arm. "No. No, my friend, surely we can work out something else?"

Stephen caught his breath and pressed one clenched fist

into his mouth. The calm voice was as familiar to him as his own.

The monk did not look up; Stephen's slight gasp must have gone unheard. "Your men are impatient, I know, waiting for their pay. As loyal subjects of King John, we of the convent would be pleased to supplement his treasury with a small loan to be applied to the pay of the army."

"How much?"

After several minutes of urgent discussion, Brother Daniel drew a purse from the sleeve of his habit and slowly counted out nine silver marks into the soldier's outstretched hand. The two of them paced the length of the nave, careful to step around the bloody heaps that littered the floor. They were talking amicably now, it seemed; Stephen heard the soldier laughing, and saw Daniel nodding in reply. Two other mercenaries followed them, one thoughtfully cleaning his sword on a fragment of an embroidered altar cloth as he walked.

The monks and the nobles who'd bought their way free of the slaughter in the cathedral gathered outside the galilee porch. Stephen slipped silently through the gallery and down the spiral stair to the level of the nave. He could get away now, while the mercenaries were busy with their prisoners, but he had to move quickly. While he'd been hiding in the secret passages of the cathedral and while the innocent who took sanctuary were being slaughtered, what had gone on on the rest of the isle? he wondered. The ice that made Ely so vulnerable would also have stripped away Aude's only protection. Of course that was what Edric had meant when he'd brought her to the convent—how could Stephen have been so stupid? How could the monks have failed to understand him? Living in the fens all his life, attuned to the weather, he would have known the signs of a hard freeze coming on, would have predicted that the ice would leave the Isle of Ely defenseless against Walter Buc and his Flemish mercenaries. That was why he'd begged shelter for Aude. Thank God he'd been denied it! She might even now be one of those shapeless bundles of bloody rags on the floor.

The pavement of the nave was sticky with the blood of slaughtered people—mostly commoners, Stephen noticed; the rich men were outside now, arranging their ransoms with their captors. The blood formed pools in the sunken grooves of the labyrinthine mosaic. In the center, where the star of peace was carved, a brown puddle of blood obscured the carving.

Stephen skirted the edges of the pattern and slipped from column to column in the dusky aisles at ground level. A gleam of white skin against the tumbled rags caught his eye and he looked in spite of himself. It was Ridel's page boy, stripped, white limbs obscenely sprawled out across the stones. It hadn't been only women, or living beings, who suffered the soldiers' lusts in the wild moments before their leader reined them in like so many hounds.

The boy's long golden hair covered his smashed-in face; if Stephen hadn't seen what had happened to him in the first moments of the fight, he might have thought the boy was sleeping.

"You were brave," he whispered to the still form. "You died trying to defend your master."

A master who had been offering ransom to the Flemish mercenaries while one of them was sodomizing his dead servant. Stephen felt the gush of bitterness in his mouth again. He had no time to spare; what if somebody came back into this charnel house of a church and recognized him? But he couldn't leave the dead boy like that, flung down naked on the ground. And he had to get rid of his habit; the black robes would make him far too conspicuous outside the convent. Stephen stripped off the heavy black scapular and gown, leaving only a tunic of anonymous, undyed wool. He arranged his habit over the page boy's body and moved the dead limbs into a posture of rest. In place of the robe Stephen wrapped himself in the patched cloak he'd stolen from the almoner's ambry.

A small dagger lay inches from the dead boy's outflung hand. It was almost like a toy, fit for nothing more than cutting meat at table, but he'd drawn it in the last attempt to defend his lord and lady. Stephen slid it point-first into the long sleeve of his tunic. "You won't need this anymore. And I might. Is that all right?"

Talking to the dead was one thing but waiting for them to answer was another. And thinking you heard the answer— Stephen sucked in his breath and fled his own mad fancies, running down the long aisles of the cathedral without care for the echoing noise of his pounding feet. He pushed open one of the small service doors and burst into a cold, bright world with sun reflecting off ice, air so cold it seemed to burn as he panted. No one was watching this side of the cathedral—they were still gathered outside the west porch.

Caution, and the remnants of common sense, returned in time for Stephen to avoid the groups of soldiers who patroled the town's empty streets. They rode up and down the two main streets, Steeple Row and the Gallery, they lounged in the shelter of the castle gatehouse, and sat in their muddy boots in the prior's hall. But they didn't know the backways of the town as Stephen had learned them in his one summer of stolen freedom, and they were not interested in chasing one peasant boy when there were still rich merchants and noble ladies to be ferreted out. Stephen slithered through cracks too narrow for a grown man and crawled under low eaves that dumped snow on him as he passed. He ignored screams coming from one house and crackling fire from burning timbers in another, and he reached the frozen marshes without being pursued.

The marshland was quiet. No birds moved in the frozen waste, no eels wriggled in nets, no frogs leapt from reeds to water at his coming. There was nothing but pale, straw reeds frozen in icy clumps, glassy black ice in the narrow creeks that laced through the fenland, and crackling frost forests under his feet where the earth had thrust up minute columns of frozen water. The cold entered into Stephen's bones, slowing his blood to a sluggish trickle. Head down, he trudged toward Alleford. It seemed farther than before and he felt he would be walking through this icy silence forever.

Black wisps of smoke, oily and dark against the pearl-gray morning sky, must have come from the houses in Alleford village. The thought of housewives rising to blow the coals into a morning fire, filling pots with bubbling porridge, and beginning their daily routines warmed Stephen as he covered the last slippery curves of the path. Sliding and crunching through ice and reeds, he saw his momentary pleasure give way to doubt. There was far too much smoke.... It rose in greasy columns from stables and houses. Roof beams were torn down and thatch was smoldering in puddles of melted ice. A dead man lay face down in a puddle that had frozen around him; the remains of a thin cow, butchered and hacked apart by unskilled hands, made an obscene, glistening pile in the reeds beside the dead man's burning stable.

No living thing stirred in the village; only another corpse, this one hanging upside down from the half-finished bell tower of Lord Ridel's church, jerked and swayed as gusts of wind whipped around the tower. The graceful pointed arch of the west door rose in a black line against the sky, naked without the vaulting it was to support. As Stephen skirted the church he saw that the smoothly cut voussoirs were covered with coarse, finger-painted pictures done in blood.

The peasants that weren't killed on the spot must have hidden in the reeds, Stephen thought. He halted for a moment, breath burning in his lungs, and listened intently. There was no sound, no cry to tell him where the soldiers had gone, or where they would strike next. But if they had been here, so close to Aude and Edric...

The reeds on either side of the path to Edric's hut were trampled flat, and in one place a pile of horse droppings fouled the surface of the ice. Stephen knew what to expect before he reached the low thatched hut, and braced himself for the worst.

Edric's eyes were open and staring into the light that spilled through the torn-apart thatch of his roof. One of his arms had been cut by a sword heavy enough to shear off the bone, and a pike had gone clean through his chest, pinning him to the one solid beam that held up the hut; Stephen had to work to get it out. There was blood everywhere, and the frail wattle-and-daub hut had been ripped apart by men searching for food and gold. They had kicked over and broken the clay pots full of preserved eels, torn down Edric's fowling nets, and trampled everything into a mess of blood and icy mud.

At least Edric had died quickly. Stephen laid him on the floor of the hut, arms crossed; closed the staring eyes, and this time remembered to murmur the prayers he had been taught.

Then he allowed himself to consider the one sign of hope he had been given: Aude was not there. Might she, like the peasants of Alleford, have escaped into the fens? Could she be hiding there now, shivering among the ice-coated reeds?

Stephen circled the hut, trampling down the stiff, frozen

spikes of marsh grass, slipping on the glossy patches where the water had iced over without a ripple, calling Aude's name in a low voice. A flock of starlings rose from the clumps of frozen sedge between Edric's hut and the village, thrumming their wings and swooping low over the ice before vanishing into the pink, eastern sky. Nothing else moved.

"Aude?"

The sedge rippled, crunched, and parted in pale ice-rimmed waves as a man crawled through on hands and knees. Stephen saw the glitter of mail and stepped backward.

"Hush, boy. I'm a friend—one of Ridel's men." He was young, perhaps in his early twenties, with black hair falling over a thin face. "Joffrey de Belmont. And I know you. From the convent, aren't you?"

Stephen shook his head. His tonsure hadn't been trimmed for a long time since the monks had been waiting for the Candlemas ordinations; with his hair grown out and this patched cloak, he'd counted on passing for a village boy.

"Oh, yes. I never forget a pretty face." The knight chuckled and caught his breath at the end of the laugh.

"You're hurt?" Stephen helped him up. The man's weight was heavy on his arm, and now he saw that there were brownish smears on the hem of his surcoat.

"My leg. One of the King's damned mercenaries caught it with his pike. Nothing serious, it will be all right in a day or two. Stupid thing to do, though—got this far, slid off my horse, couldn't catch it again. He went off behind the church, I think. Bay gelding—name's Autrefois. Bring me my horse and help me to mount—I'll pay you."

Stephen shook his head again. He helped de Belmont over to the side of Edric's hut, where there was a firmly set corner post that the knight could lean on. Under the strain, Stephen's back felt like fire—Coluin's bandages had slipped. "Later. I'm—I have to find someone first."

"The man who lived here? Don't waste your time. He's dead."

"No. There was a girl. I think she must have hidden in the sedge like you. Maybe you saw her? A little slip of a girl, dark curly hair, brown eyes... Her name is Aude...."

"No, no, don't bother going on, boy. She's gone." Joffrey de Belmont's face told Stephen what he didn't want to know. He bowed his head against the stinging wind.

After a few moments he felt a hand on his shoulder. He winced against the knight's heavy touch on his raw back.

De Belmont misinterpreted his involuntary movement. "Don't blame me! I couldn't help. You see how it is—I can't even stand without a wall to brace my back against. I couldn't have saved myself if they'd seen me in the sedge, much less defended the peasants."

"If I'd been there—"

"You'd have been killed, too." A heavy pause. "I'm sorry, lad. It's war. These things happen."

Stephen nodded and looked up to see the knight studying his face. He blinked back the moisture gathering in his eyes.

"You loved her?"

He nodded again.

"Well, then. What are we waiting for? Get my horse and let's go after them. There's still a chance to get her back."

"I thought you said she was dead!"

"No. The soldiers took her with them."

"If you couldn't do anything then . . ."

"Afoot, and wounded, that's one thing, but on my horse, with a good sword, I could charge and surprise them." De Belmont sounded almost cheerful now, as though he were looking forward to the fight. "Besides, there won't be so many to deal with now. They split up after they sacked the village. On horseback, I'd be more than a match for the three who went off with your girl—if we catch up in time."

"Just where did you say you left your horse?"

In his urgency to catch up with the men who'd taken Aude, Stephen didn't pause to question the inconsistencies of Joffrey de Belmont's story until they were well away from the village, heading east on a frosty peat road. He balanced behind the knight, uncomfortable on the horse's broad back, arms around Joffrey.

"I'm sorry if I squeezed you too hard," Stephen apologized after the horse shied at the sound of an alder branch cracking under its weight of ice. "I'm not used to riding, you see."

"That's perfectly all right, lad." Joffrey giggled, breathless and high-pitched like a girl, and Stephen thought that his wound must be paining him more than he would admit.

"It seems strange that the mercenaries would go east."

"Aye, well, belike they meant to take ship at Dunwich for their homeland."

"Wouldn't they wait to be paid first?"

"They probably got more gold from the convent than they'll ever see from our noble King—King John—King Lackland!" de Belmont said with a sneer.

Another thing troubled Stephen about Joffrey's story. He just couldn't see how the mercenaries would have had time to loot the convent, march to Alleford, burn the village, torture a few people, and get away by the east causeway before he himself arrived at the village. Besides, the fires that smoldered in the village had looked as if they'd been burning for some time. And the bodies Stephen saw had been cold—even Edric's. He shivered involuntarily at that memory and Joffrey de Belmont reached awkwardly behind to pat Stephen on the shoulder.

"Bad memories?" His hand moved gently down Stephen's arm, almost like a caress, and Stephen shivered with irritation. He would have moved away from the touch that was making him uncomfortable, but he was afraid to shift his position on the broad slippery back of the horse. The ground seemed so far away!

"I'm not a baby. You don't have to coddle me."

"Maybe I like coddling you." Joffrey's breathless giggle annoyed Stephen and made him inexplicably nervous.

"Do you think we'll catch up with them?"

"Don't see why not."

"Well. Edric's—" Stephen had to stop and swallow before he could go on. "Edric, the man in the hut, he was cold already. If you hadn't told me that you saw what happened, I'd have thought it was some time since the soldiers came through."

"Aye, well, bodies chill fast in this weather. Anyway, what do you know of corpses, lad?"

"Not much," Stephen admitted. "That's more your trade. But—can't we go faster?"

"On frozen ground, and carrying double? I'll not strain a good horse for your fancies, boy."

There was more than a touch of irritation in Joffrey de Belmont's voice, and Stephen held his tongue for the next miles. The sky before them gradually faded from the reflected pink of sunrise to the dull gray of another cloudy day, and rain began to fall again, turning to little needles of ice that stung his bare hands and face.

They rode through the day in silence, hunched low against the freezing wind. The few villages that they passed seemed as deserted as Alleford, but the houses were not torn down and Stephen saw no more corpses.

"The Flemings must be in a hurry to get home. They're not stopping to loot anymore."

"Aye, that must be it!" De Belmont sounded amused. Doubtless he was thinking that he didn't need a boy out of a monastery to teach him his trade. Stephen leaned into the shelter of the knight's back and tried to curb his impatience. If they didn't go faster, they might not catch up with Aude's kidnappers. But if he angered de Belmont, the knight would tell him to go on by himself and Stephen would never catch up with the soldiers—nor would he have a chance of freeing Aude. He would just have to be patient and let the knight direct their search.

By midafternoon they were in wooded country where the trees' shadows grew thick and close about the narrow road, deepening the gloom of the cloudy day. It would be good country for an ambush, Stephen thought. Shouldn't they be on the lookout for mercenaries? But he didn't want to risk annoying de Belmont a second time by trying to teach him his business.

Light flurries of snow fell through the trees and whirled about the woods like dancing figures. Stephen's eyes burned from staring too long and too hard at the white snow and the blue shadows behind the trees. His lids drooped despite his best efforts at alertness and he was startled when de Belmont turned the horse into a small clearing blanketed by snow.

"What—did you see something?"

"We've got to rest somewhere for the night. This is as good as any place. Help me to dismount."

Stephen obeyed de Belmont, but when they were both on the ground and the horse was tethered he couldn't help asking, "Is it too dark to go on? I thought we could ride for another couple of hours before sunset."

"We probably could, but there's no need to tire the horse with a long day, on top of carrying double. And no hurry, now that we're well away from Ely." De Belmont limped to the edge of the clearing, grimacing as he put his weight on his wounded leg. "Cold air helps. But the muscles are getting stiff. I'd better keep walking. You can help me. Gather some deadfalls to make a fire."

"No hurry?" When every minute Aude might be taken farther away? Stephen pulled his bundle of food off the horse's saddle and tucked it under his arm. "I'm sorry. I understand that you don't want to go on, but I have to. If you're stopping here, I suppose I'll have to walk." Stephen knew that on foot he had little chance of catching the soldiers or of getting Aude away from them. But maybe he could shame Joffrey de Belmont into continuing the quest.

"Oh, sit down a minute, boy. What are you in such a hurry for, anyway? We're far enough from Ely now. Nobody's going to come after either of us. We can relax and have a pleasant evening." De Belmont spread out his cloak in the snow and sat down heavily, favoring his left leg. "Sit down!"

"No, thank you. I have to keep looking for Aude."

"For—?" De Belmont's brow creased with genuine puzzlement for a moment, then he laughed. "Oh, your little peasant girl? Don't be a fool, boy. I just told you that story to get you to help me with the horse. You don't think I'd be riding for the seacoast if I thought there was a party of enemy mercenaries ahead?"

"The soldiers didn't take Aude?" Stephen felt slow and stupid, as if the cold and the long ride had gotten into his brain.

"They must have killed her, too, after they had their pleasure with her. There was a girl's body lying not ten feet from where I hid in the sedge." De Belmont laughed again. "But I didn't see it happen—they were gone from the village long before I got there. Must have raided it on their way to Ely."

"Then—why are we going to Dunwich?"

"I'm going to Dunwich to get a ship for France," said de Belmont. "There's no future here for a man in Stephen Ridel's service, and I don't plan to end my days in one of King John's dungeons. And you're coming along with me because you're running away, too, and because I fancied your company for the journey. I can use a boy to help with the horse and keep me warm at night."

"You think I'm going to stay here and build you a fire after you lied and tricked me?"

"Why not? You've nothing better to do." De Belmont stretched out one long arm and caught Stephen's hand. "And about the fire, no, that's not exactly what I meant. Come on down on my cloak and let's see if we can't forget the war for a while."

The sinewy strength of his hand pulled Stephen off-balance and he skidded down on one knee, tumbling against de Belmont's chest.

"Ah, that's a little friendlier? Mind my bad leg, now." De Belmont was fumbling under Stephen's cloak with his free hand, reaching down between his legs while he gave a breathless giggle again. "I thought you must know what I meant, all those monks and no women. Don't tell me one of them hasn't picked out a pretty boy like you for his own—"

He let go of Stephen's wrist to put his arm around him. When de Belmont put the weight of his mail-clad arm on Stephen's raw back, Stephen felt he had been hit with a burning stick. He gasped and jerked uncontrollably, but he couldn't get away from the encircling arms. De Belmont rolled over on top of him, pressing him to the ground, and Stephen screamed as the pain shot through his back. His hands were crushed between his body and de Belmont's. The tips of his fingers touched something cold and hard under his left wrist—the page boy's little knife. Stephen worked it free of the sleeve and twisted his hand around, his fist clenched around the hilt of the knife. The blade scraped across de Belmont's shirt of chain mail. He didn't even notice. He was still laughing, fumbling with Stephen's tunic. As he raised himself slightly to lift the tunic, Stephen thrust his hand up and the tip of the knife sank into de Belmont's throat. The knight reared back, one hand at his neck, and Stephen rolled out from under him and ran into the forest.

Snow flurries blinded him. He dodged trees and felt dry branches tugging at his cloak; in his panic, the twigs became de Belmont's hands, dragging him back to the clearing. Stephen fought wildly against invisible assailants and ran until the winter air burned in his lungs with each sobbing breath.

It was almost dark now, and the falling snow had covered his footprints. Even if he decided to give in and go back to de Belmont, to buy the knight's protection at the price of his shame, he'd never be able to find the clearing again. This was probably just as well, Stephen knew, because if de Belmont were still alive, he was likely thinking more of murder than of shameful lusts just now. Just then, Stephen realized he had left behind his bundle of food, too.

Useless fool! He hadn't been able to save Aude; if de Belmont was telling the truth, she'd been dead before Stephen even knew the King's soldiers were on the Isle of Ely. He probably wouldn't even be able to save himself. If de Belmont didn't get him, chances were that wolves or something worse would. With his monkish upbringing, he couldn't even climb trees well enough to get into the one that loomed above him, its lowest branch well out of his reach.

The blackness of his situation made Stephen feel a sort of crazy cheerfulness. "At least, if I'm not dead by morning, things can only get better," he said aloud.

Something rustled in the thick underbrush to his left, and a snow-laden branch spilled its burden to the ground. Perhaps the branch just above him was not out of reach, after all. Stephen leapt pulling dried scabs loose all across his back and sending waves of pain through him, but he didn't let go of the tree. Perched well above the ground with a stout branch between his legs and the page boy's knife tucked into his sleeve, Stephen bared his teeth at the unseen rustling menace below. There was, after all, a chance that he might live through the night. And in the morning—there was still Dunwich, and Master Brito's stoneyard—if he made it that far.

PART II

The
Journeyman

◻

1216–1221

CHAPTER

6

◫

Some days later, Stephen stood in the freezing rain below Dunwich town and gazed at the ruined little church of St. Michael. The roof of the church had gone long before. Most of the leading had been stripped away, and the rotting timber frame stood like a skeleton. Beneath the half-collapsed jumble of timbers, Stephen could see how the middle of the supporting barrel vault had given way, and the weight of the heavy center stones dragged the half-circle curve down until finally the arch had broken and the roof caved in. It wasn't the waves battering the foundation piers that caused this havoc— time and neglect had been all that was necessary. Now the church was slowly disappearing as its stones, lead gutters, and roofing were carried away by the scavenging fisherfolk, whose new colony clung precariously to the hill above the shingle strand.

The sea lapped at the church's eastern foundations and covered the beach where Stephen's childhood home had stood, while farther out to sea, a new sandbar was slowly growing across the mouth of the harbor. When the wind picked up, salt spray stung Stephen's cheeks; it was almost warm by comparison with the icy sleet that pelted his skin.

Behind Stephen was the town of Dunwich, with its

newly repaired walls, its seven churches, and its narrow streets full of strangers who knew nothing of Maud of Bliburgh or her husband, Alwin. For all anybody remembered, for all he could see before him, that damp, smoky, stinking hut on the shingle might have never existed.

The wind picked up and whipped round the church walls from the northeast, flinging salt spray at Stephen. Head bowed, he stumbled back up the path to Dunwich town. Enough staring out at the sea and thinking deep philosophical thoughts about the past—it was time to be practical. On a day like this Stephen couldn't afford to get his only tunic and cloak drenched; he'd be as stiff as a carved effigy in the cathedral at Ely before he found Master Brito's yard and begged a place at the fire to thaw out. He was cold enough already and being hungry made him feel the cold even more.

Thus far Stephen had had more good fortune on his journey than he had anticipated, beginning with his discovery of a newly cleared field in the forest not far from the tree where he'd huddled on that first bitter night. There was a small, smoky hut belonging to the man who'd made the clearing. He offered Stephen the use of his fire and a platter of thin bean soup, but never mentioned whose serf he was or whether anybody knew where his hut and clearing lay. Stephen was careful not to ask. In return for food and shelter, he spent two days repairing the thatch on the roof, cutting and bruising his hands on the sharp edges of reeds that were stiff with ice.

Then Stephen moved on toward the sea, his journey eased by a warm ride in the covered cart of a traveling peddler. After several more days of patient walking and munching on the sack of black bread and cold pease porridge the peddler had given him, Stephen finally saw the sandy dunes and the sea opening before him like a promise.

His food had run out the night before, and he was stiff from sleeping in a brush shelter where small hungry animals poked inquiringly round his cage of twigs. Any sensible person would have gone straight to Master Brito's stoneyard in the upper, more respectable part of town. But the smell of salt air and the sight of pale grass whipping across the dunes did something to Stephen's good sense.

He was home. He wanted to see his old house and find Mam. Later he could worry about looking for work.

Fat Letselina who ran the alehouse had died of a wasting fever three years before, and the new owner didn't remember Maud of Bliburgh or have much patience for ragged boys who asked questions. This hostile attitude was reflected by both the solid burghers and shivering laborers who jostled each other in the narrow sloping streets of Dunwich. As Stephen worked his way down to the Church of St. Michael and the fishing colony before it, he recognized that Dunwich was a much larger place than he remembered and that he and Maud and Alwin had been a very small, insignificant part of its life.

So it was no surprise that the sea had taken the church and all the narrow huts he remembered from childhood, effacing his past and confusing his memories.

Stephen shook his head as the salt wind whipped his long hair across his face. He tried to drive out the mocking voice of despair that jeered at him. Brother Coluin said that demons lay in wait to tempt men at their weakest hours, and most to be feared was the noonday demon who whispered of the uselessness of all the works of man. The rhythmic pull of the sea and the whispering voice of the demon worked together, convincing Stephen that all was hopeless. He was cold and tired and hungry; why not lie down and let the sea wash over him? He would soon be at peace, never to feel cold again.

Shutting his eyes against the stinging wind, Stephen turned and stumbled blindly up the path, away from the temptation of the waves. It had been stupid to come down here, for he knew his home had been washed away in the storm. His mother had never come back for him. Even Aude had left him—no, she was dead, but it felt all of a piece with his other losses now. He had no past to recapture, only a future ahead of him—work that he wanted to do, and a place to go for the night. He would find Master Brito's stoneyard, get a meal and a place to sleep, and work to keep his mind off the past.

"Try to think about something else," his mother's voice echoed, joining the silky whispers of the sea and the noonday demon. "It takes your mind off." So Stephen concentrated on the remembered shape of an arch rising clean and sharp against the sky, the springing columns pulsing with life, and the high crossing vaults of the galilee porch. He almost managed to shut out the voice of despair within him. Stopping once to ask directions, Stephen followed the man's pointing finger without really taking in the words he said, and he was soon lost in a maze of alleys leading down toward the quays. Through a gap between two sheds he came unexpectedly upon the back entrance of a stoneyard.

On this cold day the stonecutters were all working inside the long lodge that ran along the east side of the yard. Stephen could hear the chink of metal against stone, the low murmur of leisurely conversation broken by occasional laughter, the inviting crackle of the fire whose smoke rose through a clay-daubed hole in the short side of the lodge building.

He would have to go in there. What if Master Brito didn't remember him? Or hadn't meant his casual mention of work for Stephen? Or, as seemed all too likely, didn't want to risk trouble with the Church by taking on a runaway oblate? He should have thought of a story that would convince Master Brito he was free of his obligations to the convent of Ely.

The smell of roasting meat came through the wisps of smoke from the chimney. Stephen's stomach wrenched, reminding him that he had not eaten since yesterday morning. His mouth watered and he found that he was quite unable to think. His legs, numb with cold, were carrying him up to the lodge door without thought. He tapped three times on the door, and as it opened, he used the words he'd heard so many times when wandering masons came to ask for work on the Galilee porch.

"God greet the honorable masons and their master, is there work in the lodge for a traveler?"

The man who had opened the door smoothed both hands over his leather apron and stared wide-eyed at Stephen. Behind him, a second stonecutter dropped his chisel. It hit the stone cheek of an angel, chinked against an ear, chipped a fleck of stone from a marble feather, and fell with a dull thud into the rushes that lay in thick greasy layers upon the earthen floor.

Farther back in the dimly lit lodge, a fat boy, who reminded Stephen of his old schoolfellow Drogo, put hands on hips and laughed loudly.

"Who sent this ragamuffin to interrupt us? Get rid of him, Wimarc, before his lousy beggar's rags stink up the dinner."

The boy couldn't be more than an apprentice, he wasn't old enough, and he didn't even have a beard yet. Stephen expected the man called Wimarc to reprove him for speaking so rudely; instead, with disbelief, Stephen saw the door begin to swing shut in his face.

"Wait!" He thrust his body half inside the lodge before the door closed. "Is this how masons of Dunwich treat a fellow worker? I am a friend of your master's and come to you in courtesy, expecting no less than courtesy and honorable treatment in return."

"A beggar brat with a tongue as long as a chantry priest's," muttered Wimarc. He didn't try to force the door shut, but his lean, calloused hand rested on the frame like a threat, and his body blocked the entrance. "And what would such as you be knowing of the master?"

"Call Master Brito. He'll tell you that I served as his assistant doing the accounts at Ely, two summers past, and he offered me the same work here should I ever come to Dunwich."

Wimarc chuckled, not unkindly. "Nice try, lad. Who told you Master Brito was in Yarmouth for the month? Did you think we'd feed you and keep you hanging about the place for a week or more on the promise that he'd hire you when he got back? And us with barely enough work to keep ourselves this cold season?"

"Yarmouth?"

Wimarc might as well have said France. Stephen hadn't the strength to tramp up the coast to Yarmouth, nor the heart for it. The noonday demon was loud in his ears now, and the sea was a tempting solution.

Wimarc had turned his head and was talking to someone inside the lodge. Stephen paid no attention to what he was saying. Where should he go next? What should he do? There might be work somewhere else in the town, and he must start looking. His stomach was twisted from the good smell of the mutton fat dripping into the fire. He couldn't think here—better to go on.

Head lowered against the wind, he was already turning away when the door was jerked open. A hard push between his shoulder blades sent Stephen sprawling on the ground. The sharp chips of stone that littered the yard stung his hands and knees, and he was so dizzy that it was hard to get up.

"Now get out, beggar brat!"

It was the voice of the fat boy who had jeered at him. Stephen had become a cleverer fighter since that first time he'd run blindly into battle with Drogo years ago. He promised himself he'd have the satisfaction of winning this fight. He rose slowly from his crouch and spun, throwing out his hands toward the boy who stood in the doorway.

The boy cried out and clawed at his eyes. Stephen had filled his hands with the chips of stone on the ground, and the stinging cloud in his face blinded the other boy for precious seconds. Stephen leapt for his throat and knocked him to the ground before he could recover. He felt a savage, hungry exultation in his moment of victory. Drogo, the noonday demon of despair, the knight de Belmont—all were there under his hands to be throttled out of existence.

But there was solid muscle under that fat, and enough to pin Stephen down if the other boy got on top. Once he'd recovered from his initial surprise, the fat boy struck out hard. Still he was no match for Stephen's desperate fury. Straddling the boy and putting his hands round his short neck, Stephen began banging his head on the ground with rhythmic, satisfying thumps.

"All right, all right! That's enough!" The two stonemasons took Stephen by the arms and lifted him off the boy. The mist before his eyes began to clear and he saw no Drogo, no demons, only a greasy-faced boy who was bawling on the ground, making no effort to get up.

Wimarc set Stephen on his feet and let go of his arm. He ought to run now, before the men beat him and threw him out of the stoneyard. But he wasn't sure his legs would carry him. They were shaking so badly, now that the fit of anger had passed, that he could hardly stand.

"Well, now. Powerful bad temper you've got, for a beggar brat." For some reason, Wimarc didn't hit him; he just stood back, shaking his head and clicking his tongue in reproof. "Oh, *get* up, Ivo," he said over his shoulder to the 'prentice boy. "You're not hurt."

"I'm not a beggar. I came looking for honest work. And you need my services."

"What, as a clerk? Don't make me laugh, boy. It hurts

my cough. I told you already, we've no room to hire on anybody this season—and if we did, it'd be a man as knew his trade, not some brat off the streets."

"If your apprentice were doing his job, there'd have been no rubbish like those stone chips that I threw in his eyes." Stephen pointed at the ground where he and Ivo had been fighting. It was littered with chips of stone and knobs of spoilt carving, splintered bones that had been gnawed by the dogs, and dirty rags from the kitchen. "That stuff should be cleared away to the rubbish heap daily, and the spoilt stones should be put to one side in case you need chips of marble for smaller jobs." Eager to show this lean, unsmiling man how much he did know of the trade, Stephen searched his memory for all the details that he'd absorbed while doing the accounts for Brito. "Who brings you the stones and rough cuts them before you set them on the bankers? Who mixes your mortar or burns the lime? And who takes your tools to the forge for sharpening? Don't tell me you trust good chisels to that greasy lump of an apprentice! I could do all that for you—and I'd turn your meat on the kitchen fire, so you don't cook in the lodge and get smoke all over the work." By now the gut-wrenching smell of roasting meat had given way to the less tempting odor of burnt fat.

The other mason gave a howl of dismay and vanished into the lodge, followed closely by the apprentice. "The dinner's going up in smoke!"

"So, lad." Wimarc folded his lean, knobbly hands over his stained leather apron and gave Stephen a long sober stare. "It's a jack-of-all-trades you want to be now, fetching and carrying for us and burning your face as a turnspit boy? And here I thought we had an honorable master mason at our door, a lettered man and a clerk of the accounts, no less!"

Somehow the mockery didn't sting; Stephen sensed a rough kindness behind Wimarc's sarcasm. "I'll do anything I can," he said honestly. "I just want to work here and learn what I can from watching you."

The other mason appeared at the door of the lodge, mournfully regarding a blackened shape that he held aloft on the point of his knife. "Cinder-mutton we're having with our bread today," he mourned.

"All right. You can sleep in the shed over there." Wimarc

pointed at one of the two rickety daub-and-wattle build-ings at the back entrance to the stoneyard. "After dinner, you can take a barrow and spade and clear away that rubbish—and sort out the good bits of marble, like you said."

"You're not taking the brat on?" marveled the other mason.

"Ivo, go down the street to the alehouse and get us a flask apiece to wash down this charcoal formerly called mutton," Wimarc ordered. As the apprentice left, he put one arm round his comrade's shoulders. "Don't we need somebody to do the work that Ivo's too high and mighty to do? Master'll have a litter of brindle pups when he comes back and sees trash all over the yard. Or did you want to clean it up yourself? Besides—"

He glanced at Stephen and lowered his voice. Stephen just caught the words, "Been wanting to give that Ivo a good thrashing for years. Don't you think we owes the boy a few meals for that sight?" He looked back at Stephen. "Come on in the lodge then. You can start work after you've got something in that hollow middle of yours. Makes me hungry just to look at you!"

They gave him the burned bits off the outside of the mutton shoulder, and a mug of thin sour ale to wash it down with. No feast-day meal in the refectory at Ely had ever tasted so good.

During the next few days at the stoneyard, Stephen discovered several things, most good, but one so over-whelmingly bad that it outweighed all the rest and became a stifling weight on his chest each night.

The first good discovery was that there were usually five or six more masons working in the lodge. The others had been off on a job the day Stephen arrived. He was quite relieved when they came back since two masons hardly needed the services of one boy, let alone two. But six men were enough to keep him busy and guarantee that he could earn his keep doing their odd jobs and errands.

Stephen's second good discovery was that no task was too dirty or too dull for him to get some pleasure out of, as long as it had some relation to building. Wheeling barrows laden with heavy stone left him with aching shoulders, trembling arms and raw, blistered hands, but he was learning what size stone a man could shift unaided, what had to be lifted by two men with a stretcher, and what required the use of the cumbersome lifting wheel, with its creaking wooden beams and much-mended leather straps. He learned, too, mostly by being scolded for poor judgment and sent back to the yard, how to select a block of marble that would carve smooth and true, with no hidden faults to split an angel's head from cheek to chin when the mason's chisel came down on it. While the carving itself did not interest him much, he understood that a man would need to know all these other things before he could call himself a master stonemason.

Even sorting flints by hand for the creation of a new flint-and-mortar wall, which was the dreariest job imaginable and one that covered his fingers with tiny stinging cuts, could be interesting when one thought about how those flints were to be used.

"Sorting rubble!" Ivo jeered when he interrupted Stephen at this task. "That's a job for little boys. *I* wouldn't waste my time at it."

Stephen glanced up from the leather pad where he knelt before his buckets of clean-sorted flints and the small mountain of chips yet to be gone through. Ivo's taunt had interrupted the picture he was building in his mind of a wall set with flints in pleasing patterns and accented by smooth-cut stonework. He was irritated by Ivo's intrusion, but by now he knew the one bad thing about Master Brito's stoneyard, so he recited an Ave Maria to himself and answered Ivo pleasantly enough.

"I'm glad of any work I can get here, as you needn't be. And I'm learning things—" Excitement outran discretion. "Look, Ivo. We're going to mix these flints with mortar, higgledy-piggledy like an end-of-the-week stew, right? But what if we set them in the mortar one at a time, like this?" He laid out six of the biggest flints, and over them a row of little ones like diamonds, then another row of large flat stones. "They'd make a pattern and the wall would be stronger because there wouldn't be too much pressure on the mortar in any one place."

"Waste of time. You're dreaming at your work. You'd best get on with it or Wimarc will throw you out for playing games with the flints when you should be working."

Ivo kicked Stephen's pattern-row into the mound of

unsorted flints and managed, as if by accident, to knock
over one of the half-filled buckets as well. He swaggered
away, whistling between his front teeth, and Stephen
began picking up the spilled flints without a word.

The one thing wrong with working at Master Brito's,
he'd learned, was Ivo. Ivo was the shiftless apprentice,
who after three years of training still spoiled more stones
than he cut. Ivo was the bully, who didn't risk another
open fight with Stephen, but somehow managed to have
an endless series of "accidents" that resulted in pinched
fingers, trampled toes, barked shins, and spoiled work.
Ivo was Master Brito's stepson and only heir to the
stoneyard.

And Stephen had started his career at this yard by
fighting with the son and heir. That might have pleased
Wimarc, but Master Brito would feel differently. Ivo had
already made it clear to Stephen that as soon as Brito
returned, he was going to hear how Stephen had,
unprovoked, attempted to kill Ivo with a stone-breaking
hammer. After Brito heard this, Stephen could expect to
find himself back in the streets of Dunwich, with a kick in
the breech from Ivo to speed him on his way.

Three weeks of patience in the face of Ivo's teasing and
bullying hadn't improved his position at all. In those three
weeks, while listening to their casual conversation, Stephen
had learned just how hard times were for workingmen.
The three-cornered war between King John, the barons,
and the French was draining the purses of the great men
who, in better times, commissioned a chantry here and an
abbey there to save their souls. Someday, there would be
more work than all the masons in England could handle,
repairing the stone walls of castles breached or slighted
during King John's drawn-out wars with his barons. But for
now, times were tough: their best commission of the
winter had been the tomb of Sir Hubert of Stokely, and as
Wimarc said, you couldn't hope that a rich Dunwich
knight would die every week of the year. Most of the
carvings they were doing were just stock figures, angels
and saints and capering demons, to be stored away until
some country church was ready to improve its interior. It
was fortunate that Master Brito's purse was deep enough
to support them through this bad season, and even he

wouldn't be able to keep them all on if there weren't a few new building projects in the spring.

At a time when skilled carvers like Wimarc and his mates were grateful to be employed, a boy with no knowledge of the trade would be lucky indeed to find another job fetching and carrying in a stoneyard. Stephen redoubled his efforts to make himself indispensable to the masons, knowing that their wishes would never override Master Brito's. They found tools ready-sharpened and laid in their hands as soon as they reached for them, stone dust swept out of the lodge three times daily, water sprinkled to lay the inevitable small clouds of new dust, and hot, savory stews waiting for them at noon and sunset. And in between his daily chores, Stephen looked for new tasks. He begged three nails from the smithy where he took the tools to be sharpened. With those and a borrowed hammer, he braced the lifting wheel with timber scraps so that it creaked around with slightly less of an air of imminent disaster. Emboldened by that success, Stephen studied the mechanism by which it raised stones, and then he used the machinery to raise a stout timber at an angle against the sagging west wall of the mason's lodge.

His first attempt failed for lack of braces under the timber, and he nearly lost a hand when the timber fell. Stephen dusted himself off, ran to answer a call from the lodge, and spent the dinner hour pushing limp carrots around in his bowl to approximate a series of triangles. Three days later, after recklessly promising to devote all his holidays in the foreseeable future to carrying charcoal for the blacksmith, he attacked the problem again with a pocketful of fresh-made nails and a borrowed hammer. This time it wasn't just one heavy beam he raised, but a triangular network of bracing timbers, culminating in the beam that was to take the weight of the stone roof.

This time it stayed up, but the placement wasn't quite right. When Stephen was at the lifting wheel, using his own weight and muscle to raise the beam, how could he also be at the wall to push the beam a few inches so it would slip into the proper niche? He was trying to work the lifting wheel with one foot, pushing at the beam with his extended arm, when a shadow fell across his face. That would be Hugh, the journeyman who worked with Wimarc. He'd taken a passing interest in Stephen's project and had even lent him an axe to shape the supporting struts. He must have finished his dinner early and come to lend a hand—Hugh was that sort, not too proud to pitch in. Of course he wasn't a full mason yet, with the leather apron and the knowledge of the passwords, handshakes, and other secrets of the lodge that Stephen heard whispered about.

"Put your shoulder to the wheel for a minute, would you, Hugh? I've got to get the beam settled in that old putlog hole, see." Without looking behind him, Stephen moved away from the wheel as he felt the weight of another body holding it in place. He wiped the sweat and long hair out of his eyes with the back of one hand and pushed on the beam until the lifting wheel creaked, protested, and gave him the two extra inches of clearance he needed to swing the timber over. Hugh was grunting with effort, which was odd since Stephen would have thought such a strong man would be able to raise the beam with no trouble at all.

"Got it!" The beam slid into the wall niche with a quiet thunk. Stephen could feel it in himself, the way the vertical load of the stone-shingled roof now ran through the slant of the beam and into the hole where it was grounded, instead of pressing straight down on the wall and causing the posts to give way entirely. Roof to beam to earth: all the force and weight and pressure sank into solid earth. Stephen wiped his forehead again and stepped back to inspect his work. "Thanks, Hugh. She'll hold for a thousand years now."

"Don't ask for the sun and moon, lad. Another fifty would be quite sufficient."

That wasn't Hugh's voice. Stephen whirled around and saw Master Brito himself leaning against the lifting wheel, drops of sweat beading on his red forehead, massive barrel chest wheezing from the exertion.

"Master Brito!"

"The little monk from Ely! Don't tell me you're the new yardboy I've been hearing so much about?"

Stephen could imagine just what he'd heard. All his excitement and pleasure in the finished project drained away. He'd started his month in the stoneyard by fighting with Master Brito's stepson and ended it by ordering the master around like a common journeyman.

"Not a monk anymore. I've left the convent." As he would be leaving here, all too soon.

"They let you go? Oh, so you didn't take your final vows did you? You're a free man now, are you?"

Master Brito sounded genuinely interested. Well, perhaps Ivo hadn't gotten to him yet. But that was no reason for Stephen to get his hopes up. Ivo would tell soon enough, and Master Brito couldn't be expected to keep an untrained yardboy who'd been fighting with his heir.

Meanwhile, an ingrained habit of caution made Stephen answer Master Brito's questions with discretion. "No, I wasn't ordained yet. I was only an acolyte in minor orders, anyone with a bit of learning does that much. I never took the major orders." And minor orders did not prevent a man from living a full life in the world, if that were his choice.

"And you've got a good head for learning, as I recall. Did my accounts a fair treat, that summer. I'm surprised you didn't stay in the Church where you could use those brains of yours. Bit of a comedown, isn't it, from chanting psalms in a convent to getting your hands dirty on odd jobs in a mason's yard?"

"I'd rather shift stones than be a clerk." Dull, stupid words to convey the springing excitement he felt when his hands caressed a perfectly cut curving corbel or when he saw a stone arch rising against the sky with the promise of permanence.

"Oh, aye? Well, don't pack your brains away in sawdust, lad. There's room for thought in our work, too." Master Brito laid one hand on the slanting beam that Stephen had just levered into place, the other on Stephen's shoulder. "This beam, now. Why did you set it out at an angle to the wall, instead of just reinforcing the wall posts? Looks like you made a lot of extra work for yourself." He nodded at the framework of lashed and nailed saplings and short timbers that had taken Stephen a week of dinner hours to cobble together.

Stephen frowned. He was beginning to understand that most people couldn't see what was so clear to him, the lines of force that flowed through everything and that had to balance in the end, or come to solid ground, if a building were to last. But Master Brito was a builder. He must know these things.

"I—the roof—" He swallowed and started over. "The weight of the roof doesn't push straight down. It makes the posts under the wall push out sideways—I can't explain why, but you can see that it does. Look how the wall was beginning to buckle here and here. I thought, if I put a beam at an angle to absorb that sideways force, then the original wall would still be strong enough to take what's left of the thrust downwards."

Master Brito nodded slowly. "An angled buttress to take off vertical thrust. I've been trying to explain that one simple principle to Ivo for three years now. And you figured it out on your own?"

Ivo. Stephen stared down at his supporting framework. It had seemed so strong when he was lashing the saplings together with scaffolding rope and nailing short lengths of scrap wood in triangles that couldn't shift position. Now it looked like a boy's clumsy efforts which had no chance of lasting through the next strong wind.

"About Ivo—" Stephen started.

Brito held up one large hand and Stephen stared, fascinated, at the white scar that ran diagonally across the palm. "I heard about that already."

He must have been more absorbed in his project than he'd realized not to have noticed the bustle attendant on Brito's return. But then, everything would have been happening up front, in the house, where Stephen didn't go.

"I didn't know he was your son."

"Stepson."

"Stepson, then."

"I can't have people in the stoneyard who don't get along," said Brito finally. "And Ivo's not going anywhere."

"I understand that." He hadn't fought with Ivo since that first day. Was it any use asking Master Brito to give him another chance? No. Long ago he'd learned that it didn't matter what you said. If you were a nuisance they left you anyway, no matter what you promised. . . .

He'd learned, too, that it did no good to start thinking in crazy, pain-filled circles. Stephen stared at the white line running across Brito's palm until it blurred before his eyes into the high curve of a pointed arch, until the stubby upraised fingers looked like a row of columns stretching down to a point of light at one end.

He couldn't come so close and now give it all up, just because of a stupid mistake on his first day in the stoneyard. He wouldn't.

"I'm not going anywhere, either." Stephen heard how thin and reedy and unsure he sounded, and strove to put more confidence into his voice. "You don't want me to leave, Master Brito. I've been a good worker, ask anybody here. And you said yourself I understood the principle—the principle—"

Master Brito's words of praise hovered just beyond the reach of his tongue, and the noonday demon crackled at his failure. He was nothing, a runaway, foresworn, lost to God, and nobody would ever love him.

But Stephen didn't ask for love, only for a chance to learn and work. Reminding himself of that, he was able to shut out the demon. Then the words came to him and he turned to face Master Brito with logic and good sense.

"The principle of using an angled buttress to take off vertical thrust. I understand stones. I'm good at this and I would be good for your yard. I don't ask for pay, I'm happy to sleep in the hut and eat whatever's left over, and I'll keep doing all the odd jobs, but let me stay here. Let me learn. Please, you have to let me learn!"

Something terrible was happening to the logic; his naked desire was showing through. Stephen tried to reconstruct the rational arguments he was going to make, but all he could think of was how terribly much he wanted to stay. He wanted the stoneyard, the learning, and the rough companionship of masons and journeymen. And the more he longed for it, the more certain he was that he would lose it and be left alone again. The demon was perched on his shoulder, whispering that he was worthless, flawed, and not worth keeping. Master Brito still hadn't spoken. Stephen stared at the master, willing him to give in.

"I *am* good. I would be a good builder." He had nothing more to offer than that, his certainty and his love of the work. It had to be enough.

Master Brito sighed. "So I hear."

"You do?" This he hadn't expected.

"I had every mason in the yard tugging at my sleeve, all talking at once. They seem to think you're handy to have around. Shouldn't be let go, they said. Worth his keep, and more, they said. It would be good business to keep him—that was Hugh. Imagine a journeyman tryin' to tell me how to manage my affairs!"

Another pause. The wind had picked up and there was a hint of salt from the harbor. It clawed at Stephen's face as if it were trying to force tears from him.

"You'd have to promise—no more fighting—*whatever* the provocation."

That sounded like a reprieve. Was it possible Brito meant to let him stay?

"Oh, I promise. I haven't been fighting. I—Wimarc can tell you—" Wimarc probably already had told him; Stephen swallowed the confused jumble of words crowding into his throat.

"And you can't stay here on this basis. Running errands, cooking dinner for God's sake. My masons are going to get above themselves, thinking they have a personal servant."

"But then—you want me to leave?" asked Stephen, panic-stricken. For a moment he'd thought it would be all right, and now—"No. I won't go."

"Who said anything about going?" Brito was grinning, as if he'd just opened some pleasant surprise and expected Stephen to be equally delighted. "I said you're not staying on as a personal servant to my hired help. If you're to stay with me and I'm going to invest my good time in teaching you the trade, I want apprenticeship papers drawn up right and proper. Make sure you don't flit away without working out your time—I know how you boys are, this week you want to be a stonemason, next week you're mad to go sailing on a merchant ship! And shut your gaping mouth, you look like a fish begging for the hook."

Stephen shut and opened his mouth several times. It was too much. He had been preparing to go back to the streets where runaways belonged. Instead, Master Brito was offering him a priceless gift. Stephen knew what an apprenticeship was worth. It was years of training, with a chance for a decent trade at the end of it; he'd written up the papers himself from time to time, when townsfolk in Ely came to the convent looking for a clerk to do the job. Most of them paid the master in silver, or else promised him the income from a piece of land or a mill in recompense for the years when the boy was being trained and couldn't earn the cost of his keep.

"I don't have anything to pay you with," he pointed out.

Master Brito pretended to scowl. "Oh, yes, you do. You're not going to be another lazy 'prentice, swilling ale by the bucket and spoiling stones. When you're not working in the lodge, I expect you to keep my account books up to date. On your own time—nights and holidays."

"They shall be perfect," Stephen promised, glowing. "Clean parchment. Black ink. Every page balanced. You'll know the cost of every piece and the time it took to produce it, down to the last clipped farthing. I'll double your profits!"

"Hmmph. And the wall will last a thousand years, you said? I'll be content with a lodge that doesn't fall down and a set of account rolls that show a profit of any sort."

At the back door he stopped and gave Stephen a stern look. "And remember, I'll have a peaceful stoneyard. Masons are bad enough for fighting; I don't need a quarrelsome apprentice adding to the turmoil."

CHAPTER

7

◫

The next five years should have been a time of unalloyed happiness for Stephen. No one from Ely came searching for him; Master Brito cheerfully allowed him to turn his hand to any work within his growing competence; and he made friends with the masons and journeymen in the yard. Hugh became Stephen's particular friend and mentor, teaching Stephen all that guild regulations allowed as he himself advanced from journeyman to full-fledged mason with his own mark to cut on the stones.

Master Brito's stoneyard prospered during those years, too. The ruinous war between King John and his barons ended in October of the first year of Stephen's apprenticeship; the King fell ill and died, and the barons agreed to disallow the French claims in favor of the King's young son, Henry. William the Marshal, old and tired from the wars of three reigns, reluctantly assumed the regency, and under his nonpartisan leadership, the troubled land slowly returned to normal. As a part of this restoration, the castles that had been slighted by John or wrecked by the French invaders were rebuilt, and the royal treasury provided work for as many good stonemasons as Brito could find.

There were only two problems with Stephen's happy, peaceful life in the stoneyard. One was that in less than three years, Stephen learned all that Brito could teach him of the art of building, and his gratitude for the apprenticeship was mixed with the chafing desire to move on. He longed to have a hand in the creation of the great works that were going up around the land: the west facade of the church at Peterborough, the Lady Chapel at Winchester, the central tower at Gloucester. In the summers, the journeymen and masons traveled across the country to work on these projects, returning to Brito's in cold weather with tales of the magnificent buildings they had helped to raise. Stephen and Ivo, as lowly apprentices, could not go out looking for work; Brito kept them close at hand, laboring on the flint-and-mortar houses and cutting tombs to a standard pattern that represented the height of his own building skill. Finishing the Galilee porch according to the designer's plans had been the greatest achievement of his career, one he neither expected nor desired to repeat. It made a man's head hurt, he said, all those curlicues and new-fangled high vaults; you had to measure everything twice over before it was cut. Better to stick to the good old styles and get them right; that way you could do the same building over and over and never have to think about it.

"You still have a lot to learn about carving," Hugh would point out when Stephen complained of boredom. "The last angel you did had a twist to his mouth that made him look like the blacksmith's hunchbacked helper trying to smile, which would be good art if you'd intended it, but I think it was sheer clumsiness."

"I'll never make a freestone carver," Stephen agreed. "I don't want to. I want to build things."

"Aye? And what's wrong with that tower you and Brito put up for the fishing colony at Walberswick, so that they could ring a bell of warning in stormtime? Nice solid bit of flint-and-mortar work that ought to last out our time."

"I don't want to spend my life making flint towers and one-room churches for villages in the sand dunes. I want to build great things. Chapels, castles, cathedrals!" Stephen's arms stretched over his head as if to encompass the world of lordly monuments that danced in his mind.

"Fine, you do that—someday. Meanwhile, Master Brito wants a half-dozen stone cherubs in stock to replace those we installed last summer, and you're to help me. Try not to make 'em all grimace like souls in torment, will you?"

The other problem with working in the yard was Ivo's intermittent hostility. On good days, Ivo swaggered round the yard, calling all the masons good fellows and inviting Stephen to join him in a visit to the friendly girls at the alehouse in the lower town; on bad days he sulked in a corner, pretending to chip away at a stone carving and glowering at Stephen. The minor accidents that plagued Stephen from time to time always occurred on Ivo's bad days: a good bucket of mortar would unaccountably develop a leak that drained all its water, leaving the mortar to harden in the bucket; the lashings that held scaffoldings together would suddenly come loose, almost tipping Stephen over the top of the tower he was working on; a block of marble would happen to slide off a stationary barrow and come within a hairsbreadth of crushing his fingers.

There wasn't anything to be done. Since the death of his wife, Master Brito was responsible for Ivo, and Stephen learned to hunch his shoulders and endure the bad days. He also developed a caution habit, one that would stand him in good stead throughout his working life, of checking and double-checking any scaffolding or lifting crane or trestle on which someone's life and safety depended.

"Ivo's sour because he's been apprenticed seven years and hasn't been raised to journeyman yet," Hugh told Stephen. "I expect Brito's afraid to give him the responsibility. It's nothing to do with you—don't take it personally."

Stephen glanced at the swollen ankle that he sprained when a trestle table sagged and broke under his weight, and limped away without argument. Hugh was right, no doubt. And Master Brito had made it clear that his tenure in the yard depended on his ability to avoid fights with Ivo. And anger would cloud his brain so that he couldn't do Master Brito's accounts with the perfect accuracy and neatness that was his personal standard. This was the only repayment he could offer to the man who'd given him a start in life.

If only life would start! Stephen knew now that building the same thing over and over without thought or planning, as Brito did, would never satisfy him. He wanted more, but he didn't know how to get it.

In the cold February of 1219, three years after he'd come to Brito's, a teasing shaft of hope opened before him. On a dark evening when Stephen was laboring over Brito's books, the master himself appeared.

"Ivo's going to be made journeyman," Brito announced as he walked into the narrow cubicle where Stephen kept the books. A half closet walled off from the kitchen by a thin partition of scrap boards and plaster, it was tiny and smoky and smelled of cabbage, but it was also warm—a luxury Stephen appreciated on days when his hands were almost too numb to hold a pen. Brito's solid paunchy bulk filled the cubicle.

Stephen put down the pen and waited for Brito to go on. "I shall offer him my congratulations in the morning, master." It seemed an odd subject to be raising at eight of the clock on a dreary February night.

"He's been apprentice for eight years come Candlemas. I can't keep him well—that is—I won't live forever, you know. Ivo has to learn some responsibility before he takes over the yard. He's a grown man; it hurts his pride to be only an apprentice when Hugh, who's just one year older, got his mason's mark last year. By making him a journeyman, I'll show him I've some faith in his work, and he'll likely straighten out, stop wenching and drinking so much, and put his back into the work."

Nothing seemed less likely to Stephen—or less to do with him. "Very likely, master."

"Besides, I can't very well give you your journeyman's mark and leave Ivo as an apprentice, can I? Well, can I now?" Brito glowered at Stephen as though he'd been contradicted.

"Me!" His articles of apprenticeship had two more years to run. "But, master, I'm not—"

"Don't try and tell me you're not ready. You learned all I could teach you by last fall, when we finished that bell tower. If I want to keep you around here, I'll have to give you better work to do in the warm season. And I'm not about to go setting myself up as a master builder with a gang of masons to build castles and cathedrals just because I've got an ambitious apprentice yapping at my heels. So you'll have to go tramping for summer work from now on, instead of hanging about the yard eating me out of house

and home. Which means you'll have to be a journeyman,
or nobody'll take you on. Understand?"

"Yes, but what about the accounts?"

"Summer I can manage for myself, it's not so hard with
the size of the jobs I take on. And you'll still manage the
yard during the winter. That's another reason I'm making
you a journeyman. You've a good head on your shoulders,
now that you've learned to keep your temper, and I need
someone to take over from me, until Ivo's ready."

"Take over? You're not retiring?"

Brito slowly shook his massive head. "Not retiring, no.
But it's time for me to take things a little easier. It's getting
to be too much for me, going out in all weathers, inspecting
the marble sent by the quarry, and riding around the
country taking orders. You know that side of the work as
well as I do. Well? Is it agreed? You'll be made journeyman on Candlemas, your eighteenth birthday. And you
can go to work at Peterborough with Hugh, if he gets
taken on again this summer. But in the winters you'll come
back here and manage the yard for me."

"Will Ivo accept that? He's planning on taking charge
of the yard when you step down." Only one week ago
Stephen had heard him in the alehouse, boasting of the
great wealth that he would get out of the stoneyard and
predicting that his stepfather wouldn't last much longer.

"And so he shall. It's his inheritance. I promised my
woman I'd see him well cared for, and so I shall. I'm not
stepping down yet, Stephen—a long way from it! You're
going to assist me with the clerking and such, same as
before. Now get on with your work, will you? I don't know
why you're wasting all this time gossiping, you'll not be
done before dawn at this rate."

Brito tramped off to bed, and as his heavy steps receded, Stephen picked up his pen and tried to make sense of
the black figures that danced on the page before him.
Payments to the limeburner, to the blacksmith, to the
quarry that supplied marble; silver still owed them by the
Church of St.-George-by-Walberswick for the frieze of
marble vines and martyrs' heads; all the numbers ran
together in a meaningless jumble. Peterborough. In the
summer he would go to Peterborough to work with Hugh
under one of the great builders in the land. His fingers
were too cold to hold the pen properly, and the ink had

dried to a black blob on the end of the quill while he was listening to Brito; but in his head all the birds of summer were singing.

In the long months before summer work began, Stephen found that his position in the yard became even more difficult. Instead of being pleased with his own advancement, Ivo took it as a personal insult that Stephen should be raised to the grade of journeyman at the same time. Almost daily he accused Stephen of plotting to steal the stoneyard from him, of worming his way into the good graces of a senile old man, of cheating on the accounts and ruining the business of the yard. When Stephen could stand it no longer, he would go to the rubbish heap where the spoilt stones were dumped and methodically hammer a single stone into a pile of marble chips until his shoulders ached and his arms shook with exhaustion.

"Better the stone than Ivo, I suppose," Hugh commented when he found Stephen pounding on the half-carved face of an angel that had been discarded when a mason uncovered a vein of rusty red that ran through the angel's nose. "Although, I must say, some of us wouldn't mind if you gave Ivo another beating to match the one he had that first day you came to us, remember?"

"Master Brito would mind, and I owe him a lot."

"I'd say you owe Ivo something, too. Like a good thrashing. Well, if you don't care what he says, it's none of my business. We're through work for the day, and I've got some personal matters to see to." Hugh went off whistling. He was courting a girl named Avice who lived in the lower town and nothing that happened in the yard had the power over him of Avice's smiles and frowns.

Stephen rose and dusted off his hands, looking down at the angel's spoiled head and wondering just how long he would be able to keep his hands off Ivo. He was used to Ivo's malicious insinuations, but lately the other journeyman had hit on a line that genuinely worried Stephen. He had discovered that Stephen hated to be questioned about his origins. Now the lodge was filled with Ivo's "general" comments about orphan boys who came out of nowhere, who were afraid to tell honest folk why they were running away, and who probably had committed some crime too vile to be mentioned among decent people. Since his return to Dunwich, Stephen had managed to avoid telling anyone about Ely, and Master Brito had kept his own counsel about Stephen's origins. He was no longer afraid that Brother Daniel would appear out of nowhere, an avenging angel come to drag him back to keep the vows he'd repudiated. But Stephen would be damned if he would let Ivo bully his long-kept secret out of him!

A gentle rain settled the dust Stephen's furious hammering had raised and cooled his forehead. He took a deep breath and sniffed the damp, sweet evening air. It would not be long till spring was truly here. When the building season began, he'd be off to Peterborough with Hugh. Surely he could put up with another month of Ivo's heavy-handed teasing.

But what about the fall, when he returned to more of the same? Stephen put that question out of his mind. Anything might happen by fall, though he couldn't think of what would cut the double knot between his obligations to Brito and his continual, escalating clashes with Ivo.

That spring Hugh married his Avice, who was already big-bellied with their first child on the day they exchanged their vows. Just two weeks later, bemoaning the necessity to go tramping for work, he kissed his new bride good-bye and set off on the long road to Peterborough with Stephen at his side. Now it was Hugh's turn to brood, and Stephen's to whistle, as he pictured himself following the designs of the master builder who was putting up the west front of Peterborough in the grand French style. Stephen looked forward to learning how to design the high pointed arches and overarching clustered vaults that were to make this Church of St. Peter a landmark in the flat Anglian countryside.

The first days at Peterborough were a sore disappointment to Stephen. As a lowly journeyman, he worked strictly within the lodge, not even allowed to cut stone as he'd done at Master Brito's. Mostly he ran errands for Hugh and the other masons, which would have been all right, if only he'd been able to watch the masons at work and understand the master plan behind the building. But he found himself unable to make sense of the early stages of building. The foundations crisscrossed with a spider's web of strings and stakes and the columns were spaced at seemingly random intervals. The bits of drawings that were to guide the master masons were as tantalizing as the smell of roast meat without the taste of it in your mouth. A templet for a corbel, an order to deepen the foundation trenches on either side of the long facade—he couldn't make any sense of it.

Hugh was unsympathetic to his grumblings.

"Why do you need to know such stuff? By the time it comes down to us it's all bits and pieces anyway; all we have to worry about is doing our bit right. Look, Master Adam tells the master of the works that he wants two dozen corbels in this shape. Master of works copies the templet, gives me a copy, and tells me to cut a half-dozen corbels while his senior masons do the rest of them. I figure the size block I need and send you to the stone pile to get me a smooth bit of marble without any cross grains to split on me. You do your bit, I do mine, master of works does his. Nobody ruins their one little piece, nobody has to worry about anything beyond their capacity, and Adam of Lincoln makes a nice facade for the church. Everything works out, Stephen, if you'd stop complaining and let it work."

"Yes, but I can't see how it's going to work. Look at the foundation. Why did he stretch lines from corner to corner, when we're only supposed to dig trenches along the outside? Why are the portals so much bigger than the aisles of the church? What is he going to do with—"

A friendly cuff on the head from Hugh silenced Stephen. "And who are you to question a master builder? Master Adam knows what he's doing, or the clerics of Peterborough wouldn't have given him the contract. Run along and mix up another lot of mortar. We have to lay another course on the northside piers this morning before I can get back to my carving."

An entire summer went by that way, with Stephen watching and listening and trying to absorb as much of the art of building as he could. By the end of the summer, they were ready to raise the first pier stones upon the foundation trenches. Stephen could have cried when the onset of frost ended the work and they had to return to Dunwich for the winter. Brito's unfeigned pleasure at his return was some balm for his frustration, and the work of untangling the messy blots and scrawls representing the master's summer accounts kept him too busy to brood. Besides, he consoled himself, next summer he would be more experienced and therefore would have more opportunity to learn what Master Adam was really doing at Peterborough.

In the years after King John's death, during the minority of his son Henry, William Marshal used the interval of peace to strengthen the country's defenses. He poured revenues into the task of rebuilding the coastal defenses and restoring castles and city walls that had been slighted during the wars. Now that the great task was coming to an end, masons had to look elsewhere for work. For a mere journeyman like Stephen, there was no chance of finding a job at Peterborough that year. Stephen had to settle for doing repairs on the sagging apse of an old Norman church in the fen country. He learned some useful things about the tensile strength of various kinds of wood beams, and the flat, open fens were pleasant and soothing to his spirit now that he no longer felt trapped there. He thought about Aude and prayed for peace for her spirit, and then he wondered how the work at Peterborough was progressing without him.

The following building season Stephen returned to Peterborough, almost a mason but still restricted to a journeyman's duties. At twenty, Stephen felt he was the equal of any mason, yet he lacked the mark, the special sign and grip, and all the secrets of the lodge. In his craft he was a boy until he achieved those things. Brito had promised to give him his mason's mark in the fall, but only in return for Stephen's promise that he would stay on at the Dunwich stoneyard for at least another year. "I'm asking a lot, I know, lad," he'd said with the heavy wheezing sigh that seemed to get worse with each damp winter. "But I need your help, so I do. Ivo's not old enough to take on the responsibility yet."

And he never would be. Master Brito's face was gray with fatigue at the end of each long day. He was too old to sit up late over the accounts he hated, to trot round the yard supervising lazy masons, to make trips out into the country in search of new work for his men. "I'll stay as long as you need me," Stephen said at once, and then was ashamed to find himself praying that it wouldn't be so very long.

"You're a good lad." Brito's hand lay light as an autumn

leaf on Stephen's shoulder. Five winters of that cough had dried up the fat and muscle that used to weight his grip. "Have a good summer. Do well, and I'll give you your mark in the fall."

"Do well!" Stephen repeated under his breath, the week after he and Hugh had arrived at Peterborough. There was no glut of trained men this year, rather a shortage, but he was still not allowed to do anything but menial tasks. Three great arches were slowly rising. Stephen could trace their intended shapes in the sky, but he still didn't understand how Master Adam planned to join them to the body of the church. They were wider than the doors, and would have to rise far too high.

"You can't tell now what shape they'll be when they're done," Hugh said reasonably.

"Yes, I can. Their height will have to be in proportion to their width, otherwise the weight will push the columns outward—I can feel how it will go, but I can't explain why." Stephen was angered by his limitations. He could feel in his bones how the arches would have to rise, he could sketch it in the sand, but he couldn't understand the builder's intention. If he didn't know why it was done, how could he ever do it himself? He wanted to be up in the tracing room making the decisions instead of doing an apprentice's work.

After the mortar was mixed, there was a call for some unflawed marble in the carving lodge, and while Stephen was persuading the masons that the greenish grain on the block he'd brought would only enhance the beauty of their carving, a peevish, incomprehensible shout came from the tracing house.

The warden of the carving masons sighed and unlocked the tool cabinet. "Master Adam has broken another pair of dividers. Everytime he gets into an argument with the canons, he bears down too hard and breaks his dividers, and then he loses his temper and curses in what he thinks is French because he believes it's a more dignified form of blasphemy for a successful architect. Here, boy." He handed the great three-foot dividers to Stephen. "You take these and tell him it's all we've got left since he broke the hinges on all the smaller dividers and the smith is too busy with Master Adam's other rush order. No, don't tell him any of that, just give him the dividers and get out before he throws them at your head."

Instead of throwing the dividers or cursing in bastard French, Master Adam of Lincoln showed Stephen a face wreathed in smiles as he took the great dividers. "At last, someone with the intelligence to understand what we need up here! How can I trace my design on plaster with the toys that imbecile downstairs keeps sending up? Here, lad, take the little dividers back down and tell that lackwit to stop giving me the wrong tools at the wrong time. Now, good sirs, if you will step over to the plaster form, I will show you exactly how my design is to rise into the crowning beauty that will make your church the marvel of the shire."

With the next breath, Master Adam had forgotten Stephen, his irritation, and the entire question of what tools he needed. Pacing back and forth beside the slab of newly wetted plaster that held his scale drawing, he pointed, swept out a curve with the dividers, crossed the curve with two lines, and scratched a minute symbol where the lines met. All the while he was talking about the laws of proportion *ad quadratum* and *ad trigonum*, the harmony of the spheres, and the balancing properties of pinnacles set atop spires set atop pier towers.

Leave? Go back to carrying stones and mixing mortar, when at last he had a chance to hear the talk of architects in the tracing house? Not likely! Stephen slipped behind a high trestle table in the corner, and, concealed by mounted drawings, he tried to memorize everything Adam of Lincoln was saying.

It was complicated, beautiful, and incomprehensible, like the west facade slowly rising below them. Stephen didn't understand more than three words in ten of the architect's discussion, but he drank it all in as if it were his first taste of air after a lifetime under water.

Here, at last, was a man who knew what he was doing and why he was doing it, a man far beyond Master Brito and his round towers. Every gesture, every rolling and incomprehensible sentence bespoke Master Adam's superiority and his heavy, fur-trimmed sleeves and long gown gave him an air of confidence and nobility. True, this unseasonably hot day was hardly the weather for such heavy clothes, but Master Adam did not seem to feel the heat, and it was clear that he felt every bit of the dignity conferred by his fine garments.

Listening to Master Adam's discourse were three clerics in long black robes, fine-woven and lined with black silk. They reminded Stephen of the canons and obedientiaries who held high offices at Ely. They were as important in the world of Peterborough as Brother Daniel had been in Ely; yet they listened respectfully to what Master Adam of Lincoln had to say, hardly daring to interrupt with questions.

Stephen watched the faces of the clerics as Master Adam held forth. No question who was in charge here: they were grateful for his knowledge, grateful for his condescension in explaining his plans to them. The churchmen might be paying for the new west facade, but Master Adam in his fur-trimmed gown was telling them how to use their money. His brain directed the work, and when it was done, it would stand as a monument, not to the church's deep purse, but to Adam of Lincoln's sense of beauty, structure, and design.

Someday, Stephen promised himself, he too would stride across a tracing house floor, drawing lines in wet plaster that were to become things of eternal beauty in stone, imperiously dismissing the clerics with a wave of his furred gauntlets as Master Adam did now. "I trust my humble explanation was adequate, gentlemen? Good. Now, pray, allow me the solitude I need in which to complete this design. It must be done early as I am to dine with the sheriff of the county tonight. Some matter of the royal building plans. I trust I shall not be called to London to discuss the matter with the council; it would be a pity for my absence to delay the work here."

That was a master builder, a man who dined with the sheriff and discussed building plans with the King's advisers! Stephen watched, wide-eyed with awe and envy, as the three clerics tripped in their haste to leave Master Adam to his creative solitude. One of them knocked over the drawings on the trestle table in front of Stephen, and he bent to pick them up before he remembered that he wasn't supposed to be there. Kneeling on the floor, head down, he stretched out the small task until the churchmen had clattered down the outside stairway. Maybe, Master Adam would forget his presence again.

He stood up slowly to find that the master builder was

human after all. Now that his clients were out of sight, he was fumbling with his belt and stripping off the fur-lined robe that had given his gestures such dignity. The long tunic underneath was stained with sweat.

"That's better," he declared, tossing the heavy robe at Stephen. "Catch, boy. What are you still doing here, anyway? I thought I told you to take the small dividers downstairs. Never mind, you can hang up my robe before you go." Before he had finished his sentence, Master Adam was kneeling in front of the plaster slab, quite oblivious to Stephen's presence. He was muttering to himself while erasing the lines he'd just drawn with a flick of his hand. After each stab at the plaster, he stopped and consulted a small flat book that he cradled in the palm of his left hand. Stephen stole forward cautiously, until he could see every detail of the drawing for himself.

When he could make it out, he was overcome with disappointment. Expecting to see an elaborate drawing of the west facade as it would stand when completed, he found nothing but a network of intersecting arcs and lines, points labeled with strange symbols, and hen scratchings of arrows bristling like the spurs on a fighting cock.

It didn't look like a building. In fact, it didn't look like anything on God's earth. Stephen was so confused that he opened his mouth a second before he remembered that he wasn't supposed to be there.

"What *is* that?"

"Eh? What! A spy!" The book was slammed shut; a quick movement of one hand over the wet plaster erased the delicate web of lines that had taken so much concentration to create. Almost in the same motion, Master Adam was on his feet advancing toward Stephen, who backed toward the door with one hand raised before him.

"Who sent you here? Who paid you to spy on me?"

The questions shot forth like pellets from a sling. Master Adam was a small man, a head shorter than Stephen, but that did not lessen the menace Stephen felt in the barrage of questions. Confused, he stared at Master Adam's intent, glaring face and thought that he saw yet more intersecting lines and circles in the wrinkles that ran around the sharp black eyes and down either side of his long nose.

"Answer me, boy! Who's paying you?"

At last, Stephen's sense of humor returned. "Why—you,

good master. That is, I work here. You sent for me yourself. You wanted someone to bring the great dividers up, remember? And then you told me to hang up your robe. I'm one of your masons."

"You lie. You're too young. Journeyman, perhaps." Master Adam still peered up at Stephen with hostility, but the sharp edge of his suspicion was wearing off. "You're spying for someone."

"I wasn't spying. I wanted to know!"

"Know what?"

"Everything."

The master builder tried to hold his frown, but clearly he was finding it difficult. "That's rather ambitious, boy. What did you think you could learn from my tracing plaster? Secrets of the French style to pass on to my competitors?"

"I want to learn to build in the French style," Stephen admitted. "But not to pass on to anyone. For myself. Someday I'm going to be a builder."

"You've a long way to go before you have any business in the tracing house."

"I know that." Master Adam didn't seem angry or suspicious anymore. "I look at the foundations you've laid out, but I can't see how the west front is going to match the rest of the church. And I couldn't understand anything in the drawings you were making just now."

"Of course you couldn't. You'd have to understand geometry. It's the foundation of all art, especially ours."

"Geometry." Hadn't Joscelin mentioned that? It was one of the subjects of the quadrivium, that he would study at the university. But Joscelin thought it had little use, compared to the higher arts of theology, canon law, and logic. "Is that anything like logic?"

"Anything like—?" Adam of Lincoln let out a long, slow whistle. "Boy, geometry is the basis of logic and reason, what separates us from the beasts. It is also the basis of the builder's craft. How do you think I manage to keep all the proportions of this great building the same from season to season?"

Stephen thought. "Well," he said at last, "Master Brito has a foot rule that he uses to check everything. I suppose you have one, too."

Adam of Lincoln snorted. "A foot rule! Of course I have,

but what good does that do when every builder and foreman and master mason in Christendom has his own rule, and they're all different? Look, my Italian carver uses the Aragonese foot, which is shorter by an inch than any English measure. The master in your lodge has a metal ruler that he got from his master in France, and that's based on the Bordeaux foot, which is longer again than any English. I use the *pied-du-roi* of Paris, but the first builders of this church used the Norman foot, which was almost as short as the Aragonese. . . . Need I go on? A rule is good enough for a small job with only one master. It would never serve on a project like this. Nor does it solve the problem of transferring small designs to full-scale foundations. All this, journeyman, I do by the great, secret art of geometry, and no man lacking that art may aspire to the mastery of the builder's craft."

"Oh. Well," said Stephen hopefully, "I know a little logic, actually. White horses and reality and all that." He improvised from his memory of Joscelin's disputations with Coluin. The academic atmosphere of this talk was carrying him back to those peaceful days in the cloister. He forgot for a moment to be afraid of the master builder who'd caught him here. "I was rather good at logic," he lied. "Geometry can't be that much harder. Maybe you'd teach me?"

Sitting on the high stool before the trestle table, feet hooked on the lower rungs and knees splayed out, Master Adam indulged in a long laugh. "Teach you? By God, for a nameless journeyman, you've got the nerve of a bull calf bawling for its mama! I, Adam of Lincoln, spent seven years disputing with the best minds in Paris and brought the secrets of the French style to this benighted country. I am the greatest architect in England—do you think that my skill and knowledge is something I can pass on to an apprentice while he munches his bread and onions? You couldn't even read the notes in my sketchbook, for I don't write in common English, but in Latin, the language of learning. Get out of here, boy. You've given me a good laugh, but you're wasting my time. Now I have to start over with the drawing you spoiled."

Stephen thought of pointing out that Master Adam had spoiled the drawing himself, with his zealous suspicions and accusations. But there wasn't any reason to argue. He had overreached himself. Master Adam was right.

"We have a few good minds on this side of the Channel, too," Stephen said at last, thinking of Joscelin. "And even great architects have to start somewhere. You'll hear of me someday."

It had been a stupid defense—he knew that as he marched down the stairs, with the sound of Master Adam's laughter still in his ears.

CHAPTER

8

▨

That afternoon Stephen was laying heavy stones with the rest of the laborers while Hugh carved the elaborate scrolled border stones for the north pier tower, something Stephen was not permitted to yet. That was all right with Stephen; the years of making Brito's stone angels had convinced him that he was never going to be more than an indifferent stone-carver. He didn't care enough about decoration. What interested him was the master builder's ability to turn something as heavy as stone into a living, attenuated frame of light, shot through with the tension of balanced stresses and singing like music as it rose toward heaven.

"Building," he said to himself as he labored to set foundation stones in place over their bedding of crushed rock. "Building, that's what I care about."

The old man beside him grunted with effort as he levered a square-cut stone into place. "That is good. Since it is what you are being paid for."

"I'm not doing this for the pay."

"Indeed?" A bright, ironic glance speared Stephen momentarily, as the man's black eyes sparkled from a lined face tanned to the color of dark leather; then the old man lowered his head to his task again. "You have an independent income, perhaps? A gentleman of the aristocracy in disguise; amusing himself by seeing how the commoners live?"

"You don't have to make game of me, although," said Stephen as he spread mortar between the two stones, "it does seem to be a popular pastime these days. What's wrong with loving your work?"

"Nothing," agreed the old man. "As it happens, I too love the art of building—although I could wish to pursue it upon a more elevated plane." He straightened, putting one hand to the small of his back like a woman big with child. "My back, especially, wishes the same. By coincidence, I too am not working for the money—though perhaps not from pure dedication. I do not get paid."

"Why not?"

"I am a prisoner of war. Boy, we want more mortar here."

Stephen studied the tan, wrinkled face with interest while they waited for one of the day-laborer boys to bring up a fresh bucket of mortar. "You don't look French," he hazarded. But what else could a foreign prisoner of war be? he wondered. The only foreigners who had come to England in Stephen's life were the French with their doomed invasion under Louis. True, there were the Flemish mercenaries of Walter Buc, but this dark man was surely not a Fleming.

"French?" A dry laugh turned into a cough. "Stonecutter's chest," the old man gasped when his breath came back. "You'll get it, too, if you stay in this trade. We all do. No, I am not French. I am—I was Shihab ad-Din ibn Hafiz of Damascus, in the days of your King Richard."

Richard was not even a memory to Stephen; he was more of a legend, as remote and shining as Arthur and Tristan and other heros of romance. He had died, succeeded by King John, before Stephen was born. And now John was dead and his young son Henry was on the throne.

"I was his prisoner when he warred in the East. But he was a true King, young Richard, a gentleman and a scholar. My family refused to purchase my freedom since there had been some minor disagreement between my father and me over the matter of a favorite mare of his. Or was it a concubine? So long ago..." His voice trailed off for a moment and his head sunk on his chest.

"Here's your fresh mortar, masters." The boy who dropped

the bucket between them, spattering Stephen and Shihab with specks of lime, was only a year or two younger than Stephen.

"Well, I was only a fifteenth son, after all. He had sons to spare, and only one favorite concubine. To get me out of the way, he apprenticed me to a builder in Acre, and there I was taken when the Franks besieged the city. When your King Richard learned that I knew a trade, I thought he would scorn me for not being a gentleman. Instead he was delighted. He said I was the first person he'd talked to who knew anything useful, and invited me to come to England, as his prisoner but also as his guest, to consult with his architects and to teach them our secrets of building. You know Chateau Gaillard, his castle in France? I designed it. He wanted an impregnable fortress and I gave him one."

Stephen nodded and tried to look suitably impressed. But he couldn't help asking, "Didn't the French take Chateau Gaillard in the end?"

Shihab's leathery face darkened even further. "That fool de Laci let the French get miners under the bridge. That has nothing to do with the design."

"Yes, well . . ." Stephen had no real desire to argue with the old man, but he would hardly call a castle impregnable if it could be taken by miners. "Chateau Gaillard's a long way away. How did you come to be here?"

"After Richard's death, his clerks drove me out, calling me heathen and infidel and saying that no Saracen dog could teach true-born Christian Englishmen their craft. But they kept my secrets—they kept them! I taught them more of geometry than they had ever copied from their schoolmen, and they use the knowledge even now, though they despise the man who gave it to them."

Geometry. Stephen levered a new stone into place somewhat carelessly, dropping it the last half-inch so that mortar splattered out from between the stones already laid. "What is this geometry? Can you teach it to me?"

"I could have once. But now I'm too old and too tired. You should go to my people, though, if you want to learn geometry. We took the art from the Greeks and expanded it. We respect scholars, study, and good minds wherever they appear. Even in a town of traders like Acre, ruled by the Franks, there are more great mathematicians and philosophers in one back alley than you will find in all the schools of the West. And there's a real sun there, an Arab sun to warm an old man's bones. . . . Ah, Acre! I thought I was going into exile when my father sent me there. Now I would give all my remaining winters in this cold land to see its white-topped houses again, the women gossiping on the rooftops, and the bazaars where the merchants sit over baskets of dates and frails of figs. . . ."

"I saw a date once," Stephen interrupted. "A pilgrim brought it to—to a place where I was studying." Even after all these years, he still shied away from mentioning Ely. Brother Daniel's voice still echoed in his sleep sometimes, telling him that he was nothing and would always be nothing and would never succeed in his worldly ambitions, having turned away from God. "Surely you must remember something about this geometry?"

"Remember?" Shihab sighed. "I remember designing the great fortress of Tintagel for King Mark of Cornwall. Six wards it had, each guarded by keep towers that looked down on all sides, and. . . ."

Stephen remembered the names of Tintagel and King Mark from one of the romances that Joscelin used to smuggle into the convent, and his belief in Shihab began to fade. For the rest of the afternoon he pressed the old man, with ever diminishing hope, to tell him something of this art of geometry that he claimed had been invented by the Greeks, improved by the Arabs, and stolen by the Franks. All he got was a tangled string of reminiscences mixed with obvious fictions. The one thing that remained constant in Shihab's stories was his insistence that the Arab lands were full of learned men who did not have to be in the service of the Church to get learning. The talk of learning and mathematics stirred up Stephen's angry ambition and his desire to show Adam of Lincoln what a mistake he had made. There was still one avenue open to him. . . .

"Break into the tracing house? You're mad." Hugh gazed at his friend with an expression balanced between horror and laughter. "Do you want us to lose our good jobs?"

"You may think they're good but I don't. I'm learning nothing." Stephen pointed out.

"I don't know why you're complaining. Get paid regular,

don't we? And meat every day for dinner? All I want is for this good weather to hold up a little longer. Two more weeks and I'll have enough saved to pay the rent on a cottage for me and Avice. She'll be glad to leave me mum and dad's house before the next baby comes because she says the smell of slaughtered meat is making her sick." Hugh patted the leather pouch at his belt where he kept his growing store of coppers. "I'm not about to risk a good steady job just because you're bored with stonelaying and want some amusement. Go into the town and find yourself a girl, that'll be more fun than breaking into Master Adam's private quarters to get a look at some notebook you can't even read."

"I can read it," Stephen insisted. "I know Latin. I studied with a clerk before I came to Master Brito's. And I know numbers. And all the secrets of building are in that notebook, Hugh; he said so himself."

"Why do you need to know that stuff?" Hugh asked. "Do you know how much money it takes to set up as a master builder? You don't just walk into a church and say, 'God be with the honorable clerks, I'm Stephen of Dunwich and I know all there is to know about building, so why don't you pour the church funds into my hands so I can turn your gold into a beautiful new church?' You have to start off contracting your own jobs and running your own gang, which means having the silver to hire men, which you do not have on mason's pay. Ivo could do it, maybe—"

"Ivo," said Stephen, "could not put his head through the right hole in his cotte without Brito's guidance."

Hugh laughed. "You may be right. All the same, Ivo's going to be master of the yard. I'm a mason and you're going to be a mason. You don't need to know any more than you can learn on the job. What you do need is a nice girl to cheer you up. Want me to lend you a little money?"

"No. That's all right. I won't involve you—if I get caught, you can say you knew nothing about it."

Stephen slipped into the gathering shadows, ignoring Hugh's call to come back and act like a sensible man. Ever since Hugh married, all he could think of was his Avice and the string of babies she produced for him. His solution for all problems had something to do with a regular sex life. Stephen had been with girls in Dunwich, mostly out of a curiosity that was nowhere near as his powerful as his driving need to discover the secrets in Master Adam's book.

Stephen didn't suppose the girls in Peterborough had anything more to offer than those in Dunwich. They all seemed somehow lacking. He remembered full, plump bodies and high giggling voices and moments of convulsive pleasure. But across the back of his mind drifted a memory of a different sort: the smoky scent of clothes that had been hanging in an eel-catcher's hut, lips cool as the water in the mere, and a reed-slim body. Was that what he was looking for, some imitation of Aude?

Stephen shook his head. No. Aude had nothing to do with it. She was a ghost, even more so than Brother Daniel who haunted his dreams. Girls had nothing to do with this matter. He was going to find out the secrets of Master Adam's sketchbook, that was all. Why did Hugh have to complicate everything with meaningless suggestions?

At dusk, the day's work had ended, and the day laborers and the masons who lived near Peterborough went home. The others stayed to share a dinner of bread and soup in the lodge, to tell lies over mugs of pale sour ale and swap stories of the building trade until they doused the fat-spattering rush dips and settled down on their pallets to sleep. In his first days on this job, Stephen had been happy to share this fellowship of the lodge, brought in under Hugh's wing as though he were a full mason instead of just a journeyman. But by now he'd heard all the stories thrice over and the enterprise of learning Master Adam's secrets had much more appeal.

The glimmer of light around the lodge, the shadows, and the first hints of moonlight turned the building site into a world of deep mysteries and hidden obstacles. Stephen barked his shins on a sawhorse he'd avoided innumerable times in the daylight, narrowly missing stepping into a four-foot deep foundation trench, and found the outside staircase to the tracing house by running his nose up against it.

The door was not even locked so there was no need for the tools he'd hidden in his sleeve before he left the lodge. Master Adam must have trusted the prestige of his name and the awe inspired by his temper tantrums to keep curious apprentices from snooping in the tracing house.

Once inside the dark room, Stephen moved surely.

Darkness was less treacherous than shifting shadows; with only memory to guide him, and no half-light to mislead him, he was able to find his way around trestle tables, plaster slab, and high stools without a single mistake.

The leather-bound notebook was exactly where Master Adam had left it that afternoon, lying atop a stool beside the slab of plaster. Stephen's fingertips tingled as they caressed the leather binding, smooth with long use, scarred here and there with cuts from old accidents.

It was dangerous to light a candle, but it couldn't be helped. Stephen had brought flint and tinder and he remembered that the iron pricket-stand in one corner held a branch of three real wax candles so that Master Adam could work at night if necessary. But Master Adam had boasted that he would dine with the sheriff tonight. . . .

It would be easy enough to lift one candle off the stand and fix it in a corner where the high drawing board would shield it from the window. But if one candle were an inch or so shorter than the other two, Master Adam would guess that somebody had been in the room. After some brooding, Stephen decided to rotate the candles every time one had burned down as far as the breadth of his thumbnail. That task would help him keep track of time, too; when all three candles had been used for a thumbnail's worth of reading, he would have to slip out of the tracing house in case Master Adam returned early from his dinner.

He flipped through the first few pages of the sketchbook without interest: drawings of animals and soldiers, sketches for statues. A head rising out of foliage, like the Green Man who had decorated the font at St. Michael's in Dunwich, caught his attention and he lingered for a moment. He remembered how the fat priest there (what was his name?) used to harangue against the poor Green Man as a piece of pagan art, in hopes of collecting enough coppers from his impoverished audience to pay for the carving of a new font.

But that wasn't geometry. Stephen turned a few more pages and stopped before a sketch of a bearded face with a five-pointed star superimposed upon the features. Slowly, calling up his memories of his schoolboy Latin, he translated the inscription below the drawing. "Here begins the . . . method of drawing . . . as taught by the art of geometry.

And in the other sheets . . . will be : . . the method of masonry."

Stephen let out a whoop of excitement before he remembered to guard himself, then shoved the notebook directly under the candle, and turned pages again until he came to a full page of architectural drawings covered with the kinds of arcs and lines he'd seen Master Adam tracing out that afternoon. This page was crowded with annotations in the same miniscule black script he'd seen on the other pages. "How to measure the diameter of a column, only part of which is visible. How to find the midpoint of a drawn circle. How to divide a stone so that each of its halves is square . . ." Stephen frowned over that one. The picture showed a square with a smaller square inside it. If you cut a stone like that, you'd have one square block and one square doughnut, and what good would that be?

He shook the notebook in his impatience, frustrated at having all the secrets of masonry in his hands and lacking the key to understand the cryptic notes. A folded piece of parchment, thinner than the leaves of the notebook, fell out of the back pages and Stephen seized it with new hope. Perhaps this would provide an explanation. No, it was just columns of figures, with annotations scribbled beside them in an unsteady hand quite unlike the tiny, regular script of the notebook. The ink was different, too: pale and brown-hued. Both handwriting and ink reminded Stephen of the markings on the wooden templet that were sent down from the tracing house for the masons to cut by. The writing was clumsy but quite legible, and after years of doing accounts for the convent at Ely and for Brito's stoneyard, Stephen recognized the subject matter at a glance: It was an addition of prices for stones and timber and other materials used in the building of the west front.

If he could see how much material of what sort was being ordered, he might get an idea of Master Adam's plans. Stephen glanced down the page with interest and his eyes widened. There were two columns, both marked with the same dates—days of delivery in the last two weeks. The first column corresponded pretty well with what he remembered having seen delivered to the works: so many cartloads of crushed stone, so many wrought-iron cramping bars and wooden poles for scaffolding. The second column was marked with the same days, but with smaller numbers, representing about one-third the material that was shown in the first list. And beside each note in the second column was a sum in shillings and pence, except for the last item. That was marked with today's date and the annotation, "Two barrowloads crushed stone to Guilbert of Peterborough, six pence due on delivery."

Stephen began to grin as the meaning of the folded parchment, the two columns, and the two kinds of handwriting became clear to him. Master Adam was a thief. He was ordering far more stones and timber and iron than the west facade would need, and selling off the surplus to somebody—probably to small builders and tradesmen. It was a nice way to get an extra profit out of the building project, and not a small profit, either. The individual items might be small, but over the years it took to erect the west front at Peterborough, Master Adam would be cheating the church treasury of enough money to buy himself a house and land and all the fur-trimmed gowns his vanity required. And if you multiplied Peterborough by all the other projects that would be designed and supervised by an architect of his standing...

Stephen pursed his lips in a soundless whistle. "Not a retirement cottage. A country estate!"

And with the evidence of dishonesty before him, clear as a signed confession to an experienced accountant, the puzzle of the notebook was easily explained. The drawings and annotations in it were not Master Adam's. It was the record of somebody else's working life; Master Adam had gotten hold of it somehow, knew enough geometry and architecture to understand the knowledge encoded in those sketches, and had set himself up as a master builder on the strength of somebody else's secrets. Stephen began to chuckle aloud.

"Seven years disputing with the best minds in Paris, Master Adam? Indeed?"

"What amuses you so about that?"

The soft voice came from the stairway on the far side of the room, which was the only entrance. Stephen's foot kicked the candle as he scrambled up, and the flame darted toward the piles of wood scraps and old rags under the table where the templets were cut. He caught the candle in the middle of its falling arc and straightened to face Master Adam, the waxen stub of candle warm in his palm, his mind still jarred with images of puddled wax and flame and the tracing house burning around them.

Stephen had forgotten his intention to let each candle burn down only a thumbnail's width. Above his head, the two unlit candles stood cold and untouched on the pricket-stand, while the one by which he had been reading had melted to a stub in a pool of wax. The light from the candle formed a small golden circle around him, but it was not strong enough to reveal Master Adam's face. No matter, Stephen knew the voice. He tracked the architect's movements across the tracing house by the sparkles of light that reflected off his gown. When Master Adam was standing within the circle of candlelight, Stephen saw that the light had been sparkling off droplets of water.

"It must be raining outside."

"You were waiting to discuss the weather with me?"

Master Adam didn't sound as powerful as he had this afternoon. He sounded almost nervous, as he might be.

Stephen shrugged slightly and set the candle stub down on the table, grinding it down until the softened wax adhered to the wood. "I wanted to read your notebook. I told you I want to learn. I didn't think you would lend it to me."

"You were quite correct." Adam of Lincoln hoisted himself upon the tall stool beside the table; the move gave him enough height to look down at Stephen. "You're not supposed to know the secrets of masonry until you enter the guild, you know."

"I thought you might respect a man who seeks to learn from whatever source he can beg, borrow, or... steal." Stephen's eyes flickered toward the notebook, then he smiled at Master Adam.

"I might at that. Did you understand what you read?"

"Some. Not enough. I don't suppose you'd care to explain the rest to me?"

"You never stop pushing, do you?" There was unwilling admiration in Master Adam's voice. "Why should I give the secrets of the craft to a strange apprentice? Go home and learn from your master."

"He never had... the good fortune to find... a notebook."

"What a pity." Master Adam's bright black eyes were hard and opaque in the candlelight. Stephen realized that he wasn't going to shake the architect by insinuations about the origin of the notebook. After all, he had no way of knowing how Master Adam had come by it. He might have got it legitimately. His own handwriting was atrocious, so perhaps he paid a clerk to copy his own sketchbook for him. Stephen didn't believe that for a minute, any more than he believed Master Adam had studied for seven years in Paris, but he knew that the architect could come up with any number of plausible stories and Stephen wouldn't be able to disprove any of them. But there was another means of persuasion still at his command.

"Excuse me," Stephen said, politely, "I should return your property." He handed the notebook back to Master Adam. As if by accident, the folded sheet of parchment with Master Adam's double set of accounts on it fluttered down to the floor. The architect made an involuntary grasping gesture with one hand, but from his perch on the high stool he couldn't catch the paper. Stephen scooped it up before it touched the floor and took a step backward.

"If you wanted to teach me geometry," he said, "perhaps I could repay you. There's a lot of reckoning to be done in a project this size, and maybe you don't want to hand it all over to the clerks of the church. I've kept my master's books for years. I could help you with the accounts."

"How much?"

The architect's beady black eyes had not changed expression; Stephen wasn't sure he had grasped the offered bargain. "What?"

"What part of my profits would you want?"

Not only had Master Adam understood, he had offered his own bargain. The man was too fast for him. "I don't want money. I just want you to teach me what you know."

"Pure love of learning?" Master Adam began to smile. "I could almost like you, obnoxious journeyman. I knew a boy like you once, as hungry for learning as other boys are for bread, willing to beg, borrow, or . . . steal . . . to get the knowledge he needed to rise in the world."

"What happened to him?" Stephen answered the architect's smile with his own. Strange, how that expression could transfigure the man's rather ugly face. He looked almost friendly now, a good fellow, a coconspirator, a father.

"He came to a bad end." Master Adam's smile was indeed conspiratorial. "He became one of the King's architects, and achieved the dubious honor of being bothered by total strangers in the middle of the night. What's your name?"

"Stephen of Dunwich. I'm journeyman to Master Brito there. I have to go back to help him in his stoneyard in the winter, but until then I mean to stay on at Peterborough."

"I see. Well, young Stephen of Dunwich, I think I should teach you. I really do."

"You do?"

"Don't blaze up like that," said Master Adam reprovingly, "the light in your face is enough to set the tracing house afire. Yes. Anyone as hungry for learning as you are deserves to discover just what his desperation will get him. We'll start tomorrow. Now, if I might have my accounts back?"

Stephen nodded, but he couldn't quite relinquish the folded parchment that had been his passport to the world of the master builder.

"Come, come. Fellow builders must trust one another, whatever little tricks we may choose to play on the outside world, eh?" Master Adam plucked the parchment from Stephen's hands, patted him on the shoulder, and gently pushed him toward the stairs. "Go to your bed, young Stephen. You'll want a clear head for tomorrow's work."

"I will." He still couldn't believe this was happening to him. It was too wonderful. Colleagues! Stephen stumbled halfway down the stairs, then turned back to see the architect watching him from the door, a cramped black figure outlined against the faint light of the dying candle.

"I won't disappoint you," Stephen promised.

"I am sure you won't."

CHAPTER

9

◻

"**G**et moving, you lazy sods!"

The voice wasn't familiar, nor was the hard shoe of boiled leather that dug into Stephen's ribs. He grunted, rolled over on his pallet, and sat up, rubbing the sleep out of his eyes with both fists. It wasn't even dawn yet. Rush dips sizzled and hissed with the smell of bacon grease while half a dozen sturdy men strode from one end to the other, kicking masons out of bed and yanking apprentices up by their arms. At the far end of the lodge stood a black-browed, blue-chinned man wearing a coat of mail that glittered under the slit sides of his cotte. He was unrolling a narrow parchment decorated at the bottom with seals of red wax and tassles of gold cord. Beside him, the warden of the masons hopped from one foot to another, sputtering with rage.

"Cool your head, good warden," said the blue-chinned man. "I'm only culling your stock, not taking the entire flock. You've Master Adam to thank for that." He jerked his head backward and Stephen recognized the slight figure of the King's architect, standing slightly behind the other two men, where he was all but hidden in the shadows. "Over our dinner last night he persuaded me," the sheriff grinned and patted the pouch at his belt, "that the King would not wish the work at Peterborough to stop entirely. All I want is five freestone masons and five stonelayers."

"Ten men!" the warden sputtered. "You're crippling me, Sheriff!"

"Could be worse." The sheriff shook out his parchment so that all the dangling seals danced, and read the text to the sullen, sleepy men. "Henry, by the grace of God, King of England, to all the sheriffs, mayors, bailiffs, officers, and his other ministers, greeting.

"We command you as strictly as we can, that immediately on sight of these present letters, you cause to be chosen and attached within counties, whether within liberties or without, of the better and more skilled masons, forty masons for hewing freestone and forty masons for laying stone and cause them to be brought or sent with the tools belonging to their trade, to our castle at Rockingham for the performance of works to repair the damages done in the late war."

The sheriff took a deep breath and rolled up his parchment with a snap. "There you have it, gentlemen. I must find ten of those eighty masons, and you're supplying them—on pain, I remind you, of imprisonment for anybody resisting the King's orders. A mason in prison is as much lost to you as one in Rockingham, Master Warden."

The warden's resigned acknowledgment was all but drowned out in Master Adam's furious hiss. "Ten men! I paid you well to take no more than ten, and now you say that's all you needed! You cheated me!"

"Indeed! What a coincidence." The sheriff grinned. "Want to bring a court suit against me? Of course to bribe a King's officer is a crime punishable by loss of the right hand, I do believe. How good are you at drawing left-handed, Master Adam of Lincoln?"

The architect stood fuming in silence while the sheriff and warden paced up and down the two long rows of pallets, tapping the men to be taken and occasionally arguing over the choices. Stephen watched Adam of Lincoln's dark face and tried not to grin at the architect's evident fury. He wondered just how much of his ill-gotten gold Master Adam had wasted on an unnecessary bribe to the sheriff.

"What are you looking so happy for?" Hugh, standing beside him, muttered. The sheriff hadn't reached their end of the tent yet, and the men here were standing tensely as they waited. Some, perhaps, wouldn't mind

being removed from this project to rebuild a castle somewhere else. Others, like Hugh, had wives or sweethearts
or families nearby, and were praying that the choice would
not fall on them.

Stephen did his best to pull down the corners of his
mouth to match the strained expressions he saw around
him. Sure that Master Adam would not let his new
student be taken, he had forgotten that Hugh had no such
certainty and must be praying not to be separated from
Avice for the duration of the King's project.

"Where's Rockingham?" he muttered back.

"North. Far north."

No wonder Hugh was so tense. Here he could take a
long holiday, beg a ride to the coast on one of the barges
that slid through the fenland, and snatch a visit with Avice
before he returned to work at Peterborough. To be marched
off to the northern border of England and possibly kept
there for two or three years would be exile. Stephen
wished he had known last night that this impressment was
coming; he could have bargained with Master Adam to
keep Hugh here, too.

"That one and that. They look like good sturdy workers.
They'll need to be strong in Rockingham. I heard it's
colder than the devil's backside up there." The sheriff
tapped his two last choices and passed by Hugh and
Stephen without even looking at them. Hugh's long body
relaxed like an ill-built arch, sagging when the centering
frames are removed; Stephen could hear the soft exhalation of his breath.

"Wait a minute." Master Adam stepped forward and laid
one hand on Stephen's shoulder. Stephen gave him a
friendly nod and was surprised to see no smile in return.
"The two masons from Dunwich, you'll want them." He
glared at the sheriff. "You promised to let me pick the men
I could spare. I can well spare these two."

"Troublemakers? I don't need such."

"No, skilled men," Master Adam countered. "This one—"
he indicated Hugh, "is a fine carver in freestone, and his
mate is a sharp lad, very talented, ambitious, and he'll
thank you for the chance to get some experience in a
different line of building. It just so happens I've got too many
freestone-carvers on this project and I'm not ready to use
them. What I need is strong men to lay foundation blocks, so

you'd be doing me a favor by taking these two and leaving the big fellows. The King will thank you, too. It's not often you get such highly skilled gentlemen in an impressment."

"Oh, all right, all right, makes no odds to me." The sheriff pushed Hugh and Stephen toward the group of men waiting to be marched away.

"No" Hugh's face was contorted with the effort to hold back emotion. Half turning, he reached for the sheriff's sleeve. "No, please, I can't go to the north—my wife is due in two months—"

"And I'm due to have you out on the road by sunrise. Get along, there. I can't spend all day arguing." The sheriff pulled his sleeve free of Hugh's fingers and gave him another push to get him started in the right direction. "Guards! Form up around these ten. March 'em out quick, now."

The soldiers moved in quickly, formed a fence with their pikes about the ten chosen men, and hustled them out of the lodge before there was time for any more argument. Masons were known to be an unruly, quarrelsome lot, and the King's soldiers had learned to move quickly and break up groups before a serious fight could start. By the time Stephen had fully assimilated the shock of Master Adam's betrayal, the little group was already beyond the half-height paling that marked the boundaries of the Peterborough works. A crack of golden light showed along the edge of the eastern sky; behind, in the blue darkness, the remaining masons were picking up their tools and expressing their relief at having been spared. Glancing back, Stephen saw a slight figure standing at the corner of the lodge in a heavy furred gown and black hat. Master Adam meant to watch them out of sight.

"Why us?" Hugh moaned as they stumbled over the broken ground where cartwheels had churned mud into ruts and ridges that the summer sun then baked into a crazy nest of earthworks. "What's he got against us?"

"Me," said Stephen. "I'm a fool." How easily Stephen had given back that piece of parchment, his one bit of solid proof against Master Adam! "And you because you're my friend." Master Adam must have feared Stephen had told Hugh of his discoveries.

"You did it, then! And he caught you?"

"That. And more."

"No talking, you lot!" bellowed the sheriff without turn-

ing his head. "I'll not have complaints and seditious talk
behind my back."

One of the soldiers reinforced the order by swinging his
pike toward Stephen, forcing him to move away from
Hugh. They marched on in silence, with the rising sun at
their backs and a damp fog creeping in from the cold, wet
fields surrounding them. The earth smelled fresh and
sweet and the fields were rich and green with the growing
corn. Stephen wondered about the north: Did they have
summer up there at all, or were they marching into a land
of eternal ice and snow, with men dressed in furs year-
round? He was sorry for dragging Hugh into his troubles
and still angry with himself for being so easily gulled by
Master Adam. But it was not entirely bad, to be marching
into a strange land to work on the King's project. He'd
never done a castle before. There would be masons to
learn from and good work to do, even in the chilly north
country. And given that he'd been such a fool, perhaps he
ought to be grateful that Master Adam had been able to
arrange such a convenient way of getting rid of him. Ivo
had taught him how easy it was to arrange little "accidents"
on a building site, and the careless, hasty work at
Peterborough had shown him how many accidents could
happen when you didn't have somebody as steady as
Master Brito to oversee the yard. Stephen had seen men's
hands crushed beneath a stone that tilted off its stretcher
bed, fingers sliced off by a dropped chisel, scaffolding that
tilted crazily underfoot when its lashings stretched in the
morning dew. He would have had to be constantly on
guard at Peterborough, so perhaps this new project was
better after all.

At a crossroad three miles outside Peterborough, they
met another contingent of armed men, marching as if to
intercept them. The sheriff on his tall horse and the leader
of this group conferred in undertones. Stephen grew
bored while he waited, shuffled his feet in the dust to
relieve legs that grew tired with standing still, and wondered
for the thousandth time what the work in Rockingham
would be like.

"Psst! C'mon. Over to this side, quick!" Hugh grabbed
Stephen's arm and dragged him to the far left of the group
of masons, nearest the new soldiers, where a quarrel was
just ending.

"You're a damned thief and a bandit!" the sheriff was shouting. His broad forehead had turned purple and little veins bulged out on either side.

"My orders supersede yours." The other man was cool and quiet, with a voice like a cold deep stream flowing with irresistible force to the sea. The roll of parchment he held was heavier and thicker than the sheriff's orders, and so deeply encrusted with wax seals that the surface of the parchment was barely visible. "I'll have four of these men now. You can easily return to Peterborough and take a few more to replace them. It's not far."

"Why don't you go to Peterborough yourself?"

"Because, my dear sheriff, you have kindly saved me the trouble. I trust all these are guaranteed to be skilled men? Of course, of course, I know you would take only the best. I'll have these four."

The soldiers in black cottes, who marched behind the new man, came forward and separated the four leftmost masons from the rest of the group. Stephen, Hugh, and the two freemasons from Yarmouth fell into a line and marched west while the sheriff stood grumbling at the crossroad, weighing the cost of a return to Peterborough against the consequences of failing to make up his quota for Rockingham.

Hugh, just ahead of Stephen, was whistling softly as he marched, and the new soldiers made no objection. Stephen edged up as close to Hugh as he dared. "Why did you want to go with this lot?" he whispered.

"Closer to home," Hugh said out of the corner of his mouth. "Didn't you recognize the livery?"

"Whose is it?"

"Bishop's men. We're bound for Ely."

"I wish you'd stand up straight and look around," Hugh said in exasperation. "You've been slouching like an exhausted ploughman ever since we got within sight of Ely, and with that hood pulled down over your head you can't *see* anything. Look, we're going right by the cathedral. Don't you want to look at it? The Galilee porch is supposed to be one of the great works of this century. Stephen—"

"Don't shout my name out like that! And no, I don't want to look at the Galilee porch. I've seen it."

"You have? When? You never told me. Last summer?"

"Tell you later."

With his eyes fixed on the ruts in the street, Stephen pictured the porch in all its floating beauty. The nave of the cathedral would open out behind it, with the long double row of columns stretching down to the wooden stalls in choir. Stephen had carved his name on the back of one of those stalls, and been beaten for it; now he longed to slip into the cathedral and see if his name was still there. But that would be folly. If there was one place in England he should stay away from, it was Ely; and of all places in Ely, the cathedral and the close where the monks lived were most dangerous to him.

Stephen had ample time to think on the road to Ely, but no chance to escape the bishop's men who guarded the masons closely. One of the soldiers had told him, in a rare moment of fellowship, that the bishop was pressing masons to restore the walls of a small castle that had been slighted at the end of the barons' wars. At least they wouldn't be working on the convent grounds—only within sight of them.

Stephen thought he might have a chance to go unnoticed. Physically he was much changed from the boy who'd run away from Ely five years before; hard work and good food had filled out the promise of his tall frame, setting solid bands of muscle across his shoulders and covering his clerk's hands with calluses. And, after all, no one would expect to see a runaway monk among the laborers who were restoring the castle. That was his greatest protection. If he slouched a little to conceal the height that made him stand out among the masons, if he kept enough dust in his hair to cover up the golden gleam that also made him noticeable, and, above all, if he kept quiet and blended in with the others, he just might get through this summer's work without being recaptured by the convent. In fact, now that he thought about it, there was really no reason why he should be noticed at all. The good monks of Ely must have more to think about than one boy who'd vanished years ago.

That reasoning lasted until they were in the shadow of the cathedral. Then the cold stones loomed over him like a promise of eternity. And when the bells rang, they seemed to be saying, Stephen of Ely, Stephen of Ely, you belong to me.

"Oh, no, I don't," Stephen muttered.

"Don't what? Don't make any sense? I'll say! You might at least show me some gratitude for my quick thinking. Aren't you glad to be in Ely, practically at home, instead of marching up north to lay stones by day and get our throats cut by murdering Scots by night? Stephen, you're—"

"Don't shout my name!" Stephen hissed. "I'll explain later. Look, Hugh. I don't want to be recognized in Ely, all right? Call me ... oh ... Edric." He picked on the first name that came to him, and then winced at the memories it aroused. Aude's father pinned to the wall of his hut, and all that blood on the frozen ground. . . .

"Edric," Hugh repeated, and by then it was too late for Stephen to change the name without the need for even more explanations. "Edric. Oh, all right. Anybody ever tell you that you are a damned strange fellow, Ste—Edric?"

Soon they were at the work site, where masons and carpenters and laborers with barrows milled around the ruined castle, ingeniously accomplishing very little while putting on a great show of movement. The bishop's guards swore, complained, and wondered aloud why impressed men were always so worthless. Hugh joyfully engaged himself in the game of making sure that the bishop got as little work as possible for the fixed rate of daily pay offered by law to impressed men, and Stephen had a brief respite in which to rethink his promise of explaining everything to Hugh.

Hugh was a good man and a good, if somewhat plodding, mason, Stephen reasoned, but his imagination was strictly bounded by the rules laid down by king, church, and the honorable guild of freemasons. To him it was a major act of rebellion to "accidentally" tip over a full bucket of mortar on the pointed shoes of the bishop's chief clerk, and even that would be confessed at the end of the week along with the rest of his venial sins. Hugh had once confided that he wished it were not a sin to love one's wife excessively; while they were in Dunwich and he went home to Avice at night, every week he had an extra penance to say on that account.

Stephen doubted that a man who confessed to the "sin" of enjoying the marriage bed would sympathize with one who'd run away from his sacred vows—even if the vows had been taken by others, in his name, long before he was old enough to understand what was being promised.

By nightfall, Stephen had put together a vague, rambling story to satisfy Hugh's curiosity. Without telling any direct lies, he managed to leave Hugh with the impression that he was a nobleman's bastard who'd been educated for the Church, that he'd quarreled with his father and run away before taking his vows. He said he didn't want to go near the convent or the cathedral, or have his name used too loudly, for fear that one of the good monks who'd schooled him should recognize him and notify his noble father, who would be severely displeased to find even a bastard son working as a lowly journeyman to a gang of impressed masons. Stephen, of course, wanted to be free to pursue his chosen career, that part at least was quite true, and he thought it shed a romantic touch of realism over the rest of the tale.

Stephen was quite pleased with the story, as was Hugh who soaked up every hint and suggestion and put even more romance into it than Stephen. After that, Stephen's only problem with Hugh was the incessant meaningful looks, warning whispers, and hints of deep meaning with which he enlivened the boring hours of their daily work. What finally betrayed Stephen was not any hint of Hugh's—it was his own curiosity. From the castle where they worked, the masons could see the cathedral rising against the sky like a mountain of stone. Four-square, solid, an everlasting example of the power of man in the service of God, it made their puny efforts at laying walls and digging ramparts look like the scurryings of ants around a broken hill. The overarching walls beckoned to Stephen, and the bells mocked his ambitions with echoes of the words Brother Daniel used as effectively as a whip to scourge the sinful self out of him. He could not resist the cathedral: it haunted him, called to him, drew him inexorably.

Stephen held out for nearly a week. But one day, when rain clouds thickened overhead, bringing down an early dusk and a hint of drizzle, the master of the works announced an early closing on account of weather. The temptation of the free hours ahead was too much for Stephen. He approached the bishop's man and requested leave to pray in the cathedral. It was difficult for an ecclesiastic to refuse such a simple, pious request; Stephen got freedom from the works and a stern warning that he'd be in trouble if he weren't back by the time the bells rang for Compline.

At this hour, between Vespers and Compline, the monks would be in the refectory and most honest citizens would be settling down for dinner and bed. The great nave whispered with shadows and ghosts, but only a few pious pilgrims remained within. Stephen stood in the shelter of a fluted column, watching these few traverse the mosaic pattern of the labyrinth on their knees, the poor man's substitute for a journey to Jerusalem. The last time Stephen had stood here, the floor had been fouled with blood and horse dung and limbs hacked from living men, and there had been a puddle of blood at the starry center of the mosaic where the pilgrims now prayed.

For a moment he was a boy again, fretting in the endless routine and waiting with anguished hope for Mam to fetch him. Then he recalled the slow death of that hope, the years with nothing to do but wait, pray, sing in choir, and rise in the middle of the night with bare feet aching with cold to begin the day again.

Stephen shivered at the thought of those memories. What was he doing here? He didn't care if his name was still carved in the wooden stall at choir; it would be better if it had been obliterated, if all trace of his presence here had been wiped away! Stephen of Ely, the oblate monk, was dead. He had nothing to do with Stephen of Dunwich, journeyman mason, soon to be one of the great builders of the western world.

On his way out of the cathedral he found out just how true that was. Old memories betrayed him; he cut across the grounds of the cathedral close to get back to the castle works in time, and found that what had once been an open garden was now a small graveyard. He stumbled upon a mounded grave, fell quickly to his knees to say a brief prayer of contrition to the one who lay within, and froze, unbelieving, as he read the lines carved on the headstone. The remains of his schoolboy Latin were quite sufficient for this translation.

"Stephen, oblate of the convent of Ely, shamefully murdered in the last year of the reign of King John."

A prickling shiver ran down Stephen's bare arms even while he slowly reasoned out what he already knew. There had been no other monks named Stephen at the convent and no other oblates—the custom of offering children to the Church had fallen into disfavor before he was born. And he had run away in January five years ago—the last year of King John.

As nearly as might be possible for a mortal man, he was kneeling on his own grave.

"Then—who's buried here?" Stephen whispered.

The memories called up in the cathedral provided his answer. Before him he saw the body of the Lord Ridel's golden-haired page boy, sprawled on the cathedral floor in obscene nakedness. The picture was so clear it might have been an apparition in the gathering dusk. Stephen remembered straightening the boy's limbs, his eyes averted from the handsome face that had been disfigured by horse's hooves. He had covered the body with his habit, and the monks must have taken that body for Stephen's. All the years of fear and hiding had been unnecessary: there had never been any search since Stephen was thought to be dead.

He told himself that he should feel relieved at the news, but he was too shaken by the eerie feeling of kneeling on his own grave. The blue half-light of an early drizzling dusk turned the world around him into a distorted arena of strange shapes that had no meaning. When the bells of Compline began to ring, Stephen told himself to get up and hurry back to the castle works, but there was no power in his legs.

He was not even surprised to see her coming toward him, floating soundlessly over the grass, a thin, brown girl with her face framed by a tangle of dark curls. She was bearing a wreath of flowers in her uplifted hands. This was the place and the time when all the dead came together. When she touched him, would he be dead, too?

No. Stephen sucked in his breath and clenched his fists, feeling the strong pulse beat in his hands. He would not be drawn back into those shadows, not even for Aude; this was not his grave. He was Stephen of Dunwich, journeyman mason, with stone dust on his clothes and callouses on his hands from five years of hard labor. He was very much alive. The vision of Aude was so real that he could almost believe she, too, was alive as she drifted toward him. Her thin face was turned down to the pale pink flowers she held. She was so close now that Stephen could see the patches on her gown. The bells were ringing so loudly that he could not hear whether she made any noise as she stepped on the soft grass.

As she came closer, Stephen stood up. Whatever she was, spirit or living girl, he would not run and he would not meet her kneeling. At the movement, she looked up at last. Through the drizzle he could see her dark eyes shining with unshed tears; she turned and fled from him. He chased after her, shouting her name, hearing only the tolling of the great cathedral bells in his ears. She flitted ahead of him, a dim shadow in her dark, shapeless gown. Long grasses at the edge of the graveyard twined round Stephen's legs, and a jolting stumble over somebody's headstone brought him to the ground, breath and sense momentarily knocked out of him. When he raised his head, she was gone, and the sound of the bells had been replaced by the chanting of the monks in choir.

She must have been a ghost or a vision, able to disappear at will. Stephen rubbed one hand across his brow and stood up on unsteady legs. He should be grateful that he did not succeed in following her to the home of the unquiet spirits of the dead. But the sense of loss was as bitter as a winter frost within him, and it felt as though she'd died today and not five years ago. He was a fool, trying to recapture the flavor of one happy summer that had to be buried with the rest of the past. A fool who'd be late back to the workings, and in trouble with the bishop's man.

The light drizzle had stopped, but the clouds lay heavy on the western horizon, killing the glow of sunset. Stephen made his way back through the graveyard with just enough light left to guide his feet, now that he had regained his senses and knew to look where he was stepping. Deep shadows were ruts and ditches, light square ones were headstones, and the ruffle of pink softness lying in the grass. . . .

Stephen stopped and raised the broken wreath of pale pink marsh orchids in his hands. Did ghosts pick flowers, then?

CHAPTER

10

◻

Aude leaned against the wall of the narrow passage that led from the new graveyard to the prior's guesthouse. Her breath was loud in her ears, and she could hear her heart thumping against her ribs. It had been a fool's act to run like that. At first, she thought that she saw Stephen's ghost, not as the boy he had been, but as the man he would have grown into. And then she had had the crazy fancy that it was Stephen himself, somehow come back from the dead, and she couldn't face him. She would have been ashamed for him to know what had happened to her. But that was stupid, because Stephen was five years dead, and his spirit wouldn't have cared about how her body had been misused.

"And there's no good in brooding over the past," Aude said aloud. As the last tones of the bells died away, Aude picked up the basket she had set down when she entered the graveyard and peeped over the wall. There was no one there. It was dark, a storm was coming on, and the lady would be waiting for her. No doubt she imagined it all. Midsummer Eve, the kindly spirits walked, and if one of them had chosen to show himself to her in the form she had loved best on earth, was that a thing to be afraid of? Maids saw their true loves in the reflection of the waters on this evening; and she, who was no maid and would never have a love, had been granted this glimpse of what might have been.

And it *was* Midsummer Eve, and Aude wasn't about to go on without picking up the little wreath of marsh orchids she'd dropped in her panicky flight and placing it on Stephen's headstone to let him know she hadn't forgotten him. Aude retraced her steps through the vines that grew thick about the edges of this neglected little graveyard, breathing in their sharp green scent mixed with the soft dampness of the passing rain. She could not find the pale cluster of flowers anywhere along the path. Perhaps the man had taken it with him, in which case he was no spirit, but a living man. But he was not Stephen, whose grave was right before her.

Aude pulled her kirtle sleeves down over her arms with two impatient jerks, tightened the belt that held the scratchy fabric to her thin body, and marched out of the graveyard with a firm resolve to think no more of this disturbing encounter and the impossible notions it raised. She had her errand to finish, and a long walk home after that, so it wouldn't do her nerves any good to conjure up spirits of mortal men to affright her on her road back to the fens. She would simply not think of the matter again.

"You're late," Helene greeted her when she hurried into the top rooms of the prior's guesthouse. "I've had my women heating water for the bath this hour past, only waiting for you and your magic herbs."

"Not magic, my lady." It was dangerous to contradict the bishop's "niece," but Aude dared not let the whispers of witchcraft that already hung round her name grow any stronger. "Only sweet herbs and flowers to scent your bath and to make you beautiful for. . . ." Her voice trailed off; she bent her head and busied herself by pulling out the little bundles of herbs that she brought in the flat basket of marsh grass. She probably wasn't supposed to know that Lady Helene had her eye on a new lover. "I am sorry about being late." Though not for the bishop's niece with the peevish frown, she thought, but for the two thin girls who looked so tired after an hour of carrying can after can of hot water upstairs for the lady's special bath.

"And well you might be," said Helene, "considering what you owe me."

Aude raised her dark eyes to meet Helene's gray ones.

There were little lines at the corners, and the dark lashes looked thinner than before. She was aging, and unhappy over it, and worried that she wouldn't be able to attract young lovers any longer. A pity, Aude thought, that they couldn't change places. After all, she would never want to be with a man, and she already felt a thousand years old. What good was youth to her?

"I know what I owe you, my lady. And I am grateful." At least, she had been at first, when she woke from a nightmare of pain and terror to find herself sleeping between good linen sheets in a fine warm house. Helene had told her many times how she'd come across Aude unconscious in the icy reeds, all but naked, and hardly breathing. "The rest of the villagers were dead. Everyone was dead. There was nothing but death all around, and you were something I could save."

Like a drowning kitten, Aude thought when Helene reached this part of the tale. But she did her best to suppress those flashes of resentment. She'd been glad enough, at the time, to be safe and warm. It was only later that she sometimes wished that Helene had left her to freeze in the marsh. She knew her father must have died; the soldiers who dragged her out of the hut wouldn't have spared him. And Stephen was gone, too, buried before she had a chance to say good-bye to him. Even now her nights were torment—she dreamed of the soldiers who were laughing with faces like demons and using her again.

It was strange to think she owed her life to the tall, cruel monk who turned her away when Edric begged for shelter at the convent. Aude had seen him standing at the foot of her bed one night when she was still very ill, twisting and thrashing and trying to throw off the sheets that seemed to be burning her.

"Why do you trouble yourself? She'll die," he'd said with something like satisfaction in his cruel voice. It was then that Aude resolved to live, if only to spite him. From that night she took the broth Helene's maid gave her without protest and lay quietly to rest when she was told to. She even persuaded Helene to beg the infirmarian for the herbs and roots she knew would heal the infections within her. Some of them he didn't have—they were only simple marsh plants, not the expensive imported drugs the monks could afford. Coluin himself had come to talk with Aude to find out why she wanted these herbs, and he then tried the infusions on his own patients with some success. Her reputation as a healer began to grow, giving her another life to step into when she was well.

She needed that. Helene treated her like a doll, petting her, rocking her, and dressing her in ladies' clothes. She taught Aude curtsies and dance steps and all sorts of things that Aude would never use. She would clap her hands and make Aude show off a new graceful walk or a French phrase for her ladies, and they all laughed and exclaimed over how clever Helene was to train a little peasant girl so well. Sometimes they praised Aude, too, in subtly insulting phrases: how strange that a peasant should be so clever, learning to imitate Helene until she spoke French quite like a fine lady!

Aude wanted to tell them that speaking French was easy; it was being cosseted like a pet monkey that she found difficult. But she would not quarrel with Helene's friends since she owed Helene her life. To please her benefactress, she learned the manners and speech of a lady.

Aude walked every day until she was strong, and practiced being polite to the men who came to visit until she could conceal the shuddering fear that still overtook her when a man moved too quickly or laughed too loudly. When spring turned the bare branches of the willows along the water's edge gray with fuzzy buds, she thanked Helene for her kindness and informed her that she was going home.

"Home, child? Nonsense. Your home is with me. You can't possibly wish to go back to that odorous hut in the fens!"

There were tears, and accusations of ingratitude, and reminders of "all I've done for you." In the end, Aude left the fine clothes and trinkets Helene had showered on her and simply walked out, barefoot, in her old patched kirtle.

It had taken Helene a year to forgive Aude. That is, she had spent nine months visiting friends in the south of England before returning to her "uncle's" guesthouse in Ely; she'd been there eleven weeks before she found out that the fen witch-girl who supplied her maid with colored lip salves and washes to darken the eyebrows was Aude. It had taken her just three days to forgive Aude, send a servant to bring her in from her fenland hut, and establish a business relationship that had lasted until this day. Now they enjoyed something as close to friendship as could exist between an aging, fading lady of near-noble rank and a barefoot girl from the fens. Aude brought cosmetic washes and infusions to prolong youth, compliments and assurances that her lady was still enchantingly lovely; Helene paid in gossip of court doings, castoff ribbons and other gauds, and good solid copper coins.

"Child, what are you doing, dreaming over your basket like that! The water will grow cold again, and you've not stirred my herbs in!"

Helene's sharp voice shattered Aude's reverie. She started, apologized, and sprinkled the sweet dried herbs into the steaming water while Helene dropped her robe and slid gracefully into the tub. When Aude looked into the tub, she could see the reflection of her own triangular face and her unruly tangle of black hair, half covered by the swirling leaves and flowers that scented the water with a hint of marshland fragrances. In appearance, at least, she was little changed from the skinny brown girl who had shown Stephen all the secrets of the fen country. If that man had really called her name, if she hadn't imagined it . . . But it couldn't be Stephen. He was dead.

"Aude, child, you're not attending!" Helene reproved her. Aude tried to pay attention as Helene chattered on about some young law student, educated at this very convent, who was now returning from Cambridge to give a special disputation on three themes in canon law, as a way of showing his gratitude to his first school.

"I didn't know you cared about canon law, my lady! Are you going to become a scholar, then?" Aude could guess perfectly well why Helene was so excited about this young student's visit, but she also knew that the bishop's niece liked to be teased—respectfully, of course—and would enjoy the opportunity to explain what she found so fascinating about this young man's exposition of the decretals.

"Black-haired, pale, and beautiful as a demon," Helene described the young student on whom she'd cast her wandering eye. His name, she confided, was Joscelin.

Joscelin . . . Stephen had had a friend by that name. Brilliant, he'd said, a great logician going to Cambridge to study with a master of dialectic there. It must be the same person. Stephen was dead, and she was a confused girl who thought she saw his ghost everywhere. Helene was going to take this boy for a lover, Joscelin, who was scarcely older than Stephen would have been if he'd lived.... Aude burst into tears as she knelt beside Helene's bath.

"Aude, is something wrong? Oh, my dear, don't cry like that! I'm sorry I was sharp with you. What is the matter? Whatever it is, my dear child, we can set it right. Who is he?"

At another time, Helene's assumption that any problem must concern some man would have made Aude giggle. Now the offer of sympathy was all it took to make her sob out the story of her strange encounter in the graveyard. Helene listened patiently as Aude told her disconnected and contradictory story: first sitting in the cooling bath, then standing while waiting women draped linen towels around her wet body, and finally seated before the fire, where one of Aude's creams for the complexion heated.

"But really, child, you should have spoken to me in the first place," she said at last. "Now do try to be logical! A spirit would have had no use for your garland of flowers. The boy's ghost would have appeared to you as a boy, not as a grown man. This was a man you saw. Must be a newcomer to the town, or else you'd have noted his resemblance to your Stephen before this. How was he dressed? Noble or common?"

Aude searched her memory for the details. Helene's commonsense approach was already beginning to make her feel better; one couldn't think about spirits and ghosts in terms of their pointed shoes or the depth of embroidery on their cottes. "Not noble—but something more than common, I think," she said slowly. "Plain heavy shoes, and no decoration on his cotte or tunic, but the cloth draped well—good quality stuff, and not too badly worn."

"Heavy shoes? Not a merchant, then. A workingman, but skilled, much better paid than a simple laborer. Now let me see—ah, I have it!" Helene clapped her hands with pleasure. "Uncle just sent for a band of masons to rebuild the castle. The pressed men have been coming in all week. That's where we shall look for your mysterious admirer."

"Masons." Aude felt a flush burning her thin cheeks.

"Stephen always said he would be a mason, if he could get away from the convent. But, he's dead!"

"We don't know that, do we? Mistakes have been made before this. It was a very confusing time. Did I ever tell you how angry Uncle was, when he found out I'd set out for Ely in the midst of all the troubles?"

"You may have mentioned it once or twice," Aude murmured, but too softly to stop Helene as she launched into the well-worn story of her arrival in Ely, just hours after its devastation by mercenaries, and her discovery of Aude who had been left to freeze in the marshes. Aude knelt before the fire, pretending to stir the warming pot of ointment, and let her thoughts wander. Stephen... alive, and here again? No, it was too much to hope for. She would not let herself hope.

"Don't worry about a thing," Helene said when she was finally tired of gossip and reminiscence. "I'll make the inquiries. Come again in three days. I should know something more about your man by then, and"—a smile lit her face, making her look more like a mischievous girl than a fading, middle-aged wanton—"something more about my Joscelin, too!"

Aude thanked her in advance. Neither of them paused to consider that the Church might have its own interest in Stephen, oblate of Ely, if such a person were found to be alive and healthy instead of resting quietly in his grave.

"I think I've found your admirer," Helene announced when Aude came to see her at the end of the week. "There's a tall, blond mason working at the castle. He was pressed into service at Peterborough. He calls himself Edric and says he's twenty-five years old. He's been making quite a name for himself at the works, too. The other masons say he has a talent for building that has to come from God or the devil, choose one, but they don't much care so long as he stays on their side. The way Uncle has been pushing the work, there've been all sorts of accidents—but never around this Edric. Yesterday he shoved three men out of the way just before a whole great section of the old walls came crashing down where they were standing. He said he could hear the wall about to give way—did you ever hear of such a thing? But Uncle thinks maybe it's a genuine miracle of St. Audrey. He's having the chapter clergy look into it."

"Twenty-five? But Stephen would have been just twenty this summer," Aude said slowly. She had hardly heard anything Helene said after that; what did she care of the miracles worked by St. Audrey and some mason who happened to bear the same name as her father? Of course she had known better than to hope, but she had hoped anyway.

"And would Stephen have been a total idiot?"

"Of course not! He was kind, and clever, and . . ."

"And not such a fool as to walk back to Ely, calling himself by his right name and his right age, just to make it easy for the Church to catch up with him! Listen, child, I haven't spoken with him myself, but I talked to his comrades— there were four of them impressed from Peterborough together. His friend Hugh kept calling him Ste-uh-Edric. And the other two laughed into their sleeves every time he said it. Obviously this is your Stephen. He's not dead, and now he's come back to Ely to find you! It's so romantic I can hardly stand it!"

"Me, either," said Aude. In fact, she could hardly stand. And she felt most unromantically sick. If Stephen came back—and wanted her . . . No, she wasn't fit for him, not after what had happened. What would he do with a woman who got sick if a man so much as touched her, who still woke screaming at night when a cold frost settled over the fens? She clenched her hands tight, feeling the half-moon bite of the short nails against her palms, and willed the giddiness away. "I have to be sure. But I can't talk to him. Could you send for him? You could say—oh, I don't know—perhaps that your uncle wants to know more about this miracle."

"I can borrow Uncle's seal and have him sent for," said Helene slowly, "but what good will that do, if you won't talk to him? And why wouldn't you want to see a man who's run his neck into the noose for you? Oh, don't faint, Aude, I didn't mean it seriously. I don't suppose they hang men for running away from their vows."

"If I see him in the light," said Aude, "I'll know. I could hide behind the tapestry, and just peek. Please, Helene, my lady. I owe you so much already, please do this one more thing for me."

The reminder of gratitude worked, as she'd known it would; Helene liked to be a benefactress. Using that against her made Aude feel slightly guilty, but it didn't matter—nothing mattered except seeing Stephen again and knowing that he was alive.

They waited through the morning, Helene chattering while Aude alternately twisted her hair into knots and implored Helene not to speak so much of Stephen before the servants. "Oh, it doesn't matter, darling, they're all loyal to a fault," Helene assured her. "Why, I can have—visitors—up here anytime of the day or night, and Uncle never hears a thing about it!"

Protecting the bishop from hearing about Helene's lovers, Aude thought, was quite different from keeping this secret. The bishop wouldn't be overly grateful to anyone proving what he must already know about Helene. But recapturing a soul for the Church? That was another matter. She shivered in the warm rooms and implored Helene to send another messenger to the castle works, to find out what was taking so long.

"Oh, I can do better than that, darling," said Helene. "Don't you feel the need for a little exercise? I'm sure I do. We'll just stroll down to the works ourselves and see what's delaying the man."

Aude thought about having to see Stephen and speak to him again, then about the danger of calling attention to him. Presently she found herself outside with Helene, taking a meandering walk down to the castle works. The path Helene chose just happened to lead past the other guesthouse, where the young law student from Cambridge was staying, but to Helene's disappointment, there was nobody at the window.

And there was no big, blond mason at the castle works. "Yes, my lady," the warden of the works said respectfully. "Yes, we had a message from the bishop—two messages, actually. First he sent a bunch of his personal guard down to take our Edric and lock him up, then ten minutes later he sent another note saying he wanted to question Edric about this so-called miracle yesterday. Losing his memory, is he, then?"

The bishop's niece was not free to speculate on that interesting question. She was too busy supporting her maid, a thin dark-haired girl who had fainted with the heat of the day.

The cell under Ely Porta, the main gate to the convent and cathedral grounds, was technically the property of the bishop of Ely. It was built to hold dangerous malefactors who had disturbed the peace of the liberties of Ely until they could be given an appropriate trial and hanged with the bishop's blessing. The bishop was on reasonably good terms with the prior of Ely, however, and made no objection to letting him use the vacant cell as a storage place for a runaway monk.

The cell was narrow and windowless by design, dark and wet by the laws of nature; no candles were wasted on prisoners, and anything below or even close to ground level on the Isle of Ely suffered from the constant seepage of water from the fens. Built by economizing clerks in days when the bishopric of Ely had barely enough stone to use on the clergy's own quarters, the cell was just big enough to accommodate two undersized fenmen and not nearly large enough for a tall young man with a muscular build. Stephen's head knocked against the low ceiling if he stood upright, and if he lay diagonally across the sloping room— the only way he could stretch out his legs—either his head or his feet touched a puddle of slimy water that collected at the low end of the room. However he stood, sat, or lay, he felt the weight of stone pressing in around him.

"Stephen? Stephen of Ely!"

The whisper was unidentifiable in the darkness; it could have been man or woman, monk or layman. But it seemed unlikely that any of his friends would have penetrated the narrow dark stairs that led down to this room. "M'name's Edric," he mumbled, pretending the rough accents of an uneducated man. "From down Dunwich way. Dunno nothing about this Stephen fellow."

"What a pity. Stephen of Ely has some friends who'd like to speak with him. Do you remember Joscelin?"

Stephen grinned into the darkness. Did he remember Joscelin? How good were demons at chopping logic? "Which has more essence of horse," he asked the air, "a real gray horse or an imaginary white one?"

"Stephen, you idiot, the question is which has more essence of white horse." The voice was older, but the irritation was Joscelin all over. He never could believe that other people weren't being slow and stupid on purpose to annoy him. "You always did forget the most important terms."

"Joscelin! It *is* you" Stephen bounded to his feet, cracked his head against the low ceiling, and yowled in pain. "How did you get here?"

"The important question is how you're going to get out of here. And what made that awful noise, are you torturing a cat in there?" There was the welcome sound of a key turning in the stiff lock, and a moment later Stephen reveled in the dim light reflected down the steps of the staircase. Joscelin was a slim black shadow with a pale oval face; Stephen guessed he'd be as splendid in his churchman's robes as ever he'd been in lay dress. No black-dyed burel going rusty around the edges for Joscelin; the rustle of his long robes whispered of silk from the Orient and deep black fur bands to weight the hem with appropriate dignity.

"What? Oh—nothing. I banged my head. It hurt."

"If you make noises like that every time you hit your thumb with a hammer, God pity your fellow masons." Joscelin sighed loudly. "I did hope you'd have overcome your taste for low company by now, Stephen. If you'd stayed in the Church, who knows to what heights you might have risen?"

"Why, yes," Stephen said. "Look what a high place Brother Daniel has put me in even now. Joscelin, what are you doing here? Can you get me free? If you can, we'd best leave now. I don't know exactly what Brother Daniel has in mind for his runaway oblate, but I don't think I want to find out."

"Wait. The guards are still up at the top of the stairs. We can talk, that's all. You're sure it's Brother Daniel?"

Stephen nodded, then realized Joscelin could not see his gesture. "Yes. He came personally to gloat over my arrest. It was that damned 'miracle' that got his attention, of course. He came down with the clerks who were to set down an account of the whole matter and he saw me. I'd hoped he wouldn't recognize me after all this time, but, well, here I am."

"Miracle?"

"Nothing of the sort," said Stephen sharply. "I could tell

a section of wall was going over and warned some of my friends not to stand by it. That's all. You clerics are too quick to cry miracle when a man's just using his natural senses."

"Mmm. Some people might say you had an unnatural sense for buildings. Never mind, we won't quibble over mere words." Joscelin scuffed one foot along the damp floor of the cell and sniffed disdainfully. "Don't you even have any straw to sit on? Do you realize my clerk's robes are the best silk from Outremer? This muck will ruin them. Oh, well, I suppose I can lean against the wall for a while."

"I wouldn't. It's got mud from the marsh oozing through the seams. They didn't waste a lot of mortar putting this place together. Joss, how did you pass the guards and how did you know I was here, anyway?"

"A lady gave me a paper with the bishop's seal. And another lady told me about your plight."

"I don't know any ladies here."

"Oh, I think you'll remember this one. She and I together got you flogged once. Which reminds me, Stephen, I do owe you an apology for that incident."

"None indeed," said Stephen absently. Joscelin couldn't help being ambitious, any more than Stephen could help wanting to build in stone. Joscelin was generous with all he had, but he didn't have the kind of loyalty that could bear giving up his own ambition. Stephen had painfully reasoned that out in the lonely weeks following Joscelin's betrayal, and had forgiven him long ago. He was thinking about it now because he was afraid to think about what lady Joscelin might mean. Stephen was afraid to face a possibility he'd given up years ago.

"Aude?"

He waited, hands clenched, for the denial that would tell him he'd misinterpreted Joscelin's words.

"That's the one. Nice of you to remember her."

"Nice, nice?" Stephen laughed. He felt strong and young, as if he could reach out and break the walls of this cell with his bare hands. If Aude was really alive, if it wasn't a ghost he'd seen the other night, then he could do anything and life could start over again. "How could I forget her? She's the other half of my heart. But de Belmont said she was dead. Are you sure?" Stephen stopped and shook his head. Joffrey de Belmont had been a renegade and a liar. Of course he was lying about Aude, too. "Of course he was lying! I'm a damned fool for not seeing it sooner! Where is she?"

"*Dear* Stephen," said Joscelin with exaggerated patience, "your conversation is as difficult to follow as ever. I don't know anyone named de Belmont, nor do I care to. As for Aude, she's right behind—well, no, she must have stayed in the stairwell. Idiot girl. Aude! Come here. Stephen wants to see you."

Aude hadn't meant to see Stephen at all; only to make sure he was alive. Then she could quietly disappear while Joscelin did whatever magic he knew to save Stephen. But how could she leave, not knowing what was going to happen to him? And now it was too late; she'd loitered on the bottom step too long, and Joscelin's firm hand thrust her in the cell door and then Stephen was crushing her.

"I thought you were dead," he mumbled into her hair. "I thought you were dead. All these years."

He'd grown up, she realized. He wasn't the boy she'd led through the maze of the fen paths, laughing at him in one breath and scaring him with ghost stories in the next. Only twenty? But he was a man, big and broad-shouldered, with hard muscles and a rough, scratchy face, and a man's strength to hold her no matter what she did or how she fought.

But she was not fighting Stephen. There was no need to struggle. This was Stephen. He would not hurt her. Aude stood very still in Stephen's embrace, reminding herself of these simple facts, and eventually something of her cold stillness seeped through to Stephen and his arms relaxed around her.

"All right. If you're through with the joyous reunion, could we now examine your legal position?"

Joscelin put several quick, sharp questions to Stephen, concerning his age at the time when he was given to the Church, the words he remembered hearing, and what he had understood of the ceremony. He seemed pleased with most of the answers, but shook his head when Stephen told how he had carried the chalice to serve the prior's mass.

"That could signify consent."

"In a baby who didn't know what he was doing?" Aude

cried. "You great folk are all mad! You marry your children off and put them into the Church and name them to great titles while they're still in swaddling bands!"

"Not all at once," said Joscelin mildly. "The alternatives you've named are logically incompatible. And a vow is a vow."

"I thought you could help us. What's t'good of all your learning, if you can't get Stephen out of this? I should have gone to the masons. I'll go now." She should have known better than to trust to gentlefolk. Helene and Joscelin, what had they done for Stephen but make things worse with their fancy sentences that were like sticks stirring up the mud in an eel pond?

"No. Wait. I didn't say it was hopeless, you silly girl!"

"What do you mean about the masons?" Stephen's arm was heavy on Aude's shoulders, and his hand gripped hers. She couldn't go away. She wasn't sure, now, that she wanted to.

"They don't like being interfered with," Joscelin explained. "Pressing workers is one thing, locking up their mate in Ely Porta is another. There was talk of breaking into the prison after dark. They were sharpening tools when the bishop's niece came to me to stop them."

"Dear God. They'll be slaughtered."

"Or worse, thrown down here, and there's hardly room for one of you great hulking masons. I daren't think what the stench would be like with a dozen of you all squashed in together." Joscelin raised one hand to his mouth, and Aude caught the faraway odor of rich spices from the fluttering folds of his silken sleeve. "We'd do better to explore your legal options first, don't you think? It's a fascinating case. Granted, a few years ago it would have been hopeless, but the Fourth Lateran Council changed all that. The Pope and his councillors decreed that child oblation was to cease. It happened just before you ran away from Ely; I'm surprised nobody told you about it."

"I'm not," said Stephen. "Go on. Does that mean I'm free?"

"Do you feel particularly free?" Joscelin's dimly seen gesture took in the masses of stone enclosing them. "It's not that simple. You see, the old canon law governing the lifetime obligation of a child oblate has not been abrogated. It's simply in conflict with the new decrees. Of course, nobody's going to be an oblate now, so the conflict is theoretically unimportant, but you could be a special case. Borderline, you see. I don't know what would be the legal status of an oblate offered before the decree, who reached maturity and refused to confirm his vows after the decree. You're probably the only example," said Joscelin with mounting enthusiasm. "It would be a fascinating case in canon law, bearing on the whole question of resolution of contradictory and overlapping decrees, of which there happen to be a fair number—this business of oblation is a trivial example, of course—"

"Not to Stephen," Aude interrupted sharply.

"Well, no. Of course not." Joscelin sounded slightly disgruntled at having been interrupted. "But the implications for canon law are fascinating. Do you realize it could take years, positively years, to decide? We'd probably have to send memorials to the Pope himself! Me, Joscelin of Cressy, arguing a case before the Pope! I tell you, Stephen, this case could be the making of my legal career!"

"It could also ruin the best years of Stephen's life!"

"Yes. Well, there is that." Joscelin sighed. "I didn't think you'd really see it my way—still, it was worth a try. You're sure you don't want to go to court, Stephen?"

"The bishop's court? What chance do you think I'd have there?"

"We'd appeal, of course—oh, all right, all right, tell Aude not to bite me!" Joscelin stepped back toward the door of the cell, both hands raised in mock terror. "We'll have to use the other plan, then."

"The other plan?"

"My aunt's been after me to make a pilgrimage to Jerusalem in her name. She's getting old and counting up her sins, and she wants me to earn her pardon in heaven. I've explained to her that I can't break off my studies at this point, but she's being difficult. I need to go to Bologna since I've learned everything that English masters can teach me. She won't give me the money unless I go on pilgrimage for her first. If your mason friends could help us get you out of this cell—a small diversion shouldn't be too difficult to manage, and we do have the keys—you could take my place."

Stephen's whole body relaxed; Aude could feel the

change in his muscles. "If it's that easy, why the devil didn't you get me out at once?"

"I wanted to see if you'd let me be your lawyer," said Joscelin. "It would be a beautiful case—oh, all right, I understand you don't want to do it that way! It'll have to be the pilgrimage, then. We could even travel together as far as Bologna. I don't think even Sour Daniel would seek you out in Jerusalem; he's too busy trying to increase his power in Ely to go abroad."

"And your aunt, Lady Margery," Stephen remembered the name, "would she accept me as a substitute? A man who's running away from the Church?"

Joscelin let out a small exasperated breath, like a cat sighing. "Stephen. There is no need to bore Aunt Margery with a lot of irrelevant details. You'd be going in her name; your personal sins wouldn't count. And don't you see, this solves everything?"

"Not quite everything." Stephen's arm tightened round Aude. "I want Aude to come with me."

Excitement and panic warred in Aude's stomach. She felt all the breath whisk out of her lungs. "What? I can't go with you."

"We'll get married, of course," Stephen told her, as if that was what mattered. "But not in Ely, I think. Do you mind waiting until we're well away from here?"

"Stephen, I can't marry you! It's not—" Aude struggled for words that would make Stephen accept her refusal. "It's not proper. You're going to be a great builder. You ought to marry a woman who can help you rise in your career." She'd learned something, in these years of listening to Helene's gossip, about how marriages were made among the great folk in whose company master builders belonged. If a bishop's bastard daughter wasn't considered good marriage material, how much less a peasant girl from the fens! And in other ways Stephen deserved better, too. He deserved a woman who hadn't been hurt so badly that she might never have children, a woman who could stand the thought of being with a man. But she could not say that in front of Joscelin.

"Enough," Stephen interrupted her protests. "Last time I left here, I made two mistakes. I didn't go far enough, and I didn't take you with me. This time I shan't repeat either mistake."

PART III

Outremer

❖

1221–1226

CHAPTER

11

◻

Silk banners snapped in the wind and shone like jewels in the morning sun: the red lion of St. Mark, the pilgrim cross, the papal insignia, and the armorial bearings of the noblemen who traveled on this Venetian galley sparkled as brightly as the waves beneath the ship. As the galley pulled away from her moorings, the rowers sang, and on shore trumpets sounded a brassy marching tune. Aude hung over the rail, waving good-bye to Joscelin in his long clerk's robes, while the other passengers crowded close behind her to shout farewells to their friends and family.

"Bring me a flask of St. Anne's tears for the rheumatism!" bellowed a stout Englishwoman who had come this far in the company of pilgrims only to lose heart for the journey at the last moment. Her friends on the ship shouted their promises back, raising their voices to be heard over the loud, last-minute instructions of a worried Italian merchant whose son was taking this vessel to join the commune in Acre. Aude grinned. She couldn't understand a word of Italian, but the warnings of father to son were universal.

"Mind, Marco, don't get involved with those foreign women," she mimicked the merchant's worried cries. "Now, Marco, do what Uncle Girolamo tells you and don't fight with the nasty Saracens. No gambling, Marco, and stay away from foreign women."

The young man who stood beside her, sporting a head of hair as black and curly as Aude's own under his purple velvet cap, answered her smile with a sparkle in his black eyes and said something liquid and incomprehensible.

"Your pardon, messire," said Aude, "I do not speak Italian."

"It is I who should crave pardon." He switched to French with an ease and fluency that left her enviously gaping. "So well did you translate my papa's parting instructions, I thought you a mistress of the language."

Aude felt her face growing hot. "Oh. I just—fathers all give the same warnings, don't they? In any language."

"They do indeed. Did your father burden you with such warnings before you set off? Or—doubtless he accompanies you? He'd not be such a fool as to let a beautiful girl travel alone." The young Italian's eyes caressed Aude with a look that made her feel glad or sorry she wasn't traveling alone, she wasn't sure which; distinctly nervous, anyway. He hadn't said anything discourteous, but she still felt it was time to change the tone of their conversation.

"My father is dead."

"Oh. I am sorry—"

"But her husband is quite able to look after her." Stephen's hand closed over Aude's elbow and he nodded to the young Italian. "Come with me, Aude, I want to show you something, what were you doing flirting with that fellow?" he grumbled all in one breath as he pushed through the crowd of pilgrims.

"I wasn't flirting. He was merely being civil." As you are not, Aude longed to say, but she held her tongue. Ever since the galley had put off, Stephen had been looking more and more unhappy, and she was beginning to guess what the trouble might be.

"Good," said Stephen. Was he being censorious, or was he speaking through clenched teeth for a different reason? "This is no time to get embroiled with our fellow passengers, not when we're going to have to spend weeks together on this flimsy chip of wood in the middle of the ocean."

Aude wanted to point out that he, not she, had been the one whose manners could have started trouble. But as the galley leapt joyously to meet the open waves outside the harbor, Stephen groaned aloud and staggered to the side rail. She discreetly looked elsewhere for a few crucial moments and then joined him.

"You suffer from seasickness?"

"Evidently." Stephen breathed heavily through his nose. "How was I to know?"

"Funny you don't like the sea, being from Dunwich and all. And your dad a fisherman, too."

"I like the sea fine—to look at from ashore. It's boats I don't much care for. My father was drowned in a storm at sea."

So it was nerves, as much as sickness, that accounted for the sweat along Stephen's temples and the overfirm set of his chin.

"I'm not really brave like you," Stephen went on, apologetically.

Aude jumped. "Me? Brave?"

"Who else? You came with me all this way to Venice, and now you've agreed to follow me to Jerusalem, and you didn't have to leave home at all."

"Oh, yes, I did," Aude said under her breath. And that was the biggest proof of her cowardice, if Stephen only knew it. She'd been so afraid of never seeing him again, anything seemed better—even marrying him, when she knew she wasn't fit to be anyone's wife. Aude bit her lip and stared at the misty horizon where Venice was fading away behind them.

"Do you regret it?"

"No." Not for herself. But for Stephen—that was something else. "Do you?"

"No." Stephen sounded a little unsure; Aude wished desperately that she could know it was just the seasickness making his voice shaky. "Let's go look at our sleeping quarters. I can't stand this crowd on deck."

Of course, he must be regretting the impulsive marriage, Aude thought. It had started there in the cell, even before Joscelin had bribed the guards to look the other way while he and Aude smuggled Stephen out. He'd insisted on making their solemn promises to marry right then and there, with Joscelin for witness. That handfasting hadn't been enough for Joscelin's aunt Lady Margery, though; when they reached Cressy she'd called for her chaplain to solemnize the marriage. "I'll have no handfasted, betrothed, or planning-to-marry couples standing in the Church of the Holy Sepulchre in my name, thank you! And there'll be no hedge-born babies on this journey, either. I planned to send one pilgrim, Joscelin claims the weight of my sins is enough to justify two; very well, but I've not sinned enough to pay for an entire family. As for your disagreements with the monks of Ely, young man, that's your business. That place robbed me of two weirs and the fishing rights alongside my manor of Havenhill, thirty-five years past, and never an eel have I seen out of that manor to this day. I don't mind borrowing one of their strong young men in part payment. I just wish I were young enough to get a little more payment out of you than a pilgrimage! Don't look so shocked, girl, you know what men and women do in marriage, and it shouldn't be a vast surprise to you to find that some of us enjoyed it and would like to have a little more. And don't look at me like that, Father Herault, you know damn well I've lived chaste since Sir Roger died. Can I be in a state of sin now for thinking back fondly on things we did before you were born? Don't answer that."

Aude smiled at the memory of Lady Margery's endless chatter. She and Stephen had been swept along in the tide of the old lady's forceful will, with no chance to talk or express second thoughts or for her to tell him about the soldiers who attacked her. No, that wasn't true. She hadn't wanted to be parted from Stephen, and she'd fooled herself into thinking it wouldn't be so bad, not with a man she loved. Well, maybe it wouldn't be. They had had no chance to find out; the well-trodden pilgrim route from England to the ships at Venice was not known for luxurious accommodations. Most nights the three of them had shared a bed in some dusty roadside hovel, and they were lucky if there weren't two fat merchants snoring at the other end of the bed. Their first night on the road, Stephen said wryly that he could imagine better accommodations for beginning married life, and would Aude be insulted if they put off certain things until they could find a bed of their own?

He'd made it sound as if she would be doing him the favor. But Aude thought he knew how frightened she was, and how relieved she felt at this decision. Even in the crowded life of the road there were chances for a loving couple to find privacy: nights when they couldn't find an inn and made free of some farmer's haystack, mornings when they washed in a clear running stream and Joscelin would have tactfully strolled down the road. Instead they crossed half Europe like three chaste children, two brothers and a sister out to see the world. Whenever Stephen wasn't in sight, Aude wanted him so badly she ached inside and whenever he was there she was terrified, and it was all about to drive her out of her mind.

She was both relieved and disappointed to see that accommodations on the pilgrim galley offered even less privacy than the inns they'd stayed at on the way across Europe. The whole ship was less than two hundred feet long, and every inch of space was used. The high castle at the stern rose three stories to house the captain and the steersman's compass room and the noble pilgrims. From there a midlevel deck supported a kitchen, with a storeroom and a couple of pens for live pigs and chickens on the lower level. A narrow gangway ran back from the kitchen, over the rowers' benches, to a clear space of deck where pilgrims, servants, and merchants could congregate for a breath of fresh air. At the moment, this open space was occupied by gossiping pilgrims eating snacks and singing hymns, merchants discussing the price of figs in Aleppo, two boys throwing dice against the sway of the ship, and two others trying to clear a ring for a cockfight.

The sleeping quarters, one long cabin in the body of the ship, were no more spacious or private than the crowded deck. A single long chamber ran under the rowers' deck, dark except where light squeezed through the deck planking. Chalked lines divided the chamber into two long lines of narrow rectangles, eighteen inches by something less than six feet. Those passengers who owned more than the clothes on their backs could stow their possessions in locked chests set against the central gangway; those who had brought wine or provisions aboard could bury them in the hold below the cabin, presently filled with its ballast weight of damp cool sand.

Here they would unroll the bedding that their Venetian guide had brought on board earlier that morning; here, surrounded by gentle and common, religious and lay, men and women and children, they would sleep, wash, shelter from storms, and pray for a safe arrival in the Holy Land. The long dark room smelled of pitch and bilge water, and the way the slivers of light danced across the planks made Aude share a little of Stephen's queasiness. What would it be like in here, ten days out of harbor, with strong winds and people vomiting and children crying? She could only pray for a swift passage. No more than a fortnight, their Venetian guide had said; Aude mentally translated that to a month if they were lucky, two months if they weren't. Maybe more.

"I imagine the voyage will take about six weeks," Stephen said. He must have been reasoning it out as she was. He slipped his arm around Aude's waist and gave her a hug. "Well, I can wait that much longer for my wife; Jacob served fourteen years for Rachel, didn't he?"

Aude felt ashamed that she was so relieved. "Six weeks," she echoed. "Or longer, if we run into storms."

Stephen groaned. "Don't even mention storms. If I feel like this in calm weather . . . maybe I'll just get off here and walk the rest of the way."

"You'll feel better in the fresh air."

They left the dark cabin and climbed back up to the deck, where there was now ample space to sit as the pilgrims dispersed. The sketchbook in which Stephen had been recording the buildings seen in their travels was stuck in his sash; he took it out and flipped through the square sheets of parchment, frowning at his drawings. Aude sat on her legs a few feet away and studied her new husband's face, familiar, yet strange to her, with an unhappy expression. It wasn't, she thought miserably, just the fear of seasickness that made him look so grim and still.

It was her, of course. He'd been very patient, very tolerant, but what man wanted to be saddled with a scared girl who turned green every time he hinted of the marriage act? And they had never talked about it. On the road, Aude had let any excuse get in the way, Joscelin's presence, the muleteers who took them over the Alps, the crowded inns, their own fatigue at night. Now, with pilgrims and galley rowers on every side babbling in all the tongues of the Levant, they had as much solitude as they were going to get until they reached the Holy Land.

"It's me, isn't it? You shouldn't have married me. I knew that at the time. I'm sorry."

"What?" Stephen looked up from his drawing, blue eyes wide and innocent.

"I'm afraid," Aude said before she could lose even this little bit of courage. "Of. You know. You must have guessed."

"Yes." She had his full attention now.

"It's—the soldiers hurt me. I was sick a long time. I don't know if I can ever give you children. And I don't know if I can stand being hurt that way again, even for you, and I do love you, I do—" In another minute she would not be able to pretend that the wetness in her eyes was salt spray from the ocean. "You can get an annulment."

Stephen hitched himself over the deck to sit beside her, one arm pulling her head down to his shoulder, the open sketchbook temporarily forgotten. "Aude. I don't want an annulment. I want you."

"I know! And I c-can't—"

"Aude. It doesn't always hurt."

"How do you know? You're not a woman."

"No, but I've been with a few girls, and none of them cried about it. And think of Helene, and Lady Margery. They both like it a lot, and do they seem to you like the kind of women that would put up with men hurting them?"

That had puzzled Aude about Helene for a long time, until she had come to her own conclusions. "Maybe I'm different."

"You were too young," said Stephen firmly, a little too firmly, Aude thought. "You're older now. It will be all right. Anyway, I'm perfectly willing to wait until you get used to the idea." He laughed self-consciously and looked about to see if anybody was listening to them. "Especially with half the population of the Levant berthed on either side of us and listening to every move. I'm not at all sure I could. Severe embarrassment isn't good for a man. . . ." His voice trailed off and he scowled out over the blue sea, one hand clenched tight around his pen.

He was very unhappy, she thought, and it must be her fault, for he wasn't feeling seasick any longer, and what else could be troubling him?

"I am your wife," Aude said carefully. "I will do my duty. Here or in Acre, as you choose."

"I don't want your damned duty!" For a moment she was frightened by his sudden explosion of anger, then his fist unclenched and he smiled at her, gently, and Aude remembered how much she loved him. He slipped one arm round her waist, and she tried not to flinch. "Don't worry, Aude. I won't hurry you. I'm not some rutting boar of a peasant with nothing to think about but food and women. I'm . . ." He sighed, released Aude, and stared out over the blue horizon. "I don't know what I am, now. I was going to be a great builder. But I don't know geometry, and now I've broken my promise to Brito and lost my work at Peterborough and here I am heading off to the middle of nowhere instead of learning my trade."

So that was why he was so glum. "Oh, aye. Folk don't live in houses in the Holy Land, I suppose? All dwell in stables like the one Our Lord was born in?"

Stephen's mouth twitched slightly at the corners. "I suppose they must live somewhere," he allowed.

"What do you suppose they make their houses out of? Remember that pilgrim we met crossing the Alps said there wasn't a stick of wood in the Holy Land, so the peasants had to burn dung cakes for fuel."

Stephen sighed. "I remember the man but I don't see why you are bringing him up now."

"Think. If there's no wood, they must build in stone, Stephen!"

"I expect he was exaggerating."

"All the same. In some of the books Helene made me read there were tales of great churches in Jerusalem, and castles, and heathen shrines with roofs of gold, and all those would have to be made out of stone. There must be masons there."

Now Stephen was looking at her instead of squinting out to sea. "You're right, Aude. Maybe I could get work on a building project there. And there was an old Saracen prisoner of war at Peterborough. Bigger liar than that pilgrim we met. As he told it, he personally had a hand in every great castle built since the days of King Arthur. But he did claim there were learned men in the East who taught our English masons what little they knew of geometry. That was doubtless a lie. No infidel could know more science than an Englishman, but there might be some scraps of learning to be picked up, and at least," he said with a wry smile, "the infidels won't insist that I join the Church to get learning."

"Of course!" Aude applauded. "You'll build castles for the Crusader kings, and you'll learn geography—"

"Geometry."

"Geometry." She was impatient with his pettifogging corrections. "You'll learn everything there is to know from the heathens, and you'll draw fine buildings, and when we come home, you'll be Master Stephen in a fine, fur-trimmed robe. You can bore all the journeymen and masons with tales of the great things you did in the Holy Land."

"Aude, you're right. We've got a great future ahead of us and I've already got a start on it, with the sketches I made in Venice. Not many English masons have seen Italian styles of building. Did I show you that arcade I drew yesterday? Where—" Stephen's right hand patted the deck beside himself in widening circles and found only bare wood. "My sketchbook!"

Aude spotted a boy edging away from them, almost hidden by the bulky robes of a fat Italian monk and two chattering nuns. The boy was even thinner than Aude, and his bare shoulders were marked with red scars. A suspicious square bulge outlined the seat of his baggy trousers. "You! Boy! Thief! Come back here!"

Before the last words were out of Aude's mouth, the boy was scampering toward the far end of the galley. In an instant, Aude was on her feet after him. Coiled ropes lay in wait to trip her, a block swung within inches of her head; suddenly the deck dropped away beneath her as the galley heaved in the sea. She sprang for the narrow gangway between the rowers' benches. Men whistled and cheered in different languages as Aude hitched up her skirts and pounded after the thief. The drumming of blood in her head echoed the heavy beat of Stephen's feet behind her, and both were almost drowned out by the rowers' cries of appreciation. The boy glanced over his shoulder once near the end of the gangway; Aude's fingers were almost in his hair when he leapt monkeylike for the shrouds above him. He missed his grip, but the force of the leap carried him over the end of the gangway and onto the stairs leading to the captain's and noble pilgrims' quarters. Aude made the jump after him, leaping harder and farther, and came down on the boy's bare legs in a tangle of flying skirts. Her hands dug into his greasy hair and she panted with triumph. "Give—me—back—the book!"

An ironic patter of applause greeted her.

"Bravo!"

"Well done!"

"Bella figura!"

"Throw the girl a penny if she'll run back and show us her legs again!"

There was laughter, too. Aude looked up, still gripping the little thief, and saw a group of well-dressed nobles watching her from the narrow poop deck. They were applauding as if for a show; that was all the pilgrims were to them, Aude thought, a never-ending show to amuse them on the voyage.

Aude stood up, clutching the notebook, and the thief scuttled away. Stephen was close behind her, and probably angry with her for making a scene, but she was too angry herself to care. She hadn't felt such rage since the time Helene slapped her face for mispronouncing a French phrase in front of the bishop.

"Messieurs, mesdames, I thank you for your interest in our affairs," she said. Instead of her peasant's English, marred with dialect words, she used the pure French that Helene had taught her with such pains. "This book contains all the secrets of my husband's art. I hope that any of you ladies would be equally eager to protect your husbands' wealth and honor." She swept the group of nobles with a cool glance that, she hoped, adequately conveyed her opinion of them. She curtseyed with perfect grace, and turned to offer Stephen the recovered sketchbook.

"Wait! Signora, I apologize for the rudeness of my friends." It was Marco, the young merchant she met when they were leaving port. He leapt down the stairs, two at a time, to slip his hand under Aude's elbow and delay her departure. "Please don't be angry. Let me find a way to make amends. You must let me earn your forgiveness."

"It's no such great matter, sir." Aude wanted to draw away from the young Italian's grasp, but they were insecurely balanced on the narrow way; and she certainly didn't want to delight the lords and ladies up above with another scene. Stephen was coming along the planks behind her; she hoped he wouldn't be angry.

"We didn't mean to offend you." A tall, fair-haired man

dressed in the French fashion bowed at her other side. "Just—well, it was funny!" His open face and ingenuous chuckle invited her to see the best of the joke on herself. "Madame, we've all been plagued by the thieves that swarm around pilgrims. It's good to see somebody getting her property back for a change. And a lovely lady, too. You'll dine with us? And your good man, too," he added with a hasty, apologetic glance at Stephen.

Aude looked uncertainly at Stephen. He was frowning, but she could see that he too was unsure how to respond.

"It's the least you can do," said the Italian, "to show us you forgive our rudeness in Christian charity. And the best decision you could make, too. For one thing, they've already blown the trumpet for the common table. You'd have to scramble for a place now, and there wouldn't be much left over when you got there." He gave a half bow and offered his arm with a courtly gesture that Aude found irresistible. "Allow me to introduce myself. Marco Sanudo, merchant of Venice, bound for Acre. And you are . . . ?"

The noble passengers had malvoisie to drink and sponge cake after, but Aude was amused to find that their silver plates bore the same stew of fish and greens that the cook prepared for the commoners. Here in the captain's quarters, though, they sat in comfort on padded benches, and the fish stew was sauced with the same pleasant, meaningless chatter that she had heard in Helene's chambers. Aude enjoyed the banter and almost managed to ignore the fact that Stephen sat frowning and silent beside her for half the meal. Before the sweet cake was brought in, though, she'd lost the attention of one of her admirers. Marco and Stephen were drawing technical diagrams on the tabletop, using trenchers for beams and knives for pivot points. Aude was free to listen to the Frenchman, and listening was all she was called upon to do, once he got started.

They lingered on the poop deck for the rest of the day, only going below to the crowded pilgrim hall when it became too dark for Marco and Stephen to see the drawings they were sketching in the margins of his book.

"I'm glad that's over," Stephen murmured sleepily as they settled in for the night, huddled together in the narrow space where their bedding was unrolled between a Sienese monk and a family of five plump Rhenish burghers. "Who wants to waste time with those idle rich folk who have nothing to do but sit and chat? We won't be going up there again, anyway."

"You seemed to enjoy your talk with Marco." Aude wanted to go back to the poop deck. Everything seemed brighter and cleaner there; the air smelled of salt instead of the sour bilgewater stink in the pilgrim hall; colors were gay and light and people laughed instead of grousing about how much the pilgrim guides in Venice had overcharged them.

"He's not so bad," Stephen allowed. "He's intelligent, at least. But the rest of them! Idiot tittering nobles. That Frenchman who monopolized you, for instance. What a bore!"

"They're useful contacts for your line of work. Who d'you think hires builders? Rich people. We should go back. Geoffrey invited us to come back anytime we wanted to."

"Who's Geoffrey? Oh, the Frenchman?" Stephen snorted. "Contacts, ha. I know what sort of contact he wanted to make with you: leaning over you and whispering sweet words in your ear during dinner, playing little games while cutting up the trencher bread, and exchanging mazers when they poured out the new wine. And young Sanudo was just as bad, flirting at you over the gingerbread!"

"Stephen! Are you jealous?" Aude wriggled with guilty pleasure. Still, she didn't want Stephen to suffer the pangs of jealousy over her. "You don't need to be. They weren't flirting with me. Marco probably makes eyes at every girl he meets. He was really more interested in your drawings. And Geoffrey wanted to tell somebody about why he's going to the Holy Land. It's such a sad story, Stephen, and he's shy about telling the people he's traveling with because he's afraid they'll laugh at him. He said I was the first person he'd met who really understood him."

"That," said Stephen, "is probably what the serpent said before he tried to interest Eve in his recipe for apple tarts."

"He's really a very sweet person. He's looking for his sister, Stephen!"

"One of the tarts, no doubt."

"If you're going to be nasty and sarcastic I won't tell you his story. Remember when all those children marched through France to save Jerusalem, and they disappeared after they reached the sea? It was when you were still at Ely; you must have heard about it. That year all the goodwives locked up their children and stoned the traveling monk for child-stealing. Da said I had to stay by the hut all the time and he didn't want me talking to any damned religious types—that was before I met you, of course."

"I remember. So?"

Stephen's tone was not encouraging, but Aude was so excited by Geoffrey's sad, romantic story that she had to tell someone. "So his sister Madeline went with the Children's Crusade. His twin sister, Stephen. They were very close, being the youngest in the family. He's got six older brothers and they all lived to grow up, imagine that! His father wouldn't let them go after her because he said she would lose her virtue the first night and she'd be no good to him after that. His mother went into a decline and nearly died of grief and then his father relented and all seven boys went as far as Marseilles after the children, only by that time they had embarked on the ships and nobody ever heard of them again. His father said never to mention Madeline's name again and as far as he was concerned she was no longer one of the Tour Martel—that's his full name, Geoffrey de la Tour Martel. Until now."

"Huh?"

Aude realized that she might have gone a little too fast. "Now they've heard some news about the children. It seems there was another crusade, last year, I think, I don't know the details. We didn't win back Jerusalem, but we did exchange some prisoners. We let the captured Saracens go home, and they freed some of their Christian slaves."

"Oh? Maybe poor old Shihab will get to go home at last." Stephen thought fondly of the old Saracen prisoner of war, geometrician, architect, raconteur, and liar par excellence, whose tales had inspired him to steal Master Adam's geometry book.

"Some of the Christian slaves who were sent to Damietta were men and women who'd been on the Children's Crusade. They said the sea captain who offered them passage to the Holy Land never took them there. Instead he took them to Egypt and sold them as slaves. The lucky

children were those who couldn't fit on the small boat, and
were left behind in Marseilles crying when the ship sailed."

"So?"

"So Geoffrey's going to Egypt to find his sister, of
course! But since his father still won't have her name
mentioned, he had to pretend he was going on a pilgrimage to Jerusalem in order to get the money. Being a
seventh son, he hasn't got any money of his own, naturally.
After Jerusalem he means to go to Egypt, find Madeline,
and bring her home."

"To the father who won't have her name mentioned?"

"Oh, well," said Aude, "I expect he'll change his mind
when he sees her, don't you?"

Stephen snorted. "If I thought the poor girl really
existed, I'd worry about her. It's bad enough to be a slave
to the infidels, but worse to depend on that flower of
chivalry for rescue. He probably made up the whole story
because he thought it would appeal to your womanly
sympathies."

"At least it was more interesting than watching you and
that Italian boy trying to redesign the ship by finger-
painting on the tablecloth!"

"Now that," said Stephen with a familiar note of enthusiasm in his voice, "was really an interesting problem!"

Aude was prepared to be bored. Stephen's "interesting
problems" were good for helping her fall asleep, anyway.

"Did you see the crane they were using to lift bales on
board this morning? Four men were straining at the great
wheel for a load that had to weigh less than the smallest
stone you raise for a vault. Yet Marco says that's what they
use at all the ship quays. I'm trying to figure out how to
adapt one of our lifting wheels. It's tricky, see, because the
wheel has to pivot in all directions instead of just a quarter
circle, and that means the supports have to be . . . well, I
can't explain it, but if it were light, I could draw it for you.
Marco thinks it'll work."

"Good, show me in the morning," Aude murmured
sleepily, praying that Stephen would forget to do any such
thing. The weeks on the road had taught her that her
husband was fascinated not only by building, but by any
form of mechanical contrivance. They'd been late getting
out of Paris because he had to purchase a book of blank
parchment and a silverpoint pencil in the clerks' quarter

and then had to linger and draw the arch supports of the Pont Neuf in the fading light. Then they were thrown out of a little town on the border because Stephen wanted to show the priest how the bronze eagle on his lectern could, with strings and wheels, be made to move its head during the sermon; the priest had called him a witch-monger. And only Joscelin's quick tongue and a few bribes had saved them from being put in an Italian jail when Stephen's urge for sketching fortifications took him around the corner of the seawall and into a protected area where the secret mainspring of the great city gate worked.

Aude had been able to take all of this in stride—if only Stephen wouldn't try to explain it to her! She didn't have a mechanical mind. And Stephen, who seemed to feel in his bones how the keystone of an arch pressed down and out on the voussoirs on either side, expected everybody to have the same intuitive feeling for structure.

Well, she didn't have to actually listen to the explanations, did she? She would just let him talk.

And there was another thing Aude didn't want to think or talk about, but Stephen had promised to leave it until they reached the Holy Land. Maybe, she thought hopefully, the inns in the Holy Land are as crowded as those in Europe.

CHAPTER

12

◘

The voyage to the Holy Land took six weeks rather than the two their guide had so optimistically promised, but neither Stephen nor Aude minded. True, Stephen spent some days on the open sea feeling rather queasy and staring grimly over the railing, but those days had become rare. There were more merchants than pilgrims on board, and the captain traced a dawdling route that took in most of the coastal cities and island trading centers between Venice and Jerusalem. Stephen and Aude spent half of their time seeing the sights in strange ports while trade goods were loaded and unloaded, and then waiting while a local pilot carefully guided the ship out to sea again.

And such sights! Marco Sanudo, who had been on this trading route before, made a point of showing Stephen all the fortifications and famous buildings he might want to sketch; he kindly volunteered to keep Aude company if Stephen wanted to go off on his own and visit these sights. Sometimes Aude went with Stephen; other times she stayed with Marco, learning the traders' language with its Oriental words.

At Zara, Marco told Aude the sad story of how the town was taken by Crusaders in the Fourth Crusade, twenty years earlier, in partial payment for Venetian transport to the Holy Land. Aude was shocked to learn that Christians on their way to save the Holy Land could stop off and make war on other Christians just to pay the Venetians for lending them ships. Marco, as a Venetian, thought the whole affair had been a very clever arrangement. Stephen didn't care one way or another; he was absorbed in mentally rebuilding the walls destroyed by the Crusaders. If he and Shihab had designed the place, it might never have been taken. He dreamed, and Marco and Aude bickered good-naturedly, and eventually the ship sailed on to even more exotic ports.

When the ship put in at Spalato for water and supplies, Stephen and Aude set off to explore the ruins. The old Roman palace had been preserved through the centuries by city dwellers who built their houses within the thick walls. Even in places where they had torn down and rebuilt, Stephen could guess at the original construction and marvel at the tensile strength of Roman cement. "It's a strange place," he told Aude. "Quiet. I can hear the song of the stones, but this cement doesn't sing to me. It's like a dead thing."

"Then it's a good thing we've lost the secret of making it," Aude pointed out. "And don't tell anybody else the stones sing to you. Some folk might consider it peculiar."

Stephen remembered the talk of witchcraft and miracles that had driven him and Mam out of Dunwich. That was a warning Aude hadn't needed to give him.

On Crete, Marco conferred with the manager of the Sanudo warehouses about building a new quay to support the heavy but efficient lifting wheel Stephen had designed. On Cyprus, Stephen sketched Greek ruins and modern fortifications, Marco lectured him about the price of shipping stone in the Mediterranean, and Aude trailed through the bazaars collecting beads and pretty pieces of glass.

Just when they had adjusted to the dawdling pace of the voyage, the sandy beaches of the Holy Land were before them, and the rocky ridges west of Acre. The ship moved slowly through these shallow waters, inching west and north with infinite caution until reaching the safety of the deep bay. Once away from the rocky shoal, they moved surely into shore with the Church of St. Andrew for a guide.

Larger ships were anchored outside, but the small

pilgrim galley was allowed to pass into the small, safe harbor of Acre. It was almost like sailing into the heart of the city itself; they had to pass between twin watchtowers, over an iron chain that was lowered to permit the ship's passage, and into a half circle surrounded by jetties that were connected to the city walls by high vaulted roofs.

Laborers rushed on board, laying down plank bridges and pushing the chests of merchandise down to the jetty; guides jostled the passengers, each shrieking the praises of his particular hostel.

"We won't stay here," Stephen told Aude. They had both been warned that the pilgrim hostels of Acre were little better than thieves' dens, set up to fleece the dazed and seasick new arrivals from Europe. "We'll get donkeys and go on toward Jerusalem, and we'll sleep at an inn on the road somewhere."

"That you won't," said the guide who'd been tugging at Aude's sleeve. He gave them a cheerful, gap-toothed smile and explained that there would be no caravan of pilgrims departing for Jerusalem that day, perhaps not for weeks to come. There was unrest outside the Holy City, and fighting Bedouin tribes hadn't heard or didn't care about the latest treaty between Saracens and Crusaders.

Stephen and Aude were looking uncertainly at one another, deafened by the cries of dismay from other pilgrims who'd also planned to leave Acre at once, when Marco Sanudo appeared to take his leave of them. He grasped the situation in two words and solved it for them.

"But of course you won't stay at a public hostel. My family keeps a house in the *fóndaco*. You will be comfortable there. Signora Aude, please do me the favor of accepting our hospitality." He overrode Stephen's halfhearted protests with his princely assurance that the Sanudo house would have room for as many unannounced guests as he chose to bring. And he assured them that they were actually lucky to have this good excuse to stay in the mercantile capital of the Eastern Mediterranean. Acre was to Jerusalem, Marco assured them, as Venice to Petrina.

"I've never heard of Petrina," said Stephen.

"My point exactly. Jerusalem is nothing but a wide place in the road." Marco laughed, then sobered and crossed himself quickly. "Oh, of course, it's a holy place, the center of our faith, but who'd travel into the interior of this desert land if it weren't for the holy shrines there? Everything that matters is here." He waved one arm in a wide circle to take in the deep blue curve of the harbor, the crowds of shouting porters, bales and bundles of trade goods, screeching gulls above, and screeching pilgrims below. "The finest harbor in the Mediterranean. Everything comes through here. What do you want, cloth? Baldechino from Baghdad, taffeta from Persia, gold-threaded brocades from Byzantium, silk tapestries all the way from Zipangu? Perfumes, jewelry, salt, wool, wax, spices—especially spices. See this?" He stuck one hand into the half-open neck of a sack on a nearby barrow and brought out a reddish brown bark. Aude sniffed, breathing in a sweet, pungent smell far stronger than the hoarded spices she had tasted in the bishop's kitchens.

"Cinnamon," Marco said. "The price will be multiplied by ten before it reaches England, and two of those tens will stay in the pockets of our family. Sanudo," he shouted over the vendor's scream of protest, "Marco Sanudo, Venice," following up with a stream of Italian that Aude thought she understood. He had to be saying something like "Don't get so excited over a handful of bark, naturally we'll pay for your stupid cinnamon. Anyway the quality is so poor that you ought to be ashamed of selling in the open market!" Trading, like anxious relatives' injunctions, spoke a universal language.

"You're very good at this, aren't you?" Aude said. "Your father seemed worried that you wouldn't know what to do." How anxiously he had admonished Marco at the Venice quayside!

"Oh, Papa and his warnings. No, he goes on like that every trip. I've made the voyage three times now, but he still thinks I can't be trusted out of his sight. He's never forgotten the business about the three camels and the Syrian witch—well, never mind, you know how parents are." Marco Sanudo's olive skin was highlighted with a deep rosy color along the cheekbones. Aude made a mental note to find out more about the camels and the witch. Perhaps Marco would tell Stephen what he wouldn't tell her.

Their short journey to the House of Sanudo, in the part of Acre set aside for Venetian traders and their dependents, was slowed by Marco's burgeoning trading instincts and Stephen's fascination with the Eastern buildings. The Venetian quarter of Acre spread out in a crescent shape right along the harbor, but somehow Marco and Stephen managed to work in a quick tour of the sea towers, a look at the artificial breakwater that had extended Acre's harbor in the ninth century, a quick view of the Great Palace of the fóndaco, and a scattering of bankers' houses on the way there. While Marco checked rates of exchange and current market prices on Venetian goods with half a dozen different bankers, Stephen stared and marveled at the lines of buildings quite unlike anything he'd known at home. Aude could almost see his mind working, turning the flat roofs, the plastered walls, and the open loggias into a spider's web of lines and arrows for his sketchbook.

For herself, Aude was content to wander through the streets, gaping at the people who were so much more exotic and interesting than buildings or exchange rates. Saracen women were bundles of white or black, showing only dark-fringed eyes and slender, beringed brown hands. But the Latin ladies, with plaited locks hanging to the waist, were glorious in trained dresses and heavy silver bracelets and pendants. Their silver- and gold-embroidered trains and their sleeves, long enough to sweep in the dust of the streets if they had not been knotted up, were worked on fabric so fine that Helene would have reserved it for the very top of her best tunic. And the men out-peacocked the ladies, dressed in a gaudy array of yellow, rose, and turquoise silk, with enough gold buttons and silver chains to keep a small convent in food and firewood for years.

The House of Sanudo was an imposing three-story edifice, with carved lions to decorate the pillars. But once inside, the fallen plaster and ill-fitting wooden window frames made the house seem shabby. It stood opposite the Church of St. Mark, close to the center of the Venetian quarter; the square between house and church was busy with the crosstraffic of pilgrims, merchants, knights, commoners, and peasants from the countryside with their donkeys laden with wood or produce. Despite the brilliantly colored flowing robes, the dark faces of Saracens, and the tanned visages of Knights Templars in their plain armor, the babble of languages, and the smell of strange, spicy food, something about this bustling life made Aude feel at home. Foreign and rich they might be, these people of Acre, but they were still just people: buying, selling, haggling, and eating like people in the market square back home. She would do all right here.

Inside the dilapidated, high-ceilinged rooms of the House of Sanudo, Aude felt less sure of herself. The house had been built, Marco explained, some fifty years earlier, when the Venetian commune had just been granted its privileges in Acre. At that time, the Sanudos had great plans for establishing a merchant empire spanning the Mediterranean. Although he did not say it, Aude deduced that those plans had come to naught: the rooms had never been furnished to match the grandeur of their carved and painted ceilings and the delicate rich filigree of the wooden window screens. Instead of housing a generation of Sanudo merchant-bankers, the shadowy rooms were occupied by one old Arab couple, a crippled man and his wife, who came stumbling forth to greet this young Sanudo with bows and apologies for the state of the house. Marco waved aside their apologies with a lordly gesture, kissed the old woman on her withered cheek, and asked for some of her special chicken stuffed with dried apricots for dinner. He offered his guests the use of the entire third floor and disappeared with apologies of his own. Clearly the brief exchanges with traders in the street had whetted his appetite for the family business; he could rest later, he said, after he'd seen the Sanudo trade goods safely unloaded from the galley and stowed in the empty warehouses below the living quarters.

Stephen chose a room overlooking the bustling square, with latticework windows set with colored glass to soften the harsh sun and to filter out the noises of the street. There was no furniture on this deserted third floor, but a carpet, glowing with jewellike tones of red and blue and bathed in light from the filigree window screens, made this large room seem slightly more habitable than the others.

No sounds from the old couple in the kitchen reached Stephen and Aude's room and the babble of the market-place came to their ears only as a distant echo. A cloud of fine dust rose from the floor where the servant had dropped their bundle of clothes and cooking utensils, and Stephen watched the particles settle back down to the red and blue flowers of the carpet.

"Well," he said. His voice caught and almost broke on the single syllable. He made a show of coughing. "Sorry—there's dust in my throat. Well, we have privacy, don't we?"

Aude's mouth was dry, but not from the dust. She nodded, and was about to suggest that they go and explore the market, but then she thought better of it. Hadn't they been postponing this long enough?

"Don't look like that!" Stephen said irritably.

"Like what?"

"You remind me of me, going to take a flogging after I'd skipped lessons at the convent. Braced for the worst and eager to get it over with."

That was, Aude supposed, exactly how she felt, although she'd never been whipped.

"Dear heart, I promise not to hurry you." Stephen sank down cross-legged on the dusty carpet and held out his hands to Aude. "D'you suppose this is what they use for beds? It's soft enough. Come try it?"

After a moment's hesitation she took one hand and perched on his knee. His palm was hot and dry. He was nervous, too, she realized. That should have helped, but all she could think of was the soldiers and their angry haste. One of them had been young, no older than Stephen was now, and he had been sweating with fear of the enemy; the sharp smell of sweat on an icy day, and the hot smell of blood, first Edric's and then her own. . . .

"No. I won't let you go back there!" Stephen's voice was far away at first, then all around her like the warmth of his arms. "Aude, this is me, Stephen. You weren't afraid of me before, were you? Remember that summer when you showed me the fens? I would have been lost or drowned without you. Remember the day you showed me the marsh lilies in their pond? You said that was better than the stained-glass windows in the cathedral, and so it was, because they were alive and glowing and soft. You knew everything then, Aude, and I was just a little monk that you teased and led around on a string. Just stupid Stephen, who didn't know how to find his way. Remember?"

He went on talking, slow and soft like a man soothing a frightened animal, and Aude relaxed into his arms and let the warmth enfold her. After a while she was no longer thinking of anything but Stephen. When his hands slipped under her tunic and undid the knotted strings of her belt, she did not think at all. There wasn't time to be afraid, or room to remember; there was only cool shadow and warm light on her skin, with Stephen leading her into strange, secret places as once she'd led him.

When his breathing quickened and his hands were on her thighs, she stiffened involuntarily. Cruel, laughing faces from long ago crowded around her at once. Her fingers clenched Stephen's arm and he slowed his movements at once, slipping to the side so that he wouldn't oppress her with his weight.

"Dear Aude, am I going too fast for you? It doesn't matter." His voice trembled, and in the midst of her fear she gloried in the power she had over him. But Aude felt no desire herself; there was only the cold will to perform her duty and fulfill the marriage debt. The legal phrases the priests loved rang in her ears, but she closed her eyes and thought only of their secret summer in the marshes.

Stephen had been so lonely and scared then, and so unhappy. Aude traced the scars of those old floggings that crisscrossed his back. Years of growth and summers of work in the sun hadn't erased those lines.

That first summer when she'd found him lost in knots of unhappiness, she'd taken it on herself to show him how to live free; she'd given him the glory of the marsh lilies, the secret peace of the labyrinthine paths through the fens, the calm mirrorlike mere, with ripples lapping at the edge of the path, and the delicious mystery of the place where the Norman soldiers lay under the black fen-ooze. All that had been hers to give once, and was she poorer now?

"I'm not afraid, Stephen," she whispered. "I'm not afraid. I want you, come to me." And as she opened her arms to him, she gave him her land again, and thus she reclaimed it for herself with joy and without fear: reeds, willows, fen, waterways, and black shady paths, and the surprising glory of a thousand white waterfowl beating their wings in the air.

"Well?"

This time it was a challenge, laughing and confident. Aude opened her eyes and stretched, lazy as a cat in the sun. Had she really once been afraid? That seemed impossibly long ago, a child's midnight terror, nothing to do with this room where blue shadows and dancing drops of light chased one another over the red and blue lozenges of the deep, soft carpet.

"That's not much of a testimonial!"

"Fishing for compliments? Come back when I'm awake." Now that it was over and the vibrations of pleasure were slowly dying away, Aude felt desperately tired. All those weeks of crowded inns, with bodies all around her snuffling, breathing, snoring, excreting, making love, and endlessly talking. She supposed Stephen was used to communal living from the convent, but after the peace of her little hut in the fens it had been sheer torture for Aude. She loved Stephen, and she wanted to stay awake long enough to tell him so; but even more, she wanted to fall into the deep, exhausted sleep that was calling to her. What luxury to sleep alone; Aude didn't even want Stephen with her now, but to say so would hurt his feelings.

"If you want t' go explore the town," she murmured, "'s perfectly all right with me." And with that, she fell asleep.

Later they learned that beds were as common in the Kingdom of Jerusalem as in Dunwich or Ely. The ones belonging to the House of Sanudo had been dismantled and stored in the cool caverns below the house years before. Neither Marco's bodyservant nor the old couple who took care of the place had thought to set up a proper bed for the visitors until late that night.

The slow, lazy days they passed in Acre, waiting until it was safe to travel to Jerusalem, were a blessed time of peace and healing for Aude. In the daytime she explored the mysterious shops of the bazaars, with Marco to guide her whenever he could get away from his business obligations. Together they trailed through long, narrow streets lined with merchants squatting behind their sacks of spices and fruits. They watched the coppersmith pounding out delicate incised patterns on his wares and fingered the spiderweb silks and silver-stiffened brocades that came from lands even farther east than Outremer.

And at night she had Stephen, and the high-ceilinged white room at the top of the House of Sanudo.

Stephen amused himself in his own way, sometimes accompanying Marco and Aude on their expeditions through the bazaars, more often going off to sketch an ancient, ruined pillar or to study the lines of the city walls. Occasionally, Geoffrey de la Tour Martel accompanied him on these excursions; the French knight had an uncle by marriage among the maritime justices on the Court of the Chain, and Uncle Philippe was willing to give Geoffrey a pass to explore the defensive walls and the harbor of Acre.

"I think he wants to keep Geoffrey from talking to the released Christian slaves himself," Stephen said to Aude. "So to keep him busy, he's encouraging him to go around the walls with me. I don't mind. I'm getting into places I wouldn't have seen otherwise. And he's not a bad fellow, your Frenchman."

"Not mine," Aude corrected. "And why shouldn't Geoffrey talk to the slaves himself? That's why he came here."

"Yes, but he loses heart too easily. I think he expected the first Christian he met would recognize Madeline's description. So far nobody they've questioned knows anything about her."

"Well. She was how old at the time? Twelve? Stephen, a lot of things can happen to a young girl alone in this world." Aude bit her lip, forcing herself to know this day of white dust and summer heat instead of the ice and blood of her memories. "Has Geoffrey thought that he may not find her?"

"He doesn't want to think about that." Stephen touched a scrape on his cheekbone and Aude deduced that there had been a fight, or a near-fight, over that very issue. "He's been drinking too much lately. I've tried to distract him by explaining the building techniques used in the harbor quays, but it doesn't work too well. I think," he said in a wondering tone, "I suspect that Geoffrey is not really interested in architecture."

Aude was a sensible, grownup married woman now. She knew better than to laugh at her husband. She didn't even point out that Geoffrey was not alone in this peculiarity; the world was full of people who were not desperately longing to know how to build a better arch. She merely expressed a charitable wish that Geoffrey should find something that did interest him, to while away the time in Acre.

A few days later, Geoffrey did just that; though a *poulani* witch wasn't exactly what Aude had had in mind.

"What's a *poulani*?" she asked when Stephen told her about Geoffrey's new idea for finding his sister.

"A native-born Frank. This woman married a Syrian,

actually. She lives in the Syrian quarter, and we're going to have to slip in quietly while her husband is at Friday prayers in the mosque, because he doesn't approve of her calling djinns and telling the future. But she's supposed to be very good." Stephen eyed Aude warily, waiting for her to object.

"What time do we leave?"

"You're not going with us!"

"I'm not missing it."

On Friday night, when they were creeping through the back streets of the Syrian quarter in anonymous cloaks, Aude began to regret her insistence. She could almost feel the curious eyes watching them from behind the carved wooden lattices of the houses. They were too conspicuous: Aude did not know how to hold the veil properly over her mouth and nose, and Stephen and Geoffrey were so blond and big-footed compared to the neat, delicate Syrian merchants who lived on this street.

It was the tenth house on the street, Geoffrey had said, and they were to go in the back way so that the doorkeeper wouldn't have anything to report to his master. At first there was no answer to their cautious scratching at the back gate. Aude began to think that she wouldn't be terribly disappointed if no one let them in. They could be back at the House of Sanudo before dark. Whatever had made her think she wanted to see a foreign witch raise demons? And at night, too?

Then the gate in the wall opened to a darkness, scented with flowers and sounding with the splash of falling water. They held hands as they passed through the enclosed garden. Geoffrey was in front, being led by the old, veiled woman who'd opened the gate, and Aude was at the rear, feeling very grateful for the warm clasp of Stephen's big fingers around her hand. She smelled mint, sweet and pungent, mixed with the smell of other herbs she could not identify. Then there was the softness of carpet underfoot, and a subtle change in the quality of the darkness—now Aude was aware that the garden had only been covered by screens of silk and latticework. Her fingers brushed over the stone, silk hangings, the velvet draperies, and the finely woven carpets, layer upon layer enshrouding them and turning early evening into absolute night.

A blue flame danced in the air, and Aude caught her breath. The muscles in her thin calves were tensed to run, but Stephen's hand encircled her wrist, warm and steady, and Geoffrey loomed big on her other side.

"Who comes to question the spirits of the air?"

The wailing voice, like the blue flame, seemed to float in midair. Aude's tongue was a bit of dry wool stuck to the top of her mouth. Was this part of the witchcraft? She wished desperately that she were safe in the House of Sanudo, eating apricots and chicken with Marco and fending off his gentle flattery.

"Who comes?"

There was a touch of impatience in the question now, and the blue flame shot up higher as if to give point to the demand. In the momentary brightness, Aude glimpsed an obese woman lolling on cushions behind the lamp, wrapped in gold-shot tissue that flashed with gold coins. Her fair hair was braided in the Frankish style, and a light veil covered all of her face except for her wide, pale eyes.

"Ahh." The sigh came from behind them. Aude wanted to turn and see who had breathed that heavy, satisfied exhalation, but she could not move. The woman raised one hand, and the bangles on her plump wrist jingled.

"Yes, Takifiel?"

The bubbling sigh was repeated. The fine, short hairs at the back of Aude's neck stirred in the demon's breath, and her skin prickled with apprehension. Would she feel its claws on her neck in a moment?

"So. You seek the fair-haired girl who came over the water. Perhaps my little friend will help you—perhaps not." Her light witch-eyes were fixed on Geoffrey's face. Aude could just see his profile out of the corner of her eye. He looked grim and brave and noble. Or possibly he was just paralyzed with fear, as she was. She told herself that the witch could be as much a fake as some of the wise women back home. Hadn't she known already that Geoffrey was looking for his sister? And wasn't it a reasonable guess that Madeline was fair, like Geoffrey himself?

"And you?" The pale eyes singled out Stephen.

"I'm with my friend. I'm not looking for anything."

"No, you are running away from something. What is it?"

Stephen didn't answer. The air moved behind them, and

Aude thought she heard a high chittering noise, almost like bat squeaks in the sky.

"No matter." The witch dismissed him with a contemptuous flick of her hand. "Takifiel says it is a matter between you and your God. Do you think to be safe here, in the Holy Land of all the Gods?"

She laughed and her eyes settled on Aude. "And a woman." Her voice grew low, caressing. "A very little woman, and very frightened—perhaps too frightened to speak. What does she want from us, Takifiel?"

Rather than bear the heavy warmth of the demon's breath on the back of her neck, Aude found her own voice. "I did not come to ask you for anything, my lady." Was that the right way to address a witch? No matter, one might as well be as courteous as possible. "All we want is to help Geoffrey find his sister."

A soft chuckle stirred the loose curls on the back of her neck and was echoed by the fat woman behind the lamp. "So? I think not, little sister. Come to me."

She held out one monstrous, beringed paw, and Aude stumbled forward on numbed legs, sank down on the cushions beside the witch, and felt her own thin hand swallowed up in the witch's soft white fingers.

"Yes, I see you think you are telling the truth. You have given your fate to this man." She threw a contemptuous glance toward Stephen. "You're a fool. I feel the power in you. You could be as I am—stronger, even. Shall I free you to seek your true fate?"

Aude shook her head violently. "No! No!" Somewhere in the gliding, unctuous voice she sensed a threat against Stephen. Trying to pull free of the witch's grasp was like trying to cleanse her hands of sticky taffy; she felt as though thousands of clinging threads were binding them together. She freed herself and backed up to stand beside Stephen, one arm around his waist.

"As you wish, little sister. Follow your man to Jerusalem, then. He will find his fate there." A dry, rasping chuckle interrupted the witch's speech. "He will not thank me for the experience, but you need not fear for him. He is in no danger from any in this land, for Takifiel says that his bones will lie under the sea. Will you give me your hand, husband of my sister? Will you know more of your death than Takifiel has told me yet?"

Stephen shook his head.

"You bore me." The witch sighed. "Very well. He is the least interesting of you three, but if all you want is to find his foolish Madeline, I will ask Takifiel."

She cocked her head, listening to the almost inaudible sighs and stirring of the air around them. Stephen was squeezing Aude's hand so hard that her fingers were going numb. How had the witch known Madeline's name?

Whispers thick as sleep stirred the air behind them, and the witch raised her head like one listening to distant music. "What? Oh. Oh, all right," she said in the darkness, and looked at Geoffrey again. "Go to Jerusalem with these two. You are to look for a bearded Frank or a beardless Saracen—sometimes it's hard to tell exactly what Takifiel is saying—for a holy place defiled, and a prison opened."

"What does that mean?"

The witch raised fat puffy shoulders and a ripple ran through her bulk of flesh. "Takifiel does not always explain himself. He's gone now. You'd better go, too, because my man will be back from the mosque any minute."

She waved one jeweled hand, and the old woman who'd led them into the room scurried from side to side, lighting lamps and turning the witch's cavern into a perfectly ordinary, though slightly overfurnished, room. The witch herself was no more than a fat, bored woman with yellow braids and too many jewels, now speaking in an ordinary tone of voice as she instructed Geoffrey to pay her maid. "Fatima keeps the money safe for me," she explained. "I don't like to have a lot of coins in the house. My man might find them and then there would be trouble."

She was only an ordinary, overfed wife, with a husband who denied her these little amusements. Yet she had known the name of Geoffrey's sister without being told, and no tricks with lamps and voice-throwing could explain the heavy breaths of air that had hit the back of Aude's neck when the woman's familiar was speaking. Aude was eager to get out of this hot, enclosed room and away from the lamps burning heavy scented oil that made her head swim. But Geoffrey was still bowing over the woman's white hand, trying to tease and flatter her into giving another hint to help him on his search for Madeline. She pushed him away, whining that she was tired and her man would be home from prayers soon.

Then the shouting began, and a slave screamed in the garden, and men with wicked curved Saracen swords swarmed into the room. Aude wished very much that they had gotten out of the witch's house before her husband came home from the mosque.

CHAPTER

13

◻

Stephen and Aude owed their lives to Geoffrey, who sprang into action while they stood dazed by the sight of armed men pouring into the house. Grabbing Stephen by one arm and Aude by the other, he dragged them behind a tapestry, through a hidden door, and out into the walled garden.

"Where's the door?" Stephen panted as he groped in the darkness.

"No time. It's probably locked. Up!" Geoffrey grunted as he heaved Aude over the wall and right through the silken screens that roofed the garden for privacy. Stephen and Geoffrey scrambled after her, leaving behind a trail of bruised mint, trampled fruit, and splintered screens. Once safely on the other side, Stephen grasped Aude's elbow and Geoffrey half lifted her from the other side as they retreated from the Syrian quarter leaving a trail of barking dogs, bright lamps, and querulous voices in their wake. They didn't stop running till they were safely back in the Venetian quarter. Aude discovered that she was trailing a streamer of silk from the garden screens and Geoffrey tied the sandal strap that had burst when he vaulted the wall. Stephen found breath to ask how Geoffrey knew to make his escape that way.

"Habit, old man. I've encountered jealous husbands

before. Never go to visit a married woman without keeping one eye open for a backway out."

"Yes, but how did you know there was a door right behind us?"

"Felt the draft," Geoffrey replied succinctly, and Aude burst into laughter. When she caught her breath she informed Stephen that she, too, had felt the draft from the half-open door, but she'd thought it was the witch's demon breathing down her neck.

"I wonder if it was all tricks and lies?"

"I'm going to Jerusalem. She knew my sister's name," Geoffrey said. His prominent, squarish jaw set forward slightly, giving him a stubborn look. Stephen thought of bazaar gossip and how easily a woman could send her servants to find out all about two conspicuously big Frankish pilgrims; then he remembered the clip on the jaw he'd gotten for suggesting that Madeline had probably died before she even reached Marseilles, and decided not to try to reason with Geoffrey on this matter.

"Will you come with us?" Aude asked.

"After what has happened tonight, we'd best leave soon." If the *poulani* woman could find out the name of Geoffrey's lost sister, her husband would have no trouble finding the name and whereabouts of his wife's Frankish visitors. How far would honor compel him to pursue the argument? Stephen didn't want to find out. "Do you suppose we can hire a guide at this hour of the night?"

In the end it was Marco Sanudo who located a guide for them. At first he shook his head and advised them not to attempt the journey to Jerusalem alone; but after he heard the story of the night's misadventures, he agreed that they'd be safer leaving town for a while.

"But come back again," he urged as he saw them off early the next morning. "You'll have to pass through Acre to get a ship for home, anyway; and you're welcome to stay at the House of Sanudo as long as you like. We'll have a feast when you get back. I'll invite the entire quarter. You can rest and eat and tell lies about the holy shrines you visited, and Pietro Zanni can look at the relics you'll have been tricked into buying. He'll tell you that your splinters of the True Cross came from the lintel of a deserted house and your Tears of St. Anne have the mold of the great cistern under Jerusalem floating in their vial."

Geoffrey frowned at this levity. "We go for our souls' sakes, Messer Sanudo, and it's unbefitting to make jests about such matters. Surely no man would risk his own soul by selling false relics to pilgrims."

Marco rolled his eyes and whispered to Stephen that he thanked God every day for pious, bone-headed Frankish knights; they were a merchant's dream. "And more of them are born every day, bless the fertile girls of Normandy and Burgundy. When you come back..."

But the guide was impatient, and the string of donkeys had begun to kick, so Marco had to say good-bye. At the last minute he clasped Aude's hand and said, "I like Stephen."

"Yes, of course," Aude said, surprised.

"If not—oh, well. Go to Jerusalem. You should be safe enough; this man knows the dangers of the road as well as anyone. But come back, Aude!"

Geoffrey continued to grumble about Marco's impiety until Stephen reminded him that without his aid they'd have been walking to Jerusalem with neither guide nor string of donkeys to help them on their way. Their progress was slow since Geoffrey's new piety would not permit him to pass by a single shrine or holy place on the route to Jerusalem. They visited the prophet Elijah's cave in Mount Carmel and the birthplace of St. Denis in Francheville. Stephen wondered aloud how the patron saint of France happened to have been born in Palestine. Geoffrey hushed him and bought a second medal of St. Denis from the peddler at the shrine, to make up for his friend's impiety.

From there the road wound through marshy land that made Aude and Stephen think of the cool fens of Ely. Geoffrey thought mostly of the raising of Lazarus from the dead; there was a village named for Lazarus on the road, and although nobody seemed sure what the connection was, the villagers happily sold commemorative medals showing that the pilgrims had visited this dubiously holy place.

"The witch prophesied truly," Geoffrey explained his piety to Stephen that night. "One has to respect things of the spirit. I never did before. But if she could help me find Madeline...."

"You can't know that yet. We're not in Jerusalem, and I couldn't make much sense out of her ravings at the end."

Geoffrey's jaw slid forward. "I know, and you will, too, when I find Madeline. Anyway, if witches and demons have such power in this land, doesn't it stand to reason that we need the protection of God and His saints now more than ever?"

He lingered to look back on the village of St. Lazarus, while the guide whined that they must move on if they were to pass Rishpon and reach the safety of Jaffa before nightfall. "Must go through passage cut in the rock. Very favorite place for robbers, gentlemen!"

"Don't worry," said Stephen cheerfully, "I have it on the best authority that my bones are fated to lie under water. It's not getting to Jerusalem that worries me—it's the passage back to Europe. Maybe there's some way I could walk."

"You see," said Geoffrey triumphantly, "you believed her too! Now aren't you glad I have the protection of these relics and holy medals?"

Stephen thought privately that he was rather more glad of the protection offered by Geoffrey's sword, and hoped that the medallions clattering from his surcoat wouldn't impede his sword arm.

They passed the tunnel of rock without incident, and the rest of the journey to Jerusalem was calm and crowded; word had spread of their safe passage this far, and pilgrims who'd hesitated in Acre for fear of thieves and petty local wars now hurried to catch up with Stephen, Geoffrey, and Aude. By the time they reached Jerusalem, they were at the center of a bustling stream of pilgrims, and Geoffrey complained bitterly that the guide wouldn't allow him time to pray before they entered Jerusalem. For once, Stephen sympathized with him. He wasn't sure what he wanted to do exactly, pray or just think, but he was not quite prepared to be swept through the gates of the city in the midst of the laughing, quarreling, singing throng that now surrounded them. This was too important. As they reached the gate, he shut his eyes for a moment, trusting to his donkey's good sense to keep him out of trouble, and tried to compose his thoughts.

Jerusalem, the Holy City, where, according to the *poulani* witch, Stephen was to find fame, Geoffrey his long-lost sister. This sacred place drew Christian pilgrims from the farthest ends of the earth. It was the symbolic heart of the labyrinth in the floor of Ely cathedral, the mystical center of the round dances the peasants did at Easter and All Saints', the place from which God's truth had lit a flame in the hearts of men.

When he opened his eyes, he was in a shabby, half-deserted village of roofless houses and tumbledown walls.

"Well, Marco did tell us not to expect too much," Stephen said aloud. Still, he almost wanted to cry as he looked down at the stone huts built against the remains of ancient temples. What was he doing here? He was a builder, and this was a desolation.

"Marco did warn us that most of the Christians left Jerusalem when the Saracens took the city," Aude said softly.

"And the Saracens tore down the walls in the last Crusade, so that if the Franks took it, there wouldn't be any way to defend it," Geoffrey added.

"And there's not much trade this far inland, as Marco pointed out." Stephen tried to swallow his crushing disappointment. Hadn't they been warned? Aude's optimistic talk of finding work as a mason in the Holy Land had served to buoy his spirits on shipboard, but now it seemed as much a dream as his ideas of becoming a great builder. Nobody built in this land; they squatted in the ruins of the past, turned castle walls into hovels for peasants to live in, let sand sift over the treasures of the past.

As they made their way through the city, Aude and Geoffrey were cheered by the sight of all the activity around them. Jerusalem might not be a great trading port like Acre, and it might look like a pile of ruins from the distance, but there was still plenty of life within these ancient stones. They passed open squares where peasants shouted out the prices for their grain and produce, chickens tied by the legs and hung upside down squawked in protest, cattle lowed and tossed their heads about. As the street narrowed, they saw a dark-roofed area ahead, with cavelike openings on either side where men in striped robes called to the pilgrims.

"Signora, signorina, mademoiselle, young mistress!" wheedled a one-eyed boy who ran beside their party, holding up an apronful of clanking trinkets. "Flask of holy water from the Church of the Holy Sepulchre," he went on in English when Aude's involuntary start revealed her nationality. "Medal blessed by St. Peter personally, to show lady has been to the Holy City. Fragment of True Cross? Bangles for lady's wrists? Thorn from Our Lord's crown? Sweet perfume to make lady irresistible to all noble lords, specially blessed by Nestorian priest in Street of Bad Cookery, potency guaranteed by archbishop?"

Stephen brushed the boy out of his way like an annoying fly. He was replaced by half a dozen others, all offering relics, medals, food, and lodging, young girls very clean and nice to Frankish gentlemen, or guides to take them around the holy places.

At this last suggestion their guide screeched abuse in four different languages, thumping his chest and proclaiming his exclusive rights to the party, and the natives of Old Jerusalem scattered to wait for another less well-guarded group of pilgrims. Only one impudent man persisted with half-hearted attempts to interest the pilgrims in Jerusalem's shrines and holy places.

"Here, sirs, was Church of St. John the Baptist, very old, unfortunately somewhat tired also!" It looked worse than tired; it looked like a heap of rubble. Stephen scowled and kicked sand and stones away from a marble pillar at the front of the church, one of the few still standing. "What happened to the rest of the church?"

The guide shrugged and lifted the palms of his hands. "You Franks have a saying, 'A castle destroyed is half rebuilt.' Old church make very good new walls. People must live somewhere."

"Why don't they fix up some of the existing houses? Half the buildings we've passed were empty."

The guide shrugged again and tried to divert Stephen's interest to another crumbling ancient monument, while a persistent boy slipped between the men.

"Please, sirs, nice girls, blond like Frankish sir, like Franks very much!"

This time it was Geoffrey who kicked the intruder out of their way. "Madeline is blond," he muttered. "When I think of her winding up in the hands of such scum—"

"Don't they have anything in this city that is still standing on its foundations?" Stephen scowled at the guide. "Come on, show us to a hostel. A newly built one will be perfectly all right, I don't need to sleep in a bed that was first used by Judas Iscariot with straw that hasn't been changed since. Anything with four walls and a roof will do." And that, he thought glumly as the guide blithely changed direction to lead them out of the Grand Bazaar, summed up his future as a builder. Four walls and a roof. Would he ever be able to translate his dreams into the great cathedrals that men were making all over Europe? Would he get nothing from this sojourn in a dead land?

And after? He dared not return to England to finish his training under Brito, not when he'd embroiled himself both with the Church and the sheriff. From here, he and Aude would have to eke out Lady Margery's few remaining coins to get passage back to Italy; then he'd be tramping as a half-trained journeyman mason, taking any kind of work he could get to support himself and Aude, getting older and horny-handed and set in his ways while younger men built the cathedrals he dreamed of designing.

Wrapped in his gloomy prognostications, Stephen didn't notice that their party had again changed direction until Geoffrey tugged the bundle from his shoulders and he lifted his head to gaze at the first whole building he'd seen in the ruined city of Jerusalem.

Through a rounded arch he looked into a vast interior space covered by a dome. The center of the dome was open to the sky, and the brilliant Eastern light that passed into the church illuminated the painted pictures on the inside of the dome. A grave Jesus gazed down at Stephen with sorrowful eyes; to one side stood John the Baptist, and to the other side the Blessed Virgin spread out her cloak. Aude was transfixed by the living grace of the paintings. Stephen's soul exulted in the deep curve of the dome and the vast sweep of interior space carved out by this whole ambitious church. From afar, he heard the familiar chant of Latin syllables, smelled incense, and saw the glimmer of candles. For a moment the cold winters spent in the cathedral at Ely returned to him. Only now he welcomed the coolness in the heat of this dry Eastern land, and the Latin mass fell upon his ears like music. He was home again, in a place where men built great monuments to last for all generations to come.

Almost in a trance of delight, Stephen moved slowly into the great Church of the Holy Sepulchre, trying to absorb every detail at once. "We were new when your Lord's death and life again were a story told by grand-

mothers who had seen Him arise from the tomb," sang the
lowest stones of the foundation. "We were carved when
your forefathers still wore blue paint and skins," chanted
the fluted columns around him. "I was put here by Crusaders
when William the Norman was burning Hereward's wooden
castle," breathed the great dome that roofed all the sta-
tions of the cross and Christ's very tomb.

Lost in his trance, Stephen did not hear the guide
urging them to descend the stairs that led to the Holy
Sepulchre itself. Aude blinked in astonishment at the
throng of pilgrims from all over the world, men and
women in furs or silks or common camlet, drawn here to
worship. Geoffrey, rising from his impromptu prayer at the
gate, laid one hand on his sword when a Saracen growled,
"*Kumamah!*" and spat as he passed the arch.

"Damned infidels," he muttered. "Lord, forgive me that
I was tempted to draw my sword in Your church." He
crossed himself and murmured a prayer of contrition, and,
fortunately, missed the guide's cheerful explanation that
the local Moslems referred to this church as "*Kumamah,*"
or "The Dunghill."

"Damned infidels walking through here as if they owned
the place," he complained again when, halfway down the
steps, they were ordered to stand aside while a slender,
brown-faced man in robes of green silk slowly descended
the stairs in the midst of his attendants.

"They do," Aude pointed out. "Jerusalem hasn't been in
Christian hands for a long time."

"More shame to us."

"Do you know," Stephen remarked, "I believe some of
these columns are even older than the church itself. They
must have been taken from a pagan temple and used to
build the original shrine. You can tell that they used to
support a smaller arch, and the stone is much fresher on
this side." Happily oblivious, he wandered off to one side
of the crowd of praying pilgrims and began trying to
measure one of the marble columns with his fingers. It
was definitely much more worn on one side than on the
other. How many ages must it have stood in some heathen
temple, exposed to wind and sand that ground it down
before it was taken for this holy shrine? And the shrine
itself had been built when there were still men alive who
had seen Our Lord. Stephen felt dizzy with the glory of

ages past and the work of men so long dead that even their names were forgotten. Yet something of them still remained; if the mason who carved this column with its riot of leaves concealing the extra width of the base were alive today, he and Stephen would have a common language in the work of their hands.

"Lord, let me someday build something that will endure as the work of these men has endured," Stephen prayed spontaneously with bowed head. "And I ask no other immortality," he added, without thinking that he might be blaspheming against the faith that promised him eternal life.

Suddenly Stephen heard Aude's voice, raised to a shriek. Then he spotted her, screaming in the arms of one of the slaves who'd accompanied the man in green silk. He plowed through the pilgrims, shoulders hunched like a man under a heavy load, and heard merchants and ladies sputtering behind him. A priest was waving his hands and chittering in the native tongue, and there, on the ground, was Geoffrey who lay at the mercy of another slave's curved sword. Just as the slave raised his sword to strike, Geoffrey's arm twitched once and his own sword flashed through the air, breaking the force of the slave's blow. But the Saracen steel shattered the Frankish sword, which clattered on the stone pavement and broke the sudden silence. The next blow would kill him.

Stephen leapt to Geoffrey's aid without thinking, landing a kick on the kneecap of the slave who held Aude as he passed. He never felt the blow that sent him into absolute darkness.

CHAPTER

14

◻

When Stephen woke, he found himself in a darkness relieved by the pale gleam of light from a grating far overhead, the clank of mailed feet in a passageway somewhere outside, and the whisperings of his companions.

"I think he's waking up."

"How's his head?"

"Fine. I've washed it as best I could with some of that green, smelly water they gave us to drink. Scalp wounds bleed a lot, but he wasn't really hurt."

That was Aude, sounding ridiculously calm under the circumstances. "What do you mean, not really hurt?" Stephen grumbled. He sat up and his head exploded with pain. "I've got a crew of demon quarrymen in my head, trying to mine my skull for building rock."

"They should find plenty, great stupid oaf!" Aude gave him a friendly shove. "What good did you think you'd do, throwing yourself into the fight like that?"

"I was saving Geoffrey's life, if you recall," Stephen said stiffly. "And rescuing you. Both seemed like good ideas at the time."

"Excellent ideas." That was Geoffrey's voice, coming from a distance, and Stephen felt his muscles relax. So Geoffrey was alive, too. He thought he heard Geoffrey talking to Aude when he was just waking up, but he hadn't been sure; it might have been a dream. And he had been afraid to ask Aude.

"I do thank you for the gift of my life, Master Stephen," Geoffrey went on, "even if it is only temporary."

"What do you mean?" asked Stephen.

"The Egyptian wants to see us die. Slowly. For insulting him."

"What Egyptian?"

Geoffrey explained that the wealthy Saracen whose slaves had tried to kill him was an Egyptian nobleman named Kamil, here on pilgrimage from Cairo. He was annoyed by the fight in the Church of the Holy Sepulchre and wanted all three Christians executed, if not by flaying, then in some other slow and painful fashion.

"Can he do that? I thought Jerusalem was a Frankish city again."

"It may be a Frankish city," Geoffrey said, "but we are certainly in a Saracen prison. I don't know who holds power here, or how, but we are in the hands of the infidels now." Geoffrey's calm, light voice shook slightly. "Stephen, Aude, I'm sorry I got you into this. Maybe I can persuade that heathen dog to settle for making an example of me, and let you two go."

"Not if you keep calling him a heathen dog, you won't." Stephen was surprised at how calm he felt. Maybe he hadn't recovered from the blow yet. "Would you please tell me what happened? Last thing I remember, I was peacefully examining an antique column, and then suddenly there were Saracens with swords all over the place. Did the witch's husband chase us down? And what's the Egyptian got to do with this?"

Aude and Geoffrey vied to tell him, in chorus and in counterpoint, two slightly different versions of the same tale. According to Geoffrey, whose patience had been tested by the casual insults of Moslem passersby and by the discovery that Jerusalem was a heap of ruins in the hands of a second-rate Saracen overlord, the sight of Prince Kamil striding through the Church of the Holy Sepulchre as though he owned it had been the last straw. When Kamil interrupted one of the priests saying mass with a personal demand, Geoffrey could stand no more.

"Naturally I had to defend a man of the cloth," he said with some dignity.

After that both accounts got a little confused. Somebody had taken a swipe at Geoffrey with a scimitar, Aude had clawed one of the slaves in the face and had been seized before she could do further damage. About that time, Stephen had launched himself into the group with fists flying. By the time he was knocked out, Kamil had picked himself up from the far side of the altar.

"He yelled something in Saracen and the slaves stopped flashing their scimitars and I started to breathe again. Then Kamil and the priest gibber-gabbered back and forth for a while, and finally another bunch of Saracens in green robes appeared and marched us to this palatial lodging. While we were waiting for you to wake up, I shouted up the stairs until a Frankish-speaking slave came down and explained everything to me."

"It seems Kamil is a very important man in Cairo, a close friend and adviser to the Sultan, who is also named Kamil, just to make things confusing," Geoffrey commented in passing. "The Egyptian Kamil was short-tempered at the moment because he had various domestic problems: his favorite wife was with child again after having miscarried of two stillborn sons. His other wife had given Kamil nothing but daughters, so this pregnancy was of great importance to him. Kamil may have come to Jerusalem to consult physicians here."

"Dragging his wife all that way?"

"Oh, no. The slave seemed horrified when I suggested that. She could not be seen by the physicians—they are men, you see. Kamil will explain her symptoms to them and tell them exactly when she was born, and then they will prescribe after consulting the holy books of wisdom. Strange kind of medicine." Geoffrey went on to recount the slave's gossip. It was not encouraging.

"His wife's pregnancy was only one of Kamil's worries; he was also unhappy because he wanted to enlarge his palace in Cairo by adding on a great hall for meetings and celebrations. Discovery of a forgotten graveyard next to the palace, on the land where he wanted to build, had interfered with his plans. The Imam, "I gather that's something like a bishop," Geoffrey remarked parenthetically, "had gone to the Sultan who refused to grant Kamil permission to build over the bones of departed Moslems. Kamil killed the Coptic architect who drew up the plans for a meeting hall, and now he had neither land to build on nor an architect who would dare to work for him."

Stephen was whistling under his breath by the time Geoffrey finished this part of the story. "An Imam sounds very much like a bishop," he agreed. "Interfering old bastard. Well, he's done us a good turn, anyway."

It was too dark to see, but he fancied that he could hear Geoffrey's mouth dropping open. "Stephen, don't you understand? The point is that this Kamil casually kills anybody who annoys him, and gets away with it. And we've annoyed him."

"No. The point is that this Kamil needs a great architect who can create a beautiful hall for his palace within the constraints of existing space."

"That might improve his temper," Geoffrey allowed.

"Get that Frankish-speaking slave back," said Stephen with more confidence than he felt. "The great architect from England needs just a few more little details before he demands an audience with Kamil. And give me your purse. I may need to spend a little money in bribes."

He squirmed over mud to find Aude, who had been sitting very quietly with her arms round her knees during the last part of Geoffrey's long story. Stephen put one arm round her thin shoulders and held her close. "Don't worry, my love," he promised. "I've a plan to see us all safe again. Just trust me and try not to laugh when I'm telling the heathens about my years of building experience, all right?"

As he'd hoped, this raised a tentative smile from Aude. Stephen squeezed her against his chest for a moment longer, trying to share all the strength and faith that he was pretending to have. Then Geoffrey announced that he'd gotten the slave's attention, and Stephen prepared to tell a few of the biggest lies of his life.

"I never thought it would work," Geoffrey muttered.

"Shh. It hasn't worked yet. And you two have to look as if you believe what I say." Stephen glared at Geoffrey and Aude. Just because his initial round of lies had gotten them the privilege of an audience with Kamil, they were acting as if he had already saved their lives.

So far, it was true, Stephen had carried things off with a high hand. Once the audience was agreed to, he'd claimed it was beneath his dignity for him and his companions to appear before Kamil as stinking prisoners, filthy and ragged from their cell. They'd bathed in the steaming luxury of a Saracen bathhouse. They had feasted off flat copper trays piled high with strange spicy food: yellow rice, lamb stewed with apricots, purple vegetables stuffed with minced meat, and sherbets of rose-water and violet conserve to follow the meal. Their tattered pilgrim clothes with the red crosses sewn on the backs had been replaced by robes of green and white cambric in the Saracen style. The captain of the guard had even apologized for being unable to find Frankish-style clothing on such short notice.

All this luxury, doubly sweet after the hours they'd spent in a stinking cell below the streets, had raised Geoffrey and Aude's spirits to the point where they were positively silly: nudging each other and giggling like children, and telling "private" jokes in French about Stephen's sudden status as a great architect.

"In my country," Stephen told Geoffrey, "we have a proverb about giving a man enough rope to hang himself."

Geoffrey looked uninterested. "So?"

"So I hope Kamil's people don't have the same proverb, that's all." Stephen rubbed a hand over his chin and blessed the Crusader fashion of going clean-shaven; perhaps that would disguise the fact that he was hardly old enough to have grown one of the flowing beards favored by the Syrians. Still, anybody could look at him and see that he was too young to have the years of experience he claimed. Probably Kamil already knew that Stephen was a liar bluffing his way out of an impossible position. Probably all this, the baths and the food and the rich robes, were setting them up for an elaborate Saracen joke that would end with their deaths.

But maybe Stephen could spin out the joke long enough for help to arrive: Geoffrey's last few coins were used to bribe the guard into sending frantic messages to anybody in Jerusalem connected with Geoffrey's uncle Philippe or with the House of Sanudo. It seemed that all the Franks in the Holy Land knew each other and half of them were related by blood or marriage; there was a chance that a representative of some powerful Crusader family would show up to negotiate with Kamil while Stephen was still playing out his bluff.

Stephen hoped someone would come soon because there

was no chance that he would be able to fool anybody knowledgeable into thinking that he was a real architect. Oh, he had lots of ideas. He'd built a masterpiece of a hall in his head, so vivid and light and glorious that he was half surprised Geoffrey and Aude couldn't see it. But he hadn't the experience. He was only a journeyman, and just barely raised to that rank. He didn't know the masons' signs, passwords, and secrets of the lodge; any real mason would expose him in about one minute. And if Kamil took him seriously, he'd surely have his own experts in to question Stephen.

His only hope was that he could keep Kamil interested in his stories and building designs until somebody with a little power in Jerusalem took an interest in the fate of the three Christian prisoners.

The guards led Aude, Stephen, and Geoffrey through open colonnades and over polished marble walkways to an audience hall lined with raised alcoves. A platform covered with intricately woven carpets and jeweled pillows rose from the mosaic floor at one end of the hall. On this platform sat the lean, brown-skinned man Stephen had seen yesterday in the Church of the Holy Sepulchre. His black slaves, resplendent in cloth-of-gold turbans and flowing white robes, stood in a line to one side of the platform. To the other side, three musicians plucked at stringed instruments, making pleasant, random sounds like drops of water falling into a still pool. A boy knelt at Kamil's feet with a pitcher of snow-cooled water on a gilt tray.

There were no Franks in the hall to speak for them. Stephen's heart sank. He would have to keep playing the role of the great architect under Kamil's questioning. If only he knew whether Geoffrey's messages had reached anyone who could help them!

The guard standing behind Stephen hit him on the back of the knees with a pole and he knelt, as did Aude and Geoffrey. Stephen dared not turn his head to see if they had received the same gentle hint, or if Geoffrey was close to losing his temper. To save their lives, he must think or care about nothing but building.

Stephen concentrated on the marble mosaic beneath his knees. Even with his head bowed he could visualize the hall around them; that skill, developed so long ago in the choir at Ely, now stood him in good stead. In his mind he built up the audience room again, from foundation stones to arched wall-openings to painted wooden roof. The mosaics that decorated the walls and floor were bright and showy, and the bits of tinted glass set into plaster window-holes glowed with the Eastern sun, but the hall itself was a plain, uninspired square box. He could do better, Stephen thought. By God, he really could!

That knowledge inspired him. Then a voice said in lisping French, "I am the prince Kamil's interpreter for this hearing. Are you ready to defend yourself?"

Stephen took this as an invitation to lift his head again. He was glad to see that the interpreter was not the slave who'd gossiped with them in the prison, but a small brown Syrian gentleman with a henna-tipped beard, whom Stephen had never seen before. He could lie more effectively with someone he hadn't been pumping for information just hours earlier.

"The prince Kamil wishes to know why he should not flay three impudent Christians who insult him in a Moslem city."

Stephen's mind worked quickly. Where should he begin? Kamil knew already that Stephen claimed to be an architect, otherwise they'd not have won this much reprieve. And the comment about Jerusalem being a Moslem city was pure viciousness, aimed at stinging the Christians into anger. Fortunate, thought Stephen, with a conscious sense of virtue, that he wasn't hot tempered like Geoffrey!

"I understood that the prince Kamil is an intelligent man and no fool," he responded slowly, so that the interpreter could catch the near-insult, but also see that it was not quite an insult.

As the words were translated into the Saracen tongue, Stephen saw Kamil's face flush dark red along the cheekbones. Good. It was a dangerous game he was playing, but he thought he was on the right track. If the Christian prisoners were too meek and tractable, they'd be no fun, and Kamil would end the game before help arrived.

"Explain yourself, and apologize!" the interpreter rapped out in a comic mimicking of Kamil's imperious demand.

Stephen took a deep breath and prayed silently for strength and especially for wit. "Since I have not insulted the prince, no apology is necessary. And an explanation should not be necessary for a man of Prince Kamil's well-known intelligence. Does not all the world know that the gracious prince desires to enlarge his palace? And that he is in need of an architect who can cleverly work around the limitations imposed by certain short-sighted religious officials? It would be folly indeed for a man with Prince Kamil's needs to execute a master builder from the West, a man cunning in all the secrets of Frankish building, the only man in the Holy Land who can design a hall worthy of the prince's glory."

As the interpreter translated, a smile flickered across Kamil's face and he stroked his smooth chin with one finger. Stephen sighed with relief, knowing the flattery had pleased Kamil. Kamil and the interpreter conversed in the Saracen tongue, almost arguing. In the moment's respite, Stephen wondered why the Egyptian was beardless like a Frank, when all the other men of his entourage sported long beards that were carefully curled and stained black or red with henna. Perhaps he was a eunuch? No, they'd said his favorite wife was pregnant. Ah, well, who could tell why a heathen did anything? Stephen told himself to concentrate on spinning stories for the infidel and quit worrying about details of fashion.

"The palace of Prince Kamil lies in a quite restricted situation," the interpreter said. "He wishes me to inform you that if you are thinking of tearing down the houses on the east and north side of the palace, such a solution has already been proposed and found unacceptable. The tenants are distant members of the prince's own family and he refuses to dispossess them. The steward who proposed this solution," the interpreter added after a delicate pause, "was torn to death by wild donkeys. To displease the prince Kamil is to displease the Sultan, which is to displease Allah. *Allahu akbar.*"

"*Allahu akbar,*" murmured all the Saracens in chorus. "God is great."

"God forbid that I should suggest anything which would displease the great prince," said Stephen with a sincerity that carried through translation. "My idea was quite different. Ask the prince if he has considered—that is, ask him if he requires . . . " How I wish he spoke French, Stephen thought. Trying to talk through an interpreter was driving him crazy. He would just have to act as though the man weren't there. He looked directly up at Kamil and addressed him as though the Egyptian could understand what he was saying.

"The space all around your palace is limited. I understand that. But there's no reason why you can't build *up* instead of *out*, is there? Nobody owns the air on top of your house."

The air crackled with the harsh Saracen tongue in a brief exchange before the interpreter turned to Stephen.

"It is written that the earth and the sea and the sky belong to the Lord God, the indivisible, the all-powerful."

"I never heard of the Lord God going to the Sultan to stop anyone from building."

The interpreter smiled as he translated this. "The prince Kamil asks if you are a magician as well as an architect, to build upon the air? His palace is already three stories high and the foundations will support no more. Besides, the quarters of his women are on the top floor and he will not have them disturbed by noise."

"That won't be necessary." Stephen waved his hands in the air as he tried to sketch out the dimensions of his glorious plan. "The women's quarters are on the east side of the palace, right? On the west side there's only one story, the present meeting hall. We remove the roof, dig deeper foundations, raise piers to take the weight of the arches, and. . . ." Stephen could see Kamil's eyes glazing over as the interpreter translated. God only knew what nonsense the man was making of his words. "Please," he said. "Let me show you. I need something to draw on."

The Egyptian rapped out a sharp command. There was a rustle among the slaves standing behind Kamil, and something was passed from hand to hand until it reached the prince. He held it out, smiling. "Will this do?"

The question needed no translation. It was his sketchbook, battered from the fight, a few leaves falling out, but essentially intact. Stephen covered the distance from the prisoners' space to the dais in one long stride and clutched the sketchbook to his breast.

"Excellently, my lord. But I need also something to draw with. Your men didn't happen to pick up my silverpoint? Oh, well, I suppose that was too much to hope for." Stephen glanced around the hall and the interpreter handed him a stylus. "Good. Thank you very much. You see, my lord, this is what I had in mind."

Without bothering to go back to his place, Stephen began sketching the hall as he'd designed it, indenting the thick page of parchment with the sharp, narrow lines of the stylus. Stephen's design was a good one; what a pity he couldn't really build it! He almost wished Kamil would take this masquerade seriously; if only he could get away with it, it would be wonderful to see his new ideas translated into stone. But of course he didn't know nearly enough to carry out a design like this. Master Adam had shown him his ignorance, and he was hardly likely to remedy it here in this heathen land.

But the ideas were all that mattered now. The system of piers and arches that turned modern cathedral walls into pierced skeletons had been designed to bring light inside and to warm the building. In this desert climate, all the building principles that Stephen had learned were turned upside down; the object was not to bring light in but to exclude it, not to offer people a noble vista through windows, but to let in air while concealing the private life of the house behind pierced screens and twisting corridors. But here in Kamil's palace, the high, open walls of the French style could be used to give a sense of light and spaciousness to a hall with a limited amount of floor space. They could also be used to transmit light to the women's quarters, so that the new hall wouldn't turn their rooms into windowless prisons.

"You see?" The sketches were crude, and based only on the slave's vague description of the palace. Stephen indicated the present palace only as a series of blocks, lavishing his drawing skills on the meeting hall with its high ceiling and tall, slender windows.

Kamil nodded, took the sketchbook away from Stephen, and flipped through the pages. He said something to the interpreter without looking up.

"My lord says that anybody who designed the buildings shown here must surely be a great architect, in spite of your youthful appearance."

Stephen nodded and kept his lips shut, mutely taking credit for the west front of Chartres Cathedral, the dome of St. Mark's in Venice, and the other masterworks he'd recorded in his pilgrimage across Europe. He began mentally preparing a discussion of these buildings that would occupy Kamil for some time. How fortunate that the Egyptian was interested in his sketchbook! He should be able to prolong the audience until late afternoon; and by then, surely some of Geoffrey's messages would have reached powerful Franks who could speak in their behalf.

"And he is pleased with your ideas for his hall. There are some problems due to your lack of familiarity with the existing palace. Those can be corrected."

Kamil the Egyptian snapped Stephen's sketchbook shut, dropped it into a fold of his robe, and barked out a final sentence in the Saracen tongue. Without waiting for the interpreter to translate, he stood up and left the hall. Six black slaves, the boy with the pitcher of snow-cooled water, and the three musicians hurried after him.

"Wait! My sketchbook!" Stephen cried as Kamil left. Why had their audience ended so quickly? Despair swept over him. The interpreter regarded him kindly. "If the prince Kamil did not return your sketchbook, you may presume that he wishes to look at it further. It will be returned to you in Cairo, if not before. The prince," he added with heavy sarcasm, "does not require to increase his wealth by the sum of your possessions."

"In Cairo?" Stephen had grasped only one word.

"Cairo, *Al-Kahira* the triumphant, the mother of the world, the citadel of Egypt." The Syrian interpreter nodded and smiled at Stephen for the first time since the audience had begun. "My friend, you are going to Egypt to build the prince Kamil's new palace."

"Wait! What about my friends!" Saracens in the green robes of the city guard were closing in on Stephen, making a wall through which he could just glimpse Geoffrey rising to his feet in protest, and Aude reaching out her arms toward him.

"They go to Cairo, also. Their lives and yours stand surety for the success of the plans you have drawn."

CHAPTER

15

◻

The sun beat down on the dusty travelers and traced spirals of white light behind their half-closed eyelids. In their exhausted state, all they knew of Cairo was a maze of narrow streets whose stone gutters seemed to catch the day's heat and reflect it up to burn their feet. The din of coppersmiths and tinsmiths beating on their wares, water-sellers bawling out advertisements for their skins of water, flies buzzing round open trays of sweetmeats, children shouting happily blended into the general confusion.

When Stephen paused to gaze up at the Citadel of Cairo, he was pushed about by hurrying citizens who thronged the street. *"Iftah 'eynak!* Open your eyes!" shouted a cross man on a gray donkey. The boy running behind the donkey stopped beating it for a moment to slap Stephen's ankles with his supple pole. Stephen backed out of the way and was grabbed by one of Kamil's guards, who forced him back into the group that was struggling down the street after Kamil. Stephen craned his head for a last view of the Citadel, rising on its rocky promontory at the southern verge of the city's new stone walls.

"The Citadel was built by the emperor Salál Ad-dín who defeated your English king Richard," said Jewel, Kamil's Frankish speaking slave, when he noticed the direction of Stephen's gaze. A camel laden with brushwood ambled between them, interrupting Jewel's instructive speech and giving Stephen a momentary view of monstrous yellow teeth and rubbery lips. Jewel shouted a curse at the camel driver and continued as though nothing had happened. "To make it, he demolished three hundred tombs of ancient kings."

"Didn't the Imam object?" Despite heat and exhaustion, Stephen's curiosity was rising again.

Jewel waved a dismissive hand. "These were very ancient kings. They lived before the Prophet and they were not Moslems. Their tombs are interesting, though. They are big piles of stone pointing at the sky. Some of the stones in the larger tombs are so heavy that nobody has been able to figure out how to move them for new buildings. The magicians of ancient times placed them there with the help of demons. Perhaps some day you'll go to see them."

"Perhaps," Stephen agreed. If he lived—which seemed less and less likely the more he thought of it. His claim to be a master mason would be exposed by the first real mason he encountered, and then what would Kamil do? The interpreter had said his life, and Aude's and Geoffrey's, depended on the satisfaction of the Egyptian prince. Perhaps the interpreter had been exaggerating. Maybe if they were very lucky, they would simply live out their days as Christian slaves, in Cairo. He and Geoffrey would labor in the quarries, and Aude would wait on some pampered Saracen lady or be sold to the first man who fancied her.

Stephen shut his mind to that awful thought. He couldn't think about that, not if he was to stay sane and find some way to keep them all safe. He probably didn't have very long before a master mason with signs and passwords exposed him for the fraud he was; he'd do better to concentrate on finding a way to avoid that confrontation.

The "palace" of Kamil was a welcome surprise to the three Christian prisoners who were dazed by sun and heat. Without realizing it, Stephen, Aude, and Geoffrey had all thought of a palace as being like an English or French manor house, set in stately isolation amid bowers, orchards, gardens, and grazing grounds. Instead, Kamil's palace was merely a large, rambling house in the center of a crowded quarter. Later the Christians would understand that this "mere" house covered acres of ground, enclosing

walled gardens and pools for goldfish, labyrinths of hallways, and mazes of interconnecting chambers. But for now
they saw only an unimposing carved wooden door that
opened onto a busy street. Here the slave at the head of
their party stopped and banged upon the door with his
stick, bawling something in the Saracen tongue.

"A bell would be a pleasanter sound—and quieter,"
Geoffrey commented.

Stephen nodded cautiously. His own head was aching
and the slave's emphatic pounding did nothing to help.
Beneath her cocoon of Saracen veils, Aude was looking
pinched and pale and desperately homesick for the cool
marshes of Ely.

"Bells," said Jewel, "are the devil's musical instrument,
and where a bell is, the angels do not resort. That is why
you Franks hang them in your churches."

"We happen to think they bring us closer to God and
drive away evil spirits," Aude retorted.

Jewel glared at her and replied, "The Prophet has
written as I have said. It is not for women to discuss such
matters."

They passed through the door after Kamil, stumbled
down a dark, narrow passage and emerged, blinking, into
the paradise of the outer court. A sycamore tree shaded
the open court, and the mist from a nearby fountain
drifted through the air and cooled the travelers. Somewhere beyond their sight, a stringed instrument dropped
plaintive single notes into the air and a girl's voice rose in
accompaniment.

"I think we have entered Paradise," said Geoffrey blissfully.

"I hope not," said Stephen, remembering that Geoffrey
and Aude did not realize just how close they were to
leaving this life. So much depended on his lies.

"You will wait here until my master has made arrangements for you," said Jewel.

Aude sank down on the flat stone-wall surrounding the
fountain. "Very well," she said, pulling off so many veils at
once that Jewel hissed in shock, "but the least you can do
is bring us something to drink while we wait. I'm sure
your master would not approve of discourtesy toward his
guests." Geoffrey drew in a long breath of shock and Aude
gave him a cold stare. "It will do us no good to behave like
prisoners, Geoffrey," she said under her breath. "Kamil

says we're guests. If we act as though we believe it, perhaps he will, too."

Again Stephen was moved with pride and love. Aude was braver and cleverer than he was. "She's right, Geoffrey. We must not act afraid." While Aude was so brave, he could not give in to the fear and the certainty that soon his inadequacy would be exposed for all to see.

Jewel was so shocked by the unveiled woman who gave him orders that he disappeared and presently sent a house servant with rose-water sherbets and candied fruits for the whole party.

Aude and Geoffrey both felt much happier at this sign of favor, but Stephen could not dismiss his fears so easily. Their lives depended on his pretense of being a master builder—didn't they realize how easily he could be exposed?

Well, there was nothing Stephen could do about it now. Surely they would spend some days in the palace before Kamil was ready to begin work; maybe in that time Stephen would think of some ruse to conceal his ignorance. Or maybe they would be able to escape before then. To take his mind off the problem he concentrated on the fountain and tried to figure out how the mechanism worked.

Stephen had got no farther than casually removing one of the stone lion's heads from which the water fell when Kamil came striding into the courtyard. He had exchanged his heavy white traveling robes for an embroidered garment of iridescent silk, flashing blue and green and purple in the sunlight. Aude stared rapturously at the shimmering colors and made a small cooing sound.

"My apologies for keeping you waiting," he said in slow, accented, but quite passable French. Stephen blinked in shock and tried to remember what, if anything, Aude and Geoffrey had said in French when they thought they were talking in privacy. From the stunned expressions of his companions, he could guess that Aude and Geoffrey were going through the same exercise.

"It was necessary to confer with my household staff about whether you are to be housed as guests or prisoners. You," Kamil looked at Aude, "will stay in the women's quarters. The guards who protect my women will also prevent you from leaving, should you take any such foolish idea into your head. And cover yourself decently." He balled up one of Aude's discarded veils in his fist and threw it into her lap.

"You," he turned to Stephen, "will have to be housed in the guest quarters, since I expect to be discussing this project with you at length and it would be inconvenient for me to send to the slaves' area at the other end of the palace whenever I have an interesting idea. Your Frankish friend may stay with you for the time being to simplify the problem of guarding you. Also, as the guest quarters are open to the street, I regret that you will both have to wear chains. I trust that these, and the thought of your woman who would remain in my power, will serve to subdue any rash impulse to escape."

He gestured to a fat, veiled woman who had been hovering behind him. "Take the Frankish woman away."

"No," said Stephen, desperately. But suddenly there were slaves everywhere, most of them armed. A man was putting light chains on Stephen's wrists, and Aude was lost behind a whisk of veils and a hum of women's chatter. The pattering feet of the women disappeared into the inner maze of passages and Stephen felt truly weak and helpless.

"Now," said Kamil cheerfully while the smith hammered the wrist chains into shape, "you'll come and talk to my master mason. Fortunately the laborers assembled by my last architect are still in the palace, so you will be able to begin work immediately."

There was no time to prepare a ruse that would explain his ignorance, and now it was too late. As Stephen stumbled after Kamil, head aching, he thought that maybe it was just as well Aude had been sent away. She wouldn't be present to witness Kamil's wrath when he found out how Stephen had deceived him. He'd probably be cut to pieces on the spot, as soon as the master mason told Kamil that his "architect" hadn't even been initiated into the lowest grade of the lodge.

They threaded through more passageways and open courtyards, until Stephen understood how Jewel could be ignorant of the dimensions of a building he'd lived in all his life. Stephen realized that a person might spend twenty years in this labyrinth and never learn more than the pathways leading from one cluster of rooms to another.

They entered a long, low-ceilinged room lit by oil lamps. In spite of the elaborate wall designs in Saracen script, the silken rugs, and the colored-glass windows, the room felt as cramped as a cave. The lamps, which swung on chains from the ceiling, were so low that Stephen had to dodge around them; the bottom fringes of their beaded frames brushed the tops of Kamil's turban. At the end of the room stood two lines of brown-skinned, bearded men.

"My present hall," said Kamil with a wave of his hand. "You see why I am eager to have another."

"My masons." Another wave.

"Sarouf, the master mason."

The Saracen in front stepped forward, touched his forehead, lips, and chest in rapid succession, and murmured something in the Saracen tongue. Stephen held out his hand in an approximation of the secret grip he'd seen Hugh use, top two fingers pressed together, thumb ready to trace the masons' sign on the back of the other man's hand. Sarouf stared at the hand as if it were a long-dead fish.

"Sarouf does not care for Christians," Kamil said carelessly. A sentence in the Saracen tongue sent Sarouf to his knees. "He thought himself safe because my usual punishment for insolence is the removal of a finger or two, and he knows the value of his skilled hands. I have explained that if he does not obey you in all things, I will have his tongue split."

Stephen felt the weight in his chest dissolving into a bubble of light, despite the hatred that shot up at him from Sarouf's dark face. "Doesn't care for Christians, eh? I suppose this Sarouf is not familiar with any of our Christian customs, then? He probably," Stephen continued, "has not even been initiated into the lower grades of the mason's lodge."

Kamil's blank stare was confirmation of his guess. "Lodge? I do not know what that is." He put a few questions to Sarouf, who shook his head and looked equally blank.

"Sarouf knows nothing of this initiation. Is that a problem?"

"No. No, I think not." He was saved. He would not be exposed by Sarouf—at least, not until work started, and he'd be damned if he couldn't find some way to satisfy Kamil! What an idiot he'd been. Saracen masons wouldn't belong to the guild. They weren't even Christians. How would they know the system of secret passwords and handshakes with which decent Christian masons safeguarded the secrets of their craft?

There wasn't anybody in this city who could call him a liar. If he could design a building that pleased Kamil, supervise the men, and see it erected, then he was a master builder. That was all there was to it, and Stephen felt confident of his ability to do that.

On the way from the hall to the guest quarters, they passed through a courtyard shadowed on one side by a wall three stories high, with a narrow balcony on which black-veiled women crowded to stare at the two Frankish prisoners. One of the women called his name.

Stephen looked up and tried to pick Aude out of the mass of black. All he could see was a collection of foreheads and eyes. Then one of the women ripped off her veil and he recognized Aude. "Stephen," she cried again. "Stephen!" while two other women tried to push the veil back over her head.

"Are you all right?" Stephen shouted up, leaning back against the pull of his guards.

"'Course I am. You?"

"I'm a fool."

"Knew that," she called.

"And everything's going to be all right."

"Knew that too. You said so in the prison."

Then she disappeared behind the mass of women in their billowing veils, and there was nothing Stephen could do except pray—for her, for him, for the great work that Kamil was putting into his hands.

CHAPTER

16

◻

There were some advantages to the swathing veils. They concealed everything but the eyes and forehead so Aude could let her shoulders sag now, and could drop the bright, determined smile she'd shown to Stephen. She could admit to herself that she was desperately afraid but she mustn't let these heathens see it. Aude squared her shoulders again and marched along the balcony with a sturdy, determined tread that shook the wooden planks beneath her feet. They couldn't even build a good solid porch. Her Stephen would soon show them what decent Christian folk were worth, if he had time. . . . She tried to swallow the knot of fear that twisted within her.

At the end of the balcony hung a rectangle of red and orange silk, touched with fire where the sun played on its border of twisted gold wires. One of the old women pushed rudely ahead of Aude, twitched the curtain aside, and beckoned to her to follow.

Beyond the curtain was a white plastered passageway that turned back on itself twice with sharp angles. At each corner stood a tall black man, feet together, hands folded over a long nasty-looking sword. Aude flinched from the steady gaze of the first guard's eyes; the old woman who pattered ahead looked back, laughed, and said something in Saracen.

"I don't understand."

She grinned again and poked a sharp finger at the guard's ears, then shook her head. On her command, the man let his jaw drop. Aude looked once and then looked away, squeezing her fists shut and trying to command the roiling in her stomach. There was only a welt of scar tissue where the slave's tongue should have been.

With that knowledge, she was able to interpret the other gesture. Her stomach turned again at the thought of the double mutilation, but she would not show fear to these heathens. She owed it to Stephen to keep her chin high and her spirits up, and not to let the heathens see how scared she was. "Deaf-mutes," she said aloud, to be sure that her voice didn't shake. "I wonder why? Maybe it's as well I can't ask; I might be happier not knowing."

She hitched up the longest veil that was slipping off her head and trailing on the straw matting underfoot, and trudged on around two more sharp corners and past a hanging curtain of turquoise silk embroidered with pearls.

On the other side of the curtain lay a dreamland of jeweled tapestries, singing birds, and a soft, deep carpet woven in blue and gold. The walls of the room were gilt wicker cages in which captured birds sang. The magical lanterns of red and blue and green were made of colored glass, just like the window of their room in the House of Sanudo.

Apart from the carpets, the bird cages, and the colored lanterns, the room was virtually unfurnished. A group of brown-skinned girls in silk robes lounged on cushions set into a deep plaster niche, and one of the inevitable black-robed old crones was crouched over a brazier, stirring the contents of a pot. She was squatting in what looked, to Aude, like a most uncomfortable position; hadn't these pagans even learned to make a decent three-legged stool? With her was a boy of five or six, dressed from head to toe in brocade so stiff with silver thread and flashing jewels that Aude wondered how he could move. But, in fact, he moved nimbly; he was scurrying back and forth between the old woman at her brazier and a plaster niche in the wall where herbs were stored in carved wooden boxes. Aude sniffed the steam rising from the pot. It smelled like one of the potions she'd mixed for Helene to keep her hair bright. The acrid scent was the first hint of anything familiar in this fairytale world; she clung to it to keep her mind off worse things.

"What's that, something for the hair?"

Bright eyes in a wrinkled face stared impassively back at her. She pointed at the pot, then mimed dipping her hands into the substance and rubbing her hair vigorously. The old woman nodded and cackled agreement.

One of the young girls rose from her cushion and came forward. "Please, my name is Mariamu, and I am to interpret for you until you learn our tongue," she said in halting but clear French. "This is Bi Hassan. She has no Frankish."

Until she learned their heathen tongue! Aude told herself not to be frightened. These people might think she was going to stay in Cairo forever, but she knew better. Stephen would think of some way to get them back to Christian lands. If she kept believing in Stephen, everything would be all right. In the meantime, it might be better not to argue the point with these infidels.

When Aude asked Mariamu what she was expected to do here, Mariamu smiled hesitantly, shrugged, and gestured toward the pile of silken cushions.

"But what do *you* do?"

When Mariamu looked blank again, Aude tried rephrasing the question. "What is your work? How do you occupy your time?"

"We sing," Mariamu said. "We tell stories. We call Bi Hassan to paint our hands." She held up little palms decorated with intricate designs in reddish brown and explained that the process called for one to sit in the sun, palms upturned, for several hours at a time while the patterns drawn in henna paste baked dry and dyed the skin.

Aude shook her head decisively. "No, that won't do for me. I've never been idle in my life and I don't mean to start now." Idle hands left the mind free to wonder about unprofitable things—such as where Stephen was right this minute, and how he could be so sure everything was going to be all right, and how she was ever going to find him again in this maze of a palace.

Aude swallowed hard. No, she could do nothing but

trust in Stephen—and find herself something to do while
she waited. "Bi Hassan? What do you call this?" She
squatted beside the old woman who was stirring the pot
and pointed at the potion.

Using Mariamu as an interpreter, and helped out by
gestures and mime, Aude quickly found common ground
with the old lady who was, indeed, mixing a potion similar
to the ones she used to make for Helene. As she began to
learn the heathen words for the ingredients, she settled
almost happily into a technical discussion while helping to
keep a watchful eye on the simmering pot.

"That's a lot of cloves to use," she ventured as Bi Hassan
tipped a third handful of fragrant ground cloves into the
pot.

Bi Hassan said something that Aude understood without
translation.

"Yes, I know. There's nothing like cloves to give spirit
and spring to the hair. But they're so expensive!" Prince
Kamil must be very rich indeed, richer even than the
bishop. Aude was impressed in spite of herself. "You're
throwing in cinnamon and cloves as if they grew on
trees!"

Mariamu translated that comment, and Bi Hassan laughed
as though Aude had said something very funny.

As she settled down for a friendly discussion of the
virtues of marsh plants versus egg whites for thickening
the potion, Aude began to think it might not be so bad
here after all. Bi Hassan looked as if she knew all the
secrets of the earth. Aude might be able to learn something of the Saracen ways with healing and beauty potions
while she was here. She might even be able to teach them
a thing or two in return, once she learned their heathenish
names for the familiar herbs and spices.

Over the next few weeks Aude made a place for herself
in the complex, secretive world of the women's quarters:
healer, compounder of cosmetics, and wise-woman from
Frankish lands. At first, Bi Hassan treated her as a slow
and not overly competent assistant, but as Aude proved
the worth of her own recipes and learned to adapt them to
local ingredients, she assumed a position not much lower
than Bi Hassan's. Most of her time was spent with the
older woman, grinding spices, measuring ingredients, sending slaves to the market or into the countryside to gather

herbs. In her free hours, whenever she could cajole Mariamu into interpreting for her, she gossiped with the girls and slaves who waited on Prince Kamil's two wives: the lutanists, the silk-embroideress, the hair-braider, and the Nubian woman who painted delicate designs of dark red henna on the palms and the soft bare feet. The women's quarters were as fine and luxurious as the bishop's palace, and there was nearly as much gossip and intrigue to be enjoyed.

Aude's place in this ingrown little society was assured when one of her mixtures, madly improvised from memory, cured Kamil's first wife's second daughter of a feverish sore throat. Aisha herself, a gentle, sad-faced woman whose dark eyes expressed the scars of three children dead in infancy and her worries for the three living daughters, called Aude into her own private rooms. She caressed Aude's curly hair, gave her a purse of gold coins, a fine brocade sash of blue-green silk from Cathay, and two personal slave girls to do the heavy work of mixing and stirring spices for her.

"Heavy work!" Aude repeated to Bi Hassan with a burst of laughter. "My father would laugh to see how you treat me like a fine lady. At home I used to cut the reeds to rethatch our roof, and when my father's bones ached, I was the one who had to climb up and do the thatching, too!" Tears filled her eyes and she felt an unexpected jab of homesickness for the little cottage and the cool marsh.

Mariamu was no longer interpreting for Aude and Bi Hassan. Aude had learned a little of the Saracen tongue by now, and Bi Hassan knew a few French words, though she shook her head when Aude tried English. They could now have a sort of private conversation, though half of it was still based on mime and guesswork.

Bi Hassan politely looked away as Aude brushed the tears from her eyes. She scowled at the bowl in front of her and frothed up the mixture to a pale yellowish fluff.

"What's that for?"

"Number two wife. Name Deena. For skin."

"Oh." Aude had not yet met Deena who kept to her private room at the end of the long string of apartments. Rumor said she was pregnant, and sickly, and terrified of losing this baby as she'd lost the first two. She refused to move out of her room or to see anyone except her own favorite attendants. Privately Aude thought it was a mistake for the poor woman to shut herself up and brood like that, but it wasn't her place to speak. Prince Kamil would have her ears for a purse if she talked his second wife into going for a stroll and the poor lady lost her baby after all. Aude stuck her finger into the lemon-colored froth and tasted.

"Mmm. Lemon and egg whites. Helene used to plaster that stuff on, trying to keep her skin white. She tried some on me once, but I'm too brown by sun and nature ever to look like a cream-faced court lady." Aude glanced speculatively at Bi Hassan, with her wrinkled face looking like the glossy brown half of a walnut. "And for that matter, what good is it going to do your lady? Whitening pomades on a dark skin will just make her look sickly."

Bi Hassan snatched the bowl away from Aude and bent over it protectively, making hissing noises in her native language. To Aude, this speech sounded like a series of mumbles and clicks and hisses, as different from the Saracen tongue as that was from English, and far beyond her capacity to interpret. Bi Hassan's retreat to her native tongue was a signal that she did not wish to communicate. Aude nodded in resignation. "You don't want to tell me, do you? I suppose you're going to put in some secret ingredients. It's all right. You don't need to worry about me taking your place, Bi Hassan. You know ten times more than I do. And I'm not going to be here long enough to learn all the local plants and wise-woman's lore."

But her certainty about the duration of her stay in Cairo was not quite as firm as it had been. She'd lost count of the days—no, weeks it had been—that she'd been shut up in the women's quarters without setting foot outside. And all that time she had had only two glimpses of Stephen, both from a distance. Even those would have been denied her, but it was impossible to keep the women's quarters completely closed off while the west end of the palace was being demolished and rebuilt.

Stephen looked busy and happy and very much in charge of the work he was directing, and he was no longer wearing the chains. Aude didn't think she needed to worry much about his welfare. But a glimpse of your man's back wasn't the same as having him by you at night. Deena was lucky, Aude thought. At least she'd seen her husband often enough to get pregnant three times, even if she did have trouble carrying the babies to term. At this rate Aude would be past childbearing before she even got a chance to hold hands with Stephen again. "Oh, dear." She sighed, forgetting about the minor mystery of Deena's skin pomade. "I miss him so much."

Bi Hassan glanced up, her black eyes flashing under the wrinkled folds of brown skin, and then she looked down at her bowl again. Aude felt as though a message had been exchanged though she couldn't say for sure what it was.

Three days later Aude understood the message. With many nods and winks, Bi Hassan beckoned Aude into the large cupboard where plants were hung for drying. There she produced a packet wrapped in a silk scarf. Aude unrolled the scarf and spread out its contents before her: a fan, a bunch of flowers, and a sponge. Bi Hassan grinned and mimed the tapping of a mason's hammer on the plaster wall of the cupboard.

"Stephen?"

Bi Hassan's face was instantly void of expression.

"Is he all right?"

Another slow grin.

"Then . . ." Aude pushed the scraps of trash about, poking at them with her finger. "What's this got to do with him?"

The polyglot system of communication that had worked so well was no help now. Aude had the distinct feeling that Bi Hassan didn't want to understand her questions. She looked on with a benign, blank gaze as Aude turned the fan over and over, hoping to find a note from Stephen hidden in its folds. She patted Aude's hand, smiled once, and lumbered away to the lady Deena's private rooms which Aude was still forbidden to enter.

"And there's another mystery." Aude sighed.

In the end it was Mariamu, giggling, whispering, and making such a production of her secrecy that no one could have failed to notice, who explained the message to Aude. The fan meant "go some place in the evening," because the two words for fan and evening sounded alike in the Saracen tongue. The flowers came from the little walled garden opening off the rooms of Kamil's old tutor, Ibn

Masoud. And the sponge meant that Aude should use the excuse of going to the bath house to slip away.

The meaning became much clearer after Mariamu explained to Aude that there was only a loose wall of woven reeds between the bath house and Ibn Masoud's private garden. A slender girl could easily push the "wall" out of shape and slip through the narrow opening between the reeds and the solid outer wall of the palace. Unlike the women's gardens, Ibn Masoud's garden had a wall overlooking the street; the girls used to go there, Mariamu said with a giggle, to buy sweetmeats from the bazaar peddlers.

"What about this Ibn Masoud? Doesn't he object to having his private gardens used as part of the bazaar?"

Mariamu giggled. "That's the best part. Ibn Masoud is blind!"

He must also, Aude thought, be very tactful if he consistently failed to notice the cloying scents of musk and jasmine favored by the girls in the women's quarters. But that wasn't really her business. If Stephen said it was all right, it must be all right. Perhaps they were to escape this way. Should she try to steal food and clothes for a journey, or would that be too dangerous? Aude twisted her fingers together and closed her eyes. Sometimes she could feel when things were right. She'd had that feeling around Stephen, always, from the first day she fished him out of the fens where he was wandering lost and angry; it was right for her to be with Stephen, she'd always known that.

But now she could feel nothing. No certainty, no rightness, no fear.

"Then it's time to *do* nothing," she told herself, "except trust Stephen. Maybe he knows."

So she made no preparations. On Mariamu's advice, Aude sent back three black cumin seeds to let Stephen know that she would meet him on the third night from then. That would be Friday, when the good Moslems of Kamil's palace would be engaged in their devotions and it would seem quite normal for the Christian girl to take a private bath. Presumably it would also be an easy time for Stephen to get away. Mariamu offered to go with Aude to the bath house; she would sing and splash to trick the slaves who escorted them into thinking that there were two girls inside instead of one.

"It's too dangerous," Aude objected, but Mariamu's eagerness, and her certainty that Aude couldn't carry off the escapade without her help, wore down Aude's objections. It made Aude happy to think she had won a true friend in this gossipy women's world. Though she didn't want to think it, it had occurred to Aude that she and Stephen and Geoffrey might be here a very long time.

Friday was a night of bright moonlight. "Nice to see your lover by," said Mariamu. She was as excited and twittery as if she were the one making a secret rendezvous.

"Or to be seen by." Although Aude did not sense danger, she knew that this was a risky thing to do. But if she gave in to her fear of Kamil and his mute slaves, when would she ever see Stephen again? And what good would a long life in the women's quarters be if it were a life without Stephen?

Aude felt less nervous once they were in the bath house with its gleaming marble benches, its pool of steaming water, its raised floor of latticework. The lighted lamps they carried illuminated curving designs in black-and-white marble that were set off by bright squares of red tile. Outside the circles of lamplight, all was darkness and shadow.

Aude would have preferred if the slaves guarding the door had been the deaf-mutes who watched over the women's quarters, but as Mariamu said, one couldn't expect deaf-mutes to guard a place when they were forbidden to look inside.

Mariamu was nervous and excited, urging Aude to hurry. "You don't want to miss a minute with your husband, do you? We haven't got that long. Go on, now!" And her small hands lifted up the grating in the latticed floor.

"Anybody would think it was you meeting your love, instead of me," said Aude to put off the moment of crawling into that damp, dark space.

Mariamu's high-pitched laugh bounced off the marble walls. "*Will* you go on?"

It was as easy as Mariamu had promised to slip through the removable grating in the bath-house floor, glide along the wall under cover of thick bushes, and find the gap in the woven reeds that opened onto Ibn Masoud's garden. But there Aude's luck deserted her. A man was walking back and forth on the other side of the bushes—and it was not Stephen. She knew that much even in these confusing shadows. Aude crouched in the bushes until the man had paced to the other end of the garden, then crept along the base of the reed wall. The guard returned and seemed to be inspecting the gap in the fence. What if he called the alarm? Aude couldn't possibly get back while he stood—and she had to warn Stephen, who would be waiting somewhere close by! She pushed through the bushes, caught her veil on thorns that pricked her bare skin and finally emerged into a silvery-pale space bordered by marble walls.

In the center of that space, Stephen was sitting as still as a marble statue with the gleam of moonlight on his hair. Had he heard the guard, too? At the sound of her gown ripping on the thorns, he looked up sharply; his mouth opened and Aude hurried to his side before he could give them away.

"Hush!" she whispered. "There's a guard at this end of the garden. I think he saw where I came through."

Stephen laughed. "That's Geoffrey. He's keeping watch for us."

"Oh! You might have warned me."

"In a Saracen sign-letter? I didn't know how, and it might have confused the rest of the message. I think I did damned well to convey as much as I did."

"I think so, too." Aude's knees were still shaking from her fright; Stephen was a statue, a stranger, inches from her, yet impossibly far away. She wanted to throw herself into his arms and cry for joy and tell him how it had scared her to think she'd never see him again. But curiously, it was hard to take that first step toward him, perhaps because she knew that Geoffrey was somewhere in the background.

"Why don't you come and congratulate me properly, then?"

"Aren't you afraid Ibn Masoud will hear you?" Stephen had not bothered to lower his voice; she spoke in a half whisper because she couldn't forget the slaves on the far side of the bath house.

Stephen shook his head. "No. I'll explain later—but it's all right. Oh, God, Aude," he said, "I have missed you!"

And then she could move into his open arms. He was

bigger and stronger than she remembered. His cheek was scratchy with the beginnings of a beard in the Saracen style, and he smelled of stone dust and lime instead of musk and jasmine. Aude couldn't find words to tell him how much she had missed him in the past weeks.

"Come this way." His voice was rough with desire, she thought, because she was burning the same way and recognized the sounds. It was absurd to think they might find a private time and place for love in the midst of danger! And yet this garden of Ibn Masoud's had sheltered alcoves, and Stephen had led Aude into one. Soft grass was their mattress, flowering branches were their walls, and a sky more black than the women's veils, with brilliant stars, was their roof.

"Don't you think this Ibn Masoud might object to such goings-on in his garden?" she murmured some time later.

"He's blind, it's dark anyway."

"And we made a bit of noise, I think." Aude's memories of the last half hour were somewhat vague, but she did feel that she hadn't been quite as cautious as she had intended to be. And she certainly hoped Geoffrey had been watching the wall instead of looking back this way.

"Ibn Masoud is very tactful. In fact, he knows we're using his garden tonight—well, knows and doesn't know, if you understand? I was about to tell you, only something distracted me." Stephen kissed the tip of her nose and the edge of one ear, and then pushed her hair aside to kiss the nape of her neck. "Hmmm. I could get distracted all over again."

"We don't have time to be distracted again," Aude said, sitting up. "There's a limit to how long those slaves will believe a woman could spend taking a bath, and a limit to how long Mariamu can splash around and talk to herself. Stephen, what's going on? Are you really all right?"

"For the moment," said Stephen cautiously, "I seem to be in high favor. Ibn Masoud is interpreting for me. That *is* a favor, Aude, the personal services of Kamil's old tutor. And I am proceeding well enough with the destruction of the old hall." He paused, and in the silence Aude caught a hint of some trouble behind her husband's confident words.

"Then what are you worried about?"

"Nothing—now," Stephen said, a little too quickly and firmly. "I *was* worried about you. I couldn't find out what was going on in the women's quarters. Ibn Masoud helped there." And he went off on a long involved story that gave Aude no chance to question him further, telling her how Ibn Masoud had guessed at his loneliness and concern and had slyly hinted at this meeting. "He told me stories about how the women use flowers and symbols to send messages, so that nobody could be caught with incriminating evidence; and he happened to mention how he strongly suspected some of the girls used that weak bit of fence behind the bath house to slip into his private garden from time to time. Then he invited me to sit in his garden any night when I needed to meditate on the progress of the work. And finally he gave me a key to the gate on the far side, so I wouldn't have to disturb him by going through his rooms."

"He does sound nice," said Aude. "I wish there were some way we could thank him." Her preconceptions about the heathens had been all wrong, she thought, momentarily distracted from her sense that something was bothering Stephen.

"Then they are treating you well, Aude?"

He sounded anxious. She would have to go back in a few minutes, and it was terribly important to reassure him so that he wouldn't do anything rash. Aude talked quite fast and completely forgot that Stephen had problems he wasn't mentioning to her. "Of course they are treating me well, Stephen! I'm quite an important person on the women's side, I'll have you know! Bi Hassan, she's the old woman who mixes healing potions, and I think she's a bit of a witch on the side. . . ."

Aude chattered on about Bi Hassan and Mariamu and Kamil's first wife Aisha, trying to convince Stephen that she was well and safe and as happy as could be. "And the second wife, Deena, there's some mystery about her and I think it could be—well, listen. Bi Hassan was making a skin lotion for her one day and it was the exact same thing Helene used to keep her skin white, isn't that funny? And they *say* she's kept to her rooms throughout this pregnancy, but it sounds to me like she only took to her private room when we got here. She was already in her sixth month then and you know, Stephen, I've tended a lot of women at home and they're usually over the sick part by then and I was just wondering. . . ."

Mariamu's voice floated over the wall, wailing the Saracen song they'd agreed upon as a signal. Aude jumped to her feet. She'd tarried much longer than she meant to; what if Mariamu was in trouble? "Oh, never mind, it isn't important. I better get back before they decide to go in and check on the two of us."

CHAPTER

17

◧

Stephen's fingers caught in a trailing veil; Aude shed it without a pause and wriggled back through the thorny vines, past the weak fence, and out of sight.

He clenched the veil in his hands and stood tensely listening. To go crashing after her would only increase the chance of trouble. But what if she were hauled off by Kamil's slaves?

The shouts had ceased, and a moment later he heard Aude gaily singing an English song. The sweet sounds drifted back to him, dying away as she returned to the women's side, a promise that all was well. Stephen's shoulders relaxed and he sat down on the bench where he'd waited for Aude less than an hour ago. He absently smoothed the silky veil which had a sharp, fleeting fragrance that made him think of reeds and still pools and delicate flowers in the fens. That was Aude; no cloying sweet musk and jasmine for her, no exaggeration.

And she was brave. She would have to be brave to face the future: Within the month, they would have to make their escape from Kamil's palace. It was true what he'd said—the work had gone amazingly well up to this point. Stephen knew how to find the weak points in a wall, how to pull it down without danger to the workmen, and how to shore up the remaining bits of the building so that they wouldn't put undue stress on the rest of the palace. And after years of doing Master Brito's accounts, he was good at estimating the quantities of materials that would be needed for the new hall. Between demolition work and arranging for supplies, finding quarries and organizing the delivery of materials over the next months, he had managed to keep an appearance of professional expertise while spinning out the initial phases of the work as long as he dared. But the time was fast approaching when he could procrastinate no longer.

Once the ground was cleared, the teams of workmen organized, and the stone carts rumbled through the narrow streets, Stephen would have to lay the foundations. And that was part of the master builder's art that he had not been able to unravel from Master Adam's stolen sketchbook.

He could draw the hall as it should stand in finished form. He could reason downward to see where the foundation trenches should lie and where the buttresses should spring up from the ground. He could even sketch out the shape of the foundation. But how could he go from an inaccurate, hand-drawn sketch to the enormous trenches and piles that must be set in place with perfect accuracy? Even when copying his own sketches, Stephen's hand sometimes wavered and he had to smudge one side or cheat on the width of a wall to make it come out even. Those little mistakes went unnoticed in a sketchbook. In full size, they would be magnified a hundred times. And Stephen knew all too well that the slightest inaccuracy in the foundations led to horrible waverings, incomplete courses, and walls that fell down before they were finished. Master masons who knew the secrets of geometry were needed at this stage, to pace the ground with lengths of string and bits of chalk drawing lines in the earth and showing the workmen where to dig. That sort of knowledge would be needed from now on if Stephen was to turn rough drawings into foundations, and foundations into smoothly angled walls.

This problem haunted Stephen through his sleepless nights and abstracted days. How could he do the work of a master builder without knowing the secrets of geometry? All Stephen knew of geometry was that it was akin to logic, and that didn't help him much. What did white horses, gray horses, and imaginary horses have to do with laying out a wall in a straight line and positioning the buttresses accurately?

He sighed and shook his head. They would have to escape from Kamil's palace before Stephen started building on his inaccurate foundations. And how to get three fair-haired Franks out of Cairo and across the inhospitable land they'd traversed to come here was a problem that made the mysteries of geometry seem trivial by comparison.

"How I wish I'd paid more attention in school," Stephen muttered, pressing his aching forehead with both hands. "I wish Joscelin were here. He'd think of something logical to do."

"Psst! Stephen! Psst! Hey!"

It was a man's voice, a Frank's voice, and for one moment Stephen thought that Joscelin had indeed shown up to rescue him, as opportunely as he'd done in Ely. Then sanity returned. There was only one other Frankish man in Kamil's palace as far as Stephen knew, certainly only one other stupid enough to let his voice rise as Geoffrey was doing now. But what was Geoffrey doing on the wrong side of the bath house fence, with his long robe caught in the reeds?

"What took you so long?" Geoffrey asked when Stephen helped untangle him from the broken reeds of the fence. "I thought you would never hear me."

Stephen clenched his teeth and fought the temptation to hit Geoffrey. Didn't the idiot realize he was risking all their lives by sneaking over to the women's side of the fence? "You ought to be thankful I was here to rescue you from the consequences of your misdeeds," Stephen said when Geoffrey was free and he himself felt calm enough to speak. "What were you doing on the women's side?"

Geoffrey ducked his head and tried, unsuccessfully, to smooth the satisfied grin off his face. He looked so pleased with himself that it was obvious what had sent him across the fence.

"Let's get back to our quarters," Geoffrey suggested. "I have a lot to tell you."

"I'm not sure I want to hear it," Stephen said when they were seated cross-legged on silk cushions in the small, bare room that served as a sitting room and study for Stephen. Geoffrey was still looking uncommonly smug.

Stephen sighed. It was unfair to be angry with Geoffrey for pursuing a woman when he himself had just risked all to be with Aude. But there was the difference. He loved Aude and he wanted to see her to know that she was all right, not just to satisfy his lust. Geoffrey was going after Kamil's women like a poacher taking one of the King's deer, and his punishment would be far worse than any poacher's if he were caught. "Geoffrey, if you *must* seek out a woman, does she have to be the private possession of a man who'd have you impaled if he found out?"

"I can't meet any other women," Geoffrey pointed out. "And don't give me that priest-look! It's different for you. You've got your work to do and your wife to slip over the fence to be with you while I keep watch. I don't have anything to do except twiddle my thumbs and watch you scribbling designs in that sketchbook while a bunch of dirty heathens parade around Kamil's courtyard. It's asking too much of flesh and blood," he said passionately, "to make me sit and watch the women day after day and then expect me not to react when a black-eyed beauty whispers Frankish love songs in my ear. Her name's Mariamu, by the way. And when she's not interpreting for Aude and arranging your rendezvous, she serves Kamil's second wife."

"I don't care what her name is," Stephen said, relieved that at least Geoffrey hadn't seduced one of Kamil's wives. Things could be worse.

"And not only is she a beauty," Geoffrey went on rapturously, "but she's helped me fulfill my destiny. Stephen, we have to get out of here as soon as possible."

"That had occurred to me."

"Good. I should have known you'd think of something. How soon are you planning to do it?" Geoffrey asked with blithe confidence in Stephen's powers of invention. "I want to get Madeline away before her baby is born."

"Madeline?"

"Deena," Geoffrey explained. "Kamil's second wife. Her real name is Madeline. Stephen, she's my sister!"

It couldn't be true. Stephen shut his eyes for a moment. He felt truly sorry for Geoffrey's twin sister who had disappeared so many years ago on that ill-fated crusade. But he refused to accept her miraculous reappearance as a woman heavy with child who would hamper their escape.

Geoffrey had to be imagining it! "What makes you think that this Deena is your sister? Have you actually seen her? And are you sure you would know her after all these years?"

"No, no, I haven't seen her yet, but it all fits together, Stephen. Remember the witch's prophecy?"

"Yes. She said my bones were fated to lie under the sea. I hope she was right. If I could believe that prophecy, I'd feel safer here." Stephen rubbed the tense aching cords along the back of his neck.

"Not that part; I mean what she said about my search for Madeline! I was to go to Jerusalem and look for a clean-shaven Saracen and an open prison, remember? And see what happened? We met Kamil, and he doesn't wear a beard, and he got us into prison and you got us out again. We were meant to come here, Stephen, don't you see?"

Stephen had to admit that the terms of the witch's prophecy had been matched by events, though neither he nor Geoffrey had noticed at the time. "But all that happened weeks ago, Geoffrey. Why are you so excited about it now?"

"Because," said Geoffrey triumphantly, "Kamil's second wife is French!"

Stephen thought it over. Maybe he should have paid more attention to Aude's gossip. She mentioned something about lotions for white skin, and the confinement of Kamil's second wife which began just when the Christian prisoners arrived. "It is strange," he said at last, "that Mariamu speaks a little French. I suppose that could be evidence to support your notion. From what I've seen of the hea-thens, they don't encourage women to get learning."

"Stephen, it's not just a notion. Mariamu told me her mistress was a French girl who was sold as a slave with a bunch of other children who came from Marseilles on a crusade. That explains why none of the freed Christian slaves we talked to in Acre knew Madeline."

"It does?"

"Obviously she's been a prisoner of these Saracens all these years, and God sent me here to rescue her. And Kamil is making her hide because he's afraid I'll recognize her. Mariamu says he shaved his beard to please Madeline and he went into Jerusalem to ask the Christian priests to pray for the safe birth of her child. She's been so sickly and

nervous and Kamil thought it would make her feel better
to have a priest pray for her. Stephen, we have to save her
and we have to do it quickly, because in another month
she won't be able to travel."

Then Geoffrey stopped talking and his bright blue eyes
searched Stephen's face intently. Around them the heavy
silence of the Egyptian night pressed down like folds of
muffling curtains, broken only by the rustles and occasional snores of sleepers in the adjoining rooms.

Stephen stared into the oil lamp, trying to think of
something to say. He could almost believe that Kamil had
taken a Frankish wife and that he was so enamored of her
as to shave himself in Frankish style and invite a Christian
priest to pray for her safety. But it was a different matter to
identify this "Deena" with Geoffrey's long-lost Madeline.
Stephen dismissed the notion that Kamil was keeping
Deena out of sight on their account. Moslem men always
kept their wives out of sight, and Kamil had no way of
knowing about Geoffrey's mad quest. It was also under-
standable for Deena to avoid Aude since she must be
ashamed of having forgone her religion and married a
heathen. Of course she didn't want to face a decent
Christian woman.

No, there was no reason to believe that Deena had
anything to do with Geoffrey's sister, and it was a good
thing, too. Stephen hadn't yet figured out how the three of
them were going to slip out of the country before Kamil
discovered what a fraud he was. Adding a fourth Frank to
their party, a pregnant woman and favored wife, no less,
would ensure a death sentence if they were caught.

"And from what Mariamu told me, I think we can all get
away safely," Geoffrey said, still looking into Stephen's face
as if Stephen could give him a parental blessing. "Of
course, you probably have a much better escape plan."

"Tell me yours," Stephen suggested.

It was a simple plan, as good ones always are, and the
details that must necessarily be left to the last minute did
not bother Stephen very much. In fact, he felt rather a fool
for not thinking of such a plan himself. The miserable
overland journey from Jerusalem was still fresh in his
mind, and all his thoughts of escape had been based on
crossing that hot desolation again.

Mariamu's talk about the great harbor of Alexandria,

and the merchants who traded there, had given Geoffrey a better idea. If they could get a small boat here in Cairo they could simply sail up the Nile to Alexandria. According to Mariamu, trading vessels from all over the world filled the harbor; they could surely get passage to a Christian land on one of them.

"And how," Stephen inquired, "are we going to get a boat?"

Geoffrey triumphantly revealed the last gleanings of his talk with Mariamu. There was a Frankish quarter in Cairo, and the merchants had to keep their goods, storerooms and boats to transport them to and from the trading ships in Alexandria. And in that quarter was a branch of the House of Sanudo. Surely the Sanudo agent here would help them if he knew that they were friends of Marco's.

Upon hearing this news, Stephen began to hope. They might be able to escape. They might even be able to take Deena with them. For little as Stephen believed Geoffrey's fantasy that she was his long-lost sister, he did feel guilty about leaving a Christian woman captive in Kamil's palace.

There were innumerable details to work out, small problems that kept them awake until dawn streaked the walls with light and made the jewel-colored lamp look like a tawdry imitation of the true sun outside. Stephen would get money for their journey by cheating on the building accounts he showed to Kamil. "Thank you, Master Adam of Lincoln, for a worthwhile lesson," he murmured with a smile.

"Who's that?"

"It's a long story. I'll tell you someday."

Stephen would also try to get a message to the House of Sanudo through one of his suppliers. He didn't dare go to the Frankish quarter himself, but he could probably get someone else to carry a letter. There was a merchant he'd heard about who sold anything from old stones to new chisels and iron-work, and who had the reputation of being equally willing to sell his son or daughter for enough gold. Clever, unscrupulous, and greedy, he could surely be bribed to carry their letter.

They would need food for the journey, plain clothes to cover the silken robes Kamil had given them, and a host of small supplies. Aude, with her access to the kitchens and the women's clothing chests, could probably gather those things; Stephen would ask her next time they met. And on the next dark night, Geoffrey would go over the wall of Ibn Masoud's back garden to survey the streets and to plan a route that would get them to the Frankish quarter without arousing too much notice.

The plan was far from perfect. Too much was unknown: could they expect any help from the House of Sanudo? How long would it take them to get to Alexandria? How soon would Kamil start searching for them and how hard would he look? That last would probably depend on whether or not they took Deena along. Stephen admitted that it was necessary to give her the chance to escape, but he couldn't help hoping she would refuse to go.

For two long weeks of planning and waiting and fretting, life went on as usual. Stephen dragged out the preliminary stages of the work as much as he could. It would have been safe to lay out the foundation lines by eye; the inevitable errors wouldn't be spotted until the walls began to rise. But Stephen couldn't bear the thought of consciously doing bad work. He ached, too, over the prospect of leaving. That was insane. But the high hall he'd sketched for Kamil had become real in his mind: the overarching ceiling, the slender shells of walls that would be plastered white and painted with the graceful arabesques of heathen art.

The hall would have been his first great work, and he owed it to those who had unknowingly supplied him with his materials. Columns to support the lower stages of the new hall were taken from ancient churches; blocks of stone from the tombs of long-dead kings served as building material. The kings and priests didn't trouble him, but the men who'd built those tombs and churches haunted him. At night he walked the building site and caressed his growing trove of materials, marveling over the sheer bulk of a stone that was wind-scored with centuries of desert sand, or the graceful line of a capital carved when Christ was still a living memory in the hearts of men.

These stones carried all the centuries of the earth within them. They had been quarried by men whose bones had long since been buried, and shaped into buildings by masons who believed their work would last forever. In the piles of broken stone and marred columns Stephen saw his own mortality and the futility of his hopes. Had he thought, by building in stone, that he could make something to outlast love and death and his short stay on earth? The tumbled carvings mocked him, and in the painted heathen figures he saw the Dance of Death as it had appeared on the walls of St. Michael's Church in Dunwich. "As you are, so once was I; as I am, so shall you be," said the painted skeletons. The remains of old monuments whispered the same message to Stephen. "Our makers thought to live forever through us. Now we are brought low, and they are forgotten. And so shall you be forgotten!"

Stephen's palms covered the sand-worn stone, and he fancied that he felt the heat of the sun that had beaten down on these monuments for so long. One day his work would perish. And for the moment he could almost accept that—if only he could raise the buildings that arched so high in his imagination, and shape these old stones to their new use. He would honor the first builders by putting their work into a masterpiece so fair and fine that the stones would sing again.

But Stephen would never do this work. He hadn't the skill. And he had to think about saving his wife and friend from the Saracens and guarding the growing hoard of clothes and other supplies for the journey that he had locked in his tool cabinet.

Most of these supplies had come from Aude, who had become an accomplished thief out of necessity. Stephen and Aude met almost nightly by the bath house wall, usually with only time for a quick kiss while she handed him dried figs, a coarse woolen robe, a knife, a leather water bottle, or whatever she had been able to steal that day. Then she would flit back to Bi Hassan and the gossipy world of the women's quarters.

"I got in to see Deena," she reported one night. "She is one of us, or was. She's as fair as any English lady but she prays to Mahound like the rest of the heathens. She is surrounded by slaves so I never got a chance to talk to her in private. But she does not look *at all* well, Stephen. I don't think she will be able to travel very far or very fast."

"I hope," said Stephen grimly, "that she does not choose to do so."

"And what about Geoffrey?"

"Once he realizes that she is not his sister, he will not

insist on taking her. And I hope she is sensible enough to see that she shouldn't make the attempt."

Aude looked worried. "Yes, well, she doesn't talk about her past, Stephen, but I'm beginning to think— Shh! Bi Hassan's calling me." Her head jerked up, like a wild animal surprised too near men's houses, and she disappeared as quickly and silently as always.

A few days later they were ready to escape, and Geoffrey still had not seen Deena. Stephen worried about that. He would have preferred for Geoffrey to have the shock before they started out for Alexandria. On the other hand, what if Deena, when offered the chance to escape with them, not only refused but also alerted Kamil? It had to be done at the last minute and tonight was the best chance they would have for some time.

For Stephen, the combination of a moonless night and full purse made the opportunity too good to miss. The gold had come from Ibn Masoud, who said he had persuaded Kamil that Stephen should be rewarded for his excellent preliminary work instead of after the building's completion, as was customary. It seemed strange to Stephen, especially as Kamil had not even mentioned payment before. But he wasn't one to complain; Ibn Masoud was a gentleman, and Stephen was not going to question his ways, especially when they fit so conveniently with his own plans. Stephen told Aude to bring Deena down to the bath house with her the next evening, and to be prepared to leave from there.

"Can you do it without telling her about the escape? It will be a shock for her, but at least she will have no chance to betray our plans."

"Ye-es." Aude chewed on a fingertip. "She trusts me, although I still have not been private with her. But I'm in her chambers every day. I think she wants the company of another Christian woman especially now, so near her time. I think the baby will come sooner than she expected; she's very big now, and very slow, and she complains that her back hurts all the time. I will offer to treat her with a special healing oil, and I'll say the charms have to be sung when we are quite alone, and the bath house is the best place because of the steam. . . . Yes. I can do it. Bring Geoffrey. An hour after sunset."

The next day of waiting was a long torment of dust and

heat and petty details. Three times Stephen made errors
of calculation in his instructions to the workmen, and each
time Ibn Masoud caught the errors and corrected them as
he translated Stephen's orders. When the light faded until
a black thread could no longer be distinguished from a
white one, the day's work was over and Stephen felt as
thankful as any of his sweating laborers.

Only one hour to go now. Stephen had to tell Geoffrey,
collect their secret bundle of clothing and supplies, and
make his excuses to Ibn Masoud who wanted to spend the
evening telling Stephen long-winded stories about his
misspent youth. Finally it was time to go; the first stars
were out, and Deena should be in the bath house soon.

Stephen was torn between relief and sadness as he
made his way toward the bath house with Geoffrey by his
side. It would be good to have the waiting of the last few
days over with. But leaving his hall, Kamil's hall, as an
inchoate mass of stones and rubble tore at his heart. Ah,
but it would be good to stay and see it finished! Now it
never would rise, proud and airy, to arch over the flat-
roofed houses of Cairo, like a promise of a better world.
Kamil would call in a local builder whose idea of good
architecture was to build a stack of square boxes orna-
mented with mosaic tiles and gilt carving.

"Barbarians!" Stephen muttered under his breath.

"Yes. It'll be good to be among Christians again."

Stephen supposed it would be. Anyway, he hadn't the
learning to raise Kamil's hall. That part was something he
kept forgetting in these final moments.

The air in the garden was heavy with the scent of
night-blooming flowers, white waxy things whose name
Stephen had never learned. When they reached the gap in
the wall, Stephen dropped their bundle of provisions and
the traveling robes, partially covered them with some low
branches. Then he followed Geoffrey into the bath house.

This was forbidden territory. Inside the air was heavy
with scented oils and perfumes that the women used so
lavishly in their bath water. Stephen felt oppressed by the
low ceiling and the damp air. He also felt a quivering pulse
of excitement at penetrating to this secret place, something that helped him understand why Geoffrey could not
resist the call to adventures with strange, dangerous women.

Then light flared through an open lamp, and Stephen saw the most beautiful woman he had ever seen in his life.

Heavy with child, drawn and pale from illness and worry, she was still a queen in the smoky, shadowy bath house. She lifted her small, proud head above the vast ungainly bulk of her body in its layers of brocaded robes. Stephen stared at eyes that were blue pools shadowed by weariness, at a small mouth and chin set firm against the memory of pain and loneliness. He formed a vision that he was to try, years later, to translate into a carved capital representing the Blessed Virgin.

"Geoffrey?" Her incredulous whisper quavered. "My dear brother? Oh, no—it cannot be!"

Stephen snapped out of his artistic reverie. There was one other thing about this beautiful Deena that he'd been trying very hard not to notice: she could have been Geoffrey's twin. And, in fact, she was.

They were in each other's arms now, Madeline sobbing with joy while Geoffrey grumbled that she might stop calling him "little brother" just because he'd come into the world some twenty minutes after she did. Aude had retreated to a corner of the bath house, tactfully looking away from the reunion. Stephen joined her on a slatted bench, damp with condensed steam.

"You could have told me," he murmured out of the corner of his mouth.

"I tried to. Anyway, I didn't know for sure. Deena wouldn't say much."

Stephen sighed and admitted to himself that he had not really listened to Aude's hints. He had been so set on making the world the way he wanted it. It would be a rare coincidence for Deena to be Geoffrey's sister, and damned inconvenient for their escape plans, so he had refused even to consider the possibility. Now what were they going to do? Madeline looked exhausted from the short trip to the bath house. How would she ever make it from Kamil's palace to the Venetian *fóndaco* that was all the way across the city? Stephen wasn't even sure they would be able to get her over the wall that separated Ibn Masoud's garden from the street. He sighed and began revising his escape plans to include one very pregnant woman.

"We're going to have to pull down a section of the latticework between here and the garden," he whispered to Aude. "And she can't possibly crawl through the grills in the bath house floor. Is there any way you can distract the guards at the door?"

"I don't think we'll need to do that," Aude replied. "Have you been listening to those two?"

The first moments of their reunion had been filled with joyful babble as brother and sister tried to tell each other about the last eleven years. Neither was really listening to the other, and the whole conversation sounded jumbled and hardly intelligible to an outsider.

"—sold in the market at Damietta, and I thought this nasty old man was going to buy me, but Kamil outbid him—"

"—wouldn't let us mention your name in the house—"

"—the best man I ever knew, treated me like his own daughter, and Aisha, that's his first wife, so sweet—"

"—won my spurs at the tourney in Bourges—"

"—growing up, and I really didn't feel like his daughter, only I felt guilty because of Aisha, but guess what? She wanted me to marry him, she said then we would be sisters and perhaps I could give him a son—"

"—told Father I wanted to go on a pilgrimage, he doesn't know about you yet—"

Naturally Stephen hadn't been listening.

Now he saw that the conversation had become more connected, if not more sensible. Apparently Geoffrey had just announced to Madeline that he had come to take her away.

"But Geoffrey, darling," Madeline said with great sweetness, "haven't you been listening? I am happy here. I don't want to be rescued."

"You cannot be happy," Geoffrey stated categorically. "You are a slave in the hands of a heathen prince."

"I am the wife of a good, kind man who has treated me much better than our father ever did—or would, if I returned. I'm staying with Kamil, Geoffrey. I love him."

"Madeline!" Geoffrey was genuinely shocked. "You can't love an infidel. For your soul's sake, I must get you out of this pagan place. It is your duty to come back."

Madeline pressed one hand to the small of her back, sighed, and settled herself on a marble bench, as comfortably as she could. She looked up at Geoffrey with wide innocent eyes. "And where might I practice this consideration of my duty? In the home of our loving father?"

"Well—um—" Geoffrey stuttered.

"He will doubtless be so happy to see me, after I've been defiled by the embraces of a Saracen. He will recognize a brown-skinned infidel baby as his grandson?"

"Oh. Yes. Well." Clearly Geoffrey, when he imagined bringing his sister home, had not pictured this defiant virago clinging to her infidel child. "Perhaps you might not be quite happy at la Tour Martel."

Madeline nodded grimly. "You are beginning to understand."

"But a Christian land, Madeline!" Geoffrey pleaded. "We can find some place for you—perhaps a nice convent? There's the House for Repentant Magdalens at Tours—and I suppose the child could be fostered somewhere."

"Repentant! Magdalens!" Madeline spat out the words and stood up again, glaring at Geoffrey. "I knew it. You're just like the rest of them. Men! Listen carefully for once. I am not a whore and I am not repenting for anything. I am the honored and respected wife of a great man in this country and I am proud to be bearing his child and I am going to keep my son and I am going to stay right here where I am happy and loved. Is that clear?"

Stephen wondered how he could ever have imagined this screeching virago was like the Blessed Virgin. Blasphemy, it was! He buried his vision of Madeline's sad yet radiant face, so deep that he never recognized the image when he carved it years later.

"You little fool! After all I've done for you!" Geoffrey's face seemed to be turning purple, though it was hard to be sure in the light from the one oil lamp. The veins on his forehead were standing out, and his fists were clenched. It was time to distract him.

"Geoffrey, if Madeline is not coming, we'd better get on with it. We don't have very long until dawn." Stephen put a hand on his friend's arm and tried to pull him toward the open grating in the bath house floor. It was like trying to move one of those massive blocks of stone from the ancient tombs.

"She's coming. Just give me a minute to talk some sense into her!"

"No, I'm not!"

"You're coming out of this dirty heathen household if I have to tie you up in a sack and carry you over my shoulder!"

For a long moment brother and sister stood immobile, glaring at each other. Then Madeline let out a tiny shriek and sank down trembling. "My pains! Ahh, Aude, I can feel it, the baby's coming before its time!"

Aude leapt to Madeline's side and supported her, scowling up at the two men equally. "Now see what you great fools have done? Get out of here, will you, and give me a chance to repair the damage you've caused! There, there, don't be afraid. 'Tis a long time yet. See, now you're feeling better! Let's go up to your rooms before the pains come again. We'll have Bi Hassan brew a drink to soothe you."

Madeline declared that she could not walk. Geoffrey announced that he wasn't going anywhere until he had reasoned with his sister. Aude cursed them all.

Any minute Kamil's guards would hear the uproar in the bath house. Stephen felt trickles of sweat running down his back, mingling with the steamy, damp air. He stepped back into the corner and hefted the loose bar that had held the grating in place. There was one thing he could possibly do to simplify their problems. It would make escape that night impossible, of course, but he'd already given that up. In any case, they had to avoid a brawling scene in the bath house that would bring in onlookers and guards, and would dash all hope of a future escape. Stephen swung the beam lightly and prayed for the wit to strike just hard enough.

Geoffrey went down under the blow like an ox staggering under the butcher's mallet, blue eyes opened wide in surprise, knees folding under him. Stephen caught him and lowered his limp body gently to the floor. Madeline screeched, accusing Stephen of murdering her brother.

"Don't be silly," Stephen told her, "he's a French nobleman, the only creature on earth with a skull thicker than an ox's. See, he's still breathing. Aude, for God's sake calm her down, will you? I'll be back to get Geoffrey in a minute. First I want to hide our things better, in case one of Ibn Masoud's servants comes strolling into the garden. If there's any trouble before I get back, roll Geoffrey under the grating and I'll drag him out later. He should be unconscious for some time."

Stephen dropped through the hole in the floor as he spoke, praying that Aude would be able to keep Madeline under control until he got back. The darkness outside confused him; he'd been staring at the bath house lamp while Geoffrey and Madeline argued, and bright needles of light still danced in red-orange patterns on his eyelids. He felt his way through the gap in the wall, never noticing the thorns that cut his hands, and breathed a sigh of relief when he glimpsed a fuzzy white patch right where he'd left their bundles.

The top portion of the fuzzy white patch elongated, rose higher, resolved into the shape of an old man in a white turban and long white robes.

"I thought you would be returning this way, Stephen."

"Ibn Masoud." Somehow, Stephen wasn't surprised, but his legs felt weak. He sat down on the bundle the old man had vacated. "I thought you were blind."

"I am." The old man's voice was tranquil as the mirror-smooth surface of a lake in the fen country. "But not stupid, or deaf, or deprived of my sense of smell. I feared you might be planning to—shall we say—depart rather informally? I am afraid that I cannot permit such a rash move. Kamil wishes to see his hall completed; and in case it has escaped your notice, I am fond of Kamil."

Stephen felt very tired. Something hard was pressing against the underside of his thigh; he thought it was the handle of the knife Aude had stolen from the kitchens. She said you never knew when a good knife might come in handy and it seemed she was right.

"The hall won't be finished in any case," he said bluntly. "I don't know enough to do it right. I'm a fraud, not an architect."

"Ahhh." A long breath of satisfaction. "I had thought such might be the case. You are very young to have the years of experience you claimed. Kamil might not have noticed; he sees only a man's face, and to him all Frankish men look alike. I, of course, am forced to rely on other senses. Your voice is that of a young man, and one desperately unsure of himself. The very young," Ibn Masoud went on as tranquilly as though he and Stephen were enjoying one of their quiet after-dinner conversations, "the young often betray themselves by assuming a tone of overmuch authority. Fearing to be questioned, they try to intimidate. It seems to me that I have heard such a note in your voice, Stephen, when you discuss certain technical matters, the laying-out of the foundations, for instance. At other times, though, you have seemed quite enviably sure of yourself. You didn't hesitate in ordering the initial stages of the work; and your voice sings like a nightingale when you describe how the finished hall should look."

Ibn Masoud's voice provided cover for Stephen's fingers, busily working at the knotted bundle that concealed the knife. When the old man paused Stephen stopped too, afraid that the slightest sound would betray his movements to Ibn Masoud's acute ears.

"You've grasped the problem." He hoped his own voice would cover the sound of cords parting and linen rustling. "I don't know geometry. I can build, and I can see how the building should look, but I can't set it out accurately. So you see, there's no point in forcing me to stay. Kamil's not going to get his hall, not from me." The knots parted; Stephen slid one hand into the bundle and felt the hard smooth hilt of the knife under his fingers. He could stop talking now.

"Perhaps, perhaps not. A man cannot know what is written in the book of his fate until it comes to pass. But I can assure you of this much: if you attempt to escape, I shall be forced to call my servants to stop you."

Stephen's fingers tightened around the hilt of the knife and he stood up very slowly. Ibn Masoud raised his head, clearly following Stephen's movements, but he did not step back or shout for help.

"You could, of course, kill me and go on about your escape," he said calmly. "If that intriguingly lumpy bundle of stolen goods does not contain a knife, you could strangle me with your strong mason's hands. I would then present no obstacle to your plans."

It was the sensible, logical thing to do. There was Geoffrey to think of. And Aude. But there was also an old, blind man who had never shown him anything but kindness.

Stephen swore under his breath and threw the knife away. It clattered against the wall and fell into the bushes. Two birds screeched alarm and hovered above the wall for a moment before settling back down on the branch where they had been sleeping.

"All right, you win. I can't do it." He despised himself for being such a weakling. If only the old man had attacked him, reviled him for trying to escape, done something other than stand and wait to be slain! Now Aude and Geoffrey would be dragged down to share his fate because he was a convent-bred, softhearted fool who couldn't take one life to save three.

"Just one thing, before you call your servants. My wife knows nothing of this and neither does my friend Geoffrey. I meant to abandon them here and escape alone. Will you see to it that they are spared whatever—" Stephen's mouth felt dry. "Whatever punishment Kamil chooses to inflict on me, when you tell him what a fraud I am?"

His mind skittered through the horror stories of Saracen cruelty toward pilgrims and Crusaders: wild horses, boiling pitch, high walls with hooks strong enough to hold human flesh. Well, worse things were done at home to men whose crimes deserved it. Stephen was frightened of Kamil's anger, but more frightened for Aude, whom he had betrayed. If Ibn Masoud meant to see her included in his doom, he might yet find the moral courage to break the old man's neck.

"I don't think that will be necessary," said Ibn Masoud. "I should be sorry for Kamil, who was once my favorite pupil, to suffer such a disappointment. Perhaps he need not discover your shortcomings."

"You mean you'll let us go after all?" Hope flared in Stephen's breast.

"Not at all. I wish to propose something quite different. A sort of partnership, if you will. Come inside," said Ibn Masoud, "and let us discuss the matter over wine, which the Prophet will forgive me on account of my old age and infirmities, and which you as a heathen Frank are not forbidden to drink."

Once seated in his accustomed niche before the low, round table of chased brass, Ibn Masoud became less philosophical and more businesslike. In his youth he had been a mathematician of some repute, he told Stephen, and was expected to become one of the great scholars of the Arab world. An unlucky inability to concentrate, coupled with an even more unlucky fondness for alcohol, had ended his promising career before it was well begun: there'd been a scandal, Stephen gathered, a need to leave town quickly, a period of wasting his talents until finally he was lucky to find work tutoring rich men's sons instead of studying with learned men.

"Ah, well, those are all old stories now." Ibn Masoud sighed. "What do I have now? My garden, the songs of my birds, these rooms, which Kamil in his kindness gives to me. What more does a blind old man need?"

His eyes were filmed over with white milky stuff, but Stephen felt as though the old scholar were looking directly at him. "I'll tell you what, my son. Independence, that's what the old fool wants."

He would, he proposed, lend Stephen the benefit of his knowledge of geometry and other arcane arts. No one need know that Ibn Masoud was secretly tutoring him, solving by night the problems that arose during the day. They would only see the great hall of Kamil's palace grow as Stephen had envisioned it, becoming an architectural wonder that would amaze all Cairo.

"Kamil will, of course, reward you richly. And, with a little prompting from me, he will agree that you have more than earned your freedom."

"And your price?"

"Instead of using that freedom to return at once to Europe, you will remain here for—shall we say five years? If you are as talented as I believe, your work for Kamil will earn admiration and commissions for other such buildings. I still have some acquaintances among the good people of this city; I shall help to spread the word of your talent. And you, in return, will give me half of your earnings."

"Too much," Stephen protested instinctively. "The sixth part is more than enough."

"For the benefit of my great learning? A fourth part, at least."

Stephen hesitated. "Well . . ."

"Very well. I will accept a fifth part—but no less, and mind you do not try to cheat an old blind man! And now," Ibn Masoud remarked, "perhaps you would like to see to your companions. They must be growing tired with waiting in the bath house."

Of course the old man hadn't believed for a minute that Stephen was trying to escape alone. Stephen blushed. He had actually forgotten all about Aude and Geoffrey and Madeline. He must go back there at once; Aude would be beside herself with worry. Still he paused at the door. "How do you know you can trust me? What if I just pick up our things and go over the wall now?"

"Three reasons. First, you did not try to kill me when you thought you could do so safely."

"Thought?"

"Second, the servants who were concealed behind the bushes have now collected your bundle and your disguises and brought them inside."

"Oh!"

"And third," said Ibn Masoud, "if you had been planning to run away, you would hardly have bothered to bargain over my share of the proceeds from our partnership." He smiled and waved a wrinkled hand. "You have my leave to depart."

CHAPTER

18

Trailed by Ibn Masoud's servants, Stephen made his way to the bath house and found it empty. Aude might have helped Madeline back to the women's quarters, but where was Geoffrey? Surely he hadn't recovered so quickly from that blow on the head. Perhaps they'd hidden him somewhere.

"Geoffrey?"

The questioning word echoed off water-splashed tiles and wooden lattices. Lights and shadows moved confusingly, making the rooms seem inhabited, though they were quite empty.

Stephen was reluctant to go back to Ibn Masoud for help, but there was no one else to turn to. Kamil's tutor might be able to find out what was going on in the women's quarters, and he might be able to rescue Geoffrey and Aude from Kamil's anger, if they'd been caught. Stephen, the Frankish slave, had no power to do anything for his friends.

Ibn Masoud was patiently explaining the limits of his own influence over Kamil when a scream echoed through the house from the top floor where the women were kept.

"Aude!" Stephen leapt to his feet. "They're torturing her."

"I think that most unlikely," said Ibn Masoud tranquilly. His right hand flickered in a small gesture that sent his servants to the door, blocking Stephen's way. "If, as you told me, Deena has gone into labor prematurely, surely that explains the screams."

"If it was your wife up there," Stephen grunted against the restraining arms of Ibn Masoud's bodyservants, "you wouldn't be reasoning so calmly. Let me go!"

Aude came to the door of Ibn Masoud's rooms just in time to save the second bodyservant from being thrown against the wall. The first was sitting up, rubbing his head, and looking dazed.

"What are you doing here? How did you get away? Where's Geoffrey?"

Stephen was holding Aude too close and kissing her too fiercely in between questions for her to get any answers out. Finally she got back enough of her breath to say that she and Geoffrey were both all right, and Stephen relaxed slightly.

"For the moment."

"What do you mean?"

"It all depends," said Aude, "on whether the baby is all right. And Deena, of course."

Deena's groans, she explained, had alerted the guards at the bath house door. They'd broken in to find their mistress in labor and an unconscious Frank on the floor. They would have cut Geoffrey's head off then and there if Deena hadn't threatened to have them flayed alive. Instead they dragged Geoffrey off to Kamil. They'd wanted to carry Deena to her rooms, but she refused. She had walked with her hand on Aude's shoulder to Kamil's audience room, slowed by her pains, but determined to see that Geoffrey came to no harm.

Much of what followed was in the Saracen tongue and Aude hadn't understood it all at the time, but Mariamu and Deena's other ladies, who had been eavesdropping, explained it to her later. Deena had told Kamil that Geoffrey was her brother and that she would be very unhappy if anything happened to him. Did Kamil want to upset her in her present condition? Did he want her to die in labor, or to see his son born dead?

He did not. He promised by all the saints of the Moslem faith that not a hair of Geoffrey's head should be harmed. But Deena only half believed him. Even when the pains grew so bad that she could not stand or speak, she demanded that both Geoffrey and Kamil be where she could see them at all times.

Now she lay upstairs, surrounded by twittering ladies and attended by Bi Hassan with mysterious pain-relieving brews. She held Geoffrey's hand on one side and Kamil's on the other and refused to let either of them leave her sight. And Kamil, in his fear for her, had told Geoffrey that if either the baby or Deena did not live, the three Christian prisoners would pay for their plot with their lives. And before they were executed, they would beg to die.

"Good God." Stephen had been reclining in Ibn Masoud's cushioned wall niche, hugging Aude to him and taking in very little except his relief that she was safe. Now he sprang up, lifting her in the circle of his arm as if she were no heavier than one of the Saracen cloaks of fine-spun wool. "We have to get out of here."

"It's too late," Aude told him.

"What?"

"Why d'you think I was allowed to come down here? Do you think they'd let me go anywhere alone? Now?"

Aude's voice went up on the last question, tense and shrill. The door to the outer hall swung open and revealed the rows of expressionless Nubian slaves, full-armed in the Saracen style.

In the three days that followed, Deena labored and sweated to bring forth a baby that had begun its journey too early. And those days seemed longer to Stephen than any full year of his life.

"The time must be even longer," said Ibn Masoud, "for the poor lady upstairs. Try to think of something else," he counseled. Stephen remembered his Mam's voice, and returned to his geometry lessons. For minutes at a time he could lose himself in the regular, ordered beauty of mathematics as it unfolded before him: construction of a regular pentagon, an octagon, two squares enfolded one within the other. Geometry was like building, he thought: first you laid the foundations based on what you already understood, then you built upward, constructing a towering edifice of pure reason and light.

The propositions that Ibn Masoud laid before Stephen

were no dull constructions of lines and letters and Saracen symbols; they leapt off the page to surround him, walls and arches, towers and galleries, the secret heart of the stone that he loved. Mysteries that had been shrouded in the secrecy of the masons' lodge were clear to him now; work habits that Brito had drilled into him for no better reason than "us allus done it so," were now explained. In time, Stephen felt sure that he would understand the laws that ruled the stone, and then he would know how to build everything he wanted. He imagined great lacy towers, impossibly attenuated structures, slender columns, and thin walls, all upheld by the beautiful, inexorable laws that Ibn Masoud was laying out before him.

Then Deena cried out again, and Stephen was left with a tablet of spider hatchings before him, lines and symbols that made no sense and led nowhere except into a new maze of propositions.

By the third day, Deena's cries were barely audible, rasping from a throat grown raw with screaming. She was growing weaker; the end, Stephen thought, must be near. And with her death would come his own and Aude's, but not at the hands of Kamil's torturers. That much Stephen could give Aude, a clean, quick death before she had time to be afraid or hurt. He hoped that Ibn Masoud would not try to stop him from using the small knife he had taken from a writing desk. It was no sort of a weapon at all, but it was small enough to conceal in the palm of his hand and sharp enough, he hoped, to kill Aude and maybe himself before Kamil's torturers came to take them away. It was a pity about Geoffrey. . . .

One last hoarse panting cry came down to them from the women's quarters, and Aude raised her head. "I can't take any more of this. I'm going to her."

"No!" But she was marching down the long hall, and by the time Stephen caught up with her the guards closed in around them. They wouldn't let him force her back to Ibn Masoud's rooms. He had to follow her up the stairs and along the quivering balcony, through the red and gold curtain and into the dreamland of the women's quarters that he'd never seen before. No one tried to stop him; perhaps they thought it would be more convenient to have all three Franks together when the time came to kill them.

Aude went straight to Deena's rooms and knelt by the bed. Women held up panels of red and gold silk to protect the privacy of their mistress's swollen, agonized body. Only Deena's white, sunken face was visible above the sparkling screens. Sweat made her fair hair cling to her skin like seaweed that wraps its tendrils around drowned fishermen. Stephen looked at her, pallid and exhausted, and he knew she would die. This knowledge was reflected in the eyes of the men on either side of the bed; dull resignation in Geoffrey's face, living hatred in Kamil's. Neither of them was thinking of Deena, whom they had already given up to death.

Only Aude, kneeling by Deena's ear and murmuring low singsong words, looked strong and vital and alive. "You have to let go now, Madeline. It's time to let this child come into the world. You can't keep the baby safe in your womb forever."

"He'll die. He'll be born dead!" The words were a whisper, and even that must have hurt her throat. "Like the others."

"No." Aude reached under the screens of shimmering crimson silk and felt Deena's hard, round belly that flexed in the hopeless spasms of labor too long delayed. "I can feel him kicking now, Madeline. You know he is strong and ready to come into the world. Why won't you let him come?"

Geoffrey coughed and shifted his cramped position; Aude looked at him and stood up suddenly. "Oh, you fools!" she cried. "Have you two men been sitting by her side all this time with girdles tied and sandals laced and you, you donkey"—this for Kamil—"with an earring closed through the lobe of your ear? No wonder she can't loosen the baby! Has no one told you that all knots must be untied in the room of a laboring woman? Quick, quick, now, loosen your tight girdles and take off that closed ring. . . ."

Kamil and Geoffrey obeyed Aude's furious commands, loosening their clothes and untying all the knots with shaking hands. If Stephen had not been so afraid, he would have laughed to see one small woman bullying these men so.

"You too, my great ox of a husband!" And Stephen obeyed.

Still Deena sighed and panted. Bi Hassan moistened her lips with a sponge dipped in a sweet-smelling potion, and Deena's eyes rolled up in her head and her body relaxed. But her straining belly did not move.

"Something else, some kind of knot, something holding the babe in," Aude muttered, pacing up and down the length of the room. She glowered at Geoffrey and Kamil, clearly still suspecting them of somehow interfering with the natural course of the birth. "Of course. You two men!" she said in a tone of disgust. She knelt again by Deena's sweat-streaked head. "You're afraid of what will happen if the baby is marred by all this, aren't you?" Her small hand pushed the dampened tendrils of hair away from Deena's forehead; her voice was as sweet and low as if she had never raged at the foolish men who cluttered the chamber. "To lose baby and brother at once, that would be too hard. We won't let that happen, Madeline dear."

Deena's eyes lit with incredulous hope. Aude looked up at the men who sat on either side of the bed. "You see? It's your threats, Kamil, that have her afraid to bring forth the child. How can she loose the babe when this whole room is tied up with you and your anger?"

"I'd leave," said Kamil, "but she won't permit it.

"Of course not. That's not good enough. You must swear friendship with Geoffrey. That's it, isn't it, Madeline?"

The laboring woman's head moved feebly on the pillow.

"If she dies—" Kamil began an instinctive protest.

"She will not die." said Aude with a quiet, inexorable certainty. "I will not let her die. She will live and so will the child. But you must choose life for her. You must love her brother as your own. Geoffrey!" The snap of his name was like a whip cracking. "You must love Kamil as a brother. He is your brother now. Swear it!"

"He's a damned unbeliever," both men protested in one voice, staring at each other with repulsion.

"Swear it!"

"Swear," came the whisper from the bed.

Aude stood triumphantly over Deena's convulsing body as the two men clasped hands, and swore in the names of the Prophet and the Savior to be as brothers to one another forevermore.

"Now," she said when the oaths were concluded, "you

may go, all of you. The women, too. My lady Deena needs to rest."

And none of them questioned the authority Aude had seized.

Minutes after they had left the chamber, while Kamil paced up and down and the servants scurried to stay out of his way, the muezzin's call to prayer echoed among the rooftops of Cairo. High and shrill and persistent, it seemed to go on and on even after the words were finished.

"How can I pray," muttered Kamil, "when—"

Stephen raised his hand. "Listen!"

The cry came again, but this time from within the chamber they had just vacated: high and wavering at first, then it steadied into the indignant squall of an infant meeting the world for the first time.

Aude appeared at the curtained door, pale but smiling. "You have a son, Prince. A little prince . . . and Deena will be well. She's sleeping already!"

Forgetting the ritual ablutions and the spreading of his silken prayer mat, Kamil prostrated himself toward Mecca and mixed the words of the noonday prayer with a promise of seven times seven days of rejoicing for the birth of his son.

The festivities began that very day, with musicians and respected scholars quavering long passages in the Saracen tongue. "They are reciting the Koran from memory," Ibn Masoud explained. "The most learned recite a *juz*, a thirtieth part of the whole book; the others take a *hezb*, which is half a *juz*, or a *ruba*—"

"One quarter," Stephen said triumphantly. He remembered the term from his mathematical studies with Ibn Masoud.

"Excellent. I'm glad to see you retained something from our work in the last few days. It's a pity you cannot yet follow our speech well; you would benefit from hearing the words of the Prophet as well as my poor mathematical theories."

"You mean just anybody can understand what they're saying?" Stephen was used to a Church that concealed her mysteries behind incense and Latin chants. Priests knew the meaning of the holy words but it was thought better

for the laity not to trouble their minds, simply believing
without understanding. So he'd always been taught.

"Our book," Ibn Masoud said with a pitying smile for
Christian ignorance, "is in the language we speak, so that
all may learn and understand the words of the Prophet.
We are not afraid to share our holy faith."

Stephen knew there was a good reason why the Bible
was in Latin, only to be read and interpreted by learned
men, but he couldn't remember it. If Ibn Masoud hadn't
known better, he would have claimed that not only could
every peasant read the Bible but that every one had a
copy of it in his hut. "Isn't it time for us to return to
studying—er—your poor mathematical theories?"

First they watched while a squalling baby wrapped
in yards of priceless silk was brought down to hear the
musicians. The baby yowled even louder when an old man
struck a gong next to its ear, and two veiled women
shook the baby in a large sieve of woven reeds.

"That's so the child will be accustomed to noise and
movement."

"No wonder Kamil was praying for a healthy baby.
Saracen infants have to be strong to survive this treatment," Stephen grumbled. The sight of the squalling,
newborn baby disturbed him. For all their stolen evenings
together, Aude had not yet conceived. Of course Stephen
would not want her to go through pregnancy and childbirth as a prisoner in a heathen land, but sometimes he
wondered. Kamil's pride in his new young son was all but
overpowering, and Stephen was desperately envious of the
heathen prince.

The child was carried away to make the tour of the
house, preceded by a woman sprinkling salt and fennel
seeds upon the floor of each room and saying, "The
salt be in the eye of the person who doth not bless the
Prophet!"

"Blessed be Our Lord Mohammed!" repeated the assembled guests each time, shooting sidelong glances at the
big, blond unbeliever who stood by Ibn Masoud. When
Stephen decided it was time to slip away to his rooms to
study, no one tried to stop him.

For the next week the house was in a continual uproar
of feasting, musical parties, religious recitations and cere-
monies as old, said Ibn Masoud, as the tombs of the

heathen kings from which the building stones for Stephen's hall were taken. Wrapped in the mysteries of geometry, Stephen largely ignored the celebrations except when Aude popped a marzipan-stuffed date into his mouth or Geoffrey dropped by to grumble about Kamil's failure to give the baby a proper Christian baptism.

"I don't think you can expect that," Stephen said. "After all, he is a Moslem. And so is Madeline—Deena—now."

Geoffrey's big hands moved in an impatient gesture that showed all his frustration. "I don't care if Kamil goes to hell. Apparently he can't save my sister. But I'll have to do something about Raoul."

"Who?"

"Raoul, the baby. The heathens want to call him Rashid though." Geoffrey drifted off again, mumbling discontent. Stephen went back to pacing off the foundations of his hall.

The next interruption came from Kamil himself. He strode into the area of demolished walls and half-torn-down brickwork, flicking his robes away from dust and plaster and broken stones with a disgusted look.

"It will look more like a hall soon," Stephen promised.

"Yes, I hope so. We will discuss that later. Come with me."

"Why?" Stephen had been working out a tricky calculation in his head and trying to match his mental images to the reality of the space before him. He didn't want to leave.

"The *akika*." Kamil's hands twitched. "It's a very old ceremony. All males of the household must be present. Some thought it might be bad luck to have you and the other unbeliever present, but I have decided that it would be worse luck to exclude you from the sacrifice."

Stephen followed Kamil through halls, small courts, and long latticed galleries, wondering exactly what his role was to be in the ceremony Kamil had described as a sacrifice.

Kamil ignored him until they reached an open space that Stephen recognized as the central courtyard of the palace, though he had no idea how they had come to this sun-glazed place through the network of shifting wooden screens and lattices. "In there. Wait with your friend." Kamil pointed at the crowd and disappeared round another corner.

Dozens of robed and turbaned Saracens waited in patient stillness under the noonday sun that beat down on the unshaded space. Waves of heat rose off the stones, and the waiting silence grew thick. Stephen remembered the stillness of Ely on that frozen morning after the slaughter, ten years and half a world away. He shivered in spite of the heat. Then he caught sight of Geoffrey's fair head and Ibn Masoud's creased turban in a corner of the courtyard, and edged his way around to join them.

"What's going on?" he whispered to Ibn Masoud.

"Kamil has to—" Ibn Masoud stopped talking when Kamil himself stepped through a narrow door at the far end of the courtyard, arms bare to the elbows, his robe of white silk girdled tightly about him. He was followed by two slaves who manhandled a frightened and protesting goat into the center of the courtyard; a third slave handed Kamil his gleaming curved blade. Kamil glanced up at the sky, then, so swiftly Stephen almost missed the motion, drew the sharp blade across the animal's throat. As he did so, he chanted some words that Ibn Masoud translated in an undertone into Stephen's ear.

"O God, verily this is a ransom for my son; its blood for his blood, and its flesh for his flesh, and its bone for his bone, and its skin for his skin, and its hair for his hair."

On the conclusion of the prayer, the slaves dragged the goat's body out of sight. Kamil's robe was covered from waist to hem with splotches of blood, and a warm sweet smell rose from the blood that pooled in the worn stones of the courtyard.

"Disgusting," said Geoffrey as the crowd dispersed. "Pagan rites. Blood sacrifices."

"Yes," Stephen said slowly, falling into step beside his friend. "But he only wants to protect his son." Stephen was struggling with his own sense of revulsion, the sickly sweet smell of drying blood, and unbidden memories of that cold day in Ely. He remembered the dead boy whose eyes he'd closed; he had been someone's beloved son. "If you had a child, wouldn't you want to offer God anything you could to keep it safe?" *If you had a child . . .* Stephen shook his head to chase away the mocking thought and concentrated instead on an image of the great hall he meant to raise for Kamil.

"I can't let Raoul grow up like this."

"Rashid," Stephen corrected, "and I don't see that you

have any choice. He is Kamil's son, not yours." Sometimes Stephen wondered about Geoffrey's grasp on reality. There was that business with the *poulani* witch, his sudden bursts of religious enthusiasm, the fanatical search for his sister. But then, Geoffrey had found his sister.

But soon Stephen put Geoffrey and his intense enthusiasms out of his mind and went back to the more interesting business of planning his orders for the masons when they reported for work the following day.

For the next week his time was entirely taken up with the joyous task of laying out foundations and planning the walls. Now that he didn't have to lie and delay the work, it couldn't move fast enough for him. In this hot, dry air, the mortar set almost before it was laid; there was no need to wait for the courses to settle. Foundations were dug and filled in with rubble, the first courses of the walls were slapped in place, and the supporting buttresses rose along the outer lines. Kamil came daily to inspect the progress of the hall, and daily Stephen begged for more men to raise it even faster.

"You could finish your seven-times-seven days of feasting for your son in your own fine hall," he promised rashly.

Kamil's dark eyes gleamed with amusement. "Could I really? Will you wager your own head on that, Christian builder?"

"I thought my head was already at your disposal."

"Oh, no. Cairo would never forgive me if I executed the magician who is making my palace the showplace of the city. Already my guests come to see my son, but linger to admire your rising white walls. Already I have had enquiries as to when you will be free to do works of comparable magnificence for them. So do not promise completion dates you cannot meet, Stephen the Frank. I do not like to be disappointed."

Stephen flushed. "Well, by next year, when you celebrate the birth of your *second* son, the hall will surely be finished!"

And Kamil was inordinately pleased with the way Stephen had worded his promise, and the extra men and materials were forthcoming. Stephen began, against his will, to feel some liking and respect for this imperious Egyptian nobleman who had yanked him out of his own world, set him to building under the edge of a curved Saracen sword, and, accidentally, brought him to the learning he craved above all else.

"Prince Kamil is not bad for a Saracen," he grudgingly admitted to Ibn Masoud during one of their late-night planning sessions. "And I have his promise that I'll be free to work for other people in Cairo after the hall is finished. There are just two restrictions."

"Which are?"

"He wants a sixth part of the earnings."

"Reasonable. After all, he could as easily have decided you were his slave, and no one would have argued the point. I'll see if I can work him down to a tenth part, though. That is what is usual for a patron, and Kamil knows it. He thought you would be too ignorant to argue. And the other restriction?"

Stephen looked away. "Concerns no one but me. It's a rather technical matter of the design specifications."

Not so very technical, but not something Stephen wished to discuss. Kamil had gently suggested that he would be most unhappy if any of the buildings Stephen raised for future Cairene clients rivaled his own hall in daring, innovation, or magnificence. "I could, of course, ensure the uniqueness of my hall by having you buried outside it as soon as you finished," he pointed out.

Stephen grinned at him. "An architect who feared such an outcome might build a hall that would be guaranteed to fall down five years after it was raised, to provide him with a tomb of fitting magnificence."

"Could you really do such a thing?"

"Yes." Stephen could feel when a structure had been pushed to its limit, when the music of the stones changed to the high discordance of imminent failure. It would be easy to build something that felt as though it were teetering on the edge of disaster; to build into the arches that extra degree of stress that would eventually bring them crashing down again. An interesting technical problem.

"Enough! Enough!" Kamil held up his hand in mock surrender. "I don't like your face when you are thinking like that."

"Why?" Stephen was genuinely surprised; he hadn't thought Kamil a man to be troubled by fancies. "What do I look like?"

"Like a devil from the ancient tombs, built into the

stone and waiting to tear free." Kamil laughed uneasily, and Stephen saw that there was a gleam of sweat on his temples. The man had actually upset himself with his own imaginings. "There is a power in you that is not of this world, master builder. I think you draw it out of the stones and earth. But I am rich in the power of my world, gold and servants and the ear of the Sultan. So let us cry truce. You will not make my palace fall down, and I will not bury you."

They'd ended there, with superficial protestations of friendliness. But Stephen did not like to think of himself as somebody whose face could frighten grown men.

After that talk, though, Kamil's attitude changed subtly. He still visited the works regularly, but when he asked Stephen about the progress of the building, he spoke as one man to another, not as a master overseeing a possibly careless servant. The questions he asked were intelligent ones, and Stephen couldn't hold a grudge against any man who really wanted to understand how the keystones of an arch could hold all the other stones in place. Gradually he began to think of Kamil as a friend. Stephen had found his niche in the dusty chaos of the half-built hall. He belonged here just as Aude belonged with old Bi Hassan and her mysterious potions. Since the day of Rashid's birth they had both been treated as trusted servants. They were even given three rooms where they could live together. In many ways Stephen felt more free here than he had in his novitiate at Ely, or in his apprenticeship in Master Brito's stoneyard.

He seldom thought of England now. But occasionally, on a long, hot afternoon, he did remember the crash of the sea beating at Dunwich harbor, or the endless, pale sky of the flat fenlands. At such times he told himself that he was not really homesick; he remembered those scenes of his youth as one thinks of things so long past that even regret has faded.

In any case, Stephen could never go back to the fettered life of a monk. England was best forgotten; and he was happy enough under the Egyptian sun, with his great work and his wife beside him at night.

Geoffrey was not so content. For Deena's sake, Kamil tried to befriend him too, inviting him to join hunting and hawking parties and the other amusements of the nobility of Cairo. But Geoffrey could master no more than two or three words of the Saracen speech, and he couldn't relax in the company of men he'd been raised to regard as the enemies of Christendom. Kamil gradually gave up his half-hearted attempts at friendship. Unfortunately, he did not stop trying quite soon enough.

Stephen's first inkling of trouble came when Kamil strode into his rooms unannounced. His slender hands were trembling and his large, dark eyes, with their thick, silky lashes, expressed poorly disguised anger. "Get him out of here!" he commanded.

Ibn Masoud had been seated beside Stephen while they went over a mathematical problem on the wax tablets where he could feel the lines with his fingertips. He sighed and began to stand on creaky joints.

"Not you," Kamil snapped, "you can stay, for all I care. It's that . . ." He spat out a few Saracen words unfamiliar to Stephen. Apparently his Frankish vocabulary was not sufficient for the occasion. "That *Frank*," he finally said. "Not you, Stephen. My brother-in-law." His lips curled with distaste on the words, and he tugged at the short strands of the beard that he had begun to grow back after Deena's child was born.

"I'm sure Geoffrey would like nothing better than to return home," Stephen said slowly. "Do you mean that he is free to go?"

"He has always been free to go," said Kamil. "At least, since Deena made me swear friendship and brotherhood with him. Why should I want to keep him? He insulted me in Jerusalem, and now he has insulted me in my own home. Stephen, he must leave, or I will not be responsible for the consequences!"

What could Geoffrey have done? More woman trouble? Surely Kamil wouldn't be so upset if he found out that Geoffrey had seduced Mariamu or some other girl in his household. Or would he? Stephen felt as though he were wandering blindly through a maze of reeds and alder and buckthorn. He might have found work in Cairo, and a few friends, but he did not really understand these people. The world of the Saracens was as strange to him as the fenlands had been that first day when he'd got lost.

"What exactly has Geoffrey done?"

Kamil jumped to his feet and strode up and down the

room, sandals clicking against the polished mosaics in the tile floor, silk robes swishing about his legs with each angry turn. "I told you. He insulted me in my own house. He complained that the hunting here wasn't as good as in France, and I told him, as I have done many times before, the he is free to return to France at any time. He always said he wanted to stay and see a little more of his nephew, and how could I argue with that?

"Well. This time he agreed that it was time for him to go home. But do you know what he wanted to do? He wanted to take Rashid with him! He said..." Kamil's fists flexed and he had to breathe deeply for a moment before he could go on. "He said Rashid was a likely lad and deserved a good education. And he called him Raoul. Then he offered, as a favor to me, to take Rashid home to France so that he could be brought up as a good Christian knight. Can you imagine such a thing? The worst disaster that could befall me would be to have my son captured by the Franks, to be brought up with no knowledge of his religion and his noble ancestors. And this foolish Frank presses such a disaster upon me as a favor!"

Stephen understood now, and he wanted to laugh so badly that his stomach muscles ached from the effort of holding it in. They were so alike, Geoffrey and Kamil. Geoffrey so certain of the superiority of the Franks that he didn't even realize he was insulting his host; Kamil so sure of the rightness of Saracen ways that he expected Stephen to share his sense of insult.

It didn't seem like a very good time to remind Kamil that he also was one of the despised Franks. "I'll speak to Geoffrey," he said gravely. "I'll see what I can do."

Kamil accepted this half promise and left after spitting out more Saracen curses. Stephen laid his head down on the wax tablets and laughed until tears ran from his eyes.

"You're getting hair in the wax," said Ibn Masoud. "And just what do you propose to do about your tactless friend?"

Stephen pushed himself upright and dragged his sleeve across his face. "I don't know. I'll think of something. Let's finish this theorem. I need to concentrate on something straightforward and logical."

Stephen spent three days trying to think of a way to persuade Geoffrey to go home, without much success. He was vaguely aware that he might have been better able to solve the problem if he hadn't simultaneously been think-ing about the construction of Kamil's hall. Stephen spent most of his time thinking about architectural dilemmas since they were far more amenable to rational solution than the matter of Geoffrey and Kamil and baby Rashid.

In the end, the problem was solved for him, and from a most unexpected source.

CHAPTER

19

◈

"A Frankish visitor to see me?" Stephen set down the wax tablet on which he'd been engraving an image of the hall's support rafters. "But we don't know any Franks in Cairo. Are you sure that's what the messenger said?"

"I can't be sure of anything after this many tongues have garbled the tale." Aude shrugged. The doorkeeper had sent a boy to the building works, who had passed on the message to Sarouf, who had, with possibly deliberate incompetence, sent word to Aude via a black eunuch. Aude, at least, had had the sense to look for Stephen beside the trickling fountain in Ibn Masoud's garden, where the two men sat on hot evenings and went over the day's work.

"There must be some mistake. Unless it's one of Kamil's brother's friends who have come about the summerhouse they want me to build next season," Stephen said. "Some of them have taken a fancy to wearing Frankish dress, don't ask me why." Stephen found the loose, flowing robes favored by the Saracens to be much more comfortable in this climate than a hot tunic and sticky drawers. "Whoever it is, he'll be getting impatient by now. Those young nobles don't like being kept waiting. I hope somebody had the sense to invite him into the inner courtyard and offer him a sorbet. My apologies, Ibn Masoud. Perhaps we can resume our talks later." With that Stephen stretched lazily and rose to his feet, an imposing figure draped in the flowing Saracen robes.

As work on the hall progressed, Kamil showed his pleasure by having new Saracen suits laid out in Stephen's rooms, each one more gorgeous than the last. When he learned that Stephen was embarrassed by the gaudy brocades and jeweled headgear favored by most wealthy Cairenes, Kamil chose simple but expensive garments with which to honor his builder. The yellow silk of Stephen's robe was so fine that the whole garment could be passed through a finger ring, and the girdle that held his pen and knife was embroidered with a pair of griffins worked in fine gold-leaf. Stephen wore his blond hair loose to his shoulders instead of bound in a Moslem-style turban, and remained obstinately clean-shaven like a Frank. Except for that, he was dressed in every detail like a young Cairene aristocrat.

His visitor was indeed waiting in the inner courtyard, seated on the broad rim of the low wall surrounding the fountain. At first Stephen saw only a slender back, dark curly hair under a velvet cap, and a hand as white as his own waving away the servants. Something in the way the visitor tilted his head was familiar to Stephen, and as he stepped into the band of sunlight between the inner hall and the tree-shaded fountain it came to him.

"Marco! Marco Sanudo! What brings you here? Did the House of Sanudo pass on our message? It's all right now, but I'm glad to see you anyway."

Marco's head snapped round and his eyes showed bewilderment. Dazed from the sun and bored with waiting, the last thing he had expected was to be enthusiastically embraced by a tall Saracen dressed like a prince.

Stephen pounded Marco's slim back until the trader suffered a coughing fit.

"By Our Lady, Stephen, you came near startling me into a fit!" Marco complained when he'd caught his breath. "One minute I'm sitting here peacefully waiting for Geoffrey, the next I'm being pounded on the back by a giant in Saracen robes! At first I didn't know it was you; you're lucky I didn't try to defend myself."

"Geoffrey? Not me?" Stephen drew back slightly, a puzzled frown creased his sunburnt forehead.

Marco shrugged and spread out his hands, palms up. "Of course I was going to ask after you and Aude as soon as I'd delivered my message to Geoffrey. But that news is urgent, and it's taken me the devil's own time to find you. The man I sent to Jerusalem reported that the two of you had taken service with some Cairene named Kamil. He knew no more than that." Marco drew one sleeve across his sweating forehead. "Do you have any idea, Stephen, how many men in Cairo are named Kamil? Starting with the Sultan and working down."

"You wouldn't have had to work very far down to come to this Kamil," Stephen pointed out. "He's very nearly as important in Cairo as the Sultan himself, and considerably richer."

"Yes, so I heard. But that wasn't how I found you, as it turned out. All Cairo is talking of the Frankish builder who is creating a master work for this particular Kamil."

Stephen basked in the praise. "So they should. But wait. If you came because of that message we sent to the House of Sanudo, the people there should have known exactly where to find us."

"Message? They said nothing of any message from you." Marco looked puzzled.

Stephen smashed one fist into the palm of his other hand. "May that peddler be cursed to the tenth generation! I knew it, I knew he'd take our money and run off! Well, no harm done, I suppose. We didn't need any help anyway as it turned out."

"Tell me about it later," Marco advised. "It sounds like a complicated story. But with a happy ending, I trust? You seem to have done well enough for yourself. And Aude?"

"She's well, too." Though Deena was pregnant again, Aude was still as slender as a girl, and Stephen knew no way to chase the shadowed worry from her eyes. Aude blamed herself for her barrenness. Stephen found it easier to think of building. There, at least, he was in control.

"Tell me, Marco," he said before Marco could inquire further after Aude, "what brings you to Cairo, if it was not a message from us?"

"It's about Geoffrey. His father's sick. The Tour Martels'

chaplain sent a letter by the pilgrim galley that departed after ours, and eventually it came to the House of Sanudo. I was worried about you anyway. So..." Marco looked embarrassed. "I broke the seals. Geoffrey's father is ill and wants his son to come home at once, that's all I read, but it was enough. I decided it was time to find the three of you."

"And you came all the way to Cairo to deliver the news personally? Marco, we don't deserve a friend like you!"

Marco stared past Stephen's feet as if he were trying to trace the paving cracks with his eyes. "Well, actually the House of Sanudo had a ship going to Alexandria, and I thought it might be a good idea to see what the markets here were like. Our House in Cairo is as bad as the one in Acre: nobody responsible is looking after it. We hardly get any goods from Cairo except stinking thick camel's-hair rugs that I can't even sell to the peasants back home. Anyway," he finished, cheering up visibly, "I just happened to notice some fine copper work in the bazaar, and spices here cost half what they do in Acre, not to mention the linen I bought in Damietta, so it should be quite a profitable trip. And I'm always glad to do a favor to a fellow Christian, of course. Also, I thought it would be pleasant to see you... and Aude... again."

"Of course. We'd better get Geoffrey."

Geoffrey puzzled through the letter from his father's chaplain so slowly that Stephen longed to snatch it away from him and read it aloud. Geoffrey had mentioned several times, with pride, that all seven of the boys had been taught to read, a refinement of learning with which few of the knightly class bothered. He hadn't said that he hated reading and avoided it like the plague.

Finally he put down the letter with a deep sigh.

"Bad news?"

"Not good. There's been another quarrel with the abbot of Chastelvert." Geoffrey launched into a long story involving his father's illness, the abbot's visit, an old quarrel over disputed vineyards, and a string of violent incidents on both sides. Some of Geoffrey's brothers were being accused, most unjustly Geoffrey assured them, of having burned down the monastery's stables. Geoffrey's father blamed the abbot's curse for the sudden laming of his best destrier. There had been a vineyard harvested by the wrong side, a field of corn trampled by somebody's hunting party, a fight in the weekly market, a millstone stolen....

Stephen lost track of the rights and wrongs of the matter long before Geoffrey was finished.

"So everybody in the family has been excommunicated, except me, because I wasn't there. And the abbot has put the town under interdict whenever my father and brothers enter. So they can't oversee the market or collect the tolls from the mill, and the Givrault brothers are harassing their peasants. They need me to come home and take care of the property until Father can collect enough money to bribe somebody in Rome to lift the interdict." Geoffrey looked quite happy at the prospect. He'd had quite enough of being a prisoner-guest in Kamil's household. His reunion with Madeline had been more sour than sweet, his nephew was being raised as an infidel, and he felt useless. "How soon can I get a ship for France, Marco?"

"Are you going to leave Deena here, then?" asked Stephen.

Geoffrey shrugged. "Do you think she'd come with me? There's no place for me here, Stephen, and no place for Deena and Rashid in France."

When Geoffrey went off to pack his things, Stephen felt an odd sense of disappointment. To be sure, he'd just been puzzling over how to get Geoffrey out of Cairo before he and Kamil came to blows, but this was too sudden and too easy. Why had Geoffrey complained so much about Rashid's upbringing, why had he upset Kamil and Deena and Stephen so often, if the child really meant so little to him that he could leave on a day's notice?

"He can't wait to leave us," Stephen muttered, half resentfully. But he was not really surprised. Geoffrey had always been a man of mercurial enthusiasms; since his quest for his sister had ended, he'd been bored and unhappy. Taking charge of the family lands in France was his new obsession, and the old ones were forgotten by the wayside.

"Well, I suppose he is eager to get back to the work he was trained for just as you would be," Marco pointed out.

Stephen snorted. "Work! Riding through villages in armor, terrifying peasants—"

"And fighting other men in armor for the right to keep what's yours. That's work."

"I wish you weren't so fair-minded."

"Never mind Geoffrey. Why don't we go talk to Aude? I haven't seen her for a long time."

"You haven't seen me for a long time either." Geoffrey wanted to go home to France, Marco was acting as though Aude were the main attraction in Cairo; Stephen felt unwanted. "Anyway, Aude stays in the women's quarters during the day. We can't go up there." Marco looked disappointed. "What's the matter? Isn't my company good enough for you? Never mind, you'll see Aude tonight. I ought," Stephen said, "to be jealous of a man who's so eager to visit my wife."

"No, you shouldn't," said Marco, so quickly that Stephen feared for a moment he'd taken the heavy-handed teasing seriously. He was relieved when Geoffrey came back and began telling Marco the long tale of his reunion with Madeline. That story began in the cool loggia of Kamil's palace and ended, some hours later, in a remarkably sleazy wine shop in the Frankish quarter. The three of them staggered back to dine with Aude and Ibn Masoud in the old tutor's private garden. Marco, who in particular was drunk, seized Aude's hand and kissed it, lavishing so many effusive compliments upon her that Stephen said he would have been jealous of anybody else who behaved so.

"But not of me?" Marco asked.

"Naturally not," said Stephen calmly. "It would be another matter if anybody but my best friend were being so extravagant with my wife."

"I thought I was your best friend!" protested Geoffrey. He seized Aude round the waist and gave her a wine-flavored kiss. She beat him off with the soft part of her hands, laughing. Geoffrey pointed out to Stephen that he couldn't take offense now without denying their friendship.

"Have some quail stuffed with sesame paste," said Ibn Masoud, "and leave the drinking to a man too old to get himself into trouble with the ladies."

Aude stooped and kissed him on the brow. "Ah, you are more dangerous than any of these green lads, master!"

Ibn Masoud laughed and insisted that Aude sit on his knee to feed him bits of the spiced quails and pilaf.

* * *

The next day Geoffrey heard of a ship leaving from Damietta. Marco left with him, insisting that Geoffrey would get into six different kinds of trouble if allowed to travel through Moslem lands alone.

"But you've just arrived!" Aude protested.

Marco bowed and brushed his lips lightly over the back of her hand. "And yet I think I have already stayed too long. I've been burning up since I arrived; if the fever is not to consume me utterly, I'd best depart."

"You're sick! And didn't tell me?"

"Nothing serious." Marco fended off Aude's anxious queries with a crooked grin.

"The air here *is* unhealthy," Aude conceded. "But when you're feeling better will you come back to visit us again?"

"If I may . . ." He glanced at Stephen.

"Of course. Anytime." Something in this protracted leave-taking was making Stephen uncomfortable. Well, he didn't like partings and it was time he got back to his work.

In the first days after Marco and Geoffrey's departure Stephen felt a sense of loss. He threw himself into his work with redoubled energy and drove away his loneliness.

It did not occur to him to wonder if Aude were lonely; after all, she had friends in the women's quarters. He did notice, though, that she spent more and more time with Ibn Masoud. They both did. Ibn Masoud's philosophy was not so very different from the Christian teachings that Stephen had heard as a boy; but in the old man's calm acceptance of life and fate, Stephen learned a wisdom that he had been unable to take in from the monks of Ely.

By winter Stephen was too busy to think of anything but the completion of Kamil's hall. By spring the new hall was ready to be roofed over and decorated, and Stephen had commissions to draw up new buildings for two of Kamil's wealthy friends. With Ibn Masoud's advice, he achieved an elegant synthesis of Western architectural practices and Moslem taste that pleased both friends and led to yet more commissions.

At Stephen's request, Ibn Masoud handled the business matters that accompanied these commissions. "You do not know how to bargain," the old tutor told him, and when

Stephen saw the piles of gold pieces Ibn Masoud had collected, he agreed. All that money made him a little nervous. He and Aude had a roof over their heads, clothes to wear, and plenty to eat, and Stephen did not know what to do with the surplus.

"Let Marco keep it for us," Aude said when he confided his dilemma to her. And on Marco's next trading voyage to Alexandria, Stephen met him at the House of Sanudo and suggested just that. He was surprised by Marco's enthusiastic response.

"You want our trading company to hold your gold? Stephen, you wonderful man, that's just what we need to make the House of Sanudo a power in the Mediterranean again. I have ideas for expanding the business, but my uncle and father always say we must go slowly, not expand beyond the power of our purse strings. With your gold I can buy some extra bales of that Cairene weave, and, hmm, cinnamon prices are looking good, and cloves from Unguja are cheap enough here..." Marco hummed to himself for a few minutes while Stephen grew nervous. Then Marco broke off to say, "I can promise you a return of a third, or a fourth part anyway, on any money you care to invest with us."

"But that's usury! No one can lend money at interest. It wouldn't be right."

Marco sighed. "Stephen, sometimes you talk like a monk. What's the matter? You've gone dead white. Here, sit down and let me explain it to you. This is not usury. It's investment. A different thing altogether."

Marco patiently explained why taking Stephen's money and turning it into more money was not the same thing as being a Jewish moneylender, but Stephen couldn't follow the explanation. "Just keep it," he said finally, shoving the little sacks of gold coins into Marco's hands. "Keep it safe for me. Do what you want with it, but don't tell me about it. There'll probably be more by next season," he added. "I'm doing a merchant khan and a set of covered shops for the Syrians, and Ibn Masoud says they spend money like sand."

"You're lucky I'm honest," said Marco cheerfully. "Sure you don't want to know how I'm going to use the money?"

"Just let me how much I should spend back on masses

to keep us out of purgatory. There has to be something sinful about making money for having money."

On this visit to Cairo, Marco didn't see Aude, pleading pressing business and the need to oversee his rascally agents in the port city. Stephen did not insist that he visit. He felt vaguely guilty about that. But somehow it was easier being with Marco in Alexandria, where they were just two men alone in the bustling port city, than in Kamil's palace where Marco put on his fine manners and acted the gentleman for Aude's benefit.

Stephen went back to Cairo and built the Syrians a set of chambers around an open court, the lower floors open for shops, with fountains in each corner and a triple arch around the pool in the center of the courtyard. Kamil grumbled that Stephen hadn't built *him* anything as showy as the unroofed arched fountain.

"I hadn't thought of it then. At home we use arches to hold up the walls, and we want the walls to keep the cold air out. I'll probably have more ideas like this as I get used to building in your climate."

"Well, don't think of too many new things. My cousin's wife wants you to design a new palace for them, with a walled garden all around it. I do not," said Kamil emphatically, "wish to hear Aziza boasting about how her palace is finer than mine!"

"I can always tear down and rebuild the rest of your palace," Stephen suggested, and dodged the mock blow Kamil aimed at him.

The construction of Aziza's palace and walled garden occupied Stephen for three happy years, interrupted occasionally by other smaller commissions. Among them were several bits of work on Kamil's palace—at times it seemed that Kamil was taking quite literally Stephen's offer to tear down the building and raise it anew. But there were other, flattering requests for madrassahs and merchant khans, public baths and drinking fountains. He would not have accepted a commission to design a mosque, nor was he offered one. But in all other things, his Christian origins were no hindrance. He was well known in Cairo as the Frankish builder who moved in the finest Saracen society. Artists and philosophers dined at Ibn Masoud's table, and Stephen listened to their talk and occasionally contributed his own opinions. Generals and nobles visited Kamil's palace, and as Stephen listened to their conversations, he began to understand something of how a nation or a war develops. Gradually, Stephen became like the men he mingled with: subtle, cultivated, fluent in both Western and Eastern artistic idioms, both Christian and Moslem ways of thought.

The poor fisherboy of Dunwich was left far behind now, and so was the little novice of Ely. When Stephen thought of those days, he congratulated himself on how far and how fast he had risen. If Brother Daniel's cold voice sometimes whispered that he was worthless, he had his halls and khans and palaces to contradict that demonic voice.

Kamil was happy and generous in those years, as Deena continued to produce healthy children and his palace grew bit by bit into a shining structure of bricks and marble fit to rival the old palace of the Fatimid sultans. Stephen took other commissions as he wished. When Aude wanted more privacy, Kamil suggested that they might be happier in their own house, and Stephen rented a small house on the street of the Frankish merchants.

When Stephen was invited to design the Sultan's new stables, Kamil did not complain, though he did not look entirely pleased with a commission that would occupy his friend's time for a year or more. Ibn Masoud was frankly jubilant.

"Your fortune is made now," he told Stephen. "It's time you moved into a big house. You need to entertain in a manner befitting your station in Cairo."

"I suppose the Sultan pays well," Stephen said doubtfully. "But stables?"

"The Sultan's horses are better housed than Frankish kings."

And when Stephen saw the materials he was given to work with, polished marble from Italy in glorious shades of red and yellow, greenstone from the mountains of the Arabian desert, and alabaster from Asyut, he had to admit Ibn Masoud was right. By the time Stephen had finished the new stables, with their ingenious device that allowed fresh water to run continually through the buildings in marble troughs, with their latticework windows to admit fresh air, and with their carved stall doors all facing toward Mecca, he felt quite proud of the work.

"I wouldn't know about kings," said Aude when he took

her on a tour of the completed stables, "but it's better than the bishop of Ely's guesthouse." She looked at Aude. "D'you ever wish those old monks could see you now?"

"Never," said Stephen, more harshly than he'd intended. Aude changed the subject at once, wandering over to watch the mosaic workers setting out a pattern of porphyry and greenstone and mother-of-pearl inside a wooden form on the floor. "Looks pretty," she said, "but wouldn't it be better on the wall than on the floor?"

Stephen spent a happy fifteen minutes explaining the process of mosaic making to her. "It's just a decorative technique, of course," Stephen said at the end of his explanation. "Not true building. But the designs are rather pretty." It would be interesting to try something like that to decorate the columns of a tall church in the French style, but of course Stephen wasn't likely to be commissioned to build a church in Cairo.

That evening, Stephen felt his conscience plaguing him. It wasn't that he missed the fenland. Ely, to him, was a memory best wiped out. If he missed anything, it was the salt spray and the pebbled beach at Dunwich, the narrow streets of the town where he'd first learned the mason's craft, and the fellowship of Hugh and the other journeymen over the weak, bitter ale at the brewing house. . . .

He shook his head to drive away those thoughts. There was no point in thinking of England; he couldn't risk going back there. He had sent news of his pilgrimage to Jerusalem to Lady Margery, that she might know her sins were forgiven by proxy; but he had intentionally given the impression that he and Aude were still in Jerusalem. It was better to lose contact with every part of his past, even with Joscelin.

But they could go somewhere else. Perhaps Aude was not happy here. She didn't have the work that absorbed him, and she was restricted to the indoor life of an upper-class Cairo lady. Now that they lived in their own house, she got some amusement from shopping in the bazaars, and she still visited Deena and Aisha almost daily to play with the children. But was that enough for her? "Do you want to go back, Aude?"

She shook her head. "No." But there was a tinge of sadness in her voice. Stephen realized guiltily that he hadn't paid much attention to her since the Sultan commanded his work on the stables.

"But something is wrong. And what's that foul stuff you're drinking?" He took the cup from her hand and sniffed its contents. "Smells like horse dung and rotted roots."

"Something Bi Hassan mixed up. She wouldn't say what was in it."

"Do you like it?"

"No. It makes me sick. But she said it helped Deena conceive and nothing I know of has helped. . . ."

"Oh." Stephen raised the cup and casually flung it over his shoulder, so quickly that Aude hadn't time to stop him. She gave a cry of protest as the cup smashed against the tile floor, creating a sparkling mosaic of blue and silver shards mixed with the muddy pool of Bi Hassan's potion. "Well, I'm not having you dosing yourself with mysterious drinks that make you feel sick. If we're to have children, they'll come in God's own good time."

"Deena has three sons now," Aude said. Her face was turned away from him and her voice was muffled, as if she were pressing one hand over her mouth.

"Wonderful. How nice for Kamil. He cares about that. I don't," Stephen lied, going down on his knees and pulling Aude's hands away from her face. Her tears streaked the shimmering pearl-gray silk of the divan. Of course he'd envied Kamil his good fortune, and had looked forward to the day when he would have children. What man wouldn't? But it was also true that he believed in leaving such matters to nature, and that he had other things to leave after him. "Aude, Aude, I want *you.* I'm not a damned Saracen, to use a wife like a brood-mare, to have a few spare wives hanging about for more efficient breeding. I'm a builder. The palaces and khans I raise here in Cairo are my children, they will live after me. They are all the immortality I need. Do you understand?"

Aude nodded and tried to smile. Stephen would have stayed longer with her, but just then a client arrived, and Stephen had to leave with the promise to return later.

After he had gone, Aude stared at the swinging curtain that separated her private rooms from the hall leading to the public rooms at the front of the house. "The buildings are your children," she whispered. "But where are mine?"

And she cried again, very quietly, so that Stephen would not hear, and washed her face with cool water afterward so that he shouldn't see her red, swollen eyes when he came to bed.

In the next few months Stephen found his thoughts returning to the idea of going home. The *khamsin* blew through Cairo like a blast from a freshly opened oven door; they slept under dampened linen cloth by day and moved languidly through the heavy nights. Stephen kept thinking of cool, rainwashed skies and sandy dunes sprinkled with the fine spring flowers. If they went home—not to England, England was closed to him—but to France or Italy, some place with cooler skies and a gentler climate, would Aude be happier? Would she be able to conceive the child she longed for?

Other matters conspired to make Cairo less hospitable than it had once been. The Frankish prince of Antioch and the Knights Templars were making daring raids into Saracen territory. The Sultan sent aid to his fellow infidels, which was financed by extra levies on the citizens and merchants of Cairo. The Cairenes blamed all the Franks impartially for this new tax. And the foreigners living in the Frankish quarter of Cairo came to fear outbreaks of hostility in the streets. After Aude was insulted in the bazaar one day, Stephen bought a large slave from the southern deserts whose only duty was to walk behind Aude and carry her basket whenever she went out.

"It's not important," Aude told him. "Just little boys being silly."

"Big boys are getting silly, too. The Sicilian Armandi's khan was broken into yesterday. Some damn holy man is wandering around the city, preaching that they ought to cleanse Cairo of the Christians."

"Sultan Kamil won't allow that," said Aude confidently. "He needs the merchants and the ships coming to Alexandria. And he certainly won't want anyone to harm the master builder who constructed his new stables."

Stephen sighed and shook his head. "And when you go out," he asked, "do you wear a sign around your neck saying, don't hurt me, I'm the wife of Sultan Kamil's stable-builder? And it's not just the street mob, Aude. Sharif Abdallah told me yesterday not to bother bringing him the plans for the new summer house, he has decided to have it done by a local man. And he didn't pay me for the two months I spent drawing plans, either. Well, I didn't really want to do it anyway. It would have been just like every other house I've done in Cairo. These people don't have any sense of design. All they want is a nest of boxes; they think the way to make something beautiful is to stick a mosaic of precious stones all over the wall."

"Well, the mosaics are pretty."

"Yes, but they've got nothing to do with real building."

"Stephen," said Aude suddenly, "are you sure you don't want to go back?"

Stephen sighed. "It doesn't matter. We can't go back to England, can we?"

"Not to Ely, but there are other places."

"Not so many that would take on a man of twenty-five who never achieved his mason's mark."

"Oh. That's important, is it?"

"I'm too old to go back to being journeyman in somebody else's stoneyard," Stephen said. "And too used to being rich, and having my own way."

"You have always," said Aude, "expected to have your own way."

"Yes, but I get my own way here." Stephen rolled over on the soft cushions, his head hanging upside down off the edge of the divan. He reached up to catch Aude's hand. "Let's face it, love. We've come too far along this road to go back. Besides, there's Ibn Masoud. I promised him five years in partnership so he could make the money for his independence."

"The five years'll be up next hot season," said Aude thoughtfully. But she did not pursue the subject, and for that Stephen was grateful. As it was, he dreamed all night of building spires that would reach to the sky, graceful, curved vaults supporting towers of stone as light as the lace necklaces sold at St. Audrey's fair. He woke more discontented than ever with the plain designs demanded by his Cairo clients. Everything here was closed, built for privacy and shelter from the unrelenting sun. Stephen longed to feel cool wind against his face and the soft, thick grass of an English hill under his feet.

And the *khamsin* was still blowing. That hot season was hard even for those used to Cairo. There was sickness in the city; the blind holy man who'd been preaching against the Franks blamed them for bringing the fever, and Stephen forbade Aude to go out even with the escort of the slave he'd bought for her. For three hot, lonely weeks she obeyed him, and when she broke the prohibition it was for a crisis so grave that Stephen forgot to be angry with her.

"It was Rashid," she wept in his arms that night when at last he found her, after hours of calling on all their acquaintances in the Frankish quarter. Finally Stephen had located a fat, gossipy woman who told him that a slave in the red and gold silks of Kamil's household had come to their door around noon, and that Aude had taken off like a startled bird minutes later. Kamil's house was alight with torches and there was intermittent wailing from the women's quarters. Someone remembered having seen Aude but Stephen waited more than an hour before she came down with a tear-streaked face and fell weeping into his arms.

"These little ones go so fast when they catch the fever. This morning he was playing with his toy horse, and by noon he was so sick that Deena was frightened and sent for me to see if I could help Bi Hassan. Oh, Stephen, he was hot, so hot, and nothing we could do helped. . . ."

Rashid had gone into convulsions and died around sunset. Kamil had acted at once, sending Deena and Aisha and the surviving children to his country house. Aude had just been packing for them and seeing them off when Stephen arrived. Now, after the effort of staying calm for Deena's sake, she could hold herself together no longer. Stephen rocked and comforted her and was frightened to realize how thin she'd grown during this long hot season. She was so fragile, what if she got sick too? Selfishly he wished Deena had never sent for her. "There, there, my love," he said over and over. "It's all right. Rashid is in heaven now."

"Do you think so?" Aude sniffled. "I mean, he was a heathen."

"I know it," Stephen said firmly, putting out of his mind the Church's perfectly explicit teaching on the subject. Even the children of Christian parents, if they died upbaptized, could not enter into heaven. The priests would have laughed at the thought of letting in a Saracen baby. But, Stephen thought, the priests could not know everything.

Ibn Masoud came back to the house in the city with them, as he often did for a short visit. "Yes, Rashid is in Paradise now," he promised Aude. "Your holy men seem to be confused on this subject, but the Prophet has told us quite clearly how it is with the little innocent ones who die. These are the words of the Prophet!"

He sat back cross-legged on his cushion, took a sip of wine to clear his throat, and recited from memory the verses whose poetry survived even his impromptu translation into the clumsy Frankish tongue. When Ibn Masoud finished his recitation, Aude was weeping, but Stephen could tell that she felt comforted.

He himself felt better only in the morning, when Aude still showed no symptoms of the fever. It was time, he thought guiltily, to send her out of the city. He should have done it earlier, but that he dreaded parting from her. And now when he broached the subject, she refused to discuss it.

Stephen talked with Ibn Masoud about ways of persuading Aude to leave the city, but the old man was rambling that morning about long-ago parties with wine and dancing girls, and Stephen soon gave up. Ibn Masoud was flushed with the heat and swaying slightly; Stephen persuaded him to rest in the room they set aside for his visits, with a jug of iced rose-water to drink.

As soon as Stephen left him alone, Ibn Masoud called one of the house servants to take away this damned water and bring him wine.

"Wine is forbidden."

"Not to Franks."

The boy shifted uneasily from one foot to the other. Ibn Masoud smiled in the general direction of the sound. "And I am old and sick, my child, and the Prophet makes dispensations for an old blind man."

He was so thirsty that he finished the first jug of wine before the boy had gone away again, and called for more. Stephen was out, consulting with another client who'd suddenly developed a conscience about dealing with Christians; Aude was lying down after a sleepless night of grieving for little Rashid. There was no one else in the household to overrule his master's honored guest, and it was evening before Stephen returned with a fresh resolve to see that Aude left the city before the next day was over.

She met him at the courtyard gate, with a stricken expression that he attributed to Rashid's death.

"You've got to leave," he said without preamble. "Deena's gone, you can't help her now, and there are more cases of fever than yesterday."

"There's one here," she said, and led him to the back room.

Ibn Masoud's old, tough body held on to life for three long days, and during that time neither Aude nor Stephen left his side. By the third day the fever had passed through Cairo like a foul wind, taking mostly the very old and the very young. Shopkeepers raised their shutters again and nobles, looking slightly shamefaced, spoke of bringing their families back from the country by the end of the week.

At dawn on that third day, Ibn Masoud asked Stephen and Aude to send for witnesses of the Moslem faith to record his last wishes.

"There's no need," Stephen protested.

"It is not that I do not trust you, my son. But a Christian may not testify before the *qadi*, and I wish to be sure that my property is disposed of as I see fit."

"I didn't mean that. I mean you're getting better. You're going to be all right." Stephen turned to Aude. "Isn't he, Aude? Isn't he?"

She was weeping openly but silently, and tears ran down her face and darkened the pale silk of her robe. Ibn Masoud heard the stifled catch in her breathing, smiled and reached for her hand. "Don't be sad. You two have given a few interesting last years to a tired, bored old man. Now perhaps I can repay you."

The "repayment," when Ibn Masoud made it explicit before the witnesses, stunned Stephen. He wished, he said, to leave all he possessed to this Frank; and as he enumerated those possessions, Stephen and Aude gasped in surprise. A house in Alexandria, another in the country; so much gold on deposit with the merchant Hamed of Damietta, and three shares in a horse-breeding farm south of Cairo.

When the list was drawn up in the curlicued Saracen script, the witnesses departed, leaving their names and addresses with Stephen so that he might find them. Stephen stared at Ibn Masoud's shriveled face, and he opened and closed his mouth several times while he searched for words.

"Stop doing that," said Ibn Masoud irritably. "You look like one of the fat golden carp in Kamil's courtyard pool."

"I suppose you're not blind either?"

"I told you once that I was neither deaf nor stupid. I can hear your lips closing and opening like a fish waiting for a piece of bread."

"You also told me," Stephen said softly, "that you were a poor old man who wanted to go into partnership with me so that you could save a little money for your retirement."

A flickering smile crossed Ibn Masoud's face. "I had to have some pretext for the partnership. You might not have believed the truth."

"Which was?"

"I never had a son."

When Stephen could see through his tears, he noticed that Ibn Masoud's lips were still moving. He bent over him to catch the faint words.

"You and your buildings are the children of my heart. With this legacy, you can build greatly . . . wherever you wish."

"I might not stay in Cairo." Stephen hated himself for saying anything to disturb his old friend's last minutes, but he thought that Ibn Masoud would have hated dishonesty more.

"I know you will not. You and Aude have given me . . . enough years of your lives . . . already. You should go home now."

Ibn Masoud lived for several more hours, but he did not speak again. Toward dawn his fluttering breath ceased entirely, and Stephen laid out the thin limbs grown even more emaciated by the fever.

As the morning light grew strong enough to distinguish a white thread from a black one, the muezzin's call to prayer came through the heavy hot air. "Awake, ye faithful . . . Prayer is better than sleep! Prayer is better than sleep! Allah is great. Allah is great!"

Stephen climbed the stairs to the flat roof of the house, where he found Aude standing against the wall, staring into the rising sun.

"He's gone."

"I know. I felt him go." Aude's voice was thick with

unshed tears, but she was making an effort to speak levelly. "He was so good to you, and I loved him for it. And I never told him so."

"It's all right," said Stephen. "I think he knew."

As he stood beside Aude, one arm around her, he squinted into the sunrise and wondered just how many masons could be hired for the price of a house in Alexandria.

PART IV

The
Master
Builder

◻

1226–1229

CHAPTER

20

◻

It had to be France, of course. The Île-de-France itself was the very cradle of French architectural style: soaring arches, thin pierced walls, and windows full of light that superseded the Norman style of heavy columns and massive towers. The only question was where Stephen should go in his bid for work as an independent builder. Should it be Normandy, where the Abbey Church of St.-Etienne boasted a new choir with the mass of the piers transformed into clusters of slender, springing shafts? Or the rising walls of the fortress-monastery of Mont-Saint-Michel, on its rocky promontory surrounded by the northern seas? Or should he try to get work at one of the new cathedrals that were springing up all over France? Rheims, Rouen, Beauvais, Bourges? Everywhere Stephen turned, he heard of new opportunities, new ideas, and the mad competition for the highest church spire, the lightest walls, the finest bar-tracery to turn windows into networks of stone lace. As he and Aude made their way north from Marseilles, they stopped at masons' lodges that were humming with news of all the vaulting successes and crashing failures of the new wave of building.

The problems that had seemed insuperable now faded away before Stephen, much as the heavy stone walls and piers of the Norman style had melted into the delicate springing shafts and tracery-filled windows of the French work. He didn't need to know the masons' handgrip, the secret passwords, or the esoteric lore of the lodge. As a successful architect just returned from Outremer, with money to dress himself and his wife in the style of a wealthy merchant, Stephen was beyond such questioning. He didn't have to prove his right to join the lodge; he was invited in with respectful bows, questioned about the building styles of Crusaders and Saracens by young men who were eager to finish their apprenticeship and set out on their own wanderyears. No one asked Stephen how old he was or where he had studied.

As for geometry, that art of which Master Adam of Lincoln had made such a mystery, Stephen now knew more about it than any of the men he'd so envied as a boy. He was not above dropping his hints about the mysteries of Saracen science and great learning that he had acquired in the East. These hints had their effect. In the mobile, quarrelsome, gossiping community of the masons, where men were forever changing jobs or simply tramping across country to see how somebody else had solved a common building problem, news traveled faster than men. By the time Stephen reached the northern parts of France where the great cathedrals were being raised, tales were already swirling about his name.

"The builder from Outremer? Young, arrogant, and brilliant," Aude summarized what she'd overheard when they dined at the bishop's palace in Rheims. True, they'd been placed very far from the high seats at the head of the room; true, the bishop had a reputation for inviting any interesting strangers who passed through town, to such an extent that his clerics grumbled about the low company they were forced to keep. But the bishop had sent down a dish of spiced peacock with almond milk from his own table "with compliments to our visiting master builder." After Stephen had enjoyed an hour's intense technical conversation with the brilliant Jean d'Orbais, master of the works on the choir that was even now being raised for the new cathedral, he turned his attention back to Aude who began to report the gossip she'd heard.

"Young and brilliant—is that what they're saying about me? Reasonable." Stephen smoothed the new doublet of blue velvet he'd bespoken from a Paris tailor and admired the rich sheen of the fabric.

"That's what those who know I'm your wife say to me. But they are being careful to mind their tongues."

"And what do the others say?"

"That no one knows where you made your fortune and that it's not quite natural to know so much mathematics as you do. One lady mentioned Gerbert."

"Who's he? Another master builder? I haven't met him. What's he building?"

Aude sighed. She and Stephen had both learned from their lives; but where he'd devoted all his time to architecture, she had learned as much as she could about everything. First from Helene and her noble visitors in the bishop's palace, then from Christian pilgrims and Saracen princes, she had discovered the astonishing variety of the world. Like a magpie furnishing its nest with colorful scraps, she had taken whatever learning she could get, from the formulas of aristocratic French speech to the proper way to lift a long, fashionable tunic to stories of long-dead popes and emperors. "He was a wicked pope who lived a long time ago. He sold his soul to the devil to learn mathematics."

"Oh, well, more fool he." Stephen dismissed Gerbert with a wave of his hand. "He could have learned more from Ibn Masoud for considerably less price."

"Stephen, they're hinting at witchcraft. Don't you care?"

Stephen kissed her. "No." Mam had fled from such hints. He would not run away from them. "It doesn't make any difference," he told Aude. "Nobody's going to hire me to replace a man like Jean d'Orbais, and I don't want to work under him, so we're not staying at Rheims. Shall we go and see how the work at Beauvais is progressing?"

Aude thought Beauvais was a nice little town, or it would have been if it weren't for the commotion caused by gangs of laborers hauling stone from the quarries, masons cutting those stones, and foremen yelling down curses on their heads. The architect who'd promised the townsfolk of Beauvais a cathedral higher than any other in France had died of a dropsy the previous year, and all this activity was going on under the harried supervision of a master mason who virtually implored Stephen to apply for the vacant position. "I'm no clerk, to keep accounts and dine with the priests and draw pretty pictures of how the finished job will look," he moaned, and Stephen was reminded briefly of Brito. But after a tour of the just-started work he came out pale and sweating and feeling sick.

"What's the matter?" Aude asked.

"Something's wrong. I can't put my finger on it, but the design is wrong. Those vaults are going to be too high, the way this chap is building; I can't believe the architect meant it to go this way. Someone must have misunderstood the designer's drawings. The pier buttresses aren't going to be able to carry the load. And the masonry's been done carelessly—look how things don't fit properly. I don't want to try to patch up a job that's been begun so poorly. Can't you hear it?" he demanded. He pointed at a stub of pier buttress no higher than his own head. "The walls should be singing, but they sound like fingernails scraping across a new-polished slate."

Enough people overheard this, and saw Stephen's pale sweating face, to set the gossip flying again. Aude sighed and accepted that they weren't going to settle in Beauvais.

In Bourges, Stephen announced that their travels were at an end. Here the choir of a new cathedral stood alone, begun before Stephen was born and completed before he'd finished out his apprenticeship, yet it showed a technical daring and masterful sense of structure that, to him, surpassed any of the newer works he'd viewed in the last few months.

"Look at how much lighter the pier buttresses are," he told Aude enthusiastically, "compared to Chartres. They're like wings arching up to the height of the vault."

Aude looked up, somewhat nervously. She wouldn't for worlds have said so to Stephen, but the high, airy spaces of the Bourges choir made her feel the way the Beauvais cathedral had made him feel. She would prefer a good solid church with thick walls, anyday, to his nonsense about turing stone into lace or light. Stone was stone, to Aude's mind: heavy, solid, dependable. It wasn't supposed to arch over your head in shafts so slender they looked, as Stephen had said, like wings.

"It's quite pretty," she said neutrally. "Of course, so was Chartres."

"Yes, but this—" Stephen was off again, expounding on

the section depths of the outer flyers and the difference to the height of the pier buttresses that could be achieved by raising the angle of the flying buttresses. With a skill born of long experience, Aude let her mind wander to more interesting matters, such as exactly how much the innkeeper was overcharging them. She listened just enough to pick out the important points of his discourse. The building program at Bourges had languished for some years due to lack of funds, and the original master who'd designed this airy choir was dead. Now the cathedral clergy had collected enough to start work on the nave, but they had not yet selected a master of the works or an architect.

"I'll do both—first design the work and then oversee the construction." Stephen was too confident; his certainty, rising as high as the vaults supported by those slender flying buttresses, made Aude just as nervous.

"You mean, that's what you'll do if they accept you as the master builder."

"No question about that. They'd just about narrowed it down to one man. Robert de Montreuil. I talked to him this afternoon and let him know I might be looking to work under him. He showed me his designs." Stephen snorted. "He's a coward. Big, thick, clumsy piers, lowered vaults. He copies the choir and loses all the beauty of the original. They'll not waste their time with him after they see what I can do."

Stephen worked for three nights in their room, doing sketches on wax and copying them on vellum. Slowly the design grew clear and strong in his mind. At midnight, Aude would wake and roll over, burying her head under a feather pillow and murmuring a sleepy protest against Stephen's curses and his extravagant use of candles. At dawn she'd wake again to a cold, empty bed; Stephen would be out pacing the length and width of the choir, seeking inspiration.

On the fourth day, Stephen submitted his drawings. He wanted to make a short speech to the clergy, explaining how he understood the intent of the original architect and how the nave could follow the same conception with newer techniques to rise even lighter. But the roll of parchment was twitched out of his hand by a sour fellow in a subdeacon's black cope, who said the cathedral chapter had many things to consider and he would be heard in due time.

"Shall I wait here?"

"I wouldn't advise it. It could be a couple of weeks."

"Good," said Stephen, his energy undiminished, when he reported this exchange to Aude, "that'll give me time to start getting a crew together."

Aude sighed and rolled her eyes and devoted an evening to persuading Stephen that he'd best not lay out good money on workmen's wages until he knew that he'd been awarded the contract.

On the day when the committee was to announce their decision, Stephen was pacing in the outer courtyard of the cathedral close from first light, too nervous to eat or drink. He tried childish games to distract himself: the clerk of the committee would send for him when three blackbirds flew across the open square of sky framed by the empty pillars at the end of the choir, when the bells rang for Terce, when five men had passed through the colonnade before him, all right, five tall men, all right, five tall men with yellow hair and green surcoats—

"Geoffrey! Geoffrey de Tour Martel!"

For a moment Stephen thought he'd made an absolute fool of himself with that impulsive shout; the man he thought he recognized was older than Geoffrey and carried himself more soberly. Then the yellow head turned slowly, and it was his friend. But this Geoffrey was five years older and sobered by responsibility and sorrow. Stephen read that much in his eyes before the incredulous smile of welcome flashed across Geoffrey's face and transformed him briefly into the carefree youth who'd come to Outremer on an impossible quest.

"The master builder. What are you doing here? I thought you'd have turned Saracen by now, going down on your hands and knees to the black dog Mahound five times a day." Geoffrey thumped Stephen so hard on the back that he couldn't get his breath for a minute. "Come and drink wine with me like a Christian, then, and tell me what brought you back to civilization. And where's pretty Aude? Don't tell me you risk leaving her alone in a townful of lustful Frenchmen? Come on, let's get her and celebrate the reunion properly."

It was Geoffrey, all right. "I have to stay here." Stephen

briefly explained the business that had brought him to Bourges. Partly through Marco Sanudo's trading and partly through the inheritance from Ibn Masoud, Stephen told Geoffrey about how his fortune had grown and how he hoped to use some of the money to set himself up as an independent contractor to finish the cathedral here. The rest of the money, at Aude's insistence, was left with Marco as savings for the family they still hoped to have; but that secret grief and dying hope was not something to discuss, even with as old and dear a friend as Geoffrey. "But you, Geoffrey, what's been happening with you and your family? Is your father still as crusty as ever? Did you tell him about—"

Geoffrey's quick shake of the head warned Stephen, before he finished, that all was not well. "Dead. Before I got home. And the rest of them died all in one year—as if there was a curse on our family!"

"All?"

Geoffrey nodded gloomily. "Herault broke his neck in a tournament, and in the same tourney, Igwaine got a little scratch that festered, and he wouldn't let the barber cut his leg off when it started to corrupt. Mortet and Adhemar were fooling around with swords in the armory without their mail on, and managed to run each other through. Clotho's new destrier threw him—another broken neck. And Tonnel fell off a cliff—at least, it looked like an accident, but we suspected somebody's husband caught up with him." Geoffrey managed a pale imitation of a grin. "Tonnel always was my favorite brother. Anyway, that's how—I mean, why—well, I'm the Sieur de Tour Martel now. Me! It's been the devil of a lot of work: Hearing complaints, hanging poachers, and fining the peasants for not working to repair my roads. I never expected to have to do that sort of thing," he said plaintively. "And the girls in the neighborhood are no fun anymore because all the noble ones want to marry me and all the peasant ones give in without protest. It's been four long, boring years, Stephen. You'll have to come back with me and liven the place up for a while."

"So you sneaked off to Bourges for a bit of a holiday?"

Geoffrey's air of gloom returned. "Not a bit of it. I'm trying to get my brothers buried."

"But you said it was four years since they died?"

"Oh, they're underground, all right," Geoffrey assured him. "But not in the churchyard. You see, they were all still excommunicated when they died, so I couldn't lay them in holy ground. I had to find odd places around the castle to bury them. It's mostly rocky ground, of course, because the best site for a castle is on solid rock. We had to give up the herb garden and a good bit of the orchard. Anyway, I've been trying to talk the abbot into lifting the ban so I can have them properly buried in the churchyard at Chastelvert. But he said no. I thought I'd try my luck with the bishop of Bourges since he could force the Abbot Samson to give in if he wanted to."

"And?"

"He doesn't want to. There's a little thing I never noticed when I was a carefree younger son: our abbot is the bishop's brother. And the bishop says he won't have anything to do with raising the ban unless I give back—I mean, give the convent the south vineyard."

"I'm sorry about your brothers and all." A sour-faced cleric was beckoning to Stephen from the end of the colonnade. "Listen, Geoff, I've got to go now. Come see us later. We're staying at the White Griffon."

"Me, too," said Geoffrey, momentarily diverted by this coincidence. "Only place in town to stay, if you don't count my great-aunt Emilie, and she doesn't know I'm here, thank the Blessed Virgin for small favors. I'll go back and see Aude."

Stephen was gone, whisked behind the silent doors of the cathedral chapter house. Geoffrey sighed, then brightened as he recalled the excellent wine at the White Griffon. He smiled at the thought of persuading Aude to join him in testing the wine. She wouldn't, of course, but after four years as lord of his lands there would be some entertainment in finding a girl who didn't give in at once to his every wish.

These monks were talkative; Geoffrey figured he'd have a long afternoon waiting for Stephen to finish his contract negotiations with the building committee. There was time enough to sample all the White Griffon's wines in turn, then to go back and try them again to make sure.

"Now," said Geoffrey when he'd gotten through the initial greetings and explanations with Aude, and had persuaded her to sit downstairs in the private garden at the back of the hostelry, "I want you to tell me about what you've been doing since we last met." He clasped both her hands in his and gazed into her face with an intent look.

Aude giggled and withdrew her hands. "Oh, no, you don't. You'd much rather talk about yourself, and sample the landlord's wines; I hear they're excellent."

"Darling Aude, that's why I love you. You're the only woman who sees through me."

"And here comes Stephen, so you'd better order more wine."

"Stephen? Already?"

"Already." Stephen dropped down on the bench beside Aude and let his hands fall open on the table.

"Make that two goblets. And a full pitcher of the Burgundy."

"Two pitchers," Stephen corrected. He took the first one from the serving boy's hands and drained it without waiting for the goblets.

"You weren't very long talking to the committee," Geoffrey ventured after an impressed silence.

Stephen laughed and reached for the second pitcher of wine as the boy brought it. Geoffrey whisked it out of his reach. "Not until you tell us what happened."

"Nothing happened. They're not having me because they thought my design was too dangerous. They claimed that I couldn't prove to them it would be stable in a high wind."

"Well, could you?"

"Not to them! Not to you either, come to that. I love you like a brother, Geoffrey, but you don't understand geometry and you don't want to hear the details. Neither do they. I'd have done as well talking to the bishop's favorite mare."

"From what I hear," said Geoffrey, cheering up slightly, "the bishop's favorite mare is named Juliette, and he doesn't spend as much time in the saddle as she'd like, and I wouldn't mind proving a few things to her myself. . . ."

His cheerful voice trailed off under a withering look from Stephen. "Do you want to hear what happened, or not? Of course I could prove the stability of my design to anybody who understood geometry. I didn't have the luxury of an intelligent audience. I gave them the best design for a cathedral nave that's been drawn in France in twenty years, which anybody but those addled dotards would have appreciated at once. Robert de Montreuil came with two dozen letters from all his highly placed friends and relations, saying what a nice man he is and how they've never actually built anything themselves, but they're sure he'll do good work at Bourges. He brought sketches of the ugly church he put up in the Limousin and some noble's townhouse in Paris that he decorated with enough sculpture to bring the entire facade crashing down one day."

"So?"

Geoffrey had relaxed his watch over the wine pitcher; Stephen filled his goblet and drained it, repeated the motions, and breathed slowly through his nose.

"I tried to prove mathematically that my design would stand up and they said all those As and Bs and arcs on the drawing looked like circles to raise demons. I pointed out that de Montreuil's work is ugly and they said if it's good enough for the nobility of Paris, it's good enough for them. I said I'd done work for the Sultan of Egypt and they asked very politely if I'd care to invite him to the meeting to give me a reference. They'd already decided to give it to de Montreuil, they didn't want to have to think about anything new and they didn't. What happened to all the wine?"

Somewhere between the Burgundy and the white wine from the Loire country, Aude slipped away and left the men to their morose drinking. By the time they'd finished off the Loire wine and started on the heavy, sweet wine that came all the way from Monemvasia in the Morea and cost accordingly, Geoffrey and Stephen had been repeating the same complaints for so long that they were almost beginning to listen to each other.

"Actually, I wouldn't mind giving back the south vineyard," said Geoffrey for the fourth or fifth time, "but my dad made such a point of its being in the Tour Martel patrimony, and vowing he'd never give it back—I mean up—that it seems unfair to his memory. You'd think I could find something else the abbot would take in exchange."

"I've done too much to go back to building village churches to somebody's century-old pattern, like Brito did. I want important work. And the only way you get trusted to do important work is by having done some already."

"The trouble is, when the abbey lost the income from the vineyard, they couldn't afford to finish the church. No roof on the nave, no transepts, naked piers sticking up in the air. It's an eyesore and every time it rains the monks in choir get soaked and Abbot Samson curses the Tour Martels again. I can't really blame him."

"It doesn't matter how good you are, only thing that matters is who you know. De Montreuil's a lousy architect but he has all those letters. I don't know anybody."

"Yes, you do," said Geoffrey. His long face brightened. "You know me."

"I mean somebody important. Pass the Malmsey." Stephen held out his goblet.

"I am important. Remember? I'm the Sieur de Tour Martel. And I'm brilliant, too."

"No, Geoffrey. You're my old dear friend and I'm very fond of you and I'm glad we met again, but . . . Where was I?" Stephen blinked and ran a hand through his hair.

"My brilliance."

"Oh, yes. All of the above, Geoffrey, but you are not smart. You know that and I know that. Let's not fool ourselves."

"You're drunk."

"So are you."

"Yes, but it doesn't impugn—impede—I'm still brilliant. Really, Stephen. I may not be smart, but tonight I'm a genius. Maybe it's the wine that does it. I wonder if we could buy the last barrel and get it carted home to Tour Martel? We can solve both our problems at once, Stephen! I'll offer to finance the rest of the building on the Church of Chastelvert if Abbot Samson will lift the ban and let me bury my family. That'll cost me more than the revenues off the south vineyard, so he should be happy, and the land stays in the family, so my father won't come back to haunt me. See?"

"Might work."

"Damn right it'll work. Only I'm making one condition. He has to hire an architect of my choosing to complete the church." Geoffrey grinned and tapped the side of his nose. "An old friend of mine, very experienced, saved my life in Outremer, at last I've got a chance to return the favor."

"Geoffrey! You don't mean—"

"Of course I do. You're a good architect, even if you do consort with heathens. And I do owe you something for that affair in Jerusalem. Do you think I don't know that Kamil would have flayed me alive if you hadn't saved us all? Now will you admit how clever I am?"

"You're brilliant." Stephen upended his goblet and poured out the last of the Malmsey in a trickle. "But you're still not smart."

"Neither are you," said Geoffrey reprovingly, "wasting the good wine like that."

"I'll need a clear head from now on if I'm going to be your master builder."

Of course Stephen wanted to design a church of his own, from foundations to roof tiles, every line and stone and timber of his own specification. And someday he would. But the man who'd begun this church for the Cistercians of Chastelvert had done good work. There would be no shame in finishing what he'd begun. From the moment Stephen saw the half-completed church on a hill halfway up the long slope of the valley, he knew exactly how he would continue this project and how the finished church would soar toward the sky like a hymn of praise. The site was perfect; a hilltop above the great warren of monastery buildings, partially leveled by nature, then smoothed further by the first builder who'd laid the foundations deep and true. The choice of stone was right: pale golden limestone from the Loire, so soft when first dug out of the ground that it could be carved like butter, then slowly hardening to a durable stone for all weather. And the shape was right, too: the modest plans of the first builder were open enough to allow Stephen certain elaborations in the form of flying buttresses and multiple pierced walls.

He would have been happy to spend some weeks just absorbing the details of the site, thinking out such things as how best to place the windows in the semicircular apse so that they could catch the glory of the rising sun. But Stephen had learned in Outremer that the life of a master builder was one-part design and art to nine-parts organization and administration. During the first week, he was needed in six places at once. While Aude settled into the rooms Geoffrey had set aside for them at the Tour Martel, Stephen traveled around the countryside inspecting quarries, judging the grade of stone they offered, arranging for boatmen and carters to transport the materials to the valley, hiring teams of oxen for the local heavy work, interviewing skilled carvers and sculptors in every masons' lodge he could find. . . . At the end of the day his head was crowded with the details that had to be noted down immediately, and his sketchbook began to swell with the extra leaves on which he jotted down accounts, terms of contracts, and names of men as they were hired. Then Stephen would turn to the two drawings that refreshed his spirit: one quick sketch of Aude's head and one view of the unfinished church in its valley; this reminded him that he did have something to come back to when all this organization work was completed.

An established contractor would have had a master quarrier to find the best available stone and arrange transport, a master carpenter to check the stability of the woodwork, draughtsmen to enlarge his drawings into templets, and a master mason to see that the templets were handed out appropriately, the most complex work to the most skilled masons.

By the end of this project, Stephen promised himself, he too would have foremen to whom he could delegate all these tasks. But for now he made instant decisions about which men to hire, choosing this man for the line of calluses between forefinger and thumb that spoke of years holding a chisel, turing away that one because of the sour smell of old ale on his breath and the way he winced when a mallet crashed against stone. And every decision might be a mistake but there wasn't time to find out. And with so many guesses, how could he justify turning over any crucial part of the project to men he barely knew?

So Stephen told himself, and so he explained to Aude when he spent his first day back in Chastelvert not at the castle of Tour Martel, but at the church from dawn till sunset. "I had to go over the lifting cranes. They haven't been used for twenty years; we had to replace all the ropes and grease the bearings. And the carpenters are here, ready to make new scaffolding. If I hadn't shown them exactly how I like things done, they'd have wasted shaped wood on the hurdles, where poles roped together and wicker footrests would do just as well."

"And of course, nobody else on God's earth knows how to raise scaffolding!"

"Not the way I want it done. And it must be right. If I waste money and create great heavy scaffoldings of sawn lumber, every man on the project will know I'm not sure of myself. Rope-and-pole scaffolding is an art, raising it with the least wastage of wood is one of the great arts, and it's my first chance to show these workmen that I know what I'm doing. Besides, it's better than lumber. If you know how to lash the poles together properly, the scaffolding can be taken apart and used over and over again. If you go cutting planks to fit, you can't do anything else with them later."

"Mmm. Fascinating."

Stephen was immune to sarcasm, but it did dawn on him that Aude might be lonely. He reached for her hand and gathered her against him on the great bed, her dark hair fanning out across his chest, her slender body one armful for him to hold and cherish. "Listen, love, it'll be easier later on. Right now I don't know any of these men, and I don't know who I can trust. And they don't know me. It's only natural some of them would be testing me, to see what I'll put up with in the way of wastage and slack work. When I've got everything under control I'll choose foremen and let them waste their free days crawling around on ledges and checking machinery, while you and I go off—and—have fun," he finished limply, unable to think of anything specific to promise.

"We'll go hawking with Geoffrey?" Aude asked through the curtain of her tangled hair.

"If you want to, certainly." Stephen had never been closely acquainted with a hawk and saw no reason to change that. Who wanted to spend his free time carrying around a great mean-tempered bird that could claw your arm or bite your hand off if it wanted to? But Aude deserved to have some fun.

"And dance in the great hall, when Geoffrey's friends come to visit and the musicians play after dinner?"

"I suppose I can learn." At any rate it couldn't be as bad as hawking.

"And play chess?"

Stephen winced. Ibn Masoud had been fond of chess and had forced Stephen to learn the moves, saying it was good exercise for the mind. Stephen had never seen the point. If he was going to think that hard, he wanted to be thinking about something worthwhile, like a new way of removing centering frames from under a vault.

"Certainly," he said. "I don't think I've had a good game of chess since Ibn Masoud died."

Aude's shoulders began to shake. It was a moment before Stephen realized she was laughing. "Stephen, you are the love of my life, but you are a terrible liar. You don't want to do any of those things. You'd rather spend your holidays the same way you spend every other day of your life—building something!"

"I didn't say I wanted to dance, or hawk, or play chess," Stephen pointed out. "I said I would do any of those things with you, if you liked. But if it's all the same to you," he went on as Aude laughed quietly to herself, "maybe you'd like to take a little excursion instead, one of these nice days? Geoffrey was telling me about one of his neighbors who's putting up a new gate tower with the doorway arches projected forward to support the machicolations. I can't tell exactly how it works since Geoffrey has no precision of mind to describe these things. Anyway, it would be a pleasant ride and maybe you'd enjoy the outing. There! You see, I can so have fun! *Now* what's the matter?" he asked, aggrieved.

But Aude was laughing too hard to tell him, and after he began to tickle her in retaliation, she pulled him down on top of her and shoved his head into the feather-stuffed bolster, and then they both forgot what they'd been talking about.

After that initial burst of travel, Stephen found that he no longer had to tour the countryside looking for good craftsmen. Word of the new works at the abbey in Chastelvert traveled quickly, and men began to drift into the village in twos and threes, carpenters and plasterers and glaziers and masons and iron-workers. Some came only to see the new master builder from Outremer, and went away disappointed that Stephen wasn't black and that he had no plans to set a Saracen-style minaret on top of the church. Some, Stephen felt sure, came to inspect his building style so that they could pick up any new tricks and pass them on to

their own masons. Of these, a flatteringly high number
stayed on to work with him, including one master mason
with twenty years' experience. Maître Jean was a gift from
God. He quietly organized the lodge, ranked the stonemasons under him, and took over the hiring of new craftsmen
while Stephen was occupied with a new problem: keeping
the peace between Geoffrey and Abbot Samson.

The brief period of amity between church and castle
that began when the abbot accepted Geoffrey's offer lasted
barely long enough to get the excommunicated Tour Martels pardoned and buried in consecrated ground. Geoffrey
used the occasion of the funeral to wander round the open
shell of the church, swinging on Stephen's lifting cranes
and playing at walking round the big wheel where four
men at once would labor to raise the great stones of the
buttresses. The abbot managed to conceal his irritation on
that day, but as Geoffrey returned again and again with
grandiose ideas and interfering design notions, his patience grew visibly more strained. And he tended to
blame Stephen for the interference. The abbot hadn't
asked to be saddled with some young builder whose only
qualifications were his heathen connections and his friendship with the lord of Tour Martel, had he? He wasn't even
sure he wanted the church finished under these conditions. He'd known all along that a "gift" from the Tour
Martel family would be more trouble than it was worth.

With dark looks and short, snappish comments, he
conveyed these sentiments to Stephen without actually
saying anything unsuitable for a man of God. And Stephen
balanced uneasily between his spiritual and financial patrons, understanding the abbot's unhappiness but quite
unable to speak against the friend who'd given him this
wonderful chance.

In the end, though, it was Geoffrey's well-meant interference that united Stephen and Abbot Samson. They
found common ground, to their mutual surprise, on the
day when Geoffrey tried to dictate the design of the
stained-glass windows in the apse. It was a silly quarrel;
the windows wouldn't be set in for months, maybe years,
and by that time Geoffrey would surely have forgotten this
whim. But he'd proposed one too many design changes
that week, and neither his builder nor his spiritual father
could take any more.

"How are you laying out the apse?" he demanded, striding into the tracing house and interrupting Stephen and Abbot Samson where they bent over the parchments. "I thought so. That's too many arches. I want you to lay it out with space for seven windows, not nine."

"Impossible," said Abbot Samson. "There must be exactly nine windows, for nine is the number of the celestial choirs and also the number of the Virgin Mary, her root being the Trinity, or three."

Geoffrey's lower lip pushed out in a stubborn pout. "Who's paying for these windows? If you want full-colored glass instead of grisaille, you'll have a design that pleases me. I want to commemorate the tragic deaths of my brothers. We'll have windows for three of them on each side, and the one in the middle is for my father. Think of a good Bible story about six brothers dying young, and get one of your clerks to write a nice inscription underneath. Make sure their names are spelled right, too."

"Well . . ." Abbot Samson mused. "Seven *is* three plus four."

It was Geoffrey's turn to look blank. "What's that got to do with anything?"

"Three for the Trinity, four for the square which represents the relation between God the Father and God the Son. You see, God is the supreme unity, and the Son is unity begotten by unity, as the square results from the multiplication of a magnitude with itself. We can't have pictures of your brothers, of course; that would be blasphemy. But I could be reconciled to seven windows."

Geoffrey's face clouded over and he shouted that it was his money and he was going to have his church look the way he wanted, and to hell with trinities and squares! The abbot retaliated by threatening excommunication.

"Stop! Both of you! Geoffrey, you can't have seven windows," Stephen interrupted. "You can't just move the column and arches of the apse around like a child's building blocks. You'd destroy the structural and proportional unity of the church."

"Oh. Would that be a bad thing?"

"It might," said Stephen solemnly, "cause the whole church to fall down."

"Oh!"

"And, Abbot," Stephen turned to the red-faced cleric,

"if we have nine windows, as in the original design, then we are not referring to the Trinity anymore, are we? So it might not be blasphemous to commemorate the family that financed the church's building? After all, the number nine symbolizes the angelic choirs, and presumably that is where Geoffrey's father and brothers are right now."

Abbot Samson muttered that there might be some doubt about that, but he agreed to the compromise that Stephen had suggested. Geoffrey began to look happier.

"Although," Stephen said, "I am rather confused. I thought the White Monks didn't approve of stained glass. Don't they find that it's too sensual and that it distracts the eye from heaven?" The glass of the other Cistercian churches Stephen had seen was lightly tinted in silvery green or pale brown. Stephen rather approved of that practice because it let more light into the church. And he couldn't say about heaven, but those elaborate rose windows and tiny mosaics certainly distracted the eye from the real beauty of a well-designed building.

Abbot Samson sighed and agreed that the blessed Bernard of Clairvaux had seriously disapproved of such fripperies as stained-glass windows, jeweled shrines, and gold and silver utensils. "But saints have a tendency not to recognize the lesser needs of lesser men. For myself, I never feel closer to heaven than when the loveliness of the gems and ornaments upon our altar summons me to meditate upon the blessed joys of which they are but a pale reflection."

"Ah—quite so," said Geoffrey. "Then about my stained-glass windows—"

"Furthermore," continued the abbot, "does it not seem fitting to you that every costly thing should serve, first and foremost, for the administration of the Holy Eucharist? Unworthy as we are to receive the blessed blood of Christ, should we not do this precious gift honor by using golden vessels, precious stones, and whatever we most value among created things? *Abundet unusquisque in suo sensu,* let every man abound in his own sense, as St. Paul said. There is, further, a text in Hebrew bearing upon this very matter. . . ."

Geoffrey made his excuses and departed while the abbot droned on. Stephen looked at the abbot with new respect; he'd never thought of boring Geoffrey into going away. Stephen capped the text in Hebrew with the words of

Ezekiel. "Every precious stone was the covering, the sardius, the topaz, and the jasper, the chrysolite, and the onyx, and the beryl, the sapphire, and the carbuncle, and the emerald."

"Exactly," said Abbot Samson, cheering up. "I see you are a sensible young man. How did you happen to be associated with that fool Tour Martel? No, no, don't tell me, I suspect it is a highly unedifying story. We will certainly have stained glass. By the way, did what you were saying about seven arches and structural unity make any sense?"

"None whatever. But I like my design the way I originally drew it, and Geoffrey was convinced."

"I thought so. You must dine with me tonight, to continue our discussion—no, better make it tomorrow," he said, frowning. "I had forgotten."

"A sad anniversary?"

"Friday."

Stephen didn't object to fish, but he wasn't all that eager to dine with the formidable abbot, so he kept silent.

"Bread and water," the abbot said. "Penance on Fridays. That's what Saint Bernard prescribed for those of our order who insisted on keeping their stained glass windows. So let's dine tomorrow," he said, cheering up, "and there's some excellent Malmsey on which I should like your opinion." As the abbot talked on, it occurred to Stephen that Geoffrey wasn't the only one who could be bored into submission by that droning voice. He was quite grateful when a boy from the masons' lodge interrupted them with Maître Jean's request that he come to interview a new applicant.

"I thought Maître Jean was going to handle the hiring himself from now on," he said as they crossed the busy churchyard.

"He was," sniffed the apprentice. "He was going to send this drunk away with a flea in his ear. But the man claims to be a personal friend of yours."

Stephen frowned and shook his head. He had no friends in France other than Geoffrey. And it was hardly conceivable that one of the Egyptian craftsmen he'd worked with would have come this far into Christian lands. Maître Jean must have misunderstood the man.

The lodge was surrounded by a shady porch, nothing but a light structure of poles roofed over with green branches. In time the leaves would wither and the masons would be able to work outdoors in sunlight, cross-hatched by a screen of twigs. But now the fresh-cut branches still smelled of the forest, and their leaves cast shadows over the interior of the long porch. The man who came toward Stephen was none other than Ivo of Dunwich.

"Well, young Stephen," said Ivo. "For a runaway 'prentice boy, you've not done so badly for yourself."

CHAPTER

21

◧

Stephen's first impulse was to bolt before Ivo could tell the White Monks about his defection. He was afraid Abbot Samson would pass the news on to the Black Monks who would see to it that Stephen went back to the underground cell at Ely. Then Stephen pulled himself together. He was the master of the works here, not a frightened novice or a tormented apprentice. His men would think it strange to see him running from this shabby mason with red-rimmed eyes and shaking hands. Stephen breathed slowly and gradually understood, through the haze of panic that had blinded him, that Ivo was referring to nothing more than his disappearance from Master Brito's stoneyard. He knew nothing of the business in Ely, and even if he had known, it would have meant nothing to him. All that was real to Ivo was the stone in front of him, the pot of ale, and the girl at the end of the day. He was in the middle of telling Stephen how Wimarc had cheated him out of his rightful inheritance when Brito died.

"What's that? Your father's dead?" Stephen felt a sharp pang at the loss of someone he hadn't even thought about for years. Brito's solid shoulders and rolling paunch and hardy laugh had always been with him. Even though Stephen couldn't go back to England and even though he'd outgrown Brito's piece-work-to-rule systems long before he left, he'd felt that his place in the Dunwich stoneyard was always there for him. Now that too was gone.

"Aye, died of the breath-shortness not two winters after you disappeared. It was too much for him, getting on like he was, to travel all over the countryside after work and manage the piecework in the Dunwich shop as well. He needed your help." Ivo glowered at Stephen. "*I* don't know accounts and clerks' work," he added as though to stave off an unspoken accusation. "It was you he needed. He never stopped hoping you'd come back. Every time a journeyman or mason knocked at the lodge door looking for work, his face would brighten for a minute until he saw it wasn't you. He wouldn't even try to keep his own books straight that last winter. He kept saying, 'When Stephen comes back, he'll set it all straight.' He thought the world of you."

"Didn't Hugh tell everyone what happened? He must have known I wouldn't be able to come back."

"Hugh never said aught but that you'd been in a spot of trouble in Ely and thought you'd best take dog's leave from the workings there." Ivo rubbed his eyes and looked at Stephen with something bordering on respect. "Must've been bad trouble, if you had to run all the way to France. I didn't think you had it in you. I always thought you were a bit of a milksop, to tell the truth. You wouldn't fight me, after that first day."

"It wouldn't have been wise to fight with the heir to the stoneyard."

"No, I s'pose not," agreed Ivo, brightening visibly. "I was somebody in those days. Heir to the best stoneyard on the east coast. And all the girls ran after me, and not just for my property. But it's no world for honest men, Stephen. After Brito died. . . ."

He rambled on about how Wimarc inherited a half-share in the stoneyard, cozened him into signing his rights away when he was drunk, and finally threw Ivo out of his own home. Stephen could imagine Wimarc's side of the story: a hardworking master mason was saddled with the old master's lazy lout of a stepson who did no work and drank up all the profits. Legal papers were drawn up to protect the stoneyard and the people who worked there, and the wastrel, who drank away his inheritance then complained that there was no place for him among honest working men.

No doubt there was some truth on both sides. Nobody would want to have Ivo as a partner, and Wimarc's first care would have been for the business and the men. But it was also true that Wimarc must have known Ivo couldn't handle money, that he'd spend whatever was in his purse on drink and girls.

"Since then I've been tramping like a damned journeyman," Ivo whined, "one job after another, and sleeping rough in between jobs. There's nothing for a good man in England. I thought the French would appreciate my skills, but you know how hard it is to find work these days."

Stephen thought of how he'd pleaded, cajoled, and bargained to release skilled men from other projects. He thought of the busy lodges he'd visited throughout the country, and of the craze for building that was covering France with the spires of new cathedrals.

"I don't mind so much for me," Ivo added, watching Stephen's face closely, "but it's hard on my wife."

"You've married?"

"Pretty little thing, Yolande. Just fifteen. She has a waist like a sapling, and a face like a flower. She's French, but I've taught her enough English. She ran away with me— her people didn't approve. They thought she could do better for herself than an honest workingman." Ivo winked. "To tell the truth, I wasn't expecting her to follow me. I was rough-hewing stones to repair the wall around the village church. We had a little fun out in the meadows, and then the sour old priest got wind of it and made the master mason throw me off the job. I was half a league out of town when Yolande came running up, crying about how she loved me too much to let me go. What can I say?" Ivo smirked. "The girl's in love with me. So for her sake, I'd like to find some settled work." He looked out over the valley. "This is a pretty little place. There's a good view from the church, isn't there? I wouldn't mind staying here for a while."

He left it at that, not begging or whining or reminding Stephen of the debt he owed Brito—a debt he could never repay. But at least Stephen could give Ivo a place to stay and rebuild his career as Brito had once given a place to a starving runaway boy with no particular skills.

"All right," he said abruptly. "You're on the project.

Maître Jean will show you where we're setting up quarters for the married men."

"I'll need some tools. A fine chisel and a mallet."

Those were the tools of the freemasons, the most skilled masons who carved the statues and copied the graceful, flowing curves of corbels and capitals after the wooden templets sent down from the builder's drafting room. Remembering the slight tremor of Ivo's hands, Stephen doubted that he could be trusted with such work. "Maître Jean will assess your skills and allot you whatever tools you require." He wouldn't be surprised to see Ivo with a scappling hammer for smoothing rough stone. Neither, to judge from his downcast expression, would Ivo. For a moment Stephen hated himself for his own success, hated the system that set him to judge Ivo and others like him. In some ways there had been more freedom when he was just a journeyman under Brito's direction, free to boast with his fellows about how much better he would organize a project if he were in charge.

"And after work, let's go down to the village and have a pot of ale to celebrate our reunion—or wine, since these French don't understand good English brewing. It's nice to see somebody from the old days," Stephen said, and for that moment he meant it. As he left the lodge and crossed the cluttered churchyard, he even wondered whether it would be possible to ask Maître Jean to issue Ivo freemason's tools. Perhaps with trust and a chance to build up his self-respect, Ivo would do good work.

Stephen turned and went up the stairs to the tracing house. He managed to forget all about Ivo and Dunwich until the fading light made it too difficult to continue his fine drawing work. He could do accounts by candlelight, but it was difficult for him to see the fine spiderweb of lines representing the piers of the church and the arches springing from them. A few years ago, Stephen remembered, he had worked Ibn Masoud's geometrical problems in three dimensions, just as complicated, by the flickering light of a lamp set behind colored glass. Now he was squinting like an old man! And how old was he? Stephen, who could figure the curve on a voussoir by eye and could estimate the total wage bill for a hundred and twenty men all working at different piecework rates in his head, counted on his fingers to verify the sum. Just twenty-six. And here he was squinting over his work like old Master Adam of Lincoln, who might not have been so old now he thought back on it. Stephen decided it was time to get out of the tracing house for the day. He'd have a glass of wine with Ivo, for old times' sake, and then head back to la Tour Martel and Aude.

Aude and Geoffrey were waiting at the foot of the stairs when Stephen came in. Geoffrey was perching on a rough-carved block of stone watching Aude practice the dance steps she had learned under his minstrels' direction. Stephen paused on the steps and smiled at the sight of Aude bending like a gracious lady. The his gaze fell on the empty shell of the church, and his lips moved in calculation, until Aude cried out a greeting and came running up the stairs to kiss him.

"What were you thinking of, staring off at your old church like a dazed man?"

"You," said Stephen, at least half truthfully, and Aude laughed at him and called him a liar. He told her about Ivo and his promise to buy him a drink after the masons left work for the day.

Aude didn't care to join them. Geoffrey said he'd walk as far as the married men's lodgings with them, then take Aude back to la Tour Martel while Stephen and Ivo went off carousing.

They were almost at the long line of temporary huts erected to house the workers when Geoffrey halted and jibbed like a startled horse. "Who's *that*?"

"That" was a young girl, slender-waisted but with a voluptuous fullness that she carried somewhat awkwardly, as though she had just grown breasts and hips in the last year and wasn't quite sure what to do with them. Her red hair tumbled down over her shoulders, struck to fire by the setting sun, framing a pert, freckled face of no particular beauty. It wasn't her face Geoffrey was gaping at.

Though she wore her hair loose like an unmarried girl, she turned in at the last door in the row of temporary huts, where Maître Jean had told Stephen to seek out Ivo.

"That must be Yolande, my friend's wife. He said she was quite young. And rather pretty." Stephen swallowed and realized that he hadn't closed his mouth since Yolande minced across the yard.

"Indeed." Geoffrey was still gaping. "I do think it's time

I started taking a more serious interest in this project of yours, Stephen my boy. I've got to know the workers, and all that. After all, I'm the lord and while they're on the job, they're my responsibility, in a way. I really ought to know them at least as well as I know my own serfs, wouldn't you say? I should start now, wouldn't you say?"

Stephen was glad to remind him that he had promised to escort Aude home.

"Well," said Geoffrey philosophically, "plenty of other chances. Rome wasn't built in a day—and neither will this church be."

Stephen made a mental note to take Geoffrey aside, someday quite soon, and explain that the masons on the church project were not like his serfs. They were their own masters, with their own organization and justice, and they were not likely to feel honored at the local lord's singling out one of their women. He would have to make it clear to Geoffrey that playing with the craftsmen's women could result in a masons' strike or worse. In the back of his mind was the memory of Ivo's pugnacious ways. What would the Sieur de Tour Martel do to a commoner who attacked him? It would be small repayment of Brito's debt if he brought Ivo into a situation where he would get himself maimed or killed by the lord's "justice."

After that one evening with Ivo, Stephen felt no particular urge to revive old memories. As heir to Brito's stoneyard, Ivo had been a bully; as a wandering mason dependent on Stephen's favor for work, he expected Stephen to be a bully. That was his understanding of power. What worried Stephen was the temptation he felt to give in to it; to curse Ivo for ruining a fine stone that he'd not been authorized to cut, to threaten to beat him as he occasionally beat Yolande. (Stephen and others had seen the marks on her face, for Yolande spent an inordinate amount of time hanging around the masons' lodge in the first few weeks after Ivo was hired on.) Doubtless there was some truth in Ivo's complaint that his wife was too eager for any man's admiration, but that was no excuse for blacking both her eyes and bruising her mouth.

After a while, Yolande stopped running up to the works at every excuse, and Stephen assumed that Ivo's threats and beatings had had their effect. He tried to put the whole unhappy business out of his head. After all, he'd given Ivo a job, when there were plenty of men more skilled and more reliable to take the work, hadn't he? Wasn't that enough to discharge his old debt to Brito? Did he have to be Ivo's keeper as well?

That question raised disturbing echoes in his mind, of days that were best forgotten. Fortunately, the building of the church occupied him and kept him from brooding on old, unhappy days. The carpenters quarreled with the masons about who had the right to use the great wheel that lifted both stones and roof timbers; the masons complained that the smiths were botching the sharpening of their tools; the smith got into a fight with the glass-workers over some bags of charcoal that had disappeared just before the smith wanted to heat up his forge. And all the crafts joined together to complain in counterpoint and harmony about the monks who interrupted their work five times a day to hold choir services in the half-built church.

Of course, there was still the design work to be done in Stephen's spare time. Every beam, every truss and pier and window and flyer had to be drawn at least three times, once on the master plan and once to scale in the plaster floor and once on the wooden templet that would serve as a cutting guide. Every measurement had to match both the original master's measuring scheme and Stephen's personal measuring foot rule. Beyond that it had to obey the laws of proportion which assured that no part of the great structure would be too slender to bear the weight it must carry. It was complex, maddening, fascinating work, and Stephen's bills for wax candles went up as he strained his eyes to do the work in the middle of the night when he wouldn't be interrupted by quarreling craftsmen or administrative chores.

He had never been so happy in his life.

Sometimes, when his candles blazed all night in the tracing house windows, Abbot Samson would wander in with a flask of wine or some fresh-baked bread from the great monastery ovens. They would sit and talk while Stephen rubbed his tired eyes. He found that he rather enjoyed playing with logical propositions and capping quotations with Abbot Samson; the talk exercised a part of his mind that he had not used since he ran away from Ely, and it helped to erase the pictures of ribs and groin vaultings that danced behind his eyelids when he finally tried to sleep. Stephen was happy enough until the night when one of those talks led directly to a problem that threatened to pull down Stephen's church and halt the building.

"I wasn't sure about you at first," Abbot Samson said that night, abruptly breaking off one of his long-winded Biblical speeches. "I thought any friend of young Geoffrey's must be a light-minded wastrel. I was afraid you'd ruin my church."

Stephen grinned. "Maybe I will."

Abbot Samson waved a half-eaten chunk of fresh bread through the air. "No fear. Any man who understands Abelard's *Sic et Non* as well as you do has far too good a mind to do slipshod labor. There's a right way of understanding, whether you are building a logical proposition or a cathedral, and you have it. With a mind like that, it's a pity you didn't decide to go into the Church."

Stephen felt his whole body stiffen with the effort to hide his reaction. "I like building," he said after a time. "I'm happy as I am."

"Ah, well, maybe you're right. At least stone is solid. It doesn't shift positions. The way the Church changes its rules, I don't know whether I'm walking on earth or water."

"If it turns out to be water, let me know. An authenticated miracle would be good notice for this church."

"Have you heard about these new orders? Preaching friars, they call themselves. They wander around begging, exciting the peasants, and getting into trouble, then expect to be treated like real monks. One of them came to the village last Tuesday." Abbot Samson snorted. "Preaching against the church, he was. He said God didn't want to be glorified by works in stone, that true servants of God could worship in a hut made of branches and give the money to the deserving poor. Naturally all the peasants who were listening to him figured they were the deserving poor."

"Yes. I heard something about it. By the time I got down to the village to run him off, though, the peasants had already set their dogs on him. Geoffrey called the dogs off and invited him up to La Tour Martel by way of apology. He talks well enough, I have to admit, but he eats a lot for a man who makes such a big fuss about poverty and austerity. He put away half a haunch of venison with cherry sauce while telling Geoff that your monks were too well-fed. Is that how he annoyed the peasants?"

"Something similar. After he yammered for a while, it dawned on them that by the deserving poor he meant himself and the rest of his order—the Brothers of Francis, they call themselves." Abbot Samson swallowed half the wine in his flask at one gulp and laughed. "They weren't pleased, which is just as well. I'll wager that's the last time this valley is troubled with that particular brand of troublemakers. I wouldn't be surprised if the Pope declared them all heretics soon. They're all mad. They want to tear down buildings and live in mud huts and go barefoot. A man can't set a good example to the laity when he lives worse than their swine. There's a text in Isaiah..."

Stephen felt a jaw-cracking yawn rising within him. With a heroic effort he swallowed it. "I usually walk round the works once before I go to bed," he said. "Would you care to join me?" He and the abbot had ended half a dozen late-night visits this way, but he still issued the invitation in exactly the same words he'd used on the first night that the abbot joined him.

On dark nights it was no pleasure to inspect the littered building yard and the uncompleted church. Still Stephen's sense of duty sent him round with a candle behind glass, personally testing the strength of ropes and the oiled smoothness of lifting wheels, as had been his habit ever since the early days in Brito's yard. Tonight, though, the moon washed the church and yard with a light as pale and clear as thin whey, silvering rough-hewn blocks and emphasizing the lines of the open vaults with deep, sharp shadows. Stephen and the abbot paced slowly round the church. The beginnings of arches, flying buttresses without their fliers in place, piers rising to support the finished structure, rose out of the ground like the ribs of some giant beast. Along the west side, where the hill rose high and not quite level with the foundations of the church, the day laborers had been digging trenches and throwing back earth to use elsewhere. In the process of digging, they sometimes turned up strange old things, reminders that this hill had been a sacred place and a burial ground long before it belonged to the monks of the Christian church. Stephen's foot brushed against something that fell to ground with a hollow, muffled ringing like a gong struck underground.

"What's that?"

"Something the workmen dug up the other day. Too pretty to throw away." Stephen picked up the metal bowl, fingers caressing the embossed design of a face rising out of a circle of leaves. It was like the Green Men in the churches back home, but much older, and the bones they'd found with it had fallen to powder under the laborers' pickaxes. It was a pagan thing, not something Abbot Samson would want in his new church, but Stephen was thinking of asking one of the freemasons to copy the face onto a capital of some half-hidden pillar. The dead who had come before them must have their honor; the earth must be appeased. He knew these things, but felt shy of speaking them aloud, especially to a clever man like the abbot who would surely silence him with half a dozen well-chosen Biblical quotations.

"No, not that trash, over behind that wall." Abbot Samson pointed; Stephen saw nothing but rough stones.

"A trick of the light." But he was uneasy. If somebody was sneaking around his works this late at night, after he'd finished his evening prowl of inspection, he wanted to know about it. As he spoke, Stephen moved on light feet toward the far end of the heap of stones Abbot Samson had called a wall. When he was nearly there, he picked up a stone and flung it over at the far end of the wall.

A man's heavy body crashed into Stephen, knocked him over the stones and then was gone. At the other end of the wall, Abbot Samson was shouting hunting cries, sounding most unreligious as he puffed over broken ground in pursuit of another intruder.

"Here she is!" By the time Stephen had stood up and brushed the dust from his garments, the abbot had captured his prey. Holding her firmly by the arm, he dragged Yolande across the ground to face Stephen.

"A lovers' tryst?"

Yolande looked up at Stephen with big, tear-filled eyes that made her little face almost pretty. There was a smear of dust mixed with blood on her cheekbone; the abbot had tackled her with a little too much enthusiasm. Stephen used the long end of his sleeve to wipe her face.

"It's all right, Abbot. I know this girl. She's wife to one of my masons. Those huts we erected don't give them much privacy; there's no harm done if, during this hot weather, a man chooses to take his wife up the hill for a little pleasure in the cool of the evening. But tell your husband not to do it again, my girl," Stephen addressed Yolande with pretended sternness. "As you see, we patrol the building area nightly, and you might get hurt if someone took you for a thief."

When he released Yolande, she ran off down the hill without a word of thanks. "Unmannerly child," said the abbot without heat. "Really, the people we have crowding into the valley for this building work—no offense, Stephen, but your masons are a quarrelsome lot, and I don't want the monks or the villagers seeing such bad examples. And now this! Copulating in the very shadow of the church! Perhaps I should have the entire building reconsecrated!"

"I don't think they'd got that far, Abbot," said Stephen. "They were both fully clothed. Surely your church won't require reconsecration for a simple kiss, a friendly embrace between man and wife?"

"I suppose not," the abbot agreed. He sounded disappointed; but after a moment his mood eased and he began telling Stephen how many dignitaries of the Church would have come to the ceremony, if they had needed to reconsecrate the building.

"Cheer up," said Stephen, "you can do all that when we finish the church, and it'll be a much more impressive sight then."

"If we finish," muttered the abbot. "I'm sorry. I don't know why I said that. Tonight I have a premonition that I'll never live to see the church completed."

He wandered back to his rooms, muttering private worries and prayers, and Stephen set out on the walk back to La Tour Martel, congratulating himself on his quick thinking. The abbot would have been considerably more upset if he'd realized Yolande wasn't having an innocent moonlight walk with her husband. In the morning he really would have to talk with Geoffrey.

CHAPTER

22

◻

*T*he building site was beautiful in the morning. Below the churchyard, the monastery hummed with the minutely regulated life that Stephen remembered so well. When he had lived in that world, it had been a prison to him. But now that he was free of it, he could appreciate the simple, ordered beauty of life by the Rule though he knew it was not for him.

What was right for Stephen was the busy chaos surrounding the shell of the church, where work went on at a dozen different levels at once and craftsmen of all the building guilds competed for space and supplies. The clink of chisels on stone came from the masons' lodge; the deeper bell tone of the blacksmith's hammering at his forge joined in at intervals; the roar of the fire in the glassblowers' kiln added its menacing whisper of power and heat to the regulated sounds of men at work. Less obtrusive were the buzz of saws from the pit where two carpenters turned tree trunks into smooth beams for the roof, the splash of fresh water being poured over buckets of mortar to keep it from drying out, and the hiss of molten lead being cast into sheets to cover the roof as it was erected.

All these tasks were jumbled together because the original builder of the church had completed the choir, half built the nave, and left the transepts as empty ditches. Neither Stephen nor Abbot Samson nor Geoffrey could bear to wait and do things in an orderly fashion: first raising the walls of the transepts to match the height of those in the nave, then putting up arches that would have to sit over the winter for their mortar to harden, then efficiently finishing the roof and setting in all the stained-glass windows at one time. Instead they were trying to do it all at once. So quarrymen hauled blocks of stone for the transept walls, freemasons set up the arches over the nave and carved delicate twining shapes on the capitals of the columns, and glassworkers blew great sheets of blue and red and yellow glass to be turned into the sparkling mosaics that would fill the tall windows of the apse.

That winter, while the arches of the nave set hard and the transept walls were protected against frost by blankets of straw and turf, the fine carving could continue inside the church and the stained-glass artists could set thousands of tiny pieces of colored glass in their lead frames. Next spring the roof would go up over the nave and the windows there would be completed, and then, if he wished, Abbot Samson could hold his ceremonial opening of the church even while Stephen and his masons raised the transept walls to their full heights and lifted arches against the support of the pier buttresses.

Working this way meant that Stephen had to be at the works personally from dawn to dusk, juggling the demands of the different crafts and constantly planning ahead so that all the craftsmen would have their supplies.

He loved every minute of it.

And this morning the bustling churchyard seemed especially beautiful to him. The noises of the workmen blended into a song of praise no less harmonious than the voices of the monks in choir; the seeming chaos of a hundred men practicing their different crafts in a cramped space resolved, under his eye, to a complex patterned wheeling of tasks in separate orbits. This morning, surveying the churchyard and the monastery from his vantage point at the top of the east nave scaffolding, Stephen could appreciate the ordered procedures in the yard. Each band of craftsmen worked on their ordained tasks within the great scheme.

There were two men out of place, however; that confused Stephen for a moment. For some reason Ivo had left his spot in the masons' lodge to skulk behind the glass-blowers' hut. It would not be a comfortable place, with the raging heat of the kiln growing ever more fierce as the blowers brought it near to a perfect white heat. Ivo's thirst for a drink must be fierce indeed to make him hide in such a place. Stephen charitably resolved not to "discover" him at it.

The other break in the pattern was made by Geoffrey, who was wandering through the crowd, tripping over tools, absentmindedly stepping in front of two men shuffling along with a heavy stone on a litter. They had to break step and swing wide to avoid him. One of the tough women plasterers screeched curses at the stone-bearers for stepping into her mixing vat; the outcry made the blacksmith miss a blow at his forge and knock a bucket of tempering solution across the yard; two dogs, who shouldn't have been there anyway, were galvanized into fighting at the touch of the cold solution on their backs. And Geoffrey wandered on, cheerfully oblivious to the little circles of chaos that spread out behind him like ripples on a pond.

Chuckling despite his irritation, Stephen clambered down from the scaffolding.

"Good of you to come so soon," he hailed Geoffrey as his feet touched ground. "I hadn't thought you'd be up yet, much less have read the message I left for you." These days Stephen left the Tour Martel before daybreak so that he could get to the works at first light. Rather than waste precious daylight hours waiting to see Geoffrey, he'd told one of the page boys to ask his lord to meet the architect at the building grounds. But here was Geoffrey, not an hour after work had started; he must have risen about the time Stephen was leaving.

"Message? Oh, yes, of course." Geoffrey looked startled, and he kept glancing around as if he expected to see somebody else behind Stephen. "You wanted to talk to me?"

He sounded as if it were the first inkling he'd had of such a thing. He must be nervous—and Stephen thought he knew why. "It's all right," he said cheerfully, taking Geoffrey's elbow, "Abbot Samson doesn't know anything about it. This is just between you and me. Shall we take a turn around the church? You can look as if you are viewing the progress of the works."

Geoffrey jumped back when Stephen tried to draw him off toward the deserted high ground behind the apse. "Yes—well—can it wait? Actually, I've got some other things to do this morning."

"You found time to come down here, didn't you?" But Geoffrey was pulling away, looking around the building yard and refusing to meet Stephen's eyes. Stephen gave up his hopes of a slow, tactful discussion. "Now listen, Geoffrey. You mustn't seduce the craftsmen's women, really you mustn't. You are not their lord, and they will not be honored by the attention. My masons are a quarrelsome crew. I can't afford to have them throw down their tools because you've insulted one of their number."

"Oh. How did you know?"

At least he wasn't denying it.

"I recognized you last night, when Abbot Samson surprised you and Yolande behind the rubble pile and you damn near trampled me in your hurry to get away. *Not*," said Stephen, "a very knightly way to act—running off and leaving the lady to face us."

Geoffrey shrugged. "She's only a peasant, after all. They do it in ditches, like rabbits. Nothing for her to be embarrassed about."

In that moment Stephen came as near to disliking Geoffrey as he had at their first meeting on the pilgrim trip. He had to remind himself that the master builder could not knock the principal patron into a vat of freshly moistened lime mortar. He also reminded himself that Geoffrey was trained in fighting, and he wasn't, and he might well be the one to wind up in the lime mortar. Then he tried to think of some way to convince Geoffrey that he really must stay away from Yolande, who had enough problems already without being seduced by the lord of the manor.

And while he was silent, Geoffrey was making excuses about having another errand down in the building yard. "Sorry, maybe we can talk about it some other time, but," he winked as though nothing Stephen had said made the slightest impression, "can't disappoint a pretty girl, can we? Now where is the glassblowers' shed?"

"That way," said Stephen automatically, and then, "No, wait! I haven't finished yet! You can't—!"

Geoffrey was not accustomed to being told to wait. He

strode off, looking like a carefree lover on his way to an assignation, while Stephen was still stammering protests. Stephen felt like a fool and he longed more than ever to knock Geoffrey down. He stood quite still behind the apse, willing himself to a calm, logical mood appropriate to the master of the works. His eyes followed Geoffrey through the crowd of workmen and his mind pursued certain illogical tracks of its own.

Geoffrey had been surprised to find Stephen waiting for him. He hadn't had the message, then. But what else would have brought him to the works this early? He'd hinted that he was meeting Yolande, but it seemed unlikely that she would make an assignation in this busy, sweating milieu, only a few dangerous yards from where her husband worked. Had Geoffrey only said that to plague Stephen? It wouldn't be unlike him. No, something was going on. Ivo had been behind the glassworkers' shed a few minutes ago. Had he crept up there to spy on his wife with Geoffrey?

The soft roar of the fire in the glassworkers' kiln rose to a desperate howling, a sound like the waves of the sea crashing up and over houses and shore, and Stephen's body solved the puzzle before he did.

"Geoffrey! No! Don't go in there!" Geoffrey wouldn't be able to hear him over the rest of the noises that dinned upon his ears; only Stephen, who listened to the sounds of the works as a master musician listens to the harmony of a choir, had caught the new note of danger when the sound of the fire shifted key. The craftsmen around him were going about their business as usual. Stephen flung himself through the crowd, pushing and cursing those too slow to get out of the way; he threw himself at Geoffrey and pulled him down away from the hut. Before their bodies hit the ground, the world went up in a white-hot flash that deafened and blinded him.

When Stephen was conscious again, he was in darkness and somebody was removing cool damp compresses of herbs from his face. The slender, deft fingers and gentle movements could belong to only one person.

"Aude." He caught at her hand to keep her by his side.

She made a sound like a sob. "You're awake? Stephen? Do you know me?"

"Of course I know you," he said irritably. "Where are we? Is this our room? Why'd you hang tapestries over the windows? I can't see you."

"It's . . . it's night." Her voice quivered and he knew she was lying. Besides, he could see the dazzle of sunlight beyond the tapestries. . . . No, it seemed to follow the motion of his eyes, like a white sheet of flame perpetually hovering on the edge of his vision. He was too tired to puzzle it out.

"I'm thirsty." And his entire right side was hot, on fire; what fool had laid their bed next to an open fireplace, and then lit the fire, in summer?

A few drops of minty liquid trickled down his throat, and more compresses took away the worst of the fire, and he fell asleep before he could sort out these mysteries.

When he woke again there was cool blue summer twilight filling the room, and he had a sense of having slept for a long time. Aude was a pale shadow at the edge of his vision. He called to her and she hurried to bend over him.

"How did you know I was here, Stephen? Did I make a noise and wake you?"

"No, you were quiet as a mouse, but why wouldn't I recognize my own wife not three feet from our bed?"

She was crying. Stephen didn't understand why. He swung his feet over the edge of the bed and sat up, meaning to touch her face, and the world tilted sickeningly around him with a flame of pain along his right side.

"Aude?" He felt weak as a baby, confused and lost, and expecting her to make it right for him. Stephen gritted his teeth against the pain. After three long, slow breaths it was bearable. "Where are my clothes? I've got to get down to the works. You shouldn't have let me sleep all day. God knows what kind of problems they'll have got into without me. There was a fire, wasn't there?" It was all jumbled in his head, Geoffrey and Yolande and Ivo and a sheet of white sun exploding over them, but he knew something very wrong had happened and that it was his responsibility.

"Hush, dear. Lie down again. There's no hurry. See, it's almost dark, nobody is working now. You might as well rest through the night."

"No. I've got to make my evening rounds."

Because of his insistence, Aude reluctantly told him

things that she'd meant to break to him gently as he grew well. He hadn't missed one day of work, but six. He'd been burned in the fire, not badly but enough to make him feverish and delirious for a while. When he complained of the dark room before it had been broad midday with light streaming in the windows, and the physician who attended Geoffrey had shaken his head and warned Aude that Stephen might never recover his sight. That was why she'd been crying just now, with relief that he wasn't permanently blinded.

"Six days!" Stephen stood up, unwisely, and had to hold on to the wall while the waves of pain and dizziness rolled over him again. "I must get up to the church. Who's been looking after things in my absence? Maître Jean? The masons will obey him, but how has he managed the rest of the crew?"

"It's all right," said Aude. "Nothing's gone wrong. There's been no work done since the glassblowers' hut burned up."

Stephen sat back on the edge of the bed, relieved and ashamed that his shaky body was so glad of the respite. "If there's more, you'd best tell me."

Three people had died in that fire: the two glassblowers who were working at the kiln, and Ivo. It was thought that Ivo had thrown some of the glassworkers' volatile etching solution into the kiln furnace to make it blaze up, meaning to "accidentally" push Geoffrey into the flames. Only, with his lifelong ineptitude, he'd created a blaze that consumed him and the hut in one sheet of fire before Geoffrey was well within range.

"And Geoffrey owes his life to you," Aude pointed out.

But it wasn't much of a gift. Geoffrey had been far worse burned than Stephen; his hair had caught fire, he'd lost his sight in one eye, and one side of his handsome face was ruined. He was beginning to recover now; he was able to take food and give orders, but he refused to leave his room or talk to anybody but the wandering Franciscan friar who'd come through the village just before the explosion.

"At least he is alive."

In the face of so many useless deaths, Stephen couldn't feel proud of having averted only part of the tragedy. "I should have known what was going on."

Despair settled in Stephen's soul, worse even than the

fatigue and pain and sickness that already assailed him. For so long he had been happily occupied with his work that he'd managed to forget what a poor flawed thing he was. For a moment he felt cold and frightened and small, and a vision of a vast dark hall filled with towering columns came to him. Worthless indeed! If he'd been a better son, Mam wouldn't have left him. It he'd been a better friend, this tragedy might have been averted. Ivo dead; his friend maimed for life. It was all his fault. The indictment was unanswerable.

"If I guessed about Geoffrey and Yolande, I should have realized that Ivo might guess, too. I knew him. There were always strange accidents when we worked together in Brito's stoneyard; once or twice I was nearly maimed by his carelessness or malice. I should have realized he'd try something like that again."

"Don't blame yourself!" said Aude sharply. "I won't have it. And lie still. I want to put more compresses on your burns. Don't you realize that you saved Geoffrey's life? And nearly lost your eyesight in doing so? He owes you everything. And he'll realize it once he comes to his senses."

Then Aude broke the news to him that Geoffrey had ordered all work on the church stopped.

"Why?"

Aude shrugged.

"And Abbot Samson puts up with that?"

"Geoffrey," Aude pointed out, "holds the pursestrings. Besides, without you to oversee the works..."

"That's true." Stephen relaxed and allowed Aude to spread the damp bags of healing herbs over his burnt skin. For a moment Stephen had been fancying all sorts of mad things: that Geoffrey somehow blamed him for the explosion, that he didn't want the church finished. What ridiculous notions. Of course Geoffrey wouldn't want the work to go forward without Stephen there to see that all was done properly, and neither would Abbot Samson. Besides, there wasn't much the men could do without Stephen's daily decisions. It was far better to let them have a few days' holiday.

Something else was tugging at his memory. "What about Yolande? I suppose she'll go back to her people?"

"I understand she won't say where they are," said Aude.

"She's still staying in the hut she shared with Ivo. I think she's ashamed. Or maybe she thinks they won't have her back. She did run away with Ivo, after all."

"She's young. She'll marry again." If he did something to help Yolande, would that atone for his earlier carelessness? "Have you talked to her? She probably doesn't have any money, Ivo wasn't the sort to save his wages. Tell her we'll pay for her travel home, find a reliable merchant going that way."

"She wanted to see me. It might be a good idea. She might talk to a woman, where she wouldn't say anything to Geoffrey's chaplain. Only—I didn't want to leave you."

"I'm all right now. Why don't you go down to see her. Is she still in Ivo's lodgings?"

Aude put it off till the next day, on the excuse of the late hour; Stephen thought Aude was afraid he would go off to the works as soon as her back was turned. And she was right, it was too late to disturb Yolande. He wished, though, that he could shake off his brooding feeling that something else terrible was about to happen. It was probably the summer thunderclouds hanging low over the valley, darkening the evening sky, that made him feel that way.

Later Stephen wondered if it would have made any difference, if he'd persuaded Aude to go down that evening. Probably not. As it was, Yolande came to the castle before Aude went to see her. First she tried to see Geoffrey, and was refused admittance; then she interrupted Aude who was mixing a soothing drink for Stephen.

Stephen heard Aude's voice raised sharply outside the door, and a girl sobbing incoherently afterwards; he couldn't quite make out the words. Then Aude pushed the door halfway open and paused, her shoulder braced against the planks, speaking more softly now. "You can't be sure yet, and you don't want to have the sin on your conscience. Wait a few days, let me talk to Stephen. There are other solutions."

"Not for me," Yolande said. "And no more time. *He* won't see me, and if you won't help. . . ."

Aude sighed. "Wait here. I have to tend Stephen. I didn't say I wouldn't help, only I won't do what you're asking."

She backed through the door, both hands holding a wide

wooden bowl, and bumped it shut with her elbow. "Lie down. I want to change your dressings." Tears sparkled on the ends of her lashes.

"What was that about?"

"Yolande. She's got some women's troubles and she thought I might know some herbs to help her."

It had sounded like more than that, and Stephen didn't have to work hard to figure it out.

"She's carrying Geoffrey's child."

Aude straightened, the sopping compresses draped over her wrists in their long linen bands. "It could as well be Ivo's. Who'd know, if the silly girl didn't insist on telling me—and half the castle servants, no doubt—that Ivo'd been unable to do anything with her these three months past, so drink-sodden he was."

"Ah." That helped to explain Yolande's flirtatious ways, and the bruises Ivo had put on her face. The girl was desperate to prove she was desirable to somebody. Ivo must have been shamed by the loss of his manhood, and perhaps intimidated by this young, demanding girl. The tragedy had been brewing even before Geoffrey stirred it. Stephen felt a little less guilty.

"She wanted me to help her get rid of it." Aude's hands were too firm, tweaking the compresses into place, and Stephen winced. "Me! Could she not have asked somebody else? It's a mockery of my prayers for a baby of my own."

Stephen rested one hand on top of her busy fingers. "Our prayers. And they may be answered yet."

Aude turned away. "She's feared her parents would know 'twasn't Ivo's, since he's so dark and Geoffrey so fair. She says they'd turn her out for a whore. I think she just doesn't want the trouble of a child to raise."

"It's hard for a woman alone." The old hurt in his chest had nothing to do with the burns that Aude was tending. "Better she should make that decision now than later."

"Yes. But I was thinking. Only I wanted to ask you first, would you mind if—"

Then a woman screamed outside, and Aude never finished her question. Stephen threw his clothes on without feeling the pain of raw skin underneath the cloth.

Yolande had thrown herself into the deep fishpond in the castle gardens. The kitchen assistant who'd found her made no attempt to pull her out, but simply stood at the edge of the pond, screaming.

Long green weeds from the bottom of the pond wrapped around her arms and legs, weighting them down so that all Stephen saw at first was the pale face floating in its halo of swirling hair. The slight movements of her limbs, pulled down by the entangling weeds, made her look eerily alive. Death had robbed her face of color, and water had darkened her glowing red hair to a deep shadow with only the memory of fire in it. She looked lovelier and more peaceful than she ever had in her short life.

"Pull her out," shouted a rasping, unfamiliar voice behind Stephen. "Damn you for soulless dogs, why doesn't someone get her out of there!"

Stephen turned and stared at half of Geoffrey's face. The other half was covered in bandages, white linen strips soaked in fat and wrapped around and around over one eye and ear and most of his chin. The white ends flickered loose over his shoulders and he looked like a corpse bursting free of the grave wrappings. And his golden voice was gone: he must have breathed in the first blast of fiery air. All that was left was an angry, impotent rasp of command.

The knights and men-at-arms were coming to the front of the crowd, elbowing aside the servants, but no one moved to lift up Yolande. They ringed the pond, staring in shocked silence, while Geoffrey raved and wore out what remained of his voice in cursing everyone—himself, Yolande, and all the useless bystanders. Stephen looked round the circle of faces, still as statues. Geoffrey was right. Somebody had to get her out.

The shock of cool water on his burns took Stephen's breath away for a minute. But the water came only halfway up his legs, and he wasn't burned so badly there. How had Yolande drowned in this shallow margin of the pool? He bent and pulled her free of the clinging green weeds, and the answer came to him with a shock. He glanced around covertly. Had anybody else noticed how hard it was for him to free her of the weeds? He thought not.

She was slight, hardly more than a child, no weight at all once he'd lifted her out of the weeds. It was easy to hold her with one arm under her shoulders and one under her knees. As he waded back to the solid land, one of her slippers fell off and her bare foot dangled down toward the water.

As he set one foot on the bank, the chapel bell above them began pealing.

"Who's ringing that bell!" Geoffrey shouted in his thick, hoarse voice. "Who's the fool! Someone tell him to stop!"

The bell went on pealing wildly until a groom from the stables summoned up the courage to climb the chapel stairs and peek into the bell tower. He claimed there was no one there; but as soon as he laid hand on the rope, the ringing ceased. By that time the laundress and her helpers had consented to wash and clothe Yolande's body for burial, and Stephen was back in his room with Aude sobbing on his shoulder, for once oblivious of his burns.

"I would have taken the baby," she cried. "That's what I wanted to talk to you about. We have none of our own, and she didn't want the one she was going to have. How could I help her kill it? I wanted to rear that child. I wouldn't have cared whether it was true-born or a bastard. I wanted a little baby of my own to take care of, Stephen, only I thought I should ask you first. Oh, if only she'd waited! If only someone had pulled her out in time!"

Stephen rocked her trembling body and thought of many things he might say, none of them particularly helpful. He wasn't at all sure that he would have wanted to raise the child of flighty Yolande and unstable Geoffrey. And Yolande must have been determined on death. She hadn't just thrown herself into the pond as a child's dramatic display of unhappiness. Stephen would never tell anyone, but Yolande had wrapped the weeds around her body and held them there to keep herself under the water. That's why Stephen had trouble pulling her out of the water. He imagined going voluntarily into the choking coldness of the water, into the slimy embrace of the water reeds, and his own lungs ached in sympathy.

Presently, when Aude was calmer, he laid her down on the bed to sleep and went in search of the castle chaplain. A long talk and a large bribe convinced the man that Yolande had stumbled into the pond accidentally, and in her panic she had become entangled in the weeds and had drowned. She would not be considered a suicide and she would be buried in holy ground. That was all Stephen could think to do for her.

The castle lay under a pall of silence for three days. No more work was done at the church; Geoffrey had not lifted his command that the work should stop, and Abbot Samson did not feel that this was a good time to oppose him. Besides, the abbot pointed out, Stephen was still weak and should rest for a few days to make sure he didn't take a fever from his dip in the fishpond.

Every day Stephen trudged down from the castle, around the church and back up to his rooms trying to regain his strength. The empty windows in the apse and choir, the arches over the roofless nave, and the shells of walls rising from the transept foundations seemed to reproach him for his inactivity. Stephen noticed that every day there were fewer men waiting to greet him in the long rows of temporary lodgings set up beside the convent wall. The masons had stayed, kept together by Maître Jean and by their own desire to complete this bold new church. But the day laborers had gone back to ploughing and ditching and hedging on the manors around the valley, and the other skilled workers were drifting away to other jobs.

"What do you expect?" Abbot Samson sighed. "They are working men. They cannot afford to stay on here without work and without wages."

"Tell them it will only be a few days. Tell them I'll pay them out of my own own purse."

The abbot sighed again. "We do not know that it will be only a few days. And my conscience will not permit me to let you beggar yourself in the pursuit of my dream."

"What are you talking about? Geoffrey must come to his senses soon."

"I've heard things. You should talk to Geoffrey."

"He's shut himself up in his rooms and won't see anyone. *You* know that. What sort of things have you heard?"

Abbot Samson had lost weight in the last two weeks, and his loose skin was grayish and without resilience. He sat down heavily on one of the benches along the cloister wall and looked up at the shell of the church, avoiding Stephen's eyes. "I'm too old for all this. I think God is punishing me for my selfish desire to have the most beautiful church in Burgundy. Why does a White Monk of the Cistercians need beauty to seduce his eyes?"

Stephen cheered up the abbot by quoting the verses of

Suger of St. Denis. Then he set out for la Tour Martel, determined to shake Geoffrey back to life. Since the accident, Geoffrey's rooms were shut off from the rest of the castle, and the only person allowed inside was the Franciscan friar who had taken shelter at the Tour Martel after he'd annoyed the villagers. Stephen found himself, to his disgust, joining the throng of friends and servants, all of whom had urgent messages for Geoffrey. When the gaunt friar appeared with a bowl of boiled beans that was to be Geoffrey's dinner, the waiting petitioners all tried to shove in after him.

"Tell him his favorite bitch is about to whelp," implored the chief huntsman. "Doesn't he want to see whether the new litter of puppies will be as fine and healthy as the last?"

"Just bring him my special hot posset with honey. It always did pick up the boy's spirits."

"There's a small war in Berry, if he wants some amusement to take his mind off things," suggested one of Geoffrey's old friends. The castle was littered with such hangers-on, landless knights, and penniless nobles who'd hastened to help Geoffrey celebrate his good fortune four years before and had never left. It made Stephen uneasy to think he might be just another one of that lot.

He didn't even get to ask the friar to warn Geoffrey that the church was losing workmen at an appalling rate.

"Not that it would have made any difference," he grumbled to Aude. "The man's probably not delivering any of the messages."

"And a good thing, too. Geoffrey needs to be left in peace. And he *has* got some sins to think over." Aude patted Stephen's clenched fist until his fingers relaxed. "Surely he'll come to Yolande's burial tomorrow. Then he'll see for himself what's happening to the workmen, and if he doesn't notice, you can point it out tactfully."

Stephen agreed that would be the best way to approach the subject. He waited hopefully in the churchyard the next afternoon, but was disappointed to see only two figures accompanying the bearers who carried Yolande's shrouded coffin. Both men wore the rough, undyed tunics of Franciscan friars and had hoods pulled low over their bowed heads.

As they came closer, he stared at the taller friar. There

was something familiar about that tall form. Surely—no, it couldn't be....

The friar put back his hood and Stephen's suspicions were confirmed. It was Geoffrey. That is, the left side of the face was Geoffrey's; the right side was a mass of raw flesh. It looked as if his face had melted and fused together in the heat of the fire.

"I am glad to see you, Stephen." Geoffrey's voice was low and rough, but without the rasping urgency of his hysterical shouts at the fishpond. "Of all those at the Tour Martel, you are the one I most wished to bid farewell."

"Farewell," Stephen repeated. He wondered if he sounded as stupid as he felt.

"As you see," Geoffrey's hand indicated the patched tunic and his bare feet, already bleeding from the walk down from the castle, "I have decided to expiate my sins by embracing yet another mistress, Sweet Lady Poverty."

"Is hemp and homespun going to become the new livery at the Tour Martel?" It was a feeble joke, but still Stephen hoped that Geoffrey would laugh, peel off the tunic to reveal a new surcoat of brocade and fur, lift off the red mass of ruined flesh like a beggar taking off his bread-poultice sores.

"The Tour Martel, that abode of pride and vanity and foolish indulgence, is no longer my home. And I am no longer the Sieur de Tour Martel. I am only a poor friar of the Order of Francis, with no more possessions to trouble me than the tunic on my back and the cord that girdles it." Geoffrey shook back his sleeves and spread his arms. "Ah, Stephen, you do not know how wonderful is the freedom of Lady Poverty!"

"And are your servants and dependents equally delighted with Lady Poverty? I hadn't heard anything about this. Who is going to take over your manors?"

Geoffrey frowned. "I have arranged for the transfer of the property to the Order. I suppose it will be given to the poor."

"What about the people who depend on you? And what about your knight service? Who's going to take over your obligations to your liege lord? You can't desert all your obligations like this." Stephen laid a hand on Geoffrey's arm. "Come back to the castle with me, let's have some of that excellent Rhenish your steward guards so jealously and talk about this."

"I do not drink wine. Please, Stephen, do not try to tempt me."

"He is no friend who would entangle your feet in the briars of sin, when once you have set your face toward righteousness." Those were the first words Stephen had heard the wandering friar speak that day, and they were uttered in a deep, ringing tone that was full of conviction. For a moment Stephen felt guilty for trying to dissuade Geoffrey. Then he looked at the silly, beatific smile on Geoffrey's face, and redoubled his efforts.

"Geoff, look at you!"

"That penance, fortunately, is denied me. But if my face offends you, I will wear my hood closer." Geoffrey tugged the hood back over the worst of his scars. Stephen felt a wall going up between them.

"No, I don't mean that. Lady Poverty is a charming girl, but so were all the others you chased. And you know how quickly you tired of them. Look at your feet, they're cut already, you're not used to walking like a peasant. In a month you'll have sore feet and you'll be sick with gas from living on beans, and you'll have a perpetual cold from sleeping in hedgerows. Geoff, it's no fun to be poor, not when you have a choice. Poverty means starving in the months before harvest, losing fingers and toes to the frost in winter, and selling your children because you don't need another mouth to feed."

Stephen's throat closed up and for a moment he couldn't talk. He forced himself to concentrate on Geoffrey and the terrible mistake he was making. "Geoff, you won't like it, and when you want to go back to the Tour Martel it won't be there."

"We have delayed long enough," said the wandering friar in his deep, resonant voice that lent meaning to the simplest statement. "Come, Brother Geoffrey. Do not listen to the voice of the tempter."

"Wait! What are we to do about the church? How are we to pay the workers? They've been drifting off ever since the accident."

Geoffrey looked back. "Oh, the church? Don't worry about that, Stephen. It's not to be finished. My brother in Christ has shown me the folly of worshiping in tabernacles of stone. Fine buildings are not suitable for the truly humble servants of Our Lord. If the church were mine," he said without rancor, "I would have it pulled down. And I will not pay for a construction of vanity that brought such tragedy into our valley. As I told you, I have given everything I own to the poor."

CHAPTER

23

◻

"He didn't mean it," said Abbot Samson when he heard the news.

"I heard him. He meant it. And we've no recourse; he never signed a charter promising us anything." Stephen and Aude had left the Tour Martel for the hospitality of the monastery at Chastelvert on the day after Geoffrey's departure. The first thing Abbot Samson had done, on hearing the news, was to send for a man of law to find some means of getting back the lands and tolls. The results were not promising. Even if Geoffrey were to recover from his fit of religion, it was doubtful whether he could regain possession of the lands he had turned over to the Franciscan order. Apparently there'd been a number of similar cases with the alarming spread of this new preaching order. So far, none of the heirs contesting such gifts had managed to get their patrimony back. Abbot Samson and his monks were in a far weaker position since they were not heirs.

Even as Stephen and Aude left the Tour Martel, busy men in undyed robes were already inspecting the fittings. They cheerfully discussed plans for the great hall which would serve as a shelter for reformed beggars once the sinful tapestries and idolatrous carvings were removed. "I don't know how they got the news so fast," Stephen

grumbled, though he knew from his own experience that
news carried by wayfarers traveled almost as fast as any
carried by a king's messenger. "You'd think that preaching
friar had turned himself into a sparrow and flown across
the country, spreading the news."

"Mmm. They do say this Brother Francis is fond of
birds," Aude teased. "How d'you know that didn't happen?"

"Oh, hush! Do you want to give them credit for another
miracle?" The Franciscan friars were already claiming
Geoffrey's conversion as a miracle. Considering how easily
Geoffrey could be brought to believe in anything from a
new Crusade to the maunderings of a Syrian witch, Stephen
felt the friars were exaggerating.

Now he and Aude lived in two of the rooms in the long
row of temporary housing built for the workmen. There
was plenty of space; more than half the men who'd come
to the valley had drifted away by now, and the rest were
just waiting for word of a big project somewhere else. But
the rooms were so low that Stephen was continually
knocking his head on the flimsy roof, and the damp got
into his rolls of parchment and left smudges of greenish
mold on his tracings.

He met Abbot Samson in the tracing house for one last
conference, to show him where work had stopped in
relation to the grandiose plans, and to confer on how to
protect the unfinished building against the coming winter.
"Next time I'm going to bid higher and put the extra
money into decent lodgings for my men," Stephen vowed,
and then remembered that there would probably not be a
next time. Who'd give him a commission on the strength
of the work he'd barely begun here?

"You knew this was going to happen, didn't you?" he
challenged the abbot.

Samson had aged in the last few weeks, his bull-chest
sunk upon the frame of his massive shoulders and his
silver-speckled red hair faded to unremarkable gray. "I was
afraid of something like this, yes. That friar was a persuasive speaker. Young Geoffrey is like the rest of his family,
easily swayed by the last person he hears. And all the
world has heard of how these mad friars preach poverty
and live it, to the extent that they even want God's house
to be a mud hovel. I thought the friar would persuade
Geoffrey to give his money to feed the poor for a day with

bread, but I never imagined it would come to this. The last Tour Martel begging barefoot on the road!" Abbot Samson snorted. "I shouldn't be surprised if his father rises to haunt us, for letting such a thing happen. Not that we could have stopped it. The whole family was always dangerously unstable. Related to the Plantagenets, you know, that devil's brood of English kings."

"You mean the Tour Martels were all mad?"

"Something like that, yes. Or possessed by demons. The older boys seemed bent on rushing to their own destruction. I thought Geoffrey had escaped the family taint."

The mention of demons gave Stephen a faint flicker of hope. "I don't suppose an exorcism—?"

Abbot Samson waved one hand as if pushing the idea away. "Do you think the Franciscans would invite me to exorcise a demon from one of their new friars? And anyway, it's too late. He's already handed the property over."

"So that's it." Stephen glowered from the tracing house window at the skeleton of the church, with its empty window casings like eye sockets, its nave arched over with a crisscross of ribs that gave no protection against wind and rain, and its naked buttresses rising without the flyers that would anchor the slender shells of the upper walls. Stephen could complete the structure in his mind's eye: the golden limestone shell would catch the sunlight and transmute it into jeweled colors through stained-glass windows; the ribs of the high vaults would echo the rhythms of a chanted liturgy. But to a layman, it would simply be a lonely, unfinished building that gave no particular notice of the talents of the new builder from Outremer.

"It's not exactly going to establish me as an architect."

"I did think it would be nice, one winter, to sing the services without having rain lash through the nave."

"Is there any of that good Rhenish left?"

They drank silently and brooded over the fine line drawings which depicted the plan and elevation of a golden church that should have rivaled the great cathedrals of the north. Stephen was tormented by the knowledge that all his painstaking geometry, all his measurements and details would never be seen. No one would know how he had planned the proportions, from the least to the greatest, to sing together in perfect harmony.

Once, not long ago, Stephen had been drinking like this with Geoffrey, when out of his despair and Geoffrey's frustration had been born this marvelous idea. It had seemed too good to be true. And so it was.

"Well," said Stephen, trying for philosophy, "I've had some good experience here. It'll stand me in good stead elsewhere." If there was any work for him elsewhere. After having directed the construction of this church, he didn't think he could bear to work under another master, copying and tracing according to somebody else's vision.

"I suppose you can use the plans on something else. The small bits anyway." Abbot Samson pointed at the drawing of a pillar wreathed round with vines, bursting forth at the top into the face of the Green Man with his frame of leaves. The face was a copy of the ancient bowl that had been disinterred while digging the transept foundations.

"No, I won't be doing that." Stephen tried to tear the parchment, but it was too strong for him: best quality skins, newly washed and only scraped down the once. He rolled up the plan, carelessly crumpling the ends together, and flung it out the open door.

Aude had silently watched Stephen's despair for some days. All her attempts to cheer him up, to point out that there were other buildings and other work surely waiting in his future, had been received with the same polite inattention he gave to the announcement that dinner was ready or that it was raining. He was withdrawing and she was afraid that somewhere in his deep solitude he had already judged himself a failure.

Aude felt helpless. She couldn't joke about this tragedy, couldn't chide Stephen for sadness when it was so appropriate, and couldn't argue sense into someone who stared right through her. Without any answer or response from Stephen, Aude began telling her thoughts and venting her anger as she went about her household duties.

"He doesn't talk. He doesn't eat. And he blames himself for it all," Aude murmured while she was taking in the sun-dried laundry from the grass behind their rooms. "What shall I *do*? I don't know how to help him.

"It's my fault, too, of course. I don't think he'd give in to troubles quite so easily if he had somebody to take care of. If we'd ever had children. . . ."

That hurt too much to say aloud. Aude sank down on a stool with her lap full of folded linens, and pressed her hands together so hard they hurt. Until she said it, she hadn't realized that she had given up the hope of having a child. Well, they'd been married how many years now, and she still had not conceived? After what the soldiers did to her, she'd always suspected there might be trouble. But until now, she had not given up hope.

Aude thought about the money they had been saving all these years for the family that never came. Such a waste. Worse than the waste of labor that went into the church on the hill, now standing empty and desolate for lack of gold.

"Well, then," she said, "if you've really given up hope, you can give some to somebody else. And you'll do it with a blithe heart and a cheerful face, or it's no true charity."

Then she went to find Stephen.

As she trudged up the stairs to the tracing house, something pale and flapping sailed down to hit her in the face and enfold her with its outspread wings. For a moment she thought it was a bird. But when she caught it in her opened hands, she recognized Stephen's master plan for the church. This must be a sign, to show her how close to despair Stephen was, and to remind her to do what she could for him. Aude prayed for a willing heart, and prayed that Stephen wouldn't see how much what she was about to offer would cost her. When she thought about the men sitting upstairs and drinking their way into despair, she felt angry enough to carry out her plan.

Five angry steps brought her up to the door of the tracing house, out of breath and trailing parchment behind her. She glanced at the cluttered scene before her: dividers and pens pushed out of the way to make room for flagons of wine, ink spilled into the flat surface of the plaster and tracked in dirty footprints right across the hardened plaster. And in the center of this mess, the two strongest men she'd ever known were sitting with slumped shoulders and defeated faces, guzzling wine like a couple of alehouse sots.

"Here's your church plan." Aude flung the parchment down on the table between the two men, not-so-accidentally brushing one of the flagons of wine into Stephen's lap as she did so. "If you've no more use for it, at least you might pay some attention where you throw your trash. This hit me in the face as I was coming up to see you."

"So you throw wine at me in revenge?" Stephen grumbled. His lap was a red puddle; when he stood, it dripped all over the floor.

"You don't need any more to drink." Aude took the other flagon and upended it neatly over a heap of rags on the floor, careful not to pour it over the abbot. She knew just how much she could get away with here. It was necessary to insult these two until they regained their manhood, but not too much, or they'd only sulk.

"What do you know about it?" Stephen made an unsuccessful grab at her, too late to save the wine. Aude tossed the empty flagon at him and stood with her hands braced on her slender hips.

"I know this project was conceived in drink, and what a bad thing that's been for all of us. I know it was a drunken mason with half-baked plans of revenge, and a boy drunk first on sex and then on God, who brought it down in ruins. And I know that more drink will solve nothing. Look at the two of you!" Aude rolled her eyes. "Sitting in your trash like a couple of sturdy beggars who can think of nothing better to do than to pickle your brains in wine. Will that finish this church for us?"

"You've got a better idea?"

"Any number of them. To begin with, why don't we finish the church ourselves?" Aude picked her way delicately around the sopping rags and sat down beside Abbot Samson. Now that she had the attention of both men, she didn't feel the need to stand and spit sparks at them. But it seemed like a good idea to keep the width of the table between herself and Stephen for a few minutes.

"What with?"

"For a start, there's our savings. We have the rest of Ibn Masoud's legacy, and the money you've banked with Marco Sanudo."

Stephen gaped. "But ... you always ..." When he was hiring men for the project, Aude had been the one who insisted that two-thirds of their capital be kept back; one-third for emergencies, one-third to raise their children like gentlefolk.

"This is an emergency, isn't it?" Perhaps if she talked fast enough, he wouldn't mention the other part. "I can't think of anything more like an emergency than the need to pay the good men you've brought together here, so they don't drift away to other jobs. And it can't wait, can it? You said yourself, there are more men leaving every day. And that stands to reason; you can't expect them to wait on empty bellies and promises."

"And what about saving for our family?"

He had to ask. She was the one who'd always insisted on that.

"I don't see any reason to do that. We've been married six years now. If children were to come, we'd have them already." Aude hoped that her brisk and matter-of-fact tone would cover up the anguish she'd felt in the last few days of lonely mourning. As she wept for Yolande and her unborn child and for the children she herself did not have, she had come to take this death as a sign. It would have been so easy for her and Stephen to rear the child whose existence had sent Yolande into the fishpond. Wasn't it a sign that they weren't meant to have children? Wasn't it a sign that she was being selfish, clinging to a hope that showed no sign of fruition, and in the process standing in the way of Stephen's dearest wish?

"You always said that the buildings you raised were your children. So let's spend the money here. We've at least eight or nine hundred livres put aside—more by now, if I know Marco."

Abbot Samson gasped and hastily recovered himself, but Aude thought she saw a new light of hope in his eyes. Better than that, though, was the frown of concentration on Stephen's face. His mind was back at work, calculating and figuring and constructing. Aude gave a small sigh of her own. Their savings were well spent to bring Stephen back to himself.

"It's not enough." Stephen was pacing the tracing house floor, hands locked behind his back, brow creased in thought. "We've at least three years' work after this season, and it'll take six hundred livres a year just to pay the men, not to mention supplies."

"Can't the suppliers wait for their payment? Rufus the quarryman, Maître Ghilbert the ironmonger, they're men of property. They wouldn't go hungry if they waited until winter to be paid."

Stephen shook his head and Aude's heart sank. He was getting ready to explain something to her, patiently and slowly, with a logic that would take all the hope out of the world. "The suppliers might wait till winter, Aude, but they won't wait forever. And nine hundred livres just isn't enough to build a cathedral."

"Church," interrupted Abbot Samson. "Cathedrals are for bishops, Master Stephen." He was grinning. Maybe for him, the numbers worked out differently.

"Yes, but it's a simple sum. Say, three hundred livres for wages through the rest of this building season and four hundred to pay the suppliers, then six hundred livres a year for three years to cover wages and supplies...it won't be so much in future years, maybe three hundred a year, that's still..."

Aude's fingers flickered unobtrusively under the cover of her long sleeves and she came up with the sum before Stephen said it.

"Three thousand, four hundred livres!" he concluded in an awed voice. "You see, Aude? We couldn't begin to build a whole cathedral."

"Church," the abbot corrected again, unheeded.

"It's not quite like paying wages to keep a troop of masons together between engagements, my love. Ibn Masoud's legacy could do that for us. But it's no use. If only I could have found work without Geoffrey's patronage! If only somebody had believed in me!"

"Somebody does believe in you," interjected Abbot Samson. "I've seen your plans and your work, Master Stephen. Both are good. The work is thorough, well-founded, solid. The plans aspire to heaven, as would the finished church. I could ask for no better builder than the one young Geoffrey forced upon me."

A month ago this testimonial would have sent Stephen's head spinning. Now he could barely summon up a smile of thanks. "Very kind of you, Abbot. I wish I could stay and finish this project."

"Maybe you can." The abbot was still grinning, as he had been ever since Aude mentioned the sum at their disposal. "If you'll meet the wages of the men through the rest of this building season, I will have a little talk with your suppliers. Perhaps they will remit a part of their bill until next year. If not, we can always go elsewhere."

"That we cannot," snapped Stephen. "I personally selected the finest grained limestone from the best quarry on the river, and I'm not finishing this church with second-rate materials."

"Ah, but does Master Rufus know that? I thought not."

"Even if they let us put off payment for a year, what then?" Stephen challenged the abbot. "With nine hundred livres, I can just pay the workmen through the end of next building season. They we'll have two years' worth of supplies to pay for and no cash in the coffers—and the church still won't be done."

"By then," said the abbot, "we may hope to have found other sources of income for God's work."

"Prayer?"

"Don't sneer at prayer," said Abbot Samson mildly. "But I had in mind some more active ways to find the money. There are many ways to do God's work, and I pray that He will forgive me for having overlooked so many of them all these years. I fear I was so angry at the way the Tour Martel family cheated the abbey out of those vineyards, that I did not search as thoroughly as I might for other ways of financing the church construction. We will begin, as soon as this building season is over, by making a tour of the province with the holy relics from our altar. I will explain to the people about the miracles these relics have performed in times past and about the need to house the bones of these saints properly. You will describe the wonders of the house of God that we are building. Contributions from the faithful," said the abbot with a wandering eye, "have been known to swell a building fund by as much as fifty percent."

"But exactly what miracles *have* these relics performed, Abbot? St. Gudrun, isn't it, and St. Hildemar? I don't recall hearing any stories—"

"Half the left collarbone of St. Gudrun," the abbot corrected briskly, "and a milk tooth of the blessed Nevil of Vezelay, who has not yet been sanctified. You're right, we could do with some better relics. Leave that to me."

"Any other ideas?"

"Perhaps the guilds that work on the church would consent to forgo some of their wages, if they were allowed

to consecrate windows in the names of their patron saints,"
Aude suggested.

"Common men?" The abbot winced.

"As common clay as Adam's." Now it was Stephen's turn
to sound firm. "That's a good idea, Aude. The merchants
might pay well, too. I wonder if Rufus the quarryman
would like to have a lancet window. And there's the
ironmonger. He might like a nice window showing your
namesake, Abbot, bursting his iron chains."

Abbot Samson gave a faint moan. "There is also the
matter of indulgences," he said rapidly, "remission of
hearth taxes in the villages belonging to the monastery. I
could persuade a few of our wealthy neighbors that their
ancestors' souls would benefit from daily masses in the
new church. We can think of a number of ways to raise
money, Master Stephen, before we have to give over part
of the church to a—a—"

"Ironmonger," said Stephen, clearly and firmly. "A man
of property, Abbot."

"There are plenty of wellborn men of property to be
tapped first. What a pity that I didn't charge young
Geoffrey a good sum in cash for raising the excommunication on his father and brothers!"

"Never mind," said Stephen kindly, "I'm sure you'll find
somebody else to excommunicate before this affair is over."

Now the peace of the valley was rent by the sounds of
construction coming both from the church and from the
Tour Martel. At the monastery, Stephen and the men who
shamefacedly returned to work under him were twice as
busy as before. The men tried to prove their loyalty and
Stephen tried to make up for lost time, to get as much as
possible of the new building under cover before an early
frost brought an end to the building season. And at the
Tour Martel, the Franciscan brothers labored with enthusiasm to tear down crenellations and build hostels, to
remove machicolations and barbicans and spiked iron traps
in the moats in favor of welcoming open doors and wide
sunny windows. Aude invented an errand to take her up to
the castle when her curiosity got the better of her; the
brothers received her politely but without warmth, and
she found herself being escorted past the outer bailey
before she'd had more than a quick glimpse of the changes.

"They're working terribly hard, but not very efficiently, I think," she reported to Stephen. "Piles of rubble all over the place where they've torn down the defensive towers at the wall corners. I think they're weakening the inner wall and it may fall over into the stables someday. Maybe they'd hire you to do a proper job of the reconstruction."

Stephen pretended to throw a shoe at her head; Aude ducked and ran, giggling. Later, she was surprised to learn that he had indeed visited the Tour Martel as she suggested.

"Not for work?"

"I wouldn't work for them, and I doubt they'd have me. They think any building finer than a wattle hut is sinful pride. But I thought they might let me buy some of the building stone they're pulling out of the defensive walls. It's a good grade of limestone, and the blocks are already squared; we save ourselves the cost of quarrying, rough-hewing, and transporting the stone. *Chastel abatuz est demi refez.*" Stephen quoted the old proverb that a castle pulled down was already half rebuilt. He pulled on his soft working shoes and sighed with relief at shedding his stiff riding boots.

"And will they sell it to you?"

"No."

"Those selfish beasts! You ought to go back and tell them—"

"Softly, softly, love. Those new friars talk too fast for their own good, that's all. I'd not gotten above halfway through stating my errand when the man in charge interrupted and asked me to name my price for hauling the stone away, as he hadn't got all day to waste talking to rich and worldly craftsmen."

"So what did you do?"

"Named my price, of course. If they want to give me good money for taking their building stone, why should I refuse? It'll stretch our building fund that much further." Stephen stood up and massaged the stiff muscles in his thighs. "Ah, it's good to be back on my own feet again."

"You must ride. Walking is for peasants. You're a gentleman now."

"A jumped-up, worldly craftsman, you mean." Stephen stretched and grinned at Aude. "Suppose they'd pay me to haul away the rest of the castle for them? Then they could build some mud huts on the empty space and enjoy a truly sanctified poverty."

Aude treasured such brief exchanges the more for their rarity. Once again almost all of Stephen's time was spent supervising the construction. And now Aude hadn't even the slack winter season to look forward to for the end of outside building work would mark the beginning of a desperate fund-raising campaign.

Stephen and Abbot Samson went over the books on the building fund almost nightly, guarding every copper coin as jealously as a poor peddler's wife with six children to feed. But not all of their careful, cost-cutting efforts could stop the inexorable draining away of money. Abbot Samson did what he could with the monastery's internal funds, but the trickle of income he was able to add was like rainwater dropping into a sieve. This had never been a rich foundation, and forty years of infighting and feuding with the lords of the Tour Martel had eaten away at the monastery's original resources. The abbot still hoped that a court might someday restore the lands that the old lord had unjustly seized and that his son had given to the Franciscans. Stephen pointed out that they couldn't expect their creditors for stone, iron, glass, and lime to wait indefinitely for that joyful day.

In the meantime, they would have to resort to less dignified means of raising money. Begging, Stephen called it. The abbot preferred the phrase "inspiring the faithful to see how they may serve God." Aude had known a legless street beggar in Cairo who used similar ringing phrases to keep the coins of the faithful pouring into his bowl.

With the first frost, most work on the church ceased. Temporary roofs of thatch went over the newly mortared walls to keep them warm and dry through winter's rain. Tools belonging to the lodge were checked in, polished, and stored away in oil. Craftsmen departed by twos and threes for shops in town, for farms in the sunny southern provinces, for whatever work maintained them through the winter. Within a week, only a handful of rough-hewers were left in the empty churchyard, to smooth the great building blocks that would be needed for the next season's work. Maître Jean recommended one of them to Stephen as a foreman to watch over the others and keep track of their work; then he went home to the Midi and the patient wife who tended his olive trees while he worked in the building trade every summer.

"I wouldn't like to live that way," said Aude after Maître Jean had expatiated on the virtues of his good wife and her lonely farm. "Promise you'll always take me with you, wherever you're building, Stephen?"

"I promise," he said at once and kissed her. In the next breath he was saying to Abbot Samson that they could leave on the preaching tour whenever he liked.

It took three full days of preparation before the abbot was ready to travel in the style he preferred, with a gilt wagon to carry the precious relics in their carved ivory boxes, another wagon for his bed and bedding, and strings of mules to carry the supplies he found necessary for such a hazardous journey.

After Stephen and Abbot Samson left, the bustling monastery seemed like a desert to Aude. She had not realized how much she depended on them. The lonely chink of the rough-hewers' scappling hammers, the bells calling the monks to prayer, and the cries of birds flying overhead were the sounds that filled her days. Occasionally word would come back of the success or failure of the tour.

They'd been refused permission to preach in the marketplace at Flavigny. They moved east to Semur-en-Auxois, and rain had made a mud pie out of the pasture where they set up with the relics. The abbot had a bad cough and was thinking of returning. But then they'd drawn a fine crowd at Pontaubert, where the priest had let them take over the church and preach all day Sunday. Since it was the last day of the yearly fair, the townsfolk had money to spare and were eager to give it all for a touch of the holy relics. At Saulce and Menades the contributions poured in, and the lord of Chastellux had invited them to stay at his chateau. The last messenger said they might be somewhat late in returning; the lord of Chastellux had important friends who could be helpful to the monks.

Aude did not cry over this news though she did have one particularly bad day when Stephen and the abbot were still at Chastellux: a gossiping beggar told her that the lady of Chastellux was with child after touching the holy relics brought by the abbot and his master builder.

Stephen and Abbot Samson came back just before Candlemas, jubilant with their success. It seemed that their good luck was connected with the acquisition of the head of St. Quiriace, formerly at the church of Semur-en-Auxois.

"That was the place where you got rained out of the cow pasture?"

"And nobody in the village had the charity to offer us shelter, except one rich farmer whose barn shared a wall with the old church." Abbot Samson nodded. "Mean, hard-hearted folk they breed there. They didn't deserve to keep St. Quiriace."

The abbot and Stephen refused to say more about how the saint's mummified head had been transferred to their possession, but there were enough giggles and winks about master builders being able to walk through walls to give Aude a pretty clear idea what had happened.

"I'm ashamed of both of you," she told them. "How can you expect to profit from stolen relics?"

"We already have profited." The abbot said with a smile. He was on his second cup of hot spiced wine posset, and Stephen wasn't far behind.

"And the saint didn't mind. He works his miracles for us just as well as for Semur-en-Auxois, doesn't he? Isn't Ermengarde de Chastellux—" Stephen choked on his wine posset and set the cup down with a thud, suddenly sobered.

He had stopped too late. Aude was gone in a flash and the tapestries over the door swayed with the speed of her departure.

Stephen found her in the empty church, with the straw that had blown loose from the temporary roofs sticking to her gown. Her hands and cheeks were red with cold. "It's all right," she said at once, before he could begin to apologize for his careless words. She even managed a laugh. "Goodness, if I burst into tears very time somebody had a baby, I'd be able to water the valley with my weeping, wouldn't I? The peasants here are all too fertile for me to carry on so."

"They are that," Stephen agreed. "Abbot Samson tells me the village priest preaches himself blue in the face every spring, trying to keep them from their pagan dances in the woods, but not a bit of good does it do."

"We used to dance like that, in the churchyard, on the first day of spring." Aude sighed. "Seems a mortal long time ago."

"In the *churchyard*? Did you *want* to scandalize the priest?"

"It was the only bit of dry, level ground within a league," said Aude practically. "The Church took it to build on, but we had it for dancing ground long before that."

"There's been a church in Stuntney since Harald the Saxon's times," Stephen objected.

"Aye. Before that, 'twas a dancing ground." Aude's matter-of-fact tone made it impossible for Stephen to tease her about whether she personally remembered dancing in Stuntney before King Harald dedicated the church there. He was half afraid she might say yes.

"Well, I don't think it would be quite the thing for you to join the peasants here. But we might have some better dances than that, before long." Perhaps the prospect of some spring gaiety would drive that lingering sadness from her eyes. "Abbot Samson invited Godefroi of Chastellux to come and tour the cathedral when we're ready to start building again, after Candlemas. And he's bringing a group of his friends from the Limousin. They're to stay a week in the monastery guesthouse, hunting and hawking mostly I suppose, but the ladies will want some other amusements. Maybe you can help entertain them."

In fact the de Chastellux party did not visit the valley until the end of March. Abbot Samson wanted to time the visit of his noble guests so that the cathedral would be at its most impressive. When they arrived, the noble stone structure had been freed of its winter covering of thatch and straw, the yard was buzzing with activity and the masons' lodge was filling up again with the skilled craftsmen Stephen had recruited the previous year. From the point of view of a fund-raiser, it was an ideal time for a visit; while the nobles were admiring his architect's designs and the golden stone arches, they could also notice the activity of building and think about how much it must cost to erect such a structure.

From Stephen's point of view, the timing was not ideal. At Candlemas, with roads still icy and covered with frost, he would have had leisure to entertain the guests and to

show them every detail of his building. Now he was hard
pressed to find a minute between hiring men, arranging
for the stream of building supplies to start flowing again,
and juggling the inevitable bills that mounted up as he
balanced supplies against wages and both against time.
The church itself was a humming beehive that quieted
only when the monks were actually in choir; at all other
times there were stones swaying into the air, mortar
dripping off hurdles, scaffolding poles being pulled out of
their holes in the wall and lashed up a stage higher, and
men shouting instructions and insults in all the languages
of the civilized world.

"It's impossible!" Stephen complained. "Your visitors
should have come in the winter. All the building work is
starting now, and we can't afford to let these laborers sit in
idleness just so your rich friends can wander about the
cathedral. Look what's happening! Five minutes looking at
the capitals in the choir, then I have to get them out of the
way of your monks. I move them into the nave just when
there's a new lot of scaffolding going up on that very wall
and I have to take them around to look at the transepts. As
I'm showing how the transepts follow the geometry of the
original plan, one of those empty-headed young nobles
from the Limousin shouts that the sky's just cleared enough
for hawking and the lot of them take off like a stampeding
herd of wild horses."

"Perfect," said the abbot. "These—what did you call
them—these empty-headed young nobles are not capable
of paying more than five minutes' attention to anything
that has neither hooves nor feathers. If we'd had them
here at Candlemas, you'd have sent them all into a frozen
coma with your statements of architectural theory in an
open church. They're happy, Stephen. They're impressed.
And after the inspiring speech I mean to give tomorrow,
they'll contribute richly to the building fund. What more
do you want?"

"I want them to *understand,*" Stephen said, sulking.

Abbot Samson chuckled. "Yes. You are young. Now me,
I just want them to pay. And they will!"

Stephen sulked even more when the abbot ordered him
to shut down all work inside the church the next day while
he led the noble visitors on a ceremonial tour.

"For how long?" Stephen demanded.

"As long as it takes."

"Wasting good daylight. I have to pay the men anyway, you know. Why can't you do your little tour at night?"

"It wouldn't work as well."

And even Stephen had to admit that the abbot's grand tour had something that his own had lacked. Before dawn, the lay brothers of the monastery worked frantically to bring all the treasures of the convent into the apse: the gold-embroidered tapestries, the relic chests of wood inlaid with ivory and silver, the jeweled patens and chalices, and the heavy silk hangings for the altar. When they were through, that whole end of the church glittered with rich, deep colors and shining metals. Stephen winced to see how poor and naked his architecture seemed by contrast: the half-carved columns and the empty sockets of the windows.

"That," said Abbot Samson, "is the very point." Stephen began to understand when the abbot brought his noble guests in front of the altar and launched into an impromptu sermon on the need to glorify God by all the means at one's command. How poor were gold and jewels compared to the riches of the heavenly palaces where they all hoped to be someday! Their finest raiment, their richest vessels were dust before the Almighty; their only use was to lift up men's eyes and hearts so that they might be reminded, however distantly, of the glories awaiting them in their Father's house. He, Abbot Samson, had labored long in his humble way to prepare a fitting place in which to offer the mass and to house the sacred relics of his convent. Now, alas, all was likely to come to an end for lack of funds. Those connected with the church had given all that they could. He himself had given his modest personal savings. Now it only remained for him to strip himself bare of the symbols of worldly vanity which an old man, already knocking at heaven's gate, hardly needed to carry with him to the grave.

With those last words, Abbot Samson stripped the rings from his own fingers and threw them into the brass bowl which Stephen had rescued from the foundation diggings. "Can I do less?" cried the Lord of Chastellux. "In gratitude for my lady's good fortune, Abbot, may you build a worthy home for the bones of the saint who blessed us!"

The great sapphire on his little finger went into the bowl, and the gold chain round his neck. The others followed suit, each vying to make a louder and more impressive contribution than the last. The enigmatic leaf-framed face at the bottom of the bowl smiled up at the noble visitors until it was covered by rings and coins.

The visitors from Chastellux were to depart the next morning. After the abbot's grand tour of the church, most of them returned to the guesthouse to see to the packing of the gowns and cloaks, the feather mattresses and embroidered bedcovers, the cutlery and the silver-plated dishes which they brought for a week's visit as if for six months in the wilderness. One quiet gentleman with a long humorous face, a cousin by marriage to the Chastellux clan, strolled in the abbey garden and mentioned to Aude that he'd appreciate a chance to speak with Master Stephen—alone—and that there was no need to mention the matter to the abbot.

Aude searched the building works for Stephen and eventually was directed to the abbot's private chambers. It was hardly proper for her to go scampering in there, but she forgot propriety in her excitement. She had a good idea what Gabriel de Fougeres wanted to see Stephen about.

At the threshold to the abbot's chambers, she rocked back on her heels and skidded to a halt. Stephen and Abbot Samson were seated cross-legged on the floor on either side of the shallow brass bowl, sorting through the coins and jewels, and chattering like magpies about their bright trinkets.

"Look at this ruby," Stephen gloated, holding it up so that the afternoon sunlight struck red fire in the heart of the ring. "Must be worth a hundred livres, and that's just the stone, not counting the gold it's set in. I'll have it valued in Bourges."

"You will not." The abbot plucked the ring from Stephen's fingers with the deftness of a juggler, slid it onto his own hand and closed his fist over it. "That's one of the rings I threw into the bowl myself."

"Didn't you mean to give it to the church, then?" Aude asked in her shock.

"Of course, of course, dear child." The abbot smiled up at her, peaceful and content in the warm sunlight and sparkling gold. "But if Stephen sells it now, what will I have to strip off my fingers to get the next party of visitors started with their contributions?"

"Oh!" Aude felt like a child. She'd been moved to tears by the abbot's gesture of throwing his personal jewels into the bowl. "You're very clever."

"The service of God can sanctify many things," said the abbot, "even cleverness. You wished to see me?"

"Well." Somewhat tardily, she remembered that Gabriel de Fougeres hadn't wanted the abbot to know of his meeting with Stephen. "Stephen, actually..."

"Of course, of course. My apologies, child. I have been selfish with your husband's time. And tomorrow, when our noble guests leave, I suppose he'll want to plunge back into the building. It's only natural you should wish for one evening with him."

Aude accepted the abbot's tactful explanation of her request and led Stephen into the gardens before she mentioned that one of the visitors wanted to see him alone.

"Gabriel de Fougeres?" Stephen's quick frown was a shadow over the sunny afternoon. "I've hardly spoken with him. But that name's familiar from somewhere." He snapped his fingers. "One of de Montreuil's letters of reference. Remember? In Bourges? De Fougeres and the other nobles who spoke so highly of de Montreuil's work spoiled my chances of getting the cathedral contract."

"Maybe he wants to apologize." Aude thought he wanted much more than that, but there was no point in raising Stephen's hopes with her own speculations. Besides, she herself would not be entirely disappointed if all de Fougeres wanted was a couple of words in private. Abbot Samson hadn't guessed so badly; it would be nice to have one quiet hour with Stephen between visitors and construction. She gave him a little push toward the guesthouse. "Go on. He doesn't want the abbot to hear what he's got to say, much less a mere wife."

It was dark before Stephen came back to their rooms, but Aude didn't need a candle to interpret his light step and the irregular whistling. The satisfaction that glowed from him was near enough to light the rooms without use of flint and tinder, wax and tallow. She struck a light to a branch of candles anyway, for the pleasure of seeing his face.

"It went well, your meeting?"

"He's building a new town in Champagne. It will be on the river, to take advantage of the merchants going to the cloth fairs. And he wants me to design it!"

"What—the church?"

"The town. The whole town. Houses, market square, church, piers, trading booths, and streets for the crafts and trades. He says any man who can organize a hundred craftsmen in a space as small as the abbey churchyard, should find it child's play to plan a town where he'll give me all the land I need." Stephen threw his velvet-trimmed hood up against the low ceiling, caught it on one finger and twirled it like a child's whirligig. Two of the candles went out and Aude hastily moved the remaining ones back to a window niche, out of reach of Stephen's exuberance.

"And what will Abbot Samson say to this plan?" Aude asked, more sharply than she'd intended.

"Oh, it shouldn't affect the work on the church. De Fougeres isn't in any hurry. He says I can visit the site and draw up the plans next winter, after this building season is over." Next winter. And the one just past had been devoted to fund-raising. Aude knew, now, why she'd been feeling just a little sad over Stephen's good fortune.

"A whole town, Aude, just think! And everybody who goes to the cloth fairs will see it. It's just the beginning." Stephen threw his hood on the bed, seized Aude, and stamped his feet in a noisy peasant branle. His heels thudded on the floor and the ends of her curls brushed the ceiling when he lifted her and spun her around at the end of the improvised dance.

CHAPTER

24

◩

*I*t was, indeed, just the beginning. All through that summer's building season, Abbot Samson tirelessly exploited his contacts with nobles and highly placed churchmen, inviting them to tour the golden church rising over the monastery. Again and again the scene with the rings was repeated, until Aude said she was surprised the great ruby hadn't been scratched to a dull finish from being thrown into the bowl so many times. Abbot Samson was immune to her sarcasm; he and Stephen and the goldsmith from Bourges who transmuted the offerings into cash were happy with accounts that looked infinitely healthier than the rows of debts they'd been struggling with the previous year.

Gabriel de Fougeres wasn't the only visitor to be struck by the talent and energy of Abbot Samson's young architect. Before building ceased for the winter, Stephen had three firm contracts in hand, in addition to the commission to design Gabriel de Fougeres's new town. He spent the winter months riding from one site to another. By spring, Stephen acquired the ability to sit on a horse without excessive discomfort, and had hired foremen to manage the initial foundations of Gabriel's town. He was negotiating with his other three clients about the amount of time he would actually be expected to spend on site at each project.

"What about the church?" Aude asked, meaning, what about me? "Aren't you going to spend any time here, this building season?"

Stephen collapsed on the bed with a sigh, rubbing his back that ached from hours of bending over the drafting table. "It's mostly finishing work. Windows, carpentry details, fine carving. Maître Jean can oversee that as well as I can. And I've got to go down into Berry to see about hiring somebody to manage the town hall I've designed. It's hard to find good people. I'll have to spend every other week on site until I get someone."

Aude remembered the beginning of the work on Abbot Samson's church, the frenetic days when Stephen had exhausted himself and everybody around him by insisting on overseeing every detail personally. Those days had been tiring, but now Aude almost wished that they could go back to that time. This man, who spent more time at the drafting table than out on the building site and who tried to manage so many projects that he didn't know what his workmen were doing, didn't seem like Stephen.

And the more successful he grew, the worse it got. He spent the winter in Paris, not Chastelvert, claiming that he made more useful contacts in Paris. Aude had accompanied him in hopes of attending feasts and winter balls where the ladies sparkled with jewels and all the men were young and handsome. But she found that spring dances in the churchyard, with the priest in a red-faced rage and threatening them all with excommunication, had been more fun than the winter festivities in Paris.

Aude returned to Chastelvert before Candlemas, with Stephen promising to follow her within a week. Instead he sent messages, and Aude and Abbot Samson celebrated Stephen's twenty-eighth birthday with a quiet dinner at which the guest of honor was not present.

Stephen was in and out of Chastelvert that summer, approving the final work on the church. But he seemed distracted and his mind was already wandering to his new castles and cathedrals. Stephen didn't even come to Abbot Samson's commencement ceremony for the church; instead, he sent his apologies from Coutances and asked Aude to stand in his place.

"Coutances! What's he doing there!"

"He says a commission of architects is to rule on the stability of the present cathedral and to select a man who will do whatever repairs are needed." Aude plucked listlessly at the gold threads in the hem of her right sleeve. Stephen had sent the fabric with his letter. She would rather have had him than all the baudekins and brocades in the world.

Once upon a time Stephen would have been the one petitioning for the job of repairing the cathedral, and fulminating against those men who dared to sit in judgment on him. Now, dressed in long velvet robes trimmed with fur, he was one of those master "builders" who never took off his gloves to strike a blow on stone, but only pointed and told lesser men where to cut. And he was not yet thirty! It was wonderful, Aude supposed, for Stephen to have all this success; why didn't she have the good grace to feel happy for him?

When Stephen did come back, it was only for a whirlwind week between projects. The fool who'd been left in charge of Gabriel de Fougeres's new town in Champagne had dared to inflict his own design on the main street, and Stephen was bound for Champagne to explain quite clearly just who the master builder of this town was. Then, a group of rich burghers from the Low Countries wanted to give him the contract for their new town hall; he'd be traveling on north from Champagne to talk with them.

"Why don't I come with you?" Aude suggested.

"I have to travel too fast. There are too many people to see, too far apart." Stephen rubbed his eyes. "When did we get this house?"

"Maître Jean built it for me when it came time to tear down the temporary lodgings for the masons." Aude nudged Stephen in the ribs with the pointed toe of her shoe. "Remember? Maître Jean? Your master mason?"

"Of course I remember. I just don't remember asking him to build us a house. Never mind, it's a good idea. You'll need some place to stay while I'm traveling."

And that was the end of the discussion. Six weeks later, Stephen was back, complaining about the incompetence of one of his master carpenters. When Aude asked if he had to keep traveling so much, he explained that it was absolutely necessary for him to make personal appearances at each building project, just to make sure nobody had changed his plans. "Besides, the clients are paying for my attention and expertise. They like to see me."

"Well, then, maybe you shouldn't take on so many contracts. Wasn't it easier when you just had Abbot Samson's church to look after?"

Stephen gave her a pitying look. "You don't get to be a famous builder by doing one project at a time. It takes too long. With the work I'm doing now, my name will be known all over France and the Low Countries before I'm thirty-five."

"Yes, but how much of it are *you* doing?"

"What do you mean?"

"Parchment!" Aude swept an armload of papers off the table. "You don't have time to walk the foundations of your new buildings. You don't have time to see them put up. You're not there when the problems arise and new solutions have to be worked out. You don't even have time to make new designs anymore! Look at this wall of high windows for the new town hall; it's exactly the same as the north transept wall in Abbot Samson's church. You're not a builder or even a designer. You're copying somebody much more talented than you."

"And just who might that be?"

Stephen's eyes were hard and cold. Aude knew she'd gone too far, but it was too late to back down.

"A young man called Stephen of Dunwich. The one who ran away from a monastery and risked death and starvation just for the privilege of working in Brito's stoneyard. Perhaps you remember him?"

"I don't know what you're talking about. You're not making sense."

"No," said Aude, ignoring the accusation, "you wouldn't know what I'm talking about, would you? *You* wouldn't throw away worldly advantages for the love of building. You won't even turn down one or two contracts that are offered to you so that you could pay reasonable attention to the others."

Stephen gathered up the sheets of parchment she'd knocked askew, smoothing them out tenderly. "Be reasonable, Aude. You know we put everything we had into the building fund for the church. Do you want us to be beggars all our lives? In a few more years, I'll have done enough designs to be famous and we'll be rich again. I'm working for both of us."

"I never asked you to make me rich!"

Stephen's whole face was still and remote. Aude wanted to throw something, to shatter that icy calm. Her fingers closed round a heavy bronze candlestick. Before she could move, he'd spoken again.

"I'm sorry that you don't want me to be successful. Since it troubles you so much, I might as well go some place where they appreciate what I do. Hubert de Nevins doesn't think I'm a mere copyist; he paid well for my designs, and he's been pressing me to stay with him. There," said Stephen with cold cruelty, "I may find company more welcoming than my wife's."

"You do that. You'd better. For your wife might not be here to pick up the pieces next time!" Aude shouted at Stephen's retreating back. The empty threat made no impression; he didn't even look round. He was gone with no more farewell than that, leaving Aude with her fingers clamped so hard round the ring of the candlestick that she thought her own flesh might turn into bronze.

Stephen reached Berry to find well-ordered activity going on about the high church that Hubert de Nevins had commissioned. The walls had gone up even faster than Stephen had expected; he clapped his master mason on the back and told him he was quite pleased with the progress. "Double bonuses for all the workmen if we raise the spire before Lady-Day," the master mason told him.

"What? I never authorized that."

"Not you. *Him.*" The master mason jerked his head toward the hill behind the church, and Stephen recognized his client riding toward them, sweaty from a day's hunting, with his falcon perched on his wrist. "But I'm concerned we've been overusing the great wheel. Can you check—"

"Master Stephen!" Hubert de Nevins spurred his horse and waved one arm in exuberant welcome. "Come and dine with me!" His high tenor voice carried across the misty air to the church site.

"Surely you've a mechanic who can repair the wheel?

You see, I'm wanted elsewhere," Stephen said to the master mason. Then he nodded toward his impatient young client and rode away from the building site to greet de Nevins. This wouldn't have been a good time to confer with his master mason anyway. Stephen was too tired to cast his mind into the tangle of gears and weights and pulleys and levers that constituted the vast, creaky lifting wheel. He wasn't even sure he could remember how they'd planned to raise the stones for the roof pediment and the spire here; he could only recall that there'd been some problem.

But his job was to talk with clients, reassure them as to the progress of the project, and remind them how beautiful the finished work would be, not to check bindings and gears like some apprentice artisan. For a moment Stephen wished that it could be otherwise. Hadn't he been happier in his first days at Master Brito's yard, solving the problems of walls and pillars and lines of stress with his own brain and his own muscles? Wasn't that better than sitting at some spoiled nobleman's table, patiently steering his foolish client in the right direction?

Halfway up the hill, just before he would have had to put a smile on his face to greet young de Nevins, Stephen gave in to a moment of longing for the old days before his success. He reined in his horse and twisted in the saddle to look back at the church walls rising out of the valley mist.

At the top of the walls, the great wheel had been set up to raise the massive blocks of the roof pediment. It turned slowly as a dozen men walked up the inclined slope in the interior of the wheel, forcing it round with their own weight. The ropes overhead slid through the pulleys and lifted a block of stone large enough to bury them all if it slipped.

The men were moving too fast. From here on the hill they were little doll-figures, moving jerkily and without coordination. Stephen stared and understood. The wheel was moving too fast, some part of the delicate balance wrong, and the men inside were stumbling backward and trying to stop it. But it was too late, the stone they were raising had come up so fast that it was swinging back and forth in the iron clamps that held it. Back and forth, back and forth. . . .

With a wail of terror, one of the men inside the great wheel threw himself out into the air. His body fell, jerking like a puppet with half the strings cut. Two more men followed him, and one clung to the edge of the roof, scrabbling for a desperate hold on life. The wheel, free of the weight of half the team, spun crazily and tossed the remaining four men like stones in a barrel. And the pediment stone swung back in its lazy, inevitable arc, knocking the wheel into splintered fragments and smashing the men inside against the walls of the new church.

CHAPTER

25

❑

Stephen knew what had to be done after the accident, and he fought off his desperate weariness in order to perform each step properly. First, the broken bodies of the living must be rescued and brought to safety. He knew better than anyone how to move the light hurdles and poles of scaffolding so that men cast into corners of the half-built galleries could be carried carefully down.

Then there were the dead to be straightened on pallets, their eyes closed and their broken limbs folded. Two of the men had been so crushed beneath the falling stone that they had neither limbs nor bodies to arrange decently. Stephen saw to the levering away of the stone and knelt beside the remains of the two men. He whispered the prayers he had been taught so long ago at Ely, that their souls might have this much peace until a priest could be brought to do the job properly.

Then there was the tragic aftermath of the accident to clean up. Tearless, unmoved, and exhausted, Stephen gave orders for the dismantling of the great wheel and the replacement of the cracked and chipped stones. Work on that section of the roof would stop until he and his master mechanics could determine exactly what had gone wrong.

And then there were the wives of the dead men, and their lodge masters, and all the others involved.

Finally, in the dim haze of dusk, Stephen had to deal with his hysterical and petulant young client. In those first stunned moments after the tragedy, Stephen had brushed Hubert de Nevins aside, saying curtly that he would speak with him later. Now he stood in de Nevins's hall and listened with unaccustomed meekness while his client raged that the accident was all Stephen's fault, that he hadn't been present to oversee the workers, that his church design was too high, too daring, and too dangerous. He also said the cost of the construction delays incurred by this accident ought to be taken directly from the builder's fee.

"You're quite right," Stephen said when Hubert de Nevins at last paused to draw a breath. "It was entirely my fault." No matter that there'd been other men at the site with the competence to check the great wheel and the other lifting gear; the ultimate responsibility was with the master builder, and the master builder had been too tired from riding across two provinces to do his job.

"You agree?" De Nevins had been braced for argument; Stephen's ready compliance left him off-balance, a gamecock with feathers outspread and fighting spurs ready but with no opponent in the ring. "To everything? I warn you, I'm not paying to repair this damage or to hire a new crew. Nor will I pay for the new stones you'll have to bespeak from the quarry. As for the bonuses I offered for an early completion—"

"You offered those to my master mason, not to me. And it's with him you should speak about the details of payment."

With an effort, Stephen turned his mind away from the weary cycle of guilt and loss, and he tried to concentrate on finding words simple enough to explain his intention to a French noble. "I am resigning this contract in favor of the master mason, Maître Clotho. He has done most of the work on the church, and I'm sure he will finish it to your satisfaction. You may pay him the fee we agreed upon. I will personally make up any costs incurred by today's accident, so that need not enter into your dealings with Clotho."

When de Nevins understood that Stephen was serious, he let out a screech of outrage and went into another tirade lasting even longer than the first. He had contracted to have a church built by the finest architect in France, not by some unlettered mason with a crew of tramps. He had bought Stephen of Outremer, his design and his work and his name on the church, and by God, he wasn't going to let anyone break the contract!

"You've got the design," Stephen pointed out. "As for the craftsmanship, that's been Clotho's all along. And for the name on the church—" He wanted to laugh; the bitter humor of the situation was almost overwhelming. "Feel free to carve anywhere you please that Stephen of Outremer was the designer and began the building of this church. But after today, I fear that may not be such a coveted label. Do you really want to immortalize the man whose carelessness killed half his masons' crew?"

Hubert de Nevins hadn't seen it in that light before. While he was stammering and trying to decide what he thought, Stephen made his excuses and retired to spend a sleepless night keeping vigil in the unfinished, unconsecrated church where his masons' bodies lay.

He knelt on the bare earth of the church. Gentle breezes stirred through the high pierced walls; his single candle flickered on the block of stone that lay at the heads of the shrouded bodies. At Ely, Stephen and the other novices would have worked themselves into a state of terror with tales of the midnight demons waiting to catch the souls of the unwary. But here Stephen felt no fear. What need? The demons were within his soul already.

Stephen knelt between the two long shrouded bodies and prayed for them. He must do penance for his sins. But what would be right? Stephen shrank from the thought of confessing himself to Abbot Samson, that genial, worldly, comfortable man of the Church. The abbot would have many comforting and untrue things to say—that it wasn't his fault, that no man could foresee accident, that he must not take the blame for an act of God.

Stephen knew better.

"What shall I do? What must I do?" he cried aloud, as though the dead could answer him.

The cold voice that answered came from within, where his personal demons dwelled. *Of course you have failed. How could you expect anything else? You who forsook your vows?*

"Ely," Stephen whispered. "Ely. Should I go back, then?"

Slowly, half expecting the candle to rise into a roaring fire that would engulf him on the spot, Stephen shook his head. "I can't do that." To be shut in the aching cold of Ely convent in winter, to be harnessed to the mind-numbing daily routine, without a moment to be alone or a chance to think—Coluin and many others had found peace in such a life, but to Stephen it had been a living death.

Sitting among his dead workmen, Stephen could no longer hide in the pride of high position. For a while he had let himself forget who he was, and he had let the fur-lined cloak and gold-embroidered gauntlets hide the fact that he was only a common boy from Dunwich. Then, almost joyfully, Stephen seized on this thought as an alternative penance. He would not go back to Ely; but neither would he go back to the rich life of worldly success that he had worked so hard to attain. He would strip himself of all the worldly gain that had ensnared him. Farewell to the little dinners with the bishops and counts, to the meetings with building committees awaiting a sight of his brilliant drawings, to the sense of his growing fame. When he came back to Aude, he would be plain Stephen of Dunwich once more.

And until then, he did not deserve the comfort of her presence. He longed so desperately for just one day in Chastelvert that he knew it must be right to deny himself that privilege. He did not even permit himself to send a letter to Aude, for fear some hint of his need and longing would show through. Instead he wrote briefly to Abbot Samson, acquainting him with the details of the disaster in Berry and informing him of his intention to travel around France until he had transferred all his outstanding commitments to other men. He asked the abbot to tell Aude that he would be back before the end of the building season.

"I think he is making a mistake," she said, handing back the letter she read with a trembling hand. "But he did not ask my opinion."

"I thought you wanted him to work less."

"Less, but not to retire at twenty-eight!"

Abbot Samson looked startled. "Is he so young? I'd not have guessed."

"Who would?" The years of work in the Egyptian heat had aged Stephen before his time. The life they'd led since

returning to Europe had done little to restore him. Since
the tragedy of Yolande's death and Geoffrey's mutilation,
Aude had seen silver streaks appear in his golden hair.
Nights of stooping over a drafting table, working by lamplight
and candles, had left fine lines at the corners of his eyes;
days of riding about the country, flattering lords, balancing
building accounts, and trying to be in six places at once,
had left permanent signs of strain on his face.

"Success was killing him," said Aude slowly. "He's always lived as though he had only the day before him in
which to complete his life's work."

"So should we all live, in memory of our mortality."

"Yes, but not to the point of trying to make it true!"

Abbot Samson laughed, ruffled Aude's hair, and said
there was no cure for her irreverence; and if success was
killing Stephen, wasn't it a good thing he was giving it up?

"Failure," said Aude, "will finish the job."

"He's not a failure by any man's measure but his own."
Abbot Samson looked up with satisfaction at the sun-
warmed spires of the completed church that towered over
the monastery and the valley.

"And when did Stephen ever use another man's measure? Abbot, if you love him, pray God that he'll come to
his senses before he gives away all his work. For without
work," said Aude, "he won't live."

"Something is sure to turn up. One accident isn't going
to destroy all his clients' faith. There are worse accidents
every day—men say he's had the devil's own luck, to go so
long as he has without a single death on one of his sites.
You mark my words, some of these new clients will refuse
to let him go so easily."

Aude smiled and the abbot thought that she was reas-
sured. She didn't tell him that her smile was at him. Even
Abbot Samson, who had joined with Stephen in the mighty
effort to rescue their church, did not understand what her
husband could do when he was determined to accomplish
something. She knew him better. Her Stephen was not
just any builder: he was the boy who had preferred to go
alone and friendless into the worst winter of England's
history rather than make his final vows to the monastery,
the journeyman who'd turned himself into a great builder
of Cairo with nothing but talent and daring and lies, the
unknown exile who had become one of the great builders

in France in just three years. All the energy and determination he'd poured into achieving success would now be put into divesting himself of that success. If Stephen said he would return without a single contract, then she knew he would return in just that condition. The only thing she didn't know was what on earth he would do afterward.

Perhaps Abbot Samson, too, began to believe that Stephen would accomplish his goal as he had accomplished all others. As the weeks passed, news came of one building project after another left in abeyance or handed over to lesser men. The abbot's protestations to Aude began to have a hollow ring. When he invited her to dine with a party of foreign guests in his private chambers, she found just how seriously he was beginning to believe in Stephen's retirement: seriously enough to connive at giving him up for his own good. For these guests had come to see Stephen, and they had come from very far away indeed.

Aude was accustomed to living quietly during Stephen's long absences, as befitted a married woman who lived next to a community of celibate males. She filled her time gathering herbs in the summer, preparing dyes and medicines in the winter, and helping the village wisewoman to treat rheums and women's troubles. But she also visited the abbot several times a month. A woman might see her spiritual adviser; and the abbot of a monastery was expected to have strength to deal with worldly temptations. In any case, who'd have dared to whisper a breath of scandal about any of Abbot Samson's doings? At sixty, rejuvenated by the success of his church and the fame it had brought him throughout northern France, he still had a voice to strike terror into the heart of a gossipmonger who dared make remarks about his friend's wife.

So it was not unusual for Aude to be invited to dine in the abbot's chambers. He delighted in showing off his church to noble visitors, even now that there was no need to wrest the rings from their fingers. When Stephen was in the valley, he and Aude were honored guests at these gatherings; when he wasn't there, the nobles liked to meet the builder's wife and hear little anecdotes about the building of the church from her own lips.

Aude no longer felt shy about appearing before these noble visitors, as she had when she'd been Helene's little peasant protégée in Ely. In the little community of

Chastelvert, she was accounted a great lady herself, a much-traveled, sophisticated woman. But for all her hard-won experience of the world, the rowdy, flushed crew that greeted her in the abbot's chambers this evening startled her momentarily. The wide, gracious rooms seemed too narrow to hold the small dark men whose energy filled the space and bounced off the walls. When Aude arrived the abbot's guests were singing in deep vibrating tones with a barbaric catch to the beat, arms around one another's shoulders, furred capes tossed back to reveal gold and rough-cut gems that covered their chests like breastplates.

"Come in, come in," roared the man who stood in the center of the room, lifting one of the abbot's treasured ivory goblets as though it were an eggshell he meant to crush in his hand. "Just what we need, a pretty lady to civilize us!"

"*Jaj Istenem,*" breathed a younger man whose sweeping black moustache dominated his narrow, pale face. "It is a vision of the Blessed Queen of Heaven, in her blue cloak set with stars and her rose-red robe of the world's sorrows! Beautiful lady, will you come and glorify our Church of St. Michael in Varad? When it's built," he added as an after-thought. Without waiting for Aude to speak, he dropped to his knees before her like a worshipper. His long furred cloak spread out on the floor around him, making strange clicking noise against the floorboards. Aude realized with shock that the lumps at the corners of his robe, which she'd taken for tassels, were the paws of a bear. The forepaws of the bear were linked around the man's neck, held with a massive golden brooch, and the bear's head lolled back behind his own head.

"Karl, Géza," said a third man reprovingly, "you are alarming the lady. How many times must I tell you that French court ladies are not used to your rude mountain manners." He bowed to Aude and she suppressed an involuntary smile at being taken for a lady of the court.

The young man called Géza scrambled to his feet. "The lady of Chastel Fleuri liked my rude mountain manners seven times in one night, Lajos!"

"He's exaggerating, as usual," said the third man, the one called Karl.

"How do you know? Were you under the bed counting?" Géza aimed a wild blow that knocked the ivory cup out of

Karl's hand. The abbot leaped to catch it in midair. His anguished squeak of protest was all but lost in the grunts and thuds of the impromptu shoving match that broke out between Karl and Géza.

Lajos brushed the two men out of his way casually and offered his arm to Aude with a courtly bow. "Pray forgive my compatriots. They're rude children of the mountains, and somewhat disappointed by the results of our mission to France—also," he added with a flickering smile, "somewhat overwhelmed by the French wines and the French ladies."

Lajos escorted Aude to a seat at the small table where the abbot entertained his favorite guests. After she was seated in a safe corner, Lajos casually dumped a pitcher of chilled wine over his two compatriots, separated them with a few well-placed kicks, and pushed them toward the door with instructions to stick their wine-clouded heads under the pump before they dared sit in the same room as a lady. Meanwhile the abbot whispered a few commands to his servants who scurried to replace the fine service of chased silver platters and ivory cups with plain breach trenchers and wooden mazer bowls. He glanced toward Lajos with a look of apology and received an understanding smile in return.

Over dinner the two young men, slightly sobered and still dripping from the courtyard pump, vied with Lajos to tell Aude about the mission that had brought them to France.

"We are here as personal representatives of Count Jokai himself." Géza paused and stroked his flowing black moustaches, obviously expecting Aude to be impressed.

"Count Jokai," Lajos explained, "is lord of the city of Varad in the eastern part of Hungary. It is a wild province but rich with gold, silver, and salt. It's not really a bad place, and the hunting is excellent. Pleasant weather, too."

"Ha! Except in winter, when you get snow up to your—"

Karl broke off with a moan and reached down to feel his leg. Aude surmised that Lajos had kicked him under the table. Evidently she was supposed to hear only good things about Varad, but why?

The answer was not long in coming: Count Jokai had been troubled for ten years by a nephew who was asserting his prior right to the lordship of Varad on the grounds that his father had been the previous count. Worse, the boy kept assembling armies to support his claim. Last year the count had smashed the rebel armies in a pitched battle against overwhelming odds. He attributed the victory to the personal intervention of St. Michael, to whom he had vowed a church in the citadel of Varad if he should survive the battle. Now, in gratitude for that stunning victory, he was determined to make the finest church ever built in his country. He wanted it to be built in the new French style, light and airy and graceful. It would be a sign of the gracious new civilization into which he meant to lead his people.

Now Aude understood why she was being told about Varad in such glowing detail. But it was too soon to leap at this bait; besides, she had little hope that Stephen would take on the work in his present mood.

"What a prudent and farsighted man your count must be," she said. "And what did he do about his nephew?"

"Have some more almond chicken," said Lajos.

"Eight wild horses dragged him through the market square. It was a great spectacle. The strong young man took hours to—" Karl had his mouth open to elaborate on the spectacle when a squawk of pain emerged. "Devil take you, Lajos, that was my bad knee!"

"They'll both be bad," said Lajos, "if you don't learn to keep your mouth shut. More wine, my lady Aude?"

Aude accepted the wine and let Lajos tell her more about the beauties of the Varad district and the difficulties they'd had in finding an architect in France who would accept Count Jokai's commission. Most had not even wanted to discuss it; Karl thought they were cowards, afraid to travel so far from home.

"Really?" Aude pretended surprise. "It doesn't seem so far away to me. Of course, we may be unusual. My husband worked in Cairo for five years, among the Saracens. At least," she smiled, "Hungary is a Christian country."

"More or less," muttered Karl. "I don't know about the Kipchaks."

Aude never found out who the Kipchaks were; Lajos overrode Karl's mutterings to suggest his own theory: the French builders were so jealous of their national fame that they didn't want the Hungarians to have a church rivaling the French ones.

Aude casually mentioned that she and Stephen were

English in origin and had no such foolish nationalist scruples. "My husband lives to glorify God through his building. He does not believe that God is the exclusive property of one nation."

"Would that all men were so—so—" Géza stammered, trying to find an appropriate compliment. Lajos laid his small, calloused hand over Aude's. His skin was warm and dry, and his touch infused her with the same restless energy that all three Hungarians displayed. "My lady, you have no need to convince us of your husband's suitability for the project. We have already seen his work here. If he could build this church in three years, suffering under the financial strains of which the good abbot has told us, how much more could he do for us with unlimited time and virtually unlimited funds!"

Aude blushed with pleasure, which she attributed to Stephen's compliment. She certainly hoped she wasn't so silly as to be affected by a few glasses of wine and a man's hand covering her own. Lajos spoke to her with grave courtesy and deep respect, which Aude couldn't help contrasting to the superior tone Stephen had begun to use as his success grew.

"I fear," Lajos added, "that the difficulty will be the other way round—in persuading Master Stephen to accept our commission. The abbot tells us that he is not inclined to take on new work at the present time."

Unlimited time, unlimited funds, an unchecked commission to build the greatest church in Europe—once those promises would have affected Stephen like the headiest wine. But would they move the man who was presently atoning for one accident by ending his building career in France?

"Perhaps you can help us. A lovely lady's persuasions often succeed where rude men are doomed to failure."

Aude felt a tremor of fear, as though she were being asked to do something difficult and dangerous. She thought suddenly that Lajos probably had more success with women than either of his boasting compatriots—for what woman could resist a dare? But that was a thoroughly silly way to think. The dare in this case was to persuade Stephen into doing something for his own good; it was certainly nothing more than that. She grinned at Lajos. "I'll do what I can. Tell me more about Varad."

* * *

The Hungarian visitors lingered at the monastery until Stephen's return, hunting and hawking and riding around the valley. Abbot Samson accepted the game they brought to replenish the nightly raids they made on his larder. He never even complained to Aude about the expense of keeping three semibarbarian noblemen and their entourage for weeks. That was another measure of how seriously he was taking Stephen's black mood.

"I'll miss him, you know," he told Aude one day after she'd politely refused Lajos's eighth invitation to join the hawking party.

"Oh? And here I thought you were arranging this Hungarian business because you were desperate to get us out of your territory," Aude teased.

"I didn't arrange it. I just happened to hear about it through an old friend who wound up in the east. His name is Thomas, bishop of Split. We studied together with Stephen Langton, the archbishop of Canterbury, you know."

"You've mentioned it once or twice." Abbot Samson found frequent opportunities to mention his friendship with important churchmen; he'd dragged Stephen Langton's name into many a conversation.

"But I do worry about Stephen. He's been gone too long. He has handed over most of his clients to lesser men, just as he said he would do. Is he really going to end his career because of one mistake?"

"I don't know," said Aude honestly. "He's never made such a mistake before."

For the last few weeks Stephen had managed to keep himself busy enough to avoid thinking about the impulsive decision he'd made. It wasn't easy to persuade half a dozen influential clients that they'd be better off with the personal supervision of a lesser builder than with the occasional visits and casual attention that were all Stephen could offer. At each building site, Stephen went through the same ordeal: first there was the diplomatic talk with the client, then a night sitting up with the master mason on the site, drilling him on the secrets of design and making sure he understood everything he needed to know in order to complete the work. Most of his foremen and masters of works had been delighted to have a chance at running their own contracts. A few had been frightened, and several had flatly refused. That meant Stephen had to make additional trips to hire new builders for those sites.

All those details had kept his head buzzing with little practical problems, which helped him not to think. But now it was done. He was riding home to an empty future. That night in the church at Berry, Stephen had stubbornly refused to return to Ely, to give his life to God. Now he wondered what else he could do. If he was not a builder, what was he?

His tired horse took the familiar track up to the monastery lands at the head of the valley. The clouds were so low and heavy that they blocked out the sunset; rain lashed his face until the high trees closed in on either side of the path and gave him a moment's respite. In that moment, Stephen looked ahead and saw the house where Aude was waiting for him. Against the storm-gray dusk, firelight glinted red through the chinks in the shutters. He was still too far away for anyone to have heard his approach, but suddenly the door opened to silhouette a slim, curly-haired woman who peered down the hill and cried out with joy.

While he still had Aude, how could he think his life was empty?

PART V

The Kingdom of Hungary

◻

1229–1241

CHAPTER

26

◻

The next morning Aude told Stephen about the visitors from Hungary, and he felt his life opening before him again. With Aude by his side in the morning sunlight, all things seemed possible. He did not have to give up the work he loved, only the pride that had made him careless with that work. Yes, he would go to Transylvania. And this time he would not be distracted by considerations of fame, ambition, and wealth. This time, Stephen swore, he would think of nothing but building to the best of his ability. He would devote the rest of his life to raising the Church of St. Michael in Varad. And this would be his penance for the ambition that had cost him so dearly already: his masterwork would be buried deep in the forests of a barbarian nation, with none to see and admire it but savages in bearskin cloaks.

Géza and Karl broke out the wine to celebrate Stephen's acceptance of the contract. They threw their arms round one another's shoulders and began an impromptu stamping dance that shook the timbers of the abbot's guesthouse.

After the days of packing and leave-taking, Stephen and Aude bid a dignified farewell to the abbot and tearful good-byes to the village women who'd come to depend on Aude's knowledge of healing herbs and dye-plants.

The days of travel stretched into weeks, as they crossed

mountains already lightly flecked with snow and rode
through valleys where flowers still bloomed. They proceeded
into the deep silence of woods untouched since the Roman
legions hacked a road through to their northern conquests,
and Stephen felt the years of work and worry and pride
drop away from him.

He managed to be polite about the assemblages of
thatched mud huts and stone and timber boxes that the
Hungarians called cities, though not even Esztergom, the
capital and the seat of the archbishopric, would have stood
for more than a good-sized village in France. "That's all
right," Lajos said. "Esztergom's time is passing. The King
prefers Buda, which is my family's home, though I myself
was raised in the mountains where they grow real men.
One day it will be the capital. You will like Buda."

When they reached the bend of the Danube where
Buda's timber citadel stood amid the usual cluster of huts,
Stephen and Aude had to avoid each other's eyes to keep
from laughing. Lajos pointed proudly at certain crumbling
walls that he claimed were proof that Buda was founded in
Roman times. Then he skipped over a mere eight or nine
hundred years and spoke of his own distant ancestors who
had conquered the fertile Hungarian plain and set up their
own citadel here.

"Distant ancestors," Aude breathed in Stephen's ear.
"Do you suppose he means his grandfather? Or his second
cousin once removed?"

Stephen had been thinking along similar lines. The hill
topped with a wooden stockade looked like the residence of
some petty chieftain who'd taken over this strategic
point on the river too recently to have had time to
build properly.

"Marco used to call Jerusalem a wide place in the road,"
he whispered back to Aude. "What choice words do you
suppose he'd have for Buda?"

They rode east from Buda, across a plain that never
seemed to end: a circle of gently waving grass under the
sky, broken at long intervals by a clump of trees or a patch
of houses that seemed to grow out of the earth. There
were flocks of sheep moving like clouds across the grassy
plain, accompanied by two or three hulking, taciturn men
whose thick cloaks of unwashed sheepskin made them
seem closely related to their charges. When the travelers

camped at night, they would sometimes hear the quavering sound of a shepherd's pipe in the distance. Once there were wolves howling, and once the thunder of a herd of wild ponies that stampeded right up to their campfire and regarded the intruders with incurious eyes. Then the leader of the herd stamped three times with his right hoof and, as if on a prearranged signal, they all wheeled at once and took off across the plain again.

Eventually the plain gave way to low rolling hills, slowly rising toward a mountainous wooded country that seemed to go on forever.

"Szekely." Géza pointed and smiled.

"Transylvania," Karl translated.

"The mountains!" Lajos threw those words into the air before he and his two companions whooped and spurred their horses forward in a brief, mad gallop. "Almost home!" Lajos called back.

In truth they were still several days' ride from the citadel of Varad, Count Jokai's residence. When, at last, they reined in their tired horses at the top of the first low range of hills, the citadel of Varad was just visible at the eastern edge of the horizon. It was perched atop a low hill with a range of blue mountains behind the stone-walled town.

Stephen turned for his first good view of the way they had come. From the rolling hills they'd just ascended, the plain stretched on for mile after unbroken mile; the even curve where golden autumn grass met the gray sky showed no hint that behind the horizon lay the timber citadel of Buda, the stone churches of Esztergom, the river called the Duna, the castles of Germany, and the great cathedrals of France. Stephen and Aude were unimaginably far from all they knew; the plain was a greater barrier than the sea they had crossed to reach Jerusalem. Stephen reached for Aude's hand. "I did not think that you were going into exile, too."

"I'm not," Aude contradicted him brusquely. "I don't like cities. You're the one who's used to living in a hive." She lifted her head and sniffed the damp forest air with its hint of dead leaves, decaying bark, and green resinous evergreens. "I think I could be happy here."

"We both will," Stephen promised.

And in the first busy months after their arrival, the

promise seemed true enough—even though the citadel of Varad was more like a beehive than like the isolated mountain village Aude had imagined. What it might be like under normal circumstances, she couldn't guess; even before they came, Count Jokai had begun to transform Varad into a building camp. By the time they arrived, the first flakes of winter snow were cold on their faces, but the streets of Varad were crammed with a polyglot crew of workers and craftsmen from every country around Hungary. Saxon miners had been brought in to dig foundations, local Wallach carters were ready to heave great blocks of building stone to the top of the hill, houses that might stand in the way of the new church had been summarily pulled down, and a merchant's storeroom near the proposed site had been converted into a luxurious tracing house for Stephen.

"Look at this fresh parchment, in sheets big enough to make proper scale drawings. Three colors of ink, quills, and silverpoints, dividers in every size, all the tools I need—and a good north light through that window," Stephen exulted to Aude.

The masons' and carpenters' lodges were equally well equipped. All the way across the Hungarian plain Stephen had been fretting over the question of tools. He regretted that the hasty departure had prevented him from buying and packing all the hammers, handsaws, chisels, and punches his masons would need. Now he toured a wide, well-designed lodge and took a gloating inventory of tools enough to build a castle or a cathedral.

The other trades had been equally well provided for. The carpenters had pulleys, ladders, iron augers, and fine-bladed saws for cutting templets to Stephen's design. The plumbery held soldering irons, lead and tin blocks arranged by weight, ladles for pouring molten metal into the moulds, and a brass plane for smoothing the finished work. The glaziers were already supplied with their own soldering irons, clamps and tongs, blowpipes for flashing ruby glass, notched glozing irons tempered in the urine of a three-year-old goat for cutting the colored glass to shape, lead and copper for fixing the glass to the windows.

"It seems Lajos meant it when he said that Count Jokai would spare no expense," said Aude, when Stephen catalogued his wealth of tools and craftsmen to her.

"It seems so, indeed. Imagine hiring all these men, when he knew we couldn't get here in time to start work this season—even if I had plans drawn up! What a waste of money, to pay them wages all through the cold weather."

It was Lajos who pointed out that Stephen would have to revise his ideas of what was efficient and economical. "The problem here is getting men, not keeping them," he said. "The Saxons and Wallachs we recruited locally, but the skilled craftsmen, like yourself, had to come from far away. And I suspect Count Jokai has other projects to occupy them through the winter."

This turned out to be true. All the foreign workers were expected to drill with Count Jokai's private army through the winter, learning swordcraft and the management of a pike. They were taught how to stand out of the way of the archers, how to march through snowdrifts and stage sham sieges of snow-walled fortresses. Stephen actually found it difficult to find a handful of rough-hewers to begin smoothing the blocks for the foundation cornerstones. The count himself was not at Varad and the master of arms whom he'd left in charge was disinclined to grant any favors to a foreigner. Stephen had weekly arguments with Csaba, using Lajos as an interpreter.

In between arguments, Stephen put the winter months to good use, pacing over the site, drawing and measuring and laying out strings to mark foundation lines. By the time the snows melted and the sodden earth showed fresh green shoots, the Church of St. Michael in Varad had germinated in the darkness of Stephen's imagination and was ready to burst forth into life. Straight from the flat crest of the hill, it was to rise, with three arrogant spires that seemed to pierce the low clouds overhead. Every line of the supporting stonework expressed the striving for height, the attenuation of pier and wall in the service of light. This was the French style at its most extreme.

Aude, left to her own amusements, quickly learned to gossip with the ladies of Jokai's court in a simplified French laced with the words of Hungarian she was learning. Though the Hungarian ladies were amusing, and sometimes even shocking, they were no substitute for a husband. She came to the tracing house one noon after she hadn't seen Stephen awake for three days. The bowl of spicy Hungarian stew she carried for his dinner was only

an excuse. Aude was missing her husband, and she had
things to tell him. But the food cooled, forgotten, when
Stephen announced that he had finished his working drawings and was ready to present them.

Aude caught her breath in surprise when Stephen unrolled
the parchment sheets to show her his plan and elevation
sketches. She'd thought the golden limestone church of
the White Monks in the valley of Tour Martel quite lovely,
but even from the drawings Aude could see that St.
Michael-at-Varad would be something different. It would
be a church to rival the great cathedrals of the north, a
masterwork to crown Stephen's career. And yet there was
something that frightened her in the arrogant, fragile
spires and the attenuated stonework. Stephen was trying
to make stone be what only light, or clouds, or wind could
be.

"I knew you'd like it," said Stephen, taking in only the
surprise and admiration in her expression. "What do you
think of the clerestory? It should bring in much more light
because I've only got one tier of flying buttresses. You
generally have to have two tiers so that the lower ones
push back against the vaults—see, the vaults want to push
down, and the earth is in the way, so they go *out*—"
Stephen hunched his shoulders, squatted with outthrust
arms, and made an agonized grunt to represent the way
the high vaults would press out and try to burst themselves if not restrained by the lower buttresses. Aude
giggled.

"And the upper ones keep the roof stable against wind."
Stephen rose from his squat without acknowledging the
giggle. "But that's a lot of stonework framing the good
clean lines of the actual church. So I thought, why not
change the angle of the buttresses? Why not let the lower
tier reach high enough to help buttress the roof as well,
and not have an upper tier. You see, the wind and the
other forces ought to balance each other out—"

He was off again, drawing little arrows on the parchment, sketching strange geometric configurations, and
bemoaning his inability to translate into mathematics the
patterns of stress that he felt so clearly. "There ought to be
some way to make this work by rule, not intuition. But I
can't do it with geometry. Perhaps if I'd studied longer—"

Aude knew she didn't really have to listen to this part;

when Stephen got into one of these moods, all he really wanted was to talk to a nice friendly wall. But Aude did not object to playing the part of a wall with ears. She stared at the spidery lines and curlicues representing the west elevation of the church and thought about other matters—about spring, and young growing things, and the wet fertile smell of earth waiting to be plowed. She waited until Stephen finished his mathematical excursions and said something she could understand.

"And what's more, this design uses a third part less stone in the outer supports than the conventional system. That's a substantial savings in materials and transport. Even if he doesn't appreciate the beauty of my work the way you do, Count Jokai should be pleased by that, don't you think? Don't you?"

With an effort, Aude pulled her mind back from the flower-strewn fields where her imagination had carried her. She tried to concentrate on what Stephen was saying. "I don't know. Since neither of us has met this count yet, it's a bit hard to tell what he'll like. But I shouldn't think he'd care greatly about the money. Look at the way he's set up the building project! No expense spared, Lajos told us, and so far he's been right."

"Ah," said Stephen gloomily, "but that was last year. Things have been changing. Why d'you think the count hasn't been in Varad all winter?"

The court ladies with whom Aude talked had their own theories, most of them centering around the count's young Venetian wife who was discontented with the isolated snowy winters of the hill country. "I understood he took the countess south for the winter. To the Dalmatian coast, or was it Italy?"

"Whichever it was, he must have left her there. *He's* been in Buda."

Stephen told Aude what he'd learned of the political struggles that had beset Hungary in recent years, and how they might affect Count Jokai. In many ways, the story of Hungary's growth reminded him of the English wars that he remembered from his boyhood at the monastery. Just as the English barons had forced the Great Charter on King John, the Hungarian magnates had their Golden Bull, the charter of liberties for the nobles and the Church. The difference was that in England, King John had died of a flux the year after the charter was signed, leaving behind a child-ruler who was too young to fight to regain the crown's rights. Andrew, King of Hungary, was still alive ten years after the Golden Bull had been signed; he'd been gathering supporters and rebuilding his personal army. Now he wanted to revise the charter of liberties. The archbishop of Esztergom was threatening to excommunicate him if he touched a single word of the charter; the magnates were threatening rebellion, and Count Jokai was trying not to commit himself to any of the three parties until he could assess which had the stronger forces. He also wanted to be sure that his own army was ready in case of need.

"And armies cost money," said Aude.

"And wars won't wait, but St. Michael will." Stephen nodded. "And I don't want to sit through an entire building season while Count Jokai deliberates on whether God or the army needs his money the most. If I can show him that the new church will cost a third less than he thought, at least in the first few building seasons, he might be more inclined to keep his promises to St. Michael in a timely fashion."

"That sounds good. This time I don't think we should use our personal savings to supplement the building fund, the way you did at Chastelvert."

"Mmm? No, it wouldn't be much help, would it? This is a much bigger project." Stephen squatted on his heels, collecting the drawings that had cascaded from his arms when he hugged her. Aude suppressed a quick, exasperated sigh. Here she was with news that meant much more than all his talk of bulls and barons, and he was squatting among his scattered parchments, missing the point entirely. She would have to be more explicit.

"Regardless of whether the money would help your building work," she said very slowly and clearly, "we've got other uses for it now. We have to think of the future."

"Yes, yes, so you always used to say. . . ." Stephen's voice trailed off and he was very still, gripping the edges of the drawing in his hands. At last he looked up at her. "Aude . . . ?"

She nodded, lips closed, suddenly afraid she would burst out in tears that Stephen would misinterpret.

"When? Are you feeling all right? Sit down! Let me get you something to eat!"

Once again the parchments were scattered all over the floor. Stephen lifted Aude into the large chair in the tracing house and propped her feet up while she laughed at him and pointed out that the baby wouldn't be coming for many months and she felt perfectly healthy. Then she sat back and let him cosset her. After all, she was old to be having a first child. Nearly twenty-seven! A little care and cosseting wouldn't come amiss, to still the fears that tormented her in the midst of her happiness.

That first summer in Transylvania was pure gold: sun and ripening wheat and Aude growing slow and big and clumsy. The quick-paced, deft, impatient girl of the fens had become a young matron, carrying her swollen body with careful dignity, content to sit for hours in the sun with a piece of needlework dangling from one hand. Stephen marveled over the transformation, but did not have time to savor it fully; something else was being born this summer, something almost as precious to him as the child she carried (though he dared not admit it to Aude).

The Church of St. Michael-at-Varad would be his masterwork. All his work in Egypt and in France was only in preparation for this, his most ambitious project. When Stephen thought of the child, he said two prayers of gratitude: one that Aude had conceived after so many years, one that it had happened here. Stephen felt she would want to make her life in the place where her child was born. And Stephen knew, from the day the first lines were set out on the site, that he could never leave this church for lesser men to complete. There was a sense of perfection about it, from the foursquare lines of the foundation to the daring sweep of pinnacles and the single line of flying buttresses that would take shape against the brilliant blue sky. Everything he knew had gone into this design; his penance had become his reward.

As the foundation trenches were dug, the usual rubble of past times was turned up and brought to Stephen; somehow the laborers here had heard of his penchant for examining the curious things they brought out of the earth. The first trenching yielded a random collection of broken earthenware and one tarnished mirror whose handle and frame had been made of two dolphins with their backs arched and their tails blending together. Later dig-

gings turned up a row of teeth strung on a leather thong
that disintegrated in Stephen's hands, and a broad bone
incised with clearly recognizable figures of men hunting
some shaggy beast. The animal's form was indistinct, but
the arrows bristled out of its body all round, like quills on
a porcupine.

"We have good hunting in the mountains," Lajos said
when Stephen showed him this piece of artwork. "This
winter, when you have some free time, I'll take you."

"Thank you," said Stephen with such noticeable restraint that Lajos looked up sharply.

"What, don't you like hunting?"

"Not really. I understand it's necessary to keep the wild
beasts under control, but there's something about the idea
of being hunted with arrows that doesn't much appeal to
me."

Lajos gave a great shout of laughter. "Nor to me! Isn't it
fortunate we're on the right side of the arrows? You Franks
must think we're truly barbarians. We don't hunt *men*,
Stephen. Of course, if we were wild Kipchak tribesmen
instead of civilized Magyars, you might have reason to be
nervous. Ha! Not bad. Don't go hunting with Kipchaks,
eh?" He wandered off, chuckling, to tell his joke to
somebody else. Stephen put away the carved bone, the
mirror, and the bronze bowl he'd brought all the way from
France. He wondered briefly how he'd come to make such
a stupid slip of the tongue. Well, Lajos would have a new
joke by next week, and there were plenty of other things
to think about: a church to build and a baby coming. What
more could a man ask for?

Leveling the building site and digging the foundations
occupied his time for all of that first summer. Stephen
never forgot that the Church of St. Michael was to be his
penance as well as his glory; he was resolved that there
would be no shoddy or careless work. The foundations
were dug twenty feet below ground level. Lajos grumbled
that Stephen had been commissioned to build a cathedral,
not to turn the main square into a well. And what was the
purpose of the large, flat cauldron? Two of Stephen's
laborers were continuously hauling the massive tin vessel
from place to place, levering it down into the trenches and
filling it with water that Stephen then inspected like
an ancient pagan looking for auguries of good fortune.

"Leveling the site," Stephen explained. "You don't want the church to tilt to one side when it's finished, do you? Then we have to make sure the foundation diggings are exactly level everywhere. If I can pour water into this cauldron until it just reaches the brim all the way around, without a drop spilled, then the ground is level where it stands; otherwise, we have to bring out the spades again."

It seemed perfectly clear to Stephen, an elegant and beautiful solution to a problem that had been plaguing builders for centuries. But Lajos chewed the ends of his moustaches, muttered something about magic, and finally sighed and said he would leave the mysteries of building to the master builder.

"Very wise," Stephen said. "Why don't you go hawking?"

He himself returned quite happily to the task of overseeing the foundations. The trenches were finished well before the first frost, and the bottom courses of the foundations were laid. Frost came earlier here than in England, but Stephen was ready with cartloads of straw to cover his foundations against the cold. He felt a measure of satisfaction marred only by the fact that his employer still had not come to Varad to see the progress. What if Count Jokai decided that Stephen's plans for the church were too grandiose? This wasn't a cathedral; no bishop or archbishop would sit in the church of Varad. Stephen couldn't really delude himself that the people of this little border outpost needed a church to rival the great cathedrals of France and Italy. Jokai's munificence with tools and laborers had given Stephen the confidence to lay out foundations for a great church, a masterwork. But he wondered whether the Hungarian count had really wanted to commission a masterpiece and whether he had the money to complete the work.

"It makes me nervous, working for a man I've never met," he grumbled to Aude.

Aude nodded but, as usual these days, she was not really listening to him. Wrapped in her own peace, she hummed to herself, spent long hours gazing out toward the golden plains to the west, and slept a great deal.

Three weeks after the thatching was completed, Stephen came back from an afternoon's work in the tracing house to find his house full of clucking, excited matrons in embroidered holiday dresses. At the center of their excitement he found his old Aude back again: pale and quiet, with sweat dampening her hair, but with the impish grin that meant she was mighty proud of herself. And in her arms, almost invisible in its wrappings of lace-edged linens, was a small, red, squalling baby that she held up to him like the greatest treasure on earth. "We have a son, Stephen!"

"Good God," said Stephen, halting an arm's length from his wife and baby, "you've gone and bought a piglet at the Martinmas fair!"

The good wives who'd helped Aude, shrieked their merriment, and Aude gave him a dirty look. There was more bustle and cleaning up around them, and finally the women left, after Aude had assured them a good seven times that she needed no more help.

"You could have sent for me." Now that there were no onlookers to scold him for clumsiness, Stephen took the baby in his arms. He was surprisingly light. His son. This morning Stephen had been a preoccupied builder with nothing more to worry about than the geometry of the east stair, and now he was a father, and he hadn't even known it was happening. He could have lost Aude; women died in childbirth. "You should have sent for me," he said, more sternly. The baby yawned in his face and fell asleep with one fist crammed into its toothless mouth.

Aude looked wise and merry at once. "I sent you away. Why d'you think I was such a shrew this morning? It was easier on both of us. You know how you don't like blood."

"Next time," said Stephen severely, "you tell me. I want to be with you."

"Oh, aye, my lord. Whatever you say, my lord."

Aude fell asleep in the middle of her teasing, one arm resting across his knees. Stephen sat cradling the sleeping baby, afraid to move for fear of disturbing one of them. He felt that he could happily sit just like this forever.

Years ago, when they married, Stephen had told Aude that if they ever had a son he wanted to name him Edric, after her father. Now, though, he felt that a peasant name like Edric wouldn't be suitable for the firstborn son of a master builder. A French name would be better. Michael? Yes. They would call him Michael, as a tribute to the saint whose church he was building. Perhaps the name might buy a measure of the saint's protection for this precious, fragile baby.

The house still smelled of blood, though the stained cloths used in the birthing had been carried away by the matrons. Stephen's thoughts wandered; he was tired himself, half dreaming by the fire, and the heat of the flames upon his face reminded him of the hot Egyptian sun. Sun, new birth, and the smell of blood reminded Stephen of the courtyard where Kamil had slaughtered a goat for the safety of his firstborn son. But Kamil's prayers had been directed to the false god Mahound, and they had not protected little Rashid. St. Michael would do better by them.

Half asleep, he murmured the words of Kamil's prayer, as if the good saint would want to hear a pagan sacrifice. "O God, verily this is a ransom for my son; its blood for his blood, and its flesh for his flesh, and its bone for his bone, and its skin for his skin, and its hair for his hair." But there was no goat to be slaughtered here; he had nothing to offer God for his son's protection, but his own prayers.

CHAPTER

27

◻

*T*hat first successful year in Hungary set a pattern for the happy years that followed. Stephen watched the Church of St. Michael rise layer by layer above the citadel, and saw his son grow from a red-faced wailing wisp to a sturdy baby boy. He sometimes felt that he had as little to do with one as with the other. Both grew at their own rate, obeying their own laws, and all Stephen had to do was provide the space within which they existed. The church ate stone and time and thought and drawings; his son, whose name had been amplified to Michael-Béla, after a strong hint from Count Jokai that it might be wise to pay this compliment to the King's son, consumed porridge and meat pasties and apples at the same swift rate. Sometimes Stephen had to run his hands over the stonework of the church to convince himself that this creation of his own mind was actually solid stone. And sometimes, when Michael-Béla was risking his own neck and his mother's sanity by clambering out on swaying scaffolding, Stephen had to haul the boy down and give him a rough hug to assure himself that Michael-Béla was sturdy and real and able to bounce back from the thousand tumbles and scrapes he took in the course of the day.

Count Jokai was in and out of Varad a dozen times during those years, bringing a party of guests to enjoy the hunting, or inspecting the defenses of the city walls and the training of his standing army. He brought court gossip with him: King Andrew had died and was succeeded by his young son Béla, there was more talk about revising the Golden Bull, the price of silk was up because of some troubles on the Russian steppes far to the east. Usually the count made time for a brief visit to the building site and the tracing house. Stephen and Aude grew to know him as a large, hearty man who was always in a hurry. He seemed as simple and rough as the rest of his hard-drinking, hard-riding court, but his eyes suggested great intelligence.

As the years passed, Stephen became annoyed that Count Jokai never stayed long enough to talk about how he juggled the interests of court and church and barons. Instead, the count's visits followed a predictable, hurried, unsatisfying pattern. He would nod approvingly at the rising walls of the church, glance at Stephen's drawings, cut short any explanations of the structural soundness of the fragile-seeming building, ruffle Michael-Béla's hair, and steal a kiss from Aude. He never failed to make a joke about the days of his ancestors when the count of Varad would have been entitled to borrow such a pretty girl from her husband for as long as he resided in the city. Aude always ducked her head and blushed when the count made his jest, but after Jokai left the house, she would break a few pieces of crockery on the kitchen floor to relieve her feelings. Stephen noticed that she usually chose the cheapest utensils, flawed pitchers, and cracked cups; she didn't seem to feel a need to break the hand-blown Venetian glass goblets Jokai had brought on his first visit to welcome his imported architect to Varad. Stephen understood how she felt. He rather liked the count, but he usually spoiled a couple of stones in the masons' lodge on the day after one of Jokai's visits.

The count's Venetian-born wife, Bianca, remained in the south through those years. Apparently she stayed with Jokai in Buda or Esztergom for a few months of each year, when the court was gathered and life was lively. The rest of the time she found that her precarious health obliged her to live on the Dalmatian coast, where the climate was mild and there were real cities with Italian doges and merchant-bankers.

In the summer when Michael-Béla was five years old,

the prince for whom he'd been named succeeded to the throne, and Count Jokai came to Varad for a longer stay than usual. Stephen had grown used to predicting the length of Count Jokai's visits by counting the number of packhorses that carried his personal goods. This time the train stretched through the citadel and across the winding road through the hills. And so Stephen was not surprised when the count sent for him and told him that he meant to stay in Varad through the summer.

"Maybe longer. Maybe I can stay here permanently this time." Jokai looked out over the blue hills to the east and sniffed the mountain air with deep appreciation. "Young Béla's too much with the damned churchmen for my taste, but the boy's got a head on his shoulders. He knows he needs me here, guarding his eastern frontier, and not back in Buda guarding my own interests. He said as much before I left. 'Jokai,' he says to me, 'Jokai, you're a man of the mountains, you're rude but you always give me a straight answer. You be straight with me, Jokai,' he says, 'and I'll be straight with you. There'll be no trickery in Buda, no granting away of your lands and interests, as long as you're doing my work in the east.' That's what he said to me."

The count sniffed the mountain air again. "It's going to be a good year, builder. No more politics. I can go back to living a man's natural life—hunting and riding and keeping the damned Kipchaks and Saxons and Wallachs in their place. It's easy enough. Tax a Wallach, send a Saxon down the mines, and spear a Kipchak when you see him—that's my recipe for peace!"

He gave his explosive grunting laugh and looked at Stephen as if expecting some response.

"Yes, Count Jokai. Is that what you sent to tell me? Because I *was* supervising the placing of the lintel on the center portal of the west facade of the church, my lord, and I really should be getting—"

"Oh, sit down, sit down," Count Jokai interrupted him. "Don't be so damned stiff, man. After six seasons you should have trained your building crew so that they can get along without you for a few minutes—maybe even a few days, eh? If you haven't done that much yet, you're not much of a leader, even if you do draw good pictures."

Stephen agreed rather stiffly that his crew and foremen

could probably work without supervision for several days, providing that no unforeseen problems came up.

"Good. I thought so. It's time we got to know each other better—you, me, that wife of yours. Eh? Time you saw something of the country, too. Six years in Transylvania and I'll wager you've never been over a league from your precious church."

"I have indeed! I've been to the quarries at Temesvar, and the iron mines at Koloszvar, and. . . ."

The count was laughing. Stephen waited till the spluttering sounds ceased.

"I thought as much. Well, next week you're to have a holiday. We're going up into the mountains to see the ice caves. I want you and Aude to join us."

Count Jokai overrode Stephen's protests and excuses with a steely, smiling insistence that allowed no opposition. Stephen had already admitted the works could get on without him for a few days, hadn't he? Yes, of course it was the middle of the building season; midsummer was the only time to visit the ice caves. Who'd struggle through snowdrifts to look at icicles? But in midsummer, with the forest in leaf and the sun warming the shepherds' paths and wild flowers covering the hillside, it could be quite a pleasant excursion.

Stephen was rather surprised to hear Count Jokai growing lyrical about the beauties of nature. He'd never heard the count praise a forest for anything but its wolves, wild boars, bears, and stags. But as Jokai talked on, his real reason for insisting on this midsummer excursion became clear. And to his surprise, Stephen found himself feeling mildly sorry for the count.

"He's talked his wife into coming to Varad to spend the summer with him," he reported to Aude when he was breaking the news that she would have to find a neighbor to mind Michael-Béla for a week. "She should arrive in a few days. I think he wants to show her that life here can be quite civilized. And we're part of the civilization. A much-traveled architect from the West and his lovely and gracious lady."

"Better dig the stone dust out from under your nails before next week, then," Aude suggested.

Stephen peered at the black crescents under the nails of his right hand. "Oh, that? That's not dust. It's pork fat, mostly, and a few other things. I was trying out some new mixtures to lubricate the great lifting wheel."

"I'm sure that'll make all the difference to the count's lady."

The expected train of mules and horses and ladies in litters did not materialize the next week, nor the week after. Count Jokai sent messengers south to find out what was delaying his wife. Stephen stayed up late at night, drawing templets and detailed working plans far in advance of the current work, so that the building could go on without him whenever this visit to the ice caves took place. Aude was curious and impatient to meet Count Jokai's mysterious young wife. What would this fine Venetian lady be like? Aude visualized another Helene, pale and pretty and fading into fretful middle age; then she reminded herself that Bianca was quite young. She had married at fourteen to a foreign baron more than three times her age. Was it any wonder that she'd never been willing to settle down in a lonely castle overlooking the wild woods of Transylvania?

At long last, the count's lady made her appearance; Aude did not meet her, for Bianca took to her bed immediately upon arrival, complaining of the hardships of the journey. Count Jokai went ahead and made his plans for the long-awaited excursion to the ice caves as if Bianca had been perfectly well, which perhaps she was. Stephen laid aside his drafting tools with only token grumbling; he'd had long enough to get used to the idea of an enforced vacation. Aude suspected he might even be looking forward to it.

She herself had only one regret to plague her as the little cavalcade left Varad. Michael-Béla had taken all too happily to the news that he was to spend a week with Aude's fat laundress and her six or seven children—Aude had never managed to get an accurate count of them. Indeed, he seemed to be looking forward to the week. And it was the first time she'd been away even overnight! She would have thought he'd have missed her more.

Stephen laughed at her complaint. "Did you *want* him to cry and cling to you? Would that make you enjoy the trip more, thinking that you'd left him unhappy?"

Stephen was right, of course. And this time Aude could forgive him, because the first time they stopped to rest the horses he picked up a curiously shaped black stone "for Michael-Béla's collection," he explained with a slightly shamefaced air.

The lady Bianca was not with them; she had left two days earlier, with her women and her armed escort, to take a longer and easier, but less scenic, route to the ice caves. The two groups were to meet there and travel back to Varad together. So Aude had one more day of grace before she had to deal with the count's young wife. She told herself that she should enjoy the journey now; on the way back she'd probably be expected to entertain Bianca.

As they rode into the deep woods, Aude found it easier to forget Michael-Béla and enjoy the beauty of their surroundings. These dark clusters of fir and spruce all but shut out the sky; they rode on cushions of springy needles, breathing air tangy with resin and damp with the scent of old decaying branches. Count Jokai and his entourage had been noisy earlier, laughing and singing and passing around a leather skin of wine. Now they fell silent and rode warily, glancing from side to side, as if they feared attack from some unseen enemy. Aude knew they weren't worried about wild animals; Jokai was given to complaining that his young men had hunted the near slopes of the Apusenyi Mountains so thoroughly that nothing bigger than a rabbit could be found to give him sport. Rather it was the still spirit of the forest that made them nervous, the tangle of ferns and undergrowth that blocked their vision of the woods, the tall trees rising all around them that cut off any sense of the horizon.

Aude rather liked it. Her early life in the fens had accustomed her to moving along secret paths where she could never see more than a foot or two ahead. Here the path was bounded by steep slopes rather than by silent water, the slender shafts that barred the way were the tree trunks rather than golden-green reeds, and overhead there were arched branches of spruce and fir rather than the pale blue sky of the fens. But for all these differences, the spirit of the place spoke to her of stillness, secrecy, and quiet—everything she had given up when she chose to follow a young man with too much energy and too much ambition and an incomprehensible desire to build.

Aude glanced at Stephen's broad back and smiled. Was it worth it? Of course! She wouldn't choose to be any-

where but with Stephen. All the same, it was good to have
these few moments of peace, away from the clang of
stoneworkers and the shouts of street vendors and Michael-
Béla tugging at her skirts for attention.

Aude shivered unexpectedly. Was she growing too complacent? Some day she might long for the noise and
commotion she was escaping now. For a moment, she had
a vision of her future: she was an older, quieter woman in
some place where the only sound was the beating of waves
on shingle, where her only occupation was to look forever
out over the gray sea.

Her vision cleared and she saw Stephen riding ahead of
her once again. They had gone less than twenty feet along
the forest path while she was daydreaming—for that was
all it had been, a waking dream.

Almost against her will, she recalled the wailing voice of
the *poulani* witch in the Holy Land, so many years ago.
"You have the power if you will use it." And to Stephen,
"Your bones will lie under water."

Was that why she'd had that momentary vision of herself
staring out over the water? Aude shook her head so
violently that her patient horse snorted and missed a step
on the trail. No. She had been dreaming, nothing more.

All the same, the forest no longer seemed a comfortable,
silent, welcoming place. Now its secrets were dangerous
and the whispering of the wind in the firs was tinged with
malice. Aude was as happy as the rest of the party when
they emerged from the woods onto the central plateau of
the mountains.

From here on they entered into a land of fairy tales and
poetic romances. Forever after, the ice caves in the Apusenyi
Mountains would stand for all that was magical and unreal
in Aude's mind: mountains of ice and dazzling sunlight,
valleys carpeted with moss and fragile summer flowers.
And at the heart of a flower-filled abyss, the domed grotto
of ice, a torch-lit church as cold as death and as brilliant as
a cave set with sparkling gems.

Echoing from deep within the cave, Aude heard a
woman's high, tinkling laughter. What spirits haunted this
place? She started to cross herself, then realized her
mistake as loud male voices joined the woman's laughter.
There were no spirits here; it was only the count's lady
and her escort.

Here, of all places, Aude would have chosen to be silent, to let the natural wonder of their surroundings possess her spirit. She could see the irritation in Stephen's face as well when two gaily clad young nobles reeled around the curve in the ice passage, slipping and clinging to one another like men who'd had too much to drink. One of them dropped his torch and it skidded across the slick floor to Stephen's feet, miraculously never going out. He picked it up automatically and raised it above his head, and the dome of ice turned into a circle of shimmering radiance.

"My lord Jokai. We have been waiting for you here, as you see," said Bianca who followed her two young escorts.

The greeting was spoken with no more warmth than a woman would offer a near-stranger; the deep genuflection which accompanied the words seemed designed to show off the supple slenderness of the lady's graceful body. It took Aude a moment to convince herself that this was the lady Bianca, for whose benefit they'd made this whole journey.

"I trust you haven't been waiting too long? Are you bored? Are you chilled?"

Bianca turned away Jokai's clumsy, solicitous inquiries with a laugh. "If I had been bored and cold, surely you've brought with you enough company to amuse and warm me? Won't you introduce me to your friends?"

But by *friends* she clearly meant Stephen, not Aude. While Bianca and Stephen exchanged courtly pleasantries about the progress of the church and the delights of country life, Aude had time enough to observe and to think. And she did not like what she saw.

This Bianca was pale and fragile; her fair hair was piled high and sparkling with gems; her eyebrows plucked to delicate arches against snow-pale skin; her waist encircled by silver chains whose heaviness only emphasized the unworldly delicacy of her body.

Bianca was older than Aude had expected. All these years she'd imagined the count's wife as a girl of fourteen, forgetting how much time had passed since they had come to Transylvania. This was no lonely little girl for Aude to mother. She was a woman grown, a great lady of Venice, accustomed to having her wants attended to and her fancies cosseted.

And Aude, looking back and forth between her husband's gaping mouth and Bianca's warm, smiling eyes knew, with a sick certainty, just what it was the lady fancied right now.

The interplay was only between their eyes; Aude told herself she must be imagining things. There was nothing improper in Bianca's pretty words of greeting. But Aude came away from the introductions feeling somehow that she had been patronized, and so had Count Jokai even if he didn't know it. But there was nothing to account for her confused feelings in the words that had been spoken. Bianca had greeted her husband with restrained courtesy, had mentioned how eager she was to see the fine new church that Stephen was building and had said with a lingering, husky little laugh that she felt sure she had heretofore underrated the attractions of Varad; there was much in the city and environs that she had not known about and would like to know better.

She had, of course, been referring to such natural wonders as the ice caves. The fact that she kept glancing up into Stephen's eyes as she spoke meant nothing at all. Stephen was a strikingly handsome man who looked as confident and as wellborn as Jokai. Why wouldn't Bianca give him a second look? Any woman would.

It certainly didn't mean that Stephen had been looking back. Anyway, they were returning directly to Varad, and once they got home he would have plenty to do at the church and wouldn't waste time with people who knew and cared nothing about his work.

On the journey back to Varad, Aude's only satisfaction was in thinking that at last she had identified the source of the premonitions that had so troubled her in the forest. There had been trouble ahead, sure enough; but it wasn't anything serious. Just a bored, lovely, greedy woman who wanted to ride down the mountain beside Stephen, chattering to him of life in Venice and flattering him with her compliments. Well, let her. Aude wasn't foolish enough to push in and try to reclaim her husband in the midst of this jolly traveling party. She rode between the two boys who had led the guard escorting Bianca to the caves; one of them, she thought, had the look of a rejected lover. Aude exerted herself to amuse him. For most of the journey back to Varad she succeeded so well that Stephen cast annoyed glances over his shoulder. He was on the verge of riding back to tell his wife not to laugh so loudly or to sing such bordering-on-the-improper songs with Jokai's young noblemen.

But not all her laughter and flirting and singing could dispel the sense of gloom that hung over the forest. Aude was heartily glad to see the citadel of Varad rising before them at last. She did not even demur when Stephen responded to a chance comment of Bianca's by offering to go directly to the church, that she might see this great work which her husband had commissioned.

"It's the best time of day to see it, with sunset gilding the stones. The workmen will be just finishing for the day, so your ears won't be assaulted by the din of stones breaking and carpenters hammering," he assured the lady. And to Aude, "And if I know that imp Michael-Béla, he'll have slipped away from our good laundress to watch our arrival from the walls. You'll see him sooner, I'll bet, if we go to the church where he'll likely be awaiting us."

And so he was. They saw him first as a tiny stick figure moving on the unparapeted top of the eastern tower, where a fragile construction of ropes and wicker hurdles hung to let the skilled masons get to their work each day.

Stephen shaded his eyes and swore. "What's going on up there? I told the men never to work alone on the high tower. It's safer if they go up in pairs, one to work and one to watch the winds." In this unfinished state, the high towers and the roof arches were terribly vulnerable to gusts of wind from the mountains.

"It's not a workman." Aude recognized the disproportion of tiny limbs and large head before Stephen did. A cold hand clutched at her heart. "It's Michael-Béla."

"The monster!" Stephen jumped off his horse and dashed into the courtyard. "By God, I'll kill that child when I get him down again; he knows he's not allowed to climb on the works."

But he'd been doing so, without fear and without common sense, since he was old enough to toddle into the stoneyard. And he felt no fear now, only pride at having achieved the highest point in all the church.

"Look, Mama! Look, Dada!" shrieked the thin childish voice high above them. "Look where I am! I saw you coming! I saw you! I saw—"

His jigging dance of triumph carried him within inches of the flat edge of the tower roof. Stephen paused with one foot on the first woven hurdle; Aude put her knuckles into her mouth and bit down on her clenched hand. She stifled the scream that might startle Michael-Béla into a fall before he moved safely back from the edge.

He might have managed it if a workman hadn't left a beam lying across the corner of the towertop, ready for the carpenters to start the bracing and centering frames for the tall spire. Tripping over that beam interrupted Michael-Béla's triumphant dance, and sent him stumbling forward. His scream, and the sound of the small body landing on the stones of the courtyard, would echo in Aude's ears forever.

CHAPTER

28

◈

*T*he world was a cold and empty place without a small
boy's laughter, without an inquisitive little head poking into the churchyard. Stephen was alone in his despair,
unable even to put out a hand to Aude where she rocked
back and forth in her own grief. He wandered in an
endless labyrinth of memory, from the icy walls of Ely to
the burning sands around Cairo, and nowhere could he
find any comfort.

Prayer was supposed to bring peace, but he could not
pray to a God who had pushed Michael-Béla over the edge
of the tower. His prayers seemed as meaningless as Kamil's
sacrifice to Mahound for his firstborn son, and as useless.
Had Kamil felt this way after Rashid's death? Stephen
remembered the hot splash of goat's blood across a sunny
courtyard, a sacrifice that had done no good. It seemed to
Stephen that nothing one did made any difference. Nothing lasted except the stone and the work of his hands.

Even the love between him and Aude, the one certainty
in his life, was strained after Michael-Béla's death. Aude
had pulled away from him, and he did not know how to
reach her. Her days alternated between bouts of furious
weeping and hours of staring out the window that overlooked
the eastern mountains.

"What do you see that keeps you there?" Stephen asked once.

Aude turned dull empty eyes toward him. "Death and destruction."

Stephen consulted with the priest who was to serve in the new Church of St. Michael, who now crowded his parishoners into the cramped church at the bottom of the hill. "She had a bad time when we were young," he said awkwardly. "There was a war . . . the soldiers . . . well, you know the sort of thing that happens. Now it seems she can't stop thinking of it. And maybe she blames me. I wasn't there to save her." Nor had he been able to save his son. In everything that really mattered, he was powerless.

Father Thomas talked with Aude at length, laying great weight on the sin of excessive grief. She threw three kitchen bowls at his head and he retreated with his long skirts flapping about his shins.

"I don't think she blames you for anything," he said to Stephen, who was in the tracing house where he now spent most of his time. Father Thomas placed one pudgy hand over Stephen's parchment, to compel his attention. "Maybe you are blaming yourself?"

"You deduced this, I presume, from the pattern in which the bowls broke?"

"I think you should comfort each other. Other parents have lost a child and survived their grief."

Stephen did not throw the metal builder's square that he balanced on his palm; but something in his expression made the priest retreat even more precipitately than he had done from Aude's wrath.

The house on the city wall was a sad place now, and Stephen did not like to spend time there. He did not know how to comfort Aude. He was half afraid even to try. He had tried to keep Mam, tried to raise a son to manhood and he'd failed miserably. He could do no better for himself than this black emptiness where he now wandered; his only light came from the church rising on the hill. He couldn't keep those he loved by him, or keep them safe, or even comfort them in their grief. All he could do was build in stone, taking what comfort he could from the everlasting strength of the rising church. This, at least, would not vanish overnight.

Stephen took to sleeping in the tracing house most

nights, rather than going down the hill to face his desolate house. Aude did not complain about his absences. Perhaps she found it as difficult to see him as he found it to see her. When he looked at her narrow, pointed face and dark eyes, he saw Michael-Béla looking out of her eyes. Perhaps she saw their son's square frame and buttercup hair when she looked at Stephen. That was one of many things he could not ask her.

They could not talk or laugh or make love. Strong emotions had to be avoided, as a swimmer avoids the treacherous undercurrents of the sea. The sharp rocks of their grief were too powerful. Apart, they could barely meet the days with a surface of calm. Together, they remembered too much.

It was easier, and safer, to concentrate on the church.

His foremen and craftmasters accepted the amended plans he drew up after Michael-Béla's death with raised eyebrows but without open comment. Only old Béla, the Magyar master of works who bore a king's name and carried himself accordingly, ventured to criticize the new designs.

"They're too high and too frail. We didn't build to support walls like these and I'm not sure we can do it now."

Stephen gave him a cold look. "I can do it. If you doubt your technical competence, you are free to leave."

Béla's red face paled to match the iron-gray of his hair and moustaches. He had been on the project since before Stephen arrived in Varad; in six years he had not slept away from the building yard once. Stephen regretted the cruelty of his words as soon as he'd spoken.

"I didn't mean it," he said hastily. "I know you won't leave. What could I do without you, Béla? We will work together to make this the finest church in Hungary, the finest church in Christendom. Michael's church," he said softly, tracing the outline of the lacy spires on the parchment with one finger.

Béla cleared his throat. "Yes. We all wanted to say how sorry we were, sir, about your son. A fine, brave little boy. It must be a great loss to you. He would have been a credit to you, sir. Just the day before, he was up here, touring the works because, he said, you weren't here to do it, so he had to take your place."

Stephen's hands closed convulsively about his drawing tools when Béla began his confused speech. He wanted to tell him not to talk about Michael-Béla, not to awaken his grief, just to get out. But his throat closed up so that he couldn't speak, and old Béla wasn't one to be frightened away by a cold look. As the master of works rambled on, Stephen found some comfort in hearing Michael-Béla's name mentioned by someone who remembered him without the crushing grief that was destroying him and Aude.

After that day, Béla never again complained about the difficulty of executing the new designs for the upper walls of the church. And he took to dropping into the tracing house late at night to share a glass of wine with Stephen and to talk over the day's problems. He seldom mentioned Michael-Béla, but when he did, it was because the boy's name came naturally into the conversation, and there was no sense of awkwardness. Occasionally he hinted that while it was natural for him to sleep on a cot in the masons' lodge since he had no family, Stephen had a house and a wife and might be more comfortable there.

Stephen ignored such hints. What old Béla didn't understand was that he did not have a home and a wife; not really. For a little while he enjoyed the illusion of such things but now they were being taken away, as God took away everything except his work. Behind his sadness for Michael-Béla, buried under years of work and living, was a small boy's bewildered grief for Mam, who'd abandoned him. Now Stephen felt as though he'd always known that this desolation was waiting for him. To love someone was to lose that person. Mam had gone away. Michael-Béla was dead. Soon Aude would go away, too, and then his isolation would be complete. His only defense against these losses was to build his soul into perfect, unchanging walls of stone. Work was all he could trust, all he dared trust.

As weeks, then months, went by, Stephen found some assuagement for his grief in the rapid progress he was making on the church. He was no longer content to proceed at the slow pace to which he'd held himself in the first years of building, raising walls and piers and buttresses one layer of stones at a time, waiting for mortar to set and for the tensile strength of the most delicate sections to be tested by winter winds. What was the point? He knew where the lines of stress ran through the frame of the church, both the unfinished building on the hill and the completed one in his mind. He forced a faster pace on the masons, working out complex schemes of centering and bracing to hold the unset walls in place. Stephen knew that Béla and the other master craftsmen grumbled that he took too many risks, though they dared say nothing to his face. They were wrong. Stephen could feel the strains in the stone structure as surely as he felt the bones and sinews of his own body, feet planted in the earth, shoulders bearing whatever load they had to carry. When wind tugged at the rising spires of the outer pinnacles, when he tapped an interior column to judge the weight it bore from the vibrations under his hand, he heard the high, sweet music of stone under pressure. He had always known this song; others might call it a miracle, but Stephen knew it was God's gift to repay him for the happiness he was not destined to enjoy in this life.

As one building season succeeded another, he and Aude began to stay together, though the unspoken closeness they'd shared all their lives was gone. They maintained a facade of normal life; he began sleeping at home two or three nights a week and they always attended mass together in Father Thomas's overcrowded church at the bottom of the hill. But the months of estrangement had taken their toll. Stephen and Aude could not speak of Michael-Béla, and that great silence made a mockery of the little things with which they occasionally tried to break the silence of their evenings together. Aude would speak of trying a new flower she'd discovered in the hills, whose leaves made a good tisane for the headache and whose flowers made the most delicate blue dye. Stephen would mention that the carpenters were ready to take down the bracing under the transept arches, or that he had to visit the leadworkers in the mountains to see about getting the gargoyle gutterspouts made to his specifications. Then they'd fall silent again, she with a piece of needlework, he doodling triangles and squares on a blank corner of his sketchbook.

Aude hadn't left him; but their marriage was dead. On the whole, it was a relief to go from those long silences back to the bustle of the building yard and the cheerful, everyday working noises that floated in the windows of the tracing house.

One sweet-smelling summer evening, a little over a year after Michael-Béla's death, the lady Bianca drifted into the tracing house through the narrow arched door at the top of the stairs.

"My lady." Stephen stood up, a little clumsy in his surprise, and the legs of his stool scraped loudly across the floor.

Of course it was not the first time they had met since the expedition to the ice caves. Count Jokai had kept his promise to remain in Varad, but he no longer visited Stephen at home or in the tracing house to go over the progress of the church. Instead Stephen had to go to the count's public hall when he needed to consult with his patron. Sometimes while Stephen was waiting, he would see Bianca float through the hall with one arm lightly placed on some young man's sleeve, and he would hear her tinkling laughter. When she deigned to greet Stephen, it was always as the great lady to a respected but much inferior craftsman; Stephen saw nothing in her eyes of the hot predatory interest that had so bemused him on that first meeting. Doubtless she'd found other ways to satisfy that interest among Jokai's young men.

And now she was in his tracing house, unannounced and uninvited, casually brushing aside a stack of working drawings to seat herself on the one comfortable chair at the head of the table. Stephen swallowed his irritation and inquired in what way he might be of service to her.

"Service..." repeated Bianca consideringly, with a little trill of laughter. She leaned her head on the outspread fingers on one hand and regarded Stephen with wide, cool eyes. "Ah, well, there are many ways in which a man may serve, aren't there?"

"I, unfortunately, know very few," said Stephen, immediately regretting his hasty refusal of something which was not clearly offered. "I have the honor to serve your husband as his builder. That is, I fear, the limit of my poor talents."

"Oh, I think not. At least, not to hear Jokai on the subject! He finds you an amazingly talented man—did you know that?" Bianca laughed again, and shook her head so that a few pale gold curls escaped from her coif, and by some magic the atmosphere in the room changed. Any offer made had been withdrawn again, so subtly that

Stephen could not even be sure anything had happened. As Bianca went on to explain that she wanted Stephen's help in contriving an unusual saint's day gift for the count, Stephen thought he must be a vain and self-centered fool ever to have imagined that she wanted anything else.

"Jokai has told me how skilled you are with mechanical contrivances," Bianca flattered him, "and I do want to surprise him with something special for his name day. Only what is there in Varad? Peasant woodwork, and furs from the mountains, and lumps of gold from the gold panning at the river! I thought perhaps. . . ."

Stephen told her that he couldn't make a brazen head that could answer questions, a chess-playing manikin, a treeful of mechanical singing birds as she suggested. The lady had been reading too many romances. However, he did remember the book Ibn Masoud had shown him once, written by a Saracen, on the art of making a fountain in a place where there was no spring to feed it. He had studied such fountains in Kamil's palace, and later had built them to please his other patrons in Cairo. Perhaps something like that would amuse Count Jokai?

Bianca was sure that it would. She was also very curious about how Stephen had learned to read books in the Saracen tongue. Without realizing it, Stephen let the afternoon slip away as he told Bianca stories of the years he and Aude had spent in Moslem lands. She was a delightful listener, clasping her hands at tense moments, gasping with surprise or relief at unexpected twists in the story, laughing and smiling and asking just enough questions to make him remember intriguing details he'd thought long forgotten.

"Oh, if only you knew how I've missed just this!" said Bianca when at last she rose to go. "To spend an hour talking with a man who knows something of the world outside these barbarous mountains, a man who can speak a civilized language without inserting a *Jaj Istenem!* or some other Hungarian oath between every two words." Bianca sighed. "I knew I should enjoy talking to you. I thought so before, but this last year I feared you might not welcome the intrusion." She seemed almost shy, with none of the flirtatious airs that had made him nervous at first. It was easy for Stephen to reassure her that her visit had been a delightful break in the monotony of his working days.

After she left, he discovered to his surprise that it was true. For nearly two full hours he'd been able to forget his loss without throwing himself into an exhausting bout of work. He had actually laughed and talked with a pretty woman; he could actually believe that there might be some pleasure in life, even after Michael-Béla's death. And Bianca had promised to come back to see his drawings for the mechanical fountain and to discuss the details of the ornamental metalwork.

Stephen surprised Aude by spending that night at home, surprised her even more by kissing her at the door and insisting that she join him over a meal of wine and rich stew sent up from the cook shop. For once in his life he had the good sense not to tell her what had put him in such a cheerful mood.

Over the next few years the piercing pain of Michael-Béla's loss receded into the background. Sometimes Stephen would hear a little boy calling to his father in the building yard, and a pain that made work quite impossible would shoot through his chest for a moment. Sometimes he would come home to find Aude in tears, and he never needed to ask why. But Stephen and Aude did manage to resume a normal life again. Aude was always a little too quiet, a little too sad, but Stephen knew she had her herbs and potions and dye pots to keep her busy. If it helped her grief to spend most of every day in the fields outside Varad gathering plants, he certainly wouldn't object. He himself had two sources of comfort now, the daily progress on the church and the near-daily visits from the lady Bianca.

Aude heard of these visits eventually, of course, and made some rather catty remarks about the lady's great interest in architecture. Since that first day, Stephen had seen no hint in Bianca of any untoward interests, so he was able to treat these comments casually.

"She's lonely here, and who can be surprised, with no one to talk to but Jokai's rude mountain types? She wants a little civilized conversation, that's all."

"Oh? And just what do you two civilized people find to talk about?"

"Mathematics," said Stephen promptly. "The new style in building. Venice—she's lonely for her home, and happy that I know the city."

That was a tactical error; Aude pointed out that Stephen had spent a grand total of three days in Venice, just long enough to book passage on a pilgrim galley and purchase supplies for the journey. What kind of a fool would believe that a great lady of Venice would waste her time with a fisherman's son from Dunwich for the pleasure of his civilized conversation?

That remark almost caused a major quarrel. But instead of fighting, Stephen laughed and agreed that he was an ignorant rustic and that Bianca must be desperate for civilized conversation if she turned to him. It was safer not to quarrel, not to start loving and wanting and needing again. Since Michael-Béla's death, Stephen took very few risks with his heart. He preferred to turn the near-quarrel into a jest, and presently to go back to the tracing house where he could sit over his sketches and look out the window at the church's unfinished spires, luminous and ghostly in the moonlight.

CHAPTER

29

◻

*I*n the building season of 1239, Count Jokai's forces were augmented by a number of strange, squat men who came from the mountains to the east. These wandering herdsmen, who spoke a tongue similar to Magyar, were driven out of their grazing lands by invaders from even farther east. King Béla granted them and their leader asylum and gave them grazing lands on the wide, sparsely peopled grassland called the *puszta* that stretched west from Varad over half of Hungary. But some were good fighters as well as herdsmen, and chose to stay and serve Count Jokai on the frontier.

Stephen had felt a mild interest in these new recruits when he found out that they were the fabled Kipchaks, barbarians out of the east with whom nurses scared children. He found the small Kipchak men rather sad: lonely, missing their herds and the freedom of their grazing lands, forever mourning for the lands they had lost. They would never be truly accepted in Hungary, and Jokai's men had taken to making cruel Kipchak jokes. Apparently there was no question of their reclaiming their ancestral lands.

"Oh, they'll be all right in a few generations," said Jokai cheerfully when Stephen put this view to him. "They are from the same stock as the Magyars, you know. You might not think it to look at us now, but not so many years ago our people were wild horsemen who sewed themselves into their furs for the winter and made blood sacrifices to heathen gods. It's hard to believe now, I know."

Stephen caught Bianca's eye and regretted that glance of complicity; he was trying not to laugh, that was all, but a jealous husband might have taken their look for something else.

"Anyway, that wasn't what I wanted to see you about. I'm taking fifty day laborers off the church project. You pick out which ones you can spare and send them to the drill yard for Csaba."

"What? You can't. I can't spare any of them!" That would be more than half his heavy-work force. And the church was so near completion!

Jokai scowled and Stephen remembered that this man was absolute master in his domains, reporting to no one except the King in Esztergom—and King Béla was very far away and probably not interested in the troubles of one foreign architect.

"Look here, Master Stephen, I'm trying to be reasonable. I'm not taking any of your craftsmen, am I? Not yet, anyway. Just the common laborers. I'll even let you pick which ones."

"What for?"

"Kipchaks," Jokai remarked as if on a tangent, "are tough fighting men. My grandfather had to crucify a few of them on the city walls before he could persuade them to stay on the far side of the Meszes Pass."

"Yes, yes," Stephen said impatiently, "I'm sure they are most admirable people in many ways, but do you mean you want me to take them on in place of the Wallachs?" Most of Stephen's porters and hod carriers were Wallachs, serfs descended from the people who'd lived here before the Magyar invasion. The Magyars didn't like to do any work that couldn't be done from the back of a horse. But from what Stephen had seen, neither did Kipchaks. "Well, I suppose I could train them, but—"

Jokai shook his head. "No. No question of that. I'm making a new wing of my army. The Kipchaks will be light cavalry, skirmishers, with their bows and arrows. I want your laborers to train for foot soldiers."

"Why?"

"Something scared the Kipchaks enough to send them

through the Meszes Gate and beg me for shelter—me, with Kipchak skins still hanging in the strongroom after Grandsire's wars! I don't want to meet anything that scares Kipchaks that much," Jokai explained patiently, "without a very large, very well-trained army. I'm sending a detachment to camp out at the pass until the snows close it, and I'm going to ask Béla for some of his men as reinforcements. When those men come, or when the snow blocks the Meszes Gate, you can have your laborers back."

Jokai was called away at that point. As he left, he muttered some instructions to Bianca about soothing Stephen's ruffled feathers and seeing that he went back to work in a good frame of mind. Stephen heard enough to get the gist of what he was saying.

"Well?" he asked when Jokai was safely out of earshot. "Are you going to flatter me back into a good humor, as your lord commanded?"

Bianca stared at him with big gray eyes that stood out from her pale and delicate face. "It's not a matter for jesting, Stephen."

"No." Stephen knew he should try to be tactful in front of his patron's wife, but he was tired of being polite. Bianca had been sympathetic before, and he was too angry just now to watch his words. "I hate being at the mercy of a patron. On-again, off-again—they endow great projects and then discover they need the funds for something else, they try to turn hod carriers into soldiers and let the walls of my church stand open to another winter. I wonder what it will be next time? And how the devil am I supposed to get the roof over the nave raised with no one to haul timber and work the lifting wheel?" At that moment Stephen glowered at Bianca, seeing her only as another member of the ruling class that had been interfering in his life's work as long as he could remember. "You nobles don't understand real work. God Himself ordained that all should be done according to its proper season, but gentlefolk think they can take my laborers in high summer on a whim and then catch up later. What does Jokai think I'll build with in winter—blocks of ice?"

"Can't you ever think of anything but your church? Stephen, this is serious. The world is being destroyed around us, and here you are grumbling over the loss of a few peasants to carry stones. Don't you understand what

Jokai is saying? By next summer there won't be any church, any Varad, there won't be one stone left standing on another! And we're trapped here, trapped. The fool won't let me go home, he says his men will keep the Meszes Gate safe enough."

Bianca was twisting her fingers together and crying, long streaks of tears glistening on her white cheeks. It was the most natural thing in the world for Stephen to put his arms around her and comfort her.

"Hush now, hush, it's not so bad," Stephen murmured. She smelled like fresh flowers and her skin was the softest thing he'd ever touched. "It's just a border war between a couple of barbarian tribes. Now look around you, look at this fine walled city and all Jokai's soldiers; do you really think we could be in any danger? I'm sure if he thought so, he would send you away."

"No, he wouldn't, and you don't know the first thing about it! He talks of duty, and honor, and setting an example to the people. Those barbarians have already invaded Russia, Stephen. You don't know what it's like there, you're a stupid provincial peasant like Jokai and you don't understand anything outside your own home. My family are great bankers, they had agents in all the Russian kingdoms. Do you know what happened in Riazan?"

"My dear lady, I don't even know what Riazan is," said Stephen, hoping to slow down the torrent of hysterical words with a mild joke. "As you said, I'm an ignorant peasant."

"I've had letters from our agent in Novgorod. He wanted me to warn Jokai that something terrible is going to happen. We had a man in Riazan, too." Bianca started to sob again.

Between her sobs a story came out that would have been quite terrifying, if Stephen hadn't know how these tails were exaggerated from one traveler to another. Riazan had been a small independent city on the Russian border, and it was one of the first places attacked by the Mongols on their advance out of the east. It had taken them only five days to invade the walled city, and as punishment for resistance, they had slaughtered the inhabitants. Some were thrown into burning buildings, some flayed alive, some impaled. The women, of course, were raped first;

some didn't live through the first day of the attack to suffer the slow deaths the Mongols gave to the others.

Stephen shook his head. The story was exaggerated, it had to be. Very likely the prince of Riazan and his men had been killed, that made sense enough. And some women would have been raped. But nobody had an army big enough to rape all the women in a city, especially when you counted the peasants who would have taken refuge there as the army advanced. And no conqueror would be foolish enough to slaughter the peasants who grew crops and the artisans who worked in the city. Without them, a land was waste, not worth conquering. There might have been some ugly scenes when the city was looted, but it could hardly have been the total devastation Bianca was claiming.

"You don't have to stay, Stephen." Bianca was clinging to him, white soft hands gripping with surprising force, pinching the skin of his arms under the tunic. "You're French—"

"English," he corrected.

"You're a foreigner, like me. You can go home. You can take me with you. Please, Stephen? Jokai won't give me an escort, and I'm afraid to travel alone like a common woman, but with you I know I'd be safe. And you wanted to see more of Venice someday, you always said so."

Stephen held Bianca and stroked her head and hoped that nobody was listening to them in the hall or standing behind the French-woven tapestries that decorated three walls of Jokai's audience room. The count of Varad had been remarkably complacent about his wife's frequent visits to his master builder's tracing room, perhaps because the door was always open and carpenters, apprentices, and clerks wandered in and out at will. He might not be so complacent about finding his wife in Stephen's arms.

"You've always meant so much to me, Stephen," Bianca murmured, raising lovely tear-filled eyes to his face. "Without your friendship I don't think I could have survived these lonely years in Varad. I know you think I'm silly, interrupting your work and complaining about trifles."

She paused, giving Stephen a chance to contradict her. He patted her on the head and tried to remember what Jokai had said about his grandfather's habit of flaying Kipchaks alive. Even thinking about that did little to dispel the throbbing ache in his groin. It had been too long, that was the trouble. Aude had lost interest in him so long ago, and he wouldn't think of forcing her.

"We can't be private here," Bianca whispered. "I need to talk with you more." But it wasn't talk her gray eyes were promising. She blazed now with a peculiar feverish intensity, her loosened hair brilliant as fine gold wire, skin lit from within by desire as strong as his own. "I know a little room where we can be quite alone."

It sounded like an excellent idea to Stephen; or else a very bad one, he wasn't quite sure which. Something was wrong with this whole scene, but Stephen was finding it difficult to think.

Bianca's little hands fastened on the embroidered edge of his sleeve. She ran her fingertips along the corded muscles of his forearm, under the sleeve, and Stephen felt himself turning to water. "My lady countess—" He was a fool and thrice a fool, not to take what was so unmistakably being offered; what was the matter with him?

Bianca stood on tiptoe and pressed her lips to his, whispering promises that could only be fulfilled in a much more private place. Suddenly the tapestry covering the door was whisked back and Stephen saw, over Bianca's shoulder, someone much more dangerous to his peace of mind than Count Jokai.

"An urgent message from the count, was it? Or from his lady? What a pity," said Aude, "that I volunteered to bring a message from the building yard myself. I'm sure Béla's messenger boy is much more tactful when he interrupts these little scenes."

Aude was pale and thin and verging on middle age. She wore a plain overtunic stained with splashes from some of her herbal experiments. As Stephen looked back and forth between Aude and Bianca, he was struck by the contrast between them. His Aude was just that. His. Even if she'd been half a stranger in the last years, even if she'd taken no pains with her appearance this morning and was spitting mad just now, she was the one he wanted to look at. His eyes could rest on her face as a boat rested on the sea, as the straight-piled stones of a wall rested on their deep foundation. In her thin dark face was all the peace and all the love he had ever known.

And Bianca, the great lady with silk gowns and a dozen

maids to fix her hair and skin, was making a sour face.
Somebody was taking her toy away, and she was mad and
underneath that, frightened. Stephen stared, and wondered
why Bianca should be so afraid. Surely she didn't think
Aude would tell the count about this? He drew breath to
reassure her, and heard the tapestry rustling behind him.

"Aude, wait! It wasn't what you think. Come back here
and let me explain!"

Bianca clutched at his sleeve as he tried to get away.
"Don't worry about her, she won't tell. Don't let her
interfere with us!"

Stephen lost another precious second staring at Bianca,
amazed that she could be such a fool. Had she really spent
all those hours in his tracing house talking about life and
love and the fine cities of the south, and never understood
that Aude was the other part of his soul? Had the silence
between him and Aude, these last sad years, deceived
others into thinking there was nothing left between them?

Perhaps it had. For a while it had fooled Stephen
himself. Now he knew where he belonged; and it wasn't in
this room hung with rustling silks, with this pretty coward
clutching at his arms.

No one stopped Stephen on his way out of the squat
four-towered keep that Jokai styled a "castle," but Stephen's
progress was slowed by housewives, merchants, beggars,
and donkeys who filled the street. Someone shouted at
Stephen as he crossed the building yard outside the
church—something about the message Aude was to have
brought, he supposed. It didn't matter now. Nothing mattered
but catching up with Aude.

Stephen spotted her walking ahead of him down the
narrow street, but he didn't reach her until she was at the
door to their house. When he called her name she spun
round and shouted, "Go away! I don't want to talk to you!"

"Then you can not talk to me inside, not out on the
doorstep where all our neighbors are listening," said Stephen.
Taking both her wrists in one hand, he gently pushed her
into the house.

"I don't have anything to say to you." Aude was a
brooding shadow in the shuttered room, head bent, face
concealed under the dark tangle of her curly hair.

"No? Then just listen. Because I," Stephen told her,
"have quite a lot to say to you." On the way down the hill,

away from Bianca's intoxicating presence, Stephen had figured out what had been going on in the castle. Now he tried to explain it to Aude, though he was somewhat hampered when she gave affronted snorts and turned her back on him every time he mentioned the count's lady.

The first thing Stephen had to make clear was that Bianca was genuinely scared of these invaders from the east. If the reports she'd heard from Russia were even one-third true, she had some reason to be afraid.

"Poor Bianca!" Aude sniffed.

"You don't know what happened at Riazan." And Stephen wasn't about to tell her. His assurances to Bianca were only partially true. Nomads out of the east had always plagued Russia: barbarian tribes came and went as regularly as the seasons. But a tribe large enough, and organized enough, to take a walled city like Riazan? Stephen had never heard of such a thing. Count Jokai claimed the Russian princes were a quarrelsome, disorganized lot. If these barbarians chose to ride toward Hungary, would the remaining cities of Russia be able to stop them?

Bianca hadn't been overcome by a sudden passion for Stephen; she'd just been offering the only thing she had, her beautiful body, to persuade him to take her back to Italy. The temptation she posed to him was quite another matter, one Stephen didn't intend to discuss with Aude.

Nor did he intend to explain to her how much he feared a siege, and how much he would do to prevent a repetition of what had happened at Ely. In the end, Stephen only said that there might be some serious trouble with this latest army of barbarians from the east, and that he would feel better if Aude spent the next year or so in the safe valley of Chastelvert, under the benevolent eyes of Abbot Samson.

When he got to that part, Aude raised her head and looked him straight in the eye for the first time since he'd begun talking. "And what will you be doing?"

"I'll be here, finishing the church."

"No. You come with me."

"I'm not going to run away from my greatest work just because of some rumors about a border skirmish!"

"Then I'm not going either." Aude seated herself on the stool before the fireplace, somehow managing to thump herself down in a way that suggested her slender body was entirely composed of lead weights. "If there's no danger for you, there's none for me."

Stephen argued for hours, trying to convince Aude that he could safely stay in Varad, but that she must return to France immediately. She demolished all his arguments by pointing out how illogical his position was. Stephen grew impatient with Aude's stubbornness and lost his temper. Aude too was cross and they both said things they might regret later.

"Damn you," Stephen shouted at one point, "don't you understand that this church is the only thing in my life that I care about? If I run away and leave it unfinished, I have nothing—*nothing!*"

"Devil fly away with the church and its steeple," Aude shouted back, "and what do you mean, that's the only thing in your life you care about? What about me? What about Bianca, come to that?"

"She's nothing!"

"Do you always kiss nothing like that?"

"I told you what that was about."

"You told me what you wanted me to hear. I don't believe this tale about Kipchaks, Mongols, and Russians. You're exaggerating. You just want to get me out of the way so you can meet with the count's lady."

"Why should I bother to do that? Until today I'd never have guessed you would care who I met, or where. Do you know how long it's been since we shared a bed?"

"And that's my fault, I suppose!"

"Well, it certainly isn't mine!"

"I suppose I forced you to move into the tracing house?"

"You made this house cold enough to freeze me out."

Aude's face crumpled like torn parchment. "Yes. Yes, I did." She slid down to her knees, as if her legs had turned to water, and covered her face with both hands. "I was afraid. I've always been a coward. I was so afraid, Stephen."

"Of what?" Stephen sat down on the floor beside her and put his arms around her. He could feel her body trembling. He'd always known she might break one day. She'd never truly recovered from the rape at Ely and that was why she had to get out of Varad. Stephen had to make her see that. But just now there were more urgent things to settle. "What were you afraid of, Aude? Of having another child? Was it so bad, bearing Michael-Béla? I knew I should have been by you."

"Not of having another child. Of losing another one."

She wrapped her arms around her knees, withdrawing into herself, implicitly rejecting his embrace. Her voice came halting and muffled through the folds of her skirt. "They die so easily, the little ones. Women can bear six or seven children and not raise but two alive. But I thought that because we waited so long for Michael-Béla and because he was our only one, God would have mercy. I was wrong." Her voice sounded cold and angry. Stephen was almost afraid of the hardness that came through her words. "God doesn't know mercy. And I won't give Him another chance to hurt me like that."

Stephen took her hands, which were quite cold though it was high summer. He was cold himself. They'd lost so many years of loving, all because he and Aude had turned away from one another in their unspoken fear.

"I was afraid, too," he told her now. "But with the Kipchaks swarming over the southern passes, and the Mongol army not far behind them—" He laughed shakily. "I think we must trust in the mercy of Our Lord, Aude." And now Stephen was going to have to send Aude away, and they might never have a chance to make up those lost years. "I thought it was me."

"What?"

"I thought you hated me because I couldn't save him. Because—" He swallowed, but it had to be said; even if she told him, after all, that it was true. "Because I kept working on the church that killed him. You hate it now, I know that. You haven't been up the hill to look at the work since that day. Why wouldn't you hate me, too?"

"Oh, Stephen, no! No. Not you. I never hated you. You're all my life. Only you didn't want to be with me— after—and I thought that was maybe for the best."

Aude pressed her head against his chest. Stephen knew that all he wanted was Aude back again, his Aude, his fey girl who did love him after all. She was the only warm place in the world, and he needed her so badly that he didn't know if he could go slowly enough to keep from frightening her again. But she didn't resist him when he raised her to her feet and urged her back toward the other chamber, to the bed she'd kept alone all these years.

* * *

It had been a mistake. Stephen knew that when he woke at midnight. The years of estrangement had vanished and he and Aude were closer and happier than ever before. Or was it just that he'd forgotten what so much easy, unforced joy was like? Now it would be harder than ever to make Aude leave. Perhaps he was wrong, after all; perhaps the Mongols would never get this far.

But if they did? Some women survived the sack of a city, but not Aude; not a second time. He couldn't let her risk it. Anything was better than that; even making her hate him for a while. In less than a year they'd know whether Varad could hold against the Mongols. If the Mongols turned back, or if he finished his church before they came, Stephen could seek out Aude, afterwards, and try to make her understand. If Varad fell before the church was finished, Aude would forgive him for making her leave; but he probably wouldn't be around to care one way or another.

She was sleeping beside him, curled into a ball. Stephen pushed back the coverlet, slipped out of the high bed and leaned against the frame of the open window. From here he could look straight down on the turreted section of the city walls below them; beyond the walls, the land sloped away into the darkness of the eastern mountains. His imagination peopled those hills with an alien army on the march; fierce, wild men with no desire but to destroy all before them.

Would Varad stand against the barbarians who'd devastated Russia? Surely, at some point, the invading army would be stopped. They could hardly conquer the assembled might of the armies of Europe. But Varad was on the eastern edge of Europe. Would this citadel, an outpost of Western culture, veneered-over Magyars only a few generations from nomadism, stand, or would it go back to savagery under the barbarian attack?

Stephen did not know whether the Count Jokai's army could hold back these invaders at the Meszes Gate, whether the city walls of Varad would be stronger than the wooden palisades of the Russian princedoms, or whether King Béla would send reinforcements. But he knew these two things: Aude must leave. And he could not abandon his church, his masterwork that was so close to completion. If he ran away now, Jokai would never let him return to finish the church. And Stephen could not allow lesser hands to finish the work.

Very quietly and slowly, so as not to awaken her, he slipped back into bed and lay with one arm curled around his wife. He breathed in the warm spicy fragrance of her body and felt her tousled black curls against his lips. They had just this one night to enjoy being together. It must be settled in the morning; if Stephen weakened now he would never be able to send Aude away.

But how could he convince her? All his arguments had failed already. Aude wouldn't understand. She would be hurt and would refuse to go. She would think he didn't want her. Suddenly Stephen knew how to do it, and the knowledge hurt him almost as much as it would Aude.

"Not so bad for two old married folk, Stephen?"

As the golden morning light streamed in through the east window, Aude tickled Stephen's nose with a sprig of pungent mint, the leaves half-crushed between her fingers. Stephen felt a sharp stab of pain. He'd slept away those last happy hours. And now he was about to spoil the look of glowing contentment on Aude's face. Why couldn't he have waked forgetful, have drawn her back into his arms, spoiled the plan that had come to him at midnight?

But it was too late. He knew what he had to do; best get it over with quickly.

"Not bad." Deliberately, he made his voice cool and avoided her eyes. "At one time I would have found it quite enjoyable."

"At one—" Aude looked puzzled; "What do you mean?"

Stephen stretched lazily and hoped that he presented the picture of a slightly bored, perfectly relaxed husband. "Only that my tastes have changed over the last few years. I think we both forgot to allow for that."

Aude frowned and drew back from him. Stephen got up on the other side of the bed and pulled his tunic over his head. "Don't take it badly. Last night was a mistake, that's all. I've learned to like . . ." He paused and gave her a slow smile, like a man reminiscing over some special delights. "More sophisticated pleasures, you might say. It's not your fault. People do change, and I've found that, in fact, the lady Bianca and I have a lot more in common, at this point in our lives, than you and I. Perhaps we were foolish, trying to rekindle our childhood love."

Aude was quite still and pale. If she cried, Stephen knew he wouldn't be able to go on with this cruel pretense. He looked away from her, at the line of mountains outlined by the rising sun, and fancied that he saw flames rising where the sunlight glittered off bare stones and running water. He could not risk putting Aude through another siege. She had to be forced to leave now; later, if Varad held, when he'd finished his church, he would seek her out and explain why he'd done this to her.

"Don't worry," he assured her, still staring out the window, "I won't put you away. You're a good housekeeper, and I'd like you to keep this place up for me. I might find it . . . convenient to use sometimes. Bianca and I have to be discreet, you understand."

He expected a pot or a three-legged stool to smash against his head after that last, outrageous statement, but only silence greeted him. After a while, he looked round cautiously, braced against the sight of Aude's tears.

She was gone; she'd left the room so silently it was as if she'd never been there. If not for the crushed sprig of mint on the floor, he might have thought he'd imagined the whole sad scene, might have thought himself free to start again and dream it all differently.

During the morning's work, while his hands were busy with templets and his voice shouted commands, Stephen thought out how her departure could be best arranged. She would not argue with him now; he'd made cruelly sure of that.

She would need funds for travel and an escort of some sort; that shouldn't be too difficult to manage. In the years since the building of St. Michael's in Varad had begun, Varad had grown from a walled citadel in the wilderness to a trading town. The change was due in part to Stephen and the skilled craftsmen he'd imported from all over Europe. Western craftsmen, with silver in their purses, wanted goods and services hitherto unheard of in Varad; local laborers, their own purses jingling with coppers for draying, hauling, and timber-felling, spent more freely than before on comforts for themselves and their families.

Merchants had begun to find Varad a worthwhile stopping place for their inland trading journeys. They brought glass from Venice and chased silver cups from France, olive oil from Italy and fine woven cloth from Flanders; they returned to the coast laden with furs and wax and honey and rough bars of silver. Even the House of Sanudo, revitalized under Marco's energetic direction, had extended a trading finger toward Varad some years earlier. Marco himself had not yet found time to visit them, but Stephen corresponded with him by means of his agents in Ragusa, on the Dalmatian coast.

Aude could go as far as that wooded, rocky coast with the next trading caravan that bore its load of resin, charcoal, skins, and wax to Sanudo's agent in Ragusa. Stephen would see to it that she had enough money to make the rest of the journey to France by sea and merchant caravan, in comfort and safety and under the protection of Marco's agents. Probably it would be best to ask Father Thomas to make the arrangements; she might not wish to speak to him again after this morning.

Aude. Her name was a thin sliver of glass piercing his heart, hurting him with each breath he drew. Through the morning's hard labor, he was distracted as he tried to disentangle the confusion the works had fallen into the day before without his guidance. There had been a restful period of some years when he could leave management of the building project for days at a time to his clerks and to Béla, his master mason. But now, with the church so close to completion, they were back to the chaos of the early days, and Stephen was needed everywhere at once. The carpenters and masons could no longer be restricted to work on separate scaffoldings around the walls. Now they climbed to the top levels of the church through the winding stairs Stephen had incorporated in the side buttresses; they set up impromptu toolshops and work areas on the high galleries, and had infinitely more chances to collide and quarrel. Simultaneously, the rough-hewers were being nagged by the freemasons to supply quarry stones needed for the roof pediment. The free-carvers were demanding that the freemasons stand back until their statue of the Blessed Elizabeth was hoisted to its place. The ironworkers were crawling all over the stone tracery of the rose window in the west facade, measuring it and complaining about the need to install extra cramping irons for stability. Meanwhile, the Italian artist in charge of the stained glass wept that they were destroying the purity of his design only to show off their clever ironwork. There was more than enough for Stephen to do; four separate crises awaited him the moment he stepped into the ordered chaos of the building yard, and he never did find out which one had occasioned the fateful interruption of the day before.

Stephen spoke with Father Thomas about Aude at the midday break. He made his instructions quick and dry and harsh, giving the priest no chance to interrupt or question him. Afterwards, he put his shoulder to the small wheel in the yard and lifted stones like a common workman for an hour without stopping. The sweat ran down his back and the pain in his laboring lungs should have been much worse than that needle-thin sliver of glass in his chest. Then Stephen caught sight of a long dark robe in the midst of the sweaty, half-naked workmen, and at sight of the priest the glass sliver pierced him once again. He knew what Father Thomas was going to say before he left the wheel.

"She's gone."

"There was a group of merchants on their way to Ragusa—she'd arranged to join them before I caught up with her. They were in a hurry, and said they should have left at daybreak but some accident had delayed them. Master Stephen, I *asked* her—I *told* her you'd see she had funds—"

The round bald spot of the priest's tonsure was gleaming with sweat in the summer sun. He had always been a little afraid of this strange, taciturn, driven Englishman who'd come out of nowhere to build him a finer church than any bishop in the West could boast of.

"Will you go after them, Master Stephen? They've just departed, it's not too late."

"Go after them?" Stephen tasted the words like a bitter potion on his tongue. He could see Aude now, mounted on her little horse between the merchant's tall steeds, tossing a bundle behind her into one of the lumbering carts full of furs, wheels of white cheese, and other trade goods. She would draw a hood over her head to conceal the puzzled sorrow in her dark eyes for she would be too proud to let the merchants guess at the pain that had sent her running away from Varad. Stephen could still catch up with them, tonight or the next night or the next, as they made their slow way toward the rocky Dalmatian coast.

And then what? Tell Aude he'd lied, and let her come back to face the Mongols? Tell her he'd lied, and join her, a fugitive, the coward builder who abandoned his half-built church for fear of an invasion that might never come?

Stephen looked up at the towering bulk of the church, with its spires rising to a jagged unfinished line, and the majestic carved portals of the west facade lifting up peaks of stone to cradle the rose window that was to fill the church with light. It was like a song half sung, a piercing sweet melody of enchantment that, when finished, would tell him all the glory and meaning of life. For this, he had chosen to hurt Aude and send her away, knowing he might not live to come back to the valley of Chastelvert and make his peace with her.

There was no choice. He could not abandon his masterwork. And he could not let Aude stay here, in a city that might yet suffer the fate of Riazan.

Stephen knew that there was nothing for him now but the pure energy of stone, stone lifting to the sky and stone pressing down against the earth, the network of invisible forces that held every part of his beautiful airy church in a tension as strong as the heaviest pier, the thickest wall of the old-style builders. This, he understood; this, he dared love; this would not die or change.

Presently Stephen went back up to the tracing house, to look at the rising shape of the church and to draw the detailed templets for the last great stones of the roof. It was horribly precise work, requiring a scaled templet for each of the six surfaces of the stones; each one had slightly different dimensions based on its position in the roof relative to the windows and walls beneath it. Each had to be cut back to hold the topmost narrow windows, edged on the top and sides to support the gables, and grooved along the edge to fit with the stones beneath. And these stones were so large that they must be specially cut to size in the quarry, not brought rough-hewn to the yard for the freemasons to finish up; so detailed instructions must accompany each of the full-size templets that would be cut out of thin slabs of oak. The work required total concentration. He gave it that.

That day of concentration set the pattern for the long,

lonely days of work that followed. He set himself impossible problems to solve: he cast the spire a full twenty feet
higher than originally planned; he reduced the last courses
of the upper walls to no more than a tracery of stone
surrounding the colored glass of the windows; he created
brilliant on-the-spot solutions for the spider's web of carpentry work that was needed to support the high pitched
roof. And when his eyesight blurred and the fine lines of
the drawings danced like spiders across the parchment, he
went down into the yard and swung a mallet like a
common rough-hewer, until sweat blinded him and his
chest ached from breathing in the stone dust of the lodge.

Stephen could work himself to the point of exhaustion,
but as soon as he lay down upon his pallet he would start
calculating distances and times. Now she is halfway to
Ragusa. Now she is in the city. By now she will have taken
a ship across the Mediterranean to France. He had written
to Marco and to his Ragusan agent, asking them to watch
out for Aude and to provide her with every comfort, every
courtesy on her travels. The sums he'd banked with Marco
since coming to Hungary, though a pittance compared to
the fortune he had lavished on Abbot Samson's church,
would more than suffice to take Aude home in comfort and
free her from any financial worries. Marco was canny and
tactful; if she refused to accept money from Stephen, he
was perfectly capable of making up some other story that
she would believe. Aude would be in good hands now, safe
and cared for, far from the winds of disaster that were
sweeping the eastern edge of Europe. But that knowledge
was of surprisingly little comfort.

After two months, a late-traveling caravan from the coast
brought a letter from Marco, just a few terse lines to let
Stephen know that Aude had arrived and that his wishes
for her welfare were being carried out insofar as she would
permit. Reading between the lines, Stephen saw that
Marco thought him a cold-hearted bastard. He couldn't
quarrel with the judgment; he thought so himself, though
the reasons were somewhat different from what Marco and
Aude believed. It hadn't been another woman he had
chosen over Aude; it had been his church. Michael's
church.

CHAPTER

30

◻

*I*t was a bad winter, after the building stopped and Stephen no longer had his work to keep him busy. News of the Mongol armies in Russia, and of the Western reaction to this force gathering on the horizon, trickled into Varad. From the east they learned that the horrifying slaughters of the previous winter had not been repeated, at least not on civilized cities. The Russians huddled behind wooden stockades and icy stone walls for the winter, while the Mongol armies systematically destroyed the other nomadic nations of the steppes and mountains. No chroniclers told the fall of Murom and Gorodets, no Venetian trading agents escaped to tell the tale of Mongol atrocities in the Caucasus; Béla IV and the small group of Hungarian noblemen who took the Mongol threat seriously had to gauge the course of the wars from less direct information. An agent in Egypt reported that thousands of Kipchak, Circassian, and Alan were sold into slavery by the Mongols.

"They are wiping out everyone. Next year they'll polish off Russia like a greedy wolf crunching his victim to the bones, and the year after it will be our turn," Jokai predicted.

Lajos, one of the few men who dared contradict Count Jokai in his own hall, shook his head. "No, they've fallen to quarreling among themselves. Presently they'll rend their own nation, tribe by tribe, and there'll be a few more yellow-skinned slaves in the Turkoman army of Egypt. Then everything will return to normal. But if you want me to call out my men for winter exercises in the mountains"—Lajos grinned—"I'll be happy to obey. It's more fun than sitting in hall all winter, and there's a girl in the merchant quarter who might be most impressed if I brought her a bearskin cape."

"It's not a hunting party!" Jokai's voice was like a whip cracking in the close, smoky confines of his hall.

From the west came the news that the princes of Europe, secular and temporal, generally agreed with Lajos rather than Jokai. The Holy Roman Emperor, Frederick II, had committed his armies to a struggle with the Pope; the Pope, naturally enough, was more concerned with the immediate threat posed by Frederick than with tales of some menace far to the east. The rest of Christendom was delighted at the idea that the Mongols might help to destroy their old enemy, the Moslems. Peter des Roches, bishop of Winchester, advised the English king, "Let us leave these dogs to devour one another that they may all be consumed and perish; and when we proceed against the enemies of Christ who remain, we will slay them and cleanse the face of the earth, so that all the world will be subject to the one Catholic Church and there will be one shepherd and one fold." The possibility that Catholic Hungary might also be destroyed in this process was apparently an acceptable price to pay.

Only Louis, the holy king of France, showed signs of taking the Mongol threat seriously. But the resignation with which he met the danger was no more help to Hungary than Bishop Peter's Christian militancy had been. The master of the French Templars warned Louis that if the armies of Bohemia and Hungary were defeated, "these Tartars will find no one to stand against them as far as your land." Louis replied, "Then either we shall send them back to Hell where they came from, or else they will send us to Heaven, where we shall enjoy the bliss that waits for the chosen."

Louis of France sent no army to stand with Jokai's men at the Russian Gate. A few wandering knights of the French court and a few bored barons from the Holy

Roman Empire heeded the summons and set off for Hungary in search of high adventure and everlasting fame. Most of them made it no farther than Esztergom, where King Béla held court in the high stone-walled city with the great expanse of the Hungarian plains between him and the menacing barbarians.

The spring of 1240 brought warmth, renewed life, and a puzzling sense of anticlimax to the people of the eastern outposts. Still, the Russians in Kiev and Vladimir and Galicia, the Teutonic Knights in Poland and Lithuania, and the battle-ready Hungarians and Kipchaks who trained under Csaba's eye took turns to guard the passes through the Carpathians. Because of the deep snows, no news of the Mongols had reached Varad. But now that the spring thaw had begun, everyone was wondering where they were now. Batu and Subedei, the demon Mongol leaders, should have been moving their armies forward in spring. Instead there was only this puzzling silence.

Distorted stories of the Mongols had drifted west by this time, mixing the names of their commanders and the style of their battle standards with Western demon-lore and Hungarian earth-magic. The Westerners did not know that a petty squabble among the heirs of Genghis Khan was delaying the Mongol invasion. One of the Mongol princes had defied etiquette by drinking before his superior at a banquet, and the subsequent quarrel over seniority among the princes had to be referred back to Ogedei, the grand khan of all the Mongols, whose name the Westerners had not even heard. Meanwhile, the armies did not move.

If the cause of delay had been explained to the knights and barons in Count Jokai's army, they would have understood perfectly. For both sides, the idea of postponing a battle or an invasion or a crusade until some question of personal honor had been settled was perfectly natural. Only crude peasants, artisans, and merchants would be so crass as to put aside injured feelings for the good of the enterprise as a whole.

But no one knew that the Mongol destruction of the West had been delayed so that Ogedei Khan could decide whether Batu or Kuyuk should have the right of precedence at a feast. The puzzled armies first waited, then began gently twitching, and finally began to lose all discipline as boredom overcame the fear roused by the first stories out of Russia. Presently, at Father Thomas's urging, Count Jokai declared a day of thanksgiving in Varad for God's mercy in sparing them from the Mongols.

The keep and the new church at the top of the hill were deserted for this occasion, workmen and sentinels were given the day off by Jokai's express command so that they could join in this day of rejoicing. Noblemen and commoners alike crowded into the little dark church at the foot of the hill where Father Thomas was to hold a special mass of thanksgiving, as if for a victory. The carts that had rumbled into Varad the day before had been laden, not with timber for the bracing and framework of the high spire in the new church, but with branches of sharp-scented, resinous fir to strew upon the pavements of the old church. Candles blazed to compensate for the lack of natural light, the worn carvings of the old pillars were decked with garlands of flowers, and pretty girls in their multilayered, bright skirts lined the streets to throw more flowers on the count of Varad and his lady.

As it happened, they had only the count to cheer; the lady Bianca had remained above, pleading illness and the certainty that she would faint if subjected to the crush of the crowds. The people of the city did not appear unduly disturbed. Bianca was lovely, certainly, a fitting jewel for their count; but she was also a foreigner. On this day when Count Jokai had officially declared the Mongol menace over, all their relief and all their love went to the big, square-shouldered man who was one of them. They saluted him with bawdy jests in the Magyar tongue, reminded him of bears and wolves killed in hunting parties long ago, made pretense of offering him their pretty daughters. They laughed when he chose, instead, to kiss a wrinkled matron who boasted that she remembered seeing the count's grandfather bring him for christening in this very church.

Stephen too, was a foreigner, and never more conscious of it than when he stood among this ebullient, sweaty, laughing crowd. Ten years in this country had given him enough of the Magyar tongue for ordinary conversation, but hardly enough to follow the swift run of off-color jokes and obscene puns with which the people enlivened their hour of waiting before the mass began. Nor could he share their relief. If there was to be no war, then he had broken with Aude for nothing—the merest shadow of a fear.

Presently Father Thomas marched through the low arched door on the north of the choir, followed by a line of tousle-haired singing boys in hastily cobbled-together white capes. Count Jokai's decision to make a great show out of this feast day had been announced rather suddenly; Father Thomas was visibly nervous but determined to do his count and his city honor.

As the nobles in the gallery and the commoners on the pavement fell silent and dropped to their knees, the timeless chant of the mass rose through the church. The familiar Latin words and the smell of incense carried Stephen back to the icy cold of Ely cathedral in midwinter. Even in the stifling hot church where he now sat, Stephen could remember clearly how his breath and that of his fellow choristers would rise like steam before their faces.

All their singing had not stopped the soldiers. That great cathedral had been packed like this little church on the frosty morning when the black-clad mercenaries rode in and trampled the people before them. An old feeling of confinement and restlessness swept over Stephen. Muttering excuses to his nearest neighbors, he sidled through the close-packed crowd, pushing where necessary and accidentally stepping on toes, until he reached the west portal and the slightly less crowded street where the peasants from outside the city stood patiently awaiting another sight of Lord Jokai. From the street Stephen could just glimpse the golden walls of the citadel, the raw new stone spire atop his church and the shimmering blue sky above. That was where he needed to be, not stuck in this crowd.

More pushing, more polite shoving and murmuring, and at last he was free to climb the narrow cobbled streets to the building site that had been his life for the last ten years. Stephen couldn't remember when he had last seen it so silent and deserted. The tools were neatly packed away and the lodges closed up behind portable mats of reeds. Even on saints' holy days there were men who chose to stay on the job, either for the extra pence they would earn or for the sheer love of the work. Even in winter there was work to be done, carving of capitals and statues and scappling of stones for the next season's advance on the walls. For a moment Stephen felt angry at the count for cavalierly declaring a day of total holiday; then, as his ears grew accustomed to the silence, his anger turned into gratitude. It had been a long time since he'd had the leisure to stop and look at his church as a whole, by daylight, to see how the multitudinous parts he'd directed were coming together, to realize the vision with which he'd begun. Often enough Stephen prowled the works by night, but moonlight, with its way of silver-gilding some parts of the building and hiding others into black shadow, gave only partial views. It wasn't the same as looking at the church in full sunlight, without the workmen to distract him.

While work continued on the upper levels, the lower facade of the church was already finished, courses securely mortared, statues and decorative gutterspouts set in place. By Stephen's standards nothing more remained to be done. Count Jokai thought differently, and so Stephen had been forced to let a small army of gilders and painters swarm over the clean lines of the facade. The artists put gold leaf on carved saints' haloes and the crowns of the kings, and they added red and blue borders to their robes. Then they gilded the seven recessed arches of the central portal and accented the strong, straight lines of the supporting column with bars of bright color. In the sunlight the saints' halos and the kings' crowns sparkled, the stars in the Virgin's robe twinkled, and the bright stripes on the column joyfully called forth memories of the flowery hill-side outside the city walls.

Stephen drew a deep breath of satisfaction. The work was good, after all. They hadn't covered his building with meaningless decoration, like the Moslems with their daz-zling layers of mosaic and gilding and glass; they had only enhanced it. This was a part of the picture that Stephen hadn't been able to imagine; he had no sense of color, only of form. Now he felt happier about the prospect of letting these decorative artists into the interior of his church.

But not today. Today the Church of St. Michael in Varad belonged to him alone, from the solid stone-filled trenches of the foundations to the web of carpentry work supporting the beginnings of the great spire. With a feeling of deep satisfaction, Stephen began to climb the spiral staircase that rose through the interior of the great buttress on the northwest corner. Up and up he went, through shadows pierced with sunlight, for even the buttress had tall slender windows. From the topmost gallery Stephen looked down on the open space where the rose window was to go. Today the lacy structure of stone and ironwork was filled with the blue summer sky. He made his way further up the spiraling steps, until he passed the workmen's temporary lodges on the topmost levels and came out into the blazing sunlight at the top of this northwest tower. For a moment he stood half blinded, blinking to regain his vision, with only a vague sense that something here was not as he had expected it to be.

Then his eyes cleared, and he saw what was out of place. Not all the brightness came from the sky. The lady Bianca was sitting on a cushion, looking radiant in her blue silk tunic and crownless, wide-brimmed straw hat. Her golden hair, which spread out over the brim of the hat, sparkled in the sun.

"I thought you would come here," said Bianca, with a purr of creamy satisfaction in her voice.

"I did not think I would find *you* here, my lady."

"It's a good place to get sun." Bianca pushed aside the pale gold fringe of hair that had veiled her face and smiled at him. "In Venice I used to sit on top of my father's house with my sisters and cousins, while we competed to see who could stay longest under the heat of the sun and bleach her hair to the finest white-gold. I always won. I'm good at waiting."

She stretched, just the barest hint of movement, but enough to emphasize the perfect lines of her body under a robe so fine and clinging that it reminded Stephen of Saracen silks.

Stephen swallowed. He felt like the callow young apprentice who'd gone looking for girls with Ivo and Hugh, half hoping they wouldn't find any, half eager for the unknown sweetness ahead. "Were you waiting for me? How did you know I would come here?"

"You don't belong with the fools down in the church," said Bianca. "Neither do I." She waved one creamy white hand toward the edge of the tower, directing Stephen's gaze down toward the swarming ant hill of the lower town. "They think they're safer together. They think that if they all crowd into the church and tell God how kind He was to save them, He'll take the hint."

"And you think not."

"I know not." Bianca's mouth snapped shut over the last words; for a moment, her face and neck muscles tense, she was no longer young and beautiful. "I've had news from our agent in Russia. They're on the move again."

"Does Jokai know?" It seemed incredible, if this were true, that the count would have gone ahead with this feast day's rejoicing. Perhaps Bianca was exaggerating vague rumors.

"The man who brought my letters set off again for the coast as soon as he could get a fresh mount. Jokai doesn't read very quickly, and he was busy having his ceremonial belt with the gold lions let out so he could wear it to the feast." Bianca reported the details flatly, as though she no longer bothered to hide the fact that she despised her husband. "But he will have to know soon enough, even if he won't listen to my news. We'll have a handful of Russian princes joining the Kipchak refugees any day now. They've taken Pereiaslav and Chernigov."

The names were unfamiliar to Stephen. "Kiev?" It was the only Russian city he knew anything about; merchants from Byzantium had stirred his fancy with tales of a white-walled city standing above the marshes of the Dnieper, crowned with the golden domes of a hundred churches.

"Not yet. I expect that's next. And then there will be nothing between us and their army but the Carpathian Mountains."

"Well, they're a natural boundary. And Jokai is guarding the passes."

Bianca shrugged. "Riazan was guarded... and Chernigov. Russia is gone, Stephen, and we're next."

Stephen shook his head helplessly.

"What's the matter with you?" Bianca blazed into sudden fire. "Don't you understand, Stephen, we're doomed, all doomed?"

"I'm sorry," he said. "Probably you are right. I don't have a network of agents reporting to me from all over Europe and Russia, and if I did, I wouldn't be so certain how to interpret their messages. And I wasn't prepared for a detailed discussion of Jokai's strategy."

"Then let's do something else." Bianca stood in one sinuous motion and tossed her straw hat over the edge of the tower. It fluttered down on the drafts of hot summer air like a wounded bird, fighting to stay in the air and failing, giving in to the inexorable tug of earth. If Stephen watched it, he would think of a small boy falling from such a height, a boy who by now should have been taking his place beside Stephen in the craftsmen's lodge. And that thought was unbearable. So he looked at Bianca instead. The lines of her body were revealed in white and gold as she shrugged off her thin gown. Her body was soft and supple against his, and the call was as strong as the pull of the earth drawing the hat down; but he had not nearly so far to fall.

PART VI

The Fury
of the
Tartars

◻

1241–1242

CHAPTER

31

◻

*T*he fragrant branches of spruce and fir that had carpeted the old church for the mass of thanksgiving were still fresh when Prince Vasilko of Volynia and Prince Michael of Chernigov knelt to thank God for their escape from the fury of the Mongols. After praying in the church, they joined Jokai and his leading men to give a report on the fall of the Russian cities. Stephen was invited to join them; when he protested about leaving work, Jokai said bluntly that he might have to stop work on the church for a good deal longer than one day. It sounded like Varad was likely to need a good siege engineer and a catapult master more than a master builder.

"Church or no church, I want you to stay here," he added, with a bearlike one-armed hug round Stephen's shoulders. "From now on, nobody leaves Varad, particularly not a man with your training. From lifting wheels to catapults isn't such a long step. We may need you."

"I'm not going anywhere." Stephen looked back at the graceful lines of his church, now rising far above Jokai's squat sturdy keep. By the end of this building season, the roof would be ready for its layer of colored tiles if Jokai let him continue building. If Jokai let him live. He had grown to respect and like the count; their friendship had nothing to do with Bianca. But Stephen doubted if Count Jokai would feel the same way about it.

"Right," said Jokai cheerfully, "and neither is anybody else. Nobles, that is. Peasants can run if they want to, in siege time they're just extra mouths to feed. Now let's go and plan how to fight these demons."

The two Russian princes had more horror stories than practical suggestions to offer. Bianca's predictions of disaster were confirmed. And Prince Michael's account of the destruction of Chernigov sounded very much like the tales she'd relayed last year about Riazan. The defenders had been reduced to tearing the stones from their own battlements and pitching them at the invaders; the little squat horsemen had laughed and jeered that the Russians were doing their work for them. And when they did take the town, not one stone was left standing on another, not one inhabitant was spared the general massacre.

"My city is a desert," said Prince Michael. He bent his head into his cupped palms and groaned aloud.

Stephen wanted to know how a horde of nomads on horseback could take a walled city without some treachery from within.

"They have siege engines." The prince roused himself briefly from his despair. "They're devils, screaming devils from hell. Pray they don't come over the Carpathians, then you'll find out!"

"They won't," said Jokai with a glance round the hall at his lieutenants. Lajos and Géza on one side of the hall put hands to their swords and grinned. On the other side, three Kipchak commanders of light cavalry volunteered their willingness to die defending the Carpathian passes. Stephen was still unconvinced but Lajos and the count's other officers didn't seem to notice. They were engaged in an etymological discussion with the priest.

"Devils? Very true," said Father Thomas. "Their very name reveals their origin. *Tatars*—obviously a corruption of *Tartars*, the devils from Tartarus."

As several hundred like-minded churchmen and Latinists made the same derivation independently, the invaders from the steppes became known to the West as Tartars and their faraway home was called Tartary.

Stephen wanted to know how Prince Michael, who could speak competently as an eyewitness, had survived such destruction. He couldn't think of a polite way to pose that question to a Russian princeling, but he did ask who maintained the siege engines for the Tartars. Surely these leather-clad nomads didn't know how to work Western engines?

"Prisoners," said Prince Michael. "They spare skilled artisans wherever they go. They collect metalworkers, too. What are you? A builder? Not a chance. They don't understand stone buildings, and they think it's some sort of bad magic. Now if you'd been able to work gold and silver into pretty ornaments, you might have a chance of living—if you can call being a prisoner of demons living."

"What about ransoming nobles?" Lajos wanted to know.

Prince Vasilko spoke for the first time. "Oh, they collect us, too. Our heads, that is. Last I saw of my cousin Dimitri, most of him was sprawled in the mud and his head was going off on some Mongol's saddlebow, bump, bump, bump." He laughed, too shrilly and too long, and Jokai dismissed the informal council with the suggestion that his new guests might wish to rest and refresh themselves in private.

Stephen went back to his church and promptly forgot the threat of invasion. The church was so near completion now that every day seemed an intolerable period of waiting. This last building season would see the work all but finished: the last vaults were going up now; the weighted web of timber that would hang from the top spire and keep it straight was being constructed; the tall pointed windows stood ready to receive their shells of colored glass. By spring there'd be nothing left to do but remove the centering under the vaults, fill in those last windows and the Virgin's great rose over the west portal, and invite Father Thomas to hold the consecration ceremony.

"And then will you go back to England?" Bianca stretched luxuriously under Stephen's caressing hand, rubbing her bare shoulders against the furs with which he'd carpeted the upper gallery of the church. They met here nightly now, and if it was an act of sacrilege, Stephen didn't want to think about it. He was flying above the soaring arches of his church, flying over Bianca's white body, and as long as he could keep flying, he did not have to think about anything else.

"France, maybe. I can't go back to England."

"Why not?"

Stephen had never told Bianca about his troubles with the Church; he'd never told anybody in all of his travels. Aude was the only person who'd known him then. And where was she now?

"It's not important," he replied. "I have a house in France, in Chastelvert. That's where I sent Aude."

"Do you think she'll have you back?" In an unguarded moment, waking from a nightmare of demons tormenting his sweet Aude and Michael-Béla, Stephen had told Bianca how he drove Aude away for her own safety.

"I won't know until I get there, will I?" If he ever did get there. Stephen tried to conjure up a picture of the valley in harvest time, the fields of stubble and the stripped vineyards, but he couldn't believe he would ever see Chastelvert again. Dunwich was far more real to him, the small gray town clinging to the seaside and beaten daily by waves. They say that in old age men turn to thoughts of their childhood: Mam singing over the flat cakes she turned before the fire, rain, and waves pelting down on the pebbled shore. But surely he was young, yet, for his mind to wander so?

"I'm nearly forty," he said aloud.

"And randy as a lad of twenty." Bianca sighed with pleasure and pulled him down atop her, and Stephen forgot everything for a time.

That fall, while Stephen drove his few remaining masons to prodigies of achievement and Jokai drilled his soldiers to face a threat as vague and terrible as a blizzard out of the north, the fisherfolk of Dunwich were among the first people in the west to be affected by the storm sweeping over Russia. No ships from the Baltic came to the herring fair that year; the piles of silver fish mounded in Dunwich streets rotted until that town, and Yarmouth, and the whole coast of East Anglia smelled of stinking fish.

The explanation for the glut of herring and the absence of buyers came by way of one of the few foreigners who did visit Dunwich that fall, an Italian merchant who made the unprofitable trip solely to have a few hours' conversation with the Englishwoman he'd brought to Dunwich the preceding year. There'd been plenty of gossip then about a woman in her condition, looking pale and bedraggled and tragic under her rich clothes. She was installed in a good stone house by the foreigner who was off to sea again before a cat could turn around thrice. But in the months that followed, she'd lived quietly and modestly, going to church regularly and making no trouble. She demonstrated a talent with healing herbs that gradually won her neighbors over. All anybody could say against her was that no reasonable person would walk the sea cliffs in all weathers the way she did, staring east over storms and squalls and dragging the baby with her, too!

Now she looked at the Italian merchant with more warmth in her face than any of her neighbors had seen since she arrived. There were sprinkles of silver in his curling black hair, and he'd put on weight round the middle. It had been many years since they'd all journeyed to the Holy Land together.

"You shouldn't have troubled yourself to come, Marco."

"It's been a year. I wanted to see how you were doing— and my small namesake here. Is that excessive?" Marco Sanudo tickled the baby in his cradle and grinned at Aude. She was too thin, he thought, and too tired. But he could never see her properly; he was always blinded by the memory of the flashing black-haired girl hanging over the rail of a Venetian pilgrim galley, alive and breathless with the excitement of her first voyage. "It's been too long since you lived in a civilized land where I could visit you."

"Meaning a place that's accessible by merchant ship?" Aude teased. "You men always define civilization by your own convenience. Stephen considers a civilized place one he can get to without leaving dry land. Sometimes I don't know—"

Her voice quavered and Marco silently cursed Stephen and then he cursed Aude for still loving Stephen when there was another and much cleverer fellow sitting right at her feet. Marco continued to dream of a woman who'd always been his best friend's wife.

"How Stephen and I ever became friends?" he finished the sentence for her, with no trace of his inner turmoil showing on his face. "Sometimes I wonder, too. Especially since Stephen has treated you so badly."

"I don't want to talk about it."

"At least let me take you out of this miserable gray town before winter. We don't have to go to Venice. I have a villa in Ragusa now. Or you could stay at our *fondaco* in Acre—remember Acre, Aude? The white birds, and the white square houses, and the frails of dates and figs in the bazaar?"

Aude sighed. "We were young then." But she didn't respond to Marco's suggestion, and he knew why. Since the day she'd stumbled into his offices in Venice, sick and exhausted and on the verge of tears, she had steadfastly insisted that Dunwich was where she wanted to go. Not the valley of Chastelvert, where Abbot Samson would watch over her. Not Marco's palace in Venice, where he could take care of her himself. To Dunwich, Stephen's home. The gray town by the sea where he'd been born, and where the child he might never know about would be born. "If he ever decides to be himself again, just plain Stephen of Dunwich, instead of the worldly architect and great lover, he'll have to come here to find what's left of himself," she'd said with a flash of sarcasm that gave Marco his first hope of her survival. "And I'll be here."

She was wasting her life, looking over the sea cliffs for a man who had cast her off, a man who didn't deserve her and never had. Marco cursed under his breath in the street slang of Venice, stringing together imprecations that would have made Aude sick if she'd known what he was saying—until he looked up again and saw that she was laughing.

"Reverting to Italian makes no difference, Marco. I always know what you are saying, no matter what language you use. Remember?"

He laughed, too, shamefaced.

"And I don't want you talking like that in front of my son."

The baby was sleeping now, two fingers stuck in his mouth, sucking fiercely in his dreams. Marco smoothed the blanket over little Mark's cradle. "Does Stephen know about him?"

Aude's face closed like a shuttered window. "Stephen knows of nothing that has happened since I left Varad."

"Over a year now. A year and a half. You don't write to him?"

"If he changes his mind, he will come home. If he doesn't, there is no reason for me to see him again."

But she would wait forever, on the off chance that

someday he would be back, repentant and sane and loving her. Anger made Marco break the news he brought less gently than he'd meant to do. "Well, if he doesn't come soon, he won't have the opportunity. Do you know why your English herring are rotting on the shore?"

"I can hardly think it's Stephen's fault!" Aude laughed.

"No, but it may be the end of him. The ships from the Baltic haven't come, Aude, because they're ferrying the Teutonic Knights to Russia to fight the Tartars. There are hundreds of thousands of these people, more than you can imagine, and nothing stops them. They've already devastated most of Russia and they're moving on to the Carpathians. They fight in winter, even the snow won't stop them. And wherever they go, they leave complete devastation behind. If cities resist them, they massacre all the inhabitants. If they surrender, they merely massacre most of the inhabitants and enslave a lucky few. And their leader has sent a letter to King Béla of Hungary, demanding his surrender."

Marco hardly dared look at Aude's face after he'd spilled out the news he bore from his Russian agents, whose reports were similar to the ones Bianca had received. When Marco did look, he wondered if she'd understood. Her expression had hardly changed; calm, distant, patient.

"You came to tell me this?" Her voice was perfectly level, and it frightened Marco.

"Among other things—yes." Chief among those other things had been that he loved her, that he'd always loved her, that a year was more than enough time for her to mourn the bastard who'd cast her off. He was going to carry her away to Venice. But he hadn't had the courage to begin with that, and now he saw that it would be no use.

"You should have gone to Varad to tell Stephen."

"I don't think that will be necessary," said Marco. "My correspondents report that half of the Hungarian army has gone to the Carpathians, and that the country's overrun with Russian and Kipchak refugees. If Stephen chooses to stay and build churches under those circumstances—"

Aude gave a choked little laugh. "Chooses? Dear God, Marco, it's not a matter of choice. Stephen wouldn't notice an entire invading army unless they happened to stand in his light when he was sketching an elevation. You'll have to bring him home."

"Why me?"

"Who else? Oh, never mind. I'll do it myself. Will your ship take me as far as Ragusa?"

Three sentences, and she was alive again, determined and unstoppable. Apparently she had forgotten her wounded pride and her vow not to approach Stephen first. She was on her feet, pacing around and around the cradle until Mark woke and cried, and then she nursed him with a fold of an old blue cloak drawn over her breast. Later Marco blessed the baby for his interruption; even Aude could eventually understand that a woman with a baby at her breast might have some trouble making the journey from Ragusa to Varad! Eventually Aude agreed that Marco should send one of his own agents to make it perfectly clear to Stephen in what danger he—and all of Hungary—stood from the Mongol invasion.

Marco's messengers were hardly needed in Varad, so it was not a great loss that the ship carrying his letters went to the bottom of the Adriatic Sea in an early winter storm. By that time worse storms were sweeping over Russia, and Jokai's men kept a permanent winter guard over the passes in the Carpathians. In December the Mongols took Kiev, burning down the golden-domed churches, breaking open the tombs of the saints, and taking Byzantine reliquaries for saddle ornaments. The Teutonic Knights, who had sailed to Novgorod, died in the slush of mud and blood and snow before Kiev, and the Mongols stripped the shining armor off their bodies to enhance their own coats of stiffened leather. More Russian refugees crossed into Hungary and Poland.

King Béla himself came through Varad soon after Christmas, riding through snow to inspect the border forts in the Carpathians. He took half of Jokai's army to reinforce the northern passes under Count Denes; when Jokai shouted about his feudal rights, Béla fixed him with an arrogant eye and remarked that the chairs in Varad would burn as well as those in Esztergom. Jokai sputtered and stamped away without notable reverence for his king, but also without further protest.

"And what did he mean by that?" Stephen asked Bianca when next they were in private.

"When Béla succeeded to the throne six years ago, the

first thing he did was burn the chairs in the council chamber, so that the councillors would have to stand in his presence. He told them a land could have only one ruler, and he was it. Anybody who didn't like the arrangement could consider the penalties for high treason. I rather suspect," said Bianca thoughtfully, "that Jokai was not expecting Béla to be a strong king. Béla was only twenty-nine then, and Jokai had backed him because he thought the young king would do what he was told and keep the Church out of the barons' affairs. My family thought differently but they too supported Béla with their Venetian gold. A united rule in Hungary means safe trade through the Balkans. If it hadn't been for the Mongols, Béla might have made something of this country."

"Come now," said Stephen, "we're not lost yet." But Bianca's dispassionate analysis had shaken his confidence. In bed she was a pretty, silly, vain woman. When she talked about politics, she forgot to conceal her keen intelligence and the analytic way of thought she'd learned while growing up in one of the great Venetian trading families. She was as smart as Joscelin, Stephen thought, and as well-informed as Marco; she'd been predicting disaster from the beginning of the Mongol wars, and so far she'd been absolutely right. Still, Stephen reminded himself of all that stood between them and the invaders: ranks of soldiers in armor, heavy horses of Jokai's household troops and light ponies of the Kipchak cavalry, lines of small stone forts and high ranges of the mountains themselves. Could they really be in serious danger from an enemy so distant?

Stephen did not have much time, that winter, to brood on the matter. Jokai ordered him east to oversee the building of new barricades along the Carpathian passes. The laborers who'd hauled stone for the Church of St. Michael in Varad now blistered their palms swinging axes in knee-deep snow to fell the pine trees in the passes. Stephen drew sketches in the snow to dictate the placement of walls, spiked glacis, and supporting framework. By the beginning of March, when the snows began to melt, the original forts were almost buried behind three lines of wooden palisades. The fresh-cut tree trunks still oozed resin where the laborers had adzed them to sharp points. Stephen returned to Varad pleased with a job well done. He was looking forward to a peaceful spring of finishing and consecrating his church while Hungary crouched safe behind its defenses of walls and armed men.

Three days later, an exhausted, mud-splashed horseman rode into Varad, demanding water and a fresh mount. "I'm heading for Buda. And if you've any sense, you'll follow me. They've taken the Russian Gate."

"What about Denes? He was supposed to be in charge there," Jokai said.

The horseman shrugged. "There are a lot of dead. I only got out alive because they paused to cut up a few villagers."

"Denes was a fool," said Jokai as the messenger rode away. "He relied on the men Béla sent him from the plains. Those men are no good at mountain fighting and they don't know how to hold a defensive position. We've the walls you put up to keep our passes safe, Stephen, and my Kipchak cavalry in the north will keep the Mongols busy while I pull my men back to defend Varad."

But when Jokai sent a messenger to the barracks where the Kipchaks had been housed, no one was there. They had melted away in the night. Jokai cursed them for being cowards who'd been afraid to stand and fight, as well as oath-breakers who'd sworn fealty to him only to run away at the first sign of danger. As he was speaking, a messenger from Buda arrived with an explanation of their defection.

The Magyars of the plains had never been tolerant of the Kipchak refugees. Unlike Jokai, who saw in them the raw material for a doubled army, the farmers and herdsmen thought of the Kipchaks only as barbarians whose camps stunk, whose horses trampled the grain, and whose wild young men were a threat to the virtue of their girls. Now, with panic and rumors flying like a grass fire, a group of Magyar landowners and noblemen had decided that the Kipchaks were secretly in league with the Mongols, and had been sent to spy. These angry Magyars broke into the house of the Kipchak "king" Kotian. Realizing that there was no escape from the bloodthirsty nobles, Kotian killed his wives and himself while the other Kipchak leaders mounted a desperate, last-ditch defense. The battle ended when the heads of the Kipchak princes rolled in the street and the mob was satisfied.

When they heard the news, the Kipchaks in Béla's service broke out of their camp and slaughtered the soldiers of the bishop of Czanad. They began fighting their way south to Bulgaris, destroying and plundering as they went. Jokai's Kipchaks had slipped away by night to join them.

"I suppose it was a measure of loyalty that they didn't rise against us first," suggested Lajos.

"Why did I waste time on fortifying the passes?" Jokai cursed his stupidity. "They'll be on us from the north now. Lajos, send to my captain at the Meszes, tell him to withdraw his men to Varad. We'll have to settle in for a siege until Béla sends reinforcements. Stephen, forget your damned church. Make a tour of the citadel walls. I'll give you until sunset to find the weak spots, and you can spend the night drawing up plans to reinforce them. I want this citadel to be impregnable in two days."

"It is. No one has ever taken it—even the Kipchaks when they attacked your grandsire!" Lajos protested.

"Did I ask your opinion? I want it to be more impregnable!"

"What about the city itself?" Stephen asked. The low walls around Varad seemed much more in need of work than the high fortifications of the inner citadel.

"Forget the city. We can't defend the whole city. We're going to line soldiers up elbow to elbow around the citadel walls and wait until Béla sends an army to chase the Mongols off. Do you think I can fight a hundred thousand screaming demons outside the walls?" Jokai snorted. "You don't know much about warfare, Stephen. I hope—for all our sakes—you know more about siegecraft."

Stephen didn't need half a day to make his report on the citadel walls; with a builder's eye for stonework, he'd been aware of the wall's strengths and weaknesses since the day he came to Varad. Now he only had to walk round the walls to confirm his observations. The south bastion was strong, and the adjoining wall was additionally defended by the sharp slope of the hillside which ran down to the water. They need not fear direct attack there. The keep and the church were also well protected by a sequence of three walls interspersed with deep ditches. And to the west, although the citadel itself was weakly defended by a low wall, the attackers would have to fight through the narrow streets of the town.

Stephen took a tour through those streets to complete

his survey. Some of the wooden houses should be pulled down so that the invaders couldn't set them on fire, and the houses built against the citadel wall would have to go. Stephen's house, nestled into an angle between the city wall and the higher wall of the citadel, would have to be torn down, too. By nightfall it should be reduced to a heap of rubble, and the little room where Michael-Béla had been born would no longer exist.

It was strange that such distant memories should hurt so much. Stephen thought he'd long since grown accustomed to reality. Human love was not for him. Instead, he had his work. He looked up at the church's towering spire and took a measure of comfort from its strength and solidity. Light as air, fragile as lace, it was enduring as only the strength of stones could make it. Stephen might not live to see the next building season in Varad, but the church would stand as a record that he had lived and worked upon this earth. Other hands might put the last colored tiles on the roof, another master see the rose window filled in with blue and white glass, but the church was indisputably his work.

There was one last thing he wanted to do. Stephen slowed, turned in to the deserted building yard, and entered the nave. His steps echoed through the empty building. The mosaic labyrinth was already in place on the floor. It was the mystic seven-branched *chemin de Jerusalem* that the faithful would trace on their knees as they'd done at the cathedral of Ely. Stephen did not consider himself one of the faithful and he walked out over the maze, crossing tiled boundaries and ignoring the labyrinth of painted paths until he stood at the center. Here, when the church was ready to be consecrated, he'd meant to place a bronze plate to remind all comers that Stephen of Dunwich had created this masterwork. Superstition had kept him from placing that plate when the mosaic was laid; it was unlucky to put one's name on unfinished work. But now, Stephen thought, it would give him some comfort to see it there.

However, there was no time for such frivolities now; he had to report to Jokai, then organize a crew of laborers to pull down those houses. He could use their stones and timbers to shore up the few weak points in the north wall. After the siege began, there would probably be days or weeks with little to do. Stephen would have plenty of time to put his name on the church then; if no craftsmen could be found to cast the bronze, he'd take up mallet and chisel and carve it into the stone himself. That much, at least, should live after him, whatever happened here in Varad.

Crossing from church to keep, he thought he saw a cloud of dust rising over the eastern hills. That would be Lajos, returning from the Meszes pass with the men who'd been set to guard it. They were riding very quickly, Stephen noticed—too quickly. Not even a Magyar horseman could get to the Meszes and return with troops in less than a day. And that couldn't be dust rising when snow was still melting on the hillsides and the lower ground was a squishy bog. The cloud was something else. Squinting, Stephen thought he could see sparkling points of metal in the afternoon sunlight. By now, others were exclaiming and pointing, too. Stephen quickened his steps and hurried into the keep. He had something more urgent than the state of the citadel walls to report to Jokai.

Jokai took Stephen's news calmly enough. "We already know most of the army is to the north of us, at the Russian Gate. This will be a flanking movement to pin me down so that I can't help what's left of Denes's forces. They'll want to parley first," he predicted, "to keep us waiting until their main force swings down from the Russian Gate. By coincidence, that's what I want, too." His wolfish grin was momentarily reassuring. "Time can bring Béla's reinforcements. And Lajos may have some men he can bring round to nip at their heels. Meanwhile, we've got water; the river feeds a spring that rises directly under the keep. And it'll take them a long time to fight their way through the city."

CHAPTER

32

◫

Contrary to Jokai's predictions, the Mongols did not seem particularly interested in waiting for the rest of their army. The initial "parley" took no more than ten minutes. A small group of bandy-legged men in leather armor rode up to the city walls, prodding a bound captive before them with two long spears. The man looked like one of the Saxon miners from the villages near the ice caves: coarse tunic, face blackened by stone grit, red-rimmed eyes leaking tears. His hands were tied behind his back and when he stumbled, as happened several times on the walk to the city walls, he fell heavily with no chance to save himself. The horsemen thought this a great joke each time it happened. They pricked him with their spear points to make him rise and stumble on at a faster pace.

The miner called up to the citadel that the Khan Kadan, the servant of the Great Khan in Karakorum, generously permitted him to offer the people of Varad a chance to live and join the service of the Great Khan. If the city gates were opened now, those who surrendered first would be allowed the honor of becoming the Great Khan's slaves.

"Where's Karakorum?" Jokai mumbled. "I've never heard of the place. Not that it matters." He leaned over the wall and shouted curses that were punctuated by a ten-pound stone catapulted into the midst of the horsemen. Their shaggy ponies snorted and scattered, but not quite in time to avoid the spattering of the second shot. This time the catapult had been loaded with an oxskin sewn full of the scrapings from the garderobes.

One horseman, taller than the rest and mounted on a proper warhorse instead of a pony, separated from the group and rode forward. He pushed back his leather cap to show a handsome, aging face that was unmistakably Western. "That was a mistake," he shouted at Jokai in French. "Permit me to return the compliment." He nodded at the Mongols behind him who lobbed a round, irregularly shaped object into the air. It came sailing over the city wall in a perfect arc, and landed almost at Jokai's feet with a spatter of blood as the skull burst. It bounced gently on the cobblestones and came to rest face up. Even without eyes or lips, Lajos's head was quite recognizable.

The attack began ten minutes later and continued without cessation until long past nightfall. Continuous waves of foot soldiers were sent up against the city walls to die in the task of exhausting the defenders. Jokai sent men to keep the wall, and had his best siege engine—the great trebuchet—stationed just inside the city, where it might send its monster stones splashing down in the midst of the Mongols, who kept well out of crossbow range.

"They use their own people like cattle!" gasped Béla, Stephen's master mason, in a moment's respite at midafternoon. He and Stephen were working together to keep the catapults in order, replacing strained ropes, hammering bent catches back into shape, and trying to keep the throwing arm from separating into the three beams from which it had been constructed.

"Not their own people," Stephen replied from under the trebuchet. The layers of glue-soaked linen that held the throwing arm's beams together were separating in the moist spring air, and Stephen was trying to secure the fraying bonds with fresh lashings of cord at points where there was the most strain. As a geometrical problem, the repairs had a certain attraction for Stephen. But as a pressing dilemma which must be solved by guess and by eyesight before the next wave of the Mongol attack, the repair of the trebuchet was far less appealing. Stephen was somewhat short of breath; years of drawing and supervising were no preparation for such exhausting work in the heat of summer.

"If those aren't their own people, who are they?"

"Prisoners. Russians, Alans, Circassians, Kipchaks." Stephen waved one hand. "Any people they've conquered lately. Jokai's making a collection of the ones who get over the walls alive; they seem just as willing to fight on our side. They're only attacking because there's a Mongol army behind them ready to kill them if they slow down. Not," he added slowly, "that that's much help to us. Walls pulled down by unwilling hands are just as vulnerable." Stephen did not elaborate on his own reasons for curiosity about the prisoners: the tall man who had spoken in French just before the attack began seemed familiar to him. How could he possibly know someone from the depths of the unknown Eastern world? Even the Mongols' prisoners came from countries utterly beyond his ken. And yet there was something about that face he recognized.

A roar went up from outside, the rumble of falling masonry mixed with the shrieks of women as a whole section of city wall crumpled. Citizens ran past, their faces distorted by terror; as Stephen slid out from under the trebuchet, someone trampled on his hand. Béla grabbed his wrist and pulled him out. "To the citadel!"

"What about the trebuchet?" It was wheel-mounted; five or six men, working together, might be able to push it up the hill.

"No time!"

Strange, fierce men dressed in a motley assortment of furs and leathers and stolen bits of Western armor crowded in through the open wall now. A line of Jokai's guards, swords drawn, held them back, but only for the moment. Their ferocious advance was as inevitable and as deadly as the high tide that had swept away Stephen's childhood on the coast of Dunwich.

Neither Stephen nor Béla were armed and they hurried through the gates of the citadel in the midst of wailing children and frightened burghers. "Enough!" someone was yelling over the noise of the panicked crowd. "Close the gates!" It was Jokai, his voice hoarse with strain, shouting his orders from the gallery over the west portal of the church. His men drew their swords and forced a path through the people to close the great main gates of the citadel. Those left outside were irrevocably sundered from those who'd made it to safety, wives from husbands, parents from children. The gates swung shut and the three great bars, each cut from a single tree trunk, dropped into place with a triple thud as curt and final as the Doomsday judgment.

"Some of his own guardsmen are outside," Stephen protested.

Béla crossed himself. "Do you think they're still alive? The count's right. We should have done this in the beginning; now we've lost the trebuchet. And those devils will use it against us. *Jaj Istenem!* I should have wrecked it before we ran!"

"It could be worse," said Stephen. "I didn't finish rebinding the throwing arm. Unless they look at it carefully and finish the work, the arm will come apart the first time they try to use it. Maybe it will even kill some of them."

Béla looked perceptibly happier at that suggestion.

From within the citadel, the remaining defenders could see houses blazing on fire and could hear the screams of people being murdered in the streets. Driven by sick curiosity, Stephen mounted one of the wooden towers that guarded the citadel walls and looked down into the open square before the old church. Men and women were kneeling in rows, heads bent forward, while a single Mongol strode down the rows with a sword and lopped off their heads one by one. Some of the women were hysterical and he grabbed them by their long hair to bend their heads for the sword.

Only a few Mongols had bothered to join the looting of the city; most of the army was squatting on the far side of the river, comfortably lighting cooking fires and settling in for the night.

"They cracked us like a nut, between thumb and forefinger," Stephen muttered. It was a pity that they had lost the trebuchet, with its long arm and greater throwing range. Unlike the catapults, which were powered by a twisted skein, the trebuchet was based on a system of counterweights which made it a more effective long-range weapon. But perhaps they could add counterweights to the catapult arm, to increase its range?

Before Stephen could propose his idea to Jokai, a winch

screeched out of place on one of the small catapults and
Stephen was called to fix it. He cursed the soldiers for
forgetting to grease the wheels constantly, hammered the
wheel of the winch back into place with sweating hands,
and slapped a generous handful of lard over the wheel. It
didn't look quite straight; would it still aim true? "Stones
here!" he called over his shoulder, expecting a two-wheeled
stone cart to arrive with one of the ten-pound boulders the
small catapults used. Instead he saw a woman dragging a
leather bucket, which she pushed toward him wearily. It
was full of fist-sized rubble and bits of rock from a coping
that had shattered nearby.

"I need bigger stones to test the throwing arm!" he
snarled over his shoulder at the woman. "What can I do
with pebbles?"

"In Chernigov," said a cool Italian-accented voice, "they
pushed the stones of the city walls down on the Mongols.
We may yet have to do the same."

Stephen mopped sweat off his forehead and stared unbelieving at Bianca in plain linen gown and tunic. The glory
of her pale Venetian hair was hidden behind a stained
kerchief, and her palms were blistered from dragging
heavy buckets of stones across the courtyard to the catapults. Stephen had expected to find her hysterical in some
corner of the keep; instead she was calmer than many of
the knights and soldiers around her, offering Stephen her
bucket of pebbles as graciously as a hostess inviting him to
try another taste of the gilded peacock.

"What are you doing here?"

"Carrying rubble for the catapults. The stonepile is used
up and the carter is needed elsewhere. I can drag a bucket
of rocks as well as he can."

"Aren't there enough peasants to do that?"

"No," said Bianca in the same level, calm voice. "Most
of them are being massacred outside the walls. Doubtless
we shall face the same fate soon, but I have discovered a
strong disinclination for lying down before I am actually
dead. You'd better take some pebbles, they're all we have
left."

Stephen accepted a handful of stones and watched in
amazement as Bianca moved down the line of men working the small catapults. Who'd have thought that Bianca,
so hysterical at the threat of danger, would turn brave and

cool when all hope was lost? Well, despair did strange things to people. It had made a builder out of him. ....

In the scurry of soldiers around him, Stephen was alone in his own memories for a moment, a lost child in the cathedral of Ely, cold and frightened with the realization that Mam had abandoned him. No betrayal hurt as much as that first one. Why was he thinking of it at a time like this? There were more recent losses, too: Aude ... but at least Aude was safe. He had that knowledge to keep him strong; and he had his church, his masterwork. Stephen glanced over his shoulder at the church behind him, rising tall and strong out of the chaos of blood and slaughter. At least his church would live after him; and that knowledge helped Stephen to think clearly again. The cool weight of the pebbles in his hand, the problem of a trajectory over the roofs of the town were things he could deal with. Stephen would have to wait until he got some bigger ammunition to test the accuracy of the repaired catapult. In the meantime, he was pleased to find that he could aim the small pebbles directly into the courtyard around the old church.

Since the technical problem was reduced to a series of approximations on a target, his mind was free to wander again—this time not to the past, but to the doubtful future. Would Bianca understand if he told her that she was more beautiful to him now than she had been in her years of playing the Venetian fine lady? Probably not, but it hardly mattered. Amidst the blood and fire, Stephen still found the energy to ache for Bianca's body. In fact, he wanted her more desperately than ever before. They would all probably be dead before dawn so why was he wasting his last hours aiming a second-rate catapult with a bent winch that screeched its failure with every turn of the wheel?

"Well, if you must do this instead of being with Bianca, at least do it well," Stephen told himself with grim humor. "Up a little now, to the left, and a little more torsion on the rope; let's see if my repairs will hold." He concentrated on perfect aim, and his third shot knocked the head off the Mongol executioner's shoulders; it fell to the ground spattering blood over the screaming women who'd been kneeling to await their death. Stephen grinned mirthlessly at his moment of success.

Then the next wave of assaults began. Before sunset the fighting had taken on an even more desperate tone. The citadel where Jokai had planned to wait indefinitely for reinforcements might not last until dawn.

As soon as the people remaining in the city had been killed or made prisoners, the Mongols brought in their own siege engines. They had six catapults and a mangonel. The tall Westerner who had spoken at the parley was in command of the party working the mangonel. Initially the balance of power did not seem quite so bad; inside the citadel were four small catapults and one large one. The trebuchet, as Stephen had predicted, had come apart when the Mongols' prisoners tried to use it. Except for the fact that they were running out of ammunition in the citadel, they did not seem so overmatched.

As the long day faded into night, however, their disadvantages became apparent. Just before sunset Count Jokai summoned his leading knights, sweaty and blood-stained, for a brief conference in the keep. Jokai himself had a nasty cut over his half-closed eye, and the other men were hardly in better case. All their faces were set with the grim lines of will battling exhaustion. Stephen felt ashamed that he himself suffered from nothing worse than the aching of long-unused muscles, though he reminded himself that he'd faced exactly the same risks as the knights.

Jokai began talking as soon as the last man had slumped onto a bench against the tapestry-hung wall. "It's not going as well as I'd hoped. You know that. I thought we might be able to wait for Béla's army, but we can't. They'll be over the walls before reinforcements arrive. First," he summed up grimly, "they don't stop. We've only so many trained men to work the machines, and our artisans have to rest sometime. They've got Russian prisoners to work through the night. And they'll soon have another advantage: they can place flares to show up the citadel walls. We can't see to aim at their siege engines in the dark."

The irregular crash of stones pounding against the south wall of the citadel punctuated his words, sometimes drowning them out altogether.

"Second, we don't have much to aim at. If we're very lucky we may hit one of their siege engines. But those are small targets. Otherwise, our stones kill only a few men, and since the Mongols don't keep many of their own people within range, we get mostly the prisoners who are easily replaced. The Mongols, on the other hand, have a huge target and when their stones hit, we lose a piece of the walls." Jokai glared round the room with his one good eye. "So are we going to tear down the church for ammunition, work our engines until they fall apart and our men drop from exhaustion, then let the Mongols walk over the wall? Ha! There is only one thing to do. We've got to stop those siege engines. Now! Sortie! We're Magyars and we don't hide behind stone walls—we fight from horseback! Arpad and St. Stephen defend us!"

As Jokai raised his right arm, fist clenched, a current of renewed determination ran through the room. Several knights jumped up and gave long, ululating war cries. Then a man rose and began dancing with quick stamping steps, brandishing his sword in a fashion that made Stephen afraid for the ropes that held the great wheel of candles aloft. Soon the roomful of exhausted men seemed to have turned into the campfire of exultant Magyar warriors who'd ridden over the steppes themselves to conquer this land, not so many generations ago.

"Arms! Horses!" Jokai roared. As the men poured out of the room, revitalized by the prospect of some proper fighting, Jokai's long arms shot out and stopped white-haired Csaba.

"Not you, my master of arms. I need somebody with good sense to stay behind and defend the citadel in case we don't make it back. For now, keep my young men in order, get them armed and mounted and don't let them ride until I'm there to set the pace. I want a few words with my builder."

He turned to Stephen, who lingered awkwardly behind this rush of fighting men. "You take care of Bianca."

He gave Stephen a long hard stare, and Stephen looked back into the one unwinking gray eye and nodded. Jokai knew about him and Bianca. He had probably known for some time. Yet he had chosen to do nothing, when he wouldn't have been blamed for nailing his master builder's hide to the newly carved and gilded church door.

"Why?" Stephen asked.

Jokai shrugged. "Nothing *I* could do ever made her happy," he mumbled. "I thought you could keep her amused and make her want to stay here." Jokai glanced

into the courtyard where his men were assembling, armed
in the fragments of their own and dead men's armor,
waiting his word of command for the last mad ride against
the enemy. "It was a mistake, as it turned out. I should
have let her go back to Venice. You sent Aude away."

Stephen nodded. No one else had understood why he'd
had to break with Aude. Even Jokai had never mentioned
it until this moment.

"So. If they break in, don't let them have her. My pretty
Bianca is afraid of pain. She always has been. Do you
understand?"

Jokai flipped his wrist and a short dagger fell through
the air, turning end over end in a glittering wave of
pointed steel until it hit the floor. Stephen bent to pick it
up. When he straightened, Jokai was gone.

"*Dominus vobiscum*," Stephen murmured. "Go with
God." The long-forgotten blessing came easily to his tongue,
mixed with the words of the prayer for the dead. Both
Stephen and Jokai knew that few, if any, of the men who
would ride at breakneck speed out of the gate would
ever ride back in again. They were selling their lives for
the slender chance that they could disable the Mongol
siege engines, and give the garrison of the citadel a chance
of holding out until reinforcements came.

Stephen did not want to watch, but it seemed disloyal to
Jokai to do anything else. He shouldered his way past the
press of men at the gate tower, pushed up the stairs and
found Bianca, standing at the narrow window, pale and
outwardly composed as she had been since the attack
began.

"Let me see." She was not very tall and Stephen could
easily look over her head. On either side, men crowded
in, trying to get their eyes to the window slit for a better
view. Those on the parapet would have a better view still,
but they also had a task: to keep the Mongol troops pinned
down under a steady crossbow fire while Jokai and his men
hacked at the catapults. It was a good plan. The trouble
was that the range of the catapults was greater than that of
the crossbows, and the siege engines were mostly sheltered behind the remnants of houses where the archers
couldn't get a clear shot.

Stephen heard a clank from below, as the gate was

winched open, and then the drumming of hooves and the wild shouts of Jokai's men drowned out all else.

The broken walls were death to a heavy cavalry charge. Jokai's horse jumped the first wall, skirted a house in flames, disappeared behind what had been the garden wall of Father Thomas's house. Some of his men took the same route. Others could not follow them for lack of room and had to pick their own way through what had once been streets and alleys. The riders bunched together in twos and threes, their horses slipping and shying on the rounded cobblestones; impetus lost, they scattered across the burning remnants of houses and byres and gardens. No longer were they a mass of heavily armed knights pounding down upon the artisans at the catapults, but individual targets hampered by the weight of their armor and the bulk of their horses.

Géza was at the head of one string of riders, half standing in the stirrups and shouting his success at finding a clear route through the debris. Stephen shouted to warn him, knowing that his voice would not carry. With a sense of inevitability he watched as Géza galloped around the high wall of a house and into a swarm of leather-clad Mongols mounted on their little ponies. After him four other knights, galloping in a line, were unable to stop at the first cries of warning; they, too, rushed straight into the ambush.

The Mongols surrounded the Western knights like bees clustering over a honeycomb, and when the group broke apart, the Mongols were waving shining plates of armor. Géza's strong, slender black destrier was screaming on the ground, its hamstrings cut and its throat slashed.

Stephen gulped down sickness and squinted through the haze of smoke to where another handful of men were slashing the ropes of the nearest catapult. The machine itself was half hidden behind ruined houses, but through a gap in the walls he could see men in armor riding back and forth, their swords rising and falling rhythmically.

"They've taken one siege engine," he told Bianca. She was too short to look through the gap in the walls.

"Jokai?"

"Still mounted—wait!"

As Jokai's horse rounded the burning house, a Mongol arrow caught the count in the narrow space between helm and gorget. At this distance he was a tiny doll-figure, putting one hand to his throat, then toppling backward, the reins of his horse still caught in his fist as he fell. A Mongol soldier rode alongside the tall Hungarian horse, and leapt from his pony into Jokai's saddle. The horse snorted and darted forward, dragging the count's body until his fingers relaxed and the reins hung free. The Mongol turned his prize back toward the lower town with only the pressure of his knees, raising both hands in an unmistakable gesture of victory.

It was his last gesture. A crossbow quarrel from the gate tower struck him between the shoulders, tearing right through the leather jerkin and knocking him to the ground with the force of the impact.

The horse shook its head and trotted back to nuzzle Jokai's unmoving body.

Stephen had been too stiff with horror while the fight unfolded to notice what was going on around him. Now he wondered why there were not more crossbow bolts humming through the air, the covering fire that Jokai and his knights had counted on. The answer was in the trampling and the pressure all around him: men were fighting their way down the stairs and people were pushing him and Bianca against the wall. Stephen shielded her with his body, pushing outward with all the strength of his shoulders, and only then spared a glance over his shoulder to see what was happening.

The bowmen who were stationed at the top of the tower had broken from their posts, and with them came the knight who'd been in charge. "Lost, lost!" he bellowed as he pushed past Stephen and Bianca—an aging man with a full red face and wispy graying curls, a man who had expected to end his days doing easy castle guard duty in his lord's service. "Get you to the church, my lady. It's the only safe place. They've breached the wall." He pointed out the window slit. "Pray for God's help. Nothing else is left."

Stephen looked in the direction of the knights's gesture and saw what had panicked the defenders so. Jokai's brave sortie had succeeded in disabling just one catapult. The remaining siege engines, hammering at the citadel wall, had succeeded in dislodging a few lower supports and the wall crumpled in one place like a heap of wet folded cloth.

Even as Stephen watched, the stones slid a few inches, rocked perilously and settled into another pattern of folds.

"Fools," he said between his teeth. "Fools!" he shouted at the fleeing men, but the air was too thick with sounds of panic for them to hear him. "It's not breached—just weakened. If they don't hit the wall again in the same place—"

The wooden tower was empty now. No one was interested in hearing the theories of Jokai's master builder when the Mongols were about to come over the citadel wall.

Several of the archers had dropped their crossbows in the precipitous fight. Stephen snatched one up, together with the leather pouch of bolts that lay beside it, and jammed a bolt into the groove of horn at the fore-end of the stock. "Who knows how this works?" He'd never used one before and there wasn't time to think it out. He looked round for help.

There was no one left in the narrow room but Bianca. Stephen was on his own, ignorant and clumsy and untrained. If only he could loose a few shots from this arrow slit, enough to make the Mongols think the tower was still defended—enough to buy time until the shamed archers regrouped and returned to their duty!

What was wrong with the crossbow? Ah, stupid! Stephen cursed himself. No use arming it before he'd bent the bow. The bolt clattered uselessly out as he lowered the crossbow and braced both his feet on the bow. He clenched his hands around the twisted, resilient string and pulled up until it felt as though it would cut through his palms. The only result was a slight resonance through the curved layers of wood and horn under his feet.

"You can't do it that way," Bianca said, almost casually. "The crossbowmen have special things for pulling them up with. It's beyond a man's strength."

"What sort of things? Do you see any of them?"

She shook her head. "Jokai would have known. He's dead, you know."

"Yes," Stephen said gently. "I know." Bianca was past caring, past helping him. Given time, he thought, she might rediscover the strength that had brought her through the first of the siege. But how much time did any of them have? He peered out the window slit again. The Mongols were still winding up their nearest catapult for a finishing shot on the citadel wall. After the flight of the archers, they'd taken the time to move it in closer and position it well. The men working the machines were fully exposed to Stephen's view and well within crossbow range.

"A child with a pebble-sling could pick them off," he muttered under his breath, and cursed himself for not having learned the right things in his life. Just now he would have traded all the stonecraft he knew for one quick lesson in archery. And nowhere did Stephen see any devices for winding a crossbow—not that he was even sure what they looked like. Did he have time to climb up to the top of the tower and rummage among the archers' discards? Get a better shot from there, too—

"Stephen! They're about to shoot!"

With one great effort he pulled the string of the crossbow back and bent the bow, feeling the string cutting across his palms, the resistance of the bow like heated wires pulling through his arms and shoulders and shooting down his back like fire. But it was done. There were spots swimming before his eyes, so that he could barely see to aim.

"Give me a bolt." This time it slid into the groove with a perfect click. Stephen aimed the bow through the narrow window slit, pointing straight at the head of the Mongol who exposed himself to make sure the prisoners working the catapult performed their task. If he could just get that one man, there was a good chance the prisoners would flee, and then he might be able to rally a few archers to keep Mongols from getting back to that catapult again.

And then? It was a question Stephen never had to answer. As he loosed the string, the catapult's throwing arm rose in an arc too swift for the eye to follow. His bolt went wide, passing nowhere near the man he'd aimed at. The catapult's stones smashed into the sagging citadel wall and opened a gap wide enough to admit three men abreast. And suddenly there were Mongols everywhere, coming out of the ruins of houses and out from behind shattered walls. It seemed to Stephen that they were rising from the very ground of Varad like demons.

Slowly he lowered the crossbow, feeling the shaft of polished wood slip between his sweating hands. He watched the Mongols swarming through the broken walls, yet he felt oddly calm. None of this seemed real; it had happened too fast. Just that morning, Lajos had been making up a new obscene song with which to welcome the Mongols, and before sunset his head had become ammunition for their catapults. Stephen wondered where his own head would be by this time the next day, and wondered, too, why he couldn't seem to take more interest in the question.

"I suppose we had better take refuge in the church," Bianca said. Her voice was flat and calm, as she'd been since the threatened invasion had become a reality. "Everyone else is going there."

Stephen looked through the wide windows on the inner side of the tower. Bianca was right; the knights and nobles of Varad who had taken refuge in the citadel, together with a few commoners who'd managed to squeeze in before the gates were shut, were trampling together in one panic-stricken mass to the new church. Those stones that Stephen had raised folded great gray wings around the last people left alive in Varad. Common russet and shimmering silk, silver armor and golden brocade, all glowed with life in the deep red light of the dying day. All the people, forming one packed mass, struggled to get in the narrow doors under the high arches.

It was all sickeningly familiar to Stephen.

"No. No, not the church." He remembered how the frightened folk of Ely trampled and shoved each other to get in to the sanctuary of the cathedral; but the mercenaries had ridden over them anyway, fouling the floor of the cathedral with blood and leaving the high walls to echo screams of anguish. Would Mongol demons be more respectful of God's house than mercenaries from a Christian land? Stephen grasped Bianca's wrist and half dragged her away from the open stairway, back up toward the top of the tower and the walkway that connected it with the stone walls of the citadel.

"Where are we going?"

"The top of the wall."

"They're breaking it down!"

"Not now. They've got the breach they needed."

The citadel wall was topped with a narrow walkway between two parapets of stone, giving just enough space for one man to pace the length of his watch, meet his opposing number, salute and turn. When they got there, Stephen pushed Bianca down on her knees and made her crawl ahead of him, keeping well below the parapet, until they were in an angle of the wall out of sight of both watchtowers. There they lay curled into the corner of the wall, Stephen on the outside with his arm around Bianca. He could feel her quick breathing and the beat of the pulse in her throat.

The existence of such angles had been one of the things Stephen meant to talk to Jokai about; it was a serious weakness in any system of defenses to have a place on your walls that couldn't be covered by archers from another point. Now that weakness might work in their favor. Stephen hoped that any Mongols who ventured into the wooden towers would content themselves with the weapons and armor they found there and would see nothing in the bare line of the walkway to tempt them farther out. And if they did come out, the narrowness of the path would force them to come one at a time. Stephen felt the small dagger Jokai had given him, hard against his side where he'd stuck it in his belt.

The sunset faded into blue twilight, and the air above them was cooler than the sun-warmed stones where they lay. Screams echoed through the air, mixed with the high-pitched yells of the Mongols. Once, just below the wall, Stephen heard the gurgling cough of a man with a sword in his throat. He twisted round uncomfortably in the cramped space and pressed Bianca's head against his chest, trying to cover her ears with his arm. They were still singing in the church; could he have been wrong? Perhaps these Mongols were afraid to go into the church, or perhaps they were so unlike Western knights that they actually respected the law of sanctuary instead of making a perfunctory penance after breaking it. In that case, he had done Bianca the worst turn possible by keeping her from that refuge.

A few feet from their hiding place, an arrow slit pierced the inner wall of the walkway. The purpose of such slits was to allow men in the guard towers to shoot down at any besiegers who might get past the citadel walls; theoretically the invaders would then be an easy target, trapped between the walls of keep and church on one hand, and the citadel walls on the other. The theory depended, Stephen thought bitterly, on having a defending force that didn't run for the safety of the church as soon as the count fell. God curse them, living or dead.

But Stephen knew that wasn't fair. The archers might not have panicked under normal fighting conditions, with a strong body of knights to back them up and some assurance that the usual rules of war would be observed. The speed and vicious power of the Mongol onslaught, joined with the rumors that had been plaguing the city for weeks, were enough to break anyone's nerve. And Stephen reflected ruefully that he hadn't been of much use to the defense.

In any case, this was no time to be assigning blame. The questions now were, what could he see from the arrow slit, and what hope did the survival of the people in the church offer to him and Bianca?

Moving with infinite caution, an inch at a time, Stephen wriggled along the walkway until he could rise up and lean his head against the arrow slit. It was quite dark now; for a moment he could make out nothing but a few indistinct shapes moving in the darkness, a few more lying quite still. A surprising brightness of candles shone through the unglazed windows of his church.

Suddenly the brightness blazed up through the gray stone outline of the church like a saint's radiant halo, and Stephen knew that no one had lit candles after all. He groaned aloud; he could not help it.

"What is it?" Bianca was at his side.

"They're setting fire to the church. Don't look."

He tried to force her head down, to cover her ears as the first screams of comprehension interrupted the wavering hymns in the church. But she would not be protected from the terrible knowledge. And no one could have kept her from smelling the sickening odor of burning flesh that began to taint the wind as the fire took hold within the church.

"They are *my* people." Somehow, crouched beside Stephen, with her pale braided hair falling out of its coif and the stained rags of her dress wrapped around her legs, she still had the dignity of a reigning lady. "The count is dead, and I should take his place. I cannot save them, but I have to watch at least. I have to know—to tell—"

"You have to know," Stephen agreed softly, marveling again at the courage that Bianca had found only when she had lost hope.

Together they crouched at the narrow slit, watching the

death of Varad. A golden blaze of fire illuminated the
church in all its stark beauty, the grace of its form appeared
for once as only Stephen had ever seen it in his mind. It
was complete, tall, self-sufficient, stripped of all extrane-
ous gilding, carving, and painting. And before the terrible
purity of that backdrop, dark figures rose and fell like a
sorcerer's demonic automata, acting out little scenes of
hell. Two Mongols stood outside one of the portals with
short swords upraised, alternately chopping down the men
who thrust their way through until the bodies piled so
high that they blocked the exit.

The heat of the fire beat at Stephen and Bianca's faces.
The lead of the roof would be melting in that heat,
dripping down on those inside in molten gobbets that
would burn through everything they touched. Smoke
billowed from the upper, unglazed windows. A woman's
white face showed for a moment, illumined by a flare of
the fire around her, as she threw her screaming child out
of the high window. Before the church, another woman
was caught by her long unbound hair and dragged about
the courtyard by men who laughed at her screams, until
they had had enough of the jest and spread-eagled her for
their pleasure on the stones.

The roof was sagging now, interior timbers burnt away,
and lead dripped down like solid fire. The gargoyle gutter
spouts were twisted out of shape, mouths and necks even
more hideously elongated than their makers had intended.
No one who had been trapped inside could still be alive.
Stephen crossed himself and tried to remember the prayers
for the dead, but his mind was occupied by its own
calculations while his tongue tripped over the words he
had once known so well. How was it that the church still
stood? The roof timbers and the supporting beams under
the long galleries would be turning to charcoal, the mortar
in the arches would be a dry powder sifting down into the
flames. Yet still his church rose above the flames, a gaunt
silhouette held together by nothing more than the delicate
balance of forces that Stephen had drawn so long ago: the
stones of the arches rising and pressing against the keystones, each course in the walls held in place by the layers
of stones above, the piers prevented from buckling by the
inward thrust of the light buttresses that arched out like
wings on either side of the church. The empty stone

tracery of the rose window bloomed with fire; around it the church stood black and delicate as the skeleton of a leaf.

Portions of the roof crashed into the center of the fire, and were engulfed by flames. The spire was lit from below now, flickering like a stone flame against the night sky. No. It wasn't the light that trembled, but the stone. The spire crumbled and the walls of the church turned inward; the rose window collapsed in on itself and the stones roared against one another as they went down. What Stephen had built for eternity had died in a night. What he had built as Michael-Béla's monument was a tomb for the people of Varad, lying burnt and choked and crushed under the great stones.

And now there were grinning Mongols standing behind Stephen and Bianca, blocking both sides of the narrow walkway. Stephen remembered his promise to Jokai, reminded himself of the Mongols' cruelty. He could still save Bianca from the worst. But his will failed him and he hesitated for a moment too long. Just as he reached for the dagger concealed within his tunic, other hands caught and held him. The little men dragged Bianca away, screaming as her calm deserted her at last. They held her carelessly and she was able to break free for a moment. She tried to throw herself over the parapet, but it was too high and they jerked her back by her long braids.

That was the last Stephen saw of her, before the rope tied round his wrists and knotted at his neck tightened and he was dragged away. They had not bothered to search him for weapons, so the count's dagger still thumped against his ribs, but he could not reach it with his hands bound. He wondered why they had not killed him at once.

CHAPTER

33

◪

Stephen passed the remainder of the night roped together with some twenty other captives at the foot of the citadel wall. All were men, all commoners like himself. The priests and nobles and knights of Varad had died in the burning church, in the refuge to which their rank entitled them. None of the prisoners knew where the surviving women had been taken; they speculated on that and other things in uneasy whispers, whenever their captors permitted speech. Once a raw scream of disbelief and agony echoed in the night. It could have been a woman, or a man, or an animal dying in torment. Stephen crossed himself, as well as his bound hands would permit, and prayed that Bianca was dead already. He should have killed her himself when the Mongols broke into the citadel. In that, too, he had failed; as in everything. His personal failures no longer mattered, but he hoped that the awful scream had not come from Bianca, who had been so afraid when the Mongols came.

Dawn lit the smoking ruins of the church from behind, a stark gray against the sunrise. The body of the church was no more than a mass of smoldering timbers under the rubble of masonry, but some fluke had preserved an entire wall of the north transept and the arches of the nave, jutting up into empty air like the ribs of a great skeleton.

There was even part of a stained-glass window hanging perilously from the top of an arch, the bottom melted into grotesque shapes.

And there was a man up there, clinging to the quivering rib of the arch, inching forward to the pointed top where the stained-glass window glowed deep ruby and emerald and blue where it was not covered with soot from the fire. Stephen scrambled to his feet, dragging the next two prisoners with him, and shouted across the courtyard.

"You fool, get down, it's going to collapse at any minute! You thrice-cursed lackwit—" He strained forward against the ropes, shouting and waving his bound hands ineffectually. The shivering arch would collapse at any minute; it should not be standing now, and every time the man moved, a fresh wave of trembling went through the stone. Stephen could sense the barely visible vibrations as an agony in his own bones, he who'd calculated the load on each vault with exquisite precision; movement was making things worse. Why didn't the fool get down? Ah, now he was aware of his peril, clambering down with hasty movements that only increased the danger of collapse. "No! Stop! Don't move! You're making it worse!"

A tall gray-haired knight crossed the courtyard at a run and shouted something at the clinging man. At once the man froze. And the arch held—for the moment—with the climber trapped midway between point and foot. The knight turned to Stephen. "What should we do now? Can he jump safely?"

The distance was not so great; he might get away with a broken leg, but the impetus of a sudden leap could bring the whole tottering pile of masonry crashing down on him. Stephen shook his head. "Raise two ladders against one another, and let him step onto the topmost rung. Very slowly! Tell him not to move."

In the tense moments while the ladders were being raised, Stephen studied the knight who had interceded and realized why he, of all the Westerners in Varad, was not dead or a prisoner. "You! You're the filthy apostate who's working with the Mongols!"

"And you," said the knight pleasantly, "have just exerted your best efforts to save a Mongol. Why didn't you let him bring the arch crashing down on top of him?"

"I didn't think," said Stephen honestly. Until this moment he had not recognized that the man in peril wore the leather breeches and fur cap of the invading army. "I'm sorry, now, that I stopped him." Stephen should have let him die. He should have found some way to bring the remnants of the church crashing down on the whole group of Mongols.

"And how did you know that the arch was on the verge of collapse?" queried the knight, as though Stephen's personal feelings in the matter were of no interest whatsoever.

"How should I not know? Anybody except your barbarians would know that an arch with no pier to abut against is going to collapse from sideways pressure—sooner if some idiot soldier tries to dance a rigadoon on the keystone!"

"No. Not just anybody. So you're a mason, after all?"

The phrasing was strange, but Stephen had no time to think on it; the knight's staccato questions pressed him too hard. "Trained in the west? Had a hand in building that church, I suppose?"

"I made it."

The simple assertion stood uncontradicted, though the renegade knight raised his brows for a minute. The Mongol whom Stephen had saved swaggered over and asked the knight a question. The knight answered in the Mongol tongue, pointing back at the ruins of the church, and the soldier burst into raucous laughter. He called his friends to share the joke and all of them began laughing and pointing back and forth, first at Stephen and then at the church. The renegade knight ignored them and walked on down the line, asking each man his name and age and occupation. Stephen caught the knight's satisfied murmurs in between the jeering of the Mongols.

"Two metalworkers, very good... a farmer? Useless! Ah, a groom of the stables. Possibly trainable. What else, a bunch of merchants? Also useless, not worth feeding." His sword flashed through the air, separating the rope where it bound five plump, pale burghers to the rest of the prisoners.

One of the Mongols shouted something in Stephen's ear, and shoved him backwards. Stephen tripped, recovered his balance with difficulty, and came up to face a short stick poking at his throat. He raised his bound hands and tried to ward off the stick; his awkward movements tugged at the prisoners on either side of him. The Mongols laughed and cut him free of the other men. Their short, curved knives pricked him in the sides and legs, and they herded him toward the smoking rubble in the center of the church. Stephen turned, feinted, and blocked some of the mocking pinpricks with the rope that bound his wrists.

The five burghers whom the knight had pointed out were lying prostrate on the ground while a Mongol hacked at their necks. His blade was dull and he took many strokes, like a man chopping wood. The blade made a dull heavy sound as it came down, over and over again, while blood soaked through the tradesmen's gowns and puddled in the cobblestones.

The casual execution distracted Stephen from his own tormentors. His heel caught on a projecting timber and he went down, arching backwards to avoid the Mongol knives which pricked at his throat. He landed heavily on a smoldering mass of wood and masonry. His back was an agony of fire; he rolled to one side, trying to avoid the knives, and felt something soft under the lumps of stone.

It was a child's arm. The fingers were blackened lumps of flesh, but the embroidered sleeve was whole, with its fine cuff of gilt threads which had been protected from fire by the stones that had crushed the body.

Stephen retched and came up on his knees. He could not fight any longer. Why should he? It was fitting that he should die on the stones of his church which had become a sepulchre for the people of Varad. He waited for the blades to descend and finish the work.

The sun beat down on stones wet with blood. Somewhere close by, a fly buzzed; farther away, the renegade knight was instructing the remaining prisoners to search the citadel for food supplies and the bodies of the slain for jewels. Stephen listened with only mild interest. The fly circled before his eyes and lit on the trickle of blood running down his cheekbone where a Mongol knife had pricked him. Morning sun warmed the courtyard stones, and the stench of blood was overpowering. Stephen's mind wandered back to his summer in the fens, with a laughing brown girl who made fun of him.

The Mongols' knives circled delicately over his collarbone, cutting away his filthy tunic, tracing fine lines of blood on the sunburnt skin of his chest and shoulders. They looked angry that Stephen had given up, and shouted insults at him, but he couldn't understand.

"Enough!" The renegade knight strode into the midst of the group, cuffing one of the Mongols out of his way and pulling two others aside by their collars as he repeated his command in their own tongue.

"I told them you're not to be killed," he translated to Stephen. "They're not supposed to let their teasing get out of hand. If you're really a builder, I may have a use for you later. The Mongols thought it was funny, when I told them what your trade was; that's what started the trouble. They think a man who spends his life making things out of stone is building his own prison. A Mongol's notion of the good life is to be mounted on a swift horse and going someplace fast, never staying in the same place for long. They mean to tear down your cities and turn this country back into a grazing land for their horses, a place for free men to live." The knight chuckled. "You see, it is pretty funny, from their point of view." He slashed the rope that bound Stephen's wrists with the point of his sword. "Wait here. I'll be back for you. And don't worry—I've told them to leave you alone."

Stephen did not worry; he was past that. He rested on a carved capital, the remains of one of the great columns from the nave, and listened to the flies buzzing. The Mongols followed the renegade knight away, leaving Stephen alone in the ruins of the church. Alone with the dead who lay all about him, suffocated, burned and finally crushed under the weight of stone.

Thinking about the night just past hurt too much. Instead Stephen concentrated fiercely on impersonal things, calculating the geometry that kept the standing arches up, estimating the strains on the one remaining wall. If he concentrated hard enough he could see the entire courtyard as an abstract composition in lines and spaces. Even the bodies of the slaughtered tradesmen and the limbs flung out from under the fallen stones were nothing more than points of interest to balance the picture.

Presently Stephen found half an illuminated psalter near the one standing wall of the north transept. The other half of the book had been burnt completely away. Bright, beautiful tiny pictures adorned the text and seemed to come from another world than the one he and Bianca had entered yesterday: perfect orchards glowing with fruit, miniature castles with sparkling turrets, fields ready for harvest. Even the demons were a child's bright conception, tiny grinning monsters with pointed horns and tails. They were not frightening to a man who had seen the devil's work as close as Stephen had been observing it.

Stephen put Jokai's dagger to use, scraping away the useless illuminations and the meaningless prayers. Presently he found a burnt stick among the debris and settled down to show the world what real demons looked like. All he'd seen or guessed at in the last twenty-four hours was recorded: the blazing church, the child falling from the gallery with splayed-out limbs, women half buried under grinning Mongol soldiers, and men breathing the flames inside the church. As Stephen drew, he felt the horror of the memories becoming—not bearable, it would never be that—but somehow less immediate in his own mind. The slashing strokes of his improvised pen were an indictment, not of man, but of God who had permitted this and all other horrors upon His own creation.

Stephen sat over the psalter until his limbs were cramped and his hand shook with weariness. It was time to stop, but as soon as he put down his burnt stick and looked about him, it all became real again. This time, though, Stephen felt capable of some action besides stumbling like a cow to the slaughter. His hands were not bound, the knight who'd been in charge of the prisoners had disappeared, and the few Mongols who remained in view seemed more interested in poking through the rubble than in watching the movements of one beaten and exhausted prisoner. Stephen slipped the psalter into the bosom of his tunic and stood, casually, as if he intended no more than to stretch his cramped limbs.

No reaction came from the Mongols. He sidled toward the standing wall of the church, trying to look as if he were only wandering aimlessly through the ruins. In truth he was doing little more than that; he had no plan, only a vague notion that it would be good to get out of sight of his captors. After the lightning siege and the fires that had raged through the night, the city and the citadel alike were little more than a maze of rubble-strewn passages and collapsing buildings. A man could easily disappear into that maze, Stephen thought. Who'd bother to hunt down one prisoner where so many had been slaughtered? Yes, he could disappear and then, perhaps, he might be able to find out where the women prisoners had been taken. The keep was the most likely place since most of its walls were still standing and more than half the roof was intact. And then? Stephen shrugged and sidled a few more steps toward the wall. He still had Jokai's dagger. He'd make a plan later. If he could save Bianca, get her out of here alive, he would not be a complete failure.

Hope raised his chin, squared his shoulders and put a spring into his step—all fatal errors. One of the Mongols noticed the change in their prisoner, shouted to his fellows, who came ambling over to block Stephen's path through the rubble. One hand on his short sword, smiling ferociously, the Mongol said something that Stephen understood without translation.

Stephen smiled, shrugged, and spread out his empty hands. Intermixed with the Mongol's speech were a couple of words that sounded vaguely Russian. If he couldn't quietly disappear just now, another chance might present itself. Meanwhile, perhaps he could learn something by engaging his captors in conversation. He dredged up from his memory the few Russian words he'd learned from traveling merchants of Kiev and Novgorod, asked for water, and mimed taking a long swallow from his empty cupped hands.

One of the Mongols grinned and held out the leather bag that hung from his belt. Stephen was truly thirsty; he took a deep draught and felt liquid fire run down his throat. Coughing and choking, he dropped the bag and staggered in circles, eyes watering. What he'd drunk was like wine, but a thousand times more potent, and with an abominable aftertaste of sour milk.

The Mongols laughed and slapped each other on the back and pointed at Stephen, red-eyed and wheezing. His reaction to their practical joke was a huge success.

When he recovered his breath, Stephen sensed that his captors were feeling marginally more friendly toward him for the amusement he'd given them. Although he hadn't planned to act the buffoon for their benefit, he was not too proud to take advantage of the consequences. While they were still laughing and imitating his frenzied cough, he began to ask where the women prisoners had been taken.

This required quite a lot more mime to supplement his few words of Russian, but eventually he saw a spark of comprehension on their faces. Laughing uproariously as if he'd just made—or been—another excellent joke, they pushed him ahead of them and out of the citadel.

Away from the keep? Stephen slowed his steps and pointed up at the remnants of the keep tower, waggling his eyebrows and repeating the word for "woman" and the mime of bound hands. The Mongols nodded, and clapped him on the shoulder, and pushed him on down the hill. If he could understand their meaning at all, they were telling him not to worry, that the women were outside the citadel and they would take him to them. For some reason they found his request hilarious.

They led him to the open square before the old church, where he'd seen the people of the city lining up to be executed the day before. The bodies of the women, naked and stacked like wood for a kiln, lined two sides of the square. The open space was now occupied by a twisted tangle of white limbs and flowing hair, coifs pulled awry and women's bodies sprawled obscenely askew. Old grandmothers with flaccid bellies and withered breasts lay entwined with the smooth half-formed bodies of young girls. Dark trails of blood crisscrossed the pile of bodies. All the women had been raped many times; some had further been mutilated, breasts hacked off and stomachs slashed open.

"Women prisoner—no good! No work!" said the leading Mongol in strongly accented Russian. "No good except—" He made an obscene gesture and laughed anew at Stephen's expression.

Bianca was lying near the top of the pile as she had been one of the last to be captured. Stephen knew her by the long pale braids of sun-bleached gold, and by the cool gray of one staring eye. The other eye had been gouged out, and her breasts had been clawed to shreds as if by an animal. The lower half of her white body was covered with dried blood; she had bled a great deal, and must have been alive to suffer the worst of what they had done to her.

The Mongols were startled when their exhausted, beaten prisoner turned on them like a mad beast, raving and clawing and trying to kill them all. They were more startled at the dagger that flashed in his clenched fist. They were hardy fighters of the steppes and he was an aging craftsman, but the strength in his fists and the point of his blade gave them some trouble before one of them clouted him over the head with the flat of his sword. By that time one Mongol was nursing a broken arm and two others were bleeding copiously. They circled him cautiously for a full minute before one of them dashed in, kicked him in the chin, and took the dagger that fell out of his limp fingers.

Stephen lay on his back, staring up at the summer-blue sky and the curved sword that bisected it. He waited without feeling for the blow to fall. It would be a relief to have it over, and his death would be much easier than Bianca's.

Someone was shouting in the Mongol tongue, distracting Stephen's guards and prolonging his execution. Stephen felt a momentary irritation; couldn't they kill him before they had their gossip? In a few moments he would recover from the blows that had left him floating in a haze, too weak to do anything but stare at the sky and wait for death. Stephen didn't want to recover, to feel and hate and mourn again. He was ready for his life to be over. He closed his eyes and images of his childhood flashed before him: Aude's hut in the fens, Dunwich's gray sea, Ely's cold cathedral.

"Get up!"

A hand grasped his wrist and pulled violently. Stephen found himself standing on wobbling knees and facing the knight who served the Mongols as interpreter and prison guard. This time something in his memory had been jogged loose, by shock or blows or passing thoughts of the sack of Ely, and he was able to put a name to the face he saw.

"Joffrey de Belmont."

"So it *is* you." The gray-haired apostate nodded with satisfaction. "Stephen, the little novice from Ely. I'd not have known you again. But our spies had said that Count Jokai had brought in an English builder named Stephen, and somehow it stuck in my mind that I'd known a boy who was set on going to Dunwich to slave in a mason's stoneyard. I thought it would be interesting if you were the same. And the khan wanted me to save skilled men for his service anyway, so it was no extra trouble."

"You've changed." But not in any significant detail. De Belmont was grayer, thinner, but still recognizably the handsome, weak man who had deceived him as he tried to escape from Ely after the sack.

"So have you. More than I."

"I daresay." Stephen rubbed his unshaven chin. "What's your interest in me now, de Belmont? I'm not a pretty boy for your pleasure. Did you just want to talk about old times and old betrayals before your Mongol friends chop my head off? Because if so, you may as well tell them to get on with it. I'm not interested."

"Now, now, you've not been listening. I told you, the khan wanted you and the other artisans kept alive. Don't you care whether you live or die?"

Stephen shrugged. "I'm too tired." And if he let himself feel anything at all, for Bianca and all his friends dead, it would be too much to bear. At least Aude was safe, and he would take that comfort with him to the grave. "Actually," he said, "I am quite tired. Could we finish this play, do you think?"

"Don't you even want to know how a good knight like myself got into the service of the Mongols?" De Belmont sounded exasperated.

"Good knight?" Stephen repeated, and laughed. His laugh was rusty, and he could feel the bubble of hysteria rising with the pitch of his voice.

"All right. Come along, Stephen. I do wish you'd stop annoying your guards. I told them you were to be saved for the khan, but they have very little self-control. What were you doing down there, anyway? Oh, never mind, at least you're nearer the khan. Come on. He'll want to meet you."

"Who?"

De Belmont, already leading the way out of the square, looked over his shoulder and gave a harsh laugh. "You don't even know who destroyed you, do you? Khan Kadan, the leader of this wing of the Mongol army. He's the new master of Hungary, now that the border has fallen. You're going to make yourself useful to him, and that will improve my standing with the Mongols. Now come on."

They were heading out of the city. "He's not in the citadel?"

"The Mongols think that sleeping in stone buildings is bad for the health. He's in his tent on the far side of the river."

Khan Kadan was eating when Stephen was brought before him. Seated cross-legged on a carpet, he held a silver basin of boiled meat before him. Grabbing a strip of meat in his left hand, he bit down on the end of the strip, and his knife flashed past his flat nose as he sliced off a bite. Three grinding motions of his jaws, a quick gulping swallow, and the khan was ready for the next bite. While he ate, he studied Stephen with the bright-eyed curiosity of a child being offered a new plaything. De Belmont spoke briefly in the Mongol tongue, introducing Stephen; the khan put down the strip of meat in his left hand and barked out a question. De Belmont turned to Stephen.

"The church in Varad—was that your own design, or did you merely copy some building from the West?"

"I don't copy," Stephen replied. De Belmont had made Stephen believe that the Mongols did not care about the art of building. Certainly there was nothing in this sparsely furnished tent of dark blue cloth to contradict his view. On their rampage, the Mongols stole what they could carry, and burned or killed all else.

Khan Kadan asked Stephen several more questions which all seemed equally pointless. Was Stephen also a master of the mechanical arts? Could he build a cart large enough to carry a tree trunk?

"If I had to."

If supplied with silversmiths and other craftsmen to work under his direction, could he make a fountain to run with wine and *kumiss*?

"What's *kumiss*?"

"Fermented mare's milk. I understand my men gave you a taste of it earlier today."

"Certainly I could make such a fountain. It would take me some time though."

And, finally: Had Stephen been in charge of the siege engines used against the khan's army yesterday?

"I wasn't in charge," Stephen replied. "That post belonged to Csaba, the count's master of arms. But I and my master mason Béla worked with Csaba to fix the catapults when they broke down."

Khan Kadan bolted down the last remaining strips of boiled meat, popped a nut of dough and minced meat into his mouth, and sat back with his palms on his knees, looking Stephen up and down with an air of satisfaction.

Then, after he had given forth two comfortable belches, he spoke again and Joffrey de Belmont translated.

"If you are telling the truth, you will be allowed the honor of living as the slave of the khan. You will be in charge of repairing and maintaining our siege engines. You may select your own helpers out of the other prisoners from Varad. There are also some Russian prisoners from Kiev with knowledge of the engines, although not, regretably, as many as we had before your foolish defense of Varad."

Stephen had been waiting for this since Khan Kadan first mentioned the siege engines. Before he answered, he prayed for strength. So far he had been spared much; he had only witnessed the horrors inflicted on others. Now, he suspected, it would be his turn. He lowered his head and answered submissively; he had no appetite for being tortured to death if he could avoid. it. "My regrets to the great khan, but I fear my mechanical knowledge is not sufficient to aid his people in such a task. The working of siege engines is a complicated subject in its own right, quite different from the builder's art."

"You have already made it quite clear that you have mastered all the mechanical arts," de Belmont interrupted him. "You can build a giant cart or a magic fountain, you aimed and repaired catapults only yesterday, and now you plead ignorance? Either you have lied to the khan, which is an offense punishable by death, or you are refusing to serve him—which is punishable by slower death. Think again, stupid boy."

"I'm not your stupid boy. We're both grown men, de Belmont. Perhaps you've forgotten that some men won't serve their enemies." As he spoke these proud words, Stephen prayed that de Belmont did not know how little pride was in his cringing flesh. Some tortures gave a man with sufficient resolution a chance to die quickly; he hoped the Mongol amusements were of that sort.

De Belmont's face turned red and the cords stood out in his scrawny neck as he shouted threats at Stephen. Clearly he had expected to be rewarded by Kahn Kadan for bringing him such a useful prisoner. Instead, Stephen's recalcitrance was embarrassing him in front of his master and might cost both of them their lives.

When Stephen refused to respond, de Belmont lost

control and cuffed Stephen's head with wild swinging blows. Weak and dizzy from exhaustion, hunger, and the draught of *kumiss*, Stephen slipped to one knee on the khan's carpet. As he struggled to stand against de Belmont's rain of open-handed blows, the psalter he'd been using for a sketchbook slipped out of his bosom and fell open between him and Khan Kadan. De Belmont stopped with his hand upraised, shocked into stillness by the sight of Stephen's drawings.

The Mongol khan stared at the open pages of the psalter. On one page was sketched the heap of naked women as they had been piled in the square of the lower town. Facing that was a drawing of the burning church as Stephen remembered it, in the moment of its collapse: roof caving in, flames crackling about it, faces at the windows stretched into silent screams.

After a long moment of tense silence, the khan picked up the psalter and thumbed through the pages. He seemed to be smiling, perhaps because he was deciding how to execute the man who'd recorded his infamy. Finally Khan Kadan spoke to de Belmont, and as the renegade knight nodded and turned, Stephen braced himself to receive his death sentence.

"The khan is pleased with your drawings," de Belmont said stiffly. "He feels it would add to his consequence with the Great Khan in Karakorum if he could show such evidence of his great work in the West. You will be permitted to live so long as you continue to chronicle the khan's victories in this fashion."

The khan spoke again, still smiling, and de Belmont translated. "Khan Kadan predicts that eventually, when you understand that we are unconquerable, you will serve us in the matter of the siege engines of your own free will. Meanwhile, to inspire your willing service, the khan wishes his guards to show you what has been done with the two other skilled men of Varad who refused to work on our engines, and who did not have your skills in drawing to recommend them."

After the guards had hustled Stephen out of the tent, Khan Kadan indulged in the unusual luxury of explaining his intentions to someone. Usually he preferred to keep an impassive face of mystery before his officers, but de Belmont, after all, was not an officer. He was only a slave whose value would diminish as the Mongol army trained other prisoners to serve as interpreters. Meanwhile, the Khan might as well explain to de Belmont why he was about to be rewarded so lavishly for bringing in a recalcitrant prisoner; the knowledge might inspire him to collect other such artisans.

"The builder will travel with my army, as I have said, to record my victories for the Great Khan. But he will be of even more use to me later. My father Ogedei has been somewhat corrupted by the people of the cities he has conquered; he builds palaces of stone and timber and he sleeps under a roof. I do not approve, but I see that I may find favor with him by giving him an architect trained in the building arts of the West.

"When we have conquered this land, when I am through with Stephen, the builder he will be sent as a slave to the Great Khan in Karakorum."

CHAPTER

34

◻

*B*y the spring of 1242, slightly more than a year after the sack of Varad, the psalter with which Stephen had begun his history of the Mongol conquest was filled to the margins of every page. Undated and disordered, his sketches crammed the parchment as he recorded whatever he saw with whatever tools came his way. Stephen was never sure which things were real and which were visions sent to torment him, but the difference didn't seem to matter. The burning of the wooded island on the Crisul River, where refugees from Varad and neighboring villages had hoped to hide from the Mongols, was real enough, but what of the ripening fields where the peasants had worked through the summer of 1241, putting their trust in the Mongol assurances that they would not be harmed so long as they served their new lords? Stephen had seen only what happened in the village where Khan Kadan set up his own summer quarters, but he knew that the shameful story had been repeated everywhere.

When the harvest was gathered in, the Mongols invited the peasants to purchase their lives by offering their women. Fathers pushed their terrified virgin daughters into the arms of the conquerors, young husbands watched their wives being ravished on the floor of the threshing barns where the grain was gathered in. Those who resisted were killed on the spot. Those who did not resist were killed that night, after the khan had had his fill of watching the sport. First the children were slaughtered, then the women, and last the men. Then the army moved on, rich with the summer's grain, leaving a desert behind them.

In Stephen's sketchbook, the sheaves of grain piled in the fields had long waving hair and agonized faces; they became slender-waisted women, stretching out arms of straw for succor, while the Mongols slashed at them with members sharp as knives. And all around, the blood-red poppies bloomed. Actually the poppies were brown, for Stephen had used real blood in his sketches, and now it was dry and brown.

Sometimes he knew he was mad, other times he only thought so. He had seen too much for a man to bear and still retain his sanity. He had sought death by throwing himself into the Crisul River while the Mongols laughed at the people screaming from their burning island. After they fished him out Stephen simply waited for the next chance to take his life. As the Mongols shot down a village of peasants gathered into one field for slaughter, Stephen ran before their arrows.

But somehow those arrows missed him, and after that second episode he was guarded at all times, for Khan Kadan had no intention of losing his artist. When the army traveled, Stephen rode with them, hands lashed to the high canted wooden Mongol saddle; when the army camped, he lived in a cage of wooden bars that kept him from escaping or hurting himself but did not keep out the pointed sticks and curious gazes of his guards. Like the other prisoners, Stephen had a single rag to cover his nakedness and a handful of grain a day for rations. Since he was forced to live, he ate the grain and poured his life and soul into the drawings that filled his sketchbook. Someday, he assumed, the Mongol khan would grow bored with him and he would be killed like the other prisoners who had been deemed liabilities.

When he was sane, Stephen wished that day might come soon. When he was mad, he confessed his sins to the moon for lack of a priest, and the Mongol guards laughed at him as he wept and shouted his griefs aloud. But as time went on, they began to treat him with a wary respect because they believed that a man who looked at the moon for too long was in serious danger. The white Sky-walker had a noose of moonlight with which to catch the souls of such men. And they thought the mad builder must have some special knowledge that protected him.

Sometimes Joffrey de Belmont came to sit beside Stephen's cage, with small offerings of friendship: a silver-point pencil looted from the Cistercian monastery of Egres, some sheets of clean parchment to fold in with the pages of the psalter, a cup of wine or a basin of boiled meat. At first, when Stephen was still sane most of the time, he rejected the renegade's overtures. In later months, when Stephen was troubled by hallucinations, he was not always sure what he had said. Once he dreamed that he and his old friend Béla were having dinner together and talking about the bracing framework for the church spire. Suddenly Béla laughed at him and pulled his shirt open to expose the entrails oozing out of his stomach, and Stephen remembered that Béla had been gutted like a pig for refusing to help the Mongols work their captured siege engines. He screamed and Béla patted him on the shoulder, saying that he must hush his noise before he annoyed the guards. When Stephen's vision cleared, Béla turned into Joffrey de Belmont, real and very much alive. Stephen had been sharing Joffrey's meal of milk and boiled grain while chatting away to the shadows in his mind.

After that he did not try to drive Joffrey away. Amid so much horror, devastation, and cruelty, de Belmont's individual betrayals seemed hardly worth his concern. Stephen might as well let the man talk to him, since he seemed to esteem the conversation of a mad architect so highly.

Stephen began to learn a little of the Mongol tongue from de Belmont, and even gleaned some understanding of the rigid organization and perfect discipline that had turned the Mongols into a fighting machine to conquer the West. Sometimes their talk grew more personal. In fits and snatches, Joffrey de Belmont told him the story of how he came to be in the service of the khans of Tartary. It was a sorry tale, beginning with the day when de Belmont had broken his fealty to Stephen Ridel for fear of the mercenaries at Ely. Penniless and frightened, he'd tried to use Stephen out of fear and loneliness as much as lust; when that failed, de Belmont sought a new master only to find that the news of his treachery had gone before him.

A faithless knight could not expect to find a good master; de Belmont had drifted from one master to the next, each less honorable, until he escaped a life little better than an outlaw's by taking the Cross. Three days after his arrival in the Holy Land he was separated from his companions by an attack of wild bandits out of the mountains. There had followed a confused period in the service of an old potentate who used hashish, ruled the mountains as an absolute tyrant, and had a taste for pretty, fair-skinned Christian men. After some years of drink and hashish, de Belmont lost his looks and his health. He was dismissed from his position as personal servant to the old man and his guards and was sold as a slave to a tribe traveling east. He was resold again and again, until he fell into the hands of a strange man with yellow skin, flat cheekbones, and small, slanted eyes. This man was the first in many years to treat Joffrey de Belmont like a human being, and in gratitude de Belmont had told him all he knew about the lands of the West and the Western way of warfare. It was not until later that he realized he was betraying his people into the hands of a worse enemy than the Saracens.

"Don't let it trouble you," said Stephen one night when they were drinking together to blot out the memory of the preceding days, the fall of Esztergom and the usual slaughter of inhabitants and defenders. The Mongols had been irritated by the Hungarians' stubborn insistence on continuing to defend their cities even after they had been shown the example of previous slaughters. After Esztergom was taken, men had been spitted on lances and roasted in their armor like chestnuts over hot coals. Their screams still echoed in Stephen's ears.

Even de Belmont, accustomed as he was to Mongol warfare, had been shaken by this sack. He relived his past betrayals and failures again and again. After copious draughts of fermented mare's milk and looted wine, he finally reached the point of weeping over his treachery.

"Don't worry," said Stephen again. "They probably would have conquered Europe without your help."

"But don't you despise me?"

Stephen thought it over. "You're a traitor. I'm a failure and a madman. And God has sent this plague out of the east to destroy the world. If I despise anybody," he said with an attempt at a smile, "it should be God. Is there any wine left?"

"Only *kumiss*." De Belmont passed the sloshing leather bag through the bars of Stephen's cage, but he did not let go when Stephen reached for it. "Sometimes," he said, holding tightly to the strap that closed the bag, "you don't sound mad. Blasphemous, perhaps, but not mad."

"Sometimes I don't feel it. Talking with you, speaking a civilized tongue again, remembering England—" Stephen sighed. "And, of course, it's dark. That helps. When it's light again, I will see the work of the Mongols, and my madness will return. Give me a drink."

"No. I think not." De Belmont twitched the leather bag of fermented milk out of Stephen's hand and retreated a prudent distance from the cage. "If you wish to live, my friend, I would advise you to keep possession of your senses from now on. The *kumiss* won't help."

"And who told you I wished to live?" Stephen called after the retreating figure. The darkness swallowed de Belmont up and no answer came back.

In the weeks that followed, de Belmont repeated his hints that Stephen should try to act sane and useful if he wished to avoid the periodic slaughters of prisoners that took place whenever the army needed to move quickly. And they were moving very quickly these days; Buda was taken, Esztergom a smoking heap of rubble, the flower of the Hungarian army dead. King Béla had fled with his court from Buda to Zagreb, from Zagreb down to the Adriatic coast, and Khan Kadan had been given the special task of capturing the Hungarian King. Most of the prisoners were executed at a place called Sirbi in Slavonia; Stephen was one of the few who rode with the Mongols to Spalato, where Béla was reported to have taken refuge.

When the Mongols learned that Béla was not in the citadel, they rode south without even bothering to destroy Spalato. The horrors in Stephen's sketchbook were interrupted by a brief architectural drawing of the old Roman palace of Spalato as it appeared from the Mongol encampment on the hill. Stephen labored over the details of columns and brickwork and found himself, almost against his will, beginning to take some mild interest in living again. Spring was softening the land; Stephen drew a shaggy-maned Mongol pony stretching its neck to get a bite of the flowers growing out of a rocky cleft. Khan Kadan laughed at the picture, sent Stephen a new tunic, and invited him to dine in his own tent that night.

Stephen had learned something of the Mongol tongue during his year of imprisonment, enough to understand some of the quick slurred jests and grandiose plans that Kadan and his officers discussed over their bowls of meat and salty tea. At first Stephen paid little attention to the quick-flowing, obscene, triumphant chatter of the conquerors. He squatted on his heels in a corner of the tent and wished that he had brought parchment and drawing implements to record the scene: these demons with greasy faces, crouching like savages over boiled meat served in looted church vessels of silver and gold, their eyes sparkling in the light of three-foot wax tapers that had been made for a saint's day procession.

Presently Khan Kadan called jovially to ask why his mad artist didn't eat when he was given the chance. Stephen told the truth—that he would rather draw than eat—and the Khan laughed and sent a boy for Stephen's tools.

The candles dripped in the breeze that blew through the open-ended tent, the hanging tassels and the copper bells that adorned the tent pole swayed in the night wind, and Stephen labored with chilled fingers to set down what he could of the scene. The talk alternately amused and frustrated him until he lost track of his own inadequacies in his intense concentration. He was an architect, not an artist; his skills were in rendering the lines of force and the planes of carved stone, not in delineating the human figure. In the past year, as he set down what might be the only record of this plague of demons let loose upon Europe, his deficiencies as an artist had not seemed to matter. Fear and anger and shock had loosened his fingers; he drew what was before him without worrying overmuch about the execution of the work.

Now, as part of the price of returning sanity, Stephen had to struggle anew with his own clumsiness. He scraped away bad lines again and again until the parchment was worn thin as an eggshell in places. While he was thinking about how to render the demonic evil in the smiling, greasy faces before him, the meaning of their talk sank in. Stephen sat so still, seemingly so absorbed in his task, that not one of them thought to censor his words in front of a Western prisoner.

"Béla's in Trogir, the fool."

"I hear that's an island."

"Some of our prisoners say, yes, some, no. Who cares? Does he think a narrow channel of water between him and the mainland will stop us? If the prisoners won't bridge it, we'll fill the gap with their bodies. We'll take it in two days."

"Can he swim?"

"We'll let him try. But be sure to fish him out before he drowns! I want the head to take back to Subedei."

The name of Khan Kadan's master, the Mongol general who had planned and executed this whole attrack upon the West, caught Stephen's attention and he looked up. Though he strained to understand Kadan's words, he could no longer follow the Mongol sounds. He shrugged in frustration and went back to his drawing. As the night wore on, the khan's intentions emerged through the snatches of words that were intermittently clear to Stephen.

After taking Trogir and killing King Béla, Kadan's forces were to move back up the Dalmatian coast to join Subedei in Hungary. A third army had devastated Poland and was even now coming south to join forces with Kadan and Subedei. Then the three Mongol armies, joined as one, would strike a hammer blow directly into the heart of Christendom. There would be no more piecemeal conquests, moving slowly and destroying all resistance as they went. Instead they would drive a tunnel of devastation right through the Holy Roman Empire, where Frederick was too busy waging war with the Pope to give them effective opposition, and into France.

"The king of Frank-land wishes to be a saint," said Kadan through a mouthful of tough meat.

"What's that?" asked one of his officers.

"Something Christians become. But they have to be dead first. It will be my pleasure to gratify his wish."

Kadan paused, slurped noisily at a bowl of the Mongol tea with butter and salt, and beamed at his subordinates. "Frank-land is a rich country, my children. They tell me that every village has a stone caravanserai full of worked vessels like this." He tapped the silver bowl in which the meat had been brought. "And the women are fair after the

Frankish manner. We shall feast through this summer, and after the harvest we will kill the people and tear down the houses as always. Then we shall return across the other Christian lands until there is nothing but one great empty steppe for free men to ride!"

"Frank-land is far from Karakorum," murmured one of the officers.

"Meaning?" Khan Kadan's eyes were bright in the flickering candlelight.

"A khan who could conquer Frank-land might not need to return and take his orders from Karakorum."

Kadan's open hand slapped down on the ground with a crack sharp as a whip. "No such talk in this tent! 'There is one sun in the sky, and one Great Khan on earth,'" he quoted the Mongol saying that prefaced every letter sent in the name of the Great Khan to the Western rulers. "No one in this army will even think treason against my father Ogedei Khan."

"One sun in the sky—one Great Khan on earth," murmured the officers with heads bowed. The one who had angered Kadan regained his favor, a few minutes later, by discussing how a son who conquered the westernmost lands of the earth would surely be chosen as the only worthy successor to Ogedei. Kadan was pleased to hear himself referred to as the next Great Khan; his pleasure was clear even to the ignorant Westerner who crouched over his drawings in the corner.

That night sleep escaped Stephen, as it did on many of the anguished nights he had spent in Khan Kadan's train. The floor of his wooden cage was hard for a body worn thin by the scanty rations given to Mongol prisoners, and the memories that tormented him often made him fear his dreams. Voices and visions were better company than reality. But tonight, tormented by what he had heard in the khan's tent, Stephen forbade himself the easy escape into madness. He had to think.

The khan spoke of the drive forward into France as though it were an accomplished fact, a decision already made. But was it? Why would the khan be working to build up enthusiasm among his officers for a decision that his commander Subedei had already made? From what Stephen had seen for himself and what he had learned from de Belmont, such was not the Mongol way. Their army moved with a discipline unknown to the West; commands from the Great Khan were obeyed through all levels of the ranks without question. There were none of the quarrels and schisms between factions that had brought almost every crusade to failure; nor was there any personal glory-seeking that turned the charges of Western knights into a series of individual tourneys.

Stephen was sure that if the decision to invade France had been made by Subedei, Kadan would not be seeking to inflame his officers with tales of the rich loot and lovely women. He would not need to because the army would follow Subedei to France without questioning. Though Stephen was suspicious of Kadan's persuasive speeches, he could focus only on one thing: France. The place where he had sent Aude for safety. He had wounded her pride, broken his own heart, and destroyed their marriage, but it was worth it as long as Stephen knew Aude was safe. And now the Mongols were going to ride through France, through the green valley of Chastelvert. Stephen had seen their thoroughness; they devastated the land like locusts, seeking out and destroying any sign of life. Behind this army lay a landscape pitted and desolate like the face of hell. Next year, if Khan Kadan's ambitious plans succeeded, France would look the same. Aude's hidden valley would not escape. Stephen bit back a groan and clenched his thin hands together, staring at the moon, praying for inspiration. Somehow the Mongols had to be stopped. Stephen asked himself what one half-starved Mongol slave could do. This is not an ordinary army, he told himself. It is the mightiest siege engine that ever hurled a deathblow against kings and nations.

Siege engine. Stephen laughed aloud.

"Hey, slave," called a drowsy guard, "be quiet."

Stephen remembered thereafter to keep his voice down, but the plan that had come to him in a flash would not let him go that night. This idea of invading France was Kadan's plan, to serve his own ambition. Joffrey de Belmont had told him that the Great Khan was, by custom, elected by the commanders and princes of the Mongol army. When Ogedei died and the new Great Khan was elected, Kadan wanted to stand before the commanders as the man who had captured King Béla and subdued the distant nation of France.

Subedei, the leader of the whole invading army, might have different ideas. He was not a son of Ogedei; he came from a clan of the far north called the Reindeer People who were despised by the other Mongols as half-naked barbarians. Left to himself, Subedei might not be inclined to drive the army into a risky venture like the invasion of France. He might prefer to remain where he was, ruling what had been Hungary and Slavonia under the Great Khan, enjoying the profits of a successful war.

If the invasion was just Kadan's idea, then Kadan's death would end the plan. In any case, the death of one of the three leaders of the army was likely to force the Mongols to slow down and rethink their arrangements. Even if they decided to go on into the West, any delay might give the knights of England, France, and the Holy Roman Empire time to assemble a force that could stand against these devils.

Stephen's lips stretched into a smile. It was not a pretty smile, but it matched his thoughts, which were of siege engines and accidents and the possibility of persuading Khan Kadan to stand in the right place at the right time. Of course, the Mongols would kill the man responsible for crushing their leader under the wheels of a runaway catapult. But that was a matter of small importance compared with what could be gained from such an accident.

The next morning Stephen asked Joffrey de Belmont to tell Khan Kadan that his prediction had been absolutely correct: Stephen of Dunwich, once the master builder for Count Jokai of Varad, was now so impressed with the might of the Mongol army that he begged the privilege of repairing and restoring the catapults and other machines of war that the army dragged along in its train.

The catapults were battered and askew from the year's campaigning and from hard use by unskilled prisoners. Kadan accepted the offer, as Stephen had known he would.

That summer great news reached the Christian nations of the West, where quarrels and plans for another great crusade were still distracting the leaders even as they began to worry seriously about the Mongol threat. In March the Mongols prepared to besiege King Béla of Hungary in his island fortress of Trogir, then suddenly abandoned the chase and retreated back to their homeland. No reason was known for the change, no explanation was given. Louis of France ordered *Te Deum* to be sung in the cathedral of Notre Dame at Paris, as after a great victory. The churchmen of the West were quick to follow his lead and to proclaim the victory of their prayers and the intercessions of their particular saints as the weapons that had driven away the infidel armies. Since no one west of the Danube had any understanding of the Mongol nation and the reasons why it had drawn back at the very brink of victory, the Church gained prestige and offerings for the miraculous salvation of Europe.

Marco Sanudo, whose spies for the House of Sanudo were in every land known to Christendom, knew no more than the rest of Europe about the Mongols' abrupt retreat. But he had the news earlier than most, and his ships carried the word to England by the first favorable winds of the season. Marco himself traveled on the first ship, accompanied by certain young men whose task was to inform the bankers of the Sanudo House who could then make the best possible profit from having their knowledge a week or two in advance of the rest of the world. Timber and furs would be cheaper this season and the next, as the trade routes from the interior of Europe to the ports on the Adriatic opened again; iron and worked stone would be wanted for rebuilding; the prices of the luxury goods produced in Byzantium and the East would go up, now that the princes of the West felt free to spend their money on silk and gilded glassware instead of on armies and armor.

Marco himself was bound for the fishing towns of East Anglia. The herring, which had rotted on the streets of Dunwich and Yarmouth for the last two years, would be in great demand this fall. A clever merchant-banker, prepared to lend the fishing fleets money for reequipping their neglected boats and torn nets in return for the promise of their catch, could make a small fortune by reselling the herring to the Baltic traders who would be returning for the autumn fair.

This was all perfectly true, but not one soul on board supposed Marco Sanudo made the trip to Dunwich out of a passion for herring. They loved Marco, though, and they respected the passion and energy that he had brought out to the task of repairing the fortunes of the House of

Sanudo. Over the last twenty years he had turned the Sanudo concern from a dilapidated merchant venture possessing only two ships into an international consortium of merchants, bankers, and shippers with agents in every market of the known world. And in the process, Marco had given many of his employees the opportunity for fame and fortune and good hard work. If Messer Marco wanted to take a spring holiday on the English coast on the pretext of buying herring, it was entirely his right, and the least his shipmates could do was to restrain their jokes about sweet young fish and big hooks until Marco was out of hearing.

Aude herself did not question Marco's reasons for appearing in Dunwich. "You never need an excuse to visit Mark and me," she said. "You've been a good friend to us—better than we deserve, I fear. Get down, Mark!"

Two-year-old Mark, after an initial moment of shyness, was crawling over Marco's lap and poking inquisitive fingers into the crevices of his furred gown. The two of them were a study in contrasts: a sturdy, golden little boy and an aging merchant with his crown of silver-tipped black curls. Mark looked more like Stephen every day. Marco was always himself, her very dear friend. If there was more than that to his repeated visits, Aude did not want to hear it.

"Mark!" Aude cried as her son grabbed Marco's full sleeve and hoisted himself up by it. "Stop bothering the gentleman!"

Marco laughed and pointed out to Aude that a man carrying sweetcakes in his sleeves must expect to be set upon by small marauders.

"I didn't want him to be shy of me."

"No fear!" Aude tried to sigh but had to smile. "You invite us to take advantage of you."

"I wish you'd take more than you do," Marco said.

"This house, your care for us—"

"The house was bought out of Stephen's profits in the trading company." Mark's shouts of triumph punctuated their conversation as he found one cake after another and tried to cram them all into his mouth at once. Marco raised his voice slightly and balanced the baby from one knee to the other as though he were used to carrying on conversations around a squawking toddler. "I didn't want to tell you at first because I was afraid you wouldn't want to take anything from him."

"You had no right to keep that from me." Aude protested, but mildly. What did it matter whether she owed the roof over her head to Stephen or to Marco? She could only dimly remember her struggle across Slavonia to the sea-coast after that last searing night and day with Stephen. She had hated him so much then; she remembered that, but she could not recall how it had felt.

"Stephen wrote asking me to see that you were cared for. You were his wife; you had a right to use the money."

"Am. I am his wife. We don't know—" She couldn't say it. *That he's dead*. If she said it, it might be true. "We don't know what has been happening in Varad. Until I have certain word of his death, I will not give up hope." The very words made her hope seem too frail to survive.

Marco looked up briefly, and something flashed in his dark eyes that Aude could not recognize—did not want to recognize. She felt a moment of panic. The gossips of Dunwich had always been sure that Marco was more than a friend to her; Aude had been able to laugh them off as long as she was sure of her own feelings. Now she felt change in the air. If Marco wanted more, if he pressed her, how would she answer? She was truly fond of him and wanted him to be happy. But to let him take Stephen's place in her heart would be like admitting that Stephen was never coming back. It would be like killing Stephen.

Then Marco smiled and said something to young Mark, now chatting incomprehensibly through a mouthful of ginger and gilt marzipan, and Aude felt at ease again. It was only Marco, after all. Her old friend—their old friend. Why should she feel flustered at that look of his, nervous and silly as a girl?

"I honored Stephen's wishes because I thought, even then, that someday I might want to ask you for some-thing," Marco said, his dark head still bent over Mark's tousled golden-brown curls. "And I didn't want you to feel indebted to me on that day."

Aude shook her head, smiling. "Marco, you are the oldest and best friend Stephen and I have. There shouldn't be talk of debts between us. Whatever I can do for you, you know it is yours for the asking." She felt a brief chill, almost like a premonition, and shook her head again impatiently. She held out both her hands to Marco, still smiling. "What is it? A potion to make some lovely young lady in Venice run away from her noble family for you? Or some of my special lotion to touch away the silver at your temples?"

Marco rose and put young Mark, whose hands were full of cakes and crumbs, down from his knee. "Run outside and play for a moment," he told the boy, and Mark toddled off contented and sticky.

"I want you, Aude."

She stood quite still, one hand still outstretched toward him, the other at her chest where a pain had stabbed her for a moment.

"I've always loved you. You must know that, although you wouldn't see it for loyalty to Stephen. And I wouldn't say it—for loyalty to Stephen. How much longer must I wait, Aude? It has been over a year since Varad was sacked. If Stephen had lived, don't you think he would have contrived to send word, in all that time? Don't you think my agents would have learned something of him? Aude, the Mongols are retreating now. God knows why, but they're going back to whatever hellish land they sprang from. And they leave nothing behind—nothing except bones and empty fields and naked woods. Poland is gone. Half of Hungary is a desert. Aude, I can't bring Stephen alive out of that devastation for you."

"Would you if you could?"

"As God is my witness," said Marco, "I would, if only to see matters settled between the two of you. Aude, he cast you off nearly three years ago! If he were alive and in England, you would not cling to a marriage that's been dead for three years; you would get on with your life."

"Marriage *is* for life."

"It was no marriage in the first place! Stephen was a clerk vowed to the Church. He had no right to break those prior vows and marry you!" The words spilled out of Marco with desperate eager haste, betraying to Aude how long he must have turned these arguments over in his own mind. "Aude, while Stephen lived and was loyal to you, I would never have spoken of this. But I can't let you bury yourself here for the sake of a dead man who had already cast you off. If Stephen had lived we could have obtained an annulment. I have friends in Rome. It would not be difficult to arrange. As it is, that's not necessary. Aude, you are too young to end your life just because Stephen was a blind fool who refused to take his head out of a noose!"

"You're very quick to pronounce him dead."

Marco's hands were like birds darting aimlessly through the air—white hands, a merchant's hands. "Can you say honestly that you still think he lives?"

"I will not say that he is dead. Not yet."

"Then don't." Marco was as quick to strike a bargain here as ever he'd been in the markets of Acre. "We won't speak of Stephen again, not yet. All I ask is that you come with me out of England. Give me the chance to care for you. You've been sick—you're still coughing, I heard you as I came up the hill. Come to the South with me, Aude, and rest for a little while, and think what you will do. I promise I won't press you."

But pressure was implicit in every word he spoke. "I ... don't know," Aude said. She shivered. Even with the fire burning in the hearth, this cottage with its thick stone walls was cold and drafty; she felt the chill all around her. "I am so tired." Her voice was thick and sleepy. She longed to lie down and rest, to dream of Stephen in the good days before Michael-Béla died and the church consumed him, to forget all the weary years that had passed. But there was Marco to be answered, and young Mark to be cared for.

"Then let me take care of you." Marco slipped one arm around her waist, not lovingly, but merely to support her. "You needn't come to Venice yet, if you don't want to meet my family. You need to be quiet, and rest, and recover from the winter. I have a villa at Ragusa. There are roses there, and the boatman can take you up and down the coast. The Mongols never got that far, it is still beautiful along the coast. There is sunshine, and clear water like the finest glass, and pine trees dropping their long needles into the courtyard. I will come to visit whenever I can get away, and we will sit in the sunny courtyard and drink a glass of wine and be old friends together. That will be enough for me, Aude, to know that you are cared for and safe."

"I would be using you. It's not fair." But she was tempted, desperately tempted, by the word pictures Marco painted of his villa by the sea. And the touch of his arm had awakened feelings she'd thought to put aside forever. Perhaps, after all, life could hold more than one kind of love. She would never again be the young girl who had loved and feared and desired Stephen so desperately, who had put him at the center of her life. Maybe it would be sweet to have a man who put her at the center of his life, instead.

She shivered with something that was not a chill, and Marco, ever the consummate bargainer, seized his moment. "Then we may speak again of the future. But not too soon. I promised not to press you, and I will keep my promise."

Somehow, without pressure, he managed to persuade Aude that Lent of next year—two years after the sack of Varad, nearly a full year away—would be an appropriate time to 'think of their future,' as he put it. And somehow, without either of them putting it into words, Aude understood and accepted what the vague phrase really meant: if Lent of 1243 passed without news of Stephen, she would marry Marco on Easter.

CHAPTER

35

◻

While Béla of Hungary offered somewhat mystified thanks for his salvation, the Mongol army that had prepared to besiege him in Trogir moved south and east across the Balkan peninsula, leaving in their trail a wide swath of destruction. The peasants of Bosnia and Serbia were not so thankful as the rest of the Christian world for this change of plan.

To Stephen, riding wearily in the rear of the great army with his customary escort of Mongol guards, the unexpected retreat was a pleasant surprise. After Varad he would have welcomed death. Now, more than a year later, he reveled in a new knowledge of the sweetness of life. It was one thing to expect that at any moment his head would be lopped off with a Mongol sword. It was quite another to plan in cold blood an act which would inevitably result in his own lingering and painful death.

If Khan Kadan had paused in the first few days of his retreat to besiege Ragusa or the other cities of Dalmatia, his life might still have been in danger. Stephen and the other prisoners had not been told of the reason for the change of direction, and Stephen was then still resolved to trade his life for Kadan's at the first opportunity. In pursuit of that opportunity, he made a serious effort to remain sane, to think and talk sensibly and to produce drawings that would please the khan.

As a result Stephen began joining the khan's feasts on a regular basis. And there, pricking up his ears to understand the quick, slurred Mongol speech, he found out why the army had retreated on the very brink of victory: the Great Khan Ogedei was dead. Some said he died of drink, while others whispered that someone had put poison in his cup. By Mongol custom, the khans of the empire had to return to Karakorum to elect a new great khan. The destruction of Europe would have to wait for another season; Kadan, Batu, and Subedei were all bound for Karakorum, and their armies and prisoners must trail along behind them.

Kadan was in a foul mood as a result of this change of plans. He had been one of Ogedei's favored sons, but the backing of a dead Great Khan would not weigh heavily with the living commanders in charge of selecting a new leader. There were numerous other sons and grandsons favored by one party or another. And now Kadan had lost his chance to win glory in the eyes of the Mongol tribes by capturing the Hungarian king and taking the Western nations.

Khan Kadan drank heavily during the warm summer nights while the army moved slowly toward Bulgaria, where they were to rendezvous with Batu and Subedei. His temper, never good, was now so uncertain that servants and prisoners begged not to be sent to serve him. He struck one boy down with a blow of his sword for looking insolent, and had another prisoner flayed alive in a field outside Drivost for stumbling with his wine cup.

Stephen would have been happy to dispense with the khan's favor in this uncertain period. Kadan treated him with a smiling condescension that made him more nervous than open hostility, lavishing silk robes and looted treasures upon him and reminding him that he owed everything, even his own skin, to the khan's favor.

"I don't understand it," Stephen murmured to Joffrey de Belmont one evening when he had escaped the feasting in the khan's tent to share a cup of wine with the old knight. The wheel of fortune had turned; with the invasion of the West called off, de Belmont's skills were no longer valuable to the khan and he was treated little better than the other prisoners. Now it was Stephen who brought Joffrey de Belmont scraps of meat and leather bags of wine and butter, as well as bits of gossip and news about the army's plans. He had not intended to grow friendly with de Belmont; it had just happened. Somewhere in the year of horror, the comradeship of a man from his own country had come to matter more than the betrayals and failures that marked de Belmont's life.

"I don't understand it," Stephen repeated, "and it makes me nervous. Why is Kadan being so generous to me? He doesn't want my help with the catapults now. There's nothing to attack here except mud walls and twig huts. One man with a lance could walk through the defenses of any town in Serbia. And the great campaign is over. He doesn't need me to chronicle his atrocities any longer. I'm as useless to him as you are."

"He has plans for you, though."

"What?"

"Remember when I told you to keep your sanity if you didn't want to be thrown into a common grave with the rest of the surplus prisoners? Kadan wants a builder, not a madman."

"You're joking. You know how the Mongols feel about stone houses. You're the one who told me. Kadan has no more use for a builder than for a court jester—less, probably."

"Nor for himself. Kadan's like Subedei, he holds by the old way. But his father Ogedei was getting corrupted. He had started building himself a palace in Karakorum." Joffrey de Belmont snorted. "His palace was more like a stone box. Kadan was going to take you back to Karakorum as a present for his father."

"And now Ogedei's dead."

De Belmont shrugged. "We don't know yet who the next khan will be. Frankly, without this campaign in the West, Kadan hasn't much chance of getting elected, and he knows it. He may be indulging his temper now, but he's also clever enough to plan for the future. If the new Great Khan proves to be someone like Ogedei, someone who's already half seduced by Western toys, Kadan has the perfect gift—you." De Belmont drained the cup of wine in one long gulp and rose unsteadily to his feet. "I, on the other hand, am no more use to them. I'd better be getting back to the prisoners' lines before I'm missed. They'll want to have a full count of prisoners on the day when they shoot all of our useless bodies full of arrows."

"You think they'll do that?"

"Dear boy, they do it on a regular basis. Of course they will. They'll probably let us live till the fall, when they rendezvous with Subedei and Batu in Bulgaria. But then—" De Belmont passed one hand across his own throat and made an unpleasant clicking sound. "You haven't seen this army when it's moving really fast. They can't spare horses for prisoners, and they're not going to slow down to marching pace on our account. And they never, ever, let anybody go free. I don't know which of us I pity more, really," de Belmont murmured as he moved softly back into the darkness of the prisoners' lines, "me about to become a Mongol target, or you going to spend the rest of your life as a slave of the Great Khan in Karakorum."

Late in that summer, Marco Sanudo and Aude and the son Stephen had never seen landed in Ragusa. "Father here?" young Mark asked when they reached Marco's house in the city square, with its walled gardens overlooking the harbor.

"No, love. Your father is a long way from here," Aude replied.

The evasion irritated Marco. Couldn't she just admit that Stephen was dead? Marco knew it was too soon to remind her that by this time next year he would stand as a father to this boy who already had his name. He cursed to himself and took out his ill humor in a fault-finding inspection of the house and the narrow walled garden.

There were still late-blooming roses in the garden, and green vines were beginning to grow over the newly repaired walls. The view from the carved wooden loggia did not include the wooded hills of the Balkan peninsula, where an active imagination could see smoke still rising from remote homesteads. All that could be seen from the loggia was the deep blue-green Adriatic Sea and the coast of Italy on the horizon. Aude could lie on the screened terrace and breathe sea air, rest, and grow well while she looked toward Venice—her future home.

"I never looked forward to any feast day as I do to the

next Lenten season," Marco told Aude after she was settled into her rooms and had returned to the garden to visit with him.

"Is it true there are some people in town who have escaped from the Mongols?" Aude asked.

Marco made a mental note to speak to the gossiping old woman who kept the house for him. "A few peasants tell wild stories. I don't think any of them really escaped— more likely they were just on the fringes of the Mongol army, perhaps saw their homes burned and ran for the coast. Now they're begging for their bread and repaying charity by making up fantastic tales of things they never saw. I spoke with one of them who claimed that the Mongols can campaign in winter because their horses don't need fodder. They are trained to kick the snow away with their hooves and graze on whatever they can find underneath! Did you ever hear such a tale? Why, even I know that a destrier requires twenty pounds of grain and forage daily! No horse could possibly find so much under the winter snow!"

"Well," said Aude, "how do they campaign in winter, then? Because we certainly know that they can do that. I should like to talk with this man, Marco. He may have news—"

"I don't think any of the refugees came from as far away as Varad."

"All the same," Aude insisted, and Marco reluctantly agreed. After all, what harm could it do? Marco reasoned to himself. It might even help his cause. Once Aude had spoken with some of these poor broken men and had seen for herself that no one escaped from places so thoroughly under Mongol domination as Transylvania, she might be more ready to accept Stephen's death. She might even relent and agree to marriage before the second anniversary of the sack of Varad.

Marco began to think that he was a very clever fellow to have brought his Aude to Ragusa. Whistling between his teeth, he went off to give Jaroslav instructions about finding and interviewing any beggars who had really seen the Mongol army. Afterwards, he picked a great bouquet of the finest yellow roses in the garden and brought them in a brimming silver bowl to Aude's loggia.

* * *

Just as Joffrey de Belmont had predicted, early in the autumn of 1242, the Khans sent out a proclamation to the whole Mongol army, stating that all the captives who had been dragged this far might now consider themselves free to return to their own countries.

"You were wrong," said Stephen to de Belmont. "I will not be sent to build for the new Great Khan. All the prisoners will be freed."

"No. Wait and see. And *don't join the prisoners.*"

"The proclamation does not apply to this man," said a Mongol officer. "He is to return with us to Karakorum." Separated from Joffrey and the rest of the prisoners, Stephen watched the captives shuffling out of the Mongol camp. The prisoners were herded like cattle down a narrow valley leading to a plain where the Mongol horses had grazed the night before. Armed men on either side of the valley's slopes prevented the freed captives from straying.

Stephen felt a prickling uneasiness down his spine, a chill that had nothing to do with that day of early autumn sunshine. There were so many mounted, armed Mongols watching the shambling exodus of their captives. Had de Belmont been right? He squinted against the sun and was relieved to see Joffrey de Belmont's graying head between two other captives. If de Belmont thought the prisoners were to be slaughtered, surely he wouldn't have joined them? But probably he had not been given any choice in the matter. The Mongols weren't likely to ask their despised prisoners what they wanted to do.

The old knight had been sent away without his armor, without pay or thanks for his services to the Mongol army. But he was going free. Presumably that was payment enough. Stephen's throat ached with longing. Even the traitor de Belmont was going home to a Christian land while Stephen was to be dragged along behind the army to a desolate steppe full of savages. How could this happen? Stephen knew that if he went to Karakorum with the Mongols, he would never smell the resinous tang of the pine trees or the salt spray of the sea, never hear the church bells ringing or Christian voices raised in song.

In desperation, Stephen formed a plan: he would mingle with the mass of captives shuffling toward their freedom, and lose himself in the crowd. Who could pick him out of all those people? All Westerners looked alike to Mongols, just as Stephen had trouble telling the Mongols apart.

Stephen grinned at his guard and made squatting motions, mumbling the word the Mongols used for the dysentery that had plagued captives and soldiers alike whenever they camped more than a night or two in one place. The guard pinched his nose and motioned toward the narrow stand of trees behind the khan's tent. Presumably he'd been told not to take his eyes off Stephen, but he had also had enough of watching men squatting over ditches. A man with his bowels turning to burning water, in the cramps of dysentery, wasn't going to run anywhere. The guard knew he would be in trouble if he let Stephen foul the ground near the khan's tent and decided it would be better to let the prisoner retreat discreetly into the woods.

Stephen nodded and grinned his thanks and made off for the trees, not too fast to bely his mime of a man caught with the cramps. As soon as he was screened from the guard by a few low branches, he dropped to his stomach and crawled deeper into the wood.

He did not dare raise his head to look around him; he did not need to. As a boy in the choir at Ely he had whiled away the long hours of prayer and liturgy by mentally razing and rebuilding the cathedral around him. Now he applied the same trick of memory to the hills and valley of the campsite. His architect's eye had automatically noted each rise in the ground, each crevice and fold of earth that would have been a problem if the Mongols were raising stone buildings instead of blue cloth tents. Face pressed to the ground, eyes closed, he mentally recreated the entire site without looking farther than the carpet of decaying leaves and resinous needles before him.

To his left, the ground sloped upward to a high, barren ridge. There were no trees to conceal him, but there were large rocks clustered like a giant's abandoned dice. On the other side of the ridge, the woods sloped down toward the fertile plain where the Mongol prisoners were being herded. If Stephen could get over the ridge unseen, he might be able to make his way through the woods, well behind the Mongol horsemen who were keeping the prisoners from straggling. Once they reached the field, the prisoners would spread out into little groups, wandering and arguing and picking the directions they wanted to travel in. Stephen could slip out of the shelter of the woods and join a group when the Mongols were not looking. By the time Kadan noticed his disappearance, he would be just one of an innumerable ragged crowd. And the khans were in a hurry to set off for Karakorum. Stephen did not think that they would waste much time sifting through the crowd for one artisan. Kadan had plenty of other toys to take home as trophies.

His long crawl upward to the ridge was an agonizing contest of nerves against time. Any noise he made might alert the guards. A long absence might alert the guards. And what if he took so long that the prisoners had already dispersed before he reached the field? Sweat trickled down his face and old dried twigs reached out of the leaf mold to prick his skin. Twice he thought he heard the shouts of his guards only to realize that it was the Mongol horsemen urging the prisoners on.

At the top of the stony, barren ridge, Stephen abandoned caution and dashed from one great rock to another, thankful that the guards were all looking the other way. He was headed toward the stream of captives still descending to the plain and now he had only to get down this last wooded slope.

He managed it on his hands and knees, ducking behind bushes and holding his breath every time a guard twitched. He was just behind the scrubby, thorny vines at the edge of the field when the last guard's pony sniffed man-scent in the woods, snorted and pawed the ground.

There was no bush large enough to give shelter here. Stephen froze in plain sight, knowing his torn white tunic must stand out clearly against the dark brown trees and mold of the forest.

"Here, you. What are you doing off the path? Get back with the rest."

The staccato words, jerked out in the simplified speech the Mongols used for their prisoners, made Stephen freeze.

"Come on," grunted the guard with a wave of his sword, and Stephen stumbled forward through the low underbrush to join the moving column of prisoners. He could hardly believe it. But after all, there was no reason why this guard should know him for Khan Kadan's pet builder

artist. Hadn't he just been telling himself that all Westerners looked alike to the savages?

And now Stephen was free, anonymous, mixed in with
all the other emaciated, half-naked conscripts who were
being herded forward onto the flat open field at the
bottom of the valley. From here Stephen could see the
ring of cliffs that closed in three sides of the wide field.
These cliffs, four to six feet high, formed a natural fence
that made the field a good place to graze horses. But
perhaps not such a good one to send reprieved prisoners.
How would they get out? Whether they were bound
south, north, or west, they'd either have to retrace their
steps or scale the rocks—and most of them were in no
condition to do even that little bit of climbing. Maybe the
Mongols wanted them to stay here, out of the way, until
the army had broken camp and moved on. A short delay
really didn't matter to Stephen when the wide world of
freedom stretched before him. In a few weeks he would
see Aude again, and that was a dream that seemed impossible until now. A world that held Aude safe, and him alive
against all expectation, could not be otherwise than beautiful.

Stephen grinned and put one friendly arm over the thin
shoulders of the boy next to him. "It's a good day to be
alive," he said in English, not really caring whether he
was understood or not. "A good day to be free."

The boy smiled back, exposing broken teeth and an
unhealed slash down the corner of his mouth, and said
something in a Slavonic accent. It was probably the same
thing Stephen had just said. What else was there to say, on
a day like this? They smiled at each other in perfect amity,
with no need of a translator. Stephen loved the entire mass
of thin, scarred, confused captives, some of them as frightened by the prospect of freedom as they had been by their
original capture so many months before. They were all his
fellows, first in misfortune and now in freedom. And they
were also his hiding place; among them, he was invisible.

Nevertheless, general brotherly love aside, it would be
as well to team with somebody who spoke his language
and was headed his way. De Belmont, who knew something of fighting and had traveled through most of these
lands, would definitely be a good person to find before the
freed prisoners dispersed.

Stephen clapped the Slav boy on the shoulder, bade him

a cheery farewell, and made for the rocky ledges on the far side of the field. He scrambled onto a ledge that was just inches wide but already two or three feet off the ground, and scanned the crowd for de Belmont's gray head and erect back.

Stephen was still standing there, peering under the shade of his hand, when the guards drew their swords and charged into the standing mass of men. All the horses that had been waiting on the slopes, perhaps a tenth part of the Mongol army, thundered into the valley in a screaming cavalry charge of men and horses and flickering sharp blades.

There was nowhere to run; the people were packed in the field as close as standing corn, and the Mongol blades mowed them down like corn in harvest time. The Mongol ponies trampled the fallen with their sharp hooves, indifferent to blood and screams as good war-horses should be. The rocky ledge was hard against Stephen's back, the top of the ledge inches above his reach. There were panic-stricken men and boys clawing at the narrow shelf where he stood as though two feet in height could lift them out of reach of the Mongol swords. There were girls, too; Stephen saw one who had been pretty when she was carried off from her village a few months earlier. He remembered that day, for some reason—the girl's fat tear-streaked cheeks and her blond braids bouncing. Now she was no longer fat, her braids were a snarl of matted grease, and her mouth was stretched into a round shape of terror. And she hadn't been pretty since the night after the raid on the village, when the Mongol who took her lost interest and threw her out for his comrades to enjoy. But she'd lived through that night and the next and the next, and she wanted desperately to live now. Stephen reached out his hand and pulled her up beside him, with some confused notion of shielding her body behind his. But it was too late; the Mongol cavalry had reached the rocks. Even as the girl gasped her thanks, a sword sliced her naked throat. The downward motion of the blade caught Stephen on the shoulder; as the girl's body fell heavily against him, knocking him off balance, the blade came up again in a vicious slashing arc that sent sheets of fire through his right thigh. Stephen fell heavily on the bodies of those who'd been clutching at his knees a moment ago, and the girl fell over him, drenching him in blood.

To his left, someone groaned, *"Bozhe! Bo—"*

One stroke of a sword cut off the Slav's cry to God. Stephen lay very still. His face was pressed against the face of a dead man whose wide-open blue eyes were fixed with the terror and confusion he must have felt as his freedom turned to death. Above Stephen, the girl's body was a light, stiffening, intolerable weight that filled him with horror. If he threw her off, the Mongols would know that someone still lived in this mass of corpses, and one of them would ride over to finish the work. Stephen gritted his teeth and lay in agony, not daring to move. His right leg throbbed and he could not tell how much of the blood that soaked him was his and how much came from the girl on top of him. The sun was rising, burning off the last of the morning mists, and the sweet stench of blood filled his nostrils until he thought he would retch with every shallow breath. Stephen could still hear the Mongols calling to one another, crossing the field of blood on their fast ponies to make sure that no one had escaped the slaughter.

He lay in the heap of bodies while the morning turned to blazing noon, suffering both from the sun's heat and from the burning of his wound. There were a few signs of life: occasionally a prisoner groaned; the Mongols were striking camp on the hilltop; someone was turning over corpses with the butt end of his feathered lance. As the morning wore on, Stephen's mind wandered and sometimes he thought he was back in the little church in Dunwich, waiting for the sea to rise up and flood the town; then his mind jumped to the present, for here he was burning with yellow-faced demons poking at the bodies of the damned. No, there was no fire here. He must be thinking of Ely. The black-suited Brabantines riding into the cathedral . . . a burning church . . . no, that was wrong, they didn't burn the church, that was somewhere else, some other time, and there had been a woman with him . . .

"Bianca!"

The straining of his throat in a soundless scream jerked him out of the vivid dream, trembling with cold in the middle of this hot autumn day. Had he really screamed? Stephen lay quite still, waiting to feel a Mongol lance driven into his back. Nothing happened. His body had been encased in a tight suit of armor that crackled when he moved and pulled at his skin. The buzzing of the flies was becoming intolerable; the feel of their tiny feet crawling across his face was worse than the agony in his thigh. He had to breathe. Very slowly, with infinite caution, Stephen raised his head a few inches until he could peer out across the field.

There was no movement but the crawling black masses of flies clustering over the open wounds of the dead; no noise but the buzzing of their wings. The narrow pass leading up to the Mongol camp was empty, and the sounds of clinking gear and whinnying ponies had disappeared.

When Stephen tried to crawl out of the mass of bodies where he lay, his right leg crumpled beneath him and his head swam with pain. For a moment, maybe longer, the world was black and he was too weak to move.

The next time, he moved more cautiously, in a crablike sideways crawl that took all the weight on his left knee while the useless right leg dragged behind him. His skin cracked and stung as the coat of dried blood that had covered him broke open. He ignored this as well as his aching left shoulder and terrible thirst. Trailing his leg behind him, Stephen crawled over bloody bodies and limbs to get to the edge of the woods where there was a little stream. He fainted three more times on his slow progress across the field; the third time he woke with his face in the mud at the edge of the stream, staring at the water that was just out of reach.

"Want a drink?"

Stephen started upward like a fish that feels the net around it, cried out with pain as he jerked his right leg forward, and sank down again with his fists clenched around two handfuls of mud and pebbles.

"Not so loud," said Joffrey de Belmont reprovingly. "I'm not absolutely sure all the devils have left. And do try not to claw up the ground like that. Sometimes they come back looking for the trails of wounded men. They do a thorough job."

He dipped his shirt into the stream and wrung it out over Stephen's head. Drops of water, flavored with the sweat and dirt in the linen, trickled into his mouth and soaked into the furrowed dry surface of his tongue, the sweetest draught he had ever tasted.

"I don't know why you keep turning up," said de Belmont as Stephen sucked at the last drops of moisture in his shirt. "I suppose I must be meant to save you. It seems to be a repeated factor in our relationship." He pulled the shirt out of Stephen's weak grasp. "And now," he went on, tearing the linen into strips as he spoke, "before it gets dark, let's have a look at that nasty wound on your thigh. Have a stick to bite on; I don't want you making any more noise."

When de Belmont bound the first strip of damp linen about his thigh, the world went black. Stephen tried to speak, to tell de Belmont that it was already too dark, but there was a piece of wood stuck between his jaws and de Belmont's face was already too far away, receding through the funnel of darkness.

PART VII

Closing
the Circle

◪

1241–1250

CHAPTER

36

*U*pon waking, the first thing Stephen felt was the pain. A rhythmic shower of fiery sparks scorched his leg. Something terrible had happened, or was about to happen, and Stephen had to stop it. No. He was too late. There had been an explosion in the glassblowers' shed. "Tell them to put out the fire," Stephen mumbled. "Where's Geoffrey?"

"Quiet!" There was a hand over his mouth, a man bending over him. Stephen struggled for breath, moved his leg and lost consciousness. The next time he woke, it was daylight, and he knew where he was, but he could not remember how he had got there or what Joffrey de Belmont was doing beside him. Stephen's vision was blurred: there seemed to be two of de Belmont, and behind him the trees were dancing. In his dreams there'd been swords, and people screaming, and a barren field suddenly covered with blood. Stephen concentrated fiercely until there were four Joffrey de Belmonts bending over him. "You should be dead," Stephen said.

"So should you. Keep your voice down, will you? I don't want them to hear us."

Stephen frowned. "Mongols? Aren't they gone?"

"Not the Mongols. *Them.*" De Belmont nodded downhill, toward the field of death. Stephen had the vague

impression that there was something moving there besides
flies and ravens, but he was too tired to think about
it.

For the next two days, weak as a baby and almost as
confused, Stephen obeyed Joffrey de Belmont's whispered
commands to lie still and keep quiet. He took the water
that de Belmont brought him from the brook and tried not
to think about the stench that was rising from the field.
The nights were cold and they shivered together under
the leaves, but the days were hot with the autumn sun in a
clear blue sky. The bodies in the field swelled with the
gases of their own decomposition.

"At least the stink keeps us from feeling hungry," said de
Belmont with a grim smile.

Over those two days and nights, Stephen and Joffrey
spoke in cautious whispers, comparing notes on their
experiences during the massacre. De Belmont had believed
the captives were being marched to their death and had
bribed one of the Mongol guards to let him into the steep
rocky woods that rose on either side of their path.

"What with?" asked Stephen.

De Belmont frowned. "It doesn't matter. Anyway, as
soon as I got out of sight of the Mongols, I dived into a
hollow and covered myself with leaves. I didn't dare move
until the screaming was over and the Mongol army had
left. It seemed to take forever."

"It took longer if you were lying in the field," said
Stephen, and explained how he'd pretended to be dead
until the Mongol horsemen were gone.

De Belmont hadn't been looking for Stephen when they
met at the brook that first time; he'd just been thirsty. De
Belmont pointed out that if he had thought about the
matter at all, he would have assumed that Stephen was
already on his way back to Karakorum with the Mongol
army. Who'd have thought Stephen would be so foolish as
to run away and join a bunch of prisoners destined for
slaughter?

Stephen got the distinct impression that Joffrey de
Belmont wasn't too pleased to have pulled a wounded
architect out of the stream. With a right leg that might
never work again and an intermittent fever that left him
weak, Stephen could see that he was something of a
liability to the old knight. He tried once or twice to

express his gratitude, but de Belmont seemed embarrassed and brushed his thanks aside.

On the third morning, de Belmont decreed that it was time for them to move out of the valley. They'd been keeping hidden, he told Stephen, because of certain men who had been searching the bloated and decomposing bodies in the field.

"Mongols?"

"No. Maybe worse. Human rats. A few peasants survived—a few of them always do. They must have been hiding in the woods and starving all this time."

"Like us."

"Oh? And do you propose to wade through rotting bodies, looking for food and trinkets that the Mongols may have missed? Maybe you'd like to cut yourself a bit of meat, a nice scrawny chine of captive, to roast over the campfire?"

Stephen grimaced in disgust, and de Belmont's skeletal smile flickered across his face. "So, you see," he said, "not very much like us. But we might get to be like them if we don't do something. We've got to get out of here. We need to find food and people."

De Belmont thought their best chance was to head for the coast. The Mongol army had been moving that way too fast to bother to reduce all the fortified towns and islands they passed. "Ragusa, Trogir, Kotor. We'll get a ship."

Stephen was in no condition to argue, and, in any event, he had no better plan. De Belmont ventured into the charnel house of the plain to retrieve a Mongol sword that had been thrown away after it was blunted on the bones of too many captives. He used the dull blade to hack down a sapling which would serve as a rough crutch for Stephen. Then De Belmont went back into the pile of corpses, with a strip of wet linen tied across his nose, to steal and wash some rags that they could use as cloaks on the journey.

Stephen had nothing to do but follow, on a leg whose gaping wound opened every time he swung the crutch forward, on a stomach as empty as De Belmont's after two days of living on stream water and roots.

For three more days they struggled on through the endless forest, occasionally finding an overgrown path to follow. From time to time, Joffrey climbed a tree to get a sense of their direction. "There are tall spires that way, maybe a church they didn't burn," he would report, or, "There's a break in the forest ahead—could be cultivated land," and Stephen would set off in the direction he indicated.

There was water to drink, and they experimented with anything they could chew and force into their empty stomachs, from grubs to bark. De Belmont kept some of those nasty meals down. Stephen's body rejected almost everything he tried to swallow. Even the pure, clean stream water tasted like dirty metal. That, he knew, was caused by the fever from his wound. His leg ached and swelled around Joffrey de Belmont's hasty bandaging job, and there were ominous red streaks going up into his groin and an evil smell coming from under the strips of linen. They were both afraid to open the bandages and see what lay underneath. The gnawing pain in his leg had spread throughout his whole body. Stephen limped through the forest in a shroud of fire, so hot that the chill of the nights meant nothing to him, trembling with fever and weakness, and carried only by the force of Joffrey de Belmont's will to survive.

When they reached the church spire de Belmont had spotted, it turned out to be the only standing part of the church; the rest had collapsed in a heap of charred timbers, burnt mortar, and cracked stones. There were bones scattered throughout the ashes, and a few black circles on the ground to the east of the church showed where the peasants' huts had burned to the ground.

De Belmont groaned and sank down on the ground. "They've been here, too. They've been everywhere."

"Shall we keep going?" Stephen suggested tentatively. "You said there was another break in the forest farther on. Fields, maybe."

De Belmont shook his head and refused to get up. He sat with his hands lying limply in front of him, staring at the burnt ruins of the church. "We're too weak. We'll starve before we get there, and there'll be nothing there anyway. And you'll be dead."

"Probably." But today Stephen's leg was not paining him quite so much, and there'd been a cool damp drizzle that calmed the fire burning under his skin. He was too hungry and in too much pain to sit down and give himself up to fate, as de Belmont seemed to have done. But without the knight's will to drive him on, he felt lost.

Behind one of the burnt circles, a patch of brilliant green stood out against the pale gold and gray of the autumn grasses. It caught Stephen's eye and he limped over to see what it was. There was something growing. He stared, sniffed, dropped to one knee and cried out with the agony of bending his stiffened right leg. But it was worth it, to be down on the ground, smelling the rich, dizzying, sweet, pungent odor of growing food. Stephen clawed at the earth with both hands and came up with clusters of little bulbs whose sharp smell made his mouth water. Here were the remains of a peasant's garden: garlic and onions and radishes, all growing together in the neglected earth. He crammed a double handful of the bulbs into his mouth, earth and all. Tears sprang to his eyes at the pungent burning taste. He felt stronger as soon as he'd gulped down the first mouthful.

"De Belmont," he shouted thickly through the last unchewed stems of garlic. "Over here. Food."

They gorged on the tiny sour bulbs as though they were roast peacock and almond cakes. Though their stomachs swelled with gas and growled because of the unexpected load of food, Stephen and Joffrey ate on until they had stripped the earth bare. Stephen felt his brain working with new clarity after the food. Garlic and radishes were all very well, but they had only awakened his craving for something more. These peasants would have kept pigs, but the Mongols must have driven off the pigs already. They must have been rich peasants, rich enough to build a church with a spire for their village. Some of these people would have had food stored away in case of a bad year, and it wouldn't have been kept out in the open for anybody to see and steal it. Stephen remembered Edric's and Aude's smoky hut in the fens—the strips of dried eel were concealed in the rafters and in the cunningly designed pits in the dirt floor. A man could have walked, slept, quarreled, and made love on that floor for a week without ever realizing that under his feet lay smoked fish in earth-covered jars, closely woven reed baskets full of waterfowl pieces preserved in their own fat, strings of sun-dried onions and mallow. Stephen's nose quivered with the memory of forgotten rich tastes and he struggled clumsily to his feet, swinging his crutch forward and poking at the ground inside the burnt circles.

"What y'doing?" de Belmont asked, but before Stephen could answer, he had dozed off, somnolent with his distended stomach and the weariness of the walk.

The seventh hut was not completely destroyed; a ring of stones surrounding a cooking pit showed that this peasant had been rich enough to build himself what was, for the neighborhood, a fine house. When Stephen levered the stones of the cooking pit aside with the tip of his crutch, he found treasure: a sack of coarse gritty flour, strips of dried meat, and a whole sausage, pungent with garlic.

They feasted that night, but with moderation; already bloated from their orgy of garlic and radishes, they could tolerate only a few bites of the dried meat and a little of the flour thinned to a sticky paste with cold water. A fire would have been too dangerous, even if it hadn't been too wet for de Belmont to strike sparks off the rocks with the battered Mongol blade. The last thing they wanted was to draw the attention of the fugitives or of starving bandits, like the ones who'd picked over the scene of the last massacre. They agreed to rest where they were for the night; in the morning they would look for more food caches and start toward the coast again.

The unaccustomed exertion of the day, kneeling and digging and prying at rocks, had irritated Stephen's wounded leg. Pain and fever washed over him in waves throughout the night, interrupting his sleep with waking dreams and making him toss and moan on the hard ground. His grasp on reality weakened during the night, and by the time the sky began to grow light, his hands and feet were ice cold, but he was burning everywhere else. Feverish and confused, Stephen clawed at the linen bandages that were suddenly too tight to be borne, moaning for Brother Coluin to come and tend him.

"Stephen? Stephen! Lie down, man. Your noise will bring the whole forest down on us."

"No, I won't wake the monks. The infirmary is far enough from the dorter," Stephen assured him. "But why—" He pulled at the bandages. "—Why did he beat me on the leg this time?"

"You're raving." The lean, gray face above him was not Coluin's. Stephen drifted away on a tide of confused memories. Nothing was quite real except the pain, and even that grew less real if he lay perfectly still. Why was Coluin pulling the bandages away? It hurt too much. Not Coluin—de Belmont. Not Ely—somewhere unimaginably far away from Ely. They were starving to death in the forests of Slavonia, and for some reason Joffrey de Belmont wanted to make matters worse by prodding at his wound.

Stephen batted at the hands that were probing his open wound, sending spasms of pain through his body. He was too weak to stop his tormentor.

"The leg will have to come off."

"No!"

"Don't be a stupid peasant. I've seen men die of wounds like this. Which would you rather—lose the leg, or let the corruption spread through your whole body? I'll get the sword."

"No." Panic gave Stephen the strength to clutch at de Belmont's wrist with thin, wiry fingers. "No. If you take my leg off, I'll bleed to death."

"It's quicker than waiting for the corruption to get you."

Something in de Belmont's voice told Stephen that he knew his clumsy surgery would probably kill his patient. Why was de Belmont doing this? Speed? Ah, yes. He didn't want to be stuck here, eating the food they had miraculously found, waiting and waiting for Stephen to die.

De Belmont had the Mongol blade, blunt as it was from serving as a staff and a woodchopper. There had to be some way to stop him. Stephen stared up at death in the hands of the man he'd thought of as a friend, and felt his head spin.

"Go. Leave me here. Go on to the coast—send help back," he gasped.

Sweat trickled down Stephen's forehead as de Belmont slowly lowered the blade. The point dug into the ground inches from Stephen's face as de Belmont leaned on the blade, considering. "You'll probably die here."

"I'll take my chances."

"The food?"

"Divide it. There's enough for both."

De Belmont nodded slowly. Stephen closed his eyes and fainted with relief. When he woke again, the burning in his leg was matched by the heat of the autumn sun. He was lying in full sun, far from the little stream that had provided water for them yesterday, and his tunic was gone. So were the bandages that had covered his wounded leg. So was all the food.

CHAPTER

37

❏

*T*hroughout the autumn and winter of 1242, a trickle of refugees from the Mongol wrath reached the Dalmatian coast. Faithful to his promise to Aude, Marco Sanudo told his agents to question everyone about their experiences with the Mongols, and to send him any man who might know something about the fair-haired English builder who must have died in Varad.

For months Marco learned nothing. Most of the refugees were ignorant peasants who had spent their entire lives in some valley not ten leagues from the coast. They had no information to give except that the Mongols had burned their village and killed those who could not flee into the forest quickly enough. A few refugees were captives, freed when the Mongol armies turned back to Karakorum. These men spoke of a massacre of unarmed prisoners, a field of blood where they had been struck down unconscious and had wakened to find themselves under attack by men who roamed the woods like wolves and ate the flesh of the dead to get through that starving winter.

Had anyone else survived that massacre? Did they remember a fair-haired Englishman among the prisoners? Marco questioned them patiently, but without much hope of dragging sense or information out of their shattered brains and starved bodies. Besides, it was pointless. Even if by some miracle Stephen had been taken prisoner at Varad instead of being slaughtered, even if he'd lived to follow the Mongol army on its path of destruction, he would have died in the final massacre of which these stragglers spoke. Aude's hopes were a thin ill-spun thread, frayed and strained, but never quite broken. And Marco had promised to give her time.

Finally, in the season of the Christmas feasts, a Venetian merchant in Trogir bought some jewels from a tall, emaciated, evasive man who carried himself like one used to wearing heavy armor, who walked as if it hurt his feet and his pride to be on foot instead of on horseback. The merchant questioned the man about the source of the jewels, and, to avoid being thrown into the strong sea-cave prisons of Trogir, the man admitted that he had been a captive with the Mongol army, and before that a knight in the service of an English lord.

The Venetian merchant owed some favors to the House of Sanudo. He gave the stranger wine enough to fuddle his head, promised him passage to Venice on the next ship out, and packed him drunk aboard a coasting cog headed for Ragusa, with two servants to see that he reached Marco Sanudo.

"I would have come happily to see you of my own will, if that fool in Trogir had told me what he wanted," Joffrey de Belmont said when he recovered from the combined effects of drink and seasickness and faced Marco Sanudo in the counting room at the villa in Ragusa. "A friend of Stephen the builder's! Imagine finding such a one in this godforsaken country! I thought we two had no friends but one another."

"You know Stephen?"

"Knew."

"He lives?"

De Belmont sighed. "You must have heard how the Mongols use their prisoners. When the army moves fast, captives are massacred. I tried to warn Stephen that they were lying when they promised to set us free, but he had too much faith in humanity for his own good."

"Some men survived the Field of Poppies." The scene of that last massacre had already acquired a name in Ragusa.

De Belmont looked carefully at Marco, trying to gauge

the real intentions of this dark, slender merchant with his unreadable face. "You wish to believe that your friend might have lived. One clings, of course, to any shred of hope."

Marco's face did not change, but de Belmont saw one of his fists clench convulsively under the table. "His wife prays daily for news. Certain knowledge of his death would at least end her suspense."

"Alas," said de Belmont slowly, "I must tell you that there is no possible doubt of Stephen's death."

"You saw his body with your own eyes?"

The Venetian's hands had relaxed again as his fingers smoothed out the fine velvet of the gown that hung over his knees. With his eyes on his fingers, Joffrey de Belmont spun a long and satisfying story that told how his dear friend Stephen the builder had died in his own arms of wounds incurred at the Field of Poppies. He went on to describe the close friendship that had developed between them during their captivity, the efforts he had made to see that Stephen was better clothed and fed than the rest of the prisoners, and his own intense grief when Stephen refused to heed his warnings about the upcoming massacre.

Joffrey de Belmont had learned long ago that the best lie is one that sticks close to the truth. He was entirely accurate in describing how he himself had bribed a Mongol guard to let him slip into the forest, how he'd lain there through the day of slaughter without moving, how he'd found Stephen so badly wounded that he could not walk. He even described Stephen's wounds accurately, exaggerating no more than necessary. The only lies he told were, first, that he'd gone in search of Stephen instead of accidentally stumbling over him at the stream; and second, that Stephen had died then and there rather than days later and miles closer to the coast of Dalmatia.

They were not very big lies. If Joffrey had known Stephen had been stupid enough to join the prisoners destined for slaughter, he might actually have gone to look for him. He might. One couldn't tell. And for the rest, that suppurating wound in Stephen's thigh had surely killed him weeks ago; it was only a kindness to the man's wife and friend to suppress the story of how he'd left the stubborn bastard to die on his own when he refused to let Joffrey end his sufferings more quickly.

Joffrey never even thought about the cache of food that Stephen had discovered and that he'd stolen, and the tunic and bandages that had served as extra covering for him on cold nights. Only a fool would have left such valuable things with a dead man or one who was as good as dead, and Joffrey de Belmont was no fool.

He accepted the rewards Marco pressed upon him and was out of Ragusa with a winter caravan before the end of the week. Marco's gold, and the remaining Mongol loot sewn inside his rags, would allow Joffrey to end his days in comfort in some decent Western country with a warm climate and a pleasant village church whose bells would ring daily. He asked no more; and he gave no more thought to the man he'd left to die in the forests of Dalmatia, save to thank him for having had rich and generous friends in Ragusa.

There were two more food caches that the Mongols had not found, neither as good as the first one. From a pit under the back wall of the church Stephen got more of the coarse flour and some onions, black and rotting on the outside but still sweet at the center. And at the very edge of the village, under a half-burnt huddle of twigs and stones, another pit yielded real treasure: half a moldy white cheese wrapped in a buttered linen cloth.

Those discoveries came some days after Joffrey de Belmont abandoned him to die. On the first day, Stephen had dragged himself to the stream. Dampness and shade were welcome then, before the afternoon, when clouds thickened, and the cold evening drew on. He'd shivered through the night waiting to die, had lain by the stream another day (two? three?) passing time in delirious dreams, chatting with ghosts and cursing the constant throb of pain in his leg. Brother Daniel pointed out that a boy who ran away from his vows could hardly expect a better fate than dying like an animal in the forest. Bianca floated over the trees and stretched her arms wide in longing, and Stephen shrieked, cowered, and flung an arm over his eyes to keep from seeing her poor mutilated breasts. Ghostly armies rode through the village, mercenaries and Saracens and Mongols, and the white figures of slaughtered children rose out of the ashes.

Late on a cloudy afternoon, the ghosts changed their

nature. Instead of Bianca, it was Aude who came to him, a slender figure in a patched brown tunic that blended with the trees around the stream. "But you're not dead," said Stephen stupidly.

"Neither are you."

"Wait!"

He reached for the hem of her tunic and caught hold of a gnarled brown root sticking out of the stream bank. Movement was painful. Stephen waited for the agony of the fire burning through him, the sickening pain that made him faint when he moved. It didn't come. His leg hurt, but it wasn't enough to make him swoon.

For the first time in days Stephen looked at his own wound. He'd been lying in his own filth and the leg stank and the open edges were raw and disgusting. But the smell of corruption wasn't there, and the deep muscles that had been cut almost through were closing again. Somehow the exercise of struggling through the forest, the hours of lying almost naked under the sun, and the clear running water of the stream through which he'd crawled had begun the slow process of healing.

Stephen tried to remember the words of a prayer, but his head was swimming with hunger, and the ghosts kept chattering at him. They were friendly ghosts now. Count Jokai appeared in all his weight of armor, looking young and fresh and eager for battle, not weary and bandaged, as Stephen had last seen him.

"Up, soldier!" he roared, and Stephen winced at the noise.

"Not so loud," he implored. "You'll bring the King's mercenaries down on us."

"I'll stop when you're on your feet. No man of mine lounges in the shade when there's fighting to be done!"

Just to silence the count, Stephen found a long branch to serve as a crutch and pushed himself up to lean against a tree.

"Very good," applauded Abbot Samson. "Now see if you can make it to the garden where those fine radishes grew. Remember, as St. Denis said when he walked seven leagues bearing his own head under his arm, the first step is the hardest."

The radishes Stephen found were even sweeter than they'd been that first day, when he and de Belmont had

found them just as they were on the point of giving up.
Upon finishing his meal, Stephen set out across an eternity of root-covered forest floor, down bottomless ravines and up sheer cliffs. By the end of the day his entire left side ached badly from the bruising falls he'd taken over and over again. When he looked back, Stephen realized he had only crossed one shallow valley, and the burnt-out remains of the village were still clearly visible through the naked trees.

He could have wept, but he was ashamed to let Mam and Brother Daniel see his tears. They were there on either side of him throughout the long afternoon, floating without effort over the rocks and ditches that gave him so much trouble, and they wouldn't go away when he sat down under a tree to rest through the night.

"You're a stupid lazy boy and a disgrace to the convent," Brother Daniel said, "but with God's help I will make you a fitting servant for Him."

Mam's voice was sharp and shrill. "You'd better get up. There's a great wave coming. A great wave coming. A great wave coming."

Wearily, to please her, Stephen stumbled a few paces farther and settled with his back against a rocky cliff. But that wasn't good enough. She nagged and whined until he heaved himself up onto the first ledge of the cliff and took shelter under a flaky outcropping of rock. There he curled his tired and shivering body around the food sack, too exhausted even to nibble on one of the dried onions.

During the night, a cold penetrated through Stephen's bones, and he woke to find the world transformed by snow. The threatening gray clouds of the previous day had given way to a brilliant blue sky and a sun that sparkled without giving warmth. The tree where he'd rested the night before was covered up to its first branches by a freakish drifting of powdery snow; if he'd fallen asleep there, he might never have wakened under his cold blanket.

"Thank you, Mam," he said without surprise.

"Do you know where you are now?" Her voice was sharp with angry concern for him.

"Yes, of course." But when he tried to reason it out, his head ached and he got confused again. Joffrey de Belmont had killed Aude and abandoned him here in the snow. He had to find de Belmont and kill him. Aude's spirit wanted revenge; she was crying out to him now, her long fair hair whipped by the wind that stirred up the eddies of snow like waves in the ocean.

Stephen frowned. That wasn't right . . . Aude had curly dark hair. She wasn't dead. It was somebody else. He couldn't remember. It didn't matter. De Belmont had sins to answer for, and he was going to find him and kill him. He was going to the sea.

Stephen slid off the ledge, winced as the food sack tied around his neck struck his left shoulder with a punishing thump, and set his crutch down in the snow. He took his first fall of the day when the tip of the crutch slid down into a leaf-filled hole concealed beneath the blanket of snow. Traveling in the snow was twice as hard as walking through the woods had been, and that had already seemed impossible. Now that he could not see where he was putting his crutch, walking was twice impossible.

"There's a flaw in your logic," said Joscelin, hanging in the branches of a tree where the sun glistened on ice crystals.

Ibn Masoud stroked his beard and bobbed in the next tree. "I must agree with your Western colleague. A thing cannot be more than impossible."

Stephen went on. As starvation ate away at him, the distance he could travel decreased and the swirling confusion inside his head increased. The pain of his wounded leg was no longer as bad as the hunger gnawing at his insides, the bursting cold sores on his lips and fingers, and the bruised, broken skin of his feet. If it hadn't been for Brother Daniel telling Stephen not to give up hope, he would have been seriously tempted to lie down in the snow and go to sleep.

On the day the snow ended, he had his last and greatest bit of luck. Though it didn't seem like luck at first. Unable to judge direction during the long days and nights when the sun and stars were covered, and unfit to take any but the easiest of the impassable tracks through the snow-covered land, Stephen had been surprised when he stumbled into a clearing where three white lumps rose, with smoke coming through the top of the largest beehive shape.

Equally surprised was the man who stared at him from across the clearing. The man's short, squat figure and his thick layer of warm furs made him resemble a mountain beast. His face was black with a short beard, and his wild, starved, glittering eyes rested on Stephen and saw food.

There was a short, chipped blade protruding from his clenched fist. He saw Stephen looking at it, chuckled deep in his throat, and moved forward across the clearing, keeping the snow-covered huts between them. His shoulders were working back and forth under the furs as he spiraled in closer and closer, like a hungry dog circling a tempting morsel. His face kept changing, like something seen through the mists of time, like a reflection in a rippled pool. It was a wolf's face, a skull, a knife. Stephen shook his head and forced his eyes to make sense of what was before him. Only then did the shifting features become a man's face again. Immediately Stephen recognized Joffrey de Belmont.

Stephen grinned back at Joffrey de Belmont in a bandit's furs. This was the fight Stephen had been coming to; how kind of de Belmont to meet him! He braced his left foot against a rock and grasped the crutch firmly in his right hand, ready to lift it and use it like a spear when his enemy was close enough.

The sudden, vicious rush took him by surprise. Stephen managed to get the crutch up and jab it weakly at de Belmont, but the point slipped harmlessly off the furs. When he'd torn it loose from the tree, the crutch had a sharp jagged end, but days of walking had rounded it smooth again. And now Joffrey was on him, and without the crutch he had no support. The face was not Joffrey de Belmont's handsome aging visage, but the wolf-face of a starving stranger. Stephen went crashing backward into the snow, gagging from the sour rank smell of his attacker. The man crouched on his body, a light burden of knobbly knees and elbows. As the sharp knife was raking down his unprotected side, Stephen thrashed away from the blade and brought up the crutch between them. It was too long to jab effectively at his opponent, close-locked as they were, but it was all he had. Stephen pushed the man off his chest, using the crutch in two hands like a quarterstaff, and the bandit laughed again and pulled the crutch away from him with a quick twist. Stephen held on desperately with the one hand that wasn't completely numb, and the bandit pulled, tugged, and growled like a frustrated dog.

Stephen used the strength of the man's pull against him to haul himself up on his one good leg, only to go spinning as the bandit broke the crutch in two with a lucky kick. It cracked down the middle into two long torn pieces. The bandit threw his piece away and came at Stephen again with the knife. His face was shifting again, quivering like a pool of water, de Belmont, the bandit, de Belmont, killer, killer, killer.

Stephen stabbed back with the broken end of the crutch. It sank into the mass of furs but the bandit kept coming, yellowed cracked teeth bared and hand upraised to deliver a fatal blow.

That blow never fell. Instead the man's body sagged against Stephen, pressing him into the snow, and the sweet smell of fresh blood joined the stench of his rotting teeth. The blood trickled out of his open mouth and the eyes were fixed in their gloating stare.

It was not de Belmont. Only another poor madman starving in the woods. There would be no more hunger and cold for this one, anyway. Stephen dragged himself free of the man's body and discovered what had happened. The sharp, splintered end of the spear had gone between the bulky furs and right through the bandit's ribs, killing him in the midst of his rush.

Somewhere a girl was screaming. And Stephen's leg hurt like the fires of hell. The bandit had fallen right on the wound and he'd felt something tear open, a small matter when he thought the knife was about to go into his throat, but now it troubled him. He was too weak and dizzy to fight anymore, too weak even to sit up. He lay back in the snow and watched the patterns his snowburnt eyes traced on the gray clouds above. Black sparks were wheeling and diving in orderly spirals, and Stephen wondered if the screaming girl had belonged to the man who attacked him and if she meant to kill him now.

Very slowly, creeping like insects across the trampled, bloody snow, the people of the huts came out to see what had happened while they cowered in their flimsy shelters.

CHAPTER

38

◻

They were no friends of the dead man's; that was all Stephen understood of their thick Slavic speech and friendly mime on that first night. They brought Stephen into the biggest hut, and laid him by the fire. There he sweated out the last of his fever and drank a sour gruel of herbs and grain from a wooden bowl whose rim was crusted with the remnants of many meals.

Slowly, over the weeks of his recovery, Stephen shared the family's meager supplies of food and learned a little of their story. They had fled from a village to the north and had taken refuge here, settling in the wake of the Mongol army and burying the last of their food stocks in the ground. The head of the family, a gray-haired, broad-shouldered patriarch with a beard that flowed almost down to his withered legs, had directed the move. He had also told his family not to return and cultivate the land in the summer, even though the Mongols sent out their promises that the peasants who worked the land would not be harmed; so they had escaped the autumn massacres.

They never said how they had managed to acquire food enough to survive more than a year in the forest, and Stephen never asked. There was much that was unsaid and unexplained among them, including the family relationships that he never did quite understand. There was a buxom middle-aged woman, two young girls, and a down-trodden man of indeterminate years who deferred to the crippled patriarch in everything. Who was married to whom, or descended from whom, was a puzzle that remained impenetrable through the confusion of languages and sleeping arrangements: the whole tribe burrowed together for warmth, huddling in their heap of coarse woolen rugs, telling stories, giggling, and puffing garlic-laden breath into the cold smoky air.

There were also two goats, gentle skinny milch goats who were petted and cosseted and treated like more valuable members of the family than the two young girls who did most of the heavy work. Stephen did not object to this assessment, as it was the milk from those goats that had kept him alive through the weeks when, his wound having reopened, his fever returned and his mind wandered.

He did figure out that the bandit had captured the older of the two girls when she went into the woods to gather fuel. While the rest of the family clung to one another in the big central hut, literally sitting on their food supplies, the bandit had told them that he was willing to give the girl back only if they left the huts and all the food to him and went into the forest to almost certain death. If they delayed, he would start slicing off pieces of her flesh and roast them over a fire at the edge of the clearing, where they could hear her screams.

He'd been waiting for their reply when Stephen appeared, and the bandit had forgotten the girl in his need to get rid of this threat. The girl had seen the fight and now worshipped Stephen as her savior. So did the rest of the family, all but the patriarch, who watched the amount of food Stephen consumed with a grudging eye. It was a measure of the limits of his power that he did not overrule the rest of the family in their desire to keep the stranger through the winter. Or perhaps it demonstrated that the old man thought there was enough food for the luxury of keeping one guest. Stephen never made up his mind about that, though he had time enough to consider the question. First there were the weeks he lost, chatting with ghosts and drinking the bowls of sour goat's milk they fed him, while the temporary strength of madness and anger that had carried him so far deserted him. Stephen's leg healed during those weeks, at least as much as it was ever going to heal. The muscles were tight and quite painful when he first tried to walk, and from groin to knee his skin stretched in an ugly purplish welted scar.

When he got well enough to know who he was, the snow was deep outside. It would be suicide to leave in midwinter, they told him with shrill meaningless words and eloquent gestures. Stephen would have to stay until the spring. The old man looked on with a sour smile that made Stephen uneasy, but he did not countermand his family's offer of hospitality.

Through the rest of the cold weather, Stephen exercised his stiff leg, first hobbling around the clearing until the painful muscles loosened, then following the two girls into the woods to carry the bundles of twigs and dead limbs they found in the snow. At the same time, he stretched a mind that had been cramped in much the same way, with horror and loneliness and fear. He learned enough of the peasants' dialect to communicate simple matters with them, and he gradually stopped talking to the dead. Occasionally he still saw Ibn Masoud perched incongruously in a dead tree, spreading out his fingers to illustrate the perfect geometry of a bending branch. From time to time, Brother Daniel's cold predictions of failure drowned out the chatter of the two girls. The visions were something he could live with, no more than a momentary ache of the mind echoing the pain in his leg when the weather changed. By the time the snows began to thaw, Stephen was, he supposed, as whole and sound of mind and body as he could ever expect to be.

And it was time to be moving on. His fixation on killing Joffrey de Belmont had melted with the snows, or even before. Joffrey would be long gone by now. He was good at running away.

"So are you," croaked Brother Daniel, in the form of a raven, from the branch of the dead oak at the edge of the clearing. "You ran away from Ely, and you ran away from your own guilt and failure in France, and you ran away from the Mongols."

Stephen nodded slowly. "That's all right," he told the raven. "Anybody with any sense would run from the Mongols. You would too, if you knew what they were like. And for the rest . . . I'm through running." During the weeks of illness and slow recovery, Stephen had come to his decision. All his life he'd been a fool, challenging God's omnipotence with his puny attempts at building eternity in stone. His insolence had been punished all along, but it had taken the final horror of the siege and sack of Varad, the sight of his masterwork going up in flames amid death and suffering, to finally impress God's lesson upon his mind.

His life was useless, his greatest work a heap of rubble in the desert, and he was a middle-aged man with a bad leg and a dead mistress and a wife who'd left him years ago. And he had no children.

All those years Aude longed for children, using cures and potions and miracle-working relics. Yet they'd never understood that it was Stephen's sin that was being punished. Even when God gave them Michael-Béla only to snatch him back again, even when He let Stephen's church be the instrument of his son's death, Stephen had refused to hear the message. It had to be written in letters of fire and blood across the square of the high citadel at Varad before he understood. He had no business in the world, and God was not going to let him get away from the vows that had been made in his name so long ago. He'd lost his wife and his son and his masterwork, his health and some of his sanity fighting God's will. It was time to give in.

Aude would be better off without him. It had been selfish to think of going back to her. Even if she would have him back, even if she hadn't taken a better man by now, what right did he have to cling to her in the face of God's will? It was time to stop running.

"You win," Stephen told the black bird on the tree. "I'm going back to Ely."

The raven croaked three times, approvingly, thought Stephen, and flew away. One of the girls ran into the hut, giggling, to tell her mother that the foreign magician could speak with birds.

Stephen rather thought that with the coming of spring, the growing assurance that the Mongols had truly left the land, and the renewal of his own health, the old man who ruled the huts was beginning to find him a less unwelcome guest. He still could not understand the peasants' Slavic dialect when they talked fast, but he'd caught a few mentions of fields lying untilled and the usefulness of a

man who still had some strength in him. And the girls
were beginning to giggle speculatively when they looked
at him.

It was definitely time to leave this place. And they
didn't try to stop him; the speculations hadn't gone that
far.

"You're going to the sea?"

Deep behind the peasants' gray eyes were memories of
blue skies and turquoise-blue seas, pierced by the white
limestone cliffs of the Dalmatian coast. Stephen's own
thoughts were of church bells ringing in cities the Mongols
had barely touched: Ragusa, Trogir, Kotor.

"Trogir is closest, I think," said the old man's son.

"Yes," Stephen said, swinging over his shoulder a sack
filled generously by the girls' mother when the old man
wasn't looking. He had a patched tunic to cover his back,
too, and a cloak of undyed felted wool. They had been
generous, indeed. "Yes, I'm going to the sea."

And Stephen's eyes, staring unseeing over the wooded
clearing where he'd passed the winter, saw gray skies and
gray water rolling over a pebbled shingle. He could imagine the iridescent shine of fish heaped in a net, and a gray
stone town with twenty churches ringing bells in a Christian land that had never heard of the Mongols. He would
get a ship for England, and would stop in Dunwich on his
way to Ely. He would not go to Chastelvert to beg Aude's
understanding and forgiveness; for though she might grant
it, the temptation would be too much to bear. Stephen
wanted to be with Aude so much that he could hardly
stand it; but he knew now that wherever he went, whatever he did, God's hand would be against him until he
returned to take up his vows again.

He couldn't ask Aude to share that fate. But he would
pass through Dunwich one last time before he walled
himself up in the convent.

"Must you leave?" asked the younger of the girls, crying
unashamedly as she kissed him good-bye.

"Yes," said Stephen in English, making his first creaking
attempt at the language of his faraway childhood. Before
he learned to talk to foreign masons in Saracen and
Magyar and a jumble of other languages, he had spoken
good plain English. And it was time to be through with his
pretensions of being builder, gentleman, traveler. "Yes. I

am going home. God keep you all!" He kissed her, and the girl ran into the hut crying out to her family that the foreign magician had blessed her with a magical chant. Stephen picked up the stick that supported his steps and went into the forest in the direction of the setting sun.

Even with directions, food, a stick, and a good knife, it was not an easy journey or a safe one. He took a number of detours around suspicious camps and villages, lost his way more than once and all but lost the last of his food to a pack of starving dogs that had once tended somebody's sheep on the hills above the coast. When he finally crossed the last ridge of white hills to stand above the blue sea whose salt tang had tinged the air for the past two days of his travel, the evening shadows were turning the limestone to purple, and bells were ringing in the narrow streets of the walled city below.

At the gates of the city, he learned that the bells were ringing for the feast of Good Friday. And no, the gate guard said, this was not Trogir, all the world knew that Trogir was nothing but a village compared with the great trading city of Ragusa! Where had the stranger been, that he did not know the walls of Ragusa when he saw them? With a sharp look, the guard, who hoped this thin, scarred wanderer was good for a bribe, demanded to know if the stranger had any friends in Ragusa who could vouch for him? It was getting late, and the guard said he wasn't supposed to let in suspicious-looking characters with no known business.

Stephen shook his head. "I know no one here. I've been out of the world for a long time, indeed. I'm making my way back from being held prisoner in Khan Kadan's army of Mongols."

The guard snapped to attention. There was money in this starving beggar after all. "Go to the house of Marco Sanudo. Say I sent you, mind, so's he'll know where to send the reward! Sanudo collects refugees from the Mongols," he explained kindly. "Odd sort of habit, but he's rich enough to indulge himself as he likes."

"Not anymore, he doesn't," contradicted the man arriving to take over the watch. "He quit interviewing refugees over two months ago. No, earlier. At Christmas, I think. If you didn't have your head inside a pot of ale every minute you would know these things. You're off duty now."

The first guard smiled at his fellow.

"Sanudo? Marco Sanudo of Venice?" It seemed too good to be true. "He'll want to see me," Stephen assured the guard. "And as you're going off duty now, you can take me to his house. It'll be worth your while. We're old friends. He'll be glad to see me."

All the bells in the city were ringing in Stephen's ears as he followed the guard along narrow streets and winding ways.

CHAPTER

39

◻

The tall stone houses in the old city vaulted over the narrow streets, turning the passageways into dark tunnels without light or air. Stephen felt as if he were wandering through an endless chain of vaulted crypts in a city-wide church. At every turn he expected to see a pile of skulls, a treasure chest, or a moldering reliquary full of the bones of forgotten saints. The guard knocked at the iron-studded wooden door of Marco Sanudo's house, and when they were admitted to the antechamber, Stephen felt as though he had ascended into the upper reaches of his imagined church. Here there was light and air in plenty, the gold of the sinking sun reflected off golden-white plaster walls, and the fresh salty breeze blew unobstructed through broad high windows.

"Wait here," said the servant, showing Stephen through the door at the far side of the entry hall.

He was in a narrow garden, a space walled with white native stone and decorated with a profusion of herbs and flowering plants that bloomed early in this sheltered corner. Over the stone wall Stephen could see the sparkling sea; if he closed his eyes, he could pretend that the cries of the fishermen hauling in their nets were coming from the Dunwich shore. He was very tired. Stephen rested on a white stone bench placed halfway along the garden

wall, leaned back on sun-warmed stones and let his eyes
close for just a minute. He slipped into a dream of
Dunwich on one of its rare sunny days, with the fishermen
and the children shouting to one another on the shore,
Brito's masons hammering away in the upper town, and
somewhere a woman singing a soft, haunting lullaby. . . .

Stephen's eyes flew open with shock. He sat up too
quickly, braced his hands against the wave of dizziness that
threatened his balance, and grasped desperately after the
sanity he had recaptured with such pains during the winter before. He had not heard an English lullaby. The woman
singing had not had Aude's clear, low voice. The per-
vasive scent of lavender and rosemary that wreathed
round his nostrils came from the herbs in the garden. Was
he never to be through with these visions?

But at the far end of the narrow garden was a flight of stairs
leading up to an arched doorway, and the woman standing
at the top of the stairs was no vision. She didn't float down
the stairs; she stepped carefully. And the hair that peeped
out from under her coif was touched with silver.

Stephen stood, awkward as a jointed puppet, and limped
forward to meet her at the foot of the stairs.

Yes, she was quite real. She was solid, with a slightly
thickened waist, in fact, and she wore sun-dried linen
scented with lavender and rosemary. Her face was warm, the
suppressed sobs that made her shoulders shake were real,
the tears on her cheeks tasted of salt.

"Aude."

"I never thought—" She was weeping openly now. "I
didn't guess it might be you. Another poor soul got away
from the Mongols with nothing but his skin, the gate
guard said. He might have news. Although we'd stopped
asking for news, after—and Marco was meeting with Si-
gnor Peruzzi, so I thought I might as well—"

She drew back, seeing him and believing the evidence
of her eyes for the first time. "Oh, Stephen. What have
they done to you?"

"Nothing so very much," said Stephen. "Nothing so
bad. Hush! It's all right, Aude. We're here, aren't we?" He
stroked her hair and shoulders until he could feel her
calming under his hand, and until the ache in his throat
diminished to manageable proportions. For himself, he
did not feel at all calm. He wanted to leap in the air like a

boy, which was impossible because of his leg; and to set off
explosions of Greek fire across the harbor, which would
probably not set well with the good burghers of Ragusa;
and more than anything else, he wanted some wine and
some food and, by God, some explanations. "And speaking
of that," he said at length "what are you doing here? I
thought you would go home when you left Varad."

"I did."

'Then why did Abbot Samson let you come back this
close to the Mongols?"

"What had he to do with it?"

That started a few more questions and cross-answers,
until Stephen grasped that Aude had not gone back to
their house at Chastelvert, had never had any intention of
going there, had not even (as she somewhat acerbically
pointed out) any idea that Stephen wanted her to go there.
"You wanted to be rid of me. That was all that was clear."

"No. I didn't. I wanted to make you safe, that was all."
Stephen lifted her slender hands, work-worn and sunburnt,
and kissed each finger in turn. "That much you must
believe. If you can't forgive me for lying to you, I suppose
I must bear it. But you must believe that's all it was: lies to
make you angry, to make you go away, to make you *safe*. I
never wanted any woman but you, Aude," Stephen swore,
and for the moment he believed it. "I never had any—"

He stopped, remembering the supple whiteness of Bianca's
body and his face gave away everything he was thinking.

"Hush, my love," Aude said, gently pressing her fingertips to his mouth. "I know you lied to make me safe. I
understood that much when we heard that Varad had been
taken. I don't need you to tell me any more."

They were locked together again when Marco came
whistling down the steps, talking even before he came
through the arch and saw the two of them in the garden.
"Are you still waiting in the garden, Aude? I thought I
never would get rid of Guido Peruzzi. These bankers!
They talk as if nothing mattered but their words and
promises and money. They have no thought of little things
that could maybe go wrong, like a bad wind or a shipload
of rice in a leaky hull or a minor war or . . ."

His gay voice died away. "Little things," Marco Sanudo
repeated slowly, "that could go wrong."

The man was much changed, tragically changed, but he

would have known Stephen anywhere—even if Aude hadn't been clasping him so tightly. His golden hair was a shaggy cap of silver now, his broad shoulders all bone under a miserable coarse tunic, and there was something wrong with the right leg that dragged behind him as he moved to greet Marco. There was something wrong with his eyes, too; something was not quite right behind his pale eyes.

But it was unquestionably and recognizably Stephen of Dunwich, risen from the mass graves of the Mongol dead to take Aude away from him in the very moment of victory. Marco ground his teeth and produced a pleasant smile of greeting. He wished he could feel one-tenth the joy he was pretending over his old friend's miraculous return.

It wouldn't have been so bad if Aude weren't still hanging on to the bastard's arm, all the wrongs he'd done her forgotten in an instant, nothing in the world for her now but Stephen. Marco knew that even if Stephen had never come back, he would never have had Aude. Not truly. He might have married her, but she would never have been his. It was a bitter draught to swallow, but perhaps tomorrow it would help him to accept the situation.

"Stephen. My old friend. How wonderful to see you again!" Marco said, smiling through clenched teeth. "You must tell us how you happened to survive."

Stephen drew back a little, frowning, as if he caught the undercurrent of fury that Marco was trying so hard to conceal. Marco sensed the moment of puzzled withdrawal and could not keep his eyes from flicking to Aude's face. She was staring hard at him, willing him to the silence he'd already vowed on his own account. In a moment Stephen would notice their stare of complicity, or would begin asking questions about how Aude came to be here in his house at Ragusa, and the fragile reunion between these two would be shattered. Marco told himself again that Aude could never be his. He could make Stephen suspicious and Aude unhappy, but what good would that do any of them?

Marco forced himself to embrace Stephen before the moment of tension between the three of them could draw on too long. And at the feel of his old friend's bony shoulders, Marco wanted to cry. The ogre whose return he'd been fearing was a pallid silver-haired waif with ghosts looking out of his eyes. His friend Stephen was lost among those ghosts, and Marco wanted him back; for a moment he wanted Stephen back even more than he wanted Aude.

That feeling didn't last, but the brief flash of loss and pity for his old friend was the second thing that made it possible for Marco to accept the shattering of his hopes. He managed to complete the embrace, to talk cheerfully about baths and food and rest for their traveler, and at just the right moment he caught Aude's eye and raised his chin toward the room at the top of the garden stairs.

"I daresay you've been wondering why Aude and I keep looking at one another," he said, and grinned at Aude's indrawn hiss of dismay. "No, Aude, I think Stephen's strong enough for this news. Will you bring the boy down, or shall I? Or don't you want to wake him?"

Aude's look of relief would have made him laugh, if he hadn't been so perilously near tears. "I think this once I might risk getting him up again!" She picked up her skirts and ran as lightly as a girl toward the arched doorway, and Marco placed a solicitous hand on Stephen's shoulder.

"Stephen, I think you'd better sit down. Perhaps this should have waited until you'd had something to eat, but I thought you'd want to see him. . . ."

"See who?"

Aude came back down the stairs carrying a blond bundle that stirred and made sleepy protesting noises in her arms. She sank to her knees beside Stephen and placed the burden half in his lap, half on the bench.

"You sent me away with a gift," she said, "though you didn't know it at the time. And now I can return your gift to you."

Mark opened sleepy blue eyes and Aude stiffened, expecting him to shriek with fear when he woke in the arms of a gaunt, gray-haired stranger. Instead he smiled up into Stephen's eyes. "Daddy?" he said experimentally.

Stephen's face, as he bent over the son he had not known he had, was the third thing that made it possible for Marco to bear the loss of Aude, whom he had never truly won.

By the next day, fed and washed and clothed in a clean old gown belonging to Guido Peruzzi's oversized second cousin, Stephen was already beginning to look somewhat like his old self again. There was a new calmness about him, though, an inner stillness unlike anything Marco remembered of the old, energetic, restless, ambitious Stephen. That man had always been twitching to be off on a new adventure, to explore some tumbledown old ruin from classical times, or to build the greatest church in Europe. This Stephen seemed content to sit in the pale spring sunlight, dandling his son, and talking desultorily of old times with Marco and Aude.

Perhaps he was just tired.

But Marco also noticed that he avoided talking about the recent past. Most of the starving refugees who'd straggled down to the Dalmatian coast couldn't say enough about the sufferings they'd endured and the Mongol atrocities they'd seen. Stephen never mentioned it except to say that it was best forgotten. He would then change the subject, asking if he remembered the time they'd gone out drinking with a Persian poet from the court of the Sultan in Cairo, and the wager Geoffrey made about the forty-four nightingales and the slave girls?

Aude was glowing like a ripe peach under Stephen's eyes, and the two of them were holding hands like a pair of newlyweds. She seemed to find no fault with the gentleness and restraint that made Marco so nervous.

Marco had to admit, there was something to be said for this new, calm Stephen. For one thing, he never seriously returned to the question of why Aude had come to Ragusa. He accepted without question Marco's statement that she'd been hoping for news of him. And after all, it was part of the truth. For the rest—well, it was to have been a very quiet wedding, as befitted a man in his middle years marrying a woman so recently and so tragically widowed. Marco packed away the new tunic of brocaded silk from Persia, told his cook to give the marchpane pastries and honey-flour conceits to the poor, and carefully explained to the rest of his servants that anybody mentioning the wedding plans in his presence or that of his guests would first be killed and then have his tongue cut out and then be flogged round the streets. Then Marco went back to watch the newly reunited lovers playing with their son in his garden, and to wonder just how soon he could persuade Stephen to leave without being inhospitable.

At least the wedding preparations were canceled, and

the new clothes and gifts packed away where the sight of them could not twist his heart. He kept out only the string of amber beads set in gold, Balkan work joined with Byzantine craftsmanship, that he had meant to give Aude on their wedding morning. This he casually trailed across his open hands while he sat in the garden with them, talking of nothing in particular and trying not to look at Aude.

"Pitty!" cried Mark, reaching for the string of gold and fire that glittered in the morning sun.

"Lovely," said Aude.

Marco beamed at her. "Yes, isn't it? I bought it for my bride."

"Are you getting married, Marco?" Stephen asked.

"My family has been after me for some years to start a new generation of Sanudos," Marco replied obliquely. "As if I didn't have enough cousins and nephews and bastard half-brothers. They've even picked out a nice girl for me. One of the Peruzzi, actually. A true Florentine, my father says, with hair as golden as the sun. She's only fifteen, so she should be able to give me plenty of Sanudo sons to carry on the business, don't you think? And I thought this necklace would be a good bride-gift. It will go with her hair." He'd hoped to see it entwined round the dark curls of a woman who was probably too old to have more sons. And failing that, he had hoped at least to see some blush, some hint of regret in Aude's face. At least she ought to know what she was missing.

"You're right, Marco. The necklace will make her happy. I think you will be a very good husband," Aude said quietly.

"But not, of course, as good as Stephen." He couldn't resist that little jab. But Aude scarcely heard him; she was looking at her battered, gaunt husband with a glow in her eyes that Marco had never seen there during all their plans for the Easter wedding.

Easter morning was bright and clear, with a fresh breeze from the sea to sweep away any remnants of the winter's clouds. The narrow dark streets were bright, too, with the gold brocaded trim on merchants' robes, and the chaplets of winter-preserved roses brought out of their earthen jars to bloom on girls' bare heads. On this day the poorest of the fisherfolk on the shore brought out treasured holiday dresses handed down from generation to generation, home-spun white wool, stiff with embroidery that glowed as bright as any jewels. Ragusa was one great party on Easter Day, a merry procession of burghers and peasants, nobles and commoners, all thronging the narrow streets on their way to celebrate Christ's rising from the dead and Ragusa's salvation from the Mongols.

And in the center of the laughing, pushing, shouting crowd was the Venetian shipowner Marco Sanudo, walking slowly with his two foreign guests and their little son. On any other day, in any other year, a Venetian merchant who walked the streets of Ragusa without an escort might have expected "accidental" hard shoves, some muttered curses, and perhaps a pot of something malodorous thrown from an upper window into his path. Venetian laws and restrictions were not popular with the Ragusans. But on this bright Easter Sunday, with the memory of the Mongol invaders to sharpen the sweet taste of life renewed, the citizens of Ragusa could afford to share the sunlight with one of the Venetians who so shamelessly exploited their city.

And, of course, a merchant whose guest had survived a year with the Mongols was doubly welcome for the sake of the sight he offered. Good wives pushed and elbowed to see the man who'd lived so long with the Mongol demons, and fell back crossing themselves and whispering that there was something odd about his pale eyes. Could he have learned magical arts from the demons? Was that how he'd survived? Ah, no, there could be nothing wrong with a man who had such a sweet little son! Mark had his hair ruffled and sweetmeats thrust into his hands by total strangers, all the way along the short walk from Marco's villa in the piazza to the open square before the cathedral.

From the back of the square there was more determined pushing, as a man with callused palms and squinting eyes tried to get closer to the rich nobles and burghers entering the cathedral. "I tell you, that's him! I'd know him anywhere!"

"You're seeing things," jeered his mate. "Didn't you say, yourself, he was dead? Next you'll be seeing the ghost of this wonderful church, one you say would have risen higher than the *Duomo* here."

"And so it would," the first man insisted stoutly. "Did."

He sighed. "Ah, but Mongols took the city, and I doubt there's much left of St. Michael's Church now. But that's him, all the same, and if you help me get up to the cathedral door, he'll know me, too."

But two determined men were no match for the circles of solid wives, the lines of city guards who separated noble from common at the cathedral door, and the entire press of the crowd that gathered at the door craning their necks for a sight of the holy man who was to preach there today. They would have to wait until the preaching was over and the crowd thinned.

Still exhausted from his long winter's privations, Stephen tried to get his bearings in the Easter crowd. Through the happy hours of reunion he had been nagged by his broken vows and his promise to return to Ely. Here in God's house, it was time to think. Stephen hoped he could reclaim the certainty he had felt during the lonely winter, and the knowledge that God wanted him for something other than building.

But even the thought of building led Stephen astray, into consideration of this new cathedral in which he stood. The *Duomo*, it was called, for the great dome-shaped roof that gave it such a foreign, Eastern look. There was not much of the French style here: no attempt to lift eyes and spirits along high slender columns to a multiply vaulted roof; no piercing walls with colored glass to fill the church with light. Instead darkness was lit by massed candles, and dim colored light struggling through small circular windows. The walls were covered with mosaics that told stories of saints unknown to Stephen. But it was so dark, and so crowded, that he could hardly see the pictures. He couldn't get closer to them, either: in this church men worshipped in the nave, women in the side aisles. Aude and the baby were somewhere under the low rounded aisle vaults, hemmed in by fat joking women in gold necklaces and gold-hemmed flouncy petticoats. Stephen was surrounded by dark-faced men chattering in a barbarous Slavic dialect. Even the nobles in this remote coast city were half Slav.

Marco was separated from Stephen by one of these groups of Slav noblemen, talking in low confidential tones with a man in a green velvet cap: was it one of the Peruzzi with whose banking family he was soon to ally himself?

Stephen felt nervous; last time he stood in such a crowd, it had been a hot sunny day like this today, and the open field had bloomed with red flowers of blood.

Don't think about that, Stephen told himself. It was all over now, the burning church and the massacres and the winter waste, and he stood in church to thank God for his life. He ought to concentrate on the mass that was being sung even now, the mystery celebrated with candles and incense behind the twinkling carved apertures of the rood screen. He ought to pray for some word of guidance so he would do what was right with this life that had been given back to him so unexpectedly. Had he indeed, as he'd thought in the forest, been saved so that he could go back to Ely and fulfill his vows? But then why had God let him have Aude back? Was it a test? If so, Stephen thought, I have failed. I can put aside ambition, I can give up building, but I cannot give up Aude and my new young son. Surely God wouldn't ask him to do that.

There were no signs or answers in this low, dark Byzantine cathedral, no flood of light and certainty through walls pierced like screens with huge windows. There was only darkness, and the mystery of God's presence as real and palpable as the people pressing in on Stephen from either side. The tinkle of bells signaled the end of the Easter mass, and the priest raised his hands over the crowd that had laughed and joked and gossiped its way through the happiest mass of the year. Behind him, a tall lean figure in a gray robe moved into the circle of candlelight, and slowly a respectful silence fell over the crowd. The last echoes of their chatter drowned out the first words of the priest's introduction, and Stephen missed the name and the order of the friar. The first words he heard were, "The holy man of whom you all have heard, whom God is sending to bring the heathen Mongols the blessed word of Christ, and who has been persuaded to say a few words to us on the eve of excursion."

As the friar climbed the steps of the pulpit, his gray hood fell back and a gasp went up from the crowd at the sight of his scarred face. One side of his head was fair and smooth skinned; the other side was a twisted mass of ropy, purple scars, as if the flesh had melted and run together in puddles.

Stephen felt sick and faint. He swayed and put out a

hand for support, leaning on the shoulder of one of the Slav nobles who stood between him and Marco. "Marco!" he called out. "Marco, do you see?"

Irritated whispers flew at him from all sides.

"Hush, you, the holy man is speaking."

"It's Marco Sanudo's guest-friend, the one who was prisoner of the Mongols."

"Poor fellow, no doubt the long captivity has turned his brain."

"I don't care, he's not going to have a fit here in our *Duomo* and spoil the preaching."

"Have you no charity? He's taken ill and needs air, that's all."

"No, he needs to sit down. Isn't there a stool up by the pulpit?"

Pushing and whispering and offering sympathy, the crowd parted like slow waves of a sluggish sea, and strange hands supported Stephen and urged him on to a stool directly under the pulpit. He sat there, thankful and a bit confused by all the contradictory help and advice he'd received, and more than thankful to be sitting where he could not see the Franciscan friar.

It might have been an illusion, the familiar eye and the shock of bright hair that greeted him on the unburnt side of the friar's face. He had, after all, been seeing visions not so long ago. But most ghosts didn't start back in the pulpit as though they, too, had received a shock.

From his half-hidden seat Stephen listened to a familiar gay, light voice describing the joys of Paradise and the happiness of the love of Christ and His blessed saints. Paradise, in this friar's mouth, sounded very like a glorious party that went on and on forever. The friar did not speak of sin, or redemption, or escaping the torments of hell. This sermon was quite unlike anything Stephen had ever heard before: here was the voice of a man who was confident in the love of his God, and who wanted nothing more than to share his happiness with the rest of the world—even with the Mongols.

Even when he came to speak of his mission to Tartary, and of the need for funds to help him reach his distant goal, the friar refrained form the usual hints that a contribution now could spare the giver some years of burning in purgatory later. He simply invited his listeners to open their hearts and their purses, and in return, he promised, they would feel that much closer to their Lord.

"I wish you'd stay here to preach every week," said the priest afterwards, counting contributions even as the last of the nobles in the cathedral dropped his purse onto the offering table.

Stephen had told Marco to get Aude and the baby and wait for him outside; there was somebody he needed to see in the cathedral. "I thought I recognized him," said Marco. "Are you sure he wants to see you, though?"

Stephen shrugged. He only knew he had to try. Since the sermon, Stephen had been standing in the shadows until the crowd of ecstatic, weeping people finished giving their donations and moved on to the feasts and processions that were the next Easter amusement. Now he came forward into the circle of light cast by the candles. "You've become a preacher to rival Abbot Samson, Geoffrey. If we'd had you to solicit donations for the church, it would have been finished in no time. But of course, you don't approve of fine buildings, do you?"

"I thought it was you." Geoffrey, friar of the Franciscan order, previously the seigneur of La Tour Martel, folded his hands inside his gray sleeves and gave Stephen a long level stare from his one good eye. "So you still haven't forgiven me for discovering a higher duty than your devotion to stones and mortar?"

All at once the pain of Geoffrey's betrayal seemed as silly as a child's fight over a broken toy. "Of course I have, you damned fool." Stephen hugged Geoffrey and met a body even thinner than his own under the coarse gray robes. And this emaciated man hadn't been a prisoner. "What have you been doing? Starving yourself?"

"Fasting, yes."

"Well, you won't reach the Mongols if you collapse in the streets of Ragusa from hunger."

"But I may reach God the sooner," said Geoffrey tranquilly.

Stephen tried to persuade him to come back to Marco's house, to see Marco and Aude and the baby and to have one good meal before he set off on his mission. Geoffrey shook his head, smiling. "I've given up earthly ties, Stephen. The Mongols are as much my friends as you and Aude."

"Last time I heard you talking like that, I thought you

would get over it in a few weeks. I didn't think you understood what you were saying."

"I probably did not," Geoffrey agreed with his tranquil smile. "I was new in religion then, and I thought I had to be the perfect friar to get forgiveness for my sins. I was certainly a fool, thinking I could delude God into thinking me more holy than I was by mouthing words I didn't mean."

"But you mean them now."

It wasn't a question. Geoffrey's contentment was apparent, illuminating his ravaged face. He'd truly given himself to God.

And he would not stay even an hour to visit with his old friends. A ship was leaving Ragusa with the next tide and he meant to be on it, paying his passage with the coin he'd collected in that morning's preaching. It would be a long, roundabout route to Tartary, and he did not know exactly how he would get there, but the question did not trouble him in the least. If God wanted him to preach to the Mongols, there would be money enough for the journey and ships and caravans to take him to their land. If God had some other plan in mind for him, that would become evident in the course of his travels.

"I cannot tell you, Stephen," Geoffrey said earnestly, "how pleasant it is to know that all things are in His hands, and that our worldly planning and thinking is meaningless. All we have to do is trust in Him, and all things will be made plain."

"Hmmph. If I trusted in the Lord to level a course of stones or spring an arch, instead of seeing to my own work in my own time, my buildings would fall down before they were fairly begun."

Geoffrey shook his head, smiling that dreadfully sweet one-sided smile, but would not argue the point. "We're fated to see things differently, you and I. It's just as well you were never called to the religious life, Stephen; I don't think it would fit you."

The bitter irony of that statement made Stephen laugh.

"Strange, isn't it?" said Geoffrey.

"That we were ever friends?"

"To see you again, here. I'm ashamed to admit it, but Tartary is a long way off, and it's been good to see someone I was once close to before I go."

Then a boy appeared, calling out something breathless about the change of tides, and Geoffrey was gone.

"Ashamed, huh!" Stephen muttered to himself. "What, ashamed of the last flicker of human feeling left in you? I will never understand these religious men."

Stephen's angry muttering helped to cover up the sense of desolation he felt as he suddenly found himself alone in the darkness of the *Duomo*. The candles were all out now, and the dim-colored light that came faintly through small, distant windows turned the cathedral into a lonely place of dark shadows and mysteries.

Stephen thought of how he had promised God that he would go back to just such a life, to take up again vows he'd never accepted; to give up love and warmth and humanity for the sake of something he would never understand.

But what else was there to do? God had saved him out of the crucible of Europe for some purpose, that much he knew. All his life he'd been running away from God's will, trying to set his own will against God's, to make something immortal in stone when the only true immortality was of the spirit. The crash of burning timbers and splintered stones in Varad had been God's answer to that folly. And now, what was there for Stephen, if he did not go back to Ely? How dare he even think of staying with Aude and Mark? If he grasped at this last chance of happiness, wouldn't God punish him by striking at them?

Grief and loneliness cramped his heart. If he didn't go to Ely, God would take Aude from him in punishment; if he did go, he'd lose her anyway and he would be locked away in the cold stones of the church until he died.

Stephen dropped to his knees and prayed for a sign, begging God to send some knowledge of His will. As Stephen rose and slowly walked through the dimness of the cathedral to the western portal, ablaze with the light of the spring noontide, he found his answer as he'd found it before in his childhood.

"Stephen. Master Stephen!"

He stopped and looked again at the two dark, squat men who'd been lounging on the sunlit steps. They had broad shoulders, heavy strong arms, and callused palms. The one who'd spoken had a squint, besides. They must be masons; it was from years of hammer and chisel and lifting stones that a man got such a build. And he'd seen that squint before.... "Varad." Stephen felt as though the word spoke itself. "Gianni Ragusano." It all came back to him now, as clearly as if he'd seen the man working only yesterday. Of course he knew Gianni, the man who whistled strange haunting tunes as he carved leafy capitals of delicate beauty. "The columns of the south aisle. You were the best freestone carver I ever had."

"See? See? Told you I knew 'un, didn't I?" Gianni chattered to his mate in the slangy Italian of this shore, and Stephen grinned and followed two words in three with the help of Gianni Ragusano's expressive hands. "The greatest builder in Europe, the finest church that ever was. Ah, you should have seen it, like a piece of Spalato lacework carved in stone and raised up to the sky, it was. And I was his master carver. Said so himself. I set the windows in the south transept too, and a tricky piece of work that was. Ah, Master Stephen. We thought you were dead, we did. Maybe it wasn't so bad as we heard, eh? Anything left of the church?"

Stephen shook his head. "No. The church is gone. There is nothing left."

"Ah, well..." Gianni Ragusano looked down at his toes for a moment, then brightened. "You'll be rebuilding, perhaps?"

"No. Count Jokai is dead and there is nothing left."

"Well. When you start another project and want some good freestone carving, Master Stephen, you send for me, Gianni Ragusano, and my friends here, too. They've all heard about St. Michael's in Varad. Every man here would be honored to work on any project you took in hand, Master Stephen, you bear that in mind. Just send word to the lodge of freemasons at Ragusa, any time you want us to come."

Stephen shook his head a third time. "Thank you, Gianni, but I'm not planning..."

A white pigeon fluttered across the square, seeking crumbs dropped by the morning's churchgoers, and Stephen lost his train of thought for a moment.

Not planning to build again?

And why ever not?

The church at Varad might be gone, but men still remembered it, his great work, the finest church in Europe.

Why should it be his last work? What had made him so
sure that God wanted him to give up the thing he was
good at, building in stone, for the life of prayer and
meditation that he was so supremely unfitted for? Perhaps
the two encounters of this day had been the sign he
prayed for. In Geoffrey he'd seen a man truly given over to
the service of God, doing with all his heart and all his soul
what Stephen could only imitate. And in Gianni Ragusano
he'd seen one of the hundreds of men over Europe who
were waiting for someone like him to guide the work of
their hands to God's glory.

"I'm not sure," Stephen changed his sentence, "I'm not
sure, now, just where I'll be working next. But when I get
a job, Gianni Ragusano, I'll send for you."

As he crossed the square on his way to Marco's house,
the pigeon gave a startled squawk and lifted into the air,
dropping the crust of bread it had been pecking at. Before
the bird landed again, Stephen knew where he would
raise his next spire, and why.

"I owe St. Michael a church still," he told the pigeon in
its spiraling flight, "and where better to build it, than
where he saved me the first time?"

Whistling one of the Ragusan freemason's haunting minor tunes under his breath, he made his way down to
Marco's house by the harbor, to tell Aude that they were
going home to Dunwich. Stephen had no idea how he
was going to make matters right with the Church, and
who was going to pay for his new project. But perhaps, for
once, he could borrow a little of Geoffrey's faith and leave
those matters to God, who had not let him spend thirty
years learning the art of building just so he could give it all
up in his prime. While one man in Europe remembered the
Church of St. Michael in Varad, the glory he had raised to
God was not gone; and while Stephen of Dunwich lived,
there was still time to do it again.

CHAPTER

40

⬚

Gianni Ragusano was not the only man in Europe who
remembered the great church at Varad. There were
hundreds of masons and artisans scattered across Western
Europe after the Mongol invasion. Peasants, smallholders,
gentry, and lords, who had been bound to the land they
worked and owned and protected, were trapped when the
Mongols came; free craftsmen and merchants could move
about, and did. The men whom Stephen had collected to
work at Varad had found themselves jobs in Sweden, Italy,
France, or England, wherever they could go to escape the
coming invasion. And wherever they'd gone, they had
carried tales of the Church of St. Michael-at-Varad: finer
than the chapel that the king of France was commissioning
in Paris, higher than the cathedrals of Amiens and Beauvais,
decorated inside and out with the work of the best craftsmen
in Europe. But the greatest glory of the church, they all
agreed, had been in the genius of the master builder
who'd designed that palace of light.

All across Europe, while the Mongols burned and destroyed, men in masons' lodges and glassblowers' work-
shops had been drawing sketches for their mates and
trying to recreate something of the genius they'd seen in
action. "Now if you'd raise the buttresses *here*, we'd have
room for three tall windows, *so* . . ."

"Pier shafts can be narrower. Don't tell me the rule of *ad quadratum!* I've seen it done."

"We don't need so much stone tracery in the rose. The window I was to have set in Varad would've been pretty nearly pure glass. I want to do the same here...."

Across Europe, as the word spread that Stephen of Dunwich had returned from the dead, his quiet journey homeward with Aude took on the nature of a triumphal procession. Wherever they stopped for the night, there was sure to be someone who'd worked at Varad or had heard reports of the church there. Masons, sculptors, smiths, and carpenters wanted to shake Stephen's hand and ask where he'd be building next; they wanted to introduce likely-looking sons or nephews being brought up in the craft; they wanted to sit up all night over tankards of ale, drawing sketches with their fingers in the puddles on the table and settling in their minds just how the great spire at Varad had been stabilized by its internal framework of cross-timbering. The church at Varad was destroyed, but it rose again everywhere in men's minds.

Marco accompanied them as far as Venice, and then as far as Rome when Stephen told him what he planned to do. Before he could live and work in England, Stephen wanted to settle his standing with the Church and his own conscience. Joscelin had told him once that child oblation was a thing of the past, that a clever canon lawyer might be able to prove Stephen free of those early vows. And instead of letting Joscelin test his theory, Stephen had run away. Now, he wanted it clearly understood and agreed that Stephen of Dunwich owed no more of his life to the monks of Ely. No matter how much it cost him or how long he had to spend in Rome to get it all straightened out, Stephen knew he must resolve this matter.

"You'll need money and influence to get your case settled quickly," Marco told Stephen. "You've got the money—"

"I have?"

"Remember when you told me to sell all your holdings in the merchant venture and give you the money for the Cistercian church at Chastelvert?"

Stephen nodded.

"Well, I didn't. I made you a loan out of the capital of the company instead. It never amounted to more than a third of the value of your share, and the profits from your share paid it back before you'd been in Hungary five years. That's not to mention the money you sent me from there, from time to time." Marco laughed at Stephen's expression. "You don't understand money, my friend. I couldn't bear to see you waste it, that's all. You are now a very rich man."

"Rich enough to build a church?" With this unexpected wealth, Stephen wouldn't have to waste time begging and fund-raising for the Church of St. Michael in Dunwich. His mind leapt ahead to that, and for a moment he forgot the problems that remained to be settled in Rome.

"Even," said Marco solemnly, "rich enough to bribe a secretary in the papal chancery. But you'd best let me handle it. You've got the money, but I have the influence and the knowledge of how things are done. I even," said Marco with some pride, "have a passing acquaintance with a cardinal's mistress."

As it turned out, Marco's influence and knowledge were hardly needed; nor was it necessary to further his acquaintance with the cardinal's mistress. ("What a pity," said Aude. "I wanted to see her.") On their second day in Rome, while waiting for Marco to return from the rooms at the chancery, Stephen made his excuses to Aude and went off into the audience chambers and hallways of the papal court on a search of his own.

"What are you looking for?"

"Not what. Who."

It would have seemed, to anyone who hadn't known Joscelin as a student, the longest of gambles against very long odds. But Stephen remembered Joscelin's brilliant mind, full of ambition and intellect. And he thought it wasn't so much of a gamble after all; where but Rome would Joscelin have gone?

Before noon his questions and searches narrowed down on the very hall where Marco had promised to meet him with the result of the morning's appointments and bribes. Stephen laughed to himself at the thought that he could have just sat in this high-ceilinged room all morning and have come to the same result in the end.

"He's over there," said the page who'd been well paid to bring him to this door. "Talking to Cardinal Abruzzi—"

"I see him." Stephen could just glimpse the familiar

slim, quick-moving form parting waves of minor clerics and gossiping bishops in the crowded hall. His dark hair was now streaked with gray, but his pale face and quicksilver movements had not changed. Joscelin lifted one hand to tell off the logical points of his argument to a listener, and Stephen felt years melt away. He pushed through the crowd without grace or subtlety until he was within arm's length of Joscelin. Grinning, he addressed the silk-clad back.

"I'm disappointed in you, Joscelin de Cressy. I thought you'd be Pope by now. Or a cardinal, at the very least."

It was the only time in his life Stephen had seen clever Joscelin at a loss, whirling white-faced, the thread of his argument dangling, gap-mouthed like a fish coming to the hook.

After the back-pounding and shoulder-thumping greetings and the brief summaries of the last twenty years, Joscelin and Stephen moved to a private alcove behind the hall where they could sit over wine and discuss things in more detail and privacy. Joscelin brushed aside Stephen's worry over the disposition of his case with airy assurances. "It's not so complex a thing as it used to be. The Church doesn't accept oblates any longer—that's been established these twenty years and more—and it would be embarrassing to try to force you to follow vows that are no longer taken."

"Yes, but what has that to do with how the law stands?"

Joscelin's long white fingers wove a web of air about the top of the low table. "Everything, my simple friend. Appearance is all. The canon law can be read a dozen different ways; what matters is what the present Pope chooses to make of it. The only difficulty you might possibly have encountered was in getting your case heard, before all the parties concerned died of old age. Kings and emperors have to wait months, sometimes years, for a moment of the Pope's time."

"So I've heard," said Stephen, his momentary visions of a triumphal return to England fading into the dust of dreams. "So I've heard. And as I've no kings or emperors to advance the hearing of my cause . . . how many years do you suppose it will take?"

"Oh, we should have the matter settled by, shall we say . . ." Joscelin pulled out a tiny notebook and scanned the pages, tapping various cryptic notations with one smooth white fingernail. "Hmm, Tuesday next we dine with the cardinal of Cremona, and the next two days are spoken for, but I'm free all Friday and Saturday. Shall we say a week from Monday? I would make it sooner," Joscelin apologized as Stephen gaped, "but I've a desperately busy schedule this week, and I want you and Aude and this merchant friend of yours to spend an evening with me before you go on to England. You will come, won't you? My cook is a Tuscan, with a terrible temper but a fine hand with fish sauces, and..."

"I thought you said it might take years," Stephen interrupted.

"Well." Joscelin smirked and smoothed down the flat braided border of his silk gown. "For someone else, it might. But you happen to have a friend with rather more power—in this restricted world—than a king or an emperor. I," he said proudly, "am a papal secretary."

"Enough money to bribe a secretary of the chancery, even..." Marco's words echoed in Stephen's memory. And Joscelin's tone of triumph left no doubt that he wouldn't have traded his position inside the chancery, or his chance to argue doubtful points of law, for any wealth or fame the outside world might have offered him. He was truly in the right place, using his talents as he and God both intended them to be used.

Stephen, too, would be in the right place, once he had a tracing house set up again and a group of masons at his command. And Joscelin was giving him the right to do that work in his own home with no fear of the Church.

"I can't thank you enough—" Stephen stumbled.

"Then don't try." Another airy gesture brushed aside all the invisible webs that Joscelin had been weaving over the table. "What are old friends for? Now let us talk of other matters. How is your good wife?"

Joscelin brushed aside Stephen's repeated attempts at thanks, listened a little to his stories of the Mongol invasion, and told him a great deal about the inner workings of the chancery and the politics of the religious life. Stephen came away quite confused, but he understood clearly that Joscelin had done very well for himself, indeed, and might actually be wearing a cardinal's red hat before he was much older.

Marco was looking for Stephen in the hall, downcast and

worried. "It may take a little longer than I'd hoped. The chancery is overloaded with cases—"

"Not to worry." Stephen tried to copy Joscelin's self-assured flick of the fingers. "It seems I have a friend at court."

"The sad part of meeting old friends," said Aude wistfully some months later, "is parting with them again. I never even got to see Geoffrey. And your Joscelin—I would have liked to have known him better. And I never knew Master Brito at all."

They were standing in the new burial ground at the top of the Dunwich sea cliffs, a little windswept patch of consecrated earth without even a church to shelter the graves. A few wealthy burghers, fearful that their bones would be washed into the sea as had happened to those buried in the lower town, paid good money to have this safe spot consecrated. But their extravagance had ended there, and no funds were set aside to build a church. Many of the principal contributors had died and taken up their graves before an enterprising priest could start a new collection for the building. Master Brito was buried here beside his wife, and Hugh's loving, skilled hands had erected a monumental folly of dimpled cherubs, winged angels, and grimacing monsters over the joint grave. Stephen winced everytime he looked at the four-pillared monument; it hurt him to see such skillful carving made into an atrocious design.

Master Brito would have loved it.

"You would have liked him," said Stephen, tearing his eyes away from the monument which juxtaposed beautiful details to achieve a result of surprising ugliness. "Master Brito was rather like Edric, I think. Rough-spoken, but kind."

"I would have had to love anybody who helped you so much."

"Then you've got a long list of people to love," said Stephen, thinking back over a life that was so rich in good friends and undeserved help. "Starting with yourself."

Even from his grave Master Brito had given Stephen one more bit of help: it was now obvious to Stephen where his new church would stand—safe on the sea cliffs, above the town proper. It wasn't exactly the mountain that tradition assigned to St. Michael, but it was the perfect substitute on the flat East Anglian coast. And the piece of ground was already consecrated.

Stephen and Hugh began with only half a dozen day laborers who cleared and leveled the site. Stephen paced over the ground and planned the dimensions of the modest church, while Hugh, in his old role of listener, heard Stephen's burgeoning ideas. As the building materials began to arrive and word of the work spread, the project grew. Stephen never had to look for men. They arrived on their own in a steady trickle as the word spread that Stephen of Dunwich was building again.

Most masons were sent away, disappointed, with the news that Stephen could not hire more than a handful of men for this small church. Since he was paying for the building out of his own pocket, the progress of the work depended on the profits from his shares in the Sanudo trading company. Only a few of the best and steadiest workers stayed on, and this core company of masons understood Stephen's ways of working so well that he hardly needed to direct them.

As the church rose, artisans were hired: a Saxon carpenter who'd designed the stabilizing framework for the great spire at Varad appeared one day, and Stephen made him master of the carpentry work at once, though he warned him that there wouldn't be much challenge in a small project like this.

"How high d'you want the bell tower?"

"Not," said Stephen hastily, "all that high. It won't need stabilizing with an internal frame, like the one at Varad."

He left the Saxon holding a finger into the constant sea breeze and making his own calculations. The bell tower wouldn't go up for some years, so there was time enough to alter its dimensions.

Gianni Ragusano was another who came to Dunwich for Stephen's sake, bringing a half dozen of his dark, sharp-featured compatriots. He quarreled loudly with the English masons, downed disconcertingly large quantities of English ale without showing any outward signs of intoxication, and was forgiven everything for his ability to carve.

As the exaggerated stories of the great church at Varad grew, a steady stream of visitors came to gaze at the little church of Dunwich. Some were expecting a cathedral, and were openly disappointed; others, whom Stephen learned to prize, walked round the church without saying very much but came back for a second look, and a third and a fourth.

When he was not overseeing the building or watching the visitors, Stephen found time (usually in between building seasons) to lead his crew of masons and carpenters and artisans to other projects.

"I have to keep them out of trouble," he told Aude once when he was apologizing for being away from home so much.

She laughed and told him it was more likely they wanted to keep him out of trouble, and feared what mischief he'd get into in Dunwich if they didn't find jobs to occupy his mind.

It was a quiet life, but one that suited Stephen as the old days had never done. In between building seasons he made a pilgrimage to Peterborough and saw with his trained architect's eye what he had been unable to interpret as a boy. The proportions of the west front were all wrong for the church behind the facade: great arches leading down to minuscule doors, a pompous towering front directing the eye to false expectations.

A bustling little clerk kept trying to show him round while hinting at the need for donations to the rebuilding fund. Stephen heard at least a dozen times that Master Adam of Lincoln was the great builder who'd conceived this grand west portal.

"Thank you," said Stephen, "I knew that. What's the rebuilding fund for?"

The clerk looked embarrassed and murmured something about problems with the roof work. He said he wasn't an architect himself, but offered to bring someone who could explain the problem in detail. Stephen laughed to himself and contributed generously to the fund.

Then he went to Ely, and found the Galilee porch as beautiful as he remembered it. He was surprised to discover that no one could tell him the name of the man who'd designed it. Even Master Brito, the last builder to implement the design, had been forgotten by now.

Stephen told Aude about the contrast, by way of explanation for why he didn't care about having his own name carved on the new church at Dunwich. He said the only

fame that mattered to him now was in the eyes of men
who could appreciate his work for what it was worth.

"And what did they say at Ely about your broken
vows?"

Stephen shifted uncomfortably under Aude's penetrating gaze. "No one knew me; I didn't tell them who I was."
Brother Coluin had been long dead and Stephen couldn't
think of anyone else at Ely he cared to see. Everyone from
Ely thought Stephen had been killed in the sack, and the
parchments with the papal seal on them were moldering at
the bottom of his locked chest. There'd seemed no point in
raising old quarrels.

"You told me once," said Aude, "in Ragusa it was, that
you were coming back to England to build your church
and straighten matters out about your vows. You said then
that you were through running away from things."

"So I am." Hadn't he been right here for years, solidly
based in Dunwich, reviving Master Brito's stoneyard,
building the Church of St. Michael, and acquiring a crew
of skilled men? Stephen had watched young Mark shoot
up like a weed, his height keeping pace with the slowly
rising walls of the church. What could be less like running
than this solid, centered life that he'd built for himself and
Aude?

"I wonder." Her words were no more than a breath on
the summer air; if challenged, Aude could claim she'd said
nothing at all, that it was only his guilty imagination at
work. She went back to grinding some mixture in the
wooden bowl on her lap, ostensibly giving all her care to
blending the dried herbs. But Stephen still felt as if she
were watching him, judging and measuring. Had he fallen
short of her expectations?

"Damn the woman!" Stephen said the next morning,
when after an uneasy night, he set out to retrace his steps
toward Ely. He'd wanted Aude to come with him, but
she'd refused.

"Wouldn't you like to see the fenlands again?"

She shook her head. "Not this time. This is your journey. You'll have a lot to think on."

And that he did. The week before, when he'd gone to
Peterborough and Ely as Master Stephen of Dunwich,
he'd been able to present himself as a successful builder
who merely wanted to see the works of other architects.

Stephen returned to the scenes of his childhood, a prosperous, confident, middle-aged man with a business of his own and a few good buildings scattered across France to bear witness to his life's work.

This time, Stephen put his professional interest aside and set out on a journey that aroused painful memories. In summer's heat he was once again the starved, scared oblate who'd fled across the ice with a traitor knight, who'd shivered all night in a tree while wolves were snapping at his heels. On his fine horse, in the security of his rich gown and gilt girdle, he was again the poor fisherboy out of the lower town who'd been sent by flood and famine to beg his way along the roads with Mam. And at the end of this journey, at the heart of the twisting paths through the fens, there was cold and betrayal and unimaginable loneliness.

Stephen's spirits sank as he drew closer to Ely. His horse splashed through the puddles on the low-lying causeway, and Stephen felt the reeds hemming him round. He remembered the panic of a boy used to the wide sounding horizon of ocean and shingle.

Then the cathedral rose into view like a great ship above the golden sea of reeds, a wind rustled through the sedge like the sighing of waves, and Stephen knew again the unaccountable joy that had made his first journey and first parting bearable, so many years ago. The cathedral was massive and plain by the standards of that day's more ornate building. Its heavy columns had been set by builders who feared the bulk of stone they themselves were raising. Still, it was the first great work in stone that Stephen had ever seen, and it was still the mark by which he measured all others.

A young monk, black robes flapping about his ankles, came running out to take Stephen's horse when he reached the main gate.

"You came in good time, Master. He's waiting for you in the infirmary."

"There's some mistake." Stephen dismounted, stiff from the long ride, and rubbed his aching thighs. "I'm not expected. You have taken me for someone else."

"You're Master Stephen, the builder from Dunwich," said the young man positively. "He sent for you almost as soon as he heard you'd been asking about the men who

designed the Galilee porch. He said he'd been waiting for
you and was sorry to have missed your visit, but hoped
you'd return."

"I never got a message. We must have crossed paths on
the road. Who wants to see me? Never mind, I'll talk to
him later." Perhaps the current prior or bishop had a new
building project for him to undertake. "First I have to
see..."

Stephen paused. He had told himself that all he needed
was a short interview with the prior, to show his papers
from Rome and get the man's agreement that he had no
more obligations to the convent here. But now that he
stood in the shadow of the main gate, almost over the cell
where he'd been imprisoned twenty-five years before, he
knew that he could not leave without settling matters with
the one man whose obsession had pursued him all these
years. "I'm here to see a Brother Daniel. Your treasurer
once, though he may—"

"But, of course." The young monk seemed bewildered.
"Brother Daniel, I said, he sent for you as soon as he heard
you'd been here. But he's not treasurer any longer. His
health, you understand—and age. Indeed, it's a marvel
that he's lasted this long. This way, Master Stephen. The
infirmary."

But their meeting did not take place in the infirmary,
with its rows of beds and ailing old men. For this visit,
Brother Daniel had commanded that his bed be carried
out into the cloister garden, where they could speak in
private. He was sitting there, propped on a bolster, with
his black monk's robes wrapped and folded around his frail
body.

At first Stephen thought he would not have known the
old man. Flesh had withered away from the strong bones of
his face, and his tall broad-shouldered frame had shrunk
with the years. But the essential things were the same: his
stubborn chin, his frame of light hair—once pale yellow,
now silver—and the pale frantic eyes that fixed on Stephen's
face with a hungry look.

"I've been waiting a long time for this meeting, my
son."

His voice was firm as ever, but a fit of coughing broke
the sentence and made his bony shoulders tremble.

"Not your son," said Stephen. He fumbled in his pouch

for the precious roll of parchment with the Pope's own seal on it. "I've a judgment from Rome. The vows that were taken in my name do not stand, since I rejected them as soon as I came to an age of reason. The Pope himself—"

Brother Daniel waved the parchment away with an irritable gesture. "Don't shove that thing in my face as if I were a schoolboy who needed to see the letters written clear! I am capable of taking a hint. When a boy runs away from the convent twice, and the second time stays away for more than twenty years, it's a fairly good sign that he isn't meant for the monastic life."

"You had other signs," Stephen pointed out.

"And you had vows, which you chose not to keep. Never mind. It's over now, and I am not unhappy with the way it has turned out. And I am too old to play games of assigning blame. Life is what it is, and not what either you or I would have made of it, my son . . . ." Coughing interrupted his speech for a minute.

"Don't call me your son! You haven't that right. I do not belong to the convent; you've admitted it yourself."

"No? But who has a better right? Look at me."

Stephen stared into the unblinking, pale eyes and felt a queer, dizzy sensation. Once, long ago, he'd looked into a still pool in the fens, and had seen such eyes staring back at him.

"Ah," Brother Daniel breathed with satisfaction. "I see you begin to understand what everybody else figured out long ago. Did you never wonder how you grew so tall and fair among the fisherfolk, or why you didn't look like that little dark man I paid to marry your mother? I suppose you were too young then. Other folk talked, though. And when you came to the convent, did you wonder why I showed you such special favor?"

"No," said Stephen slowly. "I do not understand. You're claiming to be my father and to have favored me? What kind of father treats a son as you did, trying to force me into a life I hated, trying to beat me into submission?"

A sardonic smile flickered across Daniel's worn face. "Many fathers do worse. If you think otherwise, you must not have been observing the world very closely. I did no worse than most fathers, Stephen: I wanted you to live my life without making the mistakes I made."

He stopped, breathing hard, and took a sip of water

from the bowl beside his bed. "Your mother was my weakness and my mistake. It never came out in the open, but people talked. When you were born, with your light eyes and yellow hair—there were rumors that kept me from advancing with the Austin Canons. When I left them to join the Black Monks, here at Ely, I thought I could leave the whole unfortunate business behind me."

Stephen clenched his fists and put them behind his back. One did not strike an old man on his deathbed, even if he had been evil enough to dismiss Mam and his son as "unfortunate business."

Daniel seemed to be gaining strength with this confessional. His voice went on, cold and steady and passionless as Stephen remembered it. "Then she came here with you. What could I do? It was a sign from God. You were my penance and I had to take you in. My sin with Maud might have been forgotten in time, but not with you there in the monastery. You were the end of my ambitions for myself. It was only fair that she should repay me by giving me your life, so that I could protect you from my mistakes. I told her I wouldn't take you otherwise, that she and you could starve in the streets for all I cared."

"So when she gave me up—"

"The vows she took in your name," said Daniel, "were part of my price for giving you shelter. Why should I take in a boy whose very existence would ruin all my plans, only to see him go off again. She promised me that she would never try to see you again. I will say this for Maud, she kept her promises."

Stephen knew then that Mam hadn't left him—not willingly. She had abandoned him because it was the only way she could take care of him. He might have understood that years ago, if the pain of loss hadn't blinded him to the truth.

The sun was on his back and the cold shadow of the cathedral interior was far away. Stephen felt as if invisible chains were breaking off his wrists.

"Where did she go?"

"How should I know? Once I had her mark on the vows, the woman was of no importance. Some years later," Daniel added, grudgingly but with no sign of regret, "when you were fourteen, I think, I did hear that she had died. She'd used her last coin to pay a peasant to take the news to Ely. I assume she thought I was fool enough to disrupt your studies with talk of a woman you'd forgotten long ago."

Stephen remembered that at about that time there had been more beatings, more pressure to dedicate his life to the Church, more talk of an early date for his final vows. The knowledge that Mam was dead and that his claim on his bastard son was undisputable must have inspired Daniel to greater cruelty.

Daniel had no more than that to say of Mam, whom he'd driven away. Such cold indifference would once have chilled Stephen to the bone, but now he felt sorry for his father. Stephen had had a life rich in love and work and good friends; Daniel's presence had been a momentary shadow falling over his boyhood, nothing more. But Daniel himself had lived an empty life, warped by ambition and devoid of humanity. He could not even grieve for the woman he'd once loved.

"Do you hate me? I only wanted your good."

"No," Stephen said. "I don't hate you. I am sorry for you." Stephen had been rich in his life whereas Daniel had nothing but bitterness and frustrated ambition. "I am even sorry," said Stephen, "that your ambitions for me failed."

"Oh, I didn't fail." Daniel's eyes were bright and calculating.

"No?" Stephen had to laugh. Would the old man never give up? "You've seen my papers. I'm free of the convent. What did you want me to be? Prior? Bishop? A cardinal? You'd have done better to pin your hopes on Joscelin de Cressy. He may yet be a prince of the Church."

"I wanted you to have a brilliant career serving God."

"Instead of which, I became a mason."

"The Cistercian church at Chastelvert. The shrine of St. Hubert in Burgundy. The abbey cloisters at ..."

Stephen listened, slack-jawed, as Daniel rattled off the names of six or seven major works he'd built or designed in Europe, ending with, "The Church of St. Michael at Varad. And, of course, the church you are presently building in Dunwich. Oh, yes," he added, "I have known where you were and what you were doing all these years. And do you really claim that in building all these shrines and churches, you were not serving God? I misread your abilities when I tried to force you to become a clerk like myself. But things have turned out for the best. I am content in you, my son," he added with a defiant look, and Stephen did not dispute the name this time.

Soon after, the new infirmarian interrupted them with Daniel's gruel and sleeping draught. He asked that the bed be moved back inside where he could keep watch over the old man during the night.

"You'll stay?"

Daniel clutched at Stephen's hand, and he could not refuse the request.

"I'll see you in the morning."

"At least," murmured Daniel as the infirmarian and two lay brothers closed round his bed, "you'll be better lodged now than you were last time you slept at Ely. Better the guesthouse than the cells, eh?"

His sardonic laughter followed Stephen through the long shadowed walk of the cloister.

In the morning, when Stephen went to pay his respects to Daniel, the infirmarian informed him that the old monk had died in the night.

"Died! But he seemed so strong yesterday."

"I hadn't seen him that strong in years," said the infirmarian. "He'd been ailing since the fall of forty-one. That was when he resigned his offices and moved into the infirmary."

That would have been when news reached England that the Mongols were in Hungary. And Daniel, who had kept track of his son's movements through all the years, would have known that Stephen was working in Varad, on the exposed eastern edge of Hungary.

Daniel's death left Stephen feeling curiously empty, as though he had been leaning into a stiff wind that suddenly failed. Daniel's cold voice that used to accuse Stephen of failure and unworthiness was silent now. Stephen had not heard it since the afternoon before, when Daniel confessed that he'd forced Mam to go away and leave Stephen behind. Ever since that disclosure, Stephen was complete and warm and secure. There was love, and life, and the work of his hands; Daniel's voice had been stilled forever.

"Perhaps it was my own fear and loneliness speaking, not Brother Daniel and not a demon," Stephen mused on the long winding road away from Ely.

The question no longer seemed to matter. Even if he

didn't have to build great monuments to prove his own worthiness, Stephen had enough to think about, enough to come home to. Ahead of him was a church half-built, a gang of masons waiting for orders, a sharp-tongued woman who was the other half of his soul, and a growing boy whose hands already showed the aptitude for stonecarving that Stephen had always lacked. Behind him, the cathedral of Ely rose out of the marshes and watched over his journey home to the sea.

EPILOGUE

Dunwich, 1328–1988

ike most of the builders of the Middle Ages, Stephen
of Dunwich achieved fame in his own generation and
was unknown to succeeding ones. His name was not
carved on any of the buildings he erected; he used to say
wryly that the memory of Master Adam's vainglory had
cured him of such urges. What if succeeding generations
found his work just such overblown folly as that? The only
immortality Stephen requested was to be buried beneath
the pavement of his own church of St. Michael at Dunwich,
on the cliff overlooking the sea.

After his death, his son Mark, who had become a noted
sculptor, defied his father's wishes and had the name of
Stephen of Dunwich carved across the lintel of the west
door of the church, where all who entered must see
it.

In 1328 the town of Dunwich was destroyed by another
storm similar to the one that had washed away the lower
town in Stephen's childhood, but even worse. The harbor
was closed up by silt, hundreds of houses were washed
away, and the high cliff on which the new Church of St.
Michael stood was eaten away until the church tumbled
into the ocean. Spire and walls and foundations all went,
and so did the graves under the center aisle; so Stephen's
bones lay beneath the sea at last.

In later years, fishermen from the neighboring port of Bliborough claimed that they could hear the bells of St. Michael's ringing under water to warn them of impending storms.

Fishermen on the East Anglian coast today still tell of hearing bells ring under water, and still blame their torn nets on the high spires of a church in a sea-drowned village.

ABOUT THE AUTHOR

MARGARET BALL was born in 1947 in Austin, Texas, where she still lives. She has a B.A. in mathematics and a Ph.D. in linguistics from the University of Texas. After doing field research in Swahili dialects, teaching linguistics and designing computer software, she turned to writing historical novels as a way to finance her hobby of reading obscure historical journals and biographies. She has written several historical romances under the pseudonyms of Catherine Lyndell and Kathleen Fraser; *A Bridge To The Sky* is her first mainstream novel.

THE LATEST IN BOOKS
AND AUDIO CASSETTES

Paperbacks

☐ 27032 **FIRST BORN** Doris Mortman $4.95

☐ 27283 **BRAZEN VIRTUE** Nora Roberts $3.95

☐ 25891 **THE TWO MRS. GRENVILLES**
Dominick Dunne $4.95

☐ 27891 **PEOPLE LIKE US** Dominick Dunne $4.95

☐ 27260 **WILD SWAN** Celeste De Blasis $4.95

☐ 25692 **SWAN'S CHANCE** Celeste De Blasis $4.50

☐ 26543 **ACT OF WILL**
Barbara Taylor Bradford $5.95

☐ 27790 **A WOMAN OF SUBSTANCE**
Barbara Taylor Bradford $5.95

Audio

☐ **THE SHELL SEEKERS** by Rosamunde Pilcher
Performance by Lynn Redgrave
180 Mins. Double Cassette 48183-9 $14.95

☐ **COLD SASSY TREE** by Olive Ann Burns
Performance by Richard Thomas
180 Mins. Double Cassette 45166-9 $14.95

☐ **PEOPLE LIKE US** by Dominick Dunne
Performance by Len Cariou
180 Mins. Double Cassette 45164-2 $14.95

☐ **CAT'S EYE** by Margaret Atwood
Performance by Kate Nelligan
180 Mins. Double Cassette 45203-7 $14.95

Bantam Books, Dept. FBS, 414 East Golf Road, Des Plaines, IL 60016

Please send me the items I have checked above. I am enclosing $_____
(please add $2.00 to cover postage and handling). Send check or money
order, no cash or C.O.D.s please. (Tape offer good in USA only.)

Mr/Ms _____

Address _____

City/State _____ Zip_____

Please allow four to six weeks for delivery.   FBS—4/90
Prices and availability subject to change without notice.